Anonymous

Proceedings of the Legislative Council of India

Vol. IV

SALZWASSER VERLAG

Anonymous

Proceedings of the Legislative Council of India

Vol. IV

Reprint of the original, first published in 1859.

1st Edition 2022 | ISBN: 978-3-37513-121-0

Verlag (Publisher): Salzwasser Verlag GmbH, Zeilweg 44, 60439 Frankfurt, Deutschland
Vertretungsberechtigt (Authorized to represent): E. Roepke, Zeilweg 44, 60439 Frankfurt, Deutschland
Druck (Print): Books on Demand GmbH, In de Tarpen 42, 22848 Norderstedt, Deutschland

PROCEEDINGS

OF THE

LEGISLATIVE COUNCIL OF INDIA,

FOR

January to December 1858.

VOL. IV.

Published by the authority of the Council.

CALCUTTA:

G. A. SAVIELLE, CALCUTTA PRINTING AND PUBLISHING COMPANY (LIMITED),
NO. 1, WESTON'S LANE, COSSITOLLAH.

1858.

ERRATA.

Column 56. After line 28, read as follows:

"THE VICE-PRESIDENT moved that the Bill be now read a third time and passed.

The motion was carried, and the Bill read a third time."

" 146. Line 9 from the bottom. For "*The President*" read "*The Vice-President.*"

" 192. After the *first* line, read "*Message No.* 138."

" 584. Omit the 24th and 25th lines from the bottom.

PROCEEDINGS

OF THE

LEGISLATIVE COUNCIL OF INDIA.

Saturday, January 2, 1858.

PRESENT:

The Honorable J. A. Dorin, *Vice-President*, in the Chair.

Hon. Major Genl. J. Low, | E. Currie, Esq.,
Hon. B. Peacock, | Hon. Sir A. W. Buller
D. Eliott, Esq., | and
P. W. LeGeyt, Esq., | H. B. Harington, Esq.

DELHI AND MEERUT.

MR. PEACOCK moved the first reading of a Bill "to remove from the operation of the General Laws and Regulations the Delhi territory and the Meerut Division, or such parts thereof as the Governor-General in Council shall place under the administration of the Chief Commissioner of the Punjab." He said, it was the intention of the Governor-General in Council to place the Delhi territory and the Meerut Division, or some portions thereof, under the administration of the Chief Commissioner of the Punjab. It was therefore necessary that those districts should be placed on the same footing as other districts of the Punjab; and, accordingly, he proposed, by the present Bill, to make them non-Regulation Provinces. Strictly speaking, the Delhi territory was not a Regulation Province, though it was subject to the jurisdiction of the Sudder Court and Board of Revenue. By Regulation V. 1832, the Office of Resident and Chief Commissioner having been abolished, the administration of the Revenue, of the Police, and of Civil and Criminal Justice was vested in the Board of Revenue and Sudder Court respectively. By a provision in that Regulation, the Governor-General in Council was authorized to extend to the Delhi territory, by an order in Council, the whole or a part of the general Regulations. He believed that they had never been extended to that territory in so many words, though they had been generally acted upon. The present Bill declared that the Delhi territory and the Meerut Division, or such portions of them as should be placed by the Governor-General in Council under the administration of the Chief Commissioner of the Punjab, should not be subject to the general Regulations. As yet, it had not been finally determined by the Governor-General in Council whether the whole of the Meerut Division should be placed under such administration; and the Bill therefore proposed to take out of the general Regulations such portions only as might be annexed to the Punjab. If only a part of the Division should be transferred, the remainder would continue subject to the Regulations.

The Bill provided that all suits and proceedings which should be pending within these districts at the time the Act should come into operation, should be transferred to the Courts and Officers which might be established or appointed for the administration of Civil and Criminal justice, and the collection of the revenues therein, according to their respective jurisdictions.

Finally, the Bill provided that the Act should come into operation from such day as should be fixed by the Governor-General in Council by notice, t be published in the Gazette.

The Bill was read a first time.

CORPORAL PUNISHMENT.

MR. PEACOCK moved the first reading of a Bill "to authorize the infliction of corporal punishment in certain cases." The Council, he said, was well aware that, in the North Western Provinces and other parts of India many of the jails had been destroyed during the late disturbances, and that in some districts there were no means of carrying out a proper system of prison-discipline. On the Arms Act being sent up to the Chief Commissioner o Agra, that Officer suggested that, in lieu of, or in addition to, the punishment of fine which might be imposed under some of the Clauses of the Act, the Magistrate should have power to award corporal punishment. He stated that, in many cases in which a fine might be imposed, it would be almost impossible to levy it; and that, if the offender should be sentenced to suffer imprisonment for the default, there would be no means of giving effect to the sentence. The Chief Commissioner said that he was assured that the only means of carrying out the provisionsof the Act would be to allow corporal punishment to be inflicted in lieu of, or in addition to the punishment of fine in cases falling within the provisions of Sections XXII and XXV of the Act. Forhis (Mr. Peacock's) own part, he did not think that corporal punishment should be inflicted in every case of unlawful possession or concealment of arms; but he would leave these offences subject to imprisonment and fine, and make it discretionary with the Magistrate to order corporal punishment not exceeding thirty stripes with a rattan to be inflicted in lieu of the fine, in the event of its not being paid. He had, certainly, agreed with the Law Commissioners who prepared the Penal Code in the general views which they had expressed on the subject of corporal punishment. They had recommended that no corporal punishment should be inflicted; and in the Code as it was last settled, there was no provision for such punishment. But recent events had very much altered his opinion on the question. It appeared to him that it was very inexpedient to overcrowd our jails with prisoners for petty offences. He had lately seen a suggestion from the Government of the North-Western Provinces that, in cases of simple theft, corporal punishment should be allowed to be inflicted when the value of the property stolen exceeded fifty Rupees. As the Law now existed, no corporal punishment could be inflicted where the value of the property stolen was above that amount. Where the value was under fifty Rupees, the Magistrate might order corporal punishment, not exceeding thirty stripes with a rattan, to be inflicted; and he might also order corporal punishment in the case of juvenile offenders. That had been extended to Bombay by Act I of 1853; and the principle of allowing corporal punishment had been discussed and determined by the Council on a recent occasion, when the Police Bill for Calcutta was before it. The Council had adopted the principle of authorizing corporal punishment in certain cases. That Act provided that, in certain cases of theft, where the value of the property stolen did not exceed fifty Rupees, the Magistrate might order corporal punishment, not exceeding thirty stripes with a rattan, to be inflicted. It appeared to him, however, that where a theft was unaccompanied by aggravating circumstances, it should be competent to Magistrates, especially in districts where there were no means of enforcing proper prison-discipline, to award corporal punishment, even if the value of the property stolen was above fifty Rupees. He had, therefore, provided by this Bill that, in cases of simple theft, it should be lawful for Magistrates to sentence the offenders to corporal punishment not exceeding thirty stripes with a rattan.

He had also provided that in any case in which a fine should be imposed under Section VIII of Act XI of 1857, or under Section XXII or XXV of Act XXVIII of 1857, the Magistrate might order corporal punishment not exceeding thirty stripes with a rattan to be substituted for it in case it should not be paid forthwith. Sections XXII and XXV of Act XXVIII of 1857 were the Sections with respect to which the Chief Commissioner of Agra had said it would be impossible to carry out the object of the Act unless corporal punishment were allowed to be inflicted in lieu of, or in addition to, the fine. Section XXII provided hard labor for a term not exceeding two years, and a fine not exceeding five thousand Rupees for wilfully neglecting to give notice of possession of ammunition &c. in certain cases; and Section XXV provided imprisonment with or without hard labor for a term not exceeding two years, in addition to any other penalty which might be awarded under the Act, for refusing to produce, or for concealing arms, ammunition, &c. when search was made. Act XI of 1857 was the Act which authorized the Executive Government to disarm, by proclamation, any person or specified class of persons in any district; and Section VIII provided a fine not exceeding fifty Rupees or imprisonment for a term not exceeding six months, for unlawful possession of arms. In cases under this Section, also, it might be very necessary and very proper, if the fine imposed was not paid, to direct corporal punishment in substitution for it instead of over-crowding the Jails by sending the offenders to prison.

He had also provided that corporal punishment not exceeding thirty stripes with a rattan might be inflicted, in case the fine imposed was not paid, for petty offences, such as abusive language, calumny, and inconsiderable assaults or affrays, which were now punishable with fine under Regulation IX. 1793.

He had further provided that nothing in the Bill should be deemed to authorize the infliction of corporal punishment on any European, or on any female. The reasons which had induced him to bring in the Bill, did not apply to Europeans; and females had always, very properly, been exempt from corporal punishment.

Lastly, he had provided that the word "Magistrate" should include any person lawfully exercising the full powers of a Magistrate, and also any Assistant to a Magistrate, or a Deputy Magistrate specially appointed by the Executive Government to exercise the powers vested in a Magistrate by this Bill.

These were the general provisions of the Bill. Doubtless, it was susceptible of improvement; and, when it came before a Select Committee and before a Committee of the whole Council, any necessary amendments might be made in it.

SIR ARTHUR BULLER asked if the duration of the Act was limited?

MR. PEACOCK replied, it was not. Possibly, the Select Committee to whom the Bill would be referred might think it right to recommend that the duration of the Bill should be limited. The question of permitting corporal punishment would be re-considered by the Select Committee on the Penal Code. If that Committee should determine that it ought not to be permitted, this Act would be repealed: if it should determine otherwise, provisions for corporal punishment would be introduced into the Code, and the Council would have an opportunity of discussing the general principle when the Code should come before it in Committee.

With these observations, he begged to move the first reading of the Bill.

The Bill was read a first time.

ESCAPED OFFENDERS.

MR. PEACOCK moved the first reading of a Bill "for the punishment of certain offenders who have escaped from jails, and of persons who shall knowingly harbour such offenders." He said, he need scarcely inform the Council that, during the recent disturbances in the North-Western Provinces and other parts of India, many of the jails had been broken open and destroyed, and the prisoners forcibly released. Many of such prisoners were, at the time of their release, undergoing sentences of imprisonment for heinous crimes, and a large number of such prisoners were still at large. He had thought it right, therefore, to bring in a Bill to subject every such person to heavy punishment if he should fail, within one month after the passing of the Act, to surrender himself to a Magistrate or Police Officer, and make true answer, to the best of his knowledge, to all such questions as should be put to him by a Magistrate touching the jail from which he had escaped, and the cause for which he had been there detained. As it was very inexpedient to over-crowd the jails, or to allow convicts of this description to remain in the country, he had provided by the Bill that every such person should, upon conviction, be sentenced to transportation for life. He did not propose to leave it to the discretion of the Court before which such an offender should be convicted, to pass a more lenient sentence. The Bill also provided that any person who had escaped from jail or other lawful custody whilst detained under a committal for trial for any heinous offence, or under a charge of being guilty of such offence, and who should not, within one month after the passing of the Act, surrender himself to a Magistrate or Police Officer, and declare from what jail he had escaped, and the nature of the charge upon which he had been detained—should, on being convicted of having escaped, and of having committed the heinous offence for which he had been detained, be subject to the same punishment. The latter provision applied to persons who had not hitherto been convicted; and, therefore, they ought not to undergo any more severe punishment than the present law allowed for escaping from prison, unless they should also be convicted of having committed the offence for which they had been detained.

The heinous offences contemplated by the Bill, were murder, attempts to murder, thuggee, dacoity, robbery, belonging or having belonged to a gang of thugs, or to a gang of dacoits, or to a wandering gang associated for the purposes of theft or robbery, and all crimes against person or property attended with great personal violence. It was very desirable that the country should be rid of offenders of this class; and, therefore, the Bill did not leave it to the discretion of the Magistrate to sentence them to transportation for life, but made it incumbent on him to do so.

He had also provided that whoever should knowingly harbour or conceal any such escaped prisoner, or, being aware of the place of concealment, should wilfully fail to give information thereof to a Magistrate or Police Officer, should be liable to imprisonment with or without hard labor for any term not exceeding seven years, and also to fine.

Many prisoners who had escaped, were not in custody for any heinous offence. He had thought it right that the Magistrate should have the power of tendering a pardon to any such prisoner, both in respect of his having escaped from custody, and of the offence for which he was detained, upon condition of his giving such information as

might lead to the apprehension and conviction of any heinous offender punishable under the Act.

The Bill provided that offences under the Act might be tried by a Sessions Judge, or by a Special Commissioner appointed under Act XIV of 1857.

Before he concluded, he desired to offer his thanks to a gentleman of great ability and of considerable experience—Mr. Edward Lautour, the Judge of the Twenty-four Pergunnahs—for many very useful suggestions. Mr. Lautour had been kind enough himself to prepare a Bill upon the subject; and although he (Mr. Peacock) had not adopted all the provisions which were contained in that Bill, he felt bound to acknowledge the valuable assistance which he had received from that gentleman as well on this as on many other occasions.

The Bill was read a first time.

COMPULSORY LABOR (MADRAS).

MR. ELIOTT moved that the Bill "to make lawful compulsory labor for the prevention of mischief by inundation, and to provide for the enforcement of customary labor on certain works of irrigation in the Presidency of Fort St. George" be now read a third time and passed.

The motion was carried, and the Bill read a third time.

PORT-DUES (CUTTACK).

MR. CURRIE moved that the Bill "for the levy of Port-dues in certain Ports in the Province of Cuttack" be now read a third time and passed.

The motion was carried, and the Bill read a third time.

COMPULSORY LABOR (MADRAS).

MR. ELIOTT moved that Mr. Peacock be requested to take the Bill "to make lawful compulsory labor for the prevention of mischief by inundation, and to provide for the enforcement of customary labor on certain works of irrigation in the Presidency of Fort St. George" to the Governor-General for his assent.

Agreed to.

PORT-DUES (CUTTACK).

MR. CURRIE moved that Mr. Peacock be requested to take the Bill "for the levy of Port-dues in certain Ports in the Province of Cuttack" to the Governor-General for his assent.

Agreed to.

NATIVE PASSENGER SHIPS.

MR. ELIOTT moved that Mr. Currie be added to the Select Committee on the Bill "for the regulation of Native Passenger Ships."

NOTICES OF MOTION.

MR. PEACOCK gave notice that he would, on Saturday the 9th Instant, move the second reading of the following Bills, namely,

The Bill "to remove from the operation of the general Laws and Regulations the Delhi Territory and the Meerut Division, or such parts thereof as the Governor-General in Council shall place under the administration of the Chief Commissioner of the Punjab."

The Bill "to authorize the infliction of corporal punishment in certain cases."

And the Bill "for the punishment of certain offenders who have escaped from Jail, and of persons who shall knowingly harbour such offenders."

Also that he would on the same day move that the Standing Orders be suspended to enable him to proceed with the above Bills.

The Council adjourned.

Saturday, January 9, 1858.

PRESENT:

The Honorable J. A. Dorin, *Vice-President*, in the Chair.

Hon. the Chief Justice,	P. W. LeGeyt, Esq.,
Hon. Major General J. Low,	E. Currie, Esq. and
Hon. B. Peacock,	H. B. Harington, Esq.
D. Eliott, Esq.	

BOMBAY WATER-WORKS.

MR. LEGEYT moved the first reading of a Bill "to give effect to an agreement between the Government of Bombay and Her Majesty's Justices of the Peace for the Town of Bombay in relation to certain Water-works in the Islands of Salsette and Bombay." The principal object of this Bill, he said, was to give the Government of Bombay some security for the repayment of a very large sum of money disbursed by it in the construction of certain water-works known as the Vehar Valley Water-works. It would be in the recollection of the Council that, on several occasions of late years, the scarcity of water in Bombay towards the end of the hot season, had produced much painful anxiety and distress; and that, only two years ago, it was called on to pass a Bill which was rendered necessary by an extreme drought in the Island at that time, and which materially affected private comfort and property.

The population of Bombay had, of late years, increased very largely and very rapidly. Within the last twenty years, it had nearly doubled, and it now amounted to about 600,000. The Island being entirely dependent for its supply of water on the periodical rains which fell from the middle of June till the end of September, any failure of those rains necessarily produced extreme scarcity and distress. This state of things had been an object of great solicitude with the Government and the Inhabitants of the Island for some years past. Several projects for remedying the want of water had been submitted from time to time to the Government, and tested by scientific enquiry. After a careful examination of several, one, in which it was proposed to collect water in a large reservoir in the neighboring Island of Salsette, and bring it into Bombay by means of iron pipes, a distance of about fourteen miles, —was found to present the most effectual and feasible results. The cost of this work was then estimated at twenty-five lakhs of Rupees. It was obvious that an outlay of this kind, being solely for the benefit of the Inhabitants of Bombay, was one which should fall, not on the general revenues of the country, but on the Inhabitants of the place who would benefit thereby. It was accordingly proposed that the sum of twenty-five lakhs should be advanced by the Government, and that a water-rate should be levied on occupiers of houses and grounds in the Island which would yield four per cent., to be paid as interest on the outlay, and one per cent., to be set apart as a sinking fund for the gradual liquidation of the capital. This scheme received the sanction of the Government of India, and of the Honorable Court of Directors. Contracts were entered into by the Honorable Court in London for pipings &c., and the reservoir was commenced upon in Salsette, and was now on the eve of completion. But, as usually happened in such matters, the estimate of cost had been considerably exceeded. Already, the outlay had been more than thirty-five lakhs, and he believed it was probable that the work, before it was finished, would cost four or five lakhs more. The Municipality was called upon to provide funds for the repayment of the whole of this sum, and of interest at the rate of four per cent. The Justices demurred to making the municipal funds responsible for more than twenty-five lakhs, and interest upon that amount, contending that the funds had been bound only to that extent. The Government of Bombay, however, and the Government of India took a different view of the case, and thought it fair that the whole sum expended should be recovered from the Inhabitants of the Island by means of a local tax. A discussion extending over a considerable space of time ensued, and the final proposal from the Justices was that the Municipality should be made responsible for the repayment of twenty-five lakhs, and half the excess over that sum. The Government of Bombay still contended that the whole should be repaid by them. On the urgent representation of the Justices, however, they had since referred the proposition to the Honorable Court of Directors with all the circumstances connected with it, with a recommendation that it should be acceded to. No answer had been received to that representation yet.

Meanwhile, the Government of India had intimated to the Government of Bombay that it was indispensable that some security should be provided for the repayment of the whole advances made, with interest at four per cent., and had called upon them to obtain with that view legislative sanction to a water-rate being levied in the Island. In conformity with that direction, the Government of Bombay had framed the Bill which he had now the honor to bring before the Council, and which was entitled "A Bill to give effect to an agreement between the Government of Bombay and Her Majesty's Justices of the Peace for the Town and Island of Bombay and Colaba, in relation to certain water-works in the Islands of Salsette and Bombay."

The Preamble of the Bill recited that—

"Whereas the Governor in Council of Bombay has contracted with Her Majesty's Justices of the Peace for the Town and Island of Bombay and Colaba to erect and complete at an estimated cost of twenty-five Lakhs of Rupees or thereabouts, certain water-works for the purpose of supplying the said Town and Island with water from the Vehar Valley in the Island of Salsette, and to procure and lay down the piping required for that purpose, and to maintain the said works and piping when completed, on the terms and conditions that the whole of the money disbursed by the Governor in Council in the provision, erection, and completion of the said works shall, whether such sum be greater or less than the said sum of twenty-five Lakhs of Rupees, be repaid with interest at the rate of four Rupees for every one hundred Rupees per annum; and that for that purpose the said Justices shall, by and out of the Municipal Fund of Bombay, pay to the said Governor in Council in each year, until the whole of the money disbursed as aforesaid shall be repaid and satisfied, a sum equal to five Rupees on every hundred of the whole sum expended by the Governor in Council in the erection and completion of the said works and piping; that is to say, a sum equal to one-twentieth part of the whole sum disbursed as aforesaid, out of which such a sum as shall be equal to interest at four per cent. upon the principal amount of the debt remaining unpaid in each year, shall be appropriated to the payment of such interest, and the residue shall be appropriated towards reduction of such principal amount; and that the said Justices shall also, in addition to the above sum so to be annually paid by them as aforesaid, pay also annually to the said Governor in Council of Bombay out of the said Municipal Fund the actual annual cost of maintaining the said works;—

"To give effect to the said agreement; it is enacted as follows:"—

The Sections which followed authorized the Justices, with the sanction of the Governor in Council, to levy a special tax on all occupiers of houses, grounds, and tenements within the Islands of Bombay and Colaba of the annual value of forty-eight Rupees and upwards at

Mr. LeGeyt

a rate not exceeding three and a half per cent., and required the Board of Conservancy, or such other persons as should for the time being have the control of the Municipal Funds, to pay therefrom to the Governor in Council, on a certain day in each year, the amount of that water-rate in payment of the sum advanced for the water-works, and interest thereon at four per cent.

It was necessary for him to state, in introducing this Bill—and he had been instructed by the Government of Bombay to state it—that it was hoped it would not be found necessary to enforce the water-rate contemplated by it if the Municipal Bill for Bombay, which was now before a Select Committee, and about to be reported on, should pass in its present shape. In that event, it was believed that ample funds would be forthcoming, not only for ordinary municipal purposes, but also for repayment of the advances for constructing these water-works; and if this should be the case, the provisions of the present Bill would not be brought into operation. The Bill, therefore, might be regarded only as providing a grant-in-aid to the Municipal Fund as it was expected to be constituted under the Municipal Bill now before the Council, in case that Fund should be found unequal to meet the demands on it for repayment and interest. But as the sources from which the funds proposed by the Municipal Bill had not yet been determined, both the Government of Bombay and the Government of India considered it indispensable that a Bill like this should be passed in the meantime, to give the former a positive security for the payment of the money which they had advanced, but for which they at present had no security.

The Bill was read a first time.

DELHI AND MEERUT.

MR. PEACOCK moved that the Bill "to remove from the operation of the general Laws and Regulations the Delhi Territory and the Meerut Division, or such portions thereof as the Governor-General in Council shall place under the administration of the Chief Commissioner of the Punjab" be read a second time.

The Motion was carried, and the Bill read a second time.

CORPORAL PUNISHMENT.

MR. PEACOCK moved that the Bill "to authorize the infliction of corporal punishment in certain cases" be read a second time.

THE CHIEF JUSTICE said, any objection or discussion which he might be inclined to raise on the Bill, would rather be with respect to particular provisions, and to the question whether the operation of the measure should be permanent and general as to locality, than to its principle of which he entirely approved. Before speaking on the motion for the second reading, therefore, he should be glad to know whether the Honorable and learned Member proposed to proceed with the Bill at once, or to refer it to a Select Committee in the first instance.

MR. PEACOCK said, he proposed to move—first that the Standing Orders be suspended in regard to the Bill, and then that the Bill be referred to a Select Committee with instructions to them to report upon it within a fortnight.

THE CHIEF JUSTICE said, the doubt which he had in his mind—but that might be discussed in Committee very well—was whether Section 1 of the Bill went far enough, and whether Section II did not perhaps go too far. Section 1 only gave the Magistrate power to inflict corporal punishment in cases of simple theft. The reason for the Bill being declared by the Preamble to be the destruction of jails, there might be many offences in the nature of felony other than cases of simple theft, but at the same time not so serious as to justify the infliction of capital punishment, or to call for that of transportation, which it might be very desirable to deal with by such summary punishment as corporal punishment. There would be the same reason derivable from the destruction of jails for authorizing such punishment in those cases as there was for authorizing it in cases of simple theft. For instance, burglary, as practised in this country, often differed very little in gravity from simple theft. In many cases, it was committed by the mere severance of a string or the cutting of a mat-wall, and was accompanied with no danger to life, or injury to person. He could put many other cases to which, for the same reason, the provision of this Section might be made applicable as well as to cases of simple theft.

With respect to Section II, he felt considerable doubt about including in it the words "or for any petty offence, such as abusive language, calumny, inconsiderable assaults or affrays." He was quite prepared, particularly if the operation of the Act were limited to certain districts, to accede to the suggestion of the Chief Commissioner of the North-Western Provinces, and to give the power of inflicting corporal punishment for offences against particular Sections of the special enactments named in the Section. Those would be offences threatening danger to the State and to the public peace. But it seemed to him very doubtful whether the Bill should give this power in the case of abusive language, calumny, and inconsiderable assaults or affrays. He could not find that, before Lord William Bentinck interfered with the infliction of corporal punishment in other cases, those offences had been, at least in this Presidency, so punishable. Section VIII of Regulation IX. 1793 provided as follows:—

"The Magistrates are empowered to hear and determine, without any reference to the Courts of Circuit, all complaints or prosecutions brought before them for petty offences, such as abusive language, calumny, inconsiderable assaults or affrays, and to punish the offender, when convicted, by committing him to prison for a term not exceeding fifteen days, or by imposing a fine upon him not exceeding fifty Sicca Rupees."

Under this, therefore, the imprisonment was limited to fifteen days, and, as far as he could see, was simple imprisonment. If a Magistrate were to inflict thirty stripes with a rattan upon a man because he was unable to pay the fine imposed, he would be punishing his poverty rather severely; for the man would doubtless feel thirty stripes with a rattan to be much more severe than simple imprisonment for fifteen days, independently of the degrading nature of the punishment.

The objections which he felt to the Bill would be very much removed if its operation were limited to those districts in which, by reason of the destruction of jails, there was an absolute necessity for administering this rough kind of justice instead of the regular punishment of imprisonment.

Mr. ELIOTT begged to direct the attention of the Honorable and learned Mover of the Bill to Standing Order No. LXX, which was as follows:—

"Any Member, however, may move a special instruction to the Select Committee immediately after its appointment, directing it to submit forthwith a preliminary Report, suggesting any alterations which it may deem expedient to make in the Bill previous to the publication thereof in the *Calcutta Gazette.* If such preliminary Report of the Committee shall be adopted by the Council, the Bill shall be amended accordingly, and published for general information."

He wished to know whether the Honorable and learned Member would consent to the Bill being referred to a Select Committee with such a special instruction. He asked this question with reference to the observations of the Honorable and learned Chief Justice, in which, for the most part, he entirely concurred, and, concurring therein, he could hardly bring himself to vote for the second reading of the Bill as it stood, except on the understanding that it would be referred to a Select Committee for a Report preliminary to publication; for those observations went to confirm his own impression that the Bill went farther than was necessary on the grounds stated for it—an impression which he believed was shared by other Members.

Mr. PEACOCK said, he did not see any necessity for referring the Bill to a Select Committee for the purpose of amending it previous to publication. He did not propose to have the Bill published.

Mr. ELIOTT said, the Bill was considered by several Members open to considerable objection, all which objections might be removed before the Council committed itself to the Bill by publishing it in the *Gazette* in its present shape.

His main objection to the Bill was that, whereas the reasons given for it in the Preamble were only local and temporary, the Bill itself was general and permanent. The first reason recited in the Preamble, was "the destruction of the jails in many parts of India, and the consequent want of prison-discipline." But this reason did not apply to the greater part or the whole of Bengal, or to Madras, or to Bombay.

The first provision contained in the Bill was a provision authorizing the infliction of corporal punishment in cases of simple theft. Surely, that was a matter which, if there was no pressing reason to the contrary, had better be considered in connection with the Penal Code. The same remark applied to the provision made by Section 11, which authorized the infliction of corporal punishment for (among certain other offences) abusive language, calumny, and inconsiderable assaults or affrays. It was quite clear that no pressing reason for applying corporal punishment in these cases existed either in Bengal, or at Madras, or at Bombay, if any did exist in the North-Western Provinces. The cause of the necessity in the North-Western Provinces was stated to be the destruction of jails. But the Council did not know to what extent jails in those Provinces had been destroyed. At all events, arrangements might be made for replacing all those which had been destroyed. He thought it unadvisable, therefore, that the Council should, in such a question, commit itself to a permanent and general measure when the actual exigency could be met by a temporary and local one

THE CHIEF JUSTICE said, he confessed he thought that no great harm would be done by reading the Bill a second time now, and publishing it in the ordinary course. The questions raised by the Honorable Member for Madras might, at the same time, be considered in Committee. They were really questions of detail rather than of principle; and all were agreed that a Bill of some kind on this subject was necessary. It did appear to him, therefore, that the course he suggested might be adopted with advantage. He did not think that, in assenting to the second reading to-day, any Honorable Member would be pledged to vote for it in its present shape on the Motion for the third reading, or precluded from proposing such amendments in it in Committee as he might consider expedient.

MR. CURRIE said, he concurred with the Honorable Member for Madras in the observations which he had made. It did not seem to him that the point at issue was, as suggested by the Honorable and Learned Chief Justice, a matter of detail. It surely was not a matter of detail whether a Bill should be a temporary and local measure, or whether it should be a general and permanent one. That seemed to him to be essentially a question of principle; and, therefore, he thought that the course suggested by the Honorable Member for Madras was a right and proper one.

For his own part, he thought that corporal punishment might with advantage be substituted for imprisonment with respect to certain offences, but he did not think the offences selected in the Bill the only or perhaps the most appropriate ones to which such punishment could properly be made applicable. But the question was a large one, requiring careful consideration; and he thought that the proper opportunity for considering it would be in settling the Penal Code. If, therefore, the Bill was to be read a second time to-day, he should prefer that it be referred to a Select Committee for preliminary Report, as proposed by the Honorable Member for Madras. At any rate, it must be understood, that, in assenting to the second reading, the Council did not pledge itself to accept the Bill as a permanent and general measure, but might, if it thought expedient, insert amendments in Committee with the view of making it temporary and local

MR. PEACOCK said, he thought that the better course would be to take the opinion of the Council now as to whether the Bill should be read a second time or not. It certainly was not his intention to refer the Bill to a Select Committee for the purpose of being amended previously to publication. He did not think that there was any reason for taking it out of the usual course in that way. The only principle to which Honorable Members would be bound by voting for the second reading was that corporal punishment was a proper punishment in some cases. If any Honorable Member considered that it was an improper punishment to inflict in any case, it would be his duty to vote against the second reading; but if he considered that it was a proper punishment to inflict in certain cases, his voting for the second reading would not commit him to the opinion that it was a proper punishment to inflict in every case specified in the Bill.

With respect to the recitals in the Preamble, the first was as follows :—

"Whereas, in consequence of the destruction of the jails in many parts of India, and the consequent want of prison-discipline, it is expedient to substitute corporal punishment for imprisonment in cases of simple theft."

The Council had already recognized and adopted the principle that corporal punishment was a proper punishment in cases of theft in which the value of the property stolen did not exceed fifty Rupees. Having done that, he could not see what objection it could have to that punishment in cases of theft in which the value of the property stolen exceeded fifty Rupees. If corporal punishment was improper in cases of theft involving more than fifty Rupees on the ground that it was a degrading punishment, surely, it was equally improper on that ground in cases of theft involving less than fifty Rupees. There was no good reason why a man who stole sixty Rupees ought not to be degraded just as much as a man who stole one Rupee. The Honorable Member for Madras was himself one of those who had voted for the insertion of the Clause authorizing corporal punishment in the Police Act.

If it were considered that the corporal punishment proposed by the Bill was improper in cases of simple theft on the ground that thirty stripes with a rattan was an insufficient punishment in which the property stolen was of large amount, that question might be further considered by a Select Committee in the ordinary course; but he did not think it necessary to refer the Bill to a Select Committee for the purpose of amending it previously to publication.

The next recital in the Preamble was as follows :—

"And whereas it is expedient in certain cases that offenders should not be imprisoned for the non-payment of small fines."

Was it right, or was it wrong, that corporal punishment should be inflicted in certain cases in lieu of imprisonment for the non-payment of small fines? He proposed that it should be inflicted in any case in which a fine should be imposed under the provisions of Section VIII Act XI of 1857, if the fine should not be paid forthwith. Section VIII Act XI of 1857 provided a fine not exceeding fifty Rupees, or imprisonment for a period not exceeding six months, for unlawful possession of arms in districts ordered by Government to be disarmed. He also proposed that it should be lawful to inflict corporal punishment in cases of non-payment of fines imposed under the provisions of Sections XXII and XXV of the Arms Act No. XXVIII of 1857. The former of these Sections provided imprisonment with or without hard labor for a term not exceeding two years, and a fine not exceeding five thousand Rupees, for wilfully neglecting to give notice of possession of ammunition in certain cases; and the latter provided imprisonment with or without hard labor for a term not exceeding two years, in addition to any other penalty which might be awarded under the Act, for not producing or for concealing arms or ammunition when search was made. Now, the question was, ought persons convicted under these Sections to be imprisoned if they did not pay the fine imposed? The Council had been told by the Chief Commissioner of the North-Western Provinces that it would be impossible to carry out these provisions in those Provinces unless corporal punishment were allowed to be inflicted in lieu of, or in addition to, fine and imprisonment. If it would be impossible to carry out these provisions in the North-Western Provinces unless corporal punishment were allowed, it would be equally impossible to carry out the provisions of Section VIII of Act XI of 1857 in any district which the Government might order to be disarmed. If the Government should think it right, under the provisions of Act XI of 1857, to prohibit the possession of arms in certain parts of the country—and he thought that it would be necessary to do so—it would be almost impossible to imprison every one who neglected to pay a fine imposed upon him for endeavoring to evade the law. The question, therefore, resolved itself into this—were such offenders to go unpunished, or was corporal punishment to be permitted, under the circumstances? He did not contend that corporal punishment was absolutely a proper punishment for refusing to deliver up arms, or for carrying them contrary to law: but under the circumstances stated by the Chief Commissioner of the North-Western Provinces, he thought that corporal punishment ought to be permitted in such cases. For the same reason, he thought that it would be better to authorize the infliction of corporal punishment in default of payment of small fines in certain cases, than to overcrowd the jails, or to inflict imprisonment, when they had not the means of carrying out a proper system of prison-discipline. Whether the Council would agree with him in this opinion, he did not know; but, in moving for the second reading of the Bill, he did not ask them to pledge themselves to the details of it. All he asked them to declare was that corporal punishment was a proper punishment to inflict in some cases, without committing themselves to any opinion as to what those cases were.

In conclusion, he would repeat that he did not think it necessary to take this Bill out of the ordinary rules, and to refer it to a Select Committee in order that they might say, before it was published, whether it went too far in some cases, or not far enough in others. That would be the duty of the Select Committee, to whom the Bill would be referred; and he thought it was not necessary that, previously to publication, the Bill should be put into such a shape that the Council might be prepared to say to the world—"Here is the Bill as we have finally determined to pass it." He should, therefore, press his Motion for the second reading.

THE CHIEF JUSTICE said, he wished, before the vote was taken, to remind Honorable Members that this discussion had been rather irregularly mooted. He did not think it was right to put it to any Honorable Member—"Will you consent to a certain something being done to the Bill after the second reading? If you will not, I shall vote against the second reading." The second reading of a Bill ought to be determined independently of any thing to be done to it at a subsequent stage. The question whether this Bill should now be read a second time, and that which the Honorable Member for Madras had raised, were two distinct questions, and ought to be determined on their own respective merits. The latter should be raised by a specific Motion, or by way of amendment on the Motion to refer the Bill to a Select Committee.

MR. PEACOCK said, he had only spoken in reply to the question which the Honorable Member for Madras had asked.

The Motion for the second reading was then put and carried, and the Bill read a second time.

ESCAPED OFFENDERS.

MR. PEACOCK moved that the Bill "for the punishment of certain offenders who have escaped from Jail, and of persons who shall knowingly harbour such offenders" be now read a second time.

The Motion was carried, and the Bill read a second time.

DELHI AND MEERUT.

MR. PEACOCK moved that the Standing Orders be suspended to enable him to proceed with the Bill "to remove from the operation of the general Laws and Regulations the Delhi Territory and the Meerut Division, or such parts thereof as the Governor-General in Council shall place under the administration of the Chief Commissioner of the Punjab."

THE CHIEF JUSTICE seconded the Motion, which was then agreed to.

MR. PEACOCK moved that the above Bill be referred to a Select Committee consisting of the Vice-President, Mr. Harington, and the Mover, with an instruction to report thereon after six weeks.

Agreed to.

ESCAPED OFFENDERS.

MR. PEACOCK moved that the Standing Orders be suspended to enable him to proceed with the Bill "for the punishment of certain offenders who have escaped from Jail, and of persons who shall knowingly harbour such offenders."

THE CHIEF JUSTICE seconded the Motion, which was then agreed to.

MR. PEACOCK moved that the above Bill be referred to a Select Committee consisting of Mr. Currie, Mr. Harington, and the Mover, with an instruction to report thereon within a fortnight.

Agreed to.

CORPORAL PUNISHMENT.

MR. PEACOCK moved that the Standing Orders be suspended to enable him to proceed with the Bill "to authorize the infliction of corporal punishment in certain cases."

THE CHIEF JUSTICE seconded the Motion, which was then agreed to.

MR. PEACOCK moved that the above Bill be referred to a Select Committee consisting of the Chief Justice, Mr. Eliott, Mr. Currie, Mr. Harington, and the Mover, with an instruction to report thereon after six weeks.

MR. ELIOTT moved as an amendment that the words "with an instruction to report thereon after six weeks" be left out of the question, and that the words "with a special instruction to submit forthwith a preliminary Report suggesting any alterations which it may deem expedient to make in the Bill previously to its publication in the *Calcutta Gazette*" be substituted for them. Though this was not an ordinary course, it certainly was not an irregular one, because it was prescribed in the Rules for Bills the general principles of which required to be maturely considered before publication. He thought this a case requiring such consideration. His objection to the Bill was that it was general and permanent, whereas he thought it should be local and temporary. It did not appear to him that it would be competent to any Member of the Select Committee to say in Committee—"I object to the Bill, because it is general and permanent, and I propose that it be altered so as to be made local and temporary," for that would be an alteration of principle. He (Mr. Eliott) agreed that the principle of corporal punishment should be adopted in certain cases; and he had intended to move as an amendment in the Penal Code that a provision making it lawful should be introduced into it. He was prepared to go farther in the application of the principle than this Bill went. He would apply it to other cases besides those of simple theft. But he would not, as at present advised, extend it, as this Bill did, to such petty offences as abusive language and inconsiderable assaults; and he thought that the proper time for considering the whole question of the expediency of adopting the principle of corporal punishment would be when the Penal Code should come up for consideration. Was there any necessity for authorizing corporal punishment over the whole of India while the Penal Code remained still unsettled? The necessity appeared to be only in the North-Western Provinces, and for special causes. These causes did not exist in Bengal, or at Madras, or at Bombay. The Preamble of the Bill said:—

"Whereas, in consequence of the destruction of the jails in many parts of India and the consequent want of prison-discipline, it is expedient to substitute corporal punishment for imprisonment in cases of simple theft."

Was the destruction of jails in the North-Western Provinces any reason for taking up the whole question of corporal punishment now? He said it was not. The Honorable and Learned Mover of the Bill, indeed, had quoted the Preamble as affirming generally that "it was expedient in certain cases that offenders should not be imprisoned for the non-payment of small fines," without reference to the destruction of the jails as a reason for it; but in his own Statement of the Objects and Reasons of the Bill, he had explained that

"It has been found desirable in the present state of the Country, and especially in the absence of the means of enforcing proper prison-discipline, in consequence of the destruction of the Jails in many of the Districts in the North-Western Provinces and other parts of India, to allow corporal punishment in case of the non-payment of fines imposed under the Sections above referred to, and also in the other cases mentioned in the Bill."

He was not prepared, at present, to go the length this Bill would go; he thought the subject required far more consideration than had been given to it; he considered that it would not be competent to the Select Committee to limit the Bill as he would limit it; and therefore he moved his amendment.

MR. CURRIE said, if the Honorable Member for Madras was correct in his belief that it would not be competent to the Select Committee to whom this Bill would be referred in the ordinary course to make the alteration—that was to say, to limit the operation of the Bill in point of time and locality, instead of leaving it, as it stood now, a permanent and general measure—then, he should certainly vote that the Select Committee be instructed to make a preliminary Report. He had understood the Honorable and learned Chief Justice to take the same objection that the Honorable Member for Madras had taken, and to intimate an opinion that it might probably be advisable to limit the operation of the Bill; and he (Mr. Currie), in speaking on the Motion for the second reading, had stated that if Members consented to it, they must be understood as reserving their opinion upon that point. But if the functions of the Select Committee to whom the Bill should be referred would be so limited that it would not be competent to the Committee to alter it from the permanent and general measure it now was, to a temporary and local one, if it should consider such alteration expedient, he should vote for a preliminary Report prior to publication.

He would add that the Honorable and learned Mover of the Bill had removed one objection of his in reference to the second reading, when he had stated that he did not propose to have the Bill published; for he should be sorry to see it published as it now stood.

THE CHIEF JUSTICE said, it appeared to him that Honorable Members were starting at a shadow of their own imagination in supposing that it would not be competent to the Select Committee to limit the Bill as the Honorable Member for Madras would limit it if they should consider it expedient to do so. Suppose this were the ordinary case of a Bill to be published for three months in the *Gazette*, and that during that period, representations were received from a particular Presidency or particular Districts shewing that it was, for reasons affecting such Presidency or such Districts, inapplicable to them. Surely, if the Select Committee felt convinced that these representations were well founded, it would have power to insert a Section limiting the operation of the Bill as desired, subject, of course, to the opinion of the Council at large when it went into a general Committee on the Bill. He had not understood the Honorable and learned Mover of this Bill to say that he did not propose to publish it.

MR. PEACOCK said, he did not propose to do so at first; but looking at the discussion which had taken place, he thought it right that the Bill should be published for six weeks.

THE CHIEF JUSTICE said, it had occurred to him that, assuming that the Bill was to be published, that was rather a reason against the course proposed by the Honorable Member for Madras, because it might be desirable, with reference to the reasons on which the Bill was founded, that it should be got through as soon as might conveniently be. If it were to be referred to the Select Committee for a special Report, and that Report were to be followed by the publication of the Bill for a period of time sufficient to admit of opinions and suggestions being sent in by the Public, the passing of the Act would be delayed to a certain extent. It seemed to him that, after the discussion which had taken place to-day, and which would go forth to the world, it would clearly appear that Honorable Members, in assenting to the second reading, were not pledged to the adoption of the Bill as a general and permanent measure; and that, therefore, there could be no objection to publishing the Bill in its present form, but that, on the contrary, that very publication would elicit opinions which might guide the Council in determining the question of limiting its operation.

MR. PEACOCK said, the Standing Orders provided that, upon a Motion for the second reading of a Bill, a debate might be taken on the general merits and principles of the Bill; and that if the motion was carried, the Bill should be referred to a Select Committee But he apprehended that any Member of the Select Committee, or any Member of the Council, who might vote in favor of the second reading, would not be precluded by his vote from changing his mind regarding even the general merits and principles of the Bill, and moving to insert such amendments in it as might, on further consideration, appear to him to be necessary, before it was read a third time and passed. It was very erroneous and unsafe, in his judgment, to suppose that he would be so precluded. The second reading of a Bill implied that the Council generally had no objection to the leading principles of the Bill. But if any Member should afterwards, in consequence of opinions elicited by the publication of the Bill, or for any other cause, change his opinion, there could be no reason why he should not present his views to the Council, and propose any amendments in the Bill which he might consider necessary. It was always more convenient that a Member should state his objections to the leading principles of the Bill at the time of the second reading. But there was nothing in the Standing Orders to prohibit him from stating his objections either to the principle or to the details of a Bill at any other stage. If the Select Committee on a Bill could not alter the principle of the Bill because its Members had voted for the second reading, a Member who brought in a Bill could not move any amendment in it which was opposed to its general principle although he might think it right to do so upon reflection, or after considering the opinions of others more intimately acquainted with the subject.

Under these circumstances, and especially for the reasons which had been adduced by the Honorable and Learned Chief Justice, it appeared to him that it would be mere waste of time to refer the Bill to a Select Committee for a preliminary Report previous to publication; and he should therefore press his original Motion.

The amendment was then put and negatived, and the original Motion was carried.

The Council adjourned.

Saturday, January 16, 1858.

PRESENT:

The Honorable J. A. Dorin, *Vice-President,* in the Chair.

Hon the Chief Justice,	P. W. LeGeyt, Esq.,
Hon. Major Genl. J. Low,	Hon. Sir A. W. Buller, and
Hon. B. Peacock,	H. B. Harington, Esq.
D. Eliott, Esq.,	

COTTON-FRAUDS (BOMBAY).

MR. LEGEYT moved the second reading of the Bill "for the better suppression of frauds in the Cotton-trade in the Presidency of Bombay."

The motion was carried, and the Bill read a second time.

IMPRESSMENT OF LABORERS, &c.

MR. PEACOCK moved that the Standing Orders be suspended to enable him to bring in and proceed with a Bill "to authorize the impressment of artisans and laborers for the erection of Buildings for the European Troops in India, and for works urgently required for military purposes."

GENERAL LOW seconded the motion, which was then carried.

MR. PEACOCK then moved the first reading of the Bill. He said, in the early part of this week, he had received a letter from the Lieutenant-Governor of the Central Provinces shewing the necessity which existed for securing compulsory labor for the erection of buildings for European troops in India. At Benares, buildings were necessary, though, according to the statement of His Honor the Lieut.-Governor, existing buildings to a great extent might be made available there. Barracks had to be provided at Mirzapore, for one Regiment; at Ghazeepore, for another; and at Allahabad, for four Regiments, and five companies of European Artillery. The buildings, to be of any use, must be constructed within the next three months, and it was almost impossible that this could be done unless some means were provided for obtaining compulsory labor. No return had been received as to the progress which had been made in the North-Western Provinces. No doubt, measures similar to those proposed by this Bill would be required there. The subject had been laid before the Governor General in Council. His Lordship in Council concurred in the views of the Lieutenant-Governor and considered that some means should be provided for securing compulsory labor. No one who knew the Lieutenant-Governor of the Central Provinces, or had listened to his speech on the Bill to amend the law regarding the impressment of carriage and supplies for Troops, could believe that he was a person to propose such a measure unless he considered it to be absolutely necessary. With respect to carts and supplies, it might be said that Government ought to provide them without impressment with the carriage necessary for troops on their march under ordinary circumstances; but no Government could have anticipated what had taken place in India during the last few months, or could have had in readiness barracks for the accommodation of the forty thousand additional European soldiers which it had been necessary to send from England for the protection of this country. That necessity had arisen; forty thousand additional troops were now here; and either they must remain during the ensuing hot weather without shelter, or barracks must be provided for them at once. He therefore now brought in a Bill to impress artisans and laborers for the erection of buildings for European troops in India and for works urgently required for Military purposes.

Section I provided that—

"In any District or place to which the provisions of this Act shall be extended by order of the Governor-General in Council or of the Executive Government of any Presidency or place, it shall be lawful for any Officer or Officers authorized in that behalf by the Governor-General in Council or by such Executive Government as aforesaid, to impress native artisans and laborers of any sort which in the judgment of such Officer or Officers may be necessary for the erection or completion of any Building required for the accommodation of European Troops, or for the collection, preparation, or manufacture of materials for that purpose, or for any other work connected with the erection or completion of such Building; and also to impress such boats, carts, bullocks, or other animals as may be necessary in that behalf: and any such artisan or laborer, boat, cart, bullock, or other animal may be so impressed whether such artisan or laborer shall be under a contract to work for, or such boat, cart, bullock, or other animal shall have been previously let to hire to, any private person or not."

Section II provided that—

"No action or other proceeding shall be commenced or prosecuted against the East India Company, or against Government, or against the Officer ordering the impressment, or against any person acting in his aid or under his orders, for any thing done in pursuance of this Act; nor shall any person who shall be impressed, or whose property shall be impressed, under the provisions of this Act, be liable to any action or proceeding for the non-performance of any contract which he shall have entered into, and which he shall be prevented from completing, by reason of such impressment or of any thing done under the authority of this Act."

This protection being extended, it was but reasonable that compensation should be made by Government for any damage which might be sustained by breaches of contract occasioned by impressment. The Bill accordingly provided that—

"If any person with whom any contract shall have been entered into for the personal labor or services of any person impressed under this Act, or for the hire of any boat, cart, bullock, or other animal which may be so impressed, shall sustain damage by reason of any breach of such contract occasioned by any such impressment, or of any thing done under the authority of this Act, he shall be entitled to full compensation for such damage, to be paid out of the General Treasury."

The Bill next provided that the claimant should send in to the Officer by whom or under whose orders the impressment should be made, a written demand stating the terms of the contract for the breach of which he claimed compensation, the period for which the contract was entered into, the amount of advances (if any) made to the persons impressed, the nature of the damage sustained, and the amount of compensation claimed; it also enacted that, in case any dispute should arise as to the amount of such compensation, it should be determined by arbitration; and he had inserted Sections regarding the appointment and proceedings of Arbitrators somewhat similar to those provided for the assessing of compensation for land taken for public purposes.

The Bill provided that every person impressed, or whose property should be impressed, under the Act, should be paid the full market-value of his labor, or of the hire of his property, as the case might be; the amount, in case of dispute, to be settled by a Magistrate.

The Bill provided a penalty for any person liable to be impressed under this Act who should abscond or conceal himself, or endeavor to abscond or conceal himself; or should be guilty of any device for the purpose of preventing the impressment of himself or of any boat, cart, bullock, or other animal; or should without reasonable cause desert the work upon which he should be employed by Government before the same should have been completed, or should refuse or wilfully neglect to bestow his labor upon such work to the best of his ability.

The operation of the Act was limited to the period of six months.

With these observations, he should move the first reading of the Bill. To carry it through its various stages in the usual course, would be to defeat the object of the Bill; and he proposed to move the second and third reading next week.

The Bill was read a first time.

At the suggestion of the Chief Justice, Mr. Peacock moved that the Bill be now read a second time

The Motion was carried, and the Bill read a second time.

MR. PEACOCK moved that the Bill be referred to a Select Committee consisting of Mr. Eliott, Mr. Harington, and the Mover, with instructions to report upon it within a week.

Agreed to.

COTTON-FRAUDS (BOMBAY).

MR. LEGEYT moved that the Bill "for the better suppression of frauds in the Cotton-trade in the Presidency of Bombay" be referred to a Select Committee consisting of Mr. Currie, Sir Arthur Buller, and the Mover.

Agreed to.

The Council adjourned.

Saturday, January 23, 1858.

PRESENT:

The Honorable J. A. Dorin, *Vice-President*, in the Chair.

Hon. the Chief Justice,	P. W. LeGeyt, Esq.,
Hon'ble Major General J. Low,	E. Currie, Esq.,
Hon'ble B. Peacock,	Hon. Sir A. W. Buller, and
D. Eliott, Esq.,	H. B. Harington, Esq.

The following Messages from the Governor-General were brought by Mr. Peacock and read:—

COMPULSORY LABOR (MADRAS).

MESSAGE No. 123.

The Governor-General informs the Legislative Council that he has given his assent to the Bill which was passed by them on the 2nd January 1858, entitled "A Bill to make lawful compulsory labor for the prevention of mischief by inundation, and to provide for the enforcement of customary labor on certain works of irrigation in the Presidency of Fort St. George."

By order of the Right Honorable the Governor-General.

CECIL BEADON,
Secy. to the Govt. of India.

FORT WILLIAM,
The 20th Jan., 1858.

PORT-DUES (CUTTACK).

MESSAGE No. 124.

The Governor-General informs the Legislative Council that he has given his assent to the Bill which was passed by them on the 2nd January 1858, entitled "A Bill for the levy of Port-dues in certain Ports in the Province of Cuttack."

By order of the Right Honorable the Governor-General.

CECIL BEADON,
Secy. to the Govt. of India.

FORT WILLIAM,
The 20th Jan., 1858.

ESCAPED OFFENDERS.

MR. PEACOCK presented the Report of the Select Committee on the Bill "for the punishment of certain offenders who have escaped from Jail, and of persons who shall knowingly harbour such offenders."

IMPRESSMENT OF LABORERS, &c.

MR. PEACOCK presented the Report of the Select Committee on the Bill "to authorize the impressment of artisans and laborers for the erection of Buildings for the European Troops in India, and for works urgently required for Military purposes."

STATE PRISONERS.

MR. LEGEYT moved the first reading of a Bill "to amend the Law relating to the arrest and detention of State Prisoners." He said, he had prepared this Bill in consequence of a communication which he had received from the Government of Bombay relative to some difficulty which had arisen in that Presidency with regard to the confinement in a neighbouring Mofussil jail of certain persons who had been arrested in the Presidency Town. The legality of such confinement had been brought into question, and it had been held by the Chief Justice of the Supreme Court of Bombay that there were great doubts respecting it. The persons in question had been arrested under Regulation XXV. 1827 of the Bombay Code, which was in effect the same as Regulation III. 1818 of the Bengal

Code. In 1850, some difficulty was experienced in Bengal in respect of prisoners arrested under Regulation III. 1818, and Act XXIV of 1850 was passed, which gave the Governor General in Council the power of directing the detention of persons arrested under that Regulation in any place or jail within the local jurisdiction of the Supreme Court. Before that Act, the Regulation had effect only in the Mofussil districts of Bengal, and the operation of Regulation XXV. 1827 was likewise limited to the Mofussil of Bombay. Doubts having now been thrown out as to the legality of the arrest of persons under these Regulations in the Presidency towns, and, therefore, of their subsequent detention in any place of confinement, it had become necessary to rectify these defects; and for that purpose he had prepared the present Bill, which he proposed, with the permission of the Council, to pass through all its stages at once by moving the suspension of the Standing Orders.

The Bill was a very short one.

The Preamble set forth that—

"Whereas doubts have been entertained whether State Prisoners confined under Regulation II. 1819, of the Madras Code, or Regulation XXV. 1827, of the Bombay Code, can be lawfully detained in any fortress, jail, or other place within the local limits of the jurisdiction of the Supreme Courts of Judicature at Madras and Bombay respectively; and it is expedient that such doubts be removed, and that the powers of the said Regulations and of Regulation III. 1818 of the Bengal Code be extended: It is enacted as follows."

He should have mentioned before that Section I of Regulation XXV. 1827 of the Bombay Code, while it authorized the apprehension and confinement of persons as State Prisoners, contained the following proviso :—"Provided that, with reference to the individual, such apprehension and confinement shall not be in breach of British Law." It was necessary that this should be rectified; because with such a proviso, the Bill, though extended to the jurisdiction of the Supreme Court, would probably give no power to arrest any inhabitant of the town of Bombay. He, therefore, proposed, by the first Section of his Bill, that the words "provided that, with reference to the individual, the apprehension and confinement shall not be in breach of British Law"—in Section I of Regulation XXV. 1827 of the Bombay Code—be repealed. They did not occur in Regulation III. 1818 of the Bengal Code, or in Regulation II. 1819 of the Madras Code.

Section II extended to the Presidency towns the provisions of the Regulations of the three Codes relating to the arrest and confinement of persons as State Prisoners.

Section III extended to the Governors of Madras and Bombay respectively all the powers for the better custody of State Prisoners vested in the Governor-General in Council by Act XXXIV of 1850.

Section IV declared all arrests or detentions of State Prisoners made prior to the passing of the Act to be lawful.

Section V empowered the Governor-General in Council to order the removal of State Prisoners in Madras and Bombay from one place of confinement to another.

He believed that the objects and reasons of the Act were sufficiently indicated in these provisions of the Bill, and it was not necessary that he should detain the Council with any further explanation at the present stage.

The Bill was read a first time.

CONFISCATION OF VILLAGES, &c.

MR. PEACOCK moved the first reading of a Bill "to authorize the confiscation of, or the imposition of fines on, Villages and other places for offences committed by the Inhabitants."

He said it appeared to him that, as soon as order should be restored, and the districts now held by rebels and mutineers should be re-occupied by Government, there ought to be some means provided for the punishment of offences proved to have been committed by the inhabitants of any village or district in cases in which the individual offenders could not be identified and brought to justice. He had, therefore, prepared for the consideration of the Council a Bill which provided that, in any case in which it should appear to a Magistrate that the inhabitants of any village or other place within his jurisdiction, or that any large number of the inhabitants of such village or place, had been guilty of rebellion, or of waging war against the State, or of any offence punishable under Act XVI of 1857, and that the offenders could not be identified and apprehended, the Magistrate might impose a fine on the inhabitants of the village, the amount of such fine to be fixed with reference to the means of the inhabitants, the nature of the offence, and the culpability of the offenders; and that if the owner of the village should not prove to the satisfaction of the Magistrate that he had used all the means in his power to restrain the inhabitants from the commission of outrages, the Magistrate might order that the village should be confiscated. The Council had already adopted, in the Act for the prevention of outrages in Malabar, the principle of fining villages for offences committed by Moplahs. By that Act, Magistrates were authorized to impose a fine upon an Umshum or village for the perpetration of an outrage by any person or persons belonging to it, and to assess the proportion in which the same should be payable by the inhabitants. But it would be found almost impossible, in the cases contemplated by this Bill, for Magistrates to assess the portion of the fine which should be paid by each particular inhabitant. The Bill, therefore, provided that the Magistrate might impose a fine upon a village; and that, if it were not paid within three months, the village might be confiscated and sold, or the fine be levied on the inhabitants by sale of their property.

He had also adopted a suggestion of the Honorable Court of Directors, and had provided by the Bill that, in case it should appear to the satisfaction of a Magistrate that any rebel, mutineer, or deserter, or any person who had been proclaimed by Government as a rebel, or for whose apprehension a reward had been offered by Government, or any person who had escaped from jail or other lawful custody, had been concealed or harboured within any village or place, or that any arms or other property belonging to Government had been concealed therein, the inhabitants should in like manner be liable to a fine. It was almost impossible that offenders of the class he had mentioned, or property belonging to Government to a great extent, could be concealed for a length of time in any village without the fact coming to the knowledge of the head man or officers of the village, and through them to the knowledge of the villagers. Provision had already been made by another Act for the punishment of individuals who concealed or harboured offenders. But that would not touch the inhabitants of a village in which offenders might be concealed or harboured. The object of the present Bill was to make it the interest of every inhabitant of a village to give information of the fact to a Magistrate; and with that view, the Magistrate was authorized to exempt from liability any person whom he might consider entitled to such exemption in consequence of his having given such information as had led, or was calculated to lead, to the apprehension and conviction of mutineers or any other heinous offenders, or to the recovery of arms or other property belonging to Government. He proposed to bring in, next week, a Bill to make persons liable to more severe and summary punishment than was at present provided by Law for knowingly receiving or concealing arms or other property belonging to the East India Company.

He had inserted another Clause in the Bill, which had also been suggested by the Honorable Court of Directors, to the effect that, wherever it should appear to a Magistrate that the Members of any particular tribe had committed a heinous offence or depredation, it should be lawful for him to impose a fine on any members of the tribe who might be residing in the neighbourhood of the place where the offence or depredation had been committed. The Honorable Court said in their Despatch:—

"With reference to the provisions of Section I Act XVI of 1857, we would further suggest the expediency of enacting that, when it shall be proved that any members of a tribe have been guilty of committing acts of violence or depredations, it shall be competent to the executive Authorities to inflict a heavy fine upon the whole tribe residing in the neighbourhood of the localities where such acts or depredations have been committed. We believe that, in the difficulty which will be experienced of procuring evidence for the conviction of individuals, a measure of the above kind will be the only means of reaching many who have taken part in the atrocities reported to have been committed by Goojurs and others in some of the North-Western Provinces."

Mr. Peacock

It appeared to him that a provision of this kind would be necessary, because there were many cases in which outrages had been committed by members of particular tribes, but in which the individual perpetrators could not be identified or brought to justice.

He would mention here that the general principle of the Bill had been submitted to, and approved of, by the Governor General in Council. He (Mr. Peacock) was responsible for the details.

In drawing the Bill, he had thought it right to provide for the case of heinous offences committed within a village, whether by the inhabitants of the village or not. Where any European was murdered or subjected to great personal violence in any village or district, and it was not proved that the inhabitants of the village or district had used all the means in their power for the prevention of the offence, or for the apprehension of the offender, the Bill provided that the whole village or district should be subject to a fine. It appeared to him that it ought to be made known throughout the length and breadth of this land, that the murder of a European was an offence which never could be forgiven or forgotten; and that if any European was murdered, or subjected to great personal violence, the inhabitants of the place where the outrage was committed should be held responsible, if the offenders were not apprehended and delivered up.

These were the main provisions of the Bill. It was unnecessary for him to detail the various Sections which he had inserted for the purpose of levying the fines which should be imposed. The Bill would be submitted to a Select Committee, and he had no doubt would receive much improvement from the experience of the Members whom he proposed to put on that Committee. As the Bill was of great importance, and required the consideration of those who were well acquainted with the practical working of measures of this description, he intended to refer it to a Select Committee of five Members, a Member for each Presidency being of the number.

The Bill was read a first time.

CONCEALMENT OF GOVERNMENT PROPERTY.

MR. PEACOCK postponed until Saturday next the Motion (which stood in the Orders of the Day) for the first reading of a Bill "for the punishment of persons who knowingly receive or conceal arms or other property belonging to the East India Company."

ESCAPED OFFENDERS.

MR. PEACOCK moved that the Council resolve itself into a Committee on the Bill "for the punishment of certain offenders who have escaped from Jail, and of persons who shall knowingly harbour such offenders;" and that the Committee be instructed to consider the Bill in the amended form in which it had been recommended by the Select Committee to be passed.

Agreed to.

MR. PEACOCK moved that the Report of the Select Committee on the Bill be read.

The Motion was carried, and the Report read at the table.

Sections I to IV of the Bill were passed as they stood.

MR. CURRIE said, after Section IV, it would be as well to provide expressly for making Zemindars and other holders of land responsible for intelligence of the resort of escaped prisoners to places within the limits of their tenures. By Regulation III. 1812 such obligation was imposed on Zemindars when lists of prisoners who had escaped were furnished to them, but it would not apply necessarily to cases under this Bill. He should, therefore, propose that the following, the wording of which he had taken partly from Regulation VI. 1810, be inserted as a new Section after Section IV:—

"All proprietors of lands, and all farmers, agents, and other persons having the charge or management of lands, are hereby declared accountable for the early communication to the Magistrates and Police Officers, of intelligence of the resort to any place within the limits of the lands held or managed by them, of any person in respect of whom there shall be reasonable suspicion of his being such convict or prisoner who has escaped as aforesaid; and every proprietor or other person as aforesaid who shall neglect to give such intelligence, shall be liable, on conviction before a Magistrate, to imprisonment for a term not exceeding six months, and to fine not exceeding two hundred Rupees commutable, if not paid, to imprisonment for a further term not exceeding six months."

A similar provision had been introduced into the Act passed by the Council a few months ago respecting the arrest of mutineers and deserters; and he thought it advisable to insert the provision in this Bill.

The Section was put and agreed to.

THE CHIEF JUSTICE said, before the Council proceeded to the next Section, he should, as the Standing Orders had been suspended, like to go back to Section II. That Section provided that persons within its purview should, on conviction of the crimes for which they had been committed for trial, be liable to be transported. The crimes referred to were "rebellion, mutiny, desertion, murder, attempts to murder, thuggee,"—all of which were capital crimes; "dacoity, robbery, belonging or having belonged to a gang of thugs, or to a gang of dacoits, or to a wandering gang associated for the purposes of theft or robbery"—all of which already by law involved the punishment of transportation for life; and "all crimes against person or property attended with great personal violence." As the Section stood, therefore, he thought that its effect might be misunderstood by persons executing the law. It would make the meaning rather clearer if the Section ran thus:—"shall, upon conviction &c., if not liable to any higher punishment, be liable to be transported for life."

Then, again, the Section as it stood, made the punishment of an escaped offender entirely dependent on his conviction of the crime for which he had been committed for trial, or in respect of which he had been charged. The consequence of this would be that a person might be guilty of having escaped from Jail, of having concealed himself from the Officers of Justice, and of having refused to make true answer to questions touching his identity, and that yet if, from want of evidence, he happened to escape conviction of the crime with which he was originally charged, he would be wholly free from punishment for having done that which it was the object of this Bill to repress. It had occurred to him, therefore, and to his Honorable and learned friend to the right (Sir Arthur Buller) that, in the event of the party not being convicted of the crime originally charged against him, he should be liable to some punishment for having committed the offences against which this Bill was directed.

MR. PEACOCK said, with respect to the first point, he thought it very desirable that some words should be added to the Section, to prevent any mistake. The point had been considered by the Select Committee, and they had thought that the Section as worded did not exempt persons convicted of capital crimes from the extreme penalty provided by the law, but only made them liable to transportation for life in case they should not be sentenced to the punishment of death. But, as the Honorable and learned Chief Justice had suggested, the meaning might possibly be misconstrued; and he should, therefore, insert an amendment in the Section which would make it clear.

With respect to the other point, the Section provided that where a person offended against the Act while only under committal for trial for any of the crimes mentioned in Section III, or while only under a charge of being guilty of any of them, he should, upon conviction of such crime, be liable to be transported for life. The person might not be convicted of the crime; and in that case, he would be liable to punishment under the existing law for having broken jail—that was to say, to imprisonment for three years; but if he was convicted of the original crime and the additional offence of breaking jail, he would, under this Section, if liable to no higher punishment, be liable to be transported for life.

The Honorable Member concluded by moving that the words "if not sentenced to the punishment of death" be inserted before the word "charged" and after the word "be" in the last line of the Section.

The amendment was agreed to, and the Section then passed.

Section V was passed as it stood.

Section VI was passed after a verbal amendment.

The Preamble and Title were passed as they stood.

The Council having resumed its sitting, the Bill was reported.

Mr. PEACOCK moved that the Bill be now read a third time and passed.

The Motion was carried, and the Bill read a third time.

IMPRESSMENT OF LABORERS, &c.

MR. PEACOCK moved that the Council resolve itself into a Committee on the Bill "to authorize the impressment of artisans and laborers for the erection of Buildings for the European Troops in India, and for works urgently required for Military purposes;" and that the Committee be instructed to consider the Bill in the amended form in which it had been recommended by the Select Committee to be passed.

Agreed to.

Mr. PEACOCK moved that the Report of the Select Committee on the Bill be read.

The Motion was carried, and the Report read at the table.

Section I of the Bill was passed as it stood.

Section II provided that no action or other proceeding should lie against Government, &c., for ordering impressment, nor against "any person who shall be impressed, or whose property shall be impressed under the provisions of this Act, or any other person."

THE CHIEF JUSTICE said, he had some doubt regarding the words "or any other person" ,which he perceived the Select Committee had introduced into the Section. He would illustrate the grounds of his doubt by supposing a case which was not very likely, perhaps, to arise in any of the districts to which this Act might be extended, but which one could still conceive to be of possible occurrence. A might be under a contract to B to deliver an article, or finish a house, on a particular day. He might be prevented from completing his contract by the impressment under this Act of the laborers on whose services he depended. B might be considerably damnified by A's failure to fulfil his contract. The Bill involved the principle of compensation; but, as it stood, compensation would not reach B, because Section II would prevent him from maintaining an action against A, his contractor, for breach of contract, since A had been prevented from completing that contract by reason of the impressment by Government; and Section IV limited the right of claiming compensation from Government to persons who had entered into contracts for the personal labor of any individual impressed under the Act, or for the hire of any boat, cart, bullock, or other animal so impressed. Therefore, although A might have recovered compensation from Government, B would be without any remedy for the damage he had sustained. It seemed to him (the Chief Justice) that it would be more just that B should be left to his action against A. If A should be cast in that action, and had really been prevented from performing his contract by the impressment of his laborers by the Government, the very payment of damages by him to B would be his ground for coming to Government for compensation under Section IV, and the amount of the damages would be the measure of the compensation he was entitled to recover. It might be considered that the probability of cases like that which he had put was rather too remote, and that the Section in its original form might lead to too many and frivolous claims for compensation. But on the other hand, the Section as amended by the Select Committee might open a door to a great number of frivolous defences. Whenever a contractor failed to perform his contract, and was sued, he might set up the case of having been prevented from performing it by the impressment of his laborers by Government. On the whole, therefore, it appeared to him that the words "or any other person" should be omitted from the Section.

MR. PEACOCK said, the amendment by the Select Committee was intended to provide for the case of persons who had entered into contracts to supply laborers. If a man contracted, as a Sirdar, to supply a certain number of laborers, and all his laborers were impressed by Government, he would be unable to perform his contract. Such a person ought not to be sued, but the Government ought to make good the loss sustained by reason of the non-performance of his contract. Probably, it would be better to limit the amendment by making it run thus:—"or any other person who may have contracted to supply laborers."

After some conversation, the Chief Justice said, there would be so much difficulty in carrying out the view of compensation which he had taken, and the Act was to have effect for so limited a period, that it would be better to leave the Section as it was.

The Section was put as it stood, and passed.

Section III provided that full market-value of labor or hire should be paid in respect of the person or property impressed.

MR. PEACOCK said, since the last Meeting of the Council, he had received a letter from Mr. Piddington, who took a great interest in coolie laborers, and had much experience in their management, respecting the mode in which persons impressed under the Act should be paid. Although the letter had been addressed to himself individually, he should bring it before the Council, because he thought that suggestions on such a subject from a gentleman of Mr. Piddington's knowledge and experience were worthy of consideration. Mr. Piddington said:—

"I make no apology for intruding this upon you in reference to the Impressment Bill, for we have all so deep an interest in its ultimate objects of providing good shelter for our brave fellows, that, trifling as any suggestion may be, it may always be worth listening to. And without some enactment as to the mode of payment, we may get coolies and workmen together, but we shall not *keep* them. And if we do keep them, it will be as unwilling workmen who require the rattan or the lash to obtain even a poor day's work from them!

"The Sircars and lower order of overseers, European, Eurasian, or Native, can, even now, double or treble their pay! And some can make a little fortune in three or five years. When they know that laborers can be impressed, they will treble or quintuple their extortions,* while the coolies and workmen will disguise and hide themselves every where to avoid the slavery and starvation to which impressment and the present system of payments by written papers will condemn them.

"I say nothing of the economy to Government of doing with 5 or 600 days' work what will now cost it a thousand; but I am sure, upon humane grounds alone, that every right-thinking man would be glad to strike a blow at the present plundering system of pen-and-ink registry of labor, which is bad enough now with voluntary labor, but will be intolerable with any system of impressment.

"I suggest then that two Sections, enacting as follows, may not only avert a vast amount of wrong, and its corresponding product of discontent, but may also be a source of great economy to Government.

A

"Every artisan, carter, workman, or other laborer who shall be impressed for employment on any Government work shall be paid, daily, for the day's work he may have earned by a metal token, of which token the number which may represent a rupee shall be on given days, three times in every month, exchanged for money, in the presence of the principal Officer superintending the work.

B

"And if any subordinate Officer in charge of any public work or duty whatsoever which is in execution by impressed artisans or laborers, shall fail, without a reasonable excuse therefor to issue daily to all such persons the tokens representing their day's work, such subordinate Officer shall be liable to a fine of one month's pay for the first offence, and to instant dismissal with the forfeiture of all pay due to him for the second offence; and such dismissed subordinate Officer shall be declared incapable of ever serving the Government again in the Department of Public Works."

This letter he had already submitted to the Select Committee, and the Select Committee, after due consideration, had come to the conclusion that it would be better to leave to the Executive Government the framing of rules for securing just and punctual payment to persons impressed under the Act; and, accordingly, they had inserted words to that effect in this Section. Daily payment had been found by experience to have worked very well. It had, during the last few months, ensured a full supply of carts for the transport of troops; and he had no doubt in his own mind that, if a proper system of payment were adopted, there would be less difficulty in obtaining laborers than was now experienced. At the same time, the Council might be throwing difficulties in the way of the Government if they definitively laid it down in the Act that laborers impressed under it should be paid daily; for there might be many circumstances to make daily payment inexpedient or impracticable.

As the Bill had been before the Public only one week, and there had not been time for suggestions from other quarters, he had thought it right not to pass by this Section without bringing Mr. Piddington's letter to the notice of the Council, and explaining why the Select Committee had not introduced the Sections suggested by that gentleman.

MR. ELIOTT said, the method by which payment to the laborers in public roads in the Madras Presidency was secured, as described in the Second Report of the Commissioners on Public Works, was well worthy of attention.

* The check of the fear of wanting victims from whom to extort being removed.

He begged to read some extracts from that Report:—

"The plan of paying laborers by means of tickets, is not new. It has been adopted by many Officers in charge of the construction of ghauts or other works where large bodies of laborers were collected, as a means of preventing the men from being cheated. But it has never, so far as we are aware, been worked so carefully, or so much reduced to a system, as in the Road Department. There are four sorts of tickets in common use, namely, the man's ticket, the woman's ticket, the cart ticket, and the quarry ticket. Bricklayers, carpenters, and stone-cutters, are also paid by tickets on large works, but not always on small ones, as workmen of these classes do not stay away, or change from one work to another, like the common laborers, and, being few in number, a nominal roll is easily kept.

"The tickets are of Card board, the several kinds divers in shape, so as to be readily distinguished, and with various particulars noted on them. The first three of the four sorts of tickets above named, do not vary in value throughout a division of road. They represent a day's hire respectively for a man, a woman, and a cart; but the quantity of any given kind of work necessary to earn a ticket, varies from place to place according to circumstances. Quarry tickets represent a certain quantity of material excavated or prepared. They vary in amount at the several quarries according to the ease or difficulty of working.

"But the nature of the material, the quantity, and the value are all noted upon the ticket. As respects the cart tickets, there is another particular to be noticed. The work done by the carts is bringing the material from the quarry to the road; but the distances to be travelled being unequal, the number of trips constituting a day's work varies at different places. Each quarry supplies a certain portion of the road; and for each quarter mile of this space, according to the distance from the quarry, there is a fixed rate of 1½ trip, 2 trips, &c. to earn a ticket. A cart-man is entitled to a ticket when he has made that number of trips; but some guarantee to him is necessary in the meanwhile that all his trips shall be counted. This want is met by subordinate tickets, styled Register Tickets, one of which is given to the cart-man on each trip; when he has made the proper number, he receives a cart ticket, and returns the register ticket. We will only add on the subject of the tickets, that all the several kinds contain such particulars noted on them respectively in initials and abbreviations as to enable the Overseer of the division not only to determine their value at a glance when presented for payment, but also to debit the proper Pygust or Conacapillay" (subordinate officers) with the amount, and to know what amount of work done or material prepared or carted to the road he ought to find as a return for the tickets cashed at every quarry, or in every mile of his division.

"The tickets are cashed immediately on being presented to the Overseer of the division, no matter by whom they are presented. If any mistake has occurred, though such seem to be extremely rare, the issuer of the tickets, and not the holder, is responsible. This instant and unfailing payment has given the tickets the value of money. They are readily taken, and they pass from hand to hand as a medium of exchange.

"Tickets are used to secure prompt and full payment to the laborers. They do secure it, and the readiness with which the men enter into the system, and the cheapness of the rate at which they willingly work—for no tahsildar or peon is ever asked to supply laborers to the Road Department, all is voluntary—fully prove the success of the plan. But it is obvious that the tickets cannot be cashed as soon as issued; for if any fit person were at hand to cash them, he might pay the laborers at once in cash, and tickets would be unnecessary"—

which, the Honorable Member said, it might be remarked in passing, would be the case in works such as were now contemplated—building at Stations, &c.

"The Overseer of each division visits every Station where work is in progress, periodically, as already said, and cashes all the tickets presented; but the holders need not wait for those visits, for the tickets are cashed whenever or wherever presented. In point of fact, however, the workmen find it more for their interest neither to retain the tickets till the Overseer's visit, nor to lose their time in going after him to get them cashed. They pay them away to the Bazaar men for the articles of their daily consumption, and they are readily taken, at a small discount, to cover the delay and trouble of getting them cashed. The greater part of the tickets are thus cashed to Bazaar men, and some of that class appear even to make a business of cashing them for the sake of the discount they gain, quite apart from the sale of goods. This arrangement is profitable to all parties, but care is required that the visits of the Overseers to cash the tickets should be more frequent than in practice they have sometimes been. To prevent misconception, it may be well to add that there does not appear to be any connection or common interest between these Bazaar men and the agents of the Department. Care should be taken, however, to watch against any such secret understanding."

This system, or something very similar, had been followed by the Railway Engineer with remarkable success. The effect was stated with a just pride by the Chief Engineer of the Railway in a Report dated 4th April 1856, an extract from which he begged to read:—

"We came as strangers, and were looked upon as strangers; but we have secured completely the confidence of the people. The difficulty which presented itself at first from our not giving advances, has completely disappeared; and we can generally command all the available labor in the district. I have known an Engineer accidentally short both of money and tickets, recall all the tickets which were out amongst any particular gang for re-issue, by merely giving in return for them an 'I. O. U. —— Rupees.' They knew the money was quite safe, all the payments being made by Europeans."

MR. CURRIE said, undoubtedly, it was very desirable that there should be a good system and proper rules for the payment of laborers; but it was to be observed that the scope of this Bill was very limited; and he apprehended that there was not the slightest intention of introducing it except in districts where a necessity for it had already been really felt—such as those of the North-Western Provinces, where the laboring classes had been dispersed, and where a large quantity of building had to be done on private account as well as on account of Government.

THE CHIEF JUSTICE said, the suggestions made were no doubt extremely valuable, and deserved to receive attention when made in the proper quarter. But the only question which the Council had to decide was, whether it should incorporate in this Act certain regulations respecting the payment of laborers, or whether it should leave it to the executive Government to lay down such regulations. He was very clear that, considering the variety of the circumstances of the districts to which this Act would be applied, it would be far more expedient to take the latter course, as the Select Committee, by the amendment they had inserted in the Section, prosposed to do, than to prescribe rules of that rigidity which must attach to every rule embodied in an Act of the Council, which nothing short of an Act of the same Council would have the power to alter.

The Section was then put, and passed as it stood.

Section IV was passed after a verbal amendment.

Sections V and VI were passed as they stood.

Section VII provided that disputes as to amount of compensation should be determined by Arbitration, and laid down rules for the appointment and revocation of the Arbitrator.

MR. CURRIE said, it seemed to him that it was hardly necessary to introduce into this Bill all the procedure for Arbitration provided by this and the ten following Sections. The cases which would arise, would be very few; and he doubted whether an Arbitration conducted in the manner provided by the Bill would be a very effectual mode of disposing of them. It was generally found very difficult to obtain awards, unless there was some Authority empowered to superintend the proceedings of the Arbitrators. The Act for the acquisition of land for public purposes, from which the Clauses in this Bill had been taken, subjected Arbitrators appointed under its provisions to the control of the Collector, and gave that Officer power to enforce the delivery of an award. It occurred to him (Mr. Currie,) that the more efficient way would be to leave all disputes as to the amount of compensation under this Bill to be determined by the Zillah Judge. At the same time, however, as the matter had no doubt been considered by the Select Committee, he should move no amendment if they were clearly of opinion that Arbitration was the proper mode of procedure for these cases.

MR. PEACOCK said, in these Clauses, he had followed as nearly as possible the provisions on the same subject in the Act for acquiring land for public purposes. Certainly, that Act empowered the Collector to compel an award; but he had not thought it necessary to insert a Clause for the same purpose in this Bill. He had thought that, if there was a dispute as to the amount of compensation, it would be satisfactory to both parties that each should appoint an Arbitrator, and that the two Arbitrators so appointed should elect a third to act in conjunction with themselves. But if the Honorable Member for Bengal, who had greater experience of the Mofussil, thought that there would be difficulty in obtaining an award, of which he (Mr. Peacock) had not been aware, he had no objection to the disputes being settled by the Zillah Judge, provided that this were done upon summary petition, and that the decision of the Judge should be final.

MR. CURRIE moved that all the words after the word "determined" in the 4th line, be omitted from the Section, in order that the following might be substituted for them:—

"in a summary way by the Zillah Judge, or other Officer exercising the powers of a Judge, on the petition of the claimant, or of the Officer under whose authority the impressment was made; and the decision of the Judge or other Officer shall be final."

The amendment was agreed to, and the Section then passed.

MR. CURRIE moved that the whole of the subsequent Sections, down to Section XVII inclusive, be omitted.

Agreed to.

The remaining Sections, and the Preamble and Title, were severally put and passed.

The Council having resumed its sitting, the Bill was reported.

MR. PEACOCK moved that the Bill be now read a third time and passed.

The Motion was carried, and the Bill read a third time.

STATE PRISONERS.

MR. LEGEYT moved that the Standing Orders be suspended, to enable him to proceed with the Bill "to amend the Law relating to the arrest and detention of State Prisoners."

SIR ARTHUR BULLER seconded the Motion.

Agreed to.

MR. LEGEYT moved that the Bill be now read a second time.

The Motion was carried, and the Bill read a second time.

MR. LEGEYT moved that the Council resolve itself into a Committee on the Bill.

Agreed to.

Section I provided as follows:—

"So much of Section I, Clause 1, of Regulation XXV. 1827, of the Bombay Code, as provides that, with reference to the individual, the apprehension and confinement therein referred to shall not be in breach of British Law, is repealed."

THE CHIEF JUSTICE said, the repeal proposed by this Section of the words in the Bombay Regulation was unquestionably necessary. These words would—even if there were not the further objection which arose upon the wording of the Act of 1850, which was in terms limited to the Bengal Regulation III. 1818—afford sufficient ground for insisting that the Bombay Regulation as it stood could not take effect within the limits of the jurisdiction of the Supreme Court of that place; because they constituted an exception which, from its terms, would embrace all the inhabitants of the Island of Bombay: all of whom, in what regarded their personal liberty, were governed by the Law of England. In the Mofussil of Bombay, in which alone the Regulation as it stood was operative, the exception would cover only British subjects. Now, it could not be intended to apply the powers in question to that class of persons; but considering their extreme susceptibility, and the possibility that the intention of the Act might be misconstrued, and that observations of that kind might find an echo in a higher legislative assembly than that which he was addressing—he thought it would be expedient to remove all possibility of misconstruction, and to qualify the repeal proposed, by adding the words "except as regards European British subjects.

MR. LEGEYT moved that the words "except so far as the said provision applies to European British subjects" be added to the Section.

The Motion was carried, and the Section then passed.

Section II was passed after a verbal amendment.

Sections III and IV were passed as they stood.

Section V was passed after an amendment.

The Preamble and Title were severally put and passed.

The Council having resumed its sitting, the Bill was reported.

MR. LEGEYT moved that the Bill be now read a third time and passed.

The Motion was carried, and the Bill read a third time.

MR. LEGEYT moved that General Low be requested to take the Bill to the Governor General for his assent.

Agreed to.

ESCAPED OFFENDERS.

MR. PEACOCK moved that General Low be requested to take the Bill "for the punishment of certain offenders who have escaped from Jail, and of persons who shall knowingly harbour such offenders" to the Governor General for his assent.

Agreed to.

IMPRESSMENT OF LABORERS, &c.

Mr. PEACOCK moved that General Low be requested to take the Bill "to authorize the impressment of artisans and laborers for the erection of Buildings for the European Troops in India, and for works urgently required for Military purposes" to the Governor General for his assent.

Agreed to.

NOTICE OF MOTION.

Mr. CURRIE gave notice that he would, on Saturday next, move for a Committee of the whole Council on the Bill "for raising Funds for making and repairing roads in the Suburbs of Calcutta and the Station of Howrah."

ADJOURNMENT.

Mr. LeGeyt moved that the Council do adjourn for ten minutes.

Agreed to.

The Council adjourned accordingly.

The Council afterwards met pursuant to adjournment.

STATE PRISONERS.

General Low returned to the Council Chamber with the Bill "to amend the Law relating to the arrest and detention of State Prisoners," and delivered it to the Vice-President, who thereupon announced that the Governor General had signified his assent to the same.

The Council adjourned.

Thursday, January 28, 1858.

An Extra-ordinary Meeting of the Legislative Council, called by order of the Governor General, was held this day.

Present:

The Honorable J. A. Dorin, *Vice-President*, in the Chair.

Hon. the Chief Justice,	P. W. LeGeyt, Esq.,
Hon'ble Major General J. Low,	E. Currie, Esq.,
Hon'ble B. Peacock,	Hon. Sir A. W. Buller, and
D. Eliott, Esq.,	H. B. Harington, Esq.

ABSENCE OF GOVERNOR GENERAL.

The VICE-PRESIDENT said, he had been entrusted with the following Message from the Governor General to the Legislative Council.

MESSAGE No. 125.

The Governor General in Council forwards to the Legislative Council extract of a Resolution passed this day, relative to the absence of the Governor General from the Council, and to the necessity for vesting the Governor General with certain powers during such absence.

By order of the Governor General in Council.

CECIL BEADON,
Secretary to the Govt. of India.

Fort William,
The 27th January 1858.

The extract from the Resolution referred to was as follows:—

Extract of a Resolution of the Government of India in the Home Department, dated the 27th January 1858.

Resolved.—That it is expedient that the Governor General should visit the North-Western Provinces of the Presidency of Fort William in Bengal, and other parts of India, unaccompanied by any Member of the Council of India.

That the Honorable Mr. Dorin be requested to take charge of and bring into the Legislative Council, with a view to its being passed into Law, a Bill to authorize the Governor General alone, during his absence, to exercise all the powers which might be exercised by the Governor General in Council in every case in which the Governor General may think it expedient to exercise those powers.

True Extract.

CECIL BEADON,
Secretary to the Govt. of India.

In accordance with this Resolution, which notified, agreeably to the requirement of the Act of Parliament, the decision of the Council of India that it was expedient that the Governor General should proceed to the North-Western Provinces unaccompanied by any Member of the Supreme Council, he had the honor to lay before the Council such a Bill as would enable his Lordship to leave Calcutta, carrying with him the full powers of the Governor General in Council; and proposed to move that the Standing Orders be suspended, in order that the Bill might be carried through all its stages forthwith.

Before doing this, however, he would state to the Council, very shortly, the circumstances under which the Governor General proposed to proceed to the North-West. The Council was aware that during the past autumn, when the communication with Agra had been entirely cut off, it was found necessary to depute a Member of the Supreme Council to assume charge of such of the districts as were accessible, for the purpose of establishing Civil Government within them. Accordingly, Mr. Grant proceeded, and took charge of those districts, under the designation of the Central Provinces. The arrangement was purely a temporary one. Shortly after, on the lamented death of the Lieutenant-Governor of the North-Western Provinces at Agra, it became necessary to make provision for the Government of the remainder of the North-Western Provinces, and it was considered desirable to do this rather in the shape of a Military Dictatorship vested in an Officer to be assisted by the Civil Power. This arrangement was also purely temporary, and was designed merely to meet the circumstances of the case as they presented themselves at the moment. Both measures had entirely answered the purpose for which they were intended; but the circumstances were totally changed, at present.

Owing to the exertions of the gallant troops under the orders of His Excellency the Commander-in-Chief, and the co-operation of Brigades from Delhi, the communications throughout the Doab were entirely re-opened, the dawk proceeded again with almost the same regularity as previously to the disturbances, and arrangements which were desirable before were now no longer necessary and were perhaps even inexpedient.

It was felt that the concentration of Civil authority in the North-Western Provinces was very desirable, and that there should be unity of action on the part of the Civil Government in aid of Military operations. In this view, it appeared to the Governor General proper that he should himself proceed and assume charge of the Government of the North-Western Provinces, and the measure would be attended with this advantage—that the Head of the Supreme Government would thus be in the vicinity of the Head Quarters of His Excellency the Commander-in-Chief, and at hand to support with the whole weight of the Supreme Government all the Military measures which the Commander-in-Chief might think it expedient to initiate.

There were other considerations which seemed to indicate that, temporarily at all events, there should be in the North-West a power larger than that exercised by a Lieutenant-Governor. It was impossible not to have observed, during the late disturbances, that Agra was not a good position for the seat of the local Government. It was completely isolated and cut off; and practically it was impossible to exercise the functions of Government from it with any effect. It would be in the recollection of some Members of the Council that, when the Governorship of the Agra Presidency was first established, the seat of the local Government was not at Agra but at Allahabad; and that it was subsequently removed to Agra, in consequence of the then Governor, Sir Charles Metcalfe (the late Lord Metcalfe), being vested with the whole of the diplomatic and political relations of the North-Western Provinces. But that reason did not hold good after Sir Charles Metcalfe vacated the Government; for, subsequent to that period, the maintenance of Agra as a separate Presidency had been held in abeyance, and the successive Lieutenant-Governors had not been charged with the political relations of the North-West and of Central India. The main causes, therefore, which had induced the establishment of Agra as the seat of Government, had long ceased to exist, and there were no other practical considerations of weight which rendered it eligible for that purpose. The intention was to remove the seat of Government to Allahabad; and the carrying of this change into effect would probably, as he had before observed, require the temporary exercise of larger powers than were possessed by a Lieutenant-Governor.

He might mention other reasons for

the progress of the Governor General; but perhaps that was unnecessary; for no one could doubt the expediency of the Governor General, vested with full powers of the Governor General in Council, being on the spot to support the Military Authorities in the great operations which were about to be undertaken.

All these considerations were of a temporary character, and he therefore proposed that the duration of the Bill should not exceed six months. The Governor-General hoped to be able to return in considerably less time; but as it was impossible to foresee precisely what might occur in these unsettled times, he thought it would be prudent to fix six months as the period during which the Bill should have effect.

With these observations, he should move that the Standing Orders be suspended, to enable him to carry the Bill through all its stages forthwith.

MR. PEACOCK seconded the Motion, which was then carried.

THE VICE-PRESIDENT then moved the first reading of the Bill.

The Bill was read a first time.

THE VICE-PRESIDENT moved that the Bill be now read a second time.

MR. LEGEYT asked, if it was not the intention of the Bill to except the power of making Laws?

THE VICE-PRESIDENT said, no such exception was expressly made in the last Act passed by the Council for the absence of the Governor General from the Supreme Council. The assent of the Governor General would be necessary to every Law, but the power of making Laws would remain in the Legislative Council.

MR. PEACOCK said, under the Charter, the Legislative Council might authorize the Governor General alone to exercise all the executive powers which might be exercised by the Governor General in Council, but it clearly could not authorize him to make Laws and Regulations.

THE CHIEF JUSTICE said, the exception of the power to make Laws and Regulations appeared in Acts similar to this passed between 1834 and 1855, but had been omitted from the Act passed in the latter year. That omission was probably in consequence of the existence of the Legislative Council as a distinct body from the Supreme Council. He was reminded by the Honorable Member for Madras, however, that the question had been considered and solemnly decided by the Council in connection with the Act of 1855; and it would be advisable to refer to the record of the proceedings.

THE VICE-PRESIDENT read the report referred to.

MR. LEGEYT said, he was not present at the debate of which the Report had been just read. Having heard the Report, he should move no amendment in the Bill before the Council.

The Motion for the second reading was then put and carried, and the Bill read a second time.

THE VICE-PRESIDENT moved that the Council resolve itself into a Committee upon the Bill.

Agreed to.

The Bill passed through Committee without amendment.

The Council having resumed its sitting, the Bill was reported.

THE VICE-PRESIDENT moved that General Low be requested to carry the Bill to the Governor General for his assent.

Agreed to.

THE VICE-PRESIDENT moved that the Council adjourn for a few minutes.

Agreed to.

The Council resumed its sitting pursuant to adjournment.

GENERAL LOW reported that the Governor General had given his assent to the Bill.

The Council adjourned.

Saturday, January 30, 1858.

PRESENT:

The Hon'ble J. A. Dorin, *Vice-President*, in the Chair.

Hon. the Chief Justice,	P. W. LeGeyt, Esq.,
Hon. Major General J. Low,	E. Currie, Esq.,
Hon. B. Peacock,	Hon. Sir A. W. Buller, and
D. Eliott, Esq.,	H. B. Harington, Esq.

The following Messages from the Governor-General were brought by General Low and read:—

ESCAPED OFFENDERS.

MESSAGE No. 126.

The Governor-General informs the Legislative Council that he has given his assent to the Bill which was passed by them on the 23rd January 1858, entitled "A Bill for the punishment of certain offenders who have escaped from Jail, and of persons who shall knowingly harbour such offenders."

By order of the Right Honorable the Governor-General.

CECIL BEADON,
Secy. to the Govt. of India.

FORT WILLIAM,
The 29th Jan., 1858.

IMPRESSMENT OF LABORERS, &c.

MESSAGE No. 127.

The Governor-General informs the Legislative Council that he has given his assent to the Bill which was passed by them on the 23rd January 1858, entitled "A Bill to authorize the impressment of artisans and laborers for the erection of Buildings for the European Troops in India, and for works urgently required for Military purposes."

By Order of the Right Honorable the Governor-General.

CECIL BEADON,
Secy. to the Govt. of India.

FORT WILLIAM,
The 29th Jan., 1858.

PORT-DUES (FORT ST. GEORGE).

MR. ELIOTT postponed the presentation of the Report of the Select Committee on the Bill "for the levy of Port-dues and fees at Ports within the Presidency of Fort St. George."

CONCEALMENT OF GOVERNMENT PROPERTY.

MR. PEACOCK moved the first reading of a Bill "for the punishment of persons who knowingly receive or conceal arms or other property belonging to the East India Company." During the rebellion, he said, a large quantity of arms and other property belonging to Government had been taken away by the mutinous Sepoys and others, and it was necessary to provide for the punishment of all persons who should be found to be knowingly in possession of any such arms or property. As the law stood at present, where any person purchased or received plundered or stolen property knowing it to have been obtained in the perpetration of robbery by open violence, or of theft, accompanied by certain aggravating circumstances described in the Regulation, the Magistrate might commit him for trial before the Sessions Court, and the Sessions Court had the power to sentence him—formerly, to fourteen years' imprisonment and corporal punishment—at present, to fourteen years' imprisonment and two years' additional imprisonment in lieu of corporal punishment. In cases in which the amount of the stolen property knowingly received exceeded the value of three hundred Rupees, the Magistrate was also bound to commit the receiver for trial before the Sessions Court. In other cases, the Magistrate had himself the power to try and punish receivers by imprisonment for a term not exceeding two years. Wherever arms, horses, or other property of that description belonging to Government had been taken away by mutineers or rebels, persons coming into possession of the property must know, or at least have good reason to believe, that the property had been obtained in that way. He had, therefore, thought it right by this Bill to authorize the punishment of such persons by transportation for life, or imprisonment for a term not exceeding fourteen years.

In order to avoid the necessity of committing offenders of this class to the Sessions Judge, he had also provided that they might be tried by a Special Commissioner appointed under Act XIV of 1857, and in cases in which a case was committed to and tried before a Sessions Court, the sentence was to be final.

The Bill was read a first time.

BOMBAY WATER-WORKS.

MR. LEGEYT moved that the Bill "to give effect to an agreement between the Government of Bombay and Her Majesty's Justices of the Peace for the Town and Island of Bombay and Colaba in relation to certain water-works in the Islands of Salsette and Bombay" be now read a second time.

MR. ELIOTT said, he begged the Honorable Member for Bombay would postpone the second reading of this Bill, in consideration of the short time for which the papers connected with it had been in circulation. The Bill was a short one; but it referred to a great controversy, the merits of which it was difficult to arrive at without a careful study of the correspondence relating to it.

MR. CURRIE said, the Bill had an immediate connection with the Bill for levying municipal taxes in Bombay. In fact, it was dependent on it. Perhaps, it might be as well to read the Bill a second time to-day, and refer it to the Select Committee on the Municipal Bill, with instructions to make a special Report upon it previous to publication.

MR. LEGEYT said, he thought the suggestion of the Honorable Member for Bengal a very good one. It was a suggestion which he had intended himself to make. Perhaps this Bill could hardly be said to be dependent on the Municipal Bill. The object of the Bombay Government was to have it passed independently of that Bill, and to let it remain standing in case the funds proposed to be raised under the Municipal Bill should fall short. But that and all other circumstances connected with the measure could be considered and made clear by the Select Committee on the Municipal Bill.

The Motion for the second reading was then carried, and the Bill read a second time.

CONFISCATION OF VILLAGES, &c.

The Order of the Day being read for the second reading of the Bill "to authorize the confiscation of, or the imposition of fines on, Villages and other places for offences committed by the Inhabitants"—

MR. PEACOCK said, it had been his intention to move the second reading of the Bill this day, and, after the suspension of the Standing Orders, to refer it to a Select Committee with instructions to report upon it before the usual time; but as he believed the Bill had been circulated only yesterday, and his Honorable friend opposite (Mr. Eliott) wished to have further time to consider it, he would postpone his Motion until next Saturday.

MR. PEACOCK gave notice that he would, on Saturday next, move that the Standing Orders be suspended to enable the Select Committee to whom the above Bill might be referred, to present their Report before the expiration of the period prescribed by Standing Order No. LXIX.

MUNICIPAL ASSESSMENT (SUBURBS OF CALCUTTA, AND HOWRAH).

MR. CURRIE moved that the Council resolve itself into a Committee on the Bill "for raising Funds for making and repairing Roads in the Suburbs of Calcutta and the Station of Howrah;" and that the Committee be instructed to consider it in the amended form in which the Select Committee had recommended it to be passed."

Agreed to.

The Bill passed through the Committee without any amendment, and, the Council having resumed its sitting, was reported.

BOMBAY WATER-WORKS.

MR. LEGEYT moved that the Bil "to give effect to an agreement between the Government of Bombay and Her Majesty's Justices of the Peace for the Town and Island of Bombay and Colaba in relation to certain Waterworks in the Islands of Salsette and Bombay" be referred to a Select Committee consisting of Mr. Eliott, Mr. Currie, Sir Arthur Buller, and the Mover, with an instruction to submit a preliminary Report on the Bill previously to its publication in the *Calcutta Gazette.*

Agreed to.

RECOVERY OF RENTS (BENGAL).

MR. CURRIE moved that a communication received by him from the Government of Bengal be laid upon the table and referred to the Select Committee on the Bill "to amend the law relating to the recovery of Rent in the Presidency of Fort William in Bengal."

Agreed to.

The Council adjourned.

Saturday, February 6, 1858.

PRESENT:

The Honorable J. A. Dorin, *Vice-President*, in the Chair.

Hon. the Chief Justice, Hon. Major General J. Low, Hon. B. Peacock, D. Eliott, Esq. P. W. LeGeyt, Esq., E. Currie, Esq., and H. B. Harington, Esq.

CORPORAL PUNISHMENT.

THE CLERK brought under the consideration of the Council a Petition of the British Indian Association against the Bill "to authorize the infliction of Corporal Punishment in certain cases."

MR. PEACOCK moved that the above Petition be referred to the Select Committee on the Bill.

Agreed to.

RESTORATION OF POSSESSION OF LANDS (N. W. P.)

THE CLERK reported to the Council that he had received a communication from the Officiating Secretary to the Government of the North-Western Provinces with the Draft of a Bill to provide for the restoring to the possession of their lands persons who have been dispossessed during the disturbances in the North-Western Provinces.

MR. HARINGTON gave notice that he would on Saturday next move the first reading of a Bill on the subject.

PORT-DUES (FORT ST. GEORGE).

MR. ELIOTT presented the Report of the Select Committee on the Bill "for the levy of Port-dues and fees at Ports within the Presidency of Fort St. George."

KURNOOL.

MR. ELIOTT moved the first reading of a Bill "for bringing the District of Kurnool under the Laws of the Presidency of Fort St. George."

The Governor-General of India in Council, he said, had given his sanction to a proposal from the Government of Fort St. George for bringing the non-Regulation district of Kurnool in that Presidency under the general Regulations, and for constituting a new Zillah, with a Judge and a Collector and Magistrate, to be composed of the said district of Kurnool, with the addition of the Talook of Punchapolliem, now belonging to the Zillah of Bellary, and the Talooks of Coilgoontla, Doopaud, and Cumbum, now comprehended in the Zillah of Cuddapah.

The Governor-General in Council, under the power vested in him by Section LIII Act VII of 1843, had authorized the establishment of a Civil and Sessions Court at Nundial in the new Zillah; and he (Mr. Eliott) had the honor to present to the Legislative Council a Bill for the repeal of Act X of 1843, under which the administration of Justice and the collection of Revenue were now conducted in Kurnool, and for bringing the general Laws of the Presidency of Fort St. George into operation therein.

The Bill was read a first time.

CONFISCATION OF VILLAGES, &c.

MR. PEACOCK moved the second reading of the Bill "to authorize the confiscation of, or the imposition of fines on Villages and other places for offences committed by the Inhabitants."

MR. CURRIE said, the only remark he wished to make touching the principle of this Bill was with regard to the time of its application. Section XI of the Bill provided that the Act should take effect only in those districts or places to which it should be extended by order of the Governor-General in Council, or of the Executive Government of any Presidency or place. He thought that the operation of the Bill should be limited in time, as well as in place. The provisions of the Bill, and indeed the principles upon which those provisions were based, were suitable to existing circumstances in certain parts of the country; but he thought they were not generally nor permanently suitable. The Bill referred to Act XVI of 1857, which was a temporary Act; and he thought that this should also be expressly a temporary Act. This modification would affect the principle of the Bill; but it might be made in Committee.

MR. PEACOCK said, he thought there was no objection to making the Act a temporary one; but the question might, of course, be considered in Committee.

The Motion for the second reading was then carried, and the Bill read a second time.

MUNICIPAL ASSESSMENT (SUBURBS OF CALCUTTA AND HOWRAH).

Mr. CURRIE postponed the Motion (which stood in the Orders of the Day) for the third reading of the Bill "for raising Funds for making and repairing roads in the Suburbs of Calcutta and the Station of Howrah."

PORT-DUES AND FEES (KURRACHEE).

Mr. LeGEYT moved that the Council do resolve itself into a Committee on the Bill "for the levy of Port-dues and fees in the Port of Kurrachee;" and that the Committee be instructed to consider the Bill in the amended form in which it had been recommended by the Select Committee to be passed.

Agreed to.

The Bill passed through Committee after the omission of Section VII. and the substitution for it (with certain necessary modifications) of Sections V and VI Act II of 1858; and, the Council having resumed its sitting, was reported.

CONFISCATION OF VILLAGES, &c.

Mr. PEACOCK moved that the Standing Orders be suspended to enable the Select Committee to whom the Bill "to authorize the confiscation of, or the imposition of fines on Villages and other places for offences committed by the Inhabitants" might be referred, to present their Report before the expiration of the period prescribed by Standing Order No. LXIX.

GENERAL LOW seconded the motion.

Agreed to.

PORT-DUES AND FEES (KURRACHEE).

Mr. LeGEYT gave notice that he would, on Saturday the 13th Instant, move the third reading of the Bill "for the levy of Port-dues and fees in the Port of Kurrachee."

CONFISCATION OF VILLAGES, &c.

Mr. PEACOCK moved that the Bill "to authorize the confiscation of, or the imposition of fines on Villages and other places for offences committed by the Inhabitants" be referred to a Select Committee consisting of Mr. Currie, Mr. Harington, and the Mover, with an instruction to present their Report thereon within a fortnight.

Agreed to.

Mr. PEACOCK moved that Mr. Eliott and Mr. LeGeyt be added to the Select Committee on the above Bill.

Agreed to.

NOTICE OF MOTION.

Mr. ELIOTT gave notice that he would, on Saturday the 13th Instant, move for a Committee of the whole Council on the Bill "for the levy of Port-dues and fees at Ports within the Presidency of Fort St. George."

The Council adjourned.

Saturday, February 13, 1858.

PRESENT:

The Honorable J. A. Dorin, *Vice-President*, in the Chair.

Hon. Chief Justice,	P. W. LeGeyt, Esq.,
Hon. Major Genl. J. Low,	E. Currie, Esq.,
Hon. B. Peacock,	Hon. Sir A. W. Buller
D. Eliott, Esq.,	and
	H. B. Harington, Esq.

RESTORATION OF POSSESSION OF LANDS (N. W. P.)

Mr. HARINGTON moved the first reading of a Bill "to facilitate the recovery of land and other real property, of which possession may have been wrongfully taken during the recent disturbances in the North-Western Provinces of the Presidency of Bengal.

In doing so, he said from the correspondence which had lately been received from the Officiating Secretary to the Chief Commissioner at Agra, as reported to the Council on Saturday last, as well as from information derived from other quarters, it appeared that, since the breaking out of the mutiny in the Native Army of Bengal in the month of May last, there had been considerable unauthorized disturbance of possession of land and other real property in some of the districts in the North-Western

Provinces. Indeed, to such an extent had this been the case, that in one of the districts through which he had passed in his recent journey from Agra to Calcutta, he had been informed that, during the comparatively short interval that had elapsed since the period just mentioned, nearly one-half of the entire Zillah had changed hands. The parties whose possession had been thus wrongfully disturbed, had been chiefly persons who had acquired their title to the property at public sales, held either for the recovery of arrears of Government Revenue, or in execution of decrees of the Civil Courts; and their title to the property so sold to them had never been called in question. The persons by whom they had been dispossessed, had been, for the most part, the old or former owners, whose proprietary right having become extinguished, they had continued to reside on the land as cultivators, though, in consideration of their former position, they had not unfrequently been allowed more favorable terms, as regarded the rate of rent taken from them, than ordinary ryots or tenants at will. These persons, probably imagining that our rule was drawing to a close, and that in all probability it would soon cease altogether, took advantage of the temporary suspension of authority to eject the parties who were in legal possession of the property which formerly belonged to themselves, and had re-established their own possession therein. In many instances, the ouster had been attended with acts of great personal violence, for which all concerned were of course liable to severe punishment; but there was reason to apprehend that great difficulty would be experienced in obtaining reliable proof for the identification and conviction of individual offenders. There could be no doubt, however, that, in nearly every case, the act of dispossession, or of assumption of possession, having been without authority of law, was wrongful; and he had, therefore, used that term in the Title of the Bill which he was desirous of introducing, in preference to the word "forcible." He might here mention that it was the opinion of several old and experienced officers, that in allowing the compulsory sale of land in satisfaction of money-decrees, we had acted unwisely, and without a due regard to native feeling and custom. It was alleged that the practice, if not altogether unknown in Native States, was rarely, if ever, resorted to in them; and the frequency with which such sales had taken place under our system, was said to have made our rule very unpopular amongst the people. It was also objected that, by removing the old landholders from the position which they had so long held, we had deprived ourselves of the support which they were able to afford us in times of trouble such as we had lately passed through; and that the new men, who had taken their places, having no local influence, and being looked upon with dislike by the old proprietors and the ryots generally, were elements rather of weakness than of strength. There might be, and, no doubt, there was some force in these objections; but this was clearly not the time for entering into the large and important questions which were involved in them. What the Council had to consider was, whether parties who, in a time of anarchy and disorder, had been wrongfully turned out of property of which they were in legal possession under a title acquired from ourselves, or in conformity with our Regulations, had not a just claim upon the Government, now that order and public tranquillity were being rapidly re-established, to be restored at once to the state in which they were at the time the mutiny broke out; and, assuming that upon this point there could be no difference of opinion, it then remained to consider and determine in what mode the redress to which these parties were entitled, could be best afforded.

The local Civil Courts, as at present constituted, were, of course, fully competent to deal with cases of this description; but if the ousted parties were left to seek their remedy in them, it was obvious that they would be subjected, not only to considerable expense under the operation of the Stamp Laws, but also to great and vexatious delay before they could hope to recover their rights—a regular action of this nature, with the appeals allowed in it, usually occupying from two to three years, and sometimes even a longer period, before it was finally disposed of. It had been suggested that, under the provisions of Act IV of 1840 of the Bengal Code, the Magistrates were competent to reinstate parties whose possession had been disturbed during the period alluded to; but the interference of a Magistrate under that Act could be exercised only on proof of forcible dispossession, and then only when the complaint was preferred within one month from the date of dispossession. There were also other reasons why, in his opinion, the Act in question could hardly be considered as sufficient to suit the present state of things.

Under these circumstances, it appeared advisable to create a special class of Courts for the trial and determination of cases of dispossession of land or other real property which had occurred during the recent disturbances, and to invest the Officers who would preside in these Courts with a summary jurisdiction which would enable them to afford speedy redress and to punish the offenders without any great expense to the complainants; and the Bill of which he was now to move the first reading, had been prepared with that view.

It proposed to give the Government authority to appoint one or more special Commissioners for the trial and determination of cases of the nature of those under consideration, and to assign to the Officers so appointed such extent of local jurisdiction as might from time to time be deemed proper. The Commissioners would be at liberty to hold a Court at any place within the limits of their respective jurisdictions which might appear convenient for the trial of cases brought before them: and during the time that their appointment lasted, the action of the local Civil Court, in respect of cases cognizable by the Commissioners, would be suspended. On entering on their duties, the Commissioners would issue a proclamation calling upon all persons who might, without authority of law, have taken possession of any land or other real property since the beginning of May last, to surrender the same to the parties then in possession; and warning them that, in the event of their failing to comply with the requisition within the period allowed, and of its being afterwards proved, on the complaint of the ousted party, that they had wrongfully seized, and that they were still in possession of the property to which the complaint related, they would not only be compelled to deliver up the property and to account for any mesne profits that might have accrued during the period of their unlawful possession, but that they would also be liable to imprisonment, which might extend to seven years, or to fine, or to both fine and imprisonment. Looking to the time when, and to the circumstances under which, the dispossession had taken place, he did not think that these penalties could be considered as too severe, or as out of place in a Bill of this nature.

The trial before the Commissioners would be of a very simple and summary character. There would be no written pleadings beyond a brief plaint setting forth the names of the parties, their description, and places of abode, the title under which the complainant claimed to be in possession of the property at the time that he was ejected therefrom, and the date of his dispossession. Before summoning the defendant, the Commissioner would examine the complainant on oath or solemn affirmation in order to satisfy himself that there was probable cause for noticing the complaint. The defendant would ordinarily be required to attend the Court of the Commissioner in person; but it would be in the discretion of the Commissioner to dispense with such personal attendance on sufficient cause shewn. The Commissioners, having the parties and their witnesses before him, would go into the proofs adduced by the parties in support of their respective statements, and would make such further enquiry as might appear necessary; and if the complaint appeared to him to be substantiated, he would order the complainant to be reinstated and maintained in possession, and proceed at once to enforce his order, calling in the aid of the Magistrate if necessary.

No institution fee would be required from the complainant in the shape of Stamp duty or otherwise. Considering the circumstances of the country at the time the dispossession had taken place, he thought that the Government might fairly be called upon to exempt parties claiming redress under the proposed Bill, from the operation of the Stamp Laws; and as the decision of the Commissioner would be confined to the question of possession, it was not intended that there should be any appeal from his order, whether in favor of or against the complainant; but if either of the parties had any claim of right, he would be at liberty to institute a regular suit to establish the same, anything in the decision of the Commissioner notwithstanding.

These were the leading provisions of the Bill, and he now begged to move its first reading.

The Bill was read a first time.

KURNOOL.

MR. ELIOTT moved the second reading of the Bill "for bringing the District of Kurnool under the Laws of the Presidency of Fort St. George."

The Motion was carried, and the Bill read a second time.

PORT-DUES (KURRACHEE).

MR. LEGEYT moved that the Bill "for the levy of Port-dues and fees in the Port of Kurrachee" be now read a third time and passed.

The Motion was carried, and the Bill read a third time.

PORT-DUES (FORT ST. GEORGE).

MR. ELIOTT moved that the Council resolve itself into a Committee on the Bill "for the levy of Port-dues and fees at Ports within the Presidency of Fort St. George"; and that the Committee be instructed to consider it in the amended form in which the Select Committee had recommended it to be passed.

Agreed to.

The Bill passed through Committee without amendment.

The Council having resumed its sitting, the Bill was reported.

KURNOOL.

MR ELIOTT moved that the Bill "for bringing the District of Kurnool under the Laws of the Presidency of Fort St. George" be referred to a Select Committee consisting of Mr. Currie, Mr. Harington, and the Mover.

Agreed to.

PORT-DUES (KURRACHEE).

MR. LEGEYT moved that General Low be requested to take the Bill "for the levy of Port-dues and fees in the Port of Kurrachee" to the President in Council, in order that it may be submitted to the Right Honorable the Governor-General for his assent.

Agreed to.

STATE OFFENCES.

MR. ELIOTT said he had received a communication from the Madras Government forwarding a letter from the Advocate General of that Presidency referring to a trial held in the Supreme Court there under Act XI of 1857 (for the prevention, trial, and punishment of offences against the State), and in which the learned gentleman called attention to what he considered were defects in the Act. It did not appear to him (Mr. Eliott) that the defects alluded to, if they were such at all, required to be corrected; and he should, therefore, only move to lay the communication on the table.

The Council adjourned.

Saturday, February 20, 1858.

PRESENT:

The Honorable J. A. Dorin, *Vice-President*, in the Chair.

Hon. the Chief Justice.	P. W. LeGeyt, Esq.,
Hon'ble Major General J. Low,	E. Currie, Esq.,
Hon'ble B. Peacock,	Hon. Sir A. W. Buller, and
D. Eliott, Esq.,	H. B. Harington, Esq.

CONFISCATION OF VILLAGES, &c.

MR. PEACOCK presented the Report of the Select Committee on the Bill "to authorize the confiscation of, or the imposition of fines on Villages and other places for offences committed by the Inhabitants."

CORPORAL PUNISHMENT.

MR. PEACOCK also presented the Report of the Select Committee on the Bill "to authorize the infliction of Corporal Punishment in certain cases."

BOMBAY WATER-WORKS.

MR. LEGEYT presented the Report of the Select Committee on the Bill "to give effect to an agreement between the Government of Bombay and Her Majesty's Justices of the Peace for the Town and Island of Bombay and Colaba in relation to certain Water-works in the Islands of Salsette and Bombay."

MUNICIPAL ASSESSMENT (BOMBAY).

MR. LEGEYT also presented the Report of the Select Committee on the Bill "for appointing Municipal Commissioners and for raising a Fund for Municipal purposes in the Town of Bombay."

PORT-DUES (GULF OF CAMBAY).

MR. LEGEYT also presented the Report of the Select Committee on the Bill "for the levy of Port-dues in certain Ports within the limits of the Gulf of Cambay."

PORT-DUES (FORT ST. GEORGE).

MR. ELIOTT moved that the Bill "for the levy of Port-dues and fees at Ports within the Presidency of Fort St. George" be now read a third time and passed.

The Motion was carried, and the Bill read a third time.

MR. ELIOTT moved that the above Bill be sent to the President in Council in order that it may be submitted to the Right Honorable the Governor-General for his assent.

Agreed to.

NOTICE OF MOTION.

MR. LEGEYT gave notice that he would, on Saturday the 27th instant, move the first reading of a Bill to repeal Regulation VI. 1831 of the Bombay Code and Act I of 1836.

LUNACY (SUPREME COURTS).

MR. CURRIE moved that a communication received by him, from the Government of Bengal be laid upon the table and referred to the Select Committee on the Bill "to regulate proceedings in Lunacy in Her Majesty's Courts of Judicature."

Agreed to.

The Council adjourned.

Saturday, February 27, 1858.

PRESENT:

The Honorable J. A. Dorin, *Vice-President*, in the Chair.

Hon. the Chief Justice,	D. Eliott, Esq.,
Hon. Major General J. Low,	P. W. LeGeyt, Esq.,
Hon. J. P. Grant,	E. Currie, Esq., and
Hon. B. Peacock,	H. B Harington, Esq.

PATENTS FOR INVENTIONS.

THE CLERK reported that he had received from the Under-Secretary to the Government of India in the Home Department, a copy of a Despatch from the Honorable the Court of Directors with respect to the Patents Act, in which the Court desire that no time be lost in laying before the Council the Draft of an Act for the protection of Inventions, and that, when the same is approved of by the Council, it be forwarded to the Court, in order that the necessary steps may be taken for obtaining thereto the sanction of the Crown.

BOMBAY LIGHT-DUES.

MR. LEGEYT moved the first reading of a Bill "to repeal the Laws relating to the levy of Light-Dues at Ports within the limits of the Gulf of Cambay." These were enactments for the levy of Light-house dues by which Light-houses were maintained in and near the Gulf of Cambay. Provision for the future levy of these dues had been made in the Bill now before the Council for the levy of Port-dues in the Gulf of Cambay; and if that Bill passed, of which there was every probability, the enactments he now wished to repeal, would be useless. The Honorable Member concluded by reading the Preamble to the Bill and the enacting Clause.

The Bill was read a first time.

MARINE POLICE (MADRAS).

MR ELIOTT moved the first reading of a Bill "for the maintenance of a Police Force for the Port of Madras." The Bill, he said, was intended to provide for the maintenance of an additional Police Force at Madras for the purpose of protecting goods in transit between the shore and the shipping. For many years, the depredations committed in the boats employed in the conveyance of cargo in the Madras Roads had been a subject of grave complaint. In 1854, the Grand Jury made a presentment on the subject, and the Chamber of Commerce addressed to the Government a letter complaining that an organized system of robbery had grown up among the boatmen, which the existing Police Force was insufficient to repress. The Chief Magistrate, having been referred to by Government, admitted the evil; and, acknowledging it to be beyond his control with the means at his disposal, proposed as a remedy the establishment of a Marine Police, to be employed partly afloat and partly ashore. The Government of Madras submitted this proposal to the Government of India, with an intimation that the Merchants of the Port were ready to contribute towards the expenses of the establishment by paying the peons of the Force while engaged in guarding goods in course of importation and exportation. A good deal of correspondence ensued between the local Government and the Government of India, and the latter finally authorized the Government of Madras to apply to the Legislative Council for an Act to provide for the maintenance of the required Force by the imposition of a tax to be levied in addition to the hire on every boat employed in the conveyance of goods to and from the shipping in the Madras Roads, provided the Government were satisfied that the sum of one thousand Rupees a month could be raised thereby.

The Government of Madras, after consultation with the Madras Chamber of Commerce, being satisfied "that the estimate given by that body at three annas the trip, is within the mark, and will suffice to meet all ordinary demands for the purposes of a Marine Police," determined to propose that the tax should be fixed at that rate, and directed the Government Law Officers to prepare the Draft of an Act to sanction the imposition of such a tax.

The Draft of an Act for this purpose, prepared and finally settled by the Advocate General at Madras, having been sent to him by the Government of Madras, he had framed from it the Bill which he now presented.

The Madras Law Officers, being of opinion that the present Police Act for Madras did not give either the Commissioner of Police or the Police Force established under its provisions any jurisdiction beyond low water-mark, their Draft was framed so as to remedy this supposed omission, and accordingly contained provisions to make it lawful for the Commissioner and the Police Force to exercise within the limits of the *Port* of Madras, all such powers as were vested in them by the Police Act within the limits of the *Town*. It appearing to him, however, that the Law Officers were mistaken on this point, and that by the existing Law the Commissioner of Police and the Police Force were virtually vested with the powers necessary to enable them to act within the limits of the Port as well as within the limits of the Town, the Magistrate of Police being expressly vested with jurisdiction over offences committed within the limits of the Port, and the Commissioner and the Police being charged by the Act with the duty of bringing before the Magistrates all offenders subject to the jurisdiction, and the power given to the Commissioner generally for the prevention of crimes and the detection and apprehension of offenders necessarily extending as far as the jurisdiction to which the offenders were amenable, he had omitted those provisions. The Bill, therefore, as altered by him, contained only the provisions which appeared to be necessary to legalize the proposed tax intended to raise a Fund for the maintenance of the additional Force to be employed under the Commissioner for the purposes of the Act, assuming that such additional Force would be merely an extension of the Police Force constituted under Act XIII of 1856, and to direct how and under what check the tax was to be levied, and accounted for; to indicate the manner in which the Force was to be employed, and to prescribe penalties for hindering Officers in the performance of their duties; also to prescribe penalties for breach of the rules regarding the levy of the tax, and the returns to be made by the persons receiving it.

The tax, proposed was three annas for every trip made by a boat carrying goods, to be paid by the person engaging the boat, in addition to the hire, to the owner of the boat, who was to account for his receipts to the Commissioner of Police; and every boat so employed was to carry in it an Officer of the Police.

It was stated that the Draft Act having been fully discussed at a Meeting of the Chamber of Commerce, at which the Honorable Company's Solicitor had attended, its several provisions had met with the entire approval of the Meeting.

The last Section of the Bill provided that the Act should take effect from the day in which it should be notified in the Official Gazette that the Police Force had been increased for the purposes of the Act.

The Bill was read a first time.

CONCEALMENT OF GOVERNMENT PROPERTY.

MR. PEACOCK moved that the Bill "for the punishment of persons who knowingly receive or conceal arms or other property belonging to the East India Company" be now read a second time.

The motion was carried, and the Bill read a second time.

MUNICIPAL ASSESSMENT (SUBURBS OF CALCUTTA, AND HOWRAH).

The Order of the Day being read for the third reading of the Bill "for raising Funds for making and repairing roads in the Suburbs of Calcutta and the Station of Howrah" —

MR. CURRIE said, before moving the third reading, he wished to recommit the Bill, for the purpose of making an addition in one of the Sections. Since the Bill had passed through Committee—indeed, within the last week—he had received a communication from the Lieutenant-Governor of Bengal, with a letter from the Magistrate of the Twenty-four Pergunnahs, in reference to it. Mr. Fergusson said:—

"There can be no doubt that the proceeds of the carriage-tax will fall far short of the amount required for the annual repair of the suburban roads, and I regret that a portion of the difference is to be levied from the inhabitants in the form of a house-tax under the provisions of the Chowkeedary Act XX of 1856."

Mr. Fergusson went on to remark on the unpopularity of that tax, and rather deprecated any addition to it, at least at present, the tax having been very recently introduced. He said:—

"It is probably too late to regret the form in which this tax is to be raised. In my letter to the Commissioner dated the 4th of April 1856, I suggested tolls as the fairest mode of raising funds for repairing roads. I am still of opinion that by means of tolls a larger sum would be raised, in a fairer way, and with less dissatisfaction, than by the proposed Bill."

Upon that, the Lieutenant-Governor remarked:—

"Mr. Fergusson appears to be mistaken in speaking of the levy of tolls as barred by the proposed Bill. Tolls may still be levied under existing Acts of the Legislature, and the words 'proceeds of tolls' might conveniently be added in Section XXI of the Bill, as a source of income to be taken into account before recourse is had to an increase of the assessment under Act XX of 1856."

Of course, in the preparation of this Bill, the question of raising funds by means of tolls had been taken into consideration; but there had appeared to be a difficulty in the establishment of toll-bars in the suburbs,—about Bhowanipore and Ballygunge especially—and the Government of India had expressed a doubt as to the expediency of levying tolls within the limits of the suburbs. He himself was still of opinion that there were considerable difficulties in the way of levying tolls on these roads; but he agreed with the Lieutenant-Governor in thinking that the question of the expediency of raising some part of the funds necessary for the repair of the roads by the levy of tolls, might be considered an open question. It was doubtful, he thought, whether under the Law by virtue of which tolls were at present levied, it would be legal, if this Bill should pass, to levy tolls upon the roads to which the Bill referred. For Act VIII of 1851 authorized the levy of tolls only on roads which were made and repaired at the expense of Government; and by Section I of this Bill, the roads to which the Bill related were to be repaired from funds contributed by the inhabitants of the suburbs. Still, it was quite possible that it might be thought advisable to levy tolls at points in the immediate neighbourhood of these roads—as on the bridges, which were repaired at the expense of Government, or on the public roads leading into the suburbs—in which case it might be considered right that some portion of the proceeds of the tolls should be appropriated to the repairs of the adjacent suburban roads. To provide for

Mr. Eliott

such a contingency, he proposed to insert words in Section XXI which would enable the Lieutenant-Governor to assign any portion, which he might think proper, of tolls levied under Act VIII of 1851 to the repair of these roads.

With these observations, he begged to move the recommittal of the Bill.

Agreed to.

MR. CURRIE moved that the words and figures "out of the proceeds of any tolls levied under Act VIII of 1851 or" be inserted after the word "purpose" in the 24th line of Section XXI.

THE CHIEF JUSTICE said, he presumed that this Bill did not touch Act VIII of 1851, and that it left the Government the power of establishing tolls in certain localities. If they exercised that power so as to raise a double tax—that was to say, if they raised a tax from owners of horses and carriages on the ground that it was they who wore out the roads, and a further tax on the same class of persons by establishing toll-bars on roads where none existed now—they would be rather smiting the public on both cheeks. If the funds for the repairs of suburban roads were to be raised by means of tolls, one did not see why horses and carriages should be taxed more than any other property for the purpose.

MR. CURRIE said, this Bill gave Government no power which it did not now possess under Act VIII of 1851. On the contrary, it rather limited the powers which that Act conferred; because, as he had endeavored to shew, by the Act, it was only roads that were constructed and maintained at the expense of the Government that could be repaired from the proceeds of tolls, and the Bill took the roads to which it referred out of that category by declaring that they should be repaired at the expense of the inhabitants. The principle which he contended for was simply this, that, if toll-bars should be established under the powers given by the Act, in places leading to the suburbs, it was no more than just that some portion of the proceeds should be applied to the repair of the suburban roads.

MR. PEACOCK said, Section VIII of Act VIII of 1857 declared that "the tolls levied under the Act shall be deemed public revenue; but the net proceeds thereof shall be applied wholly to the construction, repair, and maintenance of roads and bridges within the Presidency in which they are levied." He apprehended that, under this provision, the Lieutenant-Governor had already the power of applying any portion of the proceeds of tolls levied under the Act to suburban roads; and he did not, therefore, see any greater necessity for inserting the amendment proposed in this Bill than in the Bill for Calcutta. If tolls were established on bridges, part of the proceeds ought to be applied to the repairs of roads within the Calcutta district; for as, on the one hand, persons would pass over the bridges for the purpose of using the suburban roads, so, on the other, would persons pass over the bridges for the purpose of using the Calcutta roads.

MR. CURRIE said, if, without any special provision, the Lieutenant-Governor had the power of his own authority to assign any part of the proceeds of tolls levied under Act VIII of 1851 to the repairs of suburban roads, the addition which he proposed might not be absolutely necessary, and he would not press his motion to a division.

The Honorable Member's amendment was put, and negatived.

The Council having resumed its sitting, the Bill was reported.

MR. CURRIE moved that the Bill be now read a third time and passed. The motion was carried, and the Bill read a third time.

CONFISCATION OF VILLAGES, &c.

MR. PEACOCK moved that the Council resolve itself into a Committee on the Bill "to authorize the confiscation of, or the imposition of fines on Villages and other places for offences committed by the inhabitants;" and that the Committee be instructed to consider the Bill in the amended form in which the Select Committee had recommended it to be passed.

Agreed to.

Section I was passed as it stood.

MR. LEGEYT said, before Section II was put, he begged to propose the introduction of a new Section. It had occurred to him that this Bill would be, as far as the confiscation of villages went, inoperative in a great measure where villages were held under *Khalsa* tenure. Almost all the villages in the Bombay and Madras Presidencies were *Khalsa* villages: and as to them, of course, the provision for confiscation would be a dead letter. But in these villages, there were two classes of Officers denominated Wuttundars, who enjoyed certain rights and lands free of all rent, in consideration of performing certain village duties, the chief of which were connected with Police and Revenue. The collection of revenue was generally entrusted to them. They were called respectively *Patells*, a sort of Deputy Magistrates, and *Coolkurnees*, or Clerks. These Officers held lands, and their tenures were of very ancient date. The offices were very much prized, and many of the Officers would rather part with their lives than with the lands they so held. These persons had considerable influence over their fellow villagers; and it was to them, assisted by the village Police, that the good order and well-being of the villages were entrusted. It appeared to him that it would be very proper to make these Officers responsible for any of the offences specified in Section I, and to provide that, if they should fail to shew that they had used all the means in their power to prevent their commission, their hereditary offices and rights should be forfeited. The risk of losing what was prized so highly, would be a strong additional incentive to these men to exert themselves and perform duties in times of trouble and disturbance. At present, the law would confiscate the offices and rights if the holders were convicted of any offence before the Sessions Judge; but there was no provision for such confiscation unless a conviction was recorded in the Sessions Court. He therefore moved that the following be inserted in the Bill as a new Section after Section I:—

"In like manner, if any hereditary Village Officer employed in the collection of Land Revenue, or in the Police, should not prove to the satisfaction of a Magistrate that he used all the means in his power to prevent the commission of any of the offences mentioned or referred to in the preceding Section by the Inhabitants of any Village in which he holds such hereditary office, the Magistrate may declare such hereditary office to be forfeited, and may confiscate any land or rights held by him in virtue of such office."

The Section was agreed to.

Mr. LeGeyt

Sections II to IV were passed as they stood.

Mr. CURRIE said, he had to propose the insertion of a new Section after Section IV. Since the Bill had been settled in Committee, he had received a communication from the Bengal Government, which was to the following effect:—

"With reference to the Bill 'to authorize the confiscation of, or the imposition of fines on Villages or other places for offences committed by the inhabitants,' at present under report of the Select Committee, I am directed to forward to you the accompanying copy of a letter addressed to the Secretary to the Government of India in the Home Department on the 5th August last, No. 1163, and to state that the Lieutenant-Governor is of opinion that the Bill should be made applicable to individuals in the manner suggested in that communication."

The communication here mentioned referred to certain cases which it was unnecessary to specify, and proceeded to say:—

"There are not a few potential Zemindars in the Province of Behar who, though they notoriously possess power and influence, will probably omit to use them for the service of lawful authority, and will yet escape all punishment for this passive countenance of rebellion, because they will not be proved to have done anything actively towards its furtherance.

"It appears to the Lieutenant-Governor that the state of public affairs is such as would justify the enactment of a Law to meet such cases; so that persons known and proved to have possessed influence and power to control or prevent rebellion among their followers and dependents, and to have failed to use that influence and power in aid of lawful authority when duly called upon to do so, should be made liable to fine or forfeiture."

Now, there could be no doubt that the Zemindars referred to in this letter would have it in their power to render most material assistance to Government when the collection of sepoys at Lucknow and other places was broken up, and the men returned to their villages. Large numbers of sepoys had their homes in some of the districts of Behar, especially Shahabad; and without the active aid of the Zemindars, it would be extremely difficult to apprehend them, or to preserve the peace of those districts. It was especially with reference to that particular contingency that he thought it desirable that some such provision as that indicated by the Lieutenant-Governor should be made; and it seemed to him that it might not inappropriately be made in this Bill. He, therefore moved that the following be inserted as a new Section after Section IV :—

"If any zemindar or other proprietor of land, when duly called on by the Magistrate to render assistance in the suppression of rebellion or the arrest of rebels, mutineers, or deserters, shall refuse or neglect to use all the means in his power for rendering such assistance, the Magistrate, on proof of such refusal or neglect, may impose a fine on the person so offending, or may confiscate his estate."

MR. GRANT said, this was a very serious clause. He did not object to it; but he would put it to the Honorable Member whether it was advisable that so very important a provision should be introduced without being before the Public in time to give those whom it would affect, an opportunity of expressing their views regarding it. There were some very valuable estates in Behar, the province which had been especially alluded to; and it seemed inexpedient that they should be made liable to confiscation by an act of legislation of which the Public would have no notice.

THE CHIEF JUSTICE said, the Section proposed did not appear to be exactly within the purvieu of this Bill, which was to render a community answerable for the murder of Europeans and for other offences which had actually been committed by individuals who could not be identified. The words of the proposed Section included, not only every Zemindar, or person holding landed property paying revenue direct to Government, who was liable by the terms of his tenure to give notice of the resort of criminals to his estate—but also holders of subordinate tenures, upon whom, he believed, the same obligation did not now lie, and who had had no notice of the proposed change. He thought it would be rather better not to legislate on such a subject so hastily, or by this Bill.

MR. CURRIE said, with reference to the remarks which had fallen from the Honorable Member opposite (Mr. Grant), it was to be observed that the matter was one of the utmost urgency. If any provision was to be made for it at all, it must be made without delay. The contingency against which the Section he had proposed was intended to provide, was one which might occur immediately. It did seem to him that the obligation which the Section would impose on zemindars was, under the circumstances of the country, a manifest and imperative duty, the neglect of which should be punished with the utmost severity. There could be no doubt of the power of zemindars to render efficient service to Government in the cases adverted to; and it was also certain that, if they remained passive, the Government would have the greatest possible difficulty in preserving the peace of the district.

He was quite aware that the introduction of the Section was open to the objection suggested by the Honorable and learned Chief Justice that the purvieu of the Bill was to provide for cases in which offences had been committed by bodies of persons, and the individuals could not be identified. But the Bill also provided for the punishment of owners of villages in certain cases; and he thought that the punishment of Zemindars in the case against which his proposed Section was directed might also, not inappropriately, be provided for in this Bill. The Preamble and Title of the Bill might be slightly altered hereafter, to meet the addition.

With respect to the Honorable and learned Chief Justice's objection that the Section as worded would impose liabilities upon certain classes of landed proprietors to whom no similar liability at present attached, that was a mistake; for the Law as it now stood rendered it incumbent on landed proprietors of all classes, whether superior or subordinate, to render assistance to the Government by giving notice of the resort of criminals to their estates.

The Honorable Member here read the Section of Regulation VI. 1810 to which he referred.

MR. GRANT said, he wished to explain that he took objection, not to the principle of the measure, but to the suddenness with which it was proposed to pass it. The Council would remember that the only occasion on which a veto had been put upon an Act passed by it was in a case very inferior in importance to this, when a Clause had been inserted at the very last stage of the Bill, and it was held that it ought to have been published before it was passed, in order that those whom it would affect might have had an opportunity of making their views respecting it known to the Courcil. The present was a much stronger case; and it appeared to him that the Council would do wisely to bear in mind what had occurred before, and not to pass the proposed Section without having previously published it for general information.

MR. PEACOCK said, it was not his intention to carry the Bill through the third reading to-day; but it was important that its progress should not be delayed, and he therefore proposed to proceed with it on Saturday next. It might be published in the interim with the new Section proposed by the Honorable Member for Bengal; but he did not think that one week would be sufficient time if it were necessary to promulgate the proposed addition to the Bill.

With respect to the suddenness with which the provision, was proposed, he would observe that Act XVII of 1857, which imposed upon Zemindars the liability to communicate early intelligence of the resort to their estates of mutineers and deserters, had been passed by the Council without any previous publication, the Standing Orders having been suspended in regard to it. The Bill had been introduced and carried through all its stages, and had received the assent of the Governor-General, the same day; Section VI provided as follows:—

"That all Zemindars, talookdars, and other persons who, by Regulation VI of 1810 of the Bengal Code, are declared to be accountable for the early communication of intelligence respecting the resort to their estates of the classes of offenders therein specified, are hereby declared to be accountable for the early communication of intelligence of the resort to any place within the limits of their estates of any person against whom there shall be reasonable suspicion of his having been guilty of mutiny or desertion; and all the provisions of the said Regulation shall have the same force and effect as if persons guilty of mutiny and desertion had been specially included in the classes of offenders specified in that Regulation."

By that Bill, passed very hastily by this Council, this new obligation had been imposed upon Zemindars. The Section proposed by the Honorable Member for Bengal required Zemindars, when called upon by Government, to render assistance in the apprehension of mutineers and deserters. Seeing that they were already bound to give notice of the resort of mutineers and deserters to their estates, he did not think that it was going too far to provide that if they should refuse to assist in apprehending them when called upon to do so by Government, they should be liable to certain punishment, and that that punishment should be fine, or confiscation of their estates. He should, therefore, vote in support of the Section.

THE CHIEF JUSTICE said, he was not prepared to object to the principle of the Section, but he did object to the suddenness with which it was proposed. He could not but think, with reference to the date of the letter which the Honorable Member for Bengal had read, that it was unfortunate that some such provision as this had not been suggested in time for the consideration at least of the Select Committee.

With respect to what had been said by the Honorable Member to his right (Mr. Grant), the Council could hardly fail to recollect that, since the Act upon which the Governor-General had put his veto, it had been called upon, owing to the circumstances of the country, to pass very many Acts hastily. Hasty legislation was very much to be deprecated if it could be avoided; still, he felt the force of the Honorable Member for Bengal's argument that the occasion for acting upon the proposed Section, if it occurred at all, would occur very shortly; and he therefore would not vote against the amendment.

MR. PEACOCK said, speaking from recollection, he believed that the veto referred to had been put, not from any objection to the principle of the provision inserted without previous notice to the Public, but upon the ground that the provision affected certain religious views and prejudices of the Natives. The present was a question, not of religion at all, but of property. If a new Act were to be passed imposing the obligation created by the Section before the Council, and it was to be of any benefit at all, it would be necessary to suspend the Standing Orders in respect of it.

MR. CURRIE'S new Section was then put, and agreed to.

Section V provided that the Magistrate's order for the confiscation of a village or the imposition of a fine should be subject to revision by the Commissioner.

After an amendment to meet the additional Section introduced on the motion of Mr. LeGeyt—

MR. ELIOTT moved that the following Proviso be added to the Section :—

"Provided also that, if the order of a Magistrate for the confiscation of any rights, land, or estate be confirmed by the Commissioner, the confiscation shall not be carried into effect without the express sanction of the Government."

MR. HARINGTON said, he thought it would be hard to call upon Government to go into every case in which an order for confiscation might be made. At present, although the order of the Commissioner was final in law, the Government had the power, since the confiscation would be for its own benefit, to review his proceedings on a petition from the party against whom the order went, and to remit or disallow the confiscation if it thought fit to do so.

THE CHIEF JUSTICE said, he was rather surprised at the late light which had broken in upon the Honorable Member for Madras and the Honorable Member for Bengal on the question involved in this amendment. This Bill, which, as it stood, involved in certain cases the confiscation of villages, seemed to have been very maturely considered by the Select Committee; and they, for reasons which it was to be supposed were satisfactory to the minds of all the Members who had put their names to the Report—and he perceived that the Honorable Member for Madras and the Honorable Member for Bombay were of the number—had come to the conclusion that, in respect of these confiscations, the order of the Commissioner should be final. If the principle for which the Honorable Member for Madras now contended was a good one, he could not see why it should not be applied to an order for the confiscation of a village just as much as to an order for the sale of a Zemindary under the Clause proposed by the Honorable Member for Bengal, or the forfeiture of an hereditary right under the clause proposed by the Honorable Member for Bombay. The proprietary right in a village which it was proposed to confiscate seemed very much in the nature of a Zemindary right; that particular village might be the whole property of which the owner was possessed; and he (the Chief Justice) could not see anything in the argument advanced by the Honorable Member for Madras that the Council ought to be more careful of the larger, than it was of the smaller right. As far as the offence was concerned which was to entail the confiscation of a Zemindary, he thought that the offence of the zemindar who refused, when called upon, to give the Government all the assistance that was in his power, was more direct and personal than the offence which was to entail the confiscation of a village. The Act, as it stood, was in some measure retrospective. It was to take effect in those cases in which Europeans had heretofore been murdered; and it cast upon the proprietor of the village the burden of proving that he had done all in his power to prevent that atrocity; that he had been guilty of no negligence in the matter. That was in a manner to call upon him to prove a negative; and his laches, or whatever it might be that would entail the confiscation of his village, might be of a much more doubtful character, and the accusation against him one which it would be far more difficult to meet, than the offence and accusation with respect to which the Sections introduced by the Honorable Member for Bengal was to operate—namely, a refusal to do a specific thing which the law called upon the party to do.

Then, again, he could not distinguish between the case of the proprietor of a village and the inhabitant of a village holding an hereditary right, which latter was the class of persons contemplated by the Section proposed by the Honorable Member for Bombay. These were persons who were inhabitants of villages in which the crime had been committed, and who had therefore incurred with the ordinary inhabitants a liability to assessment for a fine, and further to forfeiture of their hereditary offices. In respect of these hereditary offices, they seemed to stand very much on the same footing as proprietors of a village; and he (the Chief Justice) did not see why, if the principle was good that the order of the Commissioner should be final in one case, the order of the Commissioner should not equally be final in the other. All the rights now affected by the Bill involved so much knowledge of the social condition of these villages—a knowledge to which he, probably, had less pretension than any whom he was addressing—that he did not feel competent to say whether the principle of the Honorable Member for Madras was in itself a good one or not; but it did appear to him that, if it was good in one case, it must be good throughout the Bill. He thought, however, that there was weight in what had been said by the Honorable Member for the North-Western Provinces, to the effect that in all these cases, although the orders of the Commissioner might be final in law, yet in such as the confiscation would ensure to the benefit of the Government, the Government would always have the power to remit the confiscation on the petition of the persons affected by it if upon a review of the proceedings of the Commissioner, or for any other reason, it saw fit so to do.

Mr. ELIOTT'S amendment was put and negatived, and the Section was carried as previously amended.

Section VI was passed as it stood.

Section VII authorized the Collector to sell a village for the amount of the assessment remaining unpaid.

Mr. CURRIE said, before the Collector proceeded to sell the village for the amount of assessment remaining unpaid, it would be advisable that he should obtain the sanction of the Commissioner. The Commissioner had the right of revision over all his Collector's proceedings; but in cases of sale, his previous sanction should be declared necessary. He therefore moved that the words "with the consent of the Commissioner" be inserted after the word "Magistrate" in the 10th line.

Mr. PEACOCK said, he did not see any necessity for the amendment. The Collector must refer his order for the assessment of the fine to the Commissioner. If the Commissioner confirmed the order, and the assessment remained unpaid, the sale of the village ought to follow without any further reference to him.

Mr. CURRIE said, he had proposed his amendment because the Bill provided two modes for the recovery of fines assessed under it—namely, distress and sale of the property of the parties liable for the fine, or sale of the village. The parties primarily liable would be the Inhabitants of the village on whom the fine would be assessed; and it was but a rough sort of justice, at the least, to sell the property of another person if they failed to pay the sums assessed upon them. It might be allowable, with reference to the relations existing between landed proprietors and their tenants in this country, that recourse should be had to the land in the last resort; but still, the sale of the village was a harsh measure, and it seemed to him that the order of the Collector to sell should have the previous sanction of the Commissioner.

Mr. PEACOCK said, it did not appear to him that it was necessary for the protection of the proprietor that the express sanction of the Commissioner should be obtained for the sale of the village after the confirmation by him of the assessment of a fine. The more references that the Bill would allow from one Officer to another, the greater would be the delay.

Mr. CURRIE'S amendment was put and negatived, and the Section passed after some verbal amendments.

Sections VIII, IX, and X were passed as they stood.

Mr. CURRIE said, with respect to what had been observed as to the interference of Government in cases of confiscation, it was very true that the Government had the power of remission or pardon; but where a confiscation took place, certain consequences followed upon it, and a mere remission would not have the effect of remedying them. If a village was confiscated, would the remission place it in the same position in which it had stood previously?

Mr. PEACOCK said, if a village was confiscated, all the under-tenures were destroyed. Where the confiscation was remitted, the under-tenures ought to be restored. It might be as well to insert a new Section expressing that this would be the effect of a remission of the confiscation, and he therefore proposed that the following be inserted as a new Section after Section X:—

"If the Governor-General in Council or the Executive Government shall see fit to remit any confiscation under this Act, all persons affected by such confiscation shall be restored to their rights as if no such confiscation had ever taken place."

The Section was agreed to.

Section XI was passed as it stood.

Section XII was passed after verbal amendments.

The remaining Sections, with the Preamble and Title, were passed as they stood.

The Council having resumed its sitting, the Bill was reported.

MR. PEACOCK moved that the Bill, as settled in Committee of the whole Council, be referred back to the former Select Committee, with an instruction to consider the Bill and to report whether any further alterations therein are necessary.

Agreed to.

MR. GRANT said, he would suggest that the Committee also take into consideration the propriety of making the Act apply to houses as well as villages and estates.

CORPORAL PUNISHMENT.

MR. PEACOCK moved that the Council resolve itself into a Committee on the Bill "to authorize the infliction of Corporal Punishment in certain cases;" and that the Committee be instructed to consider the Bill in the amended form in which the Select Committee had recommended it to be passed.

Agreed to.

Sections I and II were passed as they stood.

Section III declared that nothing contained in the Act should be held to render "any European" liable to corporal punishment.

MR. GRANT moved that the words "or American" be inserted after the words "any European."

The amendment was agreed to, and the Section then passed.

Section IV defined the meaning of the word "European" as used in the Bill. It was passed after an amendment by which the word "European" was declared to include any person usually designated "a European British subject."

The remaining Sections, with the Preamble and Title, were passed as they stood.

The Council having resumed its sitting, the Bill was reported.

MR. PEACOCK moved that the Bill be now read a third time and passed.

The Motion was carried, and the Bill read accordingly.

MR. PEACOCK moved that General Low be requested to carry the Bill to the President in Council, in order that it might be forwarded to the Governor General for his assent.

Agreed to.

MUNICIPAL ASSESSMENT (BOMBAY).

MR. LEGEYT moved that the Council resolve itself into a Committee on the Bill "for appointing Municipal Commissioners and for raising a Fund for Municipal purposes in the Town of Bombay;" and that the Committee be instructed to consider the Bill in the amended form in which the Select Committee had recommended it to be passed.

Agreed to.

The Bill passed through Committee without amendment; and, the Council having resumed its sitting, was reported.

PORT-DUES (CAMBAY).

MR. LEGEYT moved that the Council resolve itself into a Committee on the Bill "for the levy of Port-dues in certain Ports within the limits of the Gulf of Cambay;" and that the Committee be instructed to consider the Bill in the amended form in which the Select Committee had recommended it to be passed.

Agreed to.

The Bill passed through Committee without amendment; and, the Council having resumed its sitting, was reported.

BOMBAY WATER-WORKS.

MR. LEGEYT moved that the Report of the Select Committee on the Bill "to give effect to an agreement between the Government of Bombay and Her Majesty's Justices of the Peace for the Town and Island of Bombay and Colaba, in relation to certain Water-works in the Islands of Salsette and Bombay," be adopted.

Agreed to.

AFFIDAVITS, AFFIRMATIONS, AND SOLEMN DECLARATIONS.

MR. PEACOCK moved that Mr. Currie be substituted for Sir Arthur

Buller as a member of the Select Committee on the Bill "to amend the law relating to affidavits, affirmations, and solemn declarations."

Agreed to.

NOTICES OF MOTION.

Mr. LeGeyt gave notice that he would, on Saturday the 6th of March, move the second reading of the Bill "to repeal the Laws relating to the levy of Light-dues at Ports within the limits of the Gulf of Cambay."

Also that he would on the same day move the third reading of the Bill "for the levy of Port-dues in certain Ports within the limits of the Gulf of Cambay."

Also that he would on the same day move that the Standing Orders be suspended to enable him to carry the Bill "to repeal the Laws relating to the levy of Light-dues at Ports within the limits of the Gulf of Cambay" through its subsequent stages.

MUNICIPAL ASSESSMENT (BOMBAY).

Mr. LeGeyt moved that the Bill "for appointing Municipal Commissioners and for raising a Fund for Municipal purposes in the Town of Bombay," as settled in Committee of the whole Council, be published for general information, and that it be re-considered after five weeks.

Agreed to.

NOTICE OF MOTION.

Mr. Eliott gave notice that he would on Saturday the 6th of March move the second reading of the Bill "for the maintenance of a Police Force for the Port of Madras."

MUNICIPAL ASSESSMENT (SUBURBS OF CALCUTTA, AND HOWRAH).

Mr. Currie moved that General Low be requested to take the Bill "for raising funds for making and repairing roads in the Suburbs of Calcutta and the Station of Howrah" to the President in Council, in order that it may be submitted to the Governor General for his assent.

Agreed to.

NOTICE OF MOTION.

Mr. Harington gave notice that he would on Saturday the 6th of March move the second reading of the Bill "to facilitate the recovery of land and other real property, of which possession may have been wrongfully taken during the recent disturbances in the North-Western Provinces of the Presidency of Bengal."

CONCEALMENT OF GOVERNMENT PROPERTY.

Mr. Peacock moved that the Standing Orders be suspended to enable him to proceed with the Bill "for the punishment of persons who knowingly receive or conceal arms or other property belonging to the East India Company."

Mr. Grant seconded the Motion, which was then agreed to.

Mr. Peacock moved that the above Bill be referred to a Select Committee consisting of Mr. Eliott, Mr. LeGeyt, Mr. Currie, Mr. Harington, and the Mover.

Agreed to.

The Council adjourned.

Saturday, March 6, 1858.

Present:

The Honorable J. A. Dorin, *Vice-President*, in the Chair.

Hon. the Chief Justice,	E. Currie, Esq.,
Hon'ble B. Peacock,	and
D. Eliott, Esq.,	H. B. Harington,
P. W. LeGeyt, Esq.,	Esq.

CONFISCATION OF VILLAGES, &c.

Mr. Peacock presented the Report of the Select Committee on the Bill "to authorize the confiscation of, or the imposition of fines on Villages and other places for offences committed by the Inhabitants."

GOVERNMENT STAMP PAPERS.

Mr. Peacock moved the first reading of a Bill "to provide for the authentication of Government Stamp Papers." He said, during the recent disturbances, a large quantity of Government Stamped Paper had been either plundered or destroyed, and there was reason to suppose that a considerable portion of what had been plundered was now in existence. To protect Government from the unauthorized use of such Paper, it was necessary that, in future, all Stamped Paper issued since the 25th of November last should be authenticated; and it was accordingly proposed that all Stamped Paper issued subsequent to that date should bear some stamp in addition to the stamp and counter-stamp which the existing law required to be impressed upon it. This would provide for the authentication of all new Paper that would be issued. But it was necessary also to authenticate Paper that had already been issued, and which might be in the hands of private individuals. It was proposed that such Paper should be authenticated by the Collector or his Covenanted Assistant or Deputy signing his name across the stamp on being satisfied that the paper had been *bonâ fide* purchased.

MR. PEACOCK then stated the substance of the different provisions of the Bill, and concluded by remarking that they would throw no impediment in the way of the Public in regard to conveyance or documents already in existence, inasmuch as they would apply to no private conveyance or document executed before the passing of the Act, unless it should appear to have been ante-dated for the purpose of avoiding the objects of the Act.

The Bill was read a first time.

ALLUVIAL LANDS.

MR. CURRIE moved the first reading of a Bill to explain Regulation XI. 1825 of the Bengal Code. He said, the title of the Bill he had the honor to introduce was, as it now stood, "a Bill to explain Regulation XI. 1825 of the Bengal Code, and to prescribe rules for the settlement of land gained by alluvion." He would endeavor to explain as briefly and clearly as he could the circumstances connected with the introduction of the Bill; but he feared, from the nature of the details into which it would be necessary for him to enter, that his statement would be somewhat tedious; and he must bespeak the indulgence of the Council.

Clause 1 Section III of Regulation II. 1819 provided that

"All lands which, at the period of the decennial settlement, were not within the limits of any pergunnah, mouza, or other division of estates for which a settlement was concluded with the owners, not being lands for which a distinct settlement may have been made since the period above referred to, nor lands held free of assessment under a valid and legal title of the nature specified in Regulations XIX. and XXXVII. 1793, and in the corresponding Regulations subsequently enacted, are and shall be considered liable to assessment in the same manner as other unsettled mehals."

And Clause 2 of the same Section provided that

"The foregoing principles shall be deemed applicable, not only to tracts of land, such as are described to have been brought into cultivation in the Sunderbuns, but to all churs and islands formed since the period of the decennial settlement, and generally to all lands gained by alluvion or dereliction since that period, whether from an introcession of the sea, an alteration in the course of rivers, or the gradual accession of soil on their banks."

This, then, was the general law for the settlement of alluvial lands. The detailed rules of settlement were prescribed in Regulation VII. 1822, which had been extended to Bengal by Regulation IX. 1825.

The occupation of newly-formed alluvial lands had always been a fruitful source of disputes and affrays, and no rules had been laid down for determining the proprietary right in them. Regulation XI. 1825 was passed for the declared purpose of supplying this omission, and of enacting rules for the guidance of the Courts of Judicature in determining the rights of litigant parties. Section IV of that Regulation was to the following effect:—

"When land may be gained by gradual accession, whether from the recess of a river or of the sea, it shall be considered an increment to the tenure of the person to whose land or estate it is thus annexed, whether such land or estate be held immediately from Government by a Zemindar or other superior landholder, or as a subordinate tenure by any description of under-tenant whatever. Provided that the increment of land thus obtained shall not entitle the person in possession of the estate or tenure to which the land may be annexed, to a right of property or permanent interest therein beyond that possessed by him in the estate or tenure to which the land may be annexed, and shall not in any case be understood to exempt the holder of it from the payment to Government of any assessment for the public revenue to which it may be liable under the provisions of Regulation II. 1819, or of any other Regulation in force."

The Board of Revenue had lately held that the terms of this Section, not only declared and fixed the proprietary right in the alluvial land, but also constituted the land part of the original estate which it adjoined; and that, when it was assessed with Government revenue, the only condition on which the proprietor of the old estate could be admitted to engage for it was that the revenue of the new land should be added to the revenue of the old estate, and a new engagement be executed for the aggregate increased jumma. The effect of this would be to exclude from the settlement with Government the person who was declared by the law the proprietor of the land, and who, therefore, had the best right to engage; because these alluvial formations were seldom of such a permanent nature that the owner of the old land would be willing to render his permanently-settled estate liable for the revenue assessed upon the new land.

The idea now advocated by the present Board of Revenue had been put forth by the late Sudder Board some twenty years ago; but it had never, he believed, been acted upon; and very shortly after they advanced it, the Sudder Board had seen reason to change their view, and had passed a Rule expressly authorizing Collectors to settle the alluvial land as a separate estate, whenever the proprietor of the adjoining land was unwilling to incorporate it with his original estate. The Members of the present Board held that the practice authorized by this Rule was not warranted by law, and were desirous that it should be abrogated. But in maintaining their theory that the alluvial land became part of the original estate, they fell into embarrassments and inconsistencies. They held that the new land ought to be incorporated with the old estate; but they could not infringe the right of the proprietor under the permanent settlement —they could not annul his engagement, and require him to enter into a new engagement for an enhanced jumma. They were thus reduced to the alternative either of allowing the land to remain unassessed which would be a dereliction of duty, or to take an engagement from some other person. In such case, they said that a temporary lease must be given to a farmer, Malikana allowance, or allowance for right of ownership, being reserved to the proprietor. But, in the first place, there was no law which authorized the letting out of a portion of an integral estate; and, in the second place, the assessing of any land separately, and granting a lease of it to a farmer, did, by express Revenue law, constitute it a separate estate, just as much as if a separate settlement had been made with the proprietor.

Of course, the construction which had been put upon Regulation XI. 1825 by the Board of Revenue might be overruled by the Executive Government; but, unfortunately, a recent decision of the Sudder Court had given support to it. In the case to which he referred, some alluvial land had been let out in farm, with the usual reservation of Malikana allowance. During the lease, one of the proprietors sold his interest in the alluvial land, and, shortly after, the old estate was brought to sale for arrears of revenue. He (Mr. Currie) forgot what was the precise point upon which the case was taken into Court; but the Sudder held that the sale for arrears of revenue had conveyed the proprietary right, not only in the original estate which was the subject of sale, but also in the alluvial land which was not the subject of sale and which was held under a different engagement. Now, there was no law by which two estates could be sold simultaneously for arrears of revenue falling due upon only one of them; and, at the time of this sale, the proprietors were under no liability in respect of the alluvial land which had been leased to another party.

With all respect to the Sudder Court, he ventured to express the opinion that their decision in this case was erroneous; and he believed that all the difficulty and embarrassment felt in the matter had arisen from the real purpose and scope of Regulation XI. 1825 not having been accurately apprehended and recognized. That Regulation was avowedly a judicial Regulation. It had been passed expressly "for the general information of individuals as well as for the guidance of the Courts of Judicature;" and its declared object was to fix the Civil rights of ownership in alluvial lands. When those rights were ascertained, it appeared to him that it was a forced and inadmissible construction to hold that the Regulation went farther, and controlled the proceedings of the Settlement Officer, which were conducted under different laws, as expressly provided in the Regulation itself—or that it had the effect of constituting a single estate of what, by the proceedings of the Settlement Officer under the Revenue laws, had become two distinct estates.

The question was one of considerable importance, and it was very desirable that the law on the subject should be perfectly clear. In accordance with the suggestions of the Bengal Government, therefore, he had prepared this Bill, which declared the object and scope of Regulation XI. 1825 as he had before explained them, and also laid down express rules for the settlement of alluvial lands in accordance with those prescribed by the Board of Revenue in 1841.

The Bill was read a first time.

LIGHT-DUES (GULF OF CAMBAY).

MR. LEGEYT moved the second reading of the Bill "to repeal the Laws relating to the levy of Light-dues at Ports within the limits of the Gulf of Cambay."

The Motion was carried, and the Bill read a second time.

MARINE POLICE FORCE (MADRAS).

MR. ELIOTT moved the second reading of the Bill "for the maintenance of a Police Force for the Port of Madras."

MR. LEGEYT said, he could not allow this Bill to be read a second time without making some comments upon it. It appeared to him that, in its present shape, it would not be found operative in putting down the evil for the repression of which it was designed. He might mention that he had had considerable experience of this kind of depredations some years ago, when at the head of the Police in Bombay. A similar evil had been in existence in that Port for a great number of years, to a much larger extent, he had no doubt, than had been found to be the case at Madras. In 1842, the whole system was laid bare by the testimony of approvers, who, with their accomplices, had followed a systematic plan of boat-robbery the disclosure of which astonished the entire mercantile community of the Port. The papers annexed to this Bill shewed that the depredations in Madras had been large; but he had not been able to collect from them that the same organized system of plunder existed there which had existed in Bombay, and the discovery of which resulted in the transportation of fifteen men holding respectable positions in life, and the flight of forty others, on the finding of a true Bill against them by the Grand Jury.

The success in checking these depredations in Bombay, had, doubtless, been owing to the complete development of the details of the system which the approvers had furnished. The precautionary and preventive measures adopted were of a more simple character than those provided in this Bill; and for the last seventeen or eighteen years, had worked, he believed, well. A Marine Police Force was instituted; but it was worked afloat like a division of the Land Police, under a European Superintendent. This Officer was afloat on board a hulk with his policemen, and was accustomed to board any cargo boat carrying cargo between the shipping and the shore. The expense of maintaining this Force did not amount to much more than that which was required for the additional Police Force now proposed for Madras. The Superintendent and his Officers kept a sharp look out on cargo boats conveying cargo; and as the men on these boats knew that they passed to or from the shipping subject to the chance of being boarded by the Police, the effect certainly was to check, in a great measure, the depredations formerly practised.

The first objection which he felt to the present Bill had reference to the provision of Section II. That Section provided that "no boat shall convey any cargo or goods of any description to or from any ship or vessel in the Port of Madras unless accompanied by an Officer of the Police Force." This provision would be found exceedingly cumbrous, and would render the Bill really inoperative. An Officer of Police might not always be at hand. But even if that were not an objection, he thought it would be found that the "Officer of Police"—who would be a Peon on a salary of five or six Rupees a month —would be liable to such temptations to join the boatmen in their plunderings that the object of placing him in the boat would be wholly defeated. Very few men receiving salaries of five or six Rupees a month would be able to resist the temptation of a handsome present, or a participation in the profits of the pillage, to keep their eyes shut. In Bombay, books were found belonging to the dispersed gang, in which it distinctly appeared that every Officer of Police and every Officer of Customs who could and ought to have prevented the depredations, were in the regular pay of the gang, their salary from Government, whether it was five Rupees or a hundred Rupees per month, being doubled by the gang. It appeared evident to him, therefore, that there would be very little use in trusting the prevention of these depredations in Madras to single Police Officers of a subordinate class.

Then, he thought that the collection of the tax proposed for the maintenance of the Force would not be found convenient. The Bill provided that every boat-owner should give weekly returns to the Police Commissioner of the number of trips made by each of his boats. It would be exceedingly difficult to obtain correct returns. It would be very easy for an owner to under-state the number of trips his boats had made. He (Mr. LeGeyt) should prefer to see a monthly or yearly charge levied upon owners of boats, or an additional fee levied on licenses granted under Act IV of 1842. This, however, was a question which might be settled in Select Committee.

He did not wish to oppose the second reading of the Bill, if it should be understood that he would not be committed by it to the mode in which Section II proposed to work out the Bill. His opinion was, that no definite restrictions should be placed upon preventive measures taken by the Police; but this Section would restrict the Police to one single mode of preventing the depredations in question; and that mode, as he had endeavored to shew, would be utterly ineffectual.

If the Honorable Mover of the Bill would not object to the points on which he had commented being discussed in Select Committee, and to the Select Committee having power to abandon the provisions relating to them if, on consideration, they should see fit so to do, he would assent to the second reading. If not, he should feel it his duty to oppose it.

MR. PEACOCK said, he quite agreed with the Honorable Member for Bombay in his observations regarding the provision contained in Section II. It might be very inconvenient if, by legislative enactment, no cargo boat could convey cargo to or from any ship unless accompanied by a Police Officer. The provision might throw great impediment in the way of trade. Suppose a merchant was anxious to take a quantity of cargo from a ship to the shore under his own superintendence, or to send it under the superintendence of a clerk, without waiting for the arrival of a Police Officer: was there any reason why he should not be at liberty to do so? Police Officers might not always be available at the moment they were wanted; and if cargo boats were to wait until they could be got, great impediment would be thrown in the way of trade. He could see no objection to a tax being levied to meet the expense of such an increase to the Police Force as might be necessary for checking the organized system of robbery of cargo in transit between the shore and the shipping which appeared to have grown up in Madras; and it was not his intention to oppose the second reading of the Bill, the provisions of which had been considered and approved of by the Chamber of Commerce in Madras; but he did think that it was objectionable to provide that no cargo boat should carry any cargo, even with the consent of the owner of the cargo, unless it was accompanied by an Officer of Police; and, if the Bill should be read a second time to-day, it should be understood that this point, as also the others to which the Honorable Member for Bombay had adverted, would be open to discussion in Committee.

MR. ELIOTT said, as the Honorable and learned Member opposite (Mr. Peacock) had just observed, the Bill now proposed had been submitted to, and approved, of by the Chamber of Commerce in Madras, who represented the commercial community there; and the proposal that no cargo boat should convey cargo to or from any ship without having a Police Officer on board, had emanated from themselves. They had tried on their own part a system of watching cargo boats, but had found that they could not control their men sufficiently, and that the only course left was to employ disciplined members of the Police Force, under the strict control of the Police Commissioner. This Bill being the product of the collective wisdom of all persons in Madras concerned in the question—namely, the mercantile community, the Police officials, and the Government,—he thought it might be concluded that it was tolerably well suited to the circumstances of the case. The observations that had been made upon it would be reported; and he would particularly direct the attention of the Madras Government to them. The provisions to which they referred, would also be open to discussion in Select Committee. In the meanwhile, as there was no opposition to the second reading, he should renew his Motion that the Bill be read a second time.

The Motion was carried, and the Bill read a second time.

RESTORATION OF POSSESSION OF LANDS (N. W. PROVINCES).

MR. HARINGTON moved the second readingof the Bill "to facilitate the recovery of land and other real property, of which possession may have been wrongfully taken during the recent disturbances in the North-Western Provinces of the Presidency of Bengal."

The Motion was carried, and the Bill read a second time.

PORT-DUES (GULF OF CAMBAY).

MR. LEGEYT moved that the Bill "for the levy of Port-dues in certain Ports within the limits of the Gulf of Cambay" be now read a third time and passed.

The Motion was carried, and the Bill read a third time.

CONFISCATION OF VILLAGES, &c.

MR. PEACOCK moved that the Bill to "authorize the confiscation of, or the imposition of fines on Villages and other places for offences committed by the Inhabitants" be re-committed to a Committee of the whole Council; and that the Committee be instructed to consider the Bill in the amended form in which the Select Committee had recommended it to be passed.

Agreed to.

Section I being read—

MR. ELIOTT said, he wished to call the attention of the Committee to the wording of some parts of this Section, which he conceived would make its operation unfair to Defendants. He referred to those places in which it was provided that the inhabitants of villages and others should be liable to certain punishments if they did not prove to the satisfaction of the Magistrate that they had used all the means in their power to prevent the commission of certain offences. This was an *ex post facto* law, and open to the gravest objections on that account; and he confessed he had had great difficulty in reconciling it to himself on the ground of the paramount necessity, under the extraordinary circumstances of the times, of visiting with punishment all persons from whose conduct it might be concluded with moral certainty that they had been directly or indirectly, actively or passively, accessory to, or had countenanced the atrocious crimes referred to in the Bill, or had harbored the offenders. But considering the extreme severity, and the exceptionable character of the proposed law, it seemed to him that there was the more reason why the Council should take care that it should be free from the censure of not affording a fair trial to persons prosecuted under it. He took it to be essentially necessary to a fair trial that it should be distinctly notified to the accused what were the facts and circumstances on which the charge against him was founded. This condition, he submitted, was not fulfilled by the Section as it stood, but would, he thought, be fulfilled if the provisions he referred to required, not that the accused should prove that he had used all the means in his power to prevent the commission of the offence mentioned in the charge, but that it should be proved to the satisfaction of the Magistrate that he had not used all the means in his power. It would then be necessary to state and prove facts and circumstances from which the alleged omission or neglect was inferred, and the accused would know exactly what he had to meet in his defence. He might exculpate himself by shewing that it really was not in his power to do what it was averred he could and ought to have done. But he (Mr. Eliott) did not see how a man could be ready with proofs to refute an allegation that he had not done all in his power, without any specification of the instances in which he was supposed to have failed. It was unfair, in his opinion, to require it of him; and he should, therefore, move as an amendment that the words "it shall not be proved to the satisfaction of the Magistrate" after the word "and" in the 16th line of the Section be left out.

MR. PEACOCK said, he thought that this question would have been more properly submitted at the last Meeting, because the Council had already decided that the Section should stand in this respect in its original form. The Bill had been referred back to the Select Committee last Saturday for two stated reasons—the first being that the Committee should see whether any further amendments were necessary in consequence of those which had been introduced in the Committee of the whole Council; and the second, that, according to the suggestion of an Honorable Member who was not present to-day, they might consider whether the Bill should not be made applicable to houses as well as to villages. Upon these two questions, they had made their Report. The Honorable Member for Madras was a Member of the Select Committee; but no such point as that which he now raised was suggested in the Report which they had presented. He (Mr. Peacock) did not mean to say that the Honorable Member ought to have suggested it in the Report, or that he was too late in moving his amendment now; but it did appear to him (Mr. Peacock) that this was entirely a new light thrown upon the Bill, and that the Council was now asked to undo what it had done at the last Meeting. For his own part, he could not see that the Section imposed any very great hardship upon owners of villages in requiring them to give the proof to which the Honorable Member objected. As the Bill stood, the offence must first be proved to have been committed. Where a European or American had been murdered, or subjected to violent personal outrage, in a village, he thought that there was a sufficient presumption against the inhabitants to throw upon them the burden of proving that they had done everything in their power to prevent the commission of the offence. It would be much more easy for the inhabitants to prove what they had done, than for any one to prove that they had not done all in their power to prevent the offence. By the Section as it stood, the inhabitants would have to prove what they had done; and if the Magistrate was satisfied by such proof that they had done all in their power to restrain the criminals, he would acquit them. He (Mr. Peacock) should, therefore, vote against the amendment.

THE CHIEF JUSTICE said, he thought that, if the Council were to adopt the amendment moved by the Honorable Member for Madras, it would entirely alter the principle of this Bill. He admitted that what the Bill provided was of a stringent character; but before the Magistrate could act upon the provision—before he could call upon the Inhabitants of a Village to enter on the proof that they had done all in their power to prevent any of the offences in question, it must be proved to his satisfaction that the offence had been committed. Now, what was that offence? One might omit from consideration the first clause of the Section, because that was wholly independent of the provision objected to. The next clause provided thus:—"If it shall be proved to the satisfaction of a Magistrate that any European or American has been murdered, or been subjected to any violent personal outrage in any such village." These facts, therefore, must be proved to the satisfaction of the Magistrate before he would be in a condition to call on the inhabitants of the village to clear themselves by shewing that they had done all in their power to prevent the commission of the crime or outrage. If such a law as this was necessary to impress upon the inhabitants of these districts the sacredness of the lives of Europeans, against whom the fury of those engaged in the rebellion which had agitated the country, had principally been directed—it was not unreasonable to provide that, when once it was ascertained that the life of a European had been taken in a village, the proof that they had used all the means in their power to prevent the murder, should be cast upon the inhabitants. All the circumstances attendant on the crime were presumably within their knowledge, and might be in the knowledge of no other person. In many cases, there would be no survivor of the party to which the murdered man belonged. Therefore, if it was necessary to have such a provision at all, it appeared to him expedient that it should be in its present form. If the Council should alter it as proposed by the Honorable Member for Madras, it would go far to render the Bill nugatory altogether.

MR. ELIOTT'S amendment was put and negatived, and the Section then passed as it stood.

Section V, as amended by the Select Committee, empowered Darogahs or District Police Officers, as well as Magistrates, to call on Zemindars or other proprietors of land to aid in the suppression of rebellion, and the apprehension of rebels, mutineers, or deserters.

THE CHIEF JUSTICE said, unless the Select Committee to whom the Bill had been referred back last week, had very good reasons for inserting in the Section the words "or by a Darogah or District Police Officer," which were printed in italics—reasons which they had not fully stated in their Report—he should prefer the Section as it originally stood. The power which the Section gave was a new and very stringent power; and all, he thought, must admit that the class of Officers to whom its extension was now proposed, was not one to which power could be committed with a high degree of confidence that that power would not be abused. He admitted that cases were possible in which Darogahs or District Police Officers, being in search of mutineers, might find it expedient to call upon Zemindars to render them assistance without having time to obtain the previous authority of the Magistrate; but he apprehended that such cases would be of rare occurrence. In most of the cases in which this Clause would come into operation; the Magistrate would be proceeding to tranquillize the district, and to clear it of mutineers, according to some systematic course of action; and would, either of his own motion, or on the requisition of his subordinates, have time to call on the Zemindars to render them aid. In any case, he thought, it would be safer to run the risk that, in the rare cases in which a reference to the Magistrate would be impossible, Zemindars should escape from the operation of this Clause, than to give this new and extraordinary power to a class which experience had shown was prone to abuse those it already possessed. He should, therefore, move as an amendment that the words "or by a Darogah or District Police Officer" after the word "Magistrate" in the third line of the Section be left out.

MR. HARINGTON said, the words, to which the Honorable and learned Chief Justice objected, had been inserted in the Section by the Select Committee upon his Motion. He had proposed them because it appeared to him that, unless the Section as it originally stood were extended to requisitions made by Darogahs and District Police Officers, many cases might occur in which rebels and mutineers would escape merely from the want of a written order from the Magistrate requiring Zemindars to aid in their apprehension. Some of the Districts in the North-Western Provinces were of considerable extent—Goruckpore for instance; and it would frequently happen that the Magistrate was at a great distance from the spot where the aid of the Zemindar was required for the suppression of rebellion, or for the apprehension of rebels, mutineers, or deserters. If, therefore, Darogahs or District Police Officers should be compelled to obtain the written authority of the Magistrate before they could call upon Zemindars to assist them in such cases, the offenders might escape beyond the frontier or into the Lower Provinces before the order of the Magistrate was received. It was to be observed that the Section gave no power to Police Officers to punish Zemindars for refusing to afford assistance. All that they would be able to do upon such refusal would be to report the conduct of the Zemindars to the Magistrate, with whom alone it would rest to convict or acquit. Zemindars were already required to assist the Police in apprehending offenders in certain cases; and as, for the reasons he had stated, the power which the Section, as now framed, proposed to give to Darogahs and District Police Officers appeared to him to be really necessary, and he saw no reason to suppose that it would be abused, he should vote against the amendment.

MR. CURRIE said, the words inserted in the Section in Select Committee were not necessary for the particular contingency which he had in his mind when he first proposed the Section; but having heard the grounds upon which they had been introduced, he thought that it would be better to let them stand.

THE CHIEF JUSTICE'S amendment was put and negatived, and the Section then passed.

Section VI was passed as it stood.

Section VII was passed after verbal amendments.

Section VIII empowered the Magistrate to order the sale of the village for the recovery of fines assessed upon the inhabitants.

MR. CURRIE said, when this Section was under the consideration of the Council last week, he had proposed the introduction into it of words which would render the previous sanction of the Commissioner necessary to the sale of a village; but objections had been raised, and he had not pressed his Motion to a division. On consideration, however, it appeared to him that the matter was one of considerable importance; and he proposed to renew his Motion, and, if the objections taken to it on the former occasion were repeated to-day, to take the sense of the Council upon it.

The Section was intended to provide for the recovery of fines imposed upon the inhabitants of villages. The persons to be punished were those inhabitants. If a fine was not paid, the obvious course was to endeavor to recover it from the property of those who were liable for the payment of it. The Section provided this remedy; but it also provided that the amount might be recovered by the sale of the village—that was, in many cases, by the sale of the property of another person. As he had said before, although, with reference to the relations which existed between landlord and tenant in this country, the sale of the village might generally be allowable as an ultimate remedy, it would in some cases be a very harsh and severe measure. Where the village was the property of a body of cultivating proprietors who formed a large class of the inhabitants, its sale might be right and proper; but where that was not the case, it would be extremely harsh to throw the responsibility, in case of the fine assessed on the inhabitants not being paid, upon the owner of the village. He (Mr. Currie), therefore, thought that the power to sell the village should not be left to the discretion of the Magistrate, but that the order of the Magistrate should, in all cases, be subject to the previous sanction of the Commissioner. It had been said that, when the Magistrate imposed a fine, he would have to refer his order to the Commissioner, and obtain his sanction, and that therefore any further reference would be unnecessary. But in sanctioning the order for the fine, the Commissioner would not determine the mode in which payment was to be realized. He (Mr. Currie) thought, therefore, that an express reference should be made to the Commissioner before the sale of a village, and he could see no possible reason why it should not be made. He should, therefore, move as an amendment that the words "with the previous sanction of the Commissioner" be inserted after the word "Magistrate" in the 17th line of the Section.

MR. HARINGTON said, the Motion which had just been made by the Honorable Member for Bengal was identical with the one brought forward by the Honorable Member at the last Meeting of the Council. On that occasion, it was opposed by the Honorable and learned Member opposite (Mr. Peacock) and himself, and it was negatived without a division. He had attentively listened to the observations which the Honorable Member had urged to-day in support of his Motion, but they had failed to convince him that the conclusion at which the Council had arrived on this question at its last Meeting was erroneous, and he saw no reason to alter the opinion which he had then expressed. Section VI of the Bill provided that, whenever a Magistrate might impose a fine under the Act, he should report his proceedings to the Commissioner. The Commissioner might either confirm, or modify, or annul the order of the Magistrate, as he should think fit. Under this provision, the Magistrate would be able to take no steps towards recovering the amount of any fine which he might impose upon the inhabitants of a village until his order had been confirmed by the Commissioner. When a case was reported by the Magistrate, it was to be supposed that the Commissioner would go through the proceedings with the view of satisfying himself that the order made was a just and proper one. He would be aware that, in the event of his confirming the order, the confirmation might be followed by the sale of the village on the inhabitants of which the fine was imposed; and it appeared to him (Mr. Harington) that if, with this knowledge, he did confirm the Magistrate's order, he must be presumed to look forward to its possible ultimate result, and prospectively and conditionally to sanction the sale of the village, equally with the other processes authorized by the Act for the recovery of fines imposed under its provisions.

Then, again, by Section XI, all the proceedings of the Magistrate, with exception to the assessment of the fine, would be subject to the revision and control of the Commissioner. Under that Section, the Commissioner might always direct the Magistrate to postpone the sale, if he thought that further time should be allowed to the owner of the village, or he might prohibit the sale altogether—though he (Mr. Harington) hoped the instances would be rare in which the Commissioner would exercise that power.

Looking at these two Sections, he thought that the Bill afforded as large a measure of protection to owners of villages as was consistent with its principle and object. He might also observe that the reference for which the Honorable Member for Bengal contended, would not only cause delay, but, in the event of any intermediate change in the office of Commissioner, might give rise to conflicting orders—which it was very desirable to avoid; and he should, therefore, vote against the amendment.

THE CHIEF JUSTICE said, he presumed that the owner of a village would have time to make a reference to the Commissioner against the Magistrate's order for the sale of the village before the day of sale.

MR. HARINGTON replied that he would.

MR. PEACOCK said, he thought that Section XI provided sufficiently for the protection of owners of villages, and that it would be advisable not to clog the discretion of the Magistrate by making his order for the sale of a village subject to the previous sanction of the Commissioner.

THE CHIEF JUSTICE said, he thought, if the amendment of the Honorable Member for Bengal were carried, the result would be that there would very often be two references to the Commissioner—one from the Magistrate, and the other from the owner of the village; and that it might be inexpedient to commit the Commissioner to the sale of the village on the first reference, before he had heard what could be said against the sale on the second. The answer which the Honorable Member for the North-Western Provinces had given to his question, satisfied him that the owner of a village ordered by the Magistrate to be sold, would always have time to make a reference to the Commissioner before the sale took place. On the other hand, he agreed with the Honorable Member for Bengal that the confirmation of an order for the sale of a village for the non-payment of fines assessed upon the inhabitants might be quite a different question from that of confirming the order for the assessment of the fines. For instance, though the inhabitants of the village might properly be required to pay the fine, the owner of the village might be a very well affected person, whom the Commissioner might therefore be willing to exempt from liability in respect of the default of the villagers to pay that fine. But as the Bill would give the owner time to refer to the Commissioner, and as all orders and proceedings by the Magistrate were expressly made subject to the revision and control of the Commissioner, it appeared to him (the Chief Justice) that the amendment was unnecessary.

MR. CURRIE said, it did not appear to him that Section XI would give any effectual protection to owners of villages. It said—"No appeal shall lie from any order passed by a Magistrate in carrying out the provisions of this Act." It might be said that, although no appeal would lie of right, the owner of the village might make application to the Commissioner, and the Commissioner might interfere in his behalf; but the Commissioner might be at such a distance that, very possibly, the owner might not be able to obtain an order before the day fixed for the sale. Then, if the sale took place, the Commissioner would be powerless; for he could not reverse the sale. The law allowed the reversal of a sale only where the rules prescribed for conducting sales had been contravened. The sale would, therefore, be final, unless the Commissioner should find the case to be one of such extreme hardship and injustice that he would refer it to the Government for the purpose of obtaining annulment of the sale. The Commissioner might not feel disposed to go so far as to make a reference to Government in every case of hardship; and he (Mr. Currie), therefore, still thought, with submission, that every order of the Magistrate for the sale of a village should be subject to the previous sanction of the Commissioner. The only possible objection that there could be to this was the short delay that would be occasioned by the reference; but that did not seem to him a sufficient objection; and he, therefore, felt it his duty to press his Motion.

Mr. HARINGTON said, owners of villages would in every case have at least fifteen days within which to make their references to the Commissioner, and obtain an order from that Officer. This was considered a sufficient time in other cases in which the sale of land was allowed, and he did not see why it should not be sufficient in cases under this Act. He thought it unadvisable to delay the final determination of these cases. The intention of the Bill was that the owners of villages should exert themselves to induce the inhabitants to pay the amount of the fine which might be assessed upon them. If the inhabitants failed to pay, the owners would be at liberty to make good the amount, and to recover it afterwards from the persons liable for the same by distress and sale of their property.

Mr. Currie

Mr. CURRIE'S amendment being put, the Council divided:—

Ayes 2.	*Noes 5.*
Mr. Currie,	Mr. Harington,
Mr. Eliott.	Mr. LeGeyt,
	Mr. Peacock,
	The Chief Justice.
	The Chairman.

The amendment was negatived, and the Section passed as it stood.

Sections IX and X were passed as they stood.

Mr. CURRIE said, it had been mentioned to him by the Honorable and learned Member to his right (Mr. Peacock) that the Bill made no provision for the recovery of fines imposed under Section V. If no special provision were made for the purpose, of course the fines would be recoverable under the general law—namely, by distress and sale of property, or by imprisonment. But that was not a very efficient mode of recovery; and he thought that it would be better if a special provision were made. He, therefore, moved that the following be inserted as a new Section after Section X:—

"Any fine imposed under Section V of this Act, may be recovered in the manner above prescribed for the recovery of assessments, or by sale of the estate of the person liable to the fine; and such sale shall be made by the Collector on the requisition of the Magistrate and shall be subject to all the rules applicable to the sale of estates for demands recoverable by the same process as arrears of Revenue, save that it shall not in any case be necessary to obtain the sanction of the Sudder Board of Revenue or Board of Revenue to such sale."

Agreed to.

Sections XI to XVI and the Preamble and Title were passed as they stood.

The Council having resumed its sitting, the Bill was reported.

Mr. PEACOCK moved that the Bill be now read a third time and passed.

The Motion was carried, and the Bill read a third time.

Mr. PEACOCK moved that Mr. Grant be requested to take the Bill to the President in Council, in order that it might be submitted to the Governor General for his assent.

Agreed to.

LIGHT-DUES (GULF OF CAMBAY).

Mr. LeGeyt moved that the Bill "to repeal the Laws relating to the levy of Light-dues at Ports within the limits of the Gulf of Cambay" be referred to a Select Committee consisting of Mr. Eliott, Mr. Currie, and the Mover.

Agreed to.

MR. LEGEYT moved that the Standing Orders be suspended to enable the Select Committee to present their Report within the prescribed time of three months.

MR. CURRIE seconded the Motion, which was then put and carried.

PORT-DUES (GULF OF CAMBAY).

MR. LEGEYT moved that Mr. Grant be requested to take the Bill "for the levy of Port-dues in certain Ports within the limits of the Gulf of Cambay" to the President in Council, in order that it might be submitted to the Governor-General for his assent.

Agreed to.

MARINE POLICE FORCE (MADRAS).

MR. ELIOTT moved that the Bill "for the maintenance of a Police Force for the Port of Madras" be referred to a Select Committee consisting of Mr. LeGeyt, Mr. Currie, and the Mover.

Agreed to.

RESTORATION OF POSSESSION OF LANDS (N. W. PROVINCES).

MR HARINGTON moved that the Bill "to facilitate the recovery of land and other real property, of which possession may have been wrongfully taken during the recent disturbances in the North-Western Provinces of the Presidency of Bengal" be referred to a Select Committee consisting of Mr. Peacock, Mr. Currie, and the Mover.

Agreed to.

MR. HARINGTON moved that the Standing Orders be suspended to enable the Select Committee to present their Report within one month.

MR. ELIOTT seconded the Motion, which was then put and carried.

MERCHANT SEAMEN.

MR. ELIOTT moved that a communication received by him from the Madras Government, be laid upon the table and referred to the Select Committee on the Bill "for the amendment of the law relating to Merchant Seamen."

Agreed to.

The Council adjourned.

Saturday, March 13, 1858.

PRESENT:

The Honorable J. A. Dorin, *Vice-President*, in the Chair.

Hon. the Chief Justice,	P. W. LeGeyt, Esq.,
Hon'ble J. P. Grant,	E. Currie, Esq.,
Hon'ble B. Peacock,	and
D. Eliott, Esq.,	H. B. Harington, Esq.

RECOVERY OF RENTS (BENGAL).

THE CLERK brought under the consideration of the Council a Petition of Protestant Missionaries residing in or near Calcutta in favor of the Bill "to amend the law relating to the recovery of Rent in the Presidency of Fort William in Bengal." The Petitioners stated that they

"regard with deep concern the condition of the cultivators of Bengal, and therefore have observed with thankfulness the introduction of a Bill for the recovery of Rents, and the favorable reception by your Honorable Council of that just and benevolent measure."

They then proceeded to suggest the adoption of certain other measures, and concluded as follows:—

"Your Petitioners cherish the hope that the benevolent spirit of modern legislation will animate your Honorable Council in considering these necessary provisions; and they fervently pray that the Rent Bill passed into Law may be the precursor of many other and equally important measures, intended and adapted to prevent the perversion of justice in this Presidency and throughout India, and to establish and secure tranquillity and order."

MR. CURRIE said, as the Petitioners mentioned many measures besides the Rent Bill as being, in their opinion, requisite, he did not think it necessary to refer the Petition to the Select Commitee on the Bill, and should therefore only move that it be printed.

Agreed to.

PORT-DUES (FORT ST. GEORGE).

THE CLERK reported to the Council that he had received a communication from the Chief Secretary to the Government of Fort St. George relative to the Bill "for the levy of Port-dues and fees at Ports within the Presidency of Fort St. George."

CONCEALMENT OF GOVERNMENT PROPERTY.

MR. PEACOCK presented the Report of the Select Committee on the Bill "for the punishment of persons who knowingly receive or conceal arms or other property belonging to the East India Company."

PORT-DUES (ADEN).

MR. LEGEYT presented the Report of the Select Committee on the Bill "for the levy of Port-dues in the Port of Aden."

MINORS (FORT ST. GEORGE).

MR. ELIOTT presented the Report of the Select Committee on the Bill "to extend the provisions of Act XXI of 1855 in the Presidency of Fort St. George to Minors not subject to the superintendence of the Court of Wards."

CONCEALMENT OF GOVERNMENT PROPERTY.

MR. PEACOCK postponed the motion (which stood in the Orders of the Day) for a Committee of the whole Council on the Bill "for the punishment of persons who knowingly receive or conceal arms or other property belonging to the East India Company."

He said, there had been some differences of opinion amongst the Members of the Select Committee with respect to certain provisions, and the Bill and the Report had been finally settled only this day. Before he proceeded with the Bill, it would be better to print and circulate it to Honorable Members as it now stood.

INDIAN PENAL CODE.

MR. PEACOCK moved that Mr. LeGeyt be substituted for Sir Arthur Buller as a Member of the Select Committee on "The Indian Penal Code."

Agreed to.

The Council adjourned.

Saturday, March 20, 1858.

PRESENT:

The Honorable J. A. Dorin, *Vice-President*, in the Chair.

Hon. the Chief Justice,	P. W. LeGeyt, Esq.,
Hon'ble J. P. Grant,	and
Hon'ble B. Peacock,	E. Currie, Esq.,
D. Eliott, Esq.,	

THE CLERK reported to the Council that he had received from the Under-Secretary to the Government of India in the Home Department a copy of a Despatch from the Court of Directors declining to comply with the prayer of the Memorials from the British Indian Association for the disallowance by the Court of Act XX of 1856 (to make better provision for the appointment and maintenance of Police Chowkeydars in Cities, Towns, Stations, Suburbs, and Bazaars in the Presidency of Fort William in Bengal), and Act VI of 1857 (for the acquisition of land for public purposes).

The following Messages from the Governor-General were brought by the Vice-President and read:—

PORT-DUES (FORT ST. GEORGE).

MESSAGE No. 128.

The Governor-General informs the Legislative Council that he has given his assent to the Bill which was passed by them on the 20th February 1858, entitled "A Bill for the levy of Port-dues and fees at Ports within the Presidency of Fort St. George."

By order of the Right Honorable the Governor-General.

G. F. EDMONSTONE,
Secy. to the Govt. of India, with the Govr. Genl.

ALLAHABAD, *The* 1*st March* 1858.

PORT-DUES (KURRACHEE).

MESSAGE No. 129.

The Governor-General informs the Legislative Council that he has given his assent to the Bill which was passed by them on the 13th February 1858, entitled "A Bill for the levy of Port-dues and fees in the Port of Kurrachee."

By order of the Right Honorable the Governor-General.

G. F. EDMONSTONE,
Secy. to the Govt. of India, with the Govr.-Genl.

ALLAHABAD,
The 12th March 1858.

SETTLEMENT OF ALLUVIAL LANDS (BENGAL.)

On the Order of the Day being read for the second reading of the Bill "to explain Regulation XI. 1825 of the Bengal Code, and to prescribe rules for the settlement of land gained by alluvion"—

MR. CURRIE said, since he had come into the Council Chamber, it had been intimated to him that it was the wish of some Honorable Members that he should postpone his motion. The Honorable Member for the North-Western Provinces, also, who was not present to-day, was desirous of making some observations on the Bill. He should therefore postpone his Motion.

CONCEALMENT OF GOVERNMENT PROPERTY.

MR. PEACOCK moved that the Council resolve itself into a Committee on the Bill "for the punishment of persons who knowingly receive or conceal arms or other property belonging to the East India Company;" and that the Committee be instructed to consider the Bill in the amended form in which the Select Committee had recommended it to be passed.

Agreed to.

The Bill passed through Committee without amendment.

The Council resumed its sitting.

MINORS (FORT ST. GEORGE).

MR. ELIOTT moved that the Council resolve itself into a Committee on the Bill "to extend the provisions of Act XXI of 1855 in the Presidency of Fort St. George to Minors not subject to the superintendence of the Court of Wards;" and that the Committee be instructed to consider the Bill in the amended form in which the Select Committee had recommended it to be passed.

Agreed to.

The Bill passed through Committee without amendment.

The Council having resumed its sitting, the Bills passed through Committee were reported.

CONCEALMENT OF GOVERNMENT PROPERTY.

MR. PEACOCK moved that the Bill "for the punishment of persons who unlawfully possess or conceal arms or other property belonging to Her Majesty or to the East India Company," be now read a third time and passed.

The Motion was carried, and the Bill read a third time.

MR. PEACOCK moved that Mr. Grant be requested to take the above Bill to the President in Council in order that it may be submitted to the Governor-General for his assent.

Agreed to.

IMPRESSMENT OF CARRIAGE AND SUPPLIES FOR TROOPS AND TRAVELLERS (BENGAL).

MR. ELIOTT moved that a communication received by him from the Madras Government be laid upon the table and referred to the Select Committee on the Bill "to amend the law regarding the provision of carriage and supplies for troops and travellers, and to punish unlawful impressment."

Agreed to.

The Council adjourned.

Saturday March 27, 1858.

PRESENT:

The Honorable J. A. Dorin, *Vice-President*, in the Chair.

Hon. J. P. Grant, | E. Currie, Esq.,
Hon. B. Peacock, | and
D. Eliott, Esq., | H. B. Harington, Esq.
P. W. LeGeyt, Esq.,

MESSAGES.

The following Messages from the Governor-General were brought by the Vice-President and read.

PORT-DUES (GULF OF CAMBAY).

MESSAGE No. 130.

The Right Honorable the Governor-General informs the Legislative Council that he has given his assent to the Bill which was passed by them on the 6th instant, entitled "A Bill for the levy of Port-dues in certain Ports within the limits of the Gulf of Cambay."

G. F. EDMONSTONE,
Secy. to the Govt. of India with the Govr. Genl.

ALLAHABAD,
The 19th March 1858.

CONFISCATION OF VILLAGES, &c.

MESSAGE No. 131.

The Right Honorable the Governor-General informs the Legislative Council that he has given his assent to the Bill which was passed by them on the 6th instant, entitled "A Bill to authorize the confiscation of Villages, the imposition of fines, and the forfeiture of certain offices in cases of rebellion and other crimes committed by Inhabitants of Villages or by members of tribes; and also to provide for the punishment of proprietors of land who neglect to assist in the suppression of rebellion or in the apprehension of rebels, mutineers, or deserters."

G. F. EDMONSTONE,
Secy. to the Govt. of India with the Govr. Genl.

ALLAHABAD,
The 19th March 1858.

STAMPS.

THE CLERK brought under the consideration of the Council a Petition of Mahtabchand Bahadoor, Raja of Burdwan.

The Petitioner stated that he "had brought a regular suit in the Court of the Principal Sudder Ameen in Zillah Hooghly" "for the recovery of arrears of rent with interest; and that the case was dismissed on the ground that the names of the parties and witnesses to the putnee lease were not written on the same sheet of paper, but on two different sheets: the whole lease or instrument was, however, written on stamped paper of the full value required by the Law." That it was his intention "to appeal against this decision to the Court of Sudder Dewanny Adawlut, but he was advised by his Counsel that it was useless, as that Court would certainly dismiss his appeal under the authority of two cases." The Petitioner prayed that the Council "will be pleased to pass a declaratory Act to explain or alter the general rule contained in Schedule A Regulation X. 1829, by declaring that it was and is not the intention of Regulation X. 1829 to invalidate any deed, or instrument, or document specified in the said Regulation or in the Schedules thereunto annexed, and on which the full stamp-duties required by Government have been paid, although the seals and signatures of the parties and witnesses thereupon be not contained on one sheet or piece of paper."

MR. CURRIE moved that the above Petition be printed.

Agreed to.

SUBORDINATE CRIMINAL COURT AT OOTACAMUND.

MR. ELIOTT presented the Report of the Select Committee on the Bill "to extend Act XXV of 1855," (to empower the Session Judge of Coimbatore to hold Sessions at Ootacamund on the Neilghery Hills)..

ESTATE OF THE LATE NABOB OF THE CARNATIC.

MR. PEACOCK moved the first reading of a Bill "to provide for the administration of the Estate, and for the payment of the debts of the late Nabob of the Carnatic." In doing so, he said the Council was aware that, by Act I of 1844, it was enacted "that no writ or process shall at any time be sued forth or prosecuted against the person, goods, or property of His Highness the Nabob of the Carnatic, or of the Nabob Regent for the time being, or of any person whose name shall be included in any list so published in the Gazette as aforesaid, and which for the time being shall be in force and effect for the purpose of this Act, unless such writ or process shall be so sued forth or prosecuted with the consent of the Governor in Council of Fort St. George first had and obtained; and that any writ or process which shall at any time be sued forth or prosecuted against the person or goods or property of His said Highness," "without such consent as aforesaid," "shall be utterly null and void." There was every reason to believe that the property left by the late Nabob of the Carnatic would not be sufficient to pay the whole of the debts due from him at the time of his death, and it had been decided that the Government should pay in full the amount of their several debts to such of the creditors as would consent to have them estimated, in the case of monies lent, according to the actual sums advanced, with interest at six per cent., and in the case of goods sold, according to the fair marketable value of the goods. It was believed that many of the creditors of the Nabob, partly in consequence of the exemption from process provided by Act I of 1844, and partly from other reasons, had contracted for very exorbitant rates of interest, and for prices considerably higher than would have been charged to other purchasers. When, therefore, it was decided that the Government should pay the Nabob's debts, it was not considered reasonable or just that they should be liable for more than the sums which had actually been advanced, with interest at six per cent., or, where the claim was for goods sold, for more than the fair marketable value thereof. To that extent, and to that only, the Government were prepared to pay the debts of the deceased Nabob in full.

But it was considered that it would be unjust to debar any creditor from insisting upon his strict legal rights, if he wished to do so. If, for instance, a creditor should say:—"I contracted for so much interest; I am entitled to recover it; and I insist upon my right:" well and good, let him pursue his right; but in that case, he must look to the assets of the deceased Nabob's estate; and if they should be insufficient to pay the debts in full, he would recover only so much as a rateable division of the assets among the general body of the creditors would provide for his share. A question might be raised as to whether, under Act I of 1844, an action could be brought by any creditors against the representatives of the Nabob's estate without the previous consent of Government. The Council were aware that the Supreme Court at Madras had decided that that Act was merely personal to the Nabob, and that it ceased to confer any exemption upon members of his family or household after his death; but very great doubts existed whether, if a creditor sued out an execution against his estate, he would not be suing out a writ against his "goods or property" within the meaning of the Act; and if so, it could not be done without the consent of the Government of Madras. The Bill proposed to give any creditor the power of instituting a suit in the nature of an administration suit in the Supreme Court of Judicature. It would also enable creditors to recover who were willing to come in and accept payment of their claims estimated in the equitable manner he had mentioned. It provided that the Government should appoint an Officer to be called the Receiver of the Carnatic Property, whose duty it would be to collect all the assets of the estate, whether real or personal. It gave power to any creditor to institute in the Supreme Court a suit in the nature of an administration suit against such Receiver; and the Court was authorized in such suit to compel all persons holding mortgages, or liens, or other security on any part of the property, to come in and establish their claims. The Court would take an account of all debts due from the Nabob, and of all assets liable for the payment of them. A doubt might exist whether the East India Company was not entitled to all property belonging to the deceased Nabob in the nature of State or public property; but the East India Company was willing to forego any such claim for the benefit of the creditors and of the representatives of the Nabob, if there should be a surplus after payment of the creditors. It had at first been supposed that the most expedient course would be to appoint a Commission to take an account of the debts, to collect the assets, and to pay the creditors; and the Government of Madras had proceeded in the matter so far as to appoint such a Commission; but it had been subsequently suggested that the decisions of the Commission might not be satisfactory to the creditors; and the Government of Madras therefore proposed to leave it to the Supreme Court of Judicature at Madras to ascertain the amount of the debts. He would read an extract upon this subject from a letter which had been received from the Government of Madras. They said—

"It has been decided that the debts of the Carnatic Sircar shall be liquidated in a straightforward manner, and to the full extent to which they are justly due. It would be deeply to be deplored if any opportunity that could be avoided were given to arouse distrust in, or throw discredit upon the intentions and acts of Government. In proposing a Commission, and nominating the Members who were to sit upon it, this Government believed that they had suggested the most simple and expeditious mode of settling the affairs of the late Prince. Further consideration and recent information have led them to change that opinion, and they are now disposed to concur with Mr. Dale that the decision of the Commissioners would not be viewed with satisfaction."

Again, they say—

"The Government entertain no doubt that the Judges of Her Majesty's Supreme Court would prove a much more satisfactory tribunal to all parties concerned than the present Commission, or than any other that could be appointed."

The Bill, therefore, proposed to allow any creditor to institute a suit in the Supreme Court for the administration of the assets of the Nabob. Any creditor who, on being called upon to prove his claim, should come in and sign an agreement to receive payment of the full amount of his debt estimated in the equitable manner which he (Mr. Peacock) had indicated, would have a right to have his claim heard and decided by the Supreme Court at once, without waiting for the determination of the administration suit; and upon the Court's determining what amount was fairly due to him according to the principle of assessment before mentioned, the creditor would be entitled to recover such amount out of the property in the hands of the Receiver, or, if there should not be sufficient in his hands out of the Public Treasury. Those creditors, if any, who should stand upon their strict legal rights, and insist upon payment of the whole amount of their claims, would wait until the determination of the suit. If it should turn out that the assets would yield only a dividend to the creditors generally, and that the creditors who had been paid in full under this Bill had received more than they would have been entitled to as their proportion of the assets had they prosecuted their claims, the Government would make good the excess so paid. Thus, if the assets should yield only ten shillings in the pound for division amongst the creditors, taking their claims to be estimated according to the contracts entered into by the Nabob, and a creditor should come in and say—"I am willing to receive payment of my claim in full on the principle provided by the Act," and the amount of the claim estimated in that mode should be equal to fifteen shillings in the pound, the creditor would receive the whole fifteen shillings in the pound. But that would be a larger amount by five shillings in the pound than he could have recovered if he had resorted to the estate; and the Government would make good the extra five shillings in the pound by placing it in the hands of the Receiver for the benefit of the other creditors. Thus, no injustice would be done to the creditors who might stand upon their strict legal rights. They would be paid as far as the assets would go, but they could have no claim against the Government to pay them any thing beyond.

These were the general provisions of the Bill; and it appeared to him that the arrangement proposed was an exceedingly fair and liberal one. He thought it unnecessary to enter into the details of the measure. The Bill would be published for general information; and the creditors of the Nabob and others would have an opportunity of bringing before the Council any objections which they might see against it. But he thought that publication for a month or six weeks would be sufficient for this purpose; and therefore, he should probably move hereafter that the Bill be published for that period only, instead of the period of three months required by the Standing Orders. In the meantime, he should conclude by moving the first reading.

The Bill was read a first time.

SETTLEMENT OF ALLUVIAL LANDS (BENGAL).

MR. CURRIE moved the second reading of the Bill to "explain Regulation XI. 1825 of the Bengal Code, and to prescribe rules for the settlement of land gained by alluvion."

MR. PEACOCK said, though he was not so well acquainted with the Revenue system of Bengal as the Honorable Mover of the Bill, it yet appeared to him that the Bill was objectionable—first, because it was a declaratory Act; and secondly, because it would be an unjust measure, and would injuriously affect private rights and interests.

With respect to the first objection, having given the best consideration that he could to the question, it appeared to him that the Bill called upon the Council to declare the existing Law to be different from that which he really thought it was, and to say that the conclusion to which the Sudder Board of Revenue had come, and the Sudder Court had come, on the subject, was wrong. He thought, however, that before the Legislative Council declared that a decision passed by the Sudder Court, which was the highest judicial tribunal of the East India Company, was wrong, they ought to be clearly satisfied that it was so. If the law, as the Sudder Court laid it down, required amendment, the Legislative Council might amend it; but to declare that the decision of the Court was wrong, would be to act as a Court of Appeal, which was not the constitutional duty of the Legislative Council. The Bill recited that—

"Whereas Section IV Regulation XI. 1825 of the Bengal Code contains provisions for determining the right of property in alluvial land gained by gradual accession from the recess of a river or of the sea, and doubts have been entertained as to the legal effect of certain words in the said Section with respect to the connexion of such land with the estate which it adjoins, and to the conditions under which it is to be assessed for the Government Revenue; and whereas it is expedient that such doubts should be removed; it is declared and enacted as follows."

It then proceeded to declare, not that the law should be altered for the future, but what the scope and object of Section IV of Regulation XI. 1825 were. It said—

"The object and scope of Regulation XI. 1825 of the Bengal Code is merely to lay down rules for determining the right of property in alluvial land; and the declaration in Section IV of the said Regulation, that 'when land may be gained by gradual accession, whether from the recess of a river or of the sea, it shall be considered an increment to the tenure of the person to whose land or estate it is thus annexed,' and any other words in the said Section, shall not be understood as making the right of property in the said land inseparable from the right of property in the estate which it adjoins, nor as requiring that, in the assessment of the public Revenue upon the said land, it should be treated as if it were inseparable from such estate."

He apprehended that Regulation XI. 1825 was really, in effect, a declaratory Act, because it had been decided, long before that Regulation was passed, that gradual accretions became part of the estate to which they attached themselves. The Board of Revenue, in their letter to the Government of Bengal on this subject, said—

"In the cases noted in the margin" (that was to say, cases decided by the Sudder Court so far back as the years 1811 and 1819), "the Court recognized the principle that lands gained by the gradual retirement of a river were the lawful accession of the estate to which they were so annexed; and in the latter of the two, the principle is referred to as one then '*established*.' There does not appear to have been any case published from 1811 to the end of 1819 bearing upon the point.

"In 1819, the Legislature first alluded to churs; and in Clause 2 Section III Regulation II of that year it is enacted that churs which had formed since the period of the decennial settlement were liable to assessment. Nothing, however, was then said about the parties entitled to these churs."

Then came Regulation XI. 1825, Clause 1 Section IV of which was worded thus—

"When land may be gained by gradual accession, whether from the recess of a river or of the sea, it shall be considered an increment to the tenure of the person to whose land or estate it is thus annexed, whether such land or estate be held immediately from Government by a Zemindar or other superior landholder, or as a subordinate tenure by any description of under-tenant whatever. Provided that the increment of land thus obtained shall not entitle the person in possession of the estate or tenure to which the land may be annexed, to a right of property or permanent interest therein beyond that possessed by him in the estate or tenure to which the land may be annexed, and shall not in any case be understood to exempt the holder of it from the payment to Government of any assessment for the Public Revenue to which it may be liable under the provisions of Regulation II. 1819, or of any other Regulation in force."

Now, the question was, whether, when an alluvion took place, and the original estate which adjoined was thereby increased, the alluvion became an increment to the parent estate, or was so far a separate estate that the zemindar was entitled, without the consent of Government, to have it separately assessed, so that the increment could never be made responsible for the revenue assessed on the parent estate. If it was a separate estate, and not liable to be sold in the event of the non-payment of the revenue assessed on the parent estate, this difficulty would arise. An estate might be granted on the banks of a river, and its value might greatly depend on its having a river frontage; but if an alluvion took place, and such alluvion was to be treated entirely as a separate estate, then the parent estate, which had a frontage on the river, would be entirely cut off from that frontage, and its value might consequently be materially diminished. There were many estates having wharves on the banks of rivers. If an alluvion accrued to any of them, and were not to be subject to the same tenure as that under which the parent estate was held, the wharf on the parent estate would become valueless, for there would be an estate intervening between it and the river. Suppose that, an accretion took place, and that, previously to the assessment of the increment, the revenue of the parent estate fell into arrear. Was it to be said that the parent estate could alone be sold for the non-payment of the revenue, and that the zemindar might hold the increment, and insist upon having it assessed as a separate estate?

If so, the Government might have to sell the parent estate at a very greatly deteriorated value, for it might be cut off from its frontage on the river. He (Mr. Peacock) contended that in such a case the increment became a portion of the original estate, and was liable to be sold as part of that estate for the arrears of Revenue. Now, if the increment ever became a portion of the parent estate and was even liable for the revenue of that estate, the Zemindar could not possibly have the right, which this Bill proposed to give him even without the consent of the Revenue officers, to have it assessed as a separate estate and discharged from such liability.

If the Zemindar should be willing to have the increment assessed as part of his estate, the existing Law would enable him to do so. The revenue of the estate would then be increased, and the increment as well as the parent estate would be liable for the payment of such revenue. If, however, the Zemindar should object to have the increment assessed as part of his estate, the existing law would not compel him to do so. He might say—"I had rather not incorporate the revenue of the new land with the revenue of the old estate, because if the increased revenue be not paid, the whole estate will be sold;" and it would be unjust to compel him, to accept that risk. According to the decisions of the Sudder Court, the existing law would not compel him to do so. He would be at liberty to refuse; and then the increment would be let out on farming lease, and a malikhana would be reserved to him. In that case the increment could not be sold away from the parent estate for the arrears due in respect of the increment.

But there was another view to which he would direct attention. Clause I Section IV of Regulation XI. 1825 declared that the increment should be held by the same tenure as the parent estate. The words of the Clause were—

> "When land may be gained by gradual accession, whether from the recess of a river or of the sea, it shall be considered an increment to the tenure of the person to whose land or estate it is thus annexed, whether such land or estate be held immediately from Government by a Zemindar or other superior landholder, or as a subordinate tenure by any description of under-tenant whatever."

Suppose that a Zemindar should grant out a putnee talook to be held at a fixed rent in perpetuity by the lessee and his heirs for ever—that an alluvion should take place—and that the putnee talookdar should fail to pay his rent to the Zemindar, thus rendering his tenure liable to sale. It was clear that the Zemindar would have a right to sell the alluvion as well as the original estate granted out by him, because the alluvion became an increment to that estate. Now, if the Zemindar could sell both the increment and the parent estate for arrears of rent due by his putneedar to him, why should not the Government have a similar right of selling the increment as well as the parent estate for arrears of revenue due from the Zemindar? Was not the increment just as much liable to Government for arrears of revenue payable by the Zemindar, as it was to the Zemindar for arrears of rent payable to him by the putnee talookdar? But in addition to the injury which might be done to Government by giving the Zemindar a right to have the increment assessed as a separate estate without the consent of the revenue officers, thus depreciating the value of the security which the Government had for its revenue, it appeared to him that the Council might very much injure the interests of putneedars and the holders of other under-tenures, if they allowed the Zemindar to have the increment to his estate assessed as a separate estate. The putnee talook might originally have a frontage on the river: the increment might intervene between the whole of the talook and the river. But if the increment could without the consent of the talookdar be converted into a separate estate and be regarded and treated as in all respects separate from and independent of the original estate, it might be sold away from the original estate for the non-payment of the revenue separately assessed upon it, and the talookdar might be altogether deprived of his river-frontage. What would the effect be with respect to estates such as those on the banks of the Mutlah river, the value of which depended upon their abutting on the river; or estates such as those on the Strand Road, the value of which depended upon their having a frontage on the river? Mr. Beaufort, the Legal Remembrancer, said in paragraph 10 of his Letter to the Government of Bengal, "one of the conditions of a settlement is that the land is hypothecated for the revenue assessed upon it." But, under this decree of the Sudder Court, it seems that the chur is also hypothecated for the revenue of the parent estate; and it follows that the latter is also hypothecated for the revenue of the former. Now, it appeared to him (Mr. Peacock) that Mr. Beaufort was correct in saying that the land was hypothecated for the revenue assessed upon it. He thought that any increment by alluvion was also hypothecated for the revenue of the parent estate; but he failed to perceive how it followed that the parent estate would be hypothecated for the revenue of the increment, unless the Zemindar should consent to the terms of a settlement by which the parent estate and the increment should be considered as one entire estate charged with the aggregate increased jumma. If the Zemindar consented to have the increment made a part of the original estate, and the whole estate including the increment made liable for an increased jumma, there would be no hardship upon him, because he would be a consenting party. But if he refused to make the increment a part of the original estate, and the increment was let out on a farming lease, subject to a malikana allowance, the original estate would not become responsible for that malikana allowance, or for the Government revenue assessed upon the increment. It would not, therefore, be hypothecated for the Government revenue. Then, again, if the Zemindar consented to make the increment part of the parent estate, no damage would be done to the putnee talookdar, because the putnee talookdar would remain in possession, not only of the parent estate, but also of the increment. The Sudder Court, in the judgment which formed one of the annexures to the Bill, said—

"The right of Government to assess the increment is reserved by the same Clause (Clause 1 Section IV Regulation XI. 1825); and by Section V Regulation VII. of 1822, if the proprietor of the estate refuses to engage for the mehal at the rate of assessment fixed by the revenue authorities, and it consequently remains in their hands, or is farmed by them, he is entitled to receive from them an allowance of malikana, in other words, a percentage on the rent of the mehal representing or assumed to represent the net profit resulting to the proprietor after the payment of the Government revenue and certain customary deductions for the expenses of collection, risk of loss, &c."

It appeared to him that that judgment of the Sudder Court composed of Mr. Trevor, Mr. Samuells, and Mr. Money—gentlemen of great knowledge and experience—followed the decisions which had been passed upon the subject up to the year 1838, when the Circular Order was issued to which reference was made in the annexure. In his opinion that judgment was well-considered, sound, and correct. He thought that the Council ought not to be asked to declare in effect that it was wrong. If the Council should by a legislative enactment declare it to be erroneous, might not the parties to the suit apply for a review of judgment? They might say—"the Legislative Council, placing themselves in the position of an appellate Court, have pronounced that judgment to be founded upon an erroneous construction of the law; and we apply to you to correct that judgment, and to decide upon our rights, not according to the construction which you put upon the meaning of Regulation XI. 1825, but according to the construction which the Legislature has declared that the enactment ought to have received." Then, again, there might be cases of appeal at this moment depending on this very construction of Regulation XI. 1825. Were the Legislative Council to influence the result of those cases, by declaring that the intention of the Legislature of 1825, in passing Regulation XI of that year, was not that which the Sudder Court reading the Regulation had decided it to be? Regulation XI. 1825 spoke for itself; and the proper tribunal for determining its meaning was the Sudder Court, and not the Legislative Council. The Legislative Council did not sit to declare the meaning of laws. They could judge of the meaning of a law passed in 1825 only from its wording. The Sudder Court had the same means as they of judging of the intention of the Legislature of that day; and they had moreover the benefit of mature experience and, what this Council certainly had not, the advantage of hearing the question fully argued on both sides. As a general principle, he thought that laws declaratory of the meaning of former laws were not expedient, especially after the Courts of Justice had put a different construction upon the laws to be interpreted. In this case, the Sudder Board of Revenue and the Sudder Court thought one way; the Lieutenant-Governor, the Legal Remembrancer, and the Honorable Mover of this Bill thought another. The opinion of these three gentlemen was against the opinion of the Sudder Court; but that was no sufficient reason for asking the Legislative Council to declare that the opinion of the former was the correct one. Which was the constituted tribunal for determining the meaning of Acts? He had no hesitation in saying that the Sudder Court was the proper tribunal for determining the meaning of the Regulation in question, and he did not think that it was the part of the Legislative Council to declare in effect that the construction put by a Court of Justice upon a particular law was erroneous. He thought that the decisions of the Sudder Court were entitled to as much respect as the decisions of the Supreme Court; and he did not believe that, if the Supreme Court had put a construction upon an Act of Parliament or of the local Legislature from which particular Members of this Council might dissent, that any Member of the Council, except under some very extraordinary circumstance, would propose to declare that the meaning of the Act was different from that which the Court had held it to be.

It might be said that the declaratory parts of the Bill might be struck out, and the Bill be left so as only to enact what the law should be in future. If the law required amendment, he was prepared to amend it; but speaking with great deference, he did not see that any inconvenience could result from the law as it stood; on the contrary, he thought that, if the law were altered as proposed, not only might the Government be deprived of a security for its revenue which it now had in the case of estates abutting upon rivers, but very great injustice might be done to private individuals who were not before the Council. The Bill provided that—

"If it be so agreed on between the Revenue authorities and the proprietors, the land gained by alluvion may be united with the estate which it adjoins; and in such case the Revenue assessed upon the alluvial land shall be added to the jumma of the original estate, and a new engagement shall be executed for the payment of the aggregate amount."

That was the case at present. If the zemindar agreed, the alluvion might be assessed as part of the parent estate, and there was no hardship upon him, because he was a consenting party; and there was no injury to the putnee talookdar or the holder of any other under-tenure, because he would remain in possession of both the parent estate and the increment. But the new part of the proposed law was contained in the following words:—

"In cases in which such union is not agreed on, the alluvial land shall be assessed and

Mr. Peacock

settled as a separate estate with a separate jumma."

He did not see any sufficient reason for saying that, where the Zemindar did not agree to the union of the increment with the parent estate, the increment should be assessed and settled as a separate estate without the consent of Government or of the holders of under-tenures. At present, if the proprietor of the estate did not consent to the union, the increment was let out on a lease under Regulation VII. 1822, a malikana allowance being reserved to him; but it remained part of the original estate, and could not be sold separately for arrears of revenue—so that the original estate, the value of which might depend on its having a frontage on the river, could never be cut off from that frontage. This certainly seemed to him a just and sound principle.

But the proposed Bill having given the Zemindar a right to have the increment assessed as a separate estate with a separate jumma, proceeded to declare that thenceforward it "shall be regarded and treated as in all respects separate from and independent of the original estate."

If the revenue so assessed should fall into arrear, the alluvion would be sold as a separate estate, and would be taken by the purchaser as such. Then, what became of the river frontage of the putnee talookdar? He thought, it would be doubtful whether the putnee talookdar, even if he deposited the amount of arrear due to prevent the sale of the alluvion, would be entitled to recover it from the Zemindar, because the Bill declared that the alluvion should in all respects be treated and regarded as separate from and independent of the original estate. Section IX of the Sale Law of 1841 said, with respect to deposits made by any person not a proprietor of the estate in arrear,—

"if the party depositing, whose money shall have been credited as aforesaid, shall prove before a competent Civil Court that the deposit was made *in order to protect an interest of the said party* which would have been endangered or damaged by the sale of the estate, he shall be entitled to recover the amount of the deposit, with interest, from the proprietors of the said estate."

At present the interest of the talookdar depended upon its being an increment to the estate, whereas the Bill declared that it was to be regarded in all respects as separate from and independent of it. By the declaration of this Bill, therefore, that which, by the Common Law, by the Civil Law, by the decisions of the Sudder Court, was a part of the original estate, and an increment to it, might be severed for ever from the original estate and treated as in all respects separate from and independent of it. The Honorable Mover of the Bill gave no sufficient reason in his Statement of objects and reasons to shew that such an alteration of the law was necessary. The Board of Revenue, in their letter to the Government of Bengal, expressed their opinion that, whether regard be had to the law or to expediency, there was no sufficient reason for deviating from the instructions laid down in the Circular Orders of 1833 and 1838, by which they proposed that in future the Revenue authorities should be guided in the assessment and settlement of churs.

They said—

"Whether, therefore, regard be had to the law or to expediency, the Board are of opinion that there is no sufficient reason for deviating from the instructions regarding the settlement of alluvial increments laid down in the Circular Orders of 1833 and 1838, by which in future they propose that the Revenue authorities be guided in the assessment and settlement of churs."

The Circulars of 1833 and 1838 were in accordance with the principle laid down by the Sudder Court.

The Board of Revenue, therefore, did not see any necessity for the proposed change in the law, and said expressly that they did not require it. Then, why should it be made? Was there any sufficient reason given for it? It was true he had the opinion of the Legal Remembrancer? Was this Council to act on that opinion as over-ruling the Judgment of the Sudder Court upon a point of law, and the opinion of the Board of Revenue upon a point of expediency in a matter of Revenue? It appeared to him that the opinion was not correct; and he, for his own part, was not prepared to act upon it. He thought that, in making the change, the Council might be doing injustice to the interests of persons not before them, and would not be treating with proper respect the opinion of the learned Judges of the Sudder Court who had decided the question upon a different principle, —a principle which had been declared in former decisions and acted upon up to the year 1841. For these reasons he should feel it to be his duty to vote against the second reading of the Bill.

MR. CURRIE said, he rose with great deference to endeavor to answer what had been advanced against the Bill by the Honorable and earned Member. The Honorable and learned Member objected to the Bill—first, because it was a declaratory Act; and secondly, because it was unjust. He had stated some general objections to declaratory legislation, which he (Mr. Currie) did not pretend to contest; but still, it was the fact that declaratory Acts were véry frequently passed; and when the decisions of judicial Courts rendered it necessary, in the opinion of the Legislature, to change the practice which they laid down, the Legislature might make the change, either by altering the existing law, or, if they thought the construction of the Courts not to be in accordance with the proper interpretation of the law, by declaring what its meaning really was. It appeared to him that the Legislature which passed an Act was, in the last resort, the proper authority for determining its meaning. He thought that he could not well have framed this Bill except as a declaratory enactment. Still, it was not, perhaps, absolutely necessary that it should be declaratory; and if the Bill were allowed to be read a second time, and the Select Committee to whom it might be referred should be of opinion that it might be altered so as to attain the ends desired in another form, he should have no objection to such alteration being made.

But the Honorable and learned Member had further said that he considered the Bill opposed to the right interpretation of the law. From that view he must entirely dissent.

(MR. CURRIE here read Section I of the Bill.)

The object and scope of a Regulation were to be found in its Title and Preamble. The Title of Regulation XI. 1825 described it as—

"A Regulation for declaring the rules to be observed in determining claims to lands gained by alluvion, or by dereliction of a river, or the sea."

The Preamble declared that—

"The lands gained from the rivers or sea by the means above mentioned," (that was by alluvion or dereliction) "are a frequent source of contention and affray; and, although the law and custom of the country have established rules applicable to such cases, these rules not being generally known, the Courts of Justice have sometimes found it difficult to determine the rights of litigant parties claiming Churs or other lands gained in the manner above described."

Therefore—

"the Governor General in Council has deemed it proper to enact the following rules for the general information of individuals, as well as for the guidance of the Courts of Judicature."

The object of the Regulation, therefore, was to prevent a recurrence of violent affrays in consequence of opposing claimants taking possession of new alluvial formations, and to provide fixed rules by which all questions relating to the proprietary right in the formations might be determined. In order to the determination of these questions, the Regulation declared that land "gained by gradual accession, whether from the recess of a river or of the sea," "shall be considered an increment to the tenure of the person to whose land or estate it is thus annexed, whether such land or estate be held immediately from Government by a Zemindar or other superior landholder, or as a subordinate tenure by any description of undertenant whatever;" and that the right of property in it should correspond precisely with the right of property possessed in the estate to which it had accreted. Surely, the object of such an enactment was to declare who was the rightful proprietor at the time the alluvion formed, or at the time it became valuable. The Regulation did not declare that the new land should be for all future time inseparable from the estate which it adjoined. The law of the Permanent Settlement gave the proprietor of an estate free liberty to dispose of any part of it; and the purchaser, by application to the Collector, might obtain an apportionment of the jumma, and hold his purchase as a separate estate. Why might not the same thing be done with the alluvial lan supposing it to be the effect of Regulation XI. 1825 to make it a part of th old estate? Why might not the proprietor dispose of his proprietary rights and if the Collector had assessed th new land with a separate jumma, why was not the purchaser to hold it as a separate estate? The Honorable and learned Member had said that the value o an estate might depend on its river frontage; and that, if an alluvial formation between the estate and the river were settled separately, the value of the estate would be depreciated. But the alluvion could not be settled separately except with the concurrence of the proprietor himself. It could not be transferred to another person, except by some act of his; and in such case, even though the separation or transfer depreciated the value of the old estate, there appeared to be no reason why any one else should interfere. In support of the view which he took of this point, the Honorable and learned Member had put the case of a putneedar holding a putnee talook in a settled estate, to which some new land had accreted. The Honorable and learned Member had said that the putneedar would be endamaged, if the alluvial land between his talook and the river were settled as a separate estate. But he must remember that the Bill did not in any way interfere with the provisions of Regulation XI. 1825; and Clause 1 Section IV of that Regulation provided that the new land "shall be considered an increment to the tenure of the person to whose land or estate it is thus annexed, whether such land or estate be held immediately from Government by a Zemindar or other superior landholder, or as a subordinate tenure by any description of under-tenant whatever."

Of course, then, if the land to which the alluvion accreted was held in putnee, the putneedar would have a right to extend his putnee tenure over the accretion also; and, if the accretion were settled as a separate estate, he would be a putneedar in the new estate precisely in the same manner as he was in the old. That was unquestionably the case. Under Regulation VII. 1822, it was the duty of the Collector, in making a settlement, to take cognizance of all the claims of under-tenants; and in taking an engagement from the proprietor for the payment of the Government revenue, he would provide at the same time for the legal rights of the Putneedar.

So much as to the right of property in the alluvion being inseparable from the right of property in the estate which it adjoined.

Then Section I of the Bill provided that nothing contained in Section IV of Regulation XI. 1825 should be understood as requiring that, in the assessment of revenue, the alluvion should be treated as inseparable from the old estate. Regulation XI. 1825 contained no provision whatever as to the mode of assessing the new land. It left that to other laws. It said expressly that the right to the land "shall not in any case be understood to exempt the holder of it from the payment to Government of any assessment for the public Revenue, to which it may be liable under the provisions of Regulation II. 1819, or of any other Regulation in force." Now Regulation II. 1819, Clause 2, Section III, said—

"The foregoing principles shall be deemed applicable, not only to tracts of land such as are described to have been brought into cultivation in the Sunderbuns, but to all churs and islands formed since the period of the decennial settlement, and generally to all lands gained by alluvion or dereliction since that period, whether from an introcession of the sea, an alteration in the course of rivers, or the gradual accession of soil on their banks."

The principles referred to were that

"all lands which, at the period of the decennial settlement, were not included within the limits of any pergunnah, mouza, or other divisions of estates for which a distinct settlement may have been made since the period above referred to, nor lands held free of assessment under a valid and legal title of the nature specified in Regulations XIX and XXXVII. 1793, and in the corresponding Regulations subsequently enacted, are and shall be considered liable to assessment, *in the same manner as other unsettled mehals.*"

So that the letter of the law certainly authorized the settlement of alluvial lands as separate estates—that was to say, in the same mode as all other unsettled mehals.

It appeared to him, therefore, that the declaration in Section I of the Bill, both as to the right of property not being inseparable, and as to the mode of settlement, was entirely in consonance with the law.

The Honorable and learned Member had said that the late judgment of the Sudder Court followed the decisions of the Courts from time immemorial. He (Mr. Currie) was not aware of any decisions on the subject other than those quoted by the Board of Revenue, and they only went to declare, in accordance with the rules subsequently laid down in Regulation XI. 1825, that the right of property in alluvial land was vested in the proprietor of the estate to which the land was annexed. Upon this point there was no question: the Bill did not in any way interfere with those rules. He did not wish to discuss the late judgment of the Sudder Court, nor to say more respecting it than was absolutely necessary for the elucidation of the question. That judgment seemed to hold that an alluvion, if the Zemindar would not agree to consolidate it with the original estate to which it had accrued, might be let out in farm, reserving to the Zemindar a malikana allowance; and that, when it was so let out, it necessarily followed the fortunes of the original estate. That was the point on which the judgment appeared to him to be open to question.

With respect to the Revenue Laws, it was precisely the same thing whether an alluvion were separately assessed and let out in farm, or whether it were separately settled with the proprietor; in either case, it became a separate estate. The general principle was that every estate was responsible for the revenue assessed upon it. If an estate fell into arrear, it could be sold; but no second estate belonging to the same proprietor could be sold simultaneously for that arrear. Yet, that was what the judgment of the Sudder Court would seem to affirm; for it laid down that the sale of the old estate for arrears of revenue carried with it the proprietary right in the alluvial land, although that land was entered in the Collector's rent-roll as a separate estate.

The judgment of the Sudder Court seemed to imply that malikana was paid to the proprietors of the alluvial land, because they were the proprietors of the old estate. But that was not the case. Malikana was paid to them because they were the proprietors of the *Chur*, and not because they were the proprietors of the old estate. The right to the *Chur* was indeed derived from the right to the parent estate; but that did not make the one inseparable from the other.

Then, with respect to the point of injustice. The Honorable and learned Member had referred to the Circular Order issued in 1838, and the opinion given by the present Board of Revenue respecting it. It so happened that he himself was Secretary to the Board of Revenue in 1838, and that he had himself written the Circular Order in question. He, therefore, was well acquainted with all the circumstances of the case. The Honorable and learned Member had omitted to notice that there was a later Circular Order issued on this subject—a Circular Order of 1841, which has also been written by him (Mr. Currie). It had been found that the Order of 1838 was not only contrary to what had been the general practice of the Revenue Officers, but that it involved great practical difficulties; and, therefore, by the Order of 1841, the rule enjoined in it was discontinued, and the Revenue Authorities were instructed, whenever the zemindar objected to consolidate the alluvial land with his settled estate, to offer him a separate settlement of the alluvial land. That practice had continued, without intermission, up to the present time. Consequently, this Bill, in prescribing the course to be followed in the settlement of alluvial lands, was merely declaratory of what was the actual practice at the present time. The whole of the correspondence in the annexure arose out of a proposal by the Board of Revenue to the Lieutenant-Governor to rescind the Circular Order of 1841, and to discontinue the established practice. The Lieutenant-Governor, for the reasons given in Mr. Young's letter, had declined to give his assent to that proposal.

He thought he had already shewn that in the case of a Putneedar, to which the Honorable and learned Member had especially alluded, injustice could not occur, since the right of the Putneedar extended to the *chur* as well as to the parent estate. And with respect to proprietors, there could not be a doubt that to change the present practice, would be to subject them to very great hardship;

because they, whom the law declared to be the owners of the land, would, in a vast majority of cases, be shut out from engaging for it; for it would very rarely happen that a proprietor would be willing to give his settled estate as a security for the revenue assessed upon a formation which might be washed away the next year. And there were other reasons, in the peculiar character of alluvial formations in Bengal, why they should be treated as separate estates. At the mouth of the Megna, for instance, enormous *churs* frequently formed in the course of a few years. *Churs* might attach themselves to the mainland ten or twenty times the size of the adjoining estates, and only a small proportion of the whole extent might be under cultivation at the time of the assessment. This point was noticed in Mr. Young's letter, in paragraph 9, which said—

"As regards expediency, the Lieutenant-Governor cannot but think that the Circular Order of 1841 must in practice operate with more fairness and advantage to all parties than that of 1838 would do—to say nothing of the difficulties adverted to in the Sudder Board's letter of the 16th June 1841, as arising out of 'the theory of holding the original estate and the increments to be a single property.'"

(He would remark by the way that the difficulties here alluded to had actually occurred in the case decided by the Sudder Court. The sale of an old estate for an arrear which had accrued upon it had been held to convey the proprietary right, not only in that estate which was sold, but also in the new land which was not sold. If the Revenue Authorities had intended to sell the alluvion with the parent estate, they ought to have stated that intention in their proceedings. But there was no mention of it whatever in them.)

Mr. Young's letter went on to say—

"It is evident that to force a permanent settlement, on either the Government or the Zemindar, of lands of which the capabilities are altogether unknown, is always liable to operate injuriously to either one or the other. As regards the Government on the one hand, take the case, which will frequently happen, of an accretion to an estate of several miles of new *churs*, of which, at the time of assessment, only a few biggahs are under cultivation. How is it possible that a fair permanent settlement should be made in such a case? and yet the Circular of 1838 would require that the jumma of the accretion shall be added to, and included in, the Zemindar's original *takood*. Again, take the numerous cases, especially in some of the Behar Districts, in which land is formed, washed away, and re-formed almost periodically—is it to be expected that a Zemindar would choose to peril his estate (or subject himself to the risk of heavy loss) by doubling up with it so fleeting a possession? and, in default of his doing what he cannot be expected to do, is it just to refuse him the settlement when the law gives him the proprietary right?"

It appeared to him, therefore, that the objection to the Bill on the score of injustice, had no valid foundation.

In conclusion, he would only repeat with regard to the objection that the Bill was a declaratory law, that he would willingly consent to its being altered in this respect, if the Select Committee to whom it might be referred should consider it expedient to do so. But he trusted that the Council would not refuse to allow the Bill to be read a second time.

MR. GRANT said, he should move as an amendment that this debate be adjourned until the next Meeting of the Council. Very important questions had been raised in it. He did not propose to enter into them to-day. If his Motion were carried, he might perhaps address the Council upon them next Saturday; but he wished now only to state his reasons for moving an adjournment of the debate.

As he had said, the questions raised were very important. The first was the general question of the propriety of this Council passing declaratory Acts. He did not understand the Honorable and learned Member opposite (Mr. Peacock) to have gone the length of contending that the Council had not the power of passing purely declaratory Acts; but the Honorable and learned Member had said—and what he had said was worthy of all consideration—that there were grave objections to the Council passing declaratory Acts, except upon very rare and extraordinary occasions. For his own part, there was a slight doubt in his mind, and he believed that such a doubt had occurred to others much more conversant with such questions than himself, as to the power of the Council to pass a purely declaratory Act. The Council could not proceed in this matter on the analogy of the British Parliament, which had unquestionably the power to pass declaratory Acts, and exercised that power; but the British Parliament was, not only a Legislature, but a Legislature from its own inherent powers, and included within itself the highest Court of Justice in the Kingdom. This Council was not a Legislature from its own inherent powers, and was in no sense concerned with the administration of Justice. The question, whether it had authority to pass declaratory Acts, had never been raised before in this Council. It was one of very great importance, and ought to be fully discussed, as well as the question which had been raised by the Honorable and learned Member, of the propriety of the Council passing a declaratory Act, except upon very extraordinary occasions. To-day, unfortunately, the Council was deprived of two-thirds of its legal Members. Both the learned Judges of the Supreme Court who sat in it, were unavoidably absent. He thought, therefore, that the Council would take a proper course in postponing the further consideration of this question, in order that it might give a deliberate opinion upon it when it was a little stronger in its legal Members.

The second question raised—the question of Revenue law—was in itself likewise a very important one. He would say at once that, having read the papers annexed to the Bill, and given some slight consideration to the subject, his own opinion at present agreed with that held by the Lieutenant-Governor of Bengal, his Legal Remembrancer, and the Honorable Mover of the Bill. But, at the same time, the Honorable and learned Member opposite (Mr. Peacock) had brought forward arguments on the other side which, like all arguments advanced by him on such questions, were worthy of all candid, full, and deliberate consideration; and he was anxious to give them such consideration. He should be glad, for this reason also, if the debate were adjourned. The Honorable and learned Member opposite had said that, even if the Bill were amended so as not to be declaratory, it would be open to the objection that it would injuriously affect private interests, and had mentioned as an example the case of putnee talookdars. He (Mr. Grant) did not himself, as he then understood the point, see that it would do so. It rather appeared to him that it would leave putnee talookdars, under the supposed circumstances, in precisely the same position in which, in practice, they now were. They would be the holders of one putnee talook, part of which is in one assessed estate, and part in another. This is not an unfavorable position to be in. On the other hand, if the Council should reject this Bill, and give its sanction—which, by the rejection, it virtually would do—to the decision at which certain able Judges of the Sudder Court had arrived, it would injuriously affect the interests of Zemindars. For Zemindars can now, when alluvion grows upon their lands, engage for the revenue of the new soil, paying separately in respect of it a new jumma. If the jumma of the new soil were added to, and became a part of the jumma of the parent estate, each parcel of land, besides being responsible for its own revenue, would necessarily be hypothecated for the revenue assessed upon the other. This, as he understood, was not, in practice, the position of the Zemindars now. But if the Council upheld the views of the Honorable and learned Member, this would become their position.

Without entering into the merits of the questions raised, he would repeat that it did appear to him that both the questions were of such importance that the Council would not be the worse for being strengthened in its legal elements, and for a week's consideration, before it decided upon them.

MR. GRANT'S amendment was put, and carried.

AUTHENTICATION OF GOVERNMENT STAMPS.

MR. PEACOCK moved the second reading of the Bill "to provide for the authentication of Government Stamped Paper."

The Motion was carried, and the Bill read a second time.

MINORS (FORT ST. GEORGE.)

MR. ELIOTT moved that the Bill "to extend the provisions of Act XXI of 1855 in the Presidency of Fort St. George to Minors not subject to the superintendence of the Court of Wards" be now read a third time and passed.

rant

The Motion was carried, and the Bill read a third time.

PORT-DUES (ADEN).

Mr. LeGEYT moved that the Council resolve itself into a Committee on the Bill "for the levy of Port-dues in the Port of Aden;" and that the Committee be instructed to consider the Bill in the amended form in which the Select Committee had recommended it to be passed.

Agreed to.

Sections I to V were pased as they stood.

Section VI was passed after an amendment.

Section VII and the Preamble and Title were severally passed as they stood.

The Council having resumed its sitting, the Bill was reported.

MINORS (FORT ST. GEORGE).

Mr. ELIOTT moved that Mr. Grant be requested to take the Bill "to extend the provisions of Act XXI of 1855 in the Presidency of Fort St. George to Minors not subject to the superintendence of the Court of Wards" to the President in Council, in order that it might be submitted to the Governor-General for his assent.

Agreed to.

AUTHENTICATION OF GOVERNMENT STAMPS.

Mr. PEACOCK moved that the Standing Orders be suspended to enable him to proceed with the Bill "to provide for the authentication of Government Stamped Paper."

Mr. GRANT seconded the Motion, which was then agreed to.

Mr. PEACOCK moved that the Bill be referred to a Select Committee consisting of Mr. Currie, Mr. Harington, and the Mover, with an instruction to present their Report at the end of a fortnight.

Agreed to.

NOTICE OF MOTION.

Mr. LeGEYT gave notice that he would, on Saturday the 3rd of April next, move the third reading of the Bill "for the levy of Port-dues in the Port of Aden."

CIRCULAR ORDERS, &c. (PUNJAB).

Mr. HARINGTON moved that an application be made to the Supreme Government, requesting that copies of all Circular Orders and Constructions issued in the Punjab, either by the Chief Commissioner or the Judicial Commissioner, relating to the administration of Civil Justice in that Province, be laid before the Council.

Agreed to.

The Council adjourned.

Saturday, April 3, 1858.

Present:

The Honorable J. A. Dorin, *Vice-President*, in the Chair.

Hon. the Chief Justice,	P. W. LeGeyt, Esq.
Hon. J. P. Grant.	E. Currie, Esq.
Hon. B. Peacock,	and
D. Eliott, Esq.	H. B. Harington, Esq.

REGULATION OF PORTS (FORT St. GEORGE).

Mr. ELIOTT presented the Report of the Select Committee on the Bill "for the regulation of certain Ports within the Presidency of Fort St. George."

LIGHT-DUES (GULF OF CAMBAY).

Mr. LeGEYT presented the Report of the Select Committee on the Bill "to repeal the laws relating to the levy of Light-dues at Ports within the limits of the Gulf of Cambay."

SETTLEMENT OF ALLUVIAL LANDS (BENGAL).

On the Order of the Day being read for the adjourned debate on the Bill to "explain Regulation XI. 1825 of the Bengal Code, and to prescribe rules for the settlement of land gained by alluvion"—

The PRESIDENT said, he had to remind the Council that, according to the Standing Orders, Honorable Members could speak only once to the question; and that therefore those who had already spoken could not address the Council again, except in explanation.

Mr. GRANT said, as the Council had been so good as to adjourn the debate until this day upon his Motion, he had felt it his duty to go as carefully into the question at issue as he could. The question was one of very great importance; but, having given to it the most careful consideration in his power, he would say that it did not appear to him to be one of difficulty, or, speaking with deference, of doubt.

It was not the object to criticise the decision of the Sudder Court; and in speaking of it, he would wish always to be understood as speaking with the greatest respect for that high authority. But it was absolutely necessary for the Council, which had been called upon to legislate on the general subject to which the decision in question relates, to determine what the present state of the law on that subject is; for it could not legislate to any good purpose without ascertaining what the law at present is; and to ascertain what it is, it was absolutely necessary to see whether the view of the law which had been taken by the Sudder Court was a correct view or not. Therefore, the Council was constrained, whether it wished it or not, to enter into the question which was the question before the Sudder Court when they passed their decision. He had entered into it fully, and had come to the conclusion that the view of the present law taken by the Sudder Court was decidedly unsound. If it was a correct view, then our Revenue law was certainly in a most deplorable state, and had been in such a state for the last seventy years. The practice had always been contrary to the view of the law on which the decision is founded. If that view was correct, our system, not only of Permanent Settlement, but of temporary Settlement—our whole system of Settlement—our whole Revenue system, in fact, was nothing more than a delusion; and the right of property—that security in his estate which the system was intended to give, and was believed to have given to every landholder—was without support in law. This would be a very serious condition of things; and it was absolutely necessary, therefore, for the Council, when called upon to legislate in the matter, to go into the whole question at issue, and to consider whether such a condition of things actually exists or not.

He would state five fundamental principles of our Revenue law—which, he apprehended, were the elementary principles, the A. B. C. of the system. They would not be disputed, he was sure, being such as it was the first duty of every young Assistant Collector passing out of College to learn, and such as he must never forget during the whole course of his future official career. He would state them broadly, and generally; and so stated, he was convinced that no Revenue Lawyer would contest them.

The first principle was that no estate, and no portion of an estate, is liable to sale for its own arrears of revenue, unless the owner, or some one on his behalf, has engaged for that revenue. This would be admitted to be a principle of common sense and natural justice. It seemed to him hardly necessary to quote chapter and verse for so manifest a principle; but he should do so nevertheless, especially as it would draw attention to Regulation I. 1793, the foundation upon which the rights of private property of every landholder in this Presidency rest. Section VII of that Regulation provides for the sale of the lands of actual proprietors "with or on behalf of whom a settlement has been or may be concluded, or his or her heirs or successors," on their failing to discharge the public revenue assessed. Clause 5 Section VIII of that Regulation, after speaking of disqualified proprietors who are not managing their land, declares that the lands of such proprietors "will be held answerable for any arrears that are or may become due from them, on the fixed jumma which they, or any persons on their behalf, have engaged or may engage to pay." Here is the foundation of the right of the Revenue Authorities to sell land for arrears of Revenue, and the provision applies only to land for the Revenue assessed upon which the owner, or some one on his behalf, has engaged. To support this principle, if it was necessary to support so plain a principle of justice, he might refer further to the whole series of Regulations applicable to the recovery of arrears of Revenue; but he would refer only to one passage, because it explained the principle of the right of sale in a few words. The passage occurred in Regulation XI. 1822, which was the old Sale Law. That Regulation was no longer in force now; but the Section which he was about to quote was a mere statement of what the law on this point was; and what it was, so it remains. In Section XI of that Regulation, this declaration is made:—"All estates, for which a settlement shall have been made, being liable for the Revenue assessed upon them to the extent of the interests possessed by the person or persons who may have engaged with Government as ratified and confirmed by the act of settlement and by those deriving title from such person or persons, unless otherwise especially provided," no sale shall be annulled on certain pleas which are specified.

This, then, was the first principle of our Revenue system; and he had referred to the Laws by which it was supported.

The second principle he would state, was this. No estate is liable to be sold for arrears of revenue not its own, unless those arrears are due from its owner; and in this case, only the defaulter's right and interest can be sold. When an estate is sold for arrears of revenue that have accrued upon itself, it is sold out and out, and the auction-purchaser comes in and obtains the property free from all incumbrances. But when landed property is sold otherwise than for arrears that have accrued upon itself—when, for instance, it is sold because the owner owes a debt to Government in the shape of arrears of revenue due from some other estate, then nothing but the right, title, and interest of the owner are sold, as would be the case in a sale under a process for the recovery of any other personal debt. The reason of the distinction is obvious. The land itself is hypothecated for the jumma assessed upon it and engaged for by the owner; but what is due from another estate, and under a different engagement, is a mere personal debt, due by the owner to Government so far as the first-mentioned land is concerned. He would not trouble the Council by quoting the law to prove this well-known principle, but he would merely refer to the existing Sale Law, Act I of 1845, Sections V, XXVI, and XXVII.

The third principle he would state related to what constitutes an "estate," a word he had often had occasion to use. He would draw the attention of the Council particularly to this point, because he believed that the whole fallacy of the view of the law under examination arose from its not having been brought to the minds of the Judges at the time they gave their decision, what an estate, according to the technical definition of our Revenue law, really is. An estate, in Revenue language, was defined by the law—he would quote the very words of the law—as "any land being Malgoozaree, or subject to the payment of public Revenue, for the discharge of which a separate engagement has been, or may be entered into with Government." That was the original definition, given in Regulation XLVIII. 1793, Section II, Clause 2. It remained the definition for many years, and, so far as it went, was a perfectly accurate definition. But it was not broad enough; because there were, and had always been understood to be, estates, according to our interpretation of the term, for which there were no engagements with Government; namely, lands on which a separate jumma had been assessed, but which were held Khas. Regulation VIII. 1800 gave the necessary width to the definition of the term. Section XIII commenced by reciting the definition given by Regulation XLVIII. 1793, and proceeded thus:—

"But as this definition, strictly construed, would exclude estates held Khas, in consequence of the proprietors having declined to engage for the public assessment thereupon, under the option given by the rules for the permanent settlement; as well as the estates of disqualified proprietors, which, by those rules, and by Regulation X. 1793, were placed under the superintendence of the Court of Wards; as well as estates belonging to Government, for the Revenue of which no engagement may have been taken: and it being intended that all lands paying revenue to Government should be included in the registers of estates prescribed by Regulations XLVIII. 1793, and XIX. 1795, it is hereby further explained that by the term 'estate' therein used, is to be understood any land subject to the payment of Revenue, for which a separate engagement may have been executed to Government by the proprietor, or by a farmer; or which may have been separately assessed with the public Revenue, although no engagement shall have been executed to Government, as in cases where the estate may be held Khas."

The Council would observe that the claim in question falls precisely within this definition, having been separately assessed, and a separate engagement having been executed for its Revenue by a farmer.

The fourth principle he would state, was that the owner of an estate may alienate it, or any portion of it, without asking permission of any one, and that the transfer is good against all parties saving only the lien of Government on the whole land of an estate for the whole jumma assessed upon it. This, also, was a well known principle. But to place it beyond a doubt, he would refer to Regulation I. 1793 again. Section IX of this fundamental Revenue Law says :—

"That no doubt may be entertained whether proprietors of land are entitled, under the existing Regulations, to dispose of their estates without the previous sanction of Government, the Governor General in Council notifies to the Zemindars, independent talookdars, and other actual proprietors of land, that they are privileged to transfer to whomsoever they may think proper, by sale, gift, or otherwise, their proprietary rights in the whole, or any portion of their respective estates, without applying to Government for its sanction to the transfer."

Thus, in regard to all questions of property as between private parties, the sale of any specific portion of an estate, no matter what portion or how acquired, was as valid as a similar sale in England. All that remained to be done, in order to make such a sale to all intents and purposes similar to a like sale in England, was to obtain from the Revenue authorities a separate assessment of the Revenue demand upon the alienated portion, which is provided for in the next Section of the same Regulation, which he would immediately come to.

The fifth and last principle which he had to state, was that, when the Revenue Authorities allot or assess separately a specific jumma on a specific portion of an estate, thus, by the definition, creating that portion into a separate estate—whether that portion be sold privately by its owners, or whether it be sold for arrears of revenue at auction by the Collector—the hypotheca of Government is distributed separately between the portion separated and the rest of the land, the Government abandoning its lien on the whole of the original property for the whole of the original assessment, and reducing it to a lien on each part of the property for the specific jumma of that part, as newly allotted or assessed. When this is done, then to all intents and purposes —not only as between private individuals, but also as between the Government and the respective owners of the several portions of the original estate—the portion sold off becomes a separate and independent property, responsible only for what is due from itself. Section X Regulation I. 1793 declares upon what principle, in the event of one or more portions of an estate being transferred by public auction sale, or by private conveyance, the allotment and separation of the jumma shall be made, whereby what was, in Revenue language one estate, becomes two separate estates, to all intents and purposes.

These were five fundamental principles—the A. B. C. of our Revenue System, as he had called them; and he was sure that no one would dispute them. He asked the Council to apply these unquestionable and elementary principles to the case decided by the Sudder, and it would find that there was not one of them which was not contravened by the view of the law there taken. The decision confounded the tenure of property and the private right of acquisition in new land which that tenure gives in certain cases, with the lien which the Government has on the land for the protection of the public Revenue. It was impossible to imagine two things more distinct than these. For all he knew, the Rajah of Burdwan might hold the whole of his lands, paying forty lakhs of Revenue under one and the same tenure; in which case, the whole would constitute one property, and what in England we should call one estate. But, nevertheless, the Government might have assessed a separate jumma on every village within the Rajah's territory, and the Rajah might have given a separate engagement for the Revenue of each; and in that case, he would, in the language of our Revenue law, possess as many separate estates as there are villages in his Zemindarees. In that case, every village would appear under a separate number as a separate mehal upon the Towjee, and the land of each village would be responsible only for its own assessment.

In the suit determined by the Sudder Court, the Zillah Judge stated in his decision

"that a proprietary right in alluvial lands separate from and independent of a title in a substantive or parent estate, is a thing unknown in this country, and certainly unrecognized by the laws."

He (Mr. Grant) fully agreed in this. It was so. Such a proprietary right in new soil could only become the acquisition of a private person, because the private person possessed already the adjoining land. But it did not follow from that, that, after acquiring it, he might not alienate it, like any other portion of his estate; or that the Collector, in the event of arrears of Revenue accruing—even supposing the case to be one in which no separation had been completed by a separate assessment of revenue on the alluvion—might not lawfully sell only the old estate, or only the new one, just as well as he might lawfully sell any other particular portion of the integral estate if he chose to do so, instead of selling the whole. The decision of the Zillah Judge, therefore, stands upon nothing material to the issue. The judgment of the Sudder Court says that the malikana paid on a *chur* "is an asset of the Zemindaree which the defaulting proprietor has no power either to alienate or reserve, and which passes with the estate to the auction purchaser." But what estate is meant? If it is meant that malikana passes with the estate in respect of which it is payable, there is no doubt that the position is correct; but it is immaterial to the question. It does not follow that the malikana of one estate passes with another; that the malikana of an alluvion, after it has been separately assessed, and so created a new and separate estate, and has been entered as such under a new number on the Towjee, passes with the adjacent estate from which it has been severed, and with which it retains no more connexion than it may have with any other property belonging to the same owner in any other part of the country—in Bombay, for instance, or elsewhere.

The reason which the decision gives for supporting the judgment of the Court below is this. After stating most truly that the rights and interests of the old proprietors in the parent estate of Koélwar ceased and determined when that estate was passed at the Revenue sale, it is laid down that "it is quite clear that under the law the rights of those persons, whatever they were, to the alluvial increment of the talook and the malikana due therefrom, passed at the same time." This seemed to him an obvious *petitio principii*. Whether the law is so, or not, was the very point at issue: it was the very question raised in the appeal. No attempt is made to prove the position, by reference to any particular Law in support of it; and no such law can be pointed out. Had no separate assessment of the alluvion been made, the position could not have been impugned; but it is clear that the legal effect of a separate assessment of the alluvion, and of the consequent recognition of it upon the Towjee as a separate estate under a separate engagement with a distinct party was overlooked.

In selling the estate of Koélwar alone at auction, and excluding the *chur* from the Latbundee, the Revenue Officers acted quite correctly. They acted in perfect accordance with the law, and their proceedings were unimpugnable. When selling the estate, they had carefully specified that they were selling only the old estate, and had in words, not to take in purchasers, excluded its increment the *chur*, which was the parcel of land in dispute in the suit. Therefore, the decision of the Sudder Court went this length—that what had not been offered for sale, and therefore had certainly not been sold, had nevertheless been bought!

MR. CURRIE asked, if the Revenue Officers had specifically stated that the *chur* was excluded from the sale?

MR. GRANT said that what he gathered from the annexure to the Bill appeared to him to amount to a specific statement to that effect. On the old estate, there was a particular jumma assessed—a jumma of several thousand Rupees: on the *chur*, there was a new and different jumma assessed—a jumma of one thousand Rupees and odd; and moreover the *chur* must have borne a different and a much higher number on the Towjee than the old estate. The decision admitted that "the land in suit was not lotted with the parent estate."

The decision endeavored to get rid of that fact by saying—

"The proceedings of the Revenue Authorities in this case could not affect the Civil rights of the defendants, even if they bore the interpretation which the appellants have put upon them."

That seemed much like saying that what an Auctioneer sold, had nothing to do with the Civil rights of the purchaser under the sale. He maintained that the thing sold was that which the Auctioneer stated that he offered for sale. There was no other means of judging what was sold.

The Sudder Court went on to say :—

"But the fact appears to be that the land in suit was not lotted for sale with the parent estate on the two occasions alluded to, merely because it had been temporarily settled with other parties, and the proprietor had no right of entry until the expiry of the farming engagements."

The question seemed to be what the Collector did—not why he did it. But if he, Mr. Grant, were driven to assign motives for the Collector not having lotted the *chur* for sale, he could assign a much more obvious motive than that suggested by the Sudder Court. He might say that the motive of the Collector was that, if he had lotted the *chur* with the old estate, the sale would have been certainly invalid because he could not sell two separate estates simultaneously for one arrear.

There were three objections to the view of the Revenue law taken in this decision, every one of which appeared to him to be fatal, and he thought that, if Honorable Members would attentively consider them, they would eventually arrive at the same opinion.

The first objection was that the *chur* had been specifically excluded from the sale. Even admitting, therefore, for the sake of argument, that the *chur* formed one estate with the original land, and was liable to sale—it was not sold. If it was argued that the Collector had no right to exclude any portion of the integral estate when arrears of Revenue had accrued, that position could be maintained only by a forgetfulness of what the existing law was and is ; and also of what the general practice had been up to the year 1827. When the law was framed originally, it was framed in a very just and considerate spirit. It did not intend that a proprietor should lose a large estate for a small arrear of Revenue ; and, therefore, it very carefully provided that it should not be necessary to sell the whole of an estate for the recovery of an arrear, but that the Collector might sell any portion of it which he should specify. He (Mr. Grant) would refer again upon this point to Regulation I. 1793, Section VII, and Section X Clause 2. Then, to shew what the practice had been, he would refer to Regulation XIV. 1793, Section XIII, and Regulation XI. 1822, Section VI ; and also to the Circular Order of the Board of Revenue dated 22nd May 1827. So long ago as 1827, the Board of Revenue had issued this Circular, which said :—

"The Board of Revenue for the Lower Provinces have had under consideration the practice, which now generally obtains throughout all the districts under their control, of realizing arrears of Revenue by the sale of fractional portions of estates, whose Sudder jumma exceeds the sum of five hundred Rupees without previously allotting, upon specific parts or divisions of such estates, a jumma which shall bear the same proportion to the actual produce of such specific parts or divisions, as the fixed assessment upon the whole estate may bear to its actual produce, thereby creating interests in common tenancy, and opening a door to indefinite subdivisions of landed property, which have a manifest tendency to depreciate its value."

Now, that was the practice up to 1827. It was an objectionable practice to sell portions of an estate without separate allotments of jumma, because it introduced confusion between old and new purchasers ; but it is clear that even this was perfectly legal.

The sale of portions of an estate with separate allotments of jumma, was both legal and unobjectionable, if properly managed. He would add that, whilst in 1793 it was in the discretion of the Collector to sell the whole or a portion of an estate, from 1796 to 1822 even that provision was thought to be a hardship ; for Sections II and III of Regulation V. 1796 made it obligatory on the Collector to select for sale such portion of an estate in arrear as was likely to suffice for the arrear " and no more." Thus, it would be seen that what the Collector had done in the present case, was, in any view of the position of the *chur*, perfectly legal ; and it appeared to him, therefore, that the first objection to the view of the law taken by the Sudder Court was insurmountable.

The second objection was that the *chur*, being a separate estate, could not be sold with another estate, having a different Towjee number. As he had said before, the Collector could not sell

Mr. Grant

two separate estates for one arrear. Such a sale, on the face of it, would have been monstrous; but it would also have been opposed to the terms of the Sale Law, Act I of 1845, Section XIV of which provides that "Sales shall proceed in regular order, the estate to be sold bearing the lowest number on the Towjee" being put up first, and so on in regular sequence.

The third objection was that the *chur* being a separate estate, and not being in arrear, was not primarily responsible; and that, therefore, if it had been sold at all, it could not have been sold out and out, as the parent estate was sold.

He had now gone through, he feared in a very tedious manner, the arguments which had convinced his own mind that the decision of the Sudder Court did not take a correct view of the existing law. He conceived, therefore, that the law required no amendment; for not only did he think that the Sudder Court were wrong in holding that the Revenue Authorities, even when they wished to do it, were incompetent to separate the properties in the manner they had done, but he maintained that a just reading of the Regulations made it imperative upon them to assess an alluvion as a separate estate, and to assess it in no other way, whether the owner of the adjacent land sold off the alluvion or kept it. The Revenue Authorities had no power to break up the existing engagement of a Zemindar, and to force him to resign the Charter upon which he stands, and to accept another which certainly increased the extent of his liability, and might be of very inferior value. Suppose that the Zemindar's old estate were worth one thousand Rupees a year, and that a large *chur* arose from the river, and, attaching itself to that estate, became part of the property of the proprietor. The Revenue Authorities might come in, and assess the *chur* at double its value, and there would be no appeal from that assessment. The *chur* might be worth one thousand Rupees a year, and the Revenue Authorities might assess it at two thousand Rupees a year. Would it be consistent with reason to force the Zemindar either to abandon to others the management and profits of the *chur*, or to incorporate his permanently settled estate with a new estate so highly assessed that the two together would be worth nothing? Again, suppose that there should be a perfectly fair assessment on the *chur*: would it be fair to force the owner to relinquish it, or else to incorporate it with his old estate, whereby he would lose all profit from his old estate, if the *chur* were washed away the next year? This injustice had been mentioned by the Honorable Member for Bengal last Saturday, and the argument appeared to him an extremely strong one. Or still further, suppose that the owner of the parent estate were a mokurrereedar, holding at a pepper-corn revenue—a mere nominal assessment; or a lakhirajdar holding free of all assessment: would it be contended that the law, as it stands, enables the Revenue Authorities, because a *chur* accrues to the estate, to break up the mokurreree or lakhiraj tenure, and instead of it, to force upon the owner a malgoozaree tenure for both the old estate and the new alluvion? Could greater injustice be imagined? The Revenue Authorities and Government said—"We will have none of this. We will not do it. We do not think it just. We wish to give the proprietor a separate assessment, and to create a separate estate of this new soil." But the law, it is supposed, steps in, and prevents them. Where is this absurd and iniquitous law to be found? Let any person put his finger upon the Section, if he can, and when he has so proved its existence, he (Mr. Grant) would vote for its amendment. But he was satisfied that no one could point to any such law: he was satisfied that the law, as it stands, is not open to such impeachment. He had gone over all the laws on the subject, except the last, Act IX of 1847, relating to the assessment of alluvion. That Act was not passed when the auction sale of Koélwar was made, and therefore could not be imported into this discussion of the Koélwar case. But what the Council had to determine was not the particular case of Koélwar, (although that case gave rise to the discussion), but the general question of the law bearing on such cases. He had looked into the Act of 1847, and he found that it left the law upon the point at issue, where it was. It gives the Collector in certain cases power to assess new soil, but it provides that such assessment shall be made in accordance with the Regulations in force. Now, what are those Regulations? They are contained in Regulation II. 1819, Clauses 1 and 2 of Section III. In referring to them he would reverse their order for the sake of convenience. Clause 2 provides that

"the foregoing principles shall be deemed applicable not only to tracts of land such as are described to have been brought into cultivation in the Sunderbuns, but to all *churs* and islands formed since the period of the decennial settlement, and generally to all lands gained by alluvion or dereliction since that period, whether from an introcession of the sea, an alteration in the course of the rivers, or the gradual accession of soil on their banks."

Then what were the "foregoing principles" applicable to *churs?* Clause I states them as follows:—

"All lands which, at the period of the decennial settlement, were not included within the limits of any pergunnah, mouza, or other division of estates for which a settlement was concluded with the owners, not being lands for which a distinct settlement may have been made since the period above referred to, nor lands held free of assessment under a valid and legal title of the nature specified in Regulations XIX and XXXVIII. 1793, and in the corresponding Regulations subsequently enacted, are, and shall be considered liable to assessment in the same manner as other unsettled mehals."

These *churs,* therefore, were liable to assessment. And how were they liable to assessment? "In the same manner as other unsettled mehals;" and every one knows that an unsettled mehal must stand upon its own basis, being separate land, chargeable with a separate jumma. This was a most reasonable and just system. It was, he was convinced, the only system founded in law, and certainly, up to the time of the decision of the Sudder Court in the Koelwar case, it was generally observed.

Without, therefore, entering into the question of the propriety of this Council passing a declaratory Act—which he would leave, if necessary, to be discussed by more learned heads—he would say that he would agree to any alteration in the wording of this Bill which would obviate any objection felt on the ground that it flew needlessly in the face of a decision of the Court of Justice; but that he must object to any alteration which would make the security of landed proprietors in the separate holdings which the existing practice had given

Mr. Grant

them, or which would make the Bill admit the existing law to be so absurd, and unjust, and mischievous, as it would be if that decision could be supposed to take a sound view of it.

THE CHIEF JUSTICE said, he was not present at the debate held on this question last Saturday; but having understood that it had been adjourned for discussion at a fuller Meeting of the Council, he had deemed it right to read, with as much care as his other engagements would permit, the Report of it, as also the papers originally laid before the Council in support of the Bill. Having given to them the best consideration that he could, he confessed that he had come into the Council Room that day under the impression that the decision of the Sudder Court was based upon sound legal principles; and that, therefore, whatever might be the general power of the Council to pass declaratory Acts, or the considerations which should determine the exercise of that power, he ought not to assent to this Bill in so far as it was a declaratory law impugning that decision. He had, however, also come to the conclusion, notwithstanding the arguments that had been urged by the Honorable and learned Member opposite (Mr. Peacock), that the object of the Bill was wise, just, and proper, and that he ought to support any measure which, without being open to the objection of being a law directed against a decision which he thought was right, would effect that object. After hearing, however, the very able and elaborate argument which had been addressed to the Council by the Honorable Member on his right (Mr. Grant), he felt bound to admit that his confidence in the correctness of the decision of the Sudder Court was considerably shaken.

The question before the Council bore two aspects. The Council had to consider it—first, with reference to the general law of accession, and to the phraseology of one particular Regulation, namely, Regulation XI. 1825—and secondly, with reference to the general Revenue law, and the power of Government to sell a zemindaree property for arrears of Government revenue. It was with the utmost diffidence that he expressed an opinion on a question of pure Revenue law. That was a subject to which he had naturally not directed very much attention, seeing that it was one which had been, by positive Statute, withdrawn from the jurisdiction of the only Court with which he, during his career in India, whether as an Advocate or a Judge, had been conversant.

With respect to the other aspect of the question, it was as open to him as to any other Member of the Council to form and to express an opinion. Now considering this question with reference to the general law of accession, or with reference to the particular Regulation of 1825, it appeared to him that the principles laid down by the Sudder Court and the Zillah Judge in the suit relating to the estate of Koelwar, were perfectly correct. The papers printed with the Bill shewed that Regulation XI. 1825 was, in all its circumstances as well as in its terms, a declaratory enactment; and that, by at least two decisions of the Sudder Court, the law relating to alluvial formations had been declared to be consistent with the general law of Europe, which was itself derived from the Roman Civil Law. That was the state of things when the Regulation was passed; and the Regulation seemed only to adopt and to give a legislative sanction to the view taken by the Sudder Court in the two decisions to which he had referred. Now, if the effect of the Decennial or Permanent Settlement had been such that the Zemindar took his Zemindaree for better and for worse—that was liable in no case and in no event to the assessment of any further Revenue—it could not, he thought, be doubted that, according to the general law of accession, the land gained by alluvion, which that law, as established by the decision in question, gave to the proprietor of the adjacent land, would have been added to, and have become part of his original estate for all purposes. The proprietor of lakhiraj land would have taken the increment rent-free; in the hands of the proprietor of Malgoozaree lands, the increment with the original estate would have been a security for the Revenue assessed on that original estate. The difficulty in the case was introduced by the right of Government, notwithstanding the Permanent Settlement, to assess the increment either with a separate jumma, or with a jumma in addition to that payable on the original Zemindaree. He did not know whether that right had been asserted, or whether it had existed in practice before Regulation II. 1819. But that Regulation, which was anterior to Regulation XI. 1825, did undoubtedly assert that right, and Regulation XI. 1825 as undoubtedly recognized and was subject to it. He repeated, however, that it seemed to him impossible to contend independently of that right that, if the Zemindar of a malgoozaree tenure had fallen into arrear, and his estate been put up to sale, the sale would not have conveyed every right of the Zemindar, including his right in the land gained by alluvion. The question of proprietorship in accretion was really one of boundaries. The right implied the notion of a boundary shifting with the gradual recession of the river. Again, the phraseology of Regulation XI. 1825 appeared to him to strengthen the construction for which he was contending. The words, it was to be observed, were—

> "When land may be gained by gradual accession, whether from the recess of a river or of the sea, it shall be considered an increment to the tenure"—the term used was not "estate," but "tenure"—" of the person to whose land or estate it is thus annexed, whether such land or estate be held immediately from Government by a Zemindar or other superior landholder, or as a subordinate tenure by any description of under-tenant whatever."

The Regulation, therefore, treated the alluvion as an increment to the *tenure* to which it accrued. It proceeded thus—

> "Provided that the increment of land thus obtained shall not entitle the person in possession of the estate or tenure to which the land may be annexed, to a right of property or permanent interest therein beyond that possessed by him in the estate or tenure to which the land may be annexed."

Now, stopping there, consider what was the peculiar *tenure* of a Zemindar; what was the limitation on his absolute right of property in his estate. He had a right to hold the estate so long only as he paid the Government Revenue; if he failed to pay the Government Revenue, his right in that estate was liable to be put up for sale by auction, and if sold would pass to the purchaser free and clear from all incumbrances created by the defaulting proprietor, and unaffected by any of his intermediate conveyances. The reservation of the rights of the under-tenants by Regulation XI. 1825 shewed still more clearly what the nature of the accretion was—that it was treated as a mere increment to the old tenure; so that if, before the formation of a *chur*, the zemindar had mortgaged his whole zemindaree, the mortgagee would get the benefit of the accretion as an addition to his security; or if, before such formation of the *chur*, the zemindar had granted the adjacent land in putnee, the putneedar would get the benefit of the accretion, subject to whatever right to an increased rental there might exist as between the zemindar and himself. Then, to what extent, if at all, was this state of things varied, and the general consequence that the accession followed the nature of the principal thing affected by the right of Government to claim additional Revenue in respect of the accretion; and by the general Revenue law applicable to that right? The law said that, if the Government should assess a fresh revenue on the alluvion, and the Zemindar should refuse to engage for it on the condition that it should be added to the jumma of his permanently settled estate, —which, owing to the uncertain nature of the soil, seemed to be the case generally—the Revenue Authorities might either let out the alluvion in farm, or hold it khas, reserving in either case a malikana allowance to the recusant proprietor; and the principal question before the Sudder Court appeared to have been whether the right to this malikana was a right so incident to the zemindaree right in the parent estate that it passed on a sale for arrears of Revenue to the purchaser notwithstanding its previous alienation by its original owner; or whether it was to be treated as a thing separate, and so capable of being permanently severed from the parent estate by that alienation of it. The correctness of the decision necessarily turned on the correctness of the view which the Court took of the extent of the power of sale inherent in the Government; and of its actual exercise in the particular case. If there was nothing in the law which positively prohibited the exercise of the power of sale over the accretion, and all the Zemindar's right in it, as well as over the parent estate, then we had only the general principles of the law and Regulation XI. 1825 to look to; and it appeared to him that, upon those general principles, and the construction to be put on that particular Regulation, the decision to which the Sudder Court had come was a correct one.

The speech, however, of the Honorable Member on his right (Mr. Grant) had suggested two difficulties to his mind; first, that the power of sale inherent in Government was limited to the land in respect of which the arrears of revenue had accrued; and next, that a *portion* only of an estate might be sold for the arrears of the revenue assessed on that portion. The first difficulty might be met by giving to the word "estate" a different and a wider interpretation than that which the Honorable Member would assign to it—a question on which he (the Chief Justice) still thought much was to be said. But the other difficulty seemed to him to be weightier. For if the Collector had power to sell only a portion of the estate, his acts in the particular case afforded the strongest grounds for believing that he never intended to include the right to malikana in the sale. Therefore, it seemed to him very doubtful whether, if the power to sell this right to malikana existed, it had been exercised, or had ever been intended to be exercised in the particular case; and consequently very doubtful whether the purchaser had ever acquired that right.

With respect to the question of what the law ought to be, he had, from the first, been very much in favor of making it what the Honorable Member for Bengal considered it now to be. Considering the nature of the new soil, it was hard to force the Zemindar into incorporating the jumma assessed upon it with the jumma assessed upon his permanently settled estate, and thus to make the latter liable for that increased jumma, though the new land might be swept away the next year. If—which he did not think would be the case—the right to insist on a separate settlement would in any degree endanger the public revenue, he (the Chief Justice) would not object to make that arrangement subject to the consent of the Revenue Authorities; and to leave it a matter of contract between the Settlement Officer and the Zemindar. For if they should be unable to agree on a separate settlement, the alluvion might always be let out in farm, and the Zemindar would get his malikana.

With respect to the objections that had been urged by the Honorable and learned Member opposite (Mr. Peacock) in reference to the interests of under-tenants, it appeared to him that no risk would really be run by that class of landholders. Most unquestionably, the effect of Regulation XI. 1825 was to give a putneedar the same interest in the accretion which his putnee gave him in the original estate. That provision could not be altered by the settlement of the Revenue. The only difference between a settlement which incorporated the new with the old jumma, and a separate settlement, as they affected the Putneedar, was this; that on the former, a default of his zemindar in payment of the revenue might occasion the loss of the whole putnee; on the latter a sale either of the parent estate, or of the accretion might take place, and the interest of the Putneedar in the thing sold would alone be forfeited; his interest in the other would remain unaffected.

On the whole, then, he was in favor of making the law what the Honorable Member for Bengal desired it to be. Nor did he see any objection to its enacting that the consequences which would attach under its provisions to future separate settlements of alluvion, should also attach to the separate settlements which had already been made. No existing rights would be affected by that; for the purchasers at future Government sales would know what it was that they were buying. He still thought, however, that, considering the opinion which many Honorable Members held as to what was the existing law, and the respect due to the Sudder Court, it would be better not to make the law declaratory, nor in any manner to seem to impugn the decision of which so much had been said.

MR. HARINGTON said, he concurred with the Honorable and learned Member of Council opposite (Mr. Peacock) and the Honorable and learned Chief Justice in thinking that it would be very objectionable to pass any Bill in explanation of existing enactments relating to alluvial formations which would have the effect of throwing a doubt on the correctness of the decision of the Sudder Court at Calcutta in the case reported amongst the annexures of the Bill before the Council, or which might lead to the re-opening of that case and other cases of a similar character. He would not follow the Honorable Member of Council on his left (Mr. Grant) through all the objections which he had taken to the decision of the Sudder Court. He did not think that the Council had anything to do with the circumstances of the particular case in which that decision was passed. As observed by the Honorable and learned Member of Council opposite, in the speech delivered by him on Saturday last, it was not the constitutional duty of the Legislative Council to act as a Court of Appeal, or to sit in judgment upon the decisions of the Civil Courts. What the Council had to look to were the general principles involved in the decision of the Sudder Court; and if it found them opposed to what was understood to have been the intention of the particular Regulation which the Bill brought in by the Honorable Member for Bengal proposed to explain, it might pass a declaratory Act.

The general principles laid down in the decision of the Sudder Court were to be found at page 14 of the annexures to the Bill. The Court remarked—

"It is distinctly enacted, however, in that Section"—that was to say, Section V Regulation VII. 1822—that this allowance," alluding to malikana, "shall not be claimable by any except actual proprietors or persons having the right of property in the lands; and this would necessarily be so even in the absence of any enactment, as malikana is clearly nothing more or less than a particular species of rent. It is an asset of the zemindaree which the defaulting proprietor has no power either to alienate or reserve, and which passes with the estate to the auction purchaser. Now, it is admitted that the rights and interests of Doodnarain, and of his vendee Jewan Lall in the parent estate of Koelwar ceased and determined on the 2nd of July 1845, when the estate was passed at a Revenue sale to the defendants; and it is quite clear that, under the law, the rights of those persons, whatever they were, to the alluvial increment of the talook and the malikana due therefrom, passed at the same time."

What, he would ask, had been the opinion of the highest Revenue authorities in Bengal upon this point from the time of the passing of Regulation XI. 1825 up to the present date? In the Board's Circular of the 7th of August 1838, it was ordered "that, if the zemindar agrees to the terms of settlement, the jumma of the *chur* shall be added to and included in the original *tahood*, and the parent estate with its increment shall be considered a single mehal charged with the aggregate increased jumma. But, on the other hand, should the zemindar either refuse to accede to the terms of the settlement, or object to include it in his *tahood*, the land is to be let in farm for a period not exceeding ten years, the proprietor receiving a malikana at the usual rate. Should, however, the parent estate be brought to sale for arrears of Revenue, the right of property in the *chur*"—and here was the point—" will necessarily pass to the auction purchaser."

Though the Board subsequently saw reason to modify these orders, and to issue further instructions to their subordinates in respect to the settlement of alluvial formations, they did not attempt to call in question the correctness of the interpretations which had been put upon the law in the Circular of the 7th August 1838. In their Circular of 10th July 1841, they allowed "that the instructions contained in their previous Circular were legally correct, and that the mode of settlement therein prescribed was not only borne out by the law, but was the mode most consistent with the terms of the law in which the right of property in alluvial formations is defined." From what was stated in a subsequent part of the same Circular, he was led to infer that the Board would have gone up to Government for a fresh enactment, not to explain existing laws, but to obtain a modification thereof, the practice which had been introduced admittedly under a correct interpretation of those laws having been found to lead to embarrassment; but they abstained from seeking the interference of the Legislature at that time, simply because the practice which they wished to legalize in the place of the rules then in force, involved no injury or loss to the owner of the estate to which land gained by gradual accession was found to be annexed, but would be merely a voluntary relinquishment by Government of certain rights which, under the strict letter of the law, it possessed. What the rights here alluded to were, did not very clearly appear; but the right of holding an increment by alluvion, responsible equally with the parent estate for the revenue assessed upon the latter, was probably one of the rights intended. Seeing, then, that the Sudder Court and the highest Revenue authorities in Bengal had all along been agreed as to the intention and meaning of the law, it did not appear to him that the Council could say with propriety that doubts existed as to the legal effect of particular words in Regulation XI. 1825, for the removal of which a declaratory law was necessary. Any doubts which might have been entertained on the point, had been removed by the decision of a competent Court; and he should therefore vote against the second reading of the Bill brought in by the Honorable Member for Bengal, if that reading was to be followed by the publication of the Bill as it stood.

The Honorable Member of Council on his left (Mr. Grant) had, he believed, correctly stated the law as to the settlement of lands liable to be assessed to Government, and as to their sale for any arrear of revenue accruing thereon, and he concurred in the general principles laid down by the Honorable Member in his speech; but he was unable to agree with him that alluvial formations attached to the mainland could be considered an estate within the meaning of Regulation VIII. 1800, though temporarily let out to a farmer, so long as they were not formally and absolutely separated from the parent estate with the consent and by the act of the proprietor. He could find nothing in Regulation II. 1825, to lead him to suppose that the framers of that law intended that alluvial accretions should be held separately from the estate to which they were attached, unless it was in that part of Clause 1 Section IV which declared that the increment should not in any case be understood to exempt the holder of it from the payment to Government of any assessment for the public revenue to which it might be liable under the provision of Regulation II. 1819, or of any other Regulation in force. Clause 1 Section III Regulation II. 1819, however, which declared the liability to assessment of certain lands in the same manner as other unsettled estates, applied to lands actually existing at the period of the decennial settlement, though not included at that time within the limits of any estate for which a settlement was concluded with the owners; and although the principle of the rule contained in Clause 1 Section III Regulation II. 1819 had been extended by the 2nd Clause of the same Section to alluvial formations, Section VI. Act IX of 1847 had the following words—

"Whenever, on inspection of any such new map, it shall appear to the local Revenue authorities that land has been added to any estate paying revenue directly to Government, they shall without delay assess the same."

—thus shewing that the framers of the law of 1847, equally with the framers of Regulation XI 1825, looked upon alluvial accretions as properly forming part and parcel of the estate to which they had attached themselves; and, reading Section VI Act IX of 1847, with Clause 2 Section III Regulation II. 1819, he believed that the only object of the provisions contained in those Sections was to protect the interests of Government, and to secure the payment of a fair amount of revenue on alluvial formations. For his own part, he had no doubt that the framers of Regulation XI 1825 fully intended that alluvial accretions should be incorporated with, and form part of the estate to which they might be annexed, and that they should share its fate, whatever that might be. The framers of the Regulation, knowing the value attached by the natives of this country to land, and that they were nearly as ready to fight for their lands as for their lives, probably never contemplated the possibility of the owner of the parent estate refusing to allow an alluvial formation to be incorporated therewith, and they did not think it necessary therefore to provide for such a contingency. It had, however, occurred; and he agreed with the Honorable and learned Chief Justice in thinking, that it would be advisable to pass a new law to meet such cases, in which some provision might properly be introduced to protect the interests of under-tenants.

With respect to the remarks made by the Honorable and learned Member of Council opposite (Mr. Peacock), as to the depreciation in the value of an estate which would follow the loss of its river-frontage, he would only observe that any injury occurring to the owner of the parent estate from that cause would be equally experienced by him in the event of the alluvial accretion being let in farm to a stranger. During the continuance of the farming lease, the proprietor of the parent estate would be deprived of the use of the river-frontage, any benefits arising from which would belong to the farmer; and he saw no objection, therefore, on that ground, to the passing of a new law such as that proposed by the Honorable and the learned Chief Justice.

On the whole, then, he thought it better that the present Bill should not be read a second time; but if the Honorable Member for Bengal would introduce a new Bill not open to the objections which appeared to him to exist to the Bill before the Council, he should be prepared to support it.

Mr. LeGeyt said, after the very full discussion held on the Bill this day and at the last Meeting, he should not have obtruded any observations of his own upon the Council, were it not that he thought it very desirable that the principle involved in the Bill should be determined. It appeared to him that that principle was, whether this Council could discuss, and pass declaratory Acts upon decisions of the highest Court of Civil Judicature in the Mofussil of this country. If he read Regulation X 1796 aright, the interpretation of the Regulations was vested in the Sudder Court; and if that were so, he would ask the Council if the decision passed by that Court upon the question of Regulation law at issue in this case, did not definitively settle the meaning of the law. Did it not declare the law as it stood to be in conformity with the construction which is put upon it? If that were the case, this Bill would disturb the decision, and set aside the interpretation of the Sudder Court, contrary to the provision of Regulation X. 1796.

With respect to the alteration in the existing law suggested by the Honorable Member for Bengal, his own impression was that it was advisable. That impression had been strengthened by what he heard to-day; and he should be glad to see a Bill brought in to amend the law. But he could not assent to the second reading of a Bill which, in effect, made the Council a Court of Appeal from the Sudder Adawlut, and declared that that Court had given a mistaken interpretation of a law.

MR. ELIOTT said, he would make but a few observations on the interpretation of Regulation XI 1825. He wished to state his concurrence generally in the observations which had been made by the Honorable Member on his right (Mr. Harington). He had endeavored simply to look at Regulation XI 1825 by itself, and it appeared to him that it was the intention of the law that land gained by alluvion should constitute an integral part of the old estate, as held by the present Board of Revenue. He conceived that the ruling of the Sudder Court so far was perfectly correct. He could not see what other meaning could be properly given to the words of the Regulation declaring that "the increment of land thus obtained is annexed to the land or estate," the possession of which determined the right of property in it; and although it was not expressly laid down that the assessment on such land should be added to the jumma on the estate, yet that followed as a matter of course; for the new land, being made part and parcel of the old estate, the additional assessment must be equally part of the jumma on the whole. Thus, the law regarded the increment and the old land as composing one estate. The component parts, however, not being inseparable, but separable only in the manner in which any part of the integral estate could be separated and formed into a distinct property. The manner in which such a separation could be made was laid down by the law to which the Honorable Member on his left (Mr. Grant) had alluded. The only difference in such a case as this was that it was not necessary to go through the form of *butwarrah*. For the new land being already assessed distinctly, what was equivalent to a *butwarrah* had been done. If, then, the Zemindar did not choose to hold the new land as part of his estate, all he had to do was to apply to the Collector to register it as a separate estate, subject to the assessment already imposed upon it; and the Collector was bound so to register it. If this were so, the law required no amendment. According to his view, it was unnecessary to declare, as in the 2nd Section of the Bill, that the new land might be united to the old, for Regulation XI 1825 spoke of it as *ab initio* annexed thereto. And again, it was unnecessary to provide that the new land should be assessed and settled as a separate estate with a separate jumma if the zemindar was unwilling to hold it in union with the original estate, because it was already open to the zemindar to apply to the Collector so to settle it, and the Collector was bound to attend to such application. In his opinion, then, the Board of Revenue and Sudder Court were correct in saying that the alluvion was to be regarded *primâ facie* as part and parcel of the original estate. He did not know that the Sudder Court had said that it was absolutely inseparable from it. Section I of this Bill said that nothing in Section IV of Regulation XI. 1825 should be understood as making alluvion inseparable from the estate which it adjoined; but he was not sure that the Sudder Court positively asserted that there could be no division of the two lands under any circumstances. The Regulations pointed out a mode for obtaining a separate settlement of the alluvion; and if the zemindar applied in that mode, the separation must be made.

He therefore saw no occasion for a declaratory law on the subject.

MR. CURRIE said, he had already trespassed on the attention of the Council to a greater extent than he had wished to do in speaking in support of this Bill; and he proposed, therefore, to say but a very few words in reply on the present occasion.

When he framed this Bill—the object of which was simply to give legislative sanction to a practice in the Revenue Department which had obtained since the first settlement of alluvial formations, under the Orders of the Board of Revenue and the Executive Government—the idea had never occurred to him that it would meet with so much opposition, or give rise to so much discussion. On Saturday last, objections had been taken to its merits, as well as to its form. The objections to the merits of the Bill he had endeavored to answer at the time, and they had been met more completely to-day by the Honorable Gentleman opposite (Mr. Grant). But there seemed to be a more general feeling in the Council against the form of the Bill. He did not propose to occupy the time of the Council with any remarks as to the general expediency of declaratory legislation; he would say only a few words explanatory of the course which he had adopted on this occasion. He had always considered it as a recognized principle of legislation that, when a construction was put upon a law by a Court of Justice contrary to that which the Legislature intended it should bear, or which the Legislature thought it ought to bear, it was the province of the Legislature to provide a remedy either by amending the law, or, if it thought that the wording as it stood would fairly bear the construction which it wished it to bear, by passing a declaratory Act. That had certainly been the practice of the Legislature of this country for the last fifty years. The Statute Book abounded in declaratory Acts. He would select one as an example. Act II of 1847 was "An Act to declare the meaning and extent of certain words in Act V of 1840," by which oaths were abolished, and affirmations substituted for them, in the case of Hindoos and Mahomedans. In Act V of 1840, it was provided that its provisions should not extend to any of Her Majesty's Courts of Justice. They were extended to the Police Court; but on the trial of a Hindoo indicted for perjury for a false statement made at the Police upon solemn affirmation, the Supreme Court held that Police Courts came under the designation of "Her Majesty's Courts of Justice." The prisoner was accordingly acquitted; and, on the advice of the then Advocate General, Act II of 1847 was passed. The Preamble of that Act declared that—

"Whereas, by Section IV of Act V of 1840, it was amongst other things provided that the said Act should not extend to any declaration or affirmation made in any of Her Majesty's Courts of Justice, and doubts have arisen whether the words 'Her Majesty's Courts of Justice' mean and extend to the Courts of Justices of the Peace—It is hereby declared and enacted that the words 'Her Majesty's Courts of Justice' in the said Act shall be deemed not to have meant, nor extended to, and not to mean nor extend to, the Courts of the Justices of the Peace."

When, following this, and other similar precedents, he prepared this Bill in its present form, it certainly never occurred to him that he was doing anything unusual, or anything which could be construed as giving any reasonable cause of offence to the Sudder Court. Viewing the question as he did, a declaratory Act appeared to him to be the simplest and most straight-forward way of doing what he wished to do. At the same time, as a majority of the Council seemed to think that the declaratory form was objectionable, and that the same ends might be attained by an enactment in a different form, he had no objection whatever to the form being changed. But he trusted that the Council would allow the Bill to be read a second time. It might then, if it thought necessary, instruct the Select Committee to whom it should be referred, to report what alteration they considered should be made in it before it was published. He should prefer this course to withdrawing the Bill and bringing in another in a different form; because, as he had said, the Bill was now in the form which he thought it should bear, and, in altering that form, he should like to have the assistance of Honorable Members who were of opinion that that alteration was desirable.

The question having been put, the Council divided:—

Ayes 5.	Noes. 3.
Mr. Currie.	Mr. Harington.
Mr. Eliott.	Mr. LeGeyt.
Mr. Grant.	Mr. Peacock.
The Chief Justice.	
The Vice-President.	

The Bill was then read a second time.

ESTATE OF THE LATE NABOB OF THE CARNATIC.

MR. PEACOCK moved that the Bill "to provide for the administration of the Estate, and for the payment of the debts of the late Nabob of the Carnatic" be now read a second time.

The Motion was carried, and the Bill read a second time.

PORT-DUES (ADEN).

MR. LEGEYT moved the third reading of the Bill "for the levy of Port-dues in the Port of Aden"

The Motion was carried, and the Bill read a third time.

SUBORDINATE CRIMINAL COURT AT OOTACAMUND.

MR. ELIOTT moved that the Council resolve itself into a Committee on the Bill "to extend Act XXV of 1855" (to empower the Session Judge of Coimbatore to hold Sessions at Ootacamund on the Neilgherry Hills).

Agreed to.

The Bill passed through Committee without amendment; and the Council having resumed its sitting, the Bill was reported.

MR. ELIOTT then moved that the Standing Orders be suspended to admit of the Bill being read a third time and passed.

MR. HARINGTON seconded the Motion, which was then agreed to.

MR. ELIOTT moved that the Bill be now read a third time and passed.

Agreed to.

The Bill was then read a third time.

MR. ELIOTT moved that Mr. Grant be requested to take the Bill to the President in Council in order that it may be submitted to the Governor-General for his assent.

Agreed to.

PORT-DUES (ADEN).

MR. LEGEYT moved that Mr. Grant be requested to take the Bill "for the levy of Port-dues in the Port of Aden" to the President in Council in order that it may be submitted to the Governor-General for his assent.

Agreed to.

ESTATE OF THE LATE NABOB OF THE CARNATIC.

MR. PEACOCK moved that the Bill "to provide for the administration of the Estate and for the payment of the debts of the late Nabob of the Carnatic" be referred to a Select Committee consisting of the Chief Justice, Mr. Eliott and the Mover.

Agreed to.

SETTLEMENT OF ALLUVIAL LANDS (BENGAL).

MR. CURRIE moved that the Bill "to explain Regulation XI 1825 of the Bengal Code, and to prescribe rules for the settlement of land gained by alluvion" be referred to a Select Committee consisting of the Chief Justice, Mr. Eliott, Mr. Harington, and the Mover.

Agreed to.

MR. PEACOCK moved that the Select Committee on the Bill be instructed to submit a preliminary Report suggesting any alterations which they may deem expedient to make in the Bill previously to the publication thereof, and that they omit such parts as are declaratory of the existing law.

Agreed to.

The Council adjourned.

Saturday, April 10, 1858.

PRESENT:

The Honorable J. A. Dorin, *Vice-President*, in the Chair.

Hon. the Chief Justice,	P. W. LeGeyt, Esq.,
Hon'ble J. P. Grant,	E. Currie, Esq,
Hon'ble B. Peacock,	and
D. Eliott, Esq.,	H. B. Harington, Esq.

RESTORATION OF POSSESSION OF LANDS (N. W. P.)

THE CLERK brought under the consideration of the Council a Petition of the British Indian Association suggesting amendments in the Bill "to facilitate the recovery of land and other real property, of which possession may have been wrongfully taken during the recent disturbances in the North-Western Provinces of the Presidency of Bengal."

MR HARINGTON moved that the above Petition be referred to the Select Committee on the Bill.

Agreed to.

SETTLEMENT OF ALLUVIAL LANDS (BENGAL).

MR CURRIE presented the preliminary Report of the Select Committee on the Bill "to explain Regulation XI. 1825 of the Bengal Code, and to prescribe rules for the settlement of land gained by alluvion."

AUTHENTICATION OF GOVERNMENT STAMPS.

MR PEACOCK presented the Report of the Select Committee on the Bill "to provide for the authentication of Government Stamped Paper."

EXCLUSIVE PRIVILEGES TO INVENTORS.

MR PEACOCK also presented the Report of the Select Committee appointed to consider the Despatches from the Court of Directors disallowing and desiring the repeal of Act VI of 1856 (for granting exclusive privileges to Inventors.)

FORT OF TANJORE.

MR ELIOTT postponed the Motion (which stood in the Orders of the Day) for the first reading of a Bill for bringing the Fort of Tanjore and the adjacent territory under the Laws of the Presidency of Fort St. George.

REGULATION OF PORTS (FORT ST. GEORGE).

MR ELIOTT moved that the Council resolve itself into a Committee on the Bill "for the regulation of certain Ports within the Presidency of Fort St. George;" and that the Committee be instructed to consider the Bill in the amended form in which the Select Committee had recommended it to be passed

Agreed to.

The Bill passed through Committee without amendment

The Council resumed its sitting.

LIGHT-DUES (GULF OF CAMBAY).

MR LEGEYT moved that the Council resolve itself into a Committee on the Bill "to repeal the laws relating to the levy of Light-dues within the limits of the Gulf of Cambay."

Agreed to.

Section I was passed as it stood

MR LEGEYT moved that the following new Section be added to the Bill;—namely, "This Act shall commence and have effect from and after the 1st day of May 1858."

The Section was agreed to.

The Preamble and Title were passed as they stood.

The Council having resumed its sitting, the Bills settled in Committee were reported.

SETTLEMENT OF ALLUVIAL LANDS (BENGAL).

MR CURRIE moved that the Report of the Select Committee on the Bill "to explain Regulation XI. 1825 of the Bengal Code, and to prescribe rules for the settlement of land gained by alluvion" be adopted.

MR PEACOCK said, he should not object to the Motion; but in assenting to the adoption of the Report, and the publication of the Bill in the form in which it was now presented, he must not be considered as binding himself to the alterations made in the Bill by the Select Committee. The first part of Section I authorized the assessment of alluvion as part of the estate, provided the Government should agree to that arrangement; whereas it appeared to him that the zemindar had a right to insist upon such an assessment. The second part withheld from the Government the right of dissent in cases in which he thought it ought to have that right. The Section said:—

"If the proprietor or proprietors object to such an arrangement, or if the Revenue Authorities are of opinion that a settlement of the alluvial land cannot properly be made for the same term as the existing settlement of the original estate, the alluvial land shall be assessed and settled as a separate estate with a separate jumma."

So that, if the proprietor should object to the alluvion being settled as part of the original estate, the Government would be bound to settle it as a separate estate; whereas he thought that the Government ought to have the right of objecting to such a settlement where the nature of the alluvion was such that the separation would injure the original estate. It appeared to him, therefore, that the Section was wrong—first in requiring the assent of Government to settlements to which zemindars were entitled of right; and secondly, in not giving the Government a right of dissent in cases in which it might be necessary to exercise it—a right which he believed was now vested in them by law.

MR. CURRIE said, he would not discuss now the objections stated by the Honorable and learned Member. It seemed to him that this was not the time at which they could be properly discussed. The Select Committee had altered the Bill in accordance with the instruction given to them when they were appointed last Saturday; and the objections now taken seemed to him to be objections of detail, which could properly be considered hereafter by the Committee. The recommendation in their Report was, not that the Bill should be adopted by the Council in the form which it now bore, but that it should be published in that form. Upon its publication, suggestions would doubtless be received from Revenue Officers and others interested; and the Committee would then be in a position to determine whether any further alteration was necessary.

The motion was then put, and agreed to.

LIGHT-DUES (GULF OF CAMBAY).

MR LEGEYT moved that the Standing Orders be suspended to admit of the Bill "to repeal the laws relating to the levy of Light-dues within the limits of the Gulf of Cambay" being read a third time and passed.

MR. CURRIE seconded the Motion, which was agreed to.

MR. LEGEYT moved that the Bill be now read a third time and passed.

Agreed to.

The Bill was read a third time.

MR. LEGEYT moved that the Vice-President be requested to take the above Bill to the President in Council in order that it may be submitted to the Governor-General for his assent.

Agreed to.

LUNATIC ASYLUMS.

MR. ELIOTT moved that a communication received by him from the Madras Government be laid upon the table and referred to the Select Committee on the Bill "relating to Lunatic Asylums."

Agreed to.

The Council adjourned.

Mr. Currie

Saturday, April 17, 1858.

PRESENT:

The Honorable J. A. Dorin, *Vice-President,* in the Chair.

Hon. the Chief Justice,	P. W. LeGeyt, Esq.,
Hon'ble J. P. Grant,	E. Currie, Esq.,
Hon'ble Major General Sir J. Outram,	and
Hon'ble B. Peacock,	H. B. Harington, Esq.
D. Eliott, Esq.,	

The following Messages from the Governor-General were brought by the Vice-President and read:—

CORPORAL PUNISHMENT.

MESSAGE No. 132.

The Governor-General informs the Legislative Council that he has given his assent to the Bill which was passed by them on the 27th February 1858, entitled "A Bill to authorize the infliction of Corporal punishment in certain cases."

G. F. EDMONSTONE,
Secy. to the Govt. of India, with the Governor General.

ALLAHABAD,
The 4th April 1858.

MUNICIPAL ASSESSMENT (SUBURBS OF CALCUTTA, AND HOWRAH).

MESSAGE No. 133.

The Governor-General informs the Legislative Council that he has given his assent to the Bill which was passed by them on the 27th February 1858, entitled "A Bill for raising funds for making and repairing roads in the Suburbs of Calcutta and the Station of Howrah."

G. F. EDMONSTONE,
Secy. to the Govt. of India, with the Governor-General.

ALLAHABAD,
The 4th April 1858.

CONCEALMENT OF GOVERNMENT PROPERTY.

MESSAGE No. 134.

The Governor-General informs the Legislative Council that he has given his assent to the Bill which was passed by them on the 20th March 1858, entitled "A Bill for the punishment of persons who unlawfully possess or conceal arms or other property belonging to Her Majesty or the East India Company."

G. F. EDMONSTONE,
Secy. to the Govt. of India,
with the Governor-General.

ALLAHABAD,
The 4th April 1858.

FORT OF TANJORE.

MR. ELIOTT moved the first reading of a Bill "for bringing the Fort of Tanjore and the adjacent territory under the Laws of the Presidency of Fort St. George."

He said, when the Province of Tanjore was assumed by the East India Company, the Fort and some adjacent villages were left in the possession of the Rajah, and he was authorized to conduct the administration of Justice within those precincts, for which purpose he established three Civil Courts—one, a Court for the trial of original suits; the second, a Court for the decision of ordinary appeals; and the third, a Court for the decision of special appeals. He also established a Criminal Court. In consequence of the death of the Rajah without male issue, the Fort and its adjacent territory had lapsed to the East India Company; and it had become necessary to provide for those precincts being brought under the Presidency of Fort St. George; which being done, it would be expedient to appoint competent Courts in lieu of the tribunals which had hitherto exercised jurisdiction within them. It was intended to establish a District Moonsiff's Court at Tanjore for the trial of original suits, and for the exercise of Criminal jurisdiction under Act XII of 1854, which authorized the Government of Madras to vest District Moonsiffs with such jurisdiction, at their discretion. The Court, it was proposed, should be under the Zillah Court of Trichinopoly, to which the Fort and adjacent territory were to be annexed; and appeals from the decisions of the District Moonsiff would be heard by the Principal Sudder Ameen of that Zillah by reference from the Judge.

The Bill recognized the Rajah's Courts as *de facto* exercising jurisdiction until the proposed Act should come into operation.

It provided that decisions passed by such Courts in original Civil suits should be considered as final, if no appeal should have been made against them within thirty days.

Original suits, appeals other than special appeals, and proceedings in such Courts pending at the time of the Act coming into operation, would be transferred to the Courts of the District Moonsiffs.

Appeals not pending at the time the Act should come into operation, but presented within thirty days after the passing of the decisions appealed against, would be received by the Zillah Court, and disposed of in the same manner as pending appeals.

Special appeals which were pending, or which might be preferred within sixty days of the passing of the decisions appealed against, would be heard by the Zillah Judge.

Some time ago, the Government being informed that the Rajah's Courts continued to exercise jurisdiction, directed that the Commissioner should restrict their operation as much as possible; and it was probable that, since then, scarcely any original suits had been filed in them.

The Bill was read a first time.

EXCLUSIVE PRIVILEGES TO INVENTORS.

MR. PEACOCK moved the first reading of a Bill "for granting exclusive privileges to Inventors." He said, on Saturday last, he presented the Report of the Select Committee appointed to consider the subject of the Patent Laws; and he should now move the first reading of a Bill which was recommended by that Committee to be introduced in lieu of Act VI of 1856. The Council would recollect all the circumstances relating to the passing of Act VI of 1856, and to its repeal in consequence of the opinion given by the Law Officers of the Crown that it was not competent to the Council to pass an Act for granting exclusive privileges to Inventors in India, inasmuch as it affected the Prerogative of the Crown. In consequence of that opinion, the Honorable the Court of Directors issued orders that the Act should be repealed, and a new one be introduced in substitution of it, to be sent home to England for the purpose of receiving the sanction of the Crown previously to being passed, under the 16 and 17 Vict., c. 95. He, accordingly, now brought in a Bill for that purpose, and proposed that it should be read a first and second time, then published with the view of eliciting suggestions, afterwards passed through a Committee of the whole Council, and finally sent home in the appointed form for the sanction of Her Majesty.

The Bill recited that—

"Whereas Act VI of 1856, entitled 'an Act for granting exclusive privileges to Inventors,' was passed by the Legislative Council of India without the sanction of Her Majesty to the passing thereof having been previously obtained and signified in pursuance of the Statute passed in the seventeenth year of the reign of Her Majesty, entitled—'An Act to provide for the Government of India:' and whereas, Her Majesty's Law Officers having given it as their opinion that the Legislative Council of India was not competent to pass Act VI of 1856 without previously obtaining the sanction of the Crown, and the Court of Directors of the East India Company having in pursuance of the power vested in them by Law disallowed Act VI of 1856, and having signified to the Governor-General of India in Council their disallowance thereof, the said Act was repealed by Act IX of 1857: and whereas it is expedient, for the encouragement of Inventors of new manufactures, that certain exclusive privileges in their inventions should be granted to them in India, and that exclusive privileges obtained under the said Act should be protected: It is enacted as follows. (The sanction of Her Majesty to the passing of this Act having been previously obtained and signified, in pursuance of the said Statute):—"

Several suggestions had been made for the amendment of Act VI of 1856, which the Committee had taken fully into consideration; and they proposed, in consequence of those suggestions, and on a re-consideration of the whole Act, to make certain amendments. These were not many, and he would shortly describe what they were.

By the Law of England, Letters Patent were void if the inventions in respect of which they were granted were of no utility. Any person who infringed a patent, might set up as a defence to an action by the patentee that the invention was not useful; or any person might apply for a *scire facias* to rescind a patent upon the same ground. The Select Committee, having fully considered the question, had not thought it right to allow the inutility of an invention to be raised as a defence to an action for the infringement of an exclusive privilege; because if an invention was useless, there was no occasion to infringe the exclusive privilege by using it; but they thought that it would be advisable, for the purpose of preventing frivolous applications for exclusive privileges, to provide that, if an invention should appear to be perfectly useless, any person might move the Supreme Court to have the exclusive privilege granted in respect of it, revoked. They had therefore provided that the want of utility of an invention should be no defence to an action for the infringement of an exclusive privilege, but that it might be a ground upon which to set aside an exclusive privilege on an application to the Supreme Court.

Section XVI of Act VI of 1856 provided that an importer into India of a new invention should be deemed an inventor within the meaning of the Act. By the Law of England, a person importing a new invention was entitled to Letters Patent in the same way as if he were the actual inventor. But the Select Committee, after careful reconsideration, were of opinion that there was no such merit in importing new inventions at the present day as to entitle importers to exclusive privileges. If a foreign invention was really good, and was in use abroad, they thought that the Public would be sure to hear of it in these days of scientific publications and facility of inter-communication between foreign countries; and that there would, therefore, be no necessity to give any person an exclusive privilege as an inducement to import it. For instance, if there were new inventions in America in the Electric Telegraph, in steam engines, in locomotives, or in other manufactures, there could be no doubt that they would become known in this country by the means to which he had referred; and consequently, there would be no advantage in giving exclusive privileges to persons for importing them. Under this Bill, therefore, if a man was an actual inventor, he would be entitled to an exclusive privilege; but if he was only the importer of an invention, he would not be entitled to shut out the Public from the use of the invention.

By Section XVIII of Act VI of 1856, it was enacted that an invention not publicly used or known in India before the application for leave to file a specification, should be deemed a new invention within the meaning of the Act. Several objections had been made to this provision. One gentleman had said that he had intended to bring into use here an invention for wheels for locomotives which was well known in England; but that, under this Section, he would be prevented from doing so if some one else should have previously come out and patented the invention. The Select Committee thought that this would not be right, and had provided that no invention should be deemed a new invention within the meaning of the Act if it should, before the application for leave to file the specification, have been generally used in India or in any part of the United Kingdom, or been made publicly known in any part of India or of the United Kingdom by means of a printed or written publication.

By Section XIX of Act VI of 1856, it was enacted that, if an actual inventor should have taken out Letters Patent in England, his invention should be deemed a new invention within the meaning of the Act if it was not publicly known or used in India at the date of the petition for the Letters Patent, although it might have been publicly known or used in India before the time of his petitioning the Governor-General in Council under the Act for leave to file a specification thereof—provided that he filed such Petition within six calendar months from the date of the Letters Patent. The object of this provision was to extend to India the Letters Patent granted by the Crown, if the inventor applied within six months. But objections had been taken to the period of time allowed for the application. In England, a person who had obtained Letters Patent was entitled to six months within which to file a specification of the mode in which his invention was to be used; and it had been urged that, if he should be unable to complete his patent by filing a specification until shortly before the expiration of the period allowed, he would be debarred from an exclusive privilege in his invention in India. That would be an injustice; and, therefore, the Select Committee had thought it right, and had provided, that an actual inventor who had obtained Letters Patent in England, should be entitled to an exclusive privilege under the Act if he applied to the Governor-General in Council for leave to file a specification of his invention within twelve months from the date of his patent—that was to say, he would have six months within which to complete his patent in England, and six months within which to apply for its extension to this country. On the other hand, however, they thought that, if the Letters Patent should be cancelled in England in consequence of any defect, the inventor should not be entitled to any exclusive privilege here; and they had therefore provided that an exclusive privilege under the Act should not continue beyond the time during which the Letters Patent in England should be in force, and that it should cease if the Letters Patent in England were rescinded by the Crown.

The Select Committee had made one or two slight alterations in certain other Sections of the Act to which he did not think it necessary to refer particularly, as they related to mere matters of detail.

They had omitted Section XXXV of Act VI of 1856, which declared that nothing contained in the Act should—

> "abridge or affect the Prerogative of the Crown in relation to the granting, or withholding the grant, of any Letters Patent for inventions or otherwise, or affect or interfere with any Letters Patent for an invention heretofore granted, or hereafter to be granted, by the Crown."

They had not thought it necessary to insert this Section in the present Bill, because the Bill would be sent home for the sanction of the Crown before it was passed. The Council had inserted it in Act VI of 1856, considering—whether rightly or wrongly, he would not discuss now—that it would provide against any interference with the Prerogative of the Crown. The Law Officers of the Crown, however, had given it as their opinion that it would not protect the Prerogative, and that it was beyond the competency of the Council to pass the Act. The Act had been repealed in consequence; and the Bill which he now introduced in substitution of it would, previously to being passed, be sent home for the Royal sanction. It was unnecessary, therefore, that Section XXXV of Act VI of 1856 should be retained, and the Select Committee had accordingly omitted it.

The Select Committee had inserted a new Section, by which it was provided that all exclusive privileges granted under Act VI of 1856, and all remedies which that Act gave either for the infringement of an exclusive privilege, or for the purpose of setting one aside, should be continued in the same way as if the Act had not been repealed. The object of this provision was to put all persons who had obtained exclusive privileges on the faith of the Act, in precisely the same position in which they would have been if the Act had received the sanction of Her Majesty previously to its being passed.

It had also appeared proper to the Select Committee to extend the term of exclusive privileges already obtained under Act VI of 1856. The Act allowed an exclusive privilege for the term of fourteen years from the time of applying for leave to file a specification. But as the parties who had obtained exclusive privileges under it had been prevented from bringing them into effect in consequence of its repeal, it was but right that the term of fourteen years should be taken to commence, not from the date of the application for leave to file a specification, but from the date of the passing of the new Act; so that the parties should have what the Act of 1856 contemplated—the full period of fourteen years for the enjoyment of their exclusive privileges.

With these observations, which were all that he thought it necessary to make, he should move the first reading of the Bill.

The Bill was read a first time.

REGULATION OF PORTS (FORT ST. GEORGE).

MR. ELIOTT moved that the Bill "for the Regulation of certain Ports within the Presidency of Fort St. George" be now read a third time.

Mr. Peacock

The Motion was carried, and the Bill read a third time.

AUTHENTICATION OF GOVERNMENT STAMPS.

MR. PEACOCK moved that the Council resolve itself into a Committee on the Bill "to provide for the authentication of Government Stamped Paper;" and that the Committee be instructed to consider the Bill in the amended form in which the Select Committee had recommended it to be passed.

Agreed to.

The Bill passed through Committee after the omission (on the motion of Mr. Currie) of the word "Covenanted" wherever it occurred before the words "Deputy and Assistant Collector," and the addition of the following new Section at the end of the Bill:—

"The words 'Collector' or 'his Deputy or Assistant' shall be deemed to include any Officer exercising the powers of a Collector or of his Deputy or Assistant respectively."

The Council having resumed its sitting, the Bill was reported.

REGULATION OF PORTS (FORT ST. GEORGE).

MR. ELIOTT moved that Mr. Peacock be requested to take the Bill "for the Regulation of certain Ports within the Presidency of Fort St. George" to the President in Council in order that it may be submitted to the Governor-General for his assent.

Agreed to.

The Council adjourned.

Saturday, April 24, 1858.

PRESENT:

The Honorable J. A. Dorin, *Vice-President*, in the Chair.

Hon. the Chief Justice,	D. Eliott, Esq.,
Hon. J. P. Grant,	P.W.LeGeyt, Esq.,
Hon. Major Genl. Sir J. Outram,	E. Currie, Esq., and
Hon'ble B. Peacock,	H.B.Harington, Esq.

The following Messages from the Governor General were brought by the Vice-President and read :—

(MINORS) FORT ST. GEORGE.

MESSAGE No. 135.

The Governor General informs the Legislative Council that he has given his assent to the Bill which was passed by them on the 28th March 1858, entitled a Bill "to extend the provisions of Act XXI of 1855 in the Presidency of Fort St. George to Minors not subject to the superintendence of the Court of Wards."

G. F. EDMONSTONE,
Secy. to the Govt. of India with the Govr. Genl.

ALLAHABAD;
The 9th April 1858.

PORT-DUES (ADEN).

MESSAGE No. 136.

The Governor General informs the Legislative Council that he has given his assent to the Bill which was passed by them on the 3rd April 1858, entitled a Bill "for the levy of Port-dues in the Port of Aden."

G. F. EDMONSTONE,
Secy. to the Govt. of India with the Govr. Genl.

ALLAHABAD;
The 14th April 1858.

SUBORDINATE CRIMINAL COURT (OOTACAMUND).

MESSAGE No. 137.

The Governor General informs the Legislative Council that he has given his assent to the Bill which was passed by them on the 3rd April 1858, entitled a Bill "to extend Act XXV of 1855."

G. F. EDMONSTONE,
Secy. to the Govt. of India with the Govr. Genl.

ALLAHABAD;
The 14th April 1858.

RESTORATION OF POSSESSION OF LANDS (N. W. PROVINCES).

MR. HARINGTON presented the Report of the Select Committee on the Bill "to facilitate the recovery of land and other real property, of which possession may have been wrongfully taken during the recent disturbances in the North-Western Provinces of the Presidency of Bengal."

NATIVE PASSENGER SHIPS.

MR. ELIOTT presented the Report of the Select Committee on the Bill "for the regulation of Native Passenger Ships."

FORT OF TANJORE.

MR. ELIOTT moved the second reading of the Bill "for bringing the Fort of Tanjore and the adjacent territory under the Laws of the Presidency of Fort St. George."

The motion was carried, and the Bill read a second time.

EXCLUSIVE PRIVILEGES TO INVENTORS.

MR. PEACOCK moved the second reading of the Bill "for granting exclusive privileges to Inventors."

The motion was carried and the Bill read a second time.

AUTHENTICATION OF GOVERNMENT STAMPS.

MR PEACOCK moved that the Bill "to provide for the authentication of Stamped Paper issued from the Stamp Office in Calcutta" be now read a third time and passed.

The motion was carried, and the Bill read a third time.

ESTATE OF THE LATE NABOB OF THE CARNATIC.

MR. PEACOCK said, the Honorable Member for Madras had received a communication from the Madras Government requesting him to expedite as much as possible the passing of the Bill "to provide for the administration of the Estate, and for the payment of the debts, of the late Nabob of the Carnatic." The Bill had already been read a second time, and referred to a Select Committee. He (Mr. Peacock) proposed that the Committee be instructed to present their Report upon it at the first

Meeting of the Council after the 1st of June next—which would allow two months to creditors of the Nabob for making known any objections which they might have to the Bill—and that a notification to that effect be published in the *Gazette*. Accordingly, he should now move that the Standing Orders be suspended in order that the Bill might be proceeded with without delay.

MR. ELIOTT seconded the motion, which was then agreed to.

MR. PEACOCK moved that the Select Committee on the Bill be instructed to present their Report at the first Meeting of the Council after the first of June next, and that a notification to that effect be published in the *Gazette* for general information.

Agreed to.

FORT OF TANJORE.

MR. ELIOTT moved that the Bill "for bringing the Fort of Tanjore and the adjacent territory under the Laws of the Presidency of Fort St. George" be referred to a Select Committee consisting of Mr. Currie, Mr. Harington, and the Mover.

Agreed to.

EXCLUSIVE PRIVILEGES TO INVENTORS.

MR. PEACOCK moved that the Bill "for granting exclusive privileges to Inventors" be referred to a Select Committee consisting of the Chief Justice, Mr. Grant, and the Mover.

Agreed to.

The Council adjourned.

Saturday, May 1, 1858.

PRESENT:

The Hon'ble the Chief Justice, *Vice-President*, in the Chair.

Hon. J. P. Grant,	P. W. LeGeyt, Esq.
Hon. Major Genl. Sir Jas. Outram,	E. Currie, Esq. and
Hon. H. Ricketts,	H. B. Harington, Esq.
Hon. B. Peacock,	

The following Message from the Governor General was read by the Vice-President:—

LIGHT-DUES (GULF OF CAMBAY).

THE Governor General informs the Legislative Council that he has given his assent to the Bill which was passed by them on the 10th April 1858, entitled "A Bill to repeal the Laws relating to the levy of Light-dues at Ports within the limits of the Gulf of Cambay."

G. F. EDMONSTONE,
Secy. to the Govt. of India, With the Govr. Genl.

ALLAHABAD;
April 20th, 1858.

THE CLERK brought under the consideration of the Council the following Petitions:—

COTTON-FRAUDS (BOMBAY).

A Petition of certain Native Cotton Merchants and Dealers residing in the Town and Island of Bombay against Section VI of the Bill "for the better suppression of frauds in the Cotton-trade in the Presidency of Bombay."

MR. LEGEYT moved that the Petition be referred to the Select Committee on the Bill.

Agreed to.

CONSERVANCY ACT.

Also a Petition of the Bengal Bonded Warehouse Association praying for a modification of Section XXXV of Act XIV of 1856 (for the Conservancy and Improvement of the Towns of Calcutta, Madras, and Bombay, and the several stations of the Settlement of Prince of Wales' Island, Singapore, and Malacca,) relative to the powers of the Commissioners to allow projections, not exceeding a certain width, from houses.

MR. CURRIE moved that the Petition be printed.

Agreed to.

PORTRAIT OF THE MARQUIS OF DALHOUSIE.

THE CLERK reported to the Council that he had received a communication from the Secretary to the Government of India in the Home Department forwarding an Extract of a Despatch from the Court of Directors on the subject of the Marquis of Dalhousie's Portrait.

MR. GRANT moved that the communication be printed.

Agreed to.

RESTORATION OF POSSESSION OF LANDS (N. W. P.)

MR. HARINGTON moved that the Council resolve itself into a Committee on the Bill "to facilitate the recovery of land and other real property, of which possession may have been wrongfully taken during the recent disturbances in the North-Western Provinces of the Presidency of Bengal;" and that the Committee be instructed to consider the Bill in the amended form in which the Select Committee had recommended it to be passed.

MR. RICKETTS said, having been appointed a Member of this Council only within a few minutes, he was unprepared to oppose the Motion to go into Committee on this Bill; but he wished to take that, the earliest opportunity he had had, of saying that he did not think this piece-meal legislation suited to the circumstances of the North-Western Provinces, or the crisis with which the Council had to deal. Many of those Provinces were still in the possession of the rebels. Though we had recovered possession of some of them, little better than anarchy prevailed still. The condition of all those Provinces was changing day by day: the condition of no two was the same; and it appeared to him really impossible that any Act that was applicable to one or two, should be applicable to the whole. He should much prefer, either the introduction of one comprehensive Act to enlarge the powers of the Governor of the North-Western Provinces, or the suspension for a term of the operation of the Regulations now in force within them. Were our Code of Regulations acknowledged by all to be a good Code, the Council might hesitate before it suspended its operation. But the Code, especially that part of it which related to procedure, was avowedly a bad Code; the Council had been employed, now for a long time, in the preparation of one which was to supersede it; and amongst the people who lived under it, there was a very large number who would not have the slightest objection to its being suspended whilst that measure was in progress. He had seen, not long ago, a letter from an Officer employed in one of the districts lately made over to the Government of the Punjab in which the writer said—" Let what will happen, the people of these districts will never regret the rebellion, for they have escaped the blight of the accursed Code." He found that Code spoken of in the following terms in the Pamphlet recently published entitled " The Crisis in the Punjab" :—

> "The exaggerated elaboration of its routine and ramification of its legal defences, as distasteful to those who had to administer it, as incomprehensible to the people, furnished no hope that any district could be held by either moral force founded upon its merits, or on affectionate reminiscences of its points of procedure."

He would not say that that picture was not exaggerated; but he did not think that even the Honorable Mover of this Bill would say that he believed the Code to be dear to the hearts of any of the people in any part of the Provinces in the North-West. And if that was the case, surely it would be good to strengthen the hands of the local Government by suspending the operation of the Code for a period, and creating the Governor Dictator, and making his will law.

He (Mr. Ricketts) was aware that he would not have the Council with him, and he would not, therefore, oppose the motion to go into Committee upon the Bill; but he had thought it right to avail himself of the very first opportunity of expressing the views which he entertained with regard to this subject.

MR. HARINGTON said, he did not think that this was the time to go into the question as to whether existing Regulations were popular or not. That question had nothing to do with the Bill before the Council. An emergency had arisen in the North-Western Provinces for which it was necessary to make provision. That emergency consisted in many persons having been wrongfully deprived of the possession of their estates during the recent disturbances who, if left to the ordinary remedy of a regular Civil action, would be subjected to considerable delay and expense. This Bill was intended to provide for these persons an easy and speedy means of obtaining redress; and it appeared to him that the mode of procedure which it prescribed would be found equally simple and summary with anything in the Code of the Punjab which had been so highly extolled in some quarters. He, therefore, hoped that the Council would go into Committee on the Bill.

MR. PEACOCK said, the Honorable Member opposite (Mr. Ricketts) had stated that the circumstances of the various districts of the North-Western Provinces were so different that no Act applicable to one or two could be applicable to the whole of them, and he had described this Bill as piece-meal legislation. The Bill had been prepared with great care for the purpose of being adapted to districts which differed from each other in their circumstances. It would be seen upon reference to the Bill that it was not to take effect absolutely in every district of the North-Western Provinces, but only in those districts in which the Executive Government should deem it necessary to appoint Special Commissioners for the purpose of carrying out its provisions. The Act would not take effect of its own force. Where a district required the Act, the local Government would appoint Special Commissioners, who would act under a procedure provided for them, and in that district the jurisdiction of the ordinary Courts would be suspended; but in those districts in which Special Commissioners were not appointed, the ordinary rules of the existing law would continue in force. It appeared to him, therefore, that this Bill, so far from being unsuited to the circumstances of the North-Western Provinces, was entirely adapted to them. He was not standing there to support the existing Code of Regulations; but he certainly should hesitate a long time before he could assent to the proposition of the Honorable Member that it would be expedient to appoint a Dictator whose will should be law, even if he believed that the Council had the power to legalize such an appointment. In his opinion, however, the Council had no such power. By the Charter Act, the power of making Laws and Regulations was vested in the Governor General in Council, constituted in the manner provided by the Act; but they were prohibited from making any Laws or Regulations which should vary the provisions of the Act. It was, therefore, beyond their power to enable any man to make Laws and carry them into effect. He should be very sorry to see any man vested with such extensive powers in any part of these dominions—vested with powers so extensive, that his will should be law; and he did not think that even existing circumstances rendered the introduction of such a measure necessary in the North-Western Provinces.

THE VICE-PRESIDENT said, before putting the question, he would ask the permission of the Council to say a few words upon it.

In what he proposed to say, he desired to be understood as not committing himself to any opinion on the question raised by the Honorable Member who had this day taken his seat. That question, as he understood it, was not so much the propriety of appointing a Dictator to govern the North-Western Provinces at his own will, as the more moderate proposition of reducing those Provinces to the condition of a non-Regulation Province. He by no means committed himself to the opinion that it would be inexpedient to do this. All he said was that, whatever might be the expediency of doing it, he thought that the question was a very large one, and that, if brought forward, it ought to be brought forward with the full weight and authority of the Executive Government, after mature consideration by them of the propriety of establishing the system proposed in lieu of the Regulations now in force in those Provinces. This very large question of altering the whole system of law by which certain Provinces were governed, was very different from the question involved in the measure now before the Council; and it appeared to him that it would be improper to mix them up together. The measure before the Council was designed to provide a remedy for a particular evil which had arisen out of the recent disturbances—to give as simple and speedy means of redress as possible to owners of real property who had been wrongfully driven out of possession. It would be hard on that class of sufferers to delay the passing of a measure like this, while the subject of the future government of the Provinces might be under the consideration of the Government. Every day of continued dispossession was a hardship on the rightful owner, and increased, as all the world knew, the difficulty of recovering possession. Without offering any opinion, therefore, with respect to the general views expressed by the Honorable Member, he must say it appeared to him that it was not desirable to delay the passing of the present Bill.

The motion to go into Committee on the Bill was then put and agreed to.

Sections I to X were passed as they stood.

Section XI provided for the enforcement of the order restoring possession to the rightful owner, and for the adjustment and recovery of mesne profits.

MR. RICKETTS said, as he read the Section, the Collector, on a case being referred to him for the purpose of adjusting the amount of mesne profits payable, was to endeavor to ascertain what collections had been actually made by the party wrongfully in possession, and to levy the amount for the benefit of the rightful owner. If that was the intention, the enquiry would be so difficult that it would be almost impossible for the Collector in any length of time to ascertain what the collections had amounted to. It appeared to him (Mr. Ricketts) that matters would be greatly simplified if the following words were introduced into the Section after the words "In cases so referred," in the 17th line:—

"If the settlement papers of the property, or any other papers shewing the rental at the period of settlement are forthcoming, the Collector shall adjudge as mesne profits the rental of the land for the term of its dispossession, minus ten per cent. expenses of collection, and any sum that may have been paid to the British Government as Revenue. Should such papers not be forthcoming, the Collector shall adjudge the mesne profits of a whole year to be sixty Rupees on each hundred Rupees of the sudder jumma of the estate; and the profits of each month, if the period of possession has been less than a year, at one-twelfth of such sum, minus any sum that may have been paid as Revenue to the British Government; and"—

If these words were introduced, all the trouble and the many vexations of endeavoring to ascertain what had been collected, would be saved. It was true that, by adopting such a plan, the party who had wrongfully taken possession might occasionally have to pay something more than he had collected; but he (Mr. Ricketts) could see no objection to that. If a man took possession of an estate wrongfully, he could not claim to be protected from the consequences of his wrongful act. He (Mr. Ricketts) should, therefore, move as an amendment that the words he had read be inserted after the words "In cases so referred," in the 17th line of the Section.

MR. HARINGTON said, the duty which this Section would impose on the Collector would in no way differ from the duty which that Officer had to perform when a decree of the Civil Court which awarded mesne profits to the successful party was referred to him for the purpose of adjusting the amount. In such cases, no great difficulty was experienced by the Collector in ascertaining what amount of mesne profits had been realized by the party declared liable for the same; and he (Mr. Harington) did not see that it would be more difficult for that Officer to carry out the part of the Bill under consideration. It might not be wrong in principle that the person who had taken wrongful possession of an estate should be responsible to the owner for the rents of the period during which he had been in possession, whether he had collected them or not; but in the latter case, some provision would be necessary to enable him to recover the amount from the ryots, which would be decidedly objectionable; and as, upon the whole, he preferred the Section as it stood, he should vote against the amendment.

MR. GRANT said, the amendment might, contrary to the intention of the Honorable Mover, act very unfairly towards the party dispossessed; for supposing that the property had been in the possession of the wrong-doer during that period of the year when the rents are realized, in each month of which he had perhaps realized one-eighth part of the whole annual return, it would be unfair to put off the rightful owner at the rate of only one-twelfth part a month. He (Mr. Grant) thought that it would be better to leave the adjustment of mesne profits under the Bill to the discretion of the Collector, binding him by no stringent rules, but leaving him to act according to common sense in each case, when, if he could not ascertain the precise amount, he would make an award as nearly to that amount as he could under the circumstances of the case before him.

MR. PEACOCK said he did not see any reason for a new procedure for ascertaining the amount of mesne profits payable by the defendant. What the Collector would have to ascertain was the loss which the person wrongfully dispossessed had sustained during the period he was kept out of possession. The mode which the Bill as it stood provided for that purpose, involved no greater difficulty than the mode which the Collector had to adopt in the execution of a decree awarding mesne profits in a regular suit. The object of the Bill was that persons who had been forcibly dispossessed of estates during the rebellion, should be restored to possession as speedily as possible, and that they should be re-imbursed the amount which they had lost during the period of dispossession. The amendment proposed that, where a case was referred to the Collector for the purpose of adjusting the amount payable, if papers shewing the rental of the property at the period of settlement were not forthcoming, the Collector should adjudge the mesne profits of a whole year to be sixty per cent. on the sudder jumma, and the profits for each month, if the period of wrongful possession had been less than a year, to be one-twelfth of that sum, minus payments made on account of Government Revenue. The Honorable Mover of the amendment had shewn no reason why sixty per cent. of the sudder jumma should be taken as the measure of the profits. The estate might have increased or deteriorated in value since the sudder jumma was fixed: in the one case, sixty per cent. of the sudder jumma might be too little, and in the other, it would be too much.

Then, again, as the Honorable Member to his left (Mr. Grant) had pointed out, the amendment proposed that, in ascertaining the mesne profits for less than a year, they should be taken at one-twelfth of sixty per cent. on the sudder jumma for each month, whereas the profits actually received in each month might have been very much greater.

But it appeared to him that the objection to the amendment which had been pointed out by the Honorable Member for the North-Western Provinces was insuperable. If the wrong-doer was to pay sixty per cent. on the sudder jumma whether he himself had collected the rents or not, was he to be empowered to recover the amount from the under-tenants?—was the Government to recognize his right to collect the rents from them?—or was he to pay a per-centage on the sudder jumma, and yet not have the right to realize the rents from the tenants? It was impossible for the Council to say what proportion the mesne profits of an estate during any particular period bore to the sudder jumma of the estate. The amount was a question of fact which the Bill proposed to leave to the determination of the Collector.

It appeared to him that by far the better course would be to leave the Collector to determine that fact in the manner in which he now ascertained the amount of mesne profits when that question was referred to him in regular suits. He believed that at present, no great difficulty was experienced in doing so; and he should, therefore, vote against the amendment.

MR. RICKETTS said, it was quite true that the sum which the wrong-doer would have to pay under the mode of adjustment which he had proposed, might not be the exact sum which he ought to pay; but *bis dat qui citò dat.* The party who had been dispossessed would much prefer speedy payment to waiting an indefinite period for the ascertainment of the precise amount of mesne profits which should be paid to him. The Honorable Member for the North-Western Provinces had said that it would not be more difficult for the Collector to ascertain mesne profits under the Section as it stood than it was for that Officer to ascertain mesne profits in the execution of decrees. But the Honorable Member must be aware that the execution of decrees for mesne profits frequently stood over for years and years. That was the case in every district in the North-Western Provinces; and the ascertainment of mesne profits in the present state of things would be more difficult than it had ever been before.

Although the Council was against him, he should press his amendment to the vote.

The amendment being put, the Council divided.

Aye 1.	Noes 7.
Mr. Ricketts.	Mr. Harington.
	Mr. Currie.
	Mr. LeGeyt.
	Mr. Peacock.
	Sir James Outram.
	Mr. Grant.
	The Chairman.

So the motion was negatived.

MR. RICKETTS moved that, in the concluding part of the Section—which declared that all proceedings of a Collector under the Section should be subject to the control and revision of "the superior Revenue Authorities"—the words "Commissioner of Revenue whose orders shall be final" be substituted for the words "superior Revenue Authorities."

After some conversation, the Motion was by leave withdrawn.

MR. RICKETTS then moved that the words "superior Revenue Authorities" at the end of the Section be left out, and the words "next superior Revenue Authority whose order shall be final" be substituted for them.

The amendment was agreed to, and the Section then passed.

Sections XII to XIV, and the Preamble and Title, were passed as they stood.

The Council having resumed its sitting, the Bill was reported.

NATIVE PASSENGER SHIPS.

On the Order of the Day for a Committee of the whole Council on the Bill "for the regulation of Native Passenger Ships" being read, it was moved by Mr. LeGeyt that the consideration of the Bill be postponed.

Agreed to.

AUTHENTICATION OF GOVERNMENT STAMPS.

MR. PEACOCK moved that Sir James Outram be requested to take the Bill "to provide for the authentication of Stamped Paper issued from the Stamp Office in Calcutta" to the President in Council, in order that it might be submitted to the Governor General for his assent.

Agreed to.

The Council adjourned.

Saturday, May 8, 1858.

PRESENT:

The Hon'ble the Chief Justice, *Vice-President*, in the Chair.

Hon. Major General Sir James Outram,	P. W. LeGeyt, Esq.,
Hon. H. Ricketts,	E. Currie, Esq., and
Hon. B. Peacock,	H. B. Harington, Esq.

The following Message from the Governor General was read by the Vice-President:—

REGULATION OF PORTS (FORT ST. GEORGE).

MESSAGE No. 139.

The Governor General informs the Legislative Council that he has given his assent to the Bill which was passed by them on the 17th Instant, entitled "A Bill for the Regulation of certain Ports within the Presidency of Fort St. George."

By order of the Right Honorable the Governor General

G. F. EDMONSTONE,
Secy. to the Govt. of India, with the Governor General.

ALLAHABAD;
The 27th April 1858.

MERCHANT SEAMEN.

THE CLERK brought under the consideration of the Council a Petition of the Peninsular and Oriental Steam Navigation Company against Section LXVI of the Bill "for the amendment of the law relating to Merchant Seamen." The Petition objected to the space allowed to lascars, and prayed that, before the passing into law of so much of the Bill as related to providing the number of cubic feet of accommodation to all Seamen, Europeans or Asiatics, indiscriminately, the Council would allow the Petitioner to be heard by himself, his Counsel, agents, and witnesses, either before the Select Committee on the Bill, or before a Committee of the whole Council.

MR. CURRIE said, the case was one in which there did not seem to be the slightest necessity for the Petitioner to be heard by Counsel, even if it were usual for parties to be so heard. If the

Superintendent of the Peninsular and Oriental Company had stated in the Petition what he desired should be done, the Select Committee on the Bill would report his propositions to the Council. At present, he (Mr. Currie) should only move that the Petition be printed and referred to the Select Committee.

THE VICE-PRESIDENT said, h thought that this was all that was necessary at present. The Petition stated that the vessels of the Company had been built expressly to meet the requirements of the existing law in respect of accommodation for lascars; and, assuming that the Bill, in requiring larger space to be provided, would so affect the interests of the Company that the case was one in which the Superintendent of the Company might be heard by Counsel under No. XXIX of the Standing Orders, it by no means followed that, when the Select Committee on the Bill read the Petition, they would not see the propriety of making the alteration proposed. If they did not, the Petition might then be referred to the Standing Orders Committee for the purpose of considering and reporting whether it came under the Standing Order to which he had referred.

The question was put, and agreed to.

ARMY AND STATE OFFENCES: MUTINY AND DESERTION.

On the Order of the Day being read for the first reading of a Bill "to continue in force for one year Act XIV of 1857 (for the trial and punishment of certain offences relating to the Army, and of offences against the State), and Act XVII of 1857 (for the apprehension and trial of Native Officers and Soldiers for Mutiny and Desertion")—

MR. PEACOCK said, he proposed to bring in a Bill for the purpose of continuing for one year longer Act XIV of 1857 and Act XVII of 1857. The Council were aware that, when these Acts were originally passed, it was declared that they should continue in force for one year only. Act XIV would expire on the 6th, and Act XVII on the 20th of June next. Although these Acts were not so absolutely necessary now as they were at the time they were passed, it was not desirable to weaken the hands of the Government at the present moment by allowing them to expire. In point of fact, numerous trials were now going on under them, in Delhi and other places. He had in his hand a letter from the Chief Commissioner of the Punjaub, under whose control the Delhi territory was now placed, in which that Officer said—

"It might have been anticipated that at Delhi, of all other places, these prisoners"—meaning prisoners charged with offences against Acts XIV, XVI, and XVII of 1857—"would be numerous; and, accordingly, although some five hundred have been disposed of summarily, there are some fifteen hundred men awaiting trial; and although upwards of one hundred were tried last week by the Commission, yet the aggregate of prisoners has not been diminished, owing to the number of new arrests."

It appeared to him (Mr. Peacock) necessary, therefore, that Act XIV should be continued if only for the purpose of carrying on the trial of these cases.

With respect to Act XVI, it would not expire as early as Act XIV, and he did not think it necessary that it should be continued in its present form. On Saturday next, he proposed to bring in a Bill to continue it in an amended form.

Act XIV of 1857 related to the offence of seducing or endeavoring to seduce any Officer or Soldier in the service of the East India Company from his allegiance to the British Government, or his duty to the East India Company, and rendered the offender liable either to the punishment of death, or of transportation for life, or of imprisonment with hard labor for any term not exceeding fourteen years; and also to forfeiture of all his property and effects It further authorized the Governor General in Council, by an Order in Council, to empower any General or other Officer in command of Troops to appoint a Court Martial for the trial of any such offender. Another important provision of the Act was Section VII, which enacted as follows:—

"It shall be lawful for the Governor General in Council, or for the Executive Government of any Presidency or place, or for any person or persons whom the Governor General in Council may authorize so to do, from time to time to issue a Commission for the trial of all or any persons or person charged with having committed within any district described in the Commission, whether such district shall or shall not have been proclaimed to be in a state of rebellion, any offence punishable by Sections I and II of Act XI of 1857, or by this Act, or any other crime against the State, or murder, arson, robbery, or other heinous crime against person or property."

By Section VIII, the Commissioner or Commissioners appointed might hold a Court for the trial of persons guilty of these offences. As matters settled down, it would be advisable that Courts held under a Commission should consist of more than one Commissioner, especially for the trial of capital offences; but he did not propose to tie up the hands of the Executive Government by introducing any new provision into the Act requiring that every such Court should consist of more than one Commissioner. He thought that the more expedient course would be to leave it to the Executive Government to lay down rules upon the subject. The Chief Commissioner of the Punjaub had already laid down rules upon the subject in the Delhi territory. He had directed that, in the Delhi district, not less than three Officers should sit to try persons charged with offences punishable with death, or with transportation for life, or with a more lengthened term of imprisonment than three years; and in other parts, he had directed that two Officers at least should sit. He had appointed the Magistrate and the Joint Magistrate to act as Commissioners. It might be necessary in many parts of the country, where troops were now marching accompanied by Civil Officers, and in cases of emergency, that a single Officer should have power to try offenders even in cases involving the punishment of death or of lengthened imprisonment; and he therefore thought that it would be better to leave it to the Executive Government to appoint one, two, or more Commissioners in each instance, as the necessities of the case might require, than to lay down any precise rule upon the subject by the Act.

Act XVII of 1857 authorized Sessions Judges and others to try Officers and Soldiers belonging to the Native Army, who were guilty of Mutiny and Desertion; and also empowered the Executive Government to issue Special Commissions for the trial of such offenders. It might not be so necessary at the present moment as it was when the Act was passed, to authorize Civil Officers to try persons guilty of these offences; but he still thought it advisable that the Act should be continued. The Council were probably aware that Mr. Wilson and other Officers had been appointed in the North-Western Provinces for the purpose of tracing out and trying mutineers. If this Act were not continued, the functions of that Officer would altogether be suspended.

Act XVI of 1857 subjected all persons who were guilty of any of the heinous offences described in it, to the punishment of death, or of transportation for life, or of imprisonment with hard labor for any term not exceeding fourteen years; and also to forfeiture of all their property and effects. At the present time, he did not consider it necessary to continue the Act, so far as it authorized the punishment of death for some of the offences named therein; and he, therefore, proposed to bring in a Bill at the next Meeting of the Council to amend it in this respect, and extend its duration in that modified form.

That Act also allowed persons guilty of the offences specified therein, to be tried under Special Commissions. He did not see any objection to that provision being continued. The object of the Government was that all offences, except offences against the State, should as soon as possible be referred to the ordinary Civil tribunals; but at the same time, cases might arise in which it would be necessary to issue Special Commissions. It was only very lately that the Governor General had issued a direction to the Commissioner of Meerut in which His Lordship stated that the time had now arrived when, from the improving condition of the country, the functions of Special Commissioners might with advantage be restricted to the trial of offences against the State. He did not think that there was any objection to continuing to Government the power of appointing Special Commissioners for the trial of offences against Act XVI of 1857, so that it might be used if any emergency should arise

He felt certain that they would not exercise it, except in emergent cases in which it might appear necessary to do so.

With these observations, he begged to move the first reading of the Bill to continue Act XIV of 1857 and Act XVII of 1857 for a further term of one year.

The Bill was read a first time.

STAMP DUTIES (BENGAL).

Mr. PEACOCK moved the first reading of a Bill "to amend Regulation X. 1829 of the Bengal Code relating to the collection of Stamp Duties." He said, by a recent Petition from the Rajah of Burdwan, the attention of the Council had been called to a General Rule contained in Schedule A Regulation X 1829, which declared as follows :—

"If any Deed, Instrument, or Document, specified in this Schedule, shall not be contained in one sheet or piece of paper or other material, it shall suffice that one sheet shall bear the stamp, provided that the signatures or seals of the parties and witnesses be thereupon."

In the case alluded to by the Rajah of Burdwan, it appeared that a Deed was brought forward in support of a claim, in which the names of the witnesses were not written on the sheet which bore the stamp. The names of the parties to the Instrument were on that sheet, but those of the witnesses were on another. The Rule in question required that the signatures of both the parties to a Deed and of the witnesses should be written on the same sheet on which the stamp was affixed. Native Deeds were usually attested by a number of witnesses; and there might be many cases in which it would be almost impossible to comply with the Rule. There might be no room in the sheet bearing the stamp for the signatures of all the witnesses; and if the signatures of some of them should be written on another paper, the Deed would be useless. A decision of Sir Robert Barlow was referred to in the Petition, in which that learned Judge had held that the circumstance of the signatures of the witnesses not being upon the sheet bearing the stamp, ought not to invalidate the Deed. He (Mr. Peacock), however, believed that the decision of the Courts now was that the rule laid down in Regulation X. 1829 was so strict that no Deed in which it had not been complied with could be given in evidence. Probably, that was the proper construction; but, be that as it might, he believed that the ruling of the Courts had been as he had just stated it. He was not aware of the precise object of the Rule, nor did he see that any facility would be afforded for frauds against the Revenue if it were abolished. He found no such Rule in the Stamp Act relating to Calcutta. The English Stamp Acts did not require that the *ad valorem* stamp upon conveyances should be impressed upon the sheet which bore the names of the parties to the Instrument, or of the witnesses; and he was not aware that any fraud had been attempted in England in the absence of such a Rule, or that any could be attempted here if the rule in Regulation X. 1829 were abolished. He thought it advisable that it should be abolished; and that Deeds which bore the full Stamp-duties required by Government, should be admissible in evidence even though the seals or signatures of the parties thereto and of the witnesses should not be upon the sheet on which the stamp was impressed. The Bill which he now introduced provided for that object; and he begged to move its first reading.

The Bill was read a first time.

RESTORATION OF POSSESSION OF LANDS (N. W. P.)

Mr. HARINGTON moved that the Bill "to facilitate the recovery of land and other real property, of which possession may have been wrongfully taken during the recent disturbances in the North-Western Provinces of the Presidency of Bengal" be now read a third time and passed.

The Motion was carried, and the Bill read a third time.

NATIVE PASSENGER SHIPS.

Mr. LeGEYT moved that the Council resolve itself into a Committee on the Bill "for the regulation of Native Passenger Ships;" and that the Committee be instructed to consider the Bill in the amended form in which the Select Committee had recommended it to be passed.

Agreed to.

Section I was passed after a verbal amendment.

Sections II to X were passed as they stood.

Sections XI and XII were passed after verbal amendments.

Sections XIII to XIX were passed as they stood.

Section XX provided that "nothing in this Act contained" should apply to Her Majesty's or the East India Company's Ships of War, or to ships under contract with the Government of any European State, or to sea-going steam vessels conveying public mails under a contract.

MR. LEGEYT moved that the words "the foregoing provisions of" be inserted after the words "Nothing in" and before the words "this Act" in the first line of the Section. He said, he moved this amendment because, as appeared from a communication from the Government of Bombay, which had been printed as No. 8 of the Further Papers annexed to the Bill, a discussion had arisen in that Presidency in connexion with this Bill, relative to the steamers under contract with Government to convey the public mails between Bombay and Kurrachee; and it appeared to be desirable that, though the provisions preceding this Section, which were intended particularly for ships conveying Pilgrims, should not extend to the class of vessels mentioned here, the provisions contained in certain of the subsequent Sections should be made applicable to them.

The amendment was agreed to, and the Section then passed.

Section XXI (which provided that Certificates should be furnished to steam vessels intended to carry passengers on coasting voyages before they proceeded on such voyages) was passed as it stood.

Section XXII prescribed how and after what enquiries the Certificates were to be granted.

MR. LEGEYT said, the communication to which he had just referred would have shewn Honorable Members that the Commissioner of Scinde had laid some stress on steamers carrying passengers on coasting voyages being provided with boats for the safety of passengers in cases of accident. It appeared to him (Mr. LeGeyt) that it was very proper and desirable to provide for that object by this Bill; and he should therefore move that the words "and properly equipped with boats and otherwise" be inserted after the words "that such Steam-Vessel is sea-worthy" in the 14th line of the Section.

The amendment was agreed to, and the Section then passed.

Sections XXIII and XXIV were passed as they stood.

Sections XXV and XXVI were transposed.

Sections XXVII to XXIX were passed as they stood.

Section XXX was passed after a verbal amendment.

Sections XXXI and XXXII were passed as they stood.

Section XXXIII was passed after amendments.

On the Motion of Mr. Peacock, the following new Section was added to the Bill:—

"This Act shall commence and take effect from and after the 1st day of August 1858."

Agreed to.

The Preamble was passed as it stood.

The Title was passed after the addition of the words "and of Steam-Vessels intended to convey passengers on coasting voyages."

The Council having resumed its sitting, the Bill was reported.

CRIMINAL PROCEDURE (BENGAL).

MR. CURRIE moved that a communication received by him from the Bengal Government, on the subject of preventing hindrance to justice sometimes occasioned by a defect of medical evidence in criminal trials, be laid upon the table, and referred to the Select Committee on the Bill "for extending the jurisdiction of the Courts of Criminal Judicature of the East India Company in Bengal, for simplifying the Procedure thereof, and for investing other Courts with Criminal jurisdiction."

Agreed to.

RESTORATION OF POSSESSION OF LANDS (N. W. P.)

MR. HARINGTON moved that Mr. Peacock be requested to take the Bill "to facilitate the recovery of land and other real property, of which possession may have been wrongfully taken during the recent disturbances in the North-Western Provinces of the Presidency of Bengal" to the President in Council, in order that it may be submitted to the Governor General for his assent.

Agreed to.

MERCHANT SEAMEN.

MR. LEGEYT moved that a communication received by him from the Bombay Government be laid upon the table and referred to the Select Committee on the Bill "for the amendment of the law relating to Merchant Seamen."

Agreed to.

The Council adjourned.

Saturday, May 15, 1858.

PRESENT:

The Honorable the Chief Justice, *Vice-President*, in the Chair.

Hon'ble J. P. Grant,
Hon'ble Major General Sir James Outram,
Hon'ble H. Ricketts,
Hon'ble B. Peacock,
P. W. LeGeyt, Esq.,
E. Currie, Esq.,
H. B. Harington, Esq.
and
H. Forbes, Esq.

NEW MEMBER (MADRAS).

MR. FORBES was duly sworn, and took his seat as Legislative Councillor of the Council of India for the Presidency of Fort St. George.

REMOVAL OF PRISONERS.

MR. CURRIE moved the first reading of a Bill "to make further provision for the removal of Prisoners." He said, the power of removing persons under sentence of imprisonment from one place of confinement to another had always existed, though it had not always been vested in the same authority. By Regulation LIII. 1803, the Court of Nizamut Adawlut was declared competent to order the removal of all convicts under sentence of imprisonment to any jail or district within the Company's possessions in which it might be thought proper to keep or employ them during the period of their respective sentences, although no specific sentence of banishment might have been passed against them. Under this Regulation, therefore, the Sudder Court had the power of ordering the removal of a prisoner beyond the bounds of the Presidency to which the Court's jurisdiction was limited, provided the place of removal was within the Company's possessions. The Regulation had been virtually superseded by Act VII of 1850, which provided that—

"When any person is under sentence of imprisonment within the territories under the Government of the East India Company, or any other authority other than that of one of the Supreme Courts of Judicature established by Royal Charter, the Governor or Governor in Council, or other person administering the Government of the Presidency or place, may order the removal of such prisoner from the prison or place in which he is confined, to any other public prison or place of confinement within the same Presidency or Government."

Thus, the power of removal which was formerly vested in the Sudder Court, was transferred to the local Governments—with this restriction, however, that the removal must be to some public place of confinement within the same Presidency or Government.

The Lieutenant-Governor of Bengal, therefore, under the law as it now stood, might remove prisoners to Arracan; but he could not remove them to Moulmein, or any other place beyond the limits of the Bengal Presidency.

In the late troubles, when the Dinapore troops broke out into mutiny, and the prisoners had been liberated by the mutineers and rioters from two of the Jails in the Behar Division, it became necessary to consider what should be done with the prisoners at Deeghur and other places, which were or might be threatened by the rebels. It was not necessary for him to remind the Council that, when the mutineers and rebels obtained any temporary success, their first step always was to break open the jails, and liberate the prisoners, with the view of increasing the confusion; and it was, therefore, obviously the duty of Government to render such an occurrence as little injurious as possible, by removing the worse description of criminals, whose liberation, in the event of a disturbance, would be sure to aggravate and prolong it.

Mr. Harington

influenced by these considerations, the Lieutenant-Governor determined to remove the more dangerous classes of prisoners from the jails of the Behar province; and as the Alipore Jail could not accommodate them, he obtained the sanction of the Supreme Government to transfer them to the Straits of Malacca and other places.

The object of this Bill was to legalize those proceedings, and any other measures of a similar character which might still be necessary. Considering the total want of suitable places of confinement in many parts of the country, and their insecurity in others, it might often be absolutely necessary for the safe custody of criminals, and, in consequence, for the peace of the country and public security, that they should be removed to some place beyond the limits of the Government within which they were confined. The Bill therefore provided that—

"Whenever it shall be judged necessary for the safe custody of any person who has been convicted of any heinous offence, and sentenced to imprisonment for life, or for any term exceeding three years, that such person should be removed to some place of confinement beyond the limits of the Presidency or Government within which he is confined, it shall be lawful for the Governor-General in Council, or for the Executive Government of the Presidency or place, with the sanction of the Governor-General in Council, to order the removal of such person from the prison or place in which he is confined, to any other prison or place of confinement within the territories in the possession and under the Government of the East India Company."

Section II gave legality to all such removals made previously to the passing of the Act.

The Bill was read a first time.

ARMY AND STATE OFFENCES: MUTINY AND DESERTION.

MR. PEACOCK moved the second reading of the Bill "to continue in force for one year Act XIV of 1857 (for the trial and punishment of certain offences relating to the Army, and of offences against the State), and Act XVII of 1857 (for the apprehension and trial of Native Officers and Soldiers for Mutiny and Desertion)."

The Motion was carried, and the Bill read a second time.

STAMP DUTIES (BENGAL).

MR. PEACOCK moved the second reading of the Bill "to amend Regulation X. 1829 of the Bengal Code."

The Motion was carried, and the Bill read a second time.

NATIVE PASSENGER SHIPS &c.

MR. LEGEYT moved that the Bill "for the regulation of Native Passenger Ships and of Steam Vessels intended to convey passengers on coasting voyages." be now read a third time and passed.

The Motion was carried, and the Bill read a third time.

HEINOUS OFFENCES.

MR. PEACOCK moved that the Standing Orders be suspended to enable him to introduce and proceed with a Bill "to continue in force for one year Act XVI of 1857 (for the trial and punishment of heinous offences in certain Districts)."

MR. HARINGTON seconded the Motion, which was then agreed to.

MR. PEACOCK said, he had stated at the last Meeting of the Council that it was his intention to bring in this day a Bill to continue Act XVI of 1857 for a further period, but that he at that time thought it possible that the Act might be modified. He had since consulted the other Members of Government, and they considered that, under the present circumstances of the country, it would be better to continue the Act in its present shape. He, therefore, now moved the first reading of a Bill "to continue in force for one year Act XVI of 1857 (for the trial and punishment of heinous offences in certain Districts)."

The Bill was read a first time.

MR. PEACOCK said, as the Standing Orders had been suspended, he would now move the second reading of the Bill. His only object in doing this was that he might refer the Bill today to the same Select Committee to whom he was about to refer the Bill for continuing Acts XIV and XVII of 1857, so that they might consider the question as to all three Bills at one sitting. If, however, any Honorable Member considered it inexpedient to continue Act XVI of 1857 in its present form, and objected to the Bill being read a second time to-day, he should postpone his Motion until the next Meeting of the Council.

Mr. CURRIE said he was certainly under the impression that it would not be judged necessary to continue this Act for a further period, at least in its present form. The Act did not provide any special tribunals for the punishment of offences. It only provided very much severer punishment for certain specified offences. He had no disposition to oppose the second reading of the Bill, on the understanding that it would be open to the Select Committee to whom it might be referred, to consider whether modifications might not be made in the Act. Some of the offences specified were such as, he thought, ought not to be punished in the very severe manner provided by the Act.

Mr. PEACOCK'S Motion was carried, and the Bill read a second time.

ARMY AND STATE OFFENCES: HEINOUS OFFENCES: MUTINY AND DESERTION.

Mr. PEACOCK moved that the Bill "to continue in force for one year Act XIV of 1857 (for the trial and punishment of certain offences relating to the Army, and of offences against the State), and Act XVII of 1857 (for the apprehension and trial of Native Officers and Soldiers for Mutiny and Desertion)," and the Bill "to continue in force for one year Act XVI of 1857 (for the trial and punishment of heinous offences in certain Districts)"—be referred to a Select Committee consisting of Mr. Ricketts, Mr. LeGeyt, Mr. Currie, Mr. Harington, and the Mover.

Agreed to.

Mr. PEACOCK moved that the Select Committee on the above Bills be instructed to present their Report at the next Meeting of the Council.

Agreed to.

STAMP DUTIES.

Mr. PEACOCK moved that the Bill "to amend Regulation X. 1829 of the Bengal Code" be referred to a Select Committee consisting of Mr. Ricketts, Mr. LeGeyt, Mr. Currie, Mr. Harington, and the Mover.

Agreed to.

Mr. Peacock

NOTICE OF MOTION.

Mr. HARINGTON gave notice that he would, on Saturday the 22nd instant, move the first reading of a Bill for the relief of persons who, in consequence of the recent disturbances, may have been prevented from instituting or prosecuting suits or appeals in the Courts of the North-Western Provinces within the period allowed by law.

NATIVE PASSENGER SHIPS, &c.

Mr. LeGEYT moved that Sir James Outram be requested to take the Bill "for the regulation of Native Passenger Ships and of Steam Vessels intended to convey passengers on coasting voyages" to the President in Council, in order that it might be submitted to the Governor-General for his assent.

Agreed to.

CIVIL PROCEDURE (MADRAS).

Mr. PEACOCK moved that Mr. Forbes be added to the Select Committee on the Bill "for simplifying the Procedure of the Courts of Civil Judicature of the East India Company in Madras."

Agreed to.

CRIMINAL PROCEDURE (MADRAS).

Mr. PEACOCK moved that Mr. Forbes be added to the Select Committee on the Bill "for extending the jurisdiction of the Courts of Criminal Judicature of the East India Company in Madras, for simplifying the Procedure thereof, and for investing other Courts with Criminal jurisdiction."

Agreed to.

KURNOOL (MADRAS PRESIDENCY).

Mr. CURRIE moved that Mr. Forbes be added to the Select Committee on the Bill "for bringing the District of Kurnool under the Laws of the Presidency of Fort St. George."

Agreed to.

MARINE POLICE FORCE (MADRAS).

Mr. CURRIE moved that Mr. Forbes be added to the Select Committee on the Bill "for the maintenance of a Police Force for the Port of Madras."

Agreed to.

FORT OF TANJORE.

Mr. CURRIE moved that Mr. Forbes be added to the Select Committee on the Bill "for bringing the Fort of Tanjore and the adjacent Territory under the Laws of the Presidency of Fort St. George."

Agreed to.

MEERAS LANDS (BOMBAY).

Mr. LeGEYT moved that Mr. Forbes be added to the Select Committee on the Bill "to limit the period within which a Meerasdar may assert his claim to lands which he has abandoned, or for which he may have failed to pay assessment."

Agreed to.

GUARDIANSHIP OF MINORS AND COURT OF WARDS (BENGAL).

Mr. CURRIE moved that Mr. Harington be added to the Select Committee on the Bill "for making better provision for the care of the persons and property of Minors, Lunatics, and other disqualified persons in the Presidency of Fort William in Bengal," and the Bill "to explain and amend Regulation X of 1793 and Regulation LIII of 1803."

Agreed to.

The Council adjourned.

Saturday, May 22, 1858.

PRESENT:

The Hon'ble the Chief Justice, *Vice-President*, in the Chair.

Hon. Major Genl. Sir J. Outram, Hon. H. Ricketts, Hon. B. Peacock, P. W. LeGeyt, Esq., E. Currie, Esq., H. B. Harington, Esq., and H. Forbes, Esq.

AUTHENTICATION OF STAMPS.

The VICE-PRESIDENT read a Message informing the Legislative Council that the Governor-General had assented to the Bill "to provide for the authentication of Stamped Paper issued from the Stamp Office in Calcutta."

ARMY AND STATE OFFENCES; MUTINY AND DESERTION.

Mr. PEACOCK presented the Report of the Select Committee on the Bill "to continue in force for one year Act XIV of 1857 (for the trial and punishment of certain offences relating to the Army, and of offences against the State), and Act XVII of 1857 (for the apprehension and trial of Native Officers and Soldiers for Mutiny and Desertion.")

HEINOUS OFFENCES.

Mr. PEACOCK also presented the Report of the Select Committee on the Bill "to continue in force for one year Act XVI of 1857 (for the trial and punishment of heinous offences in certain Districts.)"

Mr. PEACOCK moved that the above Report be adopted.

Agreed to.

KURNOOL.

Mr. FORBES presented the Report of the Select Committee on the Bill "for bringing the district of Kurnool under the Laws of the Presidency of Fort St. George."

INSTITUTION OF SUITS AND APPEALS (N. W. PROVINCES).

Mr. HARINGTON moved the first reading of a Bill "for the relief of persons who, in consequence of the recent disturbances, may have been prevented from instituting or prosecuting suits or appeals in the Courts of the North-Western Provinces within the period allowed by law." He said, he had lately received a communication from the Secretary to the Government of the North-Western Provinces, accompanied by a Report from the Sudder Court at Agra, in which the Court referred to the entire suspension of all business for several months of the past and present years in the great majority of the Civil Courts included within their jurisdiction, consequent on the disturbed state of the country, which rendered it quite impossible for the Judges to continue their sittings, or indeed, at most stations, to remain at their posts without a certainty of being murdered—a fate which befell no less than four of the Civil or Sessions Judges employed in the districts above Allahabad, while others effected their escape to places of safety with great difficulty. With the return of order and public tranquillity, the Civil Courts in the North-Western Provinces were resuming their sittings; but during the temporary cessation of their labors, the period allowed by law for the institution of original suits and appeals must have run out in a large number of cases; and as it would not be just or proper that the complainants or appellants in the cases which were in this predicament, should suffer in consequence of a contingency which they could not have foreseen, the Court had suggested that an application should be made to the Legislature with a view to such relief being afforded to these persons, by means of a remedial Law, as, in reference to the peculiar circumstances in which they had been so unexpectedly placed, they might be considered fairly entitled to. The Bill, of which he was now about to propose the first reading, had been framed with this object. But, before proceeding to explain its provisions, it seemed proper that he should notice—which he would do as briefly as he could—such parts of the existing Regulations which limited the period for the institution of original suits or appeals as were involved in the present question, that it might be seen why it was that special legislation was necessary at this time. He must first, however, mention that, so far back as the month of December last, the Sudder Court issued a Circular to the Zillah Judges and Principal Sudder Ameens under their orders, in which they gave it as their opinion that in all appeals

"which might be presented in the Zillah Courts after the period allowed by law from decisions passed shortly before the destruction of records and interruption of business, calculation might fairly be made from the date on which the Courts resumed their regular sittings irrespective of the period during which the conduct of public business, cut short by the violence of mutineers or mobs, might have been in abeyance. In other words, that a period during which no regular business was transacted, should not be taken into account at all."

There could be no doubt, he thought, that these instructions were perfectly fair, proper, and reasonable; but they applied to appeals only; and moreover, as respected some classes of appeals, they were found to be at variance with the law as construed and laid down by the Sudder Court in several decisions; and the competency of the Court to issue the orders in question having in consequence been disputed, it was advisable to give their instructions the force of legislative sanction, in order to remove all doubts, and to prevent the legality of any decisions which might have been passed in cases admitted after the period allowed by law, on the authority of the Court's Circular, from being called in question.

And now as to the existing law. Section XIV Regulation III. 1793, which was afterwards extended to Benares and the ceded and conquered Provinces, as a general rule, fixed the period of twelve years, after which a claimant could not enforce his claim by suit. But to this rule, as to most general rules, there were exceptions, one of which allowed of its relaxation in favor of a party who could prove to the satisfaction of the Court that, either from minority or other good and sufficient cause, he was precluded from obtaining redress within the prescribed period. It might be supposed that this exception was exactly what was needed in the existing state of things in the North-Western Provinces, in so far as cases of the nature of those under consideration were concerned, and that the wording of it was sufficiently large to reach every case in which the period limited by law might have expired during the time that the sittings of the Civil Courts were suspended in consequence of the recent disturbances, or when the dangerous state of the roads rendered access to them almost impossible; and as it could scarcely be conceived that any Court would refuse to admit this excuse when pleaded in bar of the operation of the Statute of Limitations, any special legislation to meet such cases might be considered altogether unnecessary. But, according to a ruling of the Sudder Court, there were cases to which the exception which he had quoted was not applicable, and in which the period allowed for their institution could on no account be exceeded, so that, should the claimant fail to bring his action within the limited period, his right of suit was absolutely gone, whatever might have been the cause of the default. Suits brought to contest the summary awards of the Revenue Authorities in Bengal in respect to possessory titles, for the institution of which a period was specially fixed by Act XIII of 1848, were within this category; and suits instituted to try the justice of the decisions of the Collectors and their subordinates in cases relating to arrears and exactions of rent, for the admission of which only one year was allowed, would probably be held to fall within the same stringent rule; and as it seemed only just and proper to make some provision for the admission of suits of both these descriptions in which the period allowed for their institution might have run out during the recent disturbances, the lapse of time notwithstanding, the Council would probably agree with him that any rule which might be passed, instead of being restricted in its application to particular classes of cases, should be made general, in order that the benefit of it might be enjoyed as of right by all who had suffered from the same cause, and that no more than was necessary might be left to the discretion of the Courts.

The state of the law which fixed the different periods for the admission of appeals was somewhat similar to that of the Statute of Limitations in respect to original suits. Section IX Act XXV of 1837 declared that appeals from the orders or decisions of a Principal Sudder Ameen to a Zillah or City Judge, should not be received unless the same were preferred within the period of thirty days from the date of the order or decision appealed against; but the same Section went on to say, "or unless it shall be proved that the appellant was precluded by circumstances beyond his control from presenting his appeal within the period before mentioned;"—and Clause 1 Section V Act XVI of 1853 contained a similar provision in respect to petitions of special appeal which might be presented after the period allowed—that was to say, three months—either in the Sudder Court or in the Court from whose decision the appeal was made. So that, as regarded these two descriptions of appeals—that is, appeals to the Zillah Courts from the decisions of the Principal Sudder Ameens, or special appeals to the Sudder Court from decisions of the Zillah Judges and Principal Sudder Ameens passed in regular appeal—nothing was really required to be done. The case, however, of regular appeals to the Sudder Court from decisions of the Zillah Judges and Principal Sudder Ameens, and of appeals of the same description from decisions of the Sudder Ameens and Moonsiffs, was different; for although Clause 2 Section 11 Act XV of 1853 empowered the Sudder Court to extend the time fixed by Clause 2 of the same Section for the presentation of regular appeals cognizable by the Court—that was to say, six weeks—upon being satisfied that there was sufficient cause for such extension, it had been ruled by the Court that the application for any enlargement of the time allowed must be made previously to its expiration, upon the ground that a term which had already expired could not be extended;—while, as regarded appeals from the decisions of the Sudder Ameens and Moonsiffs, the Sudder Court at Agra, taking the same view as the Sudder Court at Calcutta, had held that, as the exception contained in Section IX Act XXV of 1837, which he had just quoted, was not to be found in Clause 3 Section 11 Regulation VII. 1832, which fixed the time within which regular appeals from the decisions of the Sudder Ameens and Moonsiffs must be preferred at thirty days, and Clause 4 of the same Section required that such period should be strictly adhered to, notwithstanding the intervention of Hindoo or Mahomedan holidays or the established vacations within the prescribed period, no discretion was left to the Courts, and they had no alternative but to reject the appeal if presented after time, the only exception being when, the period of appeal having expired during an adjournment of the Court on account of any holiday or vacation, the petition of appeal was presented on the re-opening of the Court. But the suspension of business in the Civil Courts during the recent disturbances, or their inaccessibility by reason of the dangerous state of the roads, though attended with precisely the same consequences, could not, strictly speaking, be considered to fall within this exception. Some provision was therefore necessary to authorize the admission of appeals of these last two descriptions, in which the appellants might have been unable to lodge their petitions of appeal, or to apply for an extension of time within the period allowed by law owing to the operation of the causes mentioned; and the reason which rendered it desirable that any new rule which might be passed in regard to original suits in consequence of late events should be of a general nature, would appear to be equally applicable to appeals.

But there was another class of cases, the parties interested in which, though not referred to by the Sudder Court in their Report to Government, would seem to be no less entitled to relief than the persons already mentioned. He alluded to original suits and appeals instituted before the commencement of the insurrection, but which, by reason thereof, could not afterwards be prosecuted. Act XXIX of 1841, which applied to appeals as well as original suits, enacted that, if a plaintiff or appellant shall at any time neglect to proceed in his suit or appeal for six weeks, the suit or appeal shall be dismissed as of course without previous notice to the plaintiff or appellant, and without any proceeding on the part of the Court, or of the defendant, or otherwise, or assignment of any reasons, unless the plaintiff or appellant upon special application shall have previously satisfied the Court of the propriety of allowing further time.

But this rule being found to operate with inconvenient severity as regarded appeals dismissed on default, which, if the rule were properly applied, could not be revived, Act XVI of 1845 was passed to enable the Court which dismissed the appeal to re-admit the same if the appellant should make application for that purpose on the stamp prescribed for miscellaneous petitions within three months after the appeal might have been dismissed by the Sudder Court, and within one month after the appeal might have been dismissed, if dismissed by any other Court; and should satisfy the Court that the dismissal was occasioned by the default of his Vakeel, or by unavoidable accident. He need scarcely say that the time here fixed for the submission of an application for the revival of an appeal, must render the law inoperative, or at least of no use as regarded the great majority of appellants whose appeals, without any fault or wilful neglect on their part, might have incurred the penalty of dismissal without a hearing, for want of prosecution when prosecution was impossible. The Act, moreover, did not apply at all to original suits dismissed on default; and as it would be exceedingly hard to compel the plaintiffs in such cases to institute fresh actions on stamp paper of the full value, which was their only remedy in the existing state of the law, it had appeared to him that it would be only just and proper to make a general provision for the relief of all persons who might have been prevented from prosecuting their suits or appeals within the time allowed by law owing to the late disturbances.

From what he had now stated, the provisions of the Bill which he was anxious to introduce would, he thought, in a great measure be gathered; and it would be sufficient for him to remark that it proposed to empower the Civil Courts in the North-Western Provinces to admit or again bring on the file all original suits and appeals, which the complainants or appellants might have been prevented from instituting or prosecuting within the period allowed by law in consequence of the late disturbances, on proof of that fact, provided that the suit or appeal, according as the case might be, was instituted upon stamp paper of the prescribed value, or, in cases in which the penalty of dismissal on default might have been incurred, the application for the re-admission of the suit or appeal on the file was presented within the period of three months from the date on which the Chief Civil Court of original jurisdiction in the district might notify by proclamation that the Courts of the districts had resumed their sittings.

The Bill also proposed to legalize all proceedings held, as well as decisions passed in any original suits or appeals which might have been admitted after the prescribed period, or again brought on the file without authority of law on the strength of the Sudder Court's Circular, or otherwise, by any Civil Court in the North-Western Provinces whose sittings might have been temporarily suspended or interrupted during the time to which the Bill related.

With these observations, he had the honor to move that the Bill, of which he had given notice on Saturday last, might now be read a first time.

The Bill was read a first time.

REMOVAL OF PRISONERS.

MR. CURRIE moved the second reading of the Bill "to make further provisions for the removal of Prisoners."

THE CHIEF JUSTICE said, before putting the question, he wished to observe that the Bill seemed to break in upon a principle which those who had dealt with the question of punishment in this country had always regarded as important—he meant, the principle on which the Natives of this country should be subjected to transportation. It had been assumed—he dared say, with reason—that the Natives of this country, particularly Hindoos, whose caste suffered by a sea-voyage, had a peculiar dread of transportation, and that it was therefore inexpedient to inflict that punishment except for life, lest the return of convicts from transportation might diminish the wholesome terror of it which existed amongst their countrymen. He believed that those who were conversant with the administration of Justice in the Mofussil, and some of those to whom the task of legislation had been chiefly committed, had rather quarrelled with the practice of the Crown Courts, which had always been in the habit of subjecting to transportation for terms Natives and Europeans alike. It seemed to him that if the principle to which he referred did exist, and was worth preserving, the Bill before the Council very much broke in upon it, and that it did so in an objectionable manner. It enabled the Lieutenant-Governor to send across seas, not only those who were under sentence of imprisonment for life, but also those who were under sentence of imprisonment for three years or upwards. It was obvious that, by sending prisoners of the latter class across the sea to the Straits of Malacca, and allowing them to return, as they would be at liberty to return, when the term of their imprisonment expired, Government would run the risk, which it had been deemed so desirable to avoid, of diminishing the terror which the Natives were supposed to have for transportation. If, again, that feeling, however irrational and founded on prejudice of caste, was really operative in the minds of Natives, the Council would, by this Bill, give to the Executive Government the power of greatly aggravating the punishment to which prisoners had been sentenced by the Courts. Therefore, it might be well worthy of the consideration of the Select Committee to whom this Bill might be referred, whether the necessities of the times, or the circumstances which had suggested this measure, were such as to require so great an extension of the power of removing term-prisoners from one place of confinement to another as would enable the Lieutenant-Governor to send term-prisoners across the sea.

MR. CURRIE said, he was perfectly aware of the objection mentioned by the Honorable and learned Chief Justice to the principle of sending beyond seas prisoners sentenced only for a term of years. It did not escape his consideration at the time when he framed the Bill. It was urged in the Report of the framers of the Penal Code, as a reason why, in adjusting the punishments under the Code, they did not provide for transportation for a term of years. But the reason of the proposal of this measure was a great State necessity. It was believed to be absolutely necessary for the security of the country to invest the Executive Government with the power of removing beyond the limits of any particular Presidency certain classes of dangerous criminals.

With respect to the grounds of the objection to transporting only for terms of years, it might be observed that the Supreme Court had always been in the habit of transporting for terms of years; so that the superstitious dread which transportation beyond seas was supposed to inspire, had been to a considerable extent done away with, and was becoming less and less every year.

However, the defence of the measure was that it was a necessary one. He hoped, therefore, that the Council would permit the Bill to be read a second time. The Select Committee to whom it might be referred could enquire further into the question raised, and report to the Council whether, in their apprehension, the exigency was such as to require that a measure of this kind should be passed.

MR. PEACOCK said, as an ordinary rule, he apprehended that a measure like this would not be introduced, but it had been found that the Alipore Jail was so crowded with desperate characters that it was dangerous to keep them there, and the Lieutenant-Governor had applied for permission to remove beyond sea prisoners sentenced in Bengal to more than three years' imprisonment. The Government of India had assented to the proposal, and had sanctioned the transfer of such prisoners to the Straits of Malacca. The Honorable Court of Directors, in their Despatch dated the 26th of January 1858, said:—

"Under the pressing emergency of the case, we entirely approve of the measure. Should it be necessary, you will consider the expediency of legalizing it."

The recital in the Preamble of the Bill shewed that it was necessary to legalize the measure, because at present the Executive Government had no power to remove prisoners beyond the limits of the Presidency. No doubt, under ordinary circumstances, it would be much better to avoid infringing the principle of not transporting prisoners for a less period than for life; but he thought that the emergency which had arisen rendered it necessary that that principle should not be adhered to, at any rate during the present time.

MR. LEGEYT said, he had long been of opinion that the Law which limited the transportation of prisoners in the Mofussil to transportation for life, was inappropriate. The place to which the prisoners were transported was always the Straits of Malacca. He felt sure that sentences of transportation are, to Natives of this country, very wholesome and effective restraints against crime. He had seen transportation for terms of years in force in the Presidency Town of Bombay for various offences, and he did not think that the punishment, because it was for a term of years, and the convict might return back to India, was really less effective or less dreaded. It was perhaps going too far to extend the power of transportation to the cases of prisoners now under sentence of imprisonment for so short a term as three years. He would suggest that it should be limited to the cases of prisoners sentenced to imprisonment for more than five years; but he considered the principle of the Bill a good one, and should vote for the second reading.

THE CHIEF JUSTICE said, he did not in the least wish to interfere with the second reading of the Bill. All he had meant to do was to point out that the Bill infringed a principle to which he himself did not attach the same importance which others did. He was rather in favor of transportation for a term of years.

The Motion was then put and carried, and the Bill read a second time.

ARMY AND STATE OFFENCES; HEINOUS OFFENCES; MUTINY AND DESERTION.

MR. PEACOCK moved that the Council resolve itself into a Committee on the Bill "to continue in force for one year Act XIV of 1857 (for the trial and punishment of certain offences relating to the Army, and of offences against the State), and Act XVII of 1857 (for the apprehension and trial of Native Officers and Soldiers for Mutiny and Desertion);" and that the Committee be instructed to consider the Bill in the amended form in which the Select Committee had recommended it to be passed.

Agreed to.

Section I was passed as it stood.

MR. PEACOCK moved the insertion of a new Section after Section I. He said, in consequence of the difficulty of enforcing sentences of imprisonment, and the danger of over-crowding the Jails in the districts to which the Acts in question had been extended, and which, it must be remarked, were the most disturbed, he considered that it would be advisable to entrust the Officers by whom sentences of imprisonment should be passed for terms exceeding three years, with the power of ordering the offenders to be transported for such terms. The Judicial Commissioner of Oude had suggested that sentences of transportation for finite terms might be passed upon deserters and other persons tried under the special Acts. The suggestion had received the approval of the Chief Commissioner of Oude, who considered that the adoption of the principle in that province was very desirable. The question had been referred to the

Governor-General. He (Mr. Peacock) had not yet learnt what opinion the Governor-General had expressed upon the subject; but it appeared to him that it was not desirable to over-crowd the Jails in those districts, and that, therefore, in every case in which a sentence of imprisonment should be passed under the special Acts for any term exceeding three years, the Judge or other Officer passing the sentence should have the power of ordering the prisoner to be transported beyond sea for such term. He thought, however, that the exercise of this power should be subject to the general control of the Governor-General in Council. Under the Bill which had been read a second time to-day, an order of Government would be necessary for the removal of prisoners sentenced to imprisonment; but he thought it very desirable that the Judge or other Officer who passed the sentence of imprisonment, and who would have a knowledge of the capabilities of the Jail and the circumstances of the district, should also have the power of ordering at the same time that the offender should be transported beyond sea. He, therefore, moved the following new Section:—

"Unless the Governor-General in Council shall otherwise order, whenever any Court or other Officer shall sentence an offender under any of the said Acts to imprisonment for a term exceeding three years, it shall be lawful for such Court or other Officer at the same time to order that the offender be transported beyond sea for such term."

He had adopted the principle of Act XIV of 1844, by which it was enacted that, whenever prisoners were sentenced to terms of imprisonment for life, the Sudder Courts should order them to be transported beyond seas. The only difference was that, in the present case, he left it discretionary with the Judge either to order transportation or not. The Section he proposed would enable the Judge or other Officer who sentenced prisoners to terms of imprisonment exceeding three years without any special authority from Government, to order them to be transported beyond seas; but if the Governor-General in Council should think fit to issue a general order to the contrary, the ordinary rule would take effect. It should be borne in mind that this was only a temporary measure, and that it would not come into force except in those districts to which the Acts in question might be extended. He thought that in those districts it was very advisable to entrust some such power to the Officers exercising jurisdiction under the Acts, subject to the general control which he proposed to give to the Governor-General in Council.

The Section was agreed to.

The Preamble and Title were passed after amendments.

The Council having resumed its sitting, the Bill was reported.

MR. PEACOCK moved the third reading of the Bill.

The Motion was carried, and the Bill read a third time.

MR. PEACOCK moved that Mr. Ricketts be requested to take the Bill to the President in Council in order that it might be submitted to the Governor-General for his assent.

Agreed to.

INSOLVENT DEBTORS (MOFUSSIL).

MR. LEGEYT said, he had received a communication from the Government of Bombay on the subject of a Law for the relief of Insolvent Debtors in the Mofussil. The Government of Bombay had desired him to inform them whether it was in the contemplation of the Legislature to deal with that most important question. The immediate cause of the reference was a Letter from Mr. Davidson, the Magistrate of Poona, and a very intelligent Officer, in which that gentleman strongly recommended a measure of the kind being introduced, stating that the local Superintendent of Police attributed the Gang-robberies which had been committed during the latter part of 1857 in the Hill districts of the Zillah, in a great measure to the extreme poverty and indebtedness of the Ramoosee and Bheel ryots, and the hardships and tyranny which they underwent at the hands of money-lenders, to whom they were bound hand and foot. Mr. Davidson said that, after enquiry, he was satisfied that this was the main cause of the late disturbances in his Magistracy. In short, it appeared to him (Mr. LeGeyt) that the case was very much what had occurred three years ago in the Sonthal districts. Mr. Davidson was of opinion that a Law for the relief of Insolvent debtors should be enacted

"for the whole country, which would afford the unfortunate and even the improvident an outlet of escape, so that a man might have a chance of making a fresh start without a millstone round his neck for his personal success and elevation in life, not only recovering himself and family from hopeless recklessness and slavery, to his own personal benefit, but to the public benefit of the Government and the country."

He (Mr. LeGeyt) found that this was by no means a new subject before the Government of India. It appeared first to have gone before the Government in the year 1845, when, after considerable discussion, references were made to Bombay and Madras, and to the Authorities here as to the advisability of a Law on the subject. The majority of the answers were decidedly in favor of the proposed Law. In Madras alone it appeared to have been thought unadvisable. He had had access to the papers in the Home Office; and he found that, after the receipt of the opinions from Madras in 1852, the discussion was dropped. It was mentioned in the List of the Projects of Law pending before the Government of India on the 20th of May 1854, with the following remarks:—

"No Act for this purpose has yet been drafted.

"The question originated in a reference from the Madras Government in connection with the Military Courts of Requests constituted under Act 3 and 4 Vic. c. 37, and Act XI of 1841, respectively. The enquiries made as to the practice of those Courts, where there might be more than one judgment-creditor against the same defendant, with insufficiency of assets to meet the claims of all, were afterwards extended to the practice of the Civil Courts, generally, of the East India Company in similar cases. Some difference of practice appears to prevail in the Military Courts of Requests in dealing with such cases.

"The Civil Courts have their own rules, but there is no provision for the protection of creditors who have not obtained judgments upon which they can proceed.

"The subject is one of much difficulty and importance."

The subject was one of great importance, and, he admitted, of some difficulty. The only Sections in the proposed Code of Civil Procedure bearing on it were taken almost word for word from the Bombay Regulation IV. 1827. No relief could be given under them except where all the property of the debtor had been attached and sold, and the debtor himself was in prison at the suit of a creditor—and the effect was to relieve him only from imprisonment, at the instance of that particular creditor. The Government of Bombay evidently did not consider that these provisions afforded a sufficient measure of relief. After the discussion which was upon record, and the difference of opinion which appeared in the papers he had read, he had not presumed to come before the Council with a Bill on the subject; but he thought that the question might with great advantage be referred to a Select Committee, who might be instructed to report whether legislation was advisable or not. He thought it would hardly do to attempt to introduce an Insolvent Act into the Code of Civil Procedure; and he, therefore, now moved that the subject of a Law for the relief of Insolvent Debtors in the Mofussil be referred to a Select Committee consisting of Mr. Peacock, Mr. Currie, Mr. Harington, Mr. Forbes, and the Mover, with instructions to report whether any legislation was advisable.

Mr. CURRIE said, he would suggest that the better course would be to refer the communication to the Select Committee on the Procedure Bills. In the Civil Procedure Code as prepared by the Commissioners in England, there was a provision to the effect that any person in confinement under a decree who was not entitled to the benefit of any Act for the relief of Insolvent or bankrupt debtors in India, might procure his enlargement by making an application to the Judge to that effect, and surrendering all his property. The Select Committee had not finally amended the Code; but, in going over it, they struck out the reference to an Insolvent Act, and appeared to consider that sufficient provision was made for Insolvent debtors in the following Sections of the Code. As, however, the Code was still before the Select Committee, they might re-consider the question with advertence to the papers which the Honorable Member for Bombay had now laid before the Council; and probably it would be more convenient to consider it in connexion with the provisions of the Code rather than as a separate measure.

Mr. LeGeyt said, he had no objection whatever to refer the Bill to the Select Committee on the Civil Procedure Code; but, as he had stated before, it had struck him that the present subject hardly came within the scope of that Code. The suggestion made by the Bombay Government was, in effect, that an Insolvent debtor in the Mofussil should obtain relief from his debts without being taken to jail and having all his property sold under a decree in the first instance. In short, it was a suggestion that the provisions of the Insolvent Act should be extended to the Inhabitants of the Mofussil. Whether the Select Committee on the Civil Procedure Code would be disposed to consider a question so very much wider than that contained in the Code as prepared by the Commissioners in England, he did not know. The Honorable and learned Chairman of the Committee would probably inform the Council. His own idea was that they would not; and as it was expedient to consider whether such a Law as had been recommended should be passed or not, he had moved for a separate Committee. If, however, the Select Committee on the Civil Procedure Code would consider the subject of a general Insolvent Law for the Mofussil in connexion with the Code, he had no objection to amend his Motion and refer it to them.

MR. PEACOCK said, the question was hardly one of procedure at all. It was a question of extending the Insolvent Act over the whole of the territories of the East India Company. There was a separate Code of Civil Procedure for each Presidency; and although, as a matter of convenience, the Select Committees on all three met together, he did not think it advisable that the subject now brought before the Council should be referred to any one of them in particular. He thought it would be better if it were considered as a separate measure.

MR. LEGEYT'S Motion was then put and agreed to.

REMOVAL OF PRISONERS.

MR. CURRIE moved that the Bill "to make further provision for the removal of Prisoners" be referred to a Select Committee consisting of the Vice-President, Mr. Peacock, Mr. LeGeyt, and the Mover.

Agreed to.

ESTATE OF THE LATE NABOB OF THE CARNATIC.

MR. PEACOCK moved that Mr. Forbes be added to the Select Committee on the Bill "to provide for the administration of the estate and for the payment of the debts of the late Nabob of the Carnatic."

Agreed to.

The Council adjourned.

Saturday, May 29, 1858.

PRESENT:

The Hon'ble the Chief Justice, *Vice-President*, in the Chair.

Hon. J. P. Grant,	P. W. LeGeyt, Esq.
Hon. Major Genl. Sir Jas. Outram,	E. Currie, Esq.
Hon. H. Ricketts,	H. B. Harington, Esq. and
Hon. B. Peacock,	H. Forbes, Esq.

ESTATE OF THE LATE NABOB OF THE CARNATIC.

THE CLERK brought under the consideration of the Council a Petition of certain Creditors of the Estate of the late Nabob of the Carnatic praying for an amendment of Section XV of the Bill "to provide for the administration of the Estate and for the payment of the debts of the late Nabob of the Carnatic."

MR. PEACOCK moved that the above Petition be referred to the Select Committee on the Bill.

Agreed to.

CONTINUANCE OF CERTAIN PRIVILEGES TO THE FAMILY &c. OF THE LATE NABOB OF THE CARNATIC.

MR. FORBES moved the first reading of a Bill "to continue certain privileges and immunities to the Family and retainers of the late Nabob of the Carnatic." In doing so, he said the Council was aware that it had always been the practice and policy of the British Government in India to confer upon Native Princes, their families, and retainers, freedom from the jurisdiction of its Criminal and Civil Courts. Among the Princes so privileged, was the late Nabob of the Carnatic; and, for many years, it was supposed that the privilege had been granted to him by a Treaty formed between him and the East India Company in 1801. But in 1843, some suits were instituted against certain Members of the Nabob's family, and it was decided by the Supreme Court of Madras that the immunities and privileges supposed to have been given by the Treaty had really no legal force, and it became necessary, therefore, if it was desirable that they should be continued, to provide some remedy by legislative enactment. The matter was reported home; the Honorable the Court of Directors gave their assent; and, accordingly, Act I of 1844 was passed by the Government of India, which provided "that no writ or process shall at any time be sued forth or prosecuted against the person, goods, or property of his Highness the Nabob of the Carnatic, or of the Nabob Regent for the time being," "unless such writ or process shall be so sued forth or prosecuted with the consent of the Governor in Council of Fort St. George first had and obtained." Under Section I of the Act, certain lists were to be published by the Government of Madras from time to time "containing the names of persons belonging to the family, household, or retinue of His Highness the Nabob of the Carnatic, or of the Nabob Regent for the time being," and these persons also were to be entitled to privilege from Civil and Criminal process. After the passing of Act I of 1844, no difficulty occurred during the life-time of the Nabob; but on the death of his Highness in 1855, it was decided that the estate and dignity of the Nabob had become vested in the East India Company. A suit was subsequently brought against the Prince who had occupied the *musnud* as Regent during the minority of his nephew the late Nabob; and, on Act I of 1844 being pleaded in bar of the Court's jurisdiction, it was decided by a Full Bench that the Act was merely personal to the Nabob, having been passed for the support of the estate and dignity of His Highness, and that that estate and dignity having become extinct, the Act had *ipso facto* ceased to have any effect. It was thereupon considered advisable by this Council to allow a period of one year to the persons whose supposed privilege the decision of the Court would affect, for the purpose of enabling them to appeal to the Privy Council. Act XVIII of 1857 was passed with that view; but circumstances had led to that Act becoming inoperative, the single suit in which the Supreme Court had given their decision not having been appealed within six months, which was the period limited for the institution of appeals to the Privy Council, and Act XVIII of 1857 itself preventing any fresh suit being brought. Act XVIII of 1857 would expire on the 4th of next July; and unless some legislative remedy were applied, the family of the Nabob would, from that date, be subject to the process of the Civil and Criminal Courts, from which it had been the policy of the Government since 1801 to exempt them. The title of Act I of 1844 described it to be an Act "for securing certain immunities and privileges to His Highness the Nabob of the Carnatic, his family, and retinue;" and the 1st Section enacted "that it shall be lawful for the Governor in Council of Fort St George to publish from time to time in the *Gazette* at Madras, lists containing the names of persons belonging to the Family, Household, or Retinue of His Highness the Nabob of the Carnatic, or of the Nabob Regent for the time being, who are to be entitled under this Act to privilege from Civil and Criminal process;" and the Council would probably have little difficulty in coming to the conclusion that, although the wording of the Act might be faulty, the intention of the Legislature was to give the exemption for life. The present Bill was intended to supply the omission in the former Bill, and there was a precedent for this in the Statute Book. Act XVIII of 1848, which was passed on the death of the Nabob of Surat, continued to the Members of the Nabob's family the exemption from the process of the Civil and Criminal Courts which they had enjoyed during his lifetime, and the present Bill had even a stronger claim on the attention of the Council. In the case of the Nabob of Surat, there were certain Courts of Justice in which creditors might have enforced their claims against the family of the Nabob. When those Courts were abolished, Act XVIII of 1848 was passed, which deprived claimants of the right to resort to any Court at all. This was not the case in the present instance. The creditors of the family, and retainers of the late Nabob of the Carnatic would be placed by the Bill which he proposed, in no worse position than they had been in all their lives, inasmuch as there had never been, since 1801, any Court in which they could have preferred their claims without the permission of Government.

The first part of the Bill gave to the uncle and chief male relative of the late Nabob, and to the female members of his family, exemption from Civil and Criminal process during the term of their respective lives; and to the other male members of his family, and to his retinue, protection from suits of which the causes of action arose during the time Act I of 1844 and Act XVIII of 1857 were in operation.

The only other provision of the Bill to which it was necessary to draw the attention of the Council was one which made a slight addition to the provision contained in Section II of Act I of 1844. That Section enacted "that no writ or process shall at any time be sued forth or prosecuted against the person, goods, or property of His Highness the Nabob of the Carnatic, or of the Nabob Regent for the time being, or of any person whose name shall be included in any list published in the *Gazette*." It had been decided by the Supreme Court of Madras that a writ of summons issued from the Plea Side of the Court was not a writ against the person within the meaning of the Act; and the effect of this decision was, in the words of the Honorable Company's Solicitor, that "a plaintiff may file a plaint, issue and serve his summons, in default of an appearance by defendant enter an appearance for him, issue and serve a rule to plead, in default of plea enter his cause for trial, *ex parte* proceed to trial, obtain a verdict, tax his costs, sign his Judgment, and issue an execution upon his Judgment, before the defendant can take any step whatever for asserting his exemption from the process and jurisdiction of the Court under Act I of 1844. In the present Bill, therefore, the words "no action shall be commenced or prosecuted" had been inserted before the words "no writ or process shall be sued forth."

With these observations, he begged to move the first reading of the Bill.

The Bill was read a first time.

KURNOOL.

MR. FORBES moved that the Council resolve itself into a Committee on the Bill "for bringing the District of Kurnool under the Laws of the Presidency of Fort St. George."

Agreed to.

Sections I and II were passed as they stood.

MR. FORBES moved that the following Preamble be inserted in the Bill:—namely—"Whereas it is expedient that the District of Kurnool should be brought under the Laws of the Presidency of Fort St. George, it is enacted as follows."

Agreed to.

The Title was passed as it stood.

The Council having resumed its sitting, the Bill was reported.

OATHS AND AFFIRMATIONS.

MR. PEACOCK said, some time ago, a Select Committee was appointed to consider and report on certain projects of Laws relating to Oaths and Affirmations, but it had not presented its report as yet. The same question had now come before the Select Committees on the Codes of Civil Procedure framed by Her Majesty's Law Commissioners in England, who recommended that witnesses should be examined without oath or affirmation; and they were unable to decide it in consequence of the other Committee not having made any Report. He should therefore move that the Select Committee on the Projects of Laws relating to Oaths and Affirmations be discharged, and that the question be referred to the Select Committees on the Bills for simplifying the Procedure of the Courts of Civil Judicature of the East India Company.

Agreed to.

MERCHANT SEAMEN.

MR. CURRIE moved that the Vice-President be added to the Select Committee on the Bill "for the amendment of the Law relating to Merchant Seamen."

Agreed to.

LUNATIC ASYLUMS.

MR. CURRIE moved that Mr. Forbes be added to the Select Committee on the Bill "relating to Lunatic Asylums"

Agreed to.

ESTATES OF LUNATICS (MOFUSSIL).

MR. CURRIE moved that Mr. Forbes be added to the Select Committee on the Bill "to make better provision for the care of the Estates of Lunatics not subject to the jurisdiction of Her Majesty's Courts of Judicature."

Agreed to.

COTTON FRAUDS (BOMBAY).

MR. LEGEYT moved that Mr. Forbes be added to the Select Committee on the Bill "for the better suppression of Frauds in the Cotton-trade in the Presidency of Bombay."

Agreed to.

The Council then adjourned, on the motion of Mr. Grant.

Saturday, June 5, 1858.

PRESENT:

The Hon'ble the Chief Justice, *Vice-President*, in the Chair.

Hon J. P. Grant,	P. W. LeGeyt, Esq.,
Hon. Major General Sir James Outram,	E. Currie, Esq.,
Hon. B. Peacock,	H. B. Harington, Esq., and
Hon. H. Ricketts,	H. Forbes, Esq.

CIVIL PROCEDURE.

THE CLERK presented to the Council a Petition from Inhabitants of Dacca offering suggestions for improving the Procedure of the Civil Courts.

MR. CURRIE moved that the Petition be referred to the Select Committees on the Bills for simplifying the Procedure of the Courts of Civil Judicature of the East India Company.

Agreed to.

RECOVERY OF RENTS (BENGAL).

THE CLERK also presented a Petition from land-holders and others residing in Dacca relative to the Bill "to amend the law relating to the recovery of Rent in the Presidency of Fort William in Bengal."

MR. CURRIE moved that the Petition be referred to the Select Committee on the Bill.

Agreed to.

ESTATE OF THE LATE NABOB OF THE CARNATIC.

THE CLERK also presented a Petition from certain creditors of the late Nabob of the Carnatic, praying for an amendment of Section XV of the Bill "to provide for the administration of the Estate and for the payment of the debts of the late Nabob of the Carnatic."

MR. PEACOCK moved that the Petition be referred to the Select Committee on the Bill.

Agreed to.

OFFENCES AGAINST THE STATE.

THE CLERK reported to the Council that he had received a communication from the Secretary to the Government of India in the Home Department, forwarding papers relative to the trial of the Zemindar of Pachete, with a view to the amendment of the law regarding preparations for levying war against the State.

RESTORATION OF POSSESSION OF LANDS—AND REGULATION OF NATIVE PASSENGER SHIPS.

THE VICE-PRESIDENT read Messages informing the Legislative Council that the Governor General had assented to the Bill "to facilitate the recovery of land and other real property of which possession may have been wrongfully taken during the recent disturbances in the North-Western Provinces of the Presidency of Bengal;" and the Bill "for the regulation of Native Passenger Ships and of Steam Vessels intended to convey passengers on coasting voyages."

OFFENCES AGAINST THE STATE.

MR. PEACOCK moved the first reading of a Bill "to make further provision for the trial and punishment of offences against the State." He said, the papers relating to the trial of the Zemindar of Pachete had been laid on the table, with a recommendation from the Government of India that the law relating to offences against the State should be amended. It was not his intention to make any remarks on that trial; but it appeared to him that the result shewed that the existing law required amendment. According to the Commissioner before whom the trial was held, there was no doubt that the Zemindar of Pachete was in a state of disaffection. He had collected arms, ammunition, and men; he had sworn his followers to secrecy, and had sent improper and insulting letters to Officers of Government. It was not for him (Mr. Peacock) to consider what conclusion might have been drawn from these acts if the question had been with what intent the Zemindar had collected these arms, ammunition, and men. The question before the Commissioner was, had he levied war against the State, or had he conspired to do so? Levying war, and conspiring to levy war against the State, were the charges upon which he was indicted; and the Commissioner stated that, upon the evidence, he could not come to the conclusion that he was guilty of those charges. If compassing to levy war, like compassing the King's death, accompanied by an overt act, had been an offence, then there might have been another question for the Commissioner to determine. Although the prisoner had not been proved to have actually levied war, or to have entered into a conspiracy to levy war against the State, still his having collected arms, ammunition, and men—his having written and sent insulting and offensive letters to Government Officers—and his having administered an oath to his followers not to disclose anything that took place in their presence, would have been facts upon which the Commissioner could have determined the question of his intention. By the law of England as it stood under the Statute 25 of Edward III., compassing or imagining the King's death was an act of treason: the act of levying war against the King was also treason; but a mere intention to levy war was not treason. The collecting of arms, ammunition, and men for the purpose of killing the King, was an overt act of compassing the death of the King, and was treason. But collecting arms, ammunition, and men with the intention of levying war, was not treason, unless war was actually levied. The mere intention, in short, to levy war, though accompanied by an overt act, was not an act of rebellion or treason. The law was amended by 11 and 12 Vic. c. 12, s. 3, which made it felony to compass the levying of war, and rendered the offence punishable with transportation for life, if the object was one of those mentioned in the Statute. The words of the Section were as follows:—

"And be it enacted that, if any person whatever, after the passing of this Act, shall, within the United Kingdom or without, compass, imagine, invent, devise, or intend to deprive or depose our most gracious Lady the Queen, her heirs, or successors, from the style, honor, or royal name of the Imperial Crown of the United Kingdom, or of any of Her Majesty's dominions and countries, or to levy war"—that was to say, or shall compass, imagine, or intend to levy war—"against Her Majesty, her heirs, or successors, within any part of the United Kingdom, in order by force or constraint to compel her or them to change her or their measures or counsels, or in order to put any force or constraint upon, or in order to intimidate or overawe both Houses or either House of Parliament, or to move any foreigner or stranger with force to invade the United Kingdom, or any other of Her Majesty's dominions or countries under the obeisance of Her Majesty, her heirs, or successors, and such compassings, imaginations, inventions, devices, or intentions, or any of them, shall express, utter, or declare, by publishing any printing or writing, or by open and advised speaking, or by any overt act or deed, every person so offending shall be guilty of felony, and being convicted thereof, shall be liable, at the discretion of the Court, to be transported beyond the seas for the term of his or her natural life, or for any term not less than seven years, or to be imprisoned for any term not exceeding two years, with or without hard labor, as the Court shall direct."

Section VII declared as follows:—

"Provided also, and be it enacted that, if the facts or matters alleged in an Indictment for any felony under this Act shall amount in

Law to treason, such Indictment shall not by reason thereof be deemed void, erroneous, or defective; and if the facts or matters proved on the trial of any person indicted for any felony under this Act shall amount to treason, such person shall not, by reason thereof, be entitled to be acquitted of such felony: but no person tried for such felony, shall be afterwards prosecuted for treason upon the same facts."

What he proposed was to make it an offence to collect arms, ammunition, or men with the intention of levying war against the State, or of being prepared to levy such war, and to make the offence punishable in the same manner as the offence of actually levying war. Under this Bill, the collection of arms, ammunition, and men for the purpose of levying war would be punishable if it should be proved to be the intention of the offender either to levy war against the State, or to be in a state of preparation to levy such war if chances should turn up in his favor. Had that been the law at present, the Commissioner who tried the Zemindar of Pachete might probably have come to the conclusion that his object in collecting arms, ammunition, and men, was either to levy war against the State, or that he might be prepared to do so if a favorable opportunity should occur. The fact of his administering an oath of secrecy was strong evidence to shew that his intention was not merely to provide for his own defence, or to render assistance to the East India Company. The Bill enacted that, if any person, owing allegiance to the British Government, should collect arms, ammunition, and men, or otherwise prepare to levy war, with the intention either of levying war, or of being prepared to levy war against the Queen or the Government of the East India Company, he should be liable, upon conviction, to the punishment of death, or to the punishment of transportation for life, or of imprisonment with hard labor for any term not exceeding fourteen years; and should also forfeit his property and effects of whatever description. These were the punishments provided by Section I of Act XI of 1857 for rebellion, or waging war against the Government. The mere fact of an individual collecting arms, ammunition, and men, with the view, not of protecting himself, or of assisting the Government, but of levying war against the Government, or of being in a state of preparation to do so whenever an opportunity might offer, was an offence almost as dangerous to the State as the actual levying of war, and he thought that it was not going too far to render it liable to the same punishment.

Section II of the Bill was directed against the harboring or concealing of offenders, and provided the same punishment as Section II of the existing Act.

He also proposed to make misprision an offence. The Bill provided that, if any person, having knowledge of the commission by another of any of the offences mentioned in Section I of Act XI of 1857, or in Section I of this Act, should conceal the fact, or neglect to make it known to the Government or to the local judicial authorities, he should be liable to imprisonment for any term not exceeding seven years, and also to fine. This was a very important Section. Persons were not to conceal offences against the State. Such concealment was an offence punishable by the law of England; he believed it was also punishable by the laws of other countries: it was certainly punishable by the law of America, which provided the same punishment for it as that proposed in this Bill. There was a Clause in the Penal Code for punishing misprision of offences against the State. He had not exactly followed that Clause, because he was not certain that the Select Committee sitting on the Penal Code might not think it necessary to amend it before they reported upon the Code to the Council.

The Bill was read a first time.

INSTITUTION OF SUITS AND APPEALS (N. W. PROVINCES).

MR. HARINGTON moved the second reading of the Bill "for the relief of persons who, in consequence of the recent disturbances, may have been prevented from instituting or prosecuting suits or appeals in the Courts of the North-Western Provinces within the period allowed by law."

MR. RICKETTS said, if only for the sake of consistency, and lest it should be supposed that the Honorable Member for the North-Western Provinces had convinced him that the view he expressed the other day in this Council was visionary and unsuited to the condition of the times, it behoved him to say that he disapproved of the little Bill now before the Council just as much as he disapproved of the little Bill introduced some weeks ago. He wished that the Honorable Member would at once say how many more of these little Bills he had in his portfolio. He must have others; for he (Mr. Ricketts) learnt that, so long ago as the 5th of March last, the Chief Commissioner of the Punjab issued a Circular Order stating that he had resolved that

"every community, section of community, or individual who may have plundered or destroyed property, real or personal, belonging to European British subjects, or European foreigners, or to Native Christians, or to the Natives of the country who threw in their lot with us, shall be made to pay the value of the same to the utmost of his or their means, and within the earliest reasonable period."

The Chief Commissioner had also resolved that it should "be the duty of the local authorities to ascertain *summarily* and estimate fairly the value of the property plundered or destroyed, under whatsoever circumstances." These rules had been issued upwards of three months ago for the Provinces of the North-West which were transferred to the administration of the Punjab. That which was good for the Provinces transferred, must also be good for the Provinces not transferred; and he (Mr. Ricketts) supposed that the Honorable Member must have a Bill somewhere for placing the latter on the same footing in this respect. It could not, he thought, be good that the Natives of the country should see a system such as that he had just read in force in the Provinces transferred, and nothing of the kind provided for the untransferred Districts. He must suppose, therefore, that the Honorable Member had another special Bill in store; and if this was to go on, we should, for many months to come, have the Honorable Member, like Oliver, constantly asking for more. He knew that the Honorable Member would not take his advice; but, nevertheless, feeling strongly on the subject as he did, he considered it his duty to tender it. His advice was that the Honorable Member should introduce a Bill of this nature:—

"A Bill to enlarge the powers of the Government of the North-Western Provinces.

"It shall be lawful for the Government of the North-Western Provinces, anything contained in any Regulation or Act notwithstanding, to remedy generally, by such means and in such manner as may be considered suitable, any losses or injuries suffered by individuals, or communities, or by the State, in the late disturbances in those Provinces: and it shall be lawful for the said Government to amend or suspend any part of the existing Code of Procedure in the Civil and Criminal Courts, and to alter the constitution, jurisdiction, and powers of any of the Civil, Criminal, and Revenue Courts of those Provinces, and to vest any European or Native Officers of Police with such powers as from time to time may appear needful."

Armed with such an Act as that, the Executive Government might forget altogether that the Legislative Council existed; and he thought it might be well that, for a time, its existence should be forgotten. He was aware that the Honorable Member and his friends at Allahabad were wedded to the system which now existed in the North-Western Provinces, and that they felt apprehensive lest any general measure of the kind he recommended, should be construed as implying that the system had broken down. He saw no reason for any sensitiveness or any anxiety on that point, though he perceived, from the papers received by the last Mail, that high authorities in England were already beginning to speak of the expediency of introducing into the North-Western Provinces the system which had been introduced with so much advantage into the Punjab. They said:—

"In our earlier administration of India, we were ignorant of the genius and character of its people. We gave to them an elaborate and complex system of Judicature which they did not understand, much less appreciate, and which has raised up a host of native attorneys, and encouraged perjury and corruption in the Courts. What the Natives of India desired and did understand, was a system like that which had been introduced into the Punjab, Pegue, and our newly-acquired territories. They did not understand that division of authority under which the Magistrate could go farther than the Collector, and the Judge go farther than the Magistrate; and, to use an old-fashioned maxim, they preferred speedy injustice to tardy justice."

He believed that they did; that speedy justice was quite as desirable in the North-Western Provinces as in the

Punjab; and he would enable the Executive Government of those Provinces to administer speedy justice, by enacting such an Act as he had read.

MR. PEACOCK asked if the Honorable Member made any motion on the subject.

MR. RICKETTS replied that he did not.

MR. PEACOCK said, he understood the Honorable Member to recommend the Honorable Member on his right (Mr. Harington) to bring in a Bill to authorize the Government of the North-Western Provinces to pass such laws as it should think necessary for the purpose of ensuring speedy justice to the inhabitants, and of rectifying defects in the present laws and administration. As the Honorable Member had only very lately become a Member of the Legislative Council, he might possibly be excused for not having thoroughly studied its constitution. Had he so studied it, he would have known that the Legislative Council had no power to pass any such Act as that which he recommended. No Executive Government in India had power to make Laws or Regulations; and it was not competent to this Council to give them such power. All Laws passed in India must be considered and passed by this assembly, and must receive the assent of the Governor General. The Charter Act 3 and 4 Wm. IV, c. 85, under which the Council sat, contained provisions to this effect; and he thought it right to call the attention of the Honorable Member to them, because, when the Honorable Member publicly expressed opinions of this nature, he thought it right that both he and the Public should understand the position in which the Council was placed. It was useless to tell the Council that the Lieutenant-Governor of the North-Western Provinces ought to be empowered to pass Laws for providing speedy justice in those Provinces, and for other matters, when the Council had no authority to give the Lieutenant-Governor any such power. The Sections of the Statute to which he alluded, were Sections XLIII and LXX. Section XLIII enacted as follows:—

"And be it enacted that the said Governor General in Council shall have power to make Laws and Regulations for repealing, amending, or altering any Laws or Regulations whatever now in force or hereafter to be in force in the said territories or any part thereof, and to make Laws and Regulations for all persons, whether British or Native, foreigners or others, and for all Courts of justice whether established by His Majesty's Charters or otherwise, and the jurisdiction thereof, and for all places and things whatsoever within and throughout the whole and every part of the said territories and for all servants of the said Company within the dominions of Princes and States in alliance with the said Company; save and except that the said Governor General in Council shall not have the power of making any Laws or Regulations which shall in any way repeal, vary, suspend, or affect any of the provisions of this Act."

Now, the provisions here referred to, were provisions which gave to the Governor-General in Council the power of making Laws, but the same Statute withheld that power from the local Governments. So far, indeed, had Parliament gone in this particular that it had provided that, when the Governor General left the Presidency unaccompanied by any Member of the Council of India, the Legislative Council might authorize him to exercise all the powers which might be exercised by the Governor General in Council, *except the power of making Laws or Regulations.* Consequently, this Council could not vest even the Governor General himself with power to make Laws. If the Governor General wished to make any Law, he must sit in this assembly. While absent at Allahabad or elsewhere, he could give his assent to Bills passed by this Council; but he could not pass any Law whatever. The Section in the Charter Act which provided this, was Section LXX. It said:—

"Whenever the Governor General in Council shall declare it is expedient that the Governor General should visit any part of India unaccompanied by any Member or Members of the Council of India, it shall be lawful for the Governor General in Council, previous to the departure of the Governor General, to nominate some Member of the Council to be its President, in whom, during the Governor General's absence from the Presidency of Fort William, the powers of the Governor General in assemblies of the Council, shall be reposed; and it shall be lawful in every such case for the Governor General in Council, by a Law or Regulation for that purpose to be made, to authorize the Governor General alone to exercise all or any of the powers which might be exercised by the Governor General in Council, except the power of making Laws or Regulations."

Therefore, it was not competent to this Council to give the Governor General himself the power of making Laws and Regulations. The Governor General was at present administering the Executive Government of the North-Western Provinces. If the Council could not give the power of making Laws and Regulations to the Governor General as Governor General, surely it could not give it to him as Lieutenant-Governor or Governor of the North-Western Provinces; and if it could not give it to him in either of those capacities, could it give it to any inferior Officer who might be appointed Lieutenant-Governor of the North-Western Provinces? He (Mr. Peacock) apprehended that the intention of the Charter Act was that no one, whether Governor General, or Governor of a Presidency, or Lieutenant-Governor, or Chief Commissioner, should have the power of making Laws. This Council had no power to pass any Law altering the provisions of the Charter Act, and it could not authorize either the Governor General himself or any other person to make Laws. Consequently, to advise the Honorable Member for the North-Western Provinces to propose a Bill which should authorize the Executive Government of the North-Western Provinces to pass such Laws as it should consider expedient, was to advise him to propose a measure which the Council must instantaneously reject as opposed to one of the fundamental principles of its constitution. If the Honorable Member opposite (Mr. Ricketts) thought that the Charter Act did not restrict the power of making Laws to the Legislative Council, he (Mr. Peacock) would recommend him to read the Despatch which was received by the Government of India from the Honorable Court of Directors in 1834, shortly after the passing of the Charter Act. That Despatch pointed out the powers and duties of the Governor General in Council in regard to making Laws, and expressly stated that the whole responsibility for every Law that might be passed, rested upon the Governor General in Council. Was this Council to authorize the Lieutenant-Governor of the North-Western Provinces, or the Governor of any Presidency, or the Chief Commissioner or Commissioner of any Province, to make any Laws he pleased, and leave the Governor General in Council responsible for them? For his own part, he could not for a moment seriously think of attempting to vest legislative functions in any person, however high his rank, or however competent he might be for the duty, in violation of the express provisions of the Charter Act, and of the constitution of this Council. If it was desirable that powers of legislation should be given to the Executive Governments, they would, doubtless, be given by Parliament; but let not any Honorable Member be constantly talking in this Council of things that ought to be done by the Council when the Council had no power to do them. If the Honorable Member opposite (Mr. Ricketts) really thought that the Executive Government of the North-Western Provinces should be authorized to legislate and to alter at its own discretion the Civil and Criminal judicature in those Provinces, why, instead of advising another Member to bring in a Bill for the purpose, did he not bring one in himself? It was perfectly open to him to introduce a Bill suspending the operation of all the Regulations now in force, and declaring the whole of the North-Western Provinces to be non-Regulation Provinces. It was quite competent to the Honorable Member to propose it; and then he would have an opportunity of taking the opinion of the Council upon his project, and seeing how far the Council went along with him in his views. But before the Honorable Member proposed to authorize the person administering the Executive Government of the North-Western Provinces to legislate for those Provinces, he would earnestly recommend him to study the Clauses of the Charter Act to which he had referred him, and the Despatch of the Honorable Court of Directors to which he had directed his attention. The Despatch was a most excellent one, well worthy of being studied; and it laid down clearly and definitively the rules and principles by which the Governor General in Council should be guided in acting upon the powers of legislation vested in him by the Charter Act.

MR. HARINGTON said, the opposition offered by the Honorable Member of Council opposite (Mr. Ricketts) to the Bill which he had asked the Council to read this day a second time, had not taken him by surprise. Indeed, he might say that, from what had fallen from the Honorable Member on the occasion of his addressing the Council for the first time after taking his seat, he had fully anticipated that the Honorable Member would make the same objection to the Bill now proposed to be passed as was made by him to the measure then under discussion, and which, having received the assent of the Right Honorable the Governor General, as intimated to the Council at the commencement of this day's proceedings, had become Law—namely, that it was piecemeal legislation. But although the opposition which the Bill now before the Council had met with from the Honorable Member was not altogether unexpected, he must be permitted to express some degree of astonishment at the silence which had been maintained by the Honorable Member up to this time since the delivery of the speech to which he had referred. In that speech, the Honorable Member had told the Council that the condition of the North-Western Provinces was such that it did not appear to him possible that any Act which might apply to one or two Districts, would be applicable to all, and that he should much prefer either that the powers of the Governor of the North-Western Provinces should be enlarged, or that the operation of the Regulations in those Provinces should be suspended for a term. Entertaining these views, he certainly thought that, as suggested by the Honorable and learned Member of Council on his left (Mr. Peacock), the Honorable Member, instead of confining himself to an abstract declaration of his opinion as to the course which it might be proper to pursue, should himself, in this interval of upwards of a month, have brought in a Bill embodying his views, in order that he might take the sense of the Council upon them, and ascertain how far they were prepared to go along with him. He could not perceive that any advantage could arise from a mere confession of faith, if he might so speak, such as was made by the Honorable Member on the occasion of his first addressing the Council; while, if the Honorable Member's views were correct, and if he had hit upon a suitable remedy for the existing state of things in the North-Western Provinces, there could be no doubt that much practical good would result from their being made the subject of legislation, and from proper measures being taken for their enforcement. Of what use, he would ask, were the Honorable Member's views if they were to appear only on the printed record of the Council's Proceedings, or in the columns of the public prints? It was from their application, if just, and not from the expression of them merely, that the people at large would benefit.

His Honorable and learned friend on his left had so fully and conclusively answered that part of the Honorable Member's speech in which he had recommended him to bring in a Bill to do that which his Honorable and learned friend had pointed out could not legally be done, that he considered it quite unnecessary to trouble the Council with any further remarks on the subject.

The Honorable Member wished to know whether he had any more small Bills of the same character as that before the Council in his portfolio, and if so, how many? The Honorable Member would be glad to learn that he had no more Bills arising out of the present state of the country in hand, and that, moreover, he did not anticipate that, in so far as the Civil Courts in the North-Western Provinces were concerned, it would be necessary to have recourse to any further legislation until the Council were called upon to pass the Code of Civil Procedure, which was now rapidly going through Committee, and would, he hoped, soon become Law.

The Honorable Member charged him and his friends at Allahabad with being so wedded to the present system that they would consent to no change. On what authority, or on what grounds he had brought forward this charge, or who were the friends to whom the Honorable Member alluded, he had no idea; but if the Honorable Member would refer to the proceedings of Government for the year 1854, he would find that he was called down to Calcutta in that year to take part with Mr. Mills, who, for some time, had a seat in this Council, in drawing up a Code of Civil Pro-

Mr. Harington

cedure, and that they had proposed a large and sweeping measure of reform which appeared to them well calculated to secure the object so earnestly advocated by the Honorable Member of Council—namely, the speedy and efficient administration of justice in our Civil Courts. They had also drawn up a Bill empowering the Government to establish Courts of Small Causes throughout India. It was no fault of his that the measures proposed by Mr. Mills and himself had not been adopted. To himself, it had, for some time, been a subject of regret that the Bill for establishing Courts of Small Causes, which had been carefully considered and amended by a Committee of the Council, had not been passed into Law long ago. It was still before the Council, and he should cordially support any motion for passing it.

The Honorable Member seemed to suppose that the Bill under discussion had originated with him; but such was not the case. As noticed in his remarks when he moved the first reading of the Bill, he had received a communication from the Government of the North-Western Provinces, accompanied by a Report from the Sudder Court at Agra, in which he was requested to adopt the necessary measures for bringing in a Bill to meet the objects specified in the Sudder Court's letter. The present Bill was framed in consequence of those directions; and as the Honorable Member of Council opposite, though he objected to the Bill, had brought forward no specific motion, it only remained for him (Mr. Harington) to express a hope that the Council would allow it to be read a second time.

The Motion for the second reading of the Bill was carried, and the Bill read a second time.

CONTINUANCE OF CERTAIN PRIVILEGES TO THE FAMILY, &c. OF THE LATE NABOB OF THE CARNATIC.

MR. FORBES moved the second reading of the Bill "to continue certain privileges and immunities to the family and retainers of the late Nabob of the Carnatic."

The Motion was carried, and the Bill read a second time.

KURNOOL.

MR. FORBES moved that the Bill "for bringing the District of Kurnool under the Laws of the Presidency of Fort St. George" be now read a third time and passed.

The Motion was carried, and the Bill read a third time.

MUNICIPAL ASSESSMENT (BOMBAY).

MR. LEGEYT moved that the Bill "for appointing Municipal Commissioners and for raising a Fund for Municipal purposes in the Town of Bombay" be referred back to a Select Committee consisting of Mr. Currie, Mr. Forbes, and the Mover, and that the Committee be instructed to take into consideration a communication on the subject recently received by him from the Government of Bombay, and to propose such further amendments in the Bill as may appear to them to be necessary.

He said he would briefly explain his object in wishing to adopt this course. On the 27th of February last, the Bombay Municipal Bill was ordered to be republished, and to be brought up for re-consideration after five weeks.

He had not been able to bring the matter forward again at the expiration of five weeks. On the 14th of March, he received a communication from the Government of Bombay requesting that further proceedings might be suspended, in order that the Government might consider the amendments made in the Bill by the Select Committee and adopted by the Council, but which, in some respects, did not seem to meet the views of the Government or the Bench of Justices. The communication from the Government of Bombay referred to in his motion, he received only yesterday. He found that the Government and the Bench of Justices did not agree to several of the alterations made in the Bill, particularly to those which related to the constitution of the Municipal Body; moreover, great annoyance was felt by the Justices at the proposal to take the control of the public works out of their hands. It was the wish of the Government of Bombay to go as much as possible hand in hand with the Bench of Justices, in this matter. The recovery of large sums advanced by the Government for the Vehar Works depended much on a good understanding being maintained between the Justices and the Government. Under these circumstances, he thought that the Bill should undergo some reconsideration, and probably it would be better that such reconsideration should be had in Select Committee, than in a Committee of the whole Council.

After some discussion as to whether the course proposed was regular, this Bill having been settled in a Committee of the whole Council, MR. LEGEYT, with the leave of the Council, withdrew his motion, stating that he would consider the several suggestions just made, and move or give notice of motion next Saturday.

INSTITUTION OF SUITS AND APPEALS (N. W. PROVINCES).

MR. HARINGTON moved that the Bill "for the relief of persons who, in consequence of the recent disturbances, may have been prevented from instituting or prosecuting suits or appeals in the Courts of the North-Western Provinces within the period allowed by law" be referred to a Select Committee consisting of Mr. LeGeyt, Mr. Currie, and the Mover.

Agreed to.

MR. HARINGTON moved that the Standing Orders be suspended to enable the Select Committee to present their Report within one month.

MR. FORBES seconded the Motion, which was then agreed to.

CONTINUANCE OF CERTAIN PRIVILEGES TO THE FAMILY, &c. OF THE LATE NABOB OF THE CARNATIC.

MR. FORBES moved that the Bill "to continue certain privileges and immunities to the family and retainers of the late Nabob of the Carnatic" be referred to a Select Committee consisting of Mr. Peacock, Mr. Harington, and the Mover.

Agreed to.

KURNOOL.

MR. FORBES moved that Mr. Ricketts be requested to take the Bill "for bringing the District of Kurnool under the Laws of the Presidency of Fort St. George" to the President in Council, in order that it might be submitted to the Governor General for his assent.

Agreed to.

INSTITUTION OF SUITS AND APPEALS (N. W. PROVINCES).

MR. HARINGTON moved that the Select Committee on the Bill "for the relief of persons who, in consequence of the recent disturbances, may have been prevented from instituting or prosecuting suits or appeals in the Courts of the North-Western Provinces within the period allowed by law" be instructed to present their Report within one month.

Agreed to.

SUSPENSION OF SUITS AGAINST THE FAMILY, &c. OF THE LATE NABOB OF THE CARNATIC.

MR. PEACOCK moved that the Standing Orders be suspended to enable him to bring in and proceed with a Bill "to continue for six months the privileges granted by Act I of 1844 to certain members of the family, household, and retinue of his late Highness the Nabob of the Carnatic." In doing so, he said the Council had already, by its vote on the Motion for the second reading of the Bill introduced by the Honorable Member for Madras on Saturday last, adopted the principle that the privileges and immunities conferred by Act I of 1844 on the family and retainers of the late Nabob of the Carnatic should be continued to them. It had not been thought right to suspend the Standing Orders for the passing of that Bill, because, as it affected the private interests of the creditors of the Nabob, and was not a mere temporary Act, it was but fair that the creditors should have an opportunity of pointing out any objections which they might have to offer against the measure. Last year, this Council passed an Act—XVIII of 1857—allowing one year to the family and retainers of the late Nabob of the Carnatic for the purpose of appealing against the decision of the Supreme Court of Madras, which declared Act I of 1844 to have ceased to have effect in consequence of the death of the Nabob. That Act would expire on the 4th of next month; and from that date, the family and retainers of the late Nabob, if no other measure were adopted, would be liable to be sued and imprisoned. It did not appear to him expedient that, after having affirmed the principle that the exemption given by Act I of 1844 should be continued to certain members of the family of the late Nabob for life, the Council should leave them to be sued and arrested between the 4th of July and the time when it would have an opportunity of fully discussing the Bill which had just been read a second time. No appeal could now be brought under Act XVIII of 1857 against the decision of the Supreme Court. But if it was right, as the Council had determined it to be, that the family and retainers of the late Nabob should have the privilege conferred upon them by Act I of 1844 continued, he thought it was also right that they should have the same protection during the progress of the Bill introduced by the Honorable Member for Madras through its several stages. He, therefore, proposed to read for a first and second time to-day a Bill to continue for six months the privileges granted by Act I of 1844 to certain member of the family, household, and retinue of his late Highness the Nabob of the Carnatic. He had fixed six months, lest any objections might come in from creditors of the Nabob which might delay the final settlement of the Bill introduced by the Honorable Member for Madras; but if Honorable Members considered six months too long, he had no objection to limit the operation of the Bill to four months.

He moved this Bill necessarily without any previous notice. He could not have given notice that he would move it, because he could not be sure that the Council would adopt the principle of the Bill which had been brought in by the Honorable Member for Madras.

MR. GRANT seconded the Motion, which was then carried.

MR. PEACOCK moved that the Bill be now read a first time.

The Bill was read a first time.

MR. PEACOCK moved that the Bill be now read a second time.

The Motion was carried, and the Bill read a second time.

MR. PEACOCK then moved that the Bill be referred to a Select Committee consisting of Mr. Harington, Mr. Forbes, and the Mover, with an instruction to report upon it at the next Meeting of the Council.

Agreed to.

The Council adjourned.

Saturday, June 12, 1858.

PRESENT:

The Hon'ble the Chief Justice, *Vice-President*, in the Chair.

Hon. J. P. Grant,	E. Currie, Esq.
Hon. H. Ricketts,	H. B. Harington, Esq.
Hon. B. Peacock,	and
P. W. LeGeyt, Esq.	H. Forbes, Esq.

ARMY AND STATE OFFENCES; HEINOUS OFFENCES; MUTINY AND DESERTION.

THE VICE-PRESIDENT read a Message informing the Legislative Council that the Governor General had assented to the Bill "to continue in force for a further period Acts XIV of 1857, XVI of 1857, and XVII of 1857, and to authorize in certain cases the transportation of offenders sentenced to imprisonment."

ESTATE OF THE LATE NABOB OF THE CARNATIC.

THE CLERK brought to the notice of the Council a Petition purporting to be "The Humble Petition of His Highness Azeem Jah Bahadoor, Nabob of the Carnatic and Subahdar of Arcot," and signed "Azeem Jah," against the Bill "to provide for the administration of the Estate and for the payment of the debts of the late Nabob of the Carnatic."

MR. GRANT said, he apprehended that the Council could not receive the Petition. There was no such title recognized as the Nabob of the Carnatic and Subahdar of Arcot. The title had lapsed in 1855.

The Petition was not received.

MR. PEACOCK said, to give the Petitioner an opportunity of presenting his Petition in a correct form, he should move that the Clerk of the Council do inform him of the grounds upon which the present Petition had been rejected.

The VICE-PRESIDENT said, he should take this opportunity of mentioning that he had reason to believe that the full Petition of Prince Azeem Jah was not yet before the Council. By the last Mail, he had received a letter from a person describing himself as Secretary of the Prince, stating that the Prince intended to present a fuller Petition, a copy of which was enclosed, headed in the same way as that which the Council had just decided to be objectionable. He understood from the Clerk that the original of this Petition had not yet been received.

MR. PEACOCK'S Motion was then put and agreed to.

SUSPENSION OF SUITS AGAINST THE FAMILY, &c. OF THE LATE NABOB OF THE CARNATIC.

MR. PEACOCK presented the Report of the Select Committee on the Bill "to continue for six months the privileges granted by Act I of 1844 to certain members of the family, household, and retinue of his late Highness the Nabob of the Carnatic."

STATE OFFENCES.

MR. PEACOCK moved the second reading of the Bill "to make further provision for the trial and punishment of offences against the State."

The Motion was carried, and the Bill read a second time.

MUNICIPAL ASSESSMENT (BOMBAY).

On the Order of the Day for the third reading of the Bill "for appointing Municipal Commissioners and for raising a Fund for Municipal purposes in the Town of Bombay" being read, Mr. LeGeyt, who had given notice of a motion to recommit the Bill under the 87th Standing Order, moved that the consideration of the Bill be postponed.

Agreed to.

SUSPENSION OF SUITS AGAINST THE FAMILY &c. OF THE LATE NABOB OF THE CARNATIC.

MR. PEACOCK moved that the Council resolve itself into a Committee on the Bill "to continue for six months the privileges granted by Act I of 1844 to certain members of the family, household, and retinue of his late Highness the Nabob of the Carnatic."

Agreed to.

The Vice-President

The Bill passed through Committee without amendment, and was reported.

MR. PEACOCK moved that the Bill be now read a third time and passed.

The Motion was carried, and the Bill read a third time.

MR. PEACOCK moved that Mr. Ricketts be requested to take the Bill to the President in Council in order that it might be submitted to the Governor General for his assent.

Agreed to.

THE INDIAN PENAL CODE.

MR. LEGEYT said, he had received a communication from the Government of Bombay enclosing a copy of a correspondence with Brigadier General Sir R. Shakespear, Political Commissioner of Guzerat, with a request that he would lay it before the Council with a view to some legislation. The subject of the correspondence was the transmission of twigs throughout the Province of Guzerat, which had been detected by Mr. Spiers, Acting Deputy Magistrate of the Ahmedabad district, at a village near Cambay, and brought to the notice of Sir R. Shakespear, who reported it to the Government as a suspicious circumstance requiring careful enquiry. Some enquiry had been made by Mr. Spiers, but it did not seem to have elicited any such information as would enable the Authorities to come to a definite conclusion. This was the second time that twigs had been lately sent through the Province. A sketch of the route by which they had passed, had been forwarded with the correspondence. It appeared that, in answer to all the enquiries made respecting them at the different villages along this route, the one universal answer given was—"We know nothing of what they mean. The tracks arrived, and, according to custom, we passed them on." The custom here referred to was a very old one throughout the Province. When a robbery took place, the footsteps of the robbers were searched for and measured by straws or twigs and then tracked from village to village, and the village at which the track stopped was held responsible for the property robbed. In this case, there had been an attempt to show that a robbery had been committed in one of the villages; but it appeared that no information had been given to the Police of any such robbery until after the enquiry regarding the twigs had been instituted, and the story of its occurrence seemed hardly deserving of credit. Under all the circumstances, and seeing that the system of carrying signs from village to village afforded great facility for disseminating secret intelligence through the country, Sir R. Shakespear and the Government of Bombay were of opinion that some legislation was necessary to prohibit all persons from taking charge of signs without the direct orders of the Government. There was no Law at present under which the transmission of signs by villagers could be treated as a penal offence, though there was a Regulation under which village Officers in the service of Government, who after prohibition disobeyed orders in passing on these signs could be dealt with. The object now was to put a stop to the transmission of such signs entirely, whether by villagers or by village Officers. He had not thought that he would be justified in preparing a special Bill upon this subject. The Government of Bombay, in forwarding the correspondence to him, had requested that he should "submit for the consideration of the Legislative Council of India the propriety of rendering the system, as applicable to India generally, a penal offence." It appeared to him that the best way of dealing with the matter was to move, as he now did, that the communication received by him from the Government of Bombay on the subject of rendering the transmission of signs from village to village a penal offence, be laid upon the table and referred to the Select Committee on "The Indian Penal Code."

Agreed to.

CRIMINAL PROCEDURE (BENGAL).

MR. CURRIE moved that a communication received by him from the Bengal Government on the subject of private prosecutions in cases of forgery be laid upon the table and referred to the Select Committee on the Bill "for extending the jurisdiction of the Courts of Criminal Judicature of the East India Company in Bengal, for simplifying the Procedure thereof, and for investing other Courts with Criminal jurisdiction."

Agreed to.

STATE OFFENCES.

MR. PEACOCK moved that the Standing Orders be suspended to enable him to proceed with the Bill "to make further provision for the trial and punishment of offences against the State."

MR. HARINGTON seconded the Motion, which was then agreed to.

MR. PEACOCK moved that the above Bill be referred to a Select Committee consisting of the Vice-President, Mr. Harington, and the Mover, with an instruction to report upon it at the next Meeting of the Council.

Agreed to.

The Council adjourned.

Saturday, June 19, 1858.

PRESENT:

The Hon'ble the Chief Justice, *Vice-President.*

Hon. B. Peacock,	H. B. Harington, Esq.
	and
E. Currie, Esq.,	H. Forbes, Esq.

The Members assembled at the Meeting did not form the quorum required by law for a Meeting of the Council for the purpose of making Laws.

Saturday, June 26, 1858.

PRESENT:

The Honorable the Chief Justice, *Vice-President,* in the Chair.

Hon J. P. Grant,	E. Currie, Esq.,
Hon. H. Ricketts,	H. B. Harington, Esq.,
Hon. B. Peacock,	and
P. W. LeGeyt, Esq.,	H. Forbes, Esq.

KURNOOL.

THE VICE-PRESIDENT read a Message informing the Legislative Council that the Governor General had assented to the Bill "for bringing the District of Kurnool under the Laws of the Presidency of Fort St. George."

MOULMEIN PORT-DUES.

THE CLERK presented a Petition from Messrs. Miller and Buchanan, merchants of Moulmein, praying for an amendment of Act XXXV of 1857 (for the levy of Port-dues in the Ports of Moulmein, Rangoon, Kyouk Phyoo, Akyab, and Chittagong), especially with respect to the duties chargeable on ships entering the Port in ballast. The Petitioners ask to have the Act assimilated to the Calcutta and Bombay Acts.

MR. GRANT moved that the Petition be printed.

Agreed to.

ESTATE OF THE LATE NABOB OF THE CARNATIC.

THE VICE-PRESIDENT said, the Clerk of the Council had brought to his notice that he had received a Petition (which appeared to be the original of that copy which he had mentioned to the Council at its last Meeting) purporting to be from "Prince Azeem Jah, Bahadoor, Nabob of the Carnatic, and Subahdar of Arcot." He apprehended that, according to the Resolution of the Council on the former occasion, this Petition could not be received. From what he had stated to the Council in reference to the copy received by himself, he believed that the Petition had been forwarded before the Resolution of the Council could have been known to the Petitioner. Still, it fell within the Resolution, and could not be received.

MALACCA LANDS.

THE CLERK reported to the Council that he had received a communication from the Governor of the Straits Settlement on the subject of a proposed enactment concerning the property in land in Malacca and to enable the local Government to dispose of the waste lands in that Station.

MR. PEACOCK moved that the above communication be printed.

Agreed to.

ESTATE OF THE LATE NABOB OF THE CARNATIC.

On the Order of the Day being read for the presentation of the Report of the Select Committee on the Bill "to provide for the administration of the Estate and for the payment of the debts of the late Nabob of the Carnatic"—

MR. PEACOCK said, the Select Committee had framed their Report, and he had intended to present it this day; but he now understood that the Agent of Prince Azeem Jah had arrived, and was now in Calcutta; and as the Council had rejected two Petitions from the Prince on the ground of an informality in their heading, he thought it better to defer presenting it until Saturday next, unless any further Petition should be forwarded to the Council before that time.

OFFENCES AGAINST THE STATE.

MR. PEACOCK presented the Report of the Select Committee on the Bill "to make further provision for the trial and punishment of offences against the State."

BOMBAY MUNICIPAL ASSESSMENT.

On the Order of the Day being read for the third reading of the Bill "for appointing Municipal Commissioners and for raising a Fund for municipal purposes in the Town of Bombay"—

MR. LEGEYT moved that the Bill be re-committed for the purpose of considering certain amendments proposed in a communication received by him from the Government of Bombay dated 29th April 1858.

Agreed to.

Section I provided as follows:—

"So much of the 158th Section of the Act of Parliament 33 Geo. III c. 52 as remains in force; so much of Chapters II and IV of Regulation XIX. 1827 of the Bombay Code as remains in force, and so much of Act VII of 1836 as relates to those Chapters; Regulation XXXII. 1827 of the same Code; and Act XI of 1845—are hereby repealed, except so far as they repeal any other Act, and except as to any assessment or tax which shall be unpaid and as to any proceeding for the recovery of the same which shall have been commenced before this Act comes into operation."

MR. LEGEYT moved that the words and figures "except Section XIII of Chapter II" be inserted after the word "force" in the 6th line of the Section. He said, the object was that that part of Regulation XIX. 1827 which related to licenses for public notices of sale, should be retained. In the official correspondence that had taken place regarding the Bill, the Bench of Justices had suggested that it would be extremely inconvenient if the present system of giving public notice of the sale of houses and other property by beat of drum were discontinued; and the Government of Bombay had concurred in their view.

MR. CURRIE said, as the Section was originally drawn, no part of Chapter II of Regulation XIX. 1827 was proposed to be repealed. It stood thus:—

"So much of the 158th Section of the Act of Parliament 33 Geo. III c. 52 as remains in force; Sections 24, 25 and 26 of Regulation XIX. 1827; Regulation XXXII. 1827 of the Bombay Code; and Act XI of 1845, are hereby repealed, except so far as they repeal any other Act, and except as to any assessment or tax which shall be unpaid, and as to any proceedings for the recovery of the same which shall have been commenced before this Act comes into operation."

The Select Committee to whom the Bill was referred, thought that Chapter II of Regulation XIX. 1827 ought also to be repealed. Chapter II contained several Sections. The first Section, which was Section IX of the Regulation, related to assessment on shops and stalls, and was superseded by a subsequent Act which was repealed by this Bill. Sections X and XI related to licenses for wedding sheds or other places of temporary amusement, and were superseded by a provision in Act XIV of 1856, the Conservancy Act for the Presidency Towns. Section XII related to licenses for using country music without doors. In Act XIII of 1856, the Police Act for the Presidency Towns, provision was made for prohibiting altogether the use of this sort of music in the streets, except under a license from the Police Commissioner. Section XII, therefore, was also superseded by the later enactment. Then came Section XIII, to which the present Motion referred. Sections XIV, XV and XVI related to fines, penalties, and forfeitures incurred under the Chapter, and were superseded by the Police Act for the Presidency Towns. There was thus only one Section of the Chapter which was not superseded, and that was Section XIII, which provided that "all persons desirous of giving public notice by beat of battakee of the sale of any house, building, land, or other immoveable property, or the sale of any goods or chattels, or of publicly offering or giving any other kind of lawful public notice by beat of battakee," should obtain a license, upon payment of certain fees. The Select Committee on this Bill were of opinion that, in revising the whole law for raising municipal revenues for the Town of Bombay, it was right that the sources of income should be restricted to those which were provided by the Bill, and by the Conservancy Act XIV of 1856; and, therefore, they had not thought it necessary to retain Section XIII of Regulation XIX. 1827. The income which it produced, must be very small. If the levy of such fees was to be retained at all, provision ought to have been made for it in the general Conservancy, or the general Police Act; but as no such fees were taken in the other Presidency towns, the Select Committee on those Bills, had thought it unnecessary to retain them specially for Bombay.

The Honorable Member had said that it would be inconvenient to prevent notices of sale being given by beat of drum. But the repeal of the Section would not prevent such notices being given. It would only prevent fees being levied on account of the notices.

It was to be observed also that, as the Bill was drawn, the retention of Section XIII of Regulation XIX. 1827 would not make the fees levied under it applicable to municipal purposes. All fees provided for by the Conservancy Act were made payable to the Municipal Commissioners: these would be paid to the Collector; and, although Act XI of 1845 declared fees realized under Chapter II of Regulation XIX. 1827 to be applicable to municipal purposes, that Act was repealed by this Bill.

On the whole, he thought there was no necessity for retaining the Section in question.

MR. LEGEYT said, as a wish had been expressed by those who were supposed to represent the Public in Bombay more than any body else could be said to do, that the practice in question should be retained, it would be a want of courtesy to reject their application. There could be no doubt that the mode provided by Section XIII Chapter II Regulation XIX. 1827 was an extremely convenient one for giving notice of such sales as the Section contemplated, to the poorer population of a large Town, who had no access to newspapers. It had been in existence in Bombay time out of mind, and he thought that its abrogation now would be felt as a hardship and inconvenience. It was very true that a person might obtain publicity for an intended sale by employing persons for the purpose; but he thought that the notices given of such sales should be under some sort of control; and that if the control hitherto in force should be withdrawn, considerable inconvenience might follow. He should therefore press the amendment he had proposed.

The question being put, the Council divided:—

Ayes 6.	*Noes* 2.
Mr. Forbes,	Mr. Currie,
Mr. Harington,	Mr. Peacock.
Mr. LeGeyt,	
Mr. Ricketts,	
Mr. Grant,	
The Chairman.	

MR. CURRIE said, he found that the Select Committee, in amending this Section, had made an oversight. It was perhaps rather late to rectify the omission now; but still he thought it necessary to bring the matter to the notice of the Council, and, unless the Council objected, to make a Motion on the subject. Another Chapter of Regulation XIX. 1827 ought to have been included in the Section;—he meant Chapter VI. It provided rules for levying fees in the Court of Petty Sessions, and in the Offices of the Magistrates of Police. He would read the list of the fees to be levied:—

	Rs.	Qr.	Rs.
For every complaint instituted when filed in the Office of a Magistrate of Police, ...	0	2	0
For every complaint instituted when filed in the Court of Petty Sessions, ...	1	0	0
For summoning each party to answer before the Magistrate, ...	0	1	0
For summoning each party to answer before the Court of Petty Sessions, ...	0	2	0
For summoning each witness to attend at the Office of the Magistrate, and for each person sworn, if the fee for summoning has not been paid, ...	0	0	50
For summoning each witness in the Court of Petty Sessions, and for each person sworn, if the fee for summoning has not been paid,	0	1	0
For every voluntary affidavit, ...	1	0	0
For granting each certificate to the Commanders of ships, on their arrival at, and departure from, the Port of Bombay, payable on the delivery of the *rôle d'équipage* of their vessels, ...	5	0	0
For every commission to a Patell, Mukadum, or Chogla of a Caste,	1	0	0
For every passport issued by the Senior Magistrate to Europeans,	2	0	0

These fees, which consisted principally of fees in cases instituted before the Magistrates of Police, in the Court of Petty Sessions, did not obtain in the other Presidency towns; and the Committee which prepared the Police Bill for the Presidency towns had been of opinion that they ought to be discontinued in Bombay. Accordingly, in the Schedule to that Bill, among the Laws to be repealed was mentioned Chapter VI of Regulation XIX. 1827. But in a Committee of the whole Council, the Honorable Member for Bombay objected to the repeal of the Chapter. He said—

"The Bombay Government had represented that the repeal of this Regulation would deprive the Municipal Revenue of that Presidency of six thousand Rupees per annum, which it could ill afford to lose, and for which nothing was substituted in the Bill. This Bill had hitherto avoided all matters which related to Municipal Revenue, and he thought that the Regulations referred to in the above Clause should be allowed to remain in force until the new Municipal Bill should come before the Council, and the revenues to be collected thereunder be considered. Six thousand Rupees per annum was a large sum for the Municipal Fund, in its present state, to lose; but if it should be determined to repeal Chapter VI of Regulation XIX. 1827 by the Municipal Bill, he hoped to have provision made in that Bill for making good from other sources the loss of the amount now realized under the Regulation."

Now, the Bill before the Council did provide ample funds for all municipal purposes; and as this Chapter had not been repealed by the Police Act solely on the ground that the municipal revenues of Bombay were not then under revision, he thought it ought to be included in Section I of the present Bill. The reason for which the Honorable Member wished it to be retained when the Police Act passed, had ceased to exist; and it ought now to be repealed. He (Mr. Currie) therefore moved

Mr. LeGeyt

that the word and figures "and VI" be inserted after the figures "IV" in the 4th line of Section 1.

MR. LEGEYT said, he thought that the Council had better leave the Section as it now stood. The income of the Bombay Municipality had undergone rigid scrutiny; and in the papers which formed the annexures to the Bill which he introduced in January last, all the items that were receivable by the Municipality had been taken into account and set against the estimated disbursements. He did not think that, upon reference to that account, the Honorable Member would find that much margin had been left, although the sum calculated upon as the income was very large. There might be a greater deficiency in the taxes to be levied under the head of Town duties than the Council was aware of; and the whole scheme might be considerably disturbed by the deduction now proposed. The charges under Chapter VI of Regulation XIX. 1827 might appear frivolous; but they had been of long standing. When it was proposed to repeal the Chapter on a former occasion, the Bombay Government urged that it should be retained; and he did not think that any advantage whatever would result from the repeal. The amount realized under this Chapter was about six thousand Rupees a year, which was not a very small sum; and he really did not see any reason for discontinuing the existing arrangements, especially as this item had been calculated in the estimate of income out of which the future disbursements for municipal purposes were to be provided.

MR. PEACOCK said, it was very inconvenient that these questions should be brought before the Council without previous notice. He had certainly been under the impression that Chapter VI of Regulation XIX. 1827 had been repealed. The fees levied under it had hitherto been appropriated to the Municipal Fund; but the Municipal Fund was provided for by the present Bill, and he thought that the fees in question ought not to go to that Fund. They were fees for the administration of Justice, and, if levied at all, they should be applied to the support of the Courts of Justice, or form part of the general revenues of the State. By the Police Act, the Council had very much increased the powers of the Magistrates. Under this extended jurisdiction, Magistrates had to deal with many more cases than before, and the fees for processes would be proportionately larger. The Council had just now, by the amendment which had been carried, put on a tax for municipal purposes for a license to give notice by beat of drum of a sale of property, and other matters. He thought that such a tax was objectionable. To impose a tax upon legal proceedings for municipal purposes appeared to him to be still more so; and he should vote in support of the Motion for repealing Chapter VI of Regulation XIX. 1827.

MR. CURRIE said, with respect to what had been stated regarding the appropriation of the fees, as the Bill stood, he did not exactly know what would become of them. Section XXXI Chapter VI of the Regulation of 1827 provided that they should be paid to the Sub Treasurer "for the benefit of the County Fund;" Act XI of 1845 directed that they should be appropriated to the Municipal Fund; but that Act would be repealed by this Bill; and the Section of this Bill which constituted the Municipal Fund, provided indeed that all fines and penalties imposed by the Court of Petty Sessions or Magistrates of Police should form part of the Fund, but it made no mention of fees levied in the Court of Petty Sessions and in the Offices of the Magistrates.

THE CHAIRMAN said, the effect of introducing the proposed amendment now would possibly be to delay the passing of the Bill, and to vary, to some slight extent, the estimate of income upon which the Government of Bombay had proceeded. He was therefore disposed to leave the Clause as it stood; although, if the amendment had been brought forward before, he should have been inclined to vote in favor of it.

MR. CURRIE said, he begged to remind the Council that the question of the repeal of Chapter VI of Regulation XIX. 1827 had been before it on a former occasion, in connection with the Police Bill for the Presidency Towns; and the only apparent reason for which the Chapter was allowed to stand in that

Bill was that the Municipal Fund of Bombay was in difficulties, and could not afford to lose the revenue derived under it until the new Municipal Bill should provide other sources of income.

THE CHAIRMAN replied that still, by inadvertence or otherwise, the present Bill had been allowed to go before the Government and the community of Bombay without any notice of the intention to insert in it an amendment repealing Chapter VI of Regulation XIX. 1827.

The Motion was then put and agreed to.

MR. LEGEYT moved that the words "the repealed portions of" be inserted after the word "to" in the 7th line of the Section.

The Motion was agreed to and the Section then passed.

Section IV provided that there should be three Commissioners, one to be appointed by the Governor in Council, and the two others to be elected by the Justices of the Peace in Sessions.

MR. LEGEYT moved that this Section be left out, and the following new Section substituted for it:—

"There shall be seven Commissioners for the purposes of this Act, and for the conservancy and improvement of the Town of Bombay. Two of such Commissioners shall be appointed by the Governor in Council. The other five Commissioners shall consist of two European and three Native residents of Bombay, who shall be elected by Her Majesty's Justices of the Peace in Sessions assembled."

The Honorable Member said, the Council would perceive that this was a return to the Section which stood in the Draft Bill, but which was altered by the Select Committee. The alteration had met with considerable disfavor from the Bench of Justices in Bombay. The Government of Bombay, when the subject first went before it for consideration, was not opposed to a reduction of the number of the Board of Conservancy; but subsequently, in a letter which they had addressed to him, dated 29th April 1858, they said—

"The Governor in Council agrees with the Bench in the opinions expressed throughout the remainder of the Acting Clerk's letter, with the exception of its 4th and 5th paragraphs. With respect to the matters to which [illegible] two paragraphs refer, the Select Com[illegible] correctly observed that Government was reluctantly brought to consent to a scheme of municipal management involving the continuance of seven Commissioners, acting under the supervision, direction, and control of the Justices; but having done so, His Lordship in Council is unwilling to retract the assent already given by him to the adoption of that scheme; and he considers the avoidance of further delay in passing the Municipal Bill so important, that he would, at any rate, feel disinclined from renewing a discussion which might possibly cause additional obstruction."

The Justices stated in their letter to the Government as follows:—

"With reference to Section IV of the Bill, I am desired to state that the Bench consider that the proposition made by them, agreed to by the Bombay Government, and embodied in the Draft Act sent from Bombay to the Legislative Council, with reference to the appointment of seven Municipal Commissioners, should be adhered to."

He had received several non-official communications on this subject from persons interested in it in Bombay; and he found the real feeling there to be this—that by the reduction of the Municipal Board from seven to three, the Natives of Bombay would lose a voice, and a strong voice in the municipal arrangements of the Town, which they considered they had enjoyed as a privilege for many years. The present Conservancy Board consisted of three Natives and four Europeans; and the Bench of Justices were anxious that this should continue to be the constitution of the Board. A Board of three Commissioners would never have more than one Native Member in it; and the sore point with them was that the Native voice would be lost in the future Conservancy arrangements of the Island.

With respect to the efficient working of a Board composed of seven Members, those who had written to him argued in their letters that the work might be divided amongst Sub-Committees of four and three Members, and would thus be done just as well as it could be by a Board of only three Members. The change in the constitution of the Board had given rise to strong feeling in Bombay, and the Government thought that the agreement which they had made with the Justices should be allowed to stand. Under all these circumstances, he had thought it right to re-introduce the original Section, providing that the Municipal Board should consist of seven Members instead of only three.

MR. CURRIE said, the objection which was said by the Honorable Member to exist to the amendment made by the Select Committee in this Section, and adopted by the Council—namely, that the Natives of Bombay would lose a voice in the Conservancy arrangements of the town—was hardly borne out by the fact. The Conservancy Board at Bombay now consisted of seven Members, of whom he believed four were Europeans, and the other three Natives. The Europeans, consequently, had now a majority in the Board. Under the new constitution as proposed by the Select Committee, and adopted by the Council, there might be, and in all probability would be, one Native and two Europeans, or there might be one European and two Natives. At any rate, it was probable that there would always be one Native at least. The Europeans had a majority in the Board at present, and they might have a majority in the Board proposed. Therefore, the objection taken to the amended Section did not seem to him to be well founded; especially as the election of the two elective Commissioners would remain in the hands of the Bench of Justices, just in the same way as the election of the five elective Members of the Conservancy Board was now vested in them.

The grounds upon which the Select Committee had proposed the amendment, were stated in their Report; and, that Report being in the hands of Honorable Members, he thought it unnecessary to go into them. They concluded by saying:—

"We concur in the opinion expressed by the Government, and by some of the Justices, that a small number of well-paid Commissioners, not subject to minute supervision and control, but acting under a sense of personal responsibility, will constitute a body much better adapted for the convenient and speedy despatch of the ordinary current work of the Conservancy, than the seven Commissioners now proposed, who may be controlled in all their proceedings by a body so numerous and so uncertain as the Justices assembled in Sessions."

It was undeniable that the Board as now constituted had not given general satisfaction. Among the printed papers connected with the Bill was an Extract from a Government Resolution dated 17th April 1855, which ran as follows:—

"That, with reference to the repeated calls which have been made upon the Worshipful Bench of Justices to expedite the submission of the Draft Act which has been now several months under consideration and discussion, and generally to the dilatoriness which has hitherto marked the proceedings of the Board of Conservancy and the Bench of Justices in Municipal matters, the Governor in Council is of opinion that some alteration in the mode of transacting Municipal business is urgently required, and possibly, that the whole Municipal constitution of Bombay may stand in need of revision."

In consequence of the dissatisfaction felt with respect to the present constitution of the Municipal body, a suggestion was made, and approved by the Government of Bombay, that the number should be reduced, and a Board constituted similar to that provided by the amended Bill. The Government did not now object to the amendment which had been made by the Select Committee and adopted by the Council. They admitted that they had given an unwilling assent to the proposal of the Justices to retain the existing constitution of the Board; but stated that, having given that assent, they were disinclined now to retract it. One Member of the Government, however, who had not been a party to this unwilling acquiescence, declared himself in favor of the Municipal Body proposed by the amended Bill. Nor did the Justices themselves appear to be at all unanimous on the subject. He found from a Report published in one of the Bombay newspapers, that at the Meeting of Justices at which this Section of the Bill was taken into consideration, there were present only twelve Justices out of sixty or seventy. The Report said:—

"At the last Meeting, Section V of the Bill, which provides that the Governor in Council shall appoint one of the Commissioners, who shall be President, and that the other two Commissioners shall be elected by Her Majesty's Justices of the Peace in Sessions assembled, was taken into consideration; and, although there were but twelve Justices present, there were no less than three different propositions regarding this Section of the Bill. Messrs. Acland and Stuart were of opinion that one

Commissioner would be more likely to carry out the provisions of the Bill with advantage to the Public than three, the number mentioned in Section IV; Messrs. Narayen Dinanath and Rustomjee Cursetjee (Members of the Board of Conservancy) were opposed to this view, and proposed as an amendment that seven Commissioners were necessary to carry out the provisions of the Bill; whilst Messrs. Winchester and Hutchinson proposed as a further amendment that the 4th Clause of the Bill be allowed to remain unaltered. The latter amendment was, on being put to the vote, lost: the same result attended the first proposition; and ultimately, the amendment of Mr. Narayen Dinanath, to continue the old Board, was carried by seven votes *versus* five."

He thought, therefore, that the statement made on this point in the letter of the Acting Clerk of the Peace could hardly be accepted as the collective voice of the Bench of Justices—the more so as among the connected papers was a Petition to the Council signed by Mr. Gilmore and twelve other Justices, expressly approving of a Municipal Board composed of three Members, in preference to one composed of seven. He thought, therefore, that there was really no ground for the Council changing the resolution to which it had already come upon this question.

Mr. PEACOCK said, he did not see any reason for making the proposed change. The Bill had been settled by a Committee of the whole Council on the Report of the Select Committee to whom it had been referred. Originally, Section III stood as the Honorable Member for Bombay now proposed; but the Select Committee had altered it, and the alteration had been adopted by the Council in Committee. The Council ought, therefore, to have some very strong reason to induce it to change the resolution to which it had already come upon the question. He did not know whether the Honorable Member for Bombay proposed, if he carried his amendment, to alter Section VIII of the Bill. As the Bill now stood, there were to be three Commissioners, and these were to be paid. Section VIII provided that they

"may receive such allowances out of the funds to be raised under this Act as shall be, from time to time, fixed by the Governor in Council. Provided that the allowances for any Commissioner shall not exceed the rate of ten thousand Rupees a year if the Commissioner holds no other appointment or occupation; or the rate of four thousand Rupees a year if he holds any other appointment or occupation."

That provision adopted the principle laid down by the Council in the Municipal Bill for Calcutta. If there were to be seven Commissioners, he should like to know whether the Honorable Member for Bombay would have all of them paid Commissioners, or all of them unpaid Commissioners, or some of them paid and some unpaid. If all were to be paid, it would be an important question whether the Municipal Fund could afford to pay £7,000 a year instead of £3,000 a year for the purpose. The only public ground upon which the Honorable Member proposed the change in the Bill, was stated in the letter from the Acting Clerk of the Peace in Bombay to the Secretary to the Government of Bombay. Mr. Leathes said:—

"With reference to Section IV of the Bill, I am desired to state that the Bench consider that the proposition made by them, agreed to by the Bombay Government, and embodied in the Draft Act sent from Bombay to the Legislative Council, with reference to the appointment of seven Municipal Commissioners, should be adhered to."

But the Bench gave no reason why the proposition made by them should be adhered to.

The Acting Clerk of the Peace proceeded to say, in the next para. of his letter—

"The Bench consider, with reference to Section IX of the Bill, that the Municipal Commissioners should be under the supervision, direction, and control of Her Majesty's Justices in Sessions assembled, as proposed in Section X of the original Draft Bill."

But the Bench gave no reason for this opinion. The question of placing the Commissioners under the supervision and control of the Justices had been considered by the Select Committee on this Bill, and they made the following remarks on the subject in their original Report:—

"In considering the constitution of the Municipal body at Bombay, and the several communications on this subject which have from time to time been printed, we have felt ourselves bound to advert to the different aspect which this question has now assumed in consequence of the important duties connected with the drainage of the Town not being undertaken by the Government, as was contemplated when the scheme proposed by the Bill was discussed between the Government and the Justices. We concur in the opinion expressed by the Government and by some of the Justices, that a small number of well-paid Commissioners, not subject to minute supervision and control, but acting under a sense of personal responsibility, will constitute a body much better adapted for the convenient and speedy despatch of the ordinary current work of the Conservancy, than the seven Commissioners now proposed, who may be controlled in all their proceedings by a body so numerous and so uncertain as the Justices assembled in Sessions.

We therefore propose that there shall be at Bombay (as there is in each of the two other Presidency Towns) only three Commissioners, of whom one shall be an Officer appointed by Government, and two shall be elected by the Justices, and paid out of the Municipal Fund. We think that the Justices, who are presumed at Bombay in some degree to represent the whole body of rate-payers, should have both the privilege and the responsibility of electing two fit persons for this important office. We propose that the three Commissioners should ordinarily not be subject to check or control by the Justices; but with respect to new works involving a large expenditure of the Municipal Funds, we think that the Commissioners may with advantage be required to lay their proposals before the Justices before they are submitted to the Governor in Council for sanction; and we have so provided by Section IX of the Amended Bill."

The Select Committee, therefore, of whom the Honorable Member for Bombay was one, having duly weighed all the communications that had been placed before them on the subject, had recommended to the Council that the Commissioners should not be subject to the control of the Justices; and, in accordance with that recommendation, had inserted in the Bill the Section which now stood as Section IX, and which enacted as follows:—

"In the execution of this Act and the Incorporated Act, and of Act XIV of 1856, the Commissioners shall not be subject to any check or control on the part of the Justices. Provided that, in respect of any work for the execution of which the consent or sanction of the local Government is necessary under any of the said Acts, and in respect of the regulation of the salaries of Officers appointed under any of the said Acts, the Commissioners shall, before making application to Government, submit a plan of the work or a Schedule of the salaries for the approval of the Justices. When any such plan or Schedule is disapproved by the Justices, the Commissioners, if they see fit, may refer the matter for the decision of the Governor in Council."

The Council had adopted this Section in a Committee of the whole Council, as also Section IV of the amended Bill, which provided that the number of Commissioners should be three, and that of these, one should be appointed by the local Government, and the other two be elected by the Justices,—and Section VIII, which provided that the Commissioners should receive salaries for their services. He thought that the views taken by the Select Committee were correct, and that no sufficient ground had been shewn for inducing the Council to change the resolution to which it had already come with respect to them. The Government of Bombay themselves did not advocate the change very strongly. They said:—

"The Governor in Council agrees with the Bench in the opinions expressed throughout the remainder of the Acting Clerk's letter, with the exception of its 4th and 5th paragraphs. With respect to the matters to which these two paragraphs refer, the Select Committee correctly observed that Government was reluctantly brought to consent to a scheme of Municipal management involving the continuance of seven Commissioners, acting under the supervision, direction, and control of the Justices; but having done so, his Lordship in Council is unwilling to retract the assent already given by him to the adoption of that scheme; and he considers the avoidance of further delay in passing the Municipal Bill so important, that he would, at any rate, feel disinclined from renewing a discussion which might possibly cause additional obstruction."

These were the only reasons before the Council in support of the proposed alteration. They were followed by a paragraph which was against it. The paragraph said:—

"I am, however, directed to state that the Honorable Mr. Reeves, who was not a Member of this Government when the matter was originally discussed, wishes that you should be made aware of his opinion that the substitution of seven Commissioners for the three proposed in the Select Committee's Amended Draft Act, would most injuriously affect the Municipal Constitution of Bombay."

He (Mr. Peacock) was certainly of the same opinion; and he thought that the Council, having once come to the conclusion in a Committee of the whole Council that there should be only three Commissioners, should require some stronger reasons than those which had as yet been brought forward to induce it to vary its opinion.

MR. LEGEYT'S Motion was then put and negatived, and the Section passed as it stood.

Section IX provided that the Commissioners should not be under the control of the Justices.

MR. LEGEYT said, after the resolution to which the Council had just come, it would perhaps be superfluous to press an alteration which he intended to propose in this Section. The object of that alteration was to restore the control of the Justices over the proceedings of the Commissioners. When the question was discussed in Select Committee, he did not oppose the reduction of the number of the Board of Commissioners from seven to three; but he did oppose the removal of the Commissioners from the control of the Justices, and he still continued of opinion that such a measure was not likely to be attended by any particular good. He was also satisfied that it would create a strong feeling of disfavor among the Natives of Bombay. The Justices had exercised control over the Municipal disbursements and arrangements of the Island for many years. That they had done so with good effect in the main, was universally admitted. They had also lately come forward in a most liberal manner, and suggested the imposition of new taxes upon themselves and the community at large for improvements which would place Bombay far beyond any other town in India as far as municipal advantages were concerned. It was now proposed to deprive them of all control over the Commissioners; and they naturally said—"We have done all this for Bombay; we have swayed the community by our influence to assent to a town duty which will raise large funds; we have done all that the authorities have asked of us; and what do we get in return? We are pushed aside; we are told—'We do not want you any longer; we will deprive you of that voice which you have hitherto had in the management of the municipal funds, and in the supervision of public works which have hitherto been carried out with those funds under your control.'" It appeared to him that, under the circumstances, the Justices had considerable reason to complain. As he had said just now, the belief in Bombay was that, if the Board should be reduced to three Commissioners, the control over public works in the Island would altogether pass away from the body which had hitherto exercised such control over it. And he must say a very happy influence it had been; because it had enabled the Board of Conservancy to carry out improvements without any of those petty acts of opposition which check such improvements beyond anything else, to a surprising extent. When the provision for removing the Commissioners from the control of the Justices was promulgated in Bombay, a universal cry was raised there against it amongst the Natives. He did not say that there was a unanimous feeling in the Bench of Justices, that the present state of things should be retained. The Bench consisted partly of European and partly of Native Justices; and the Europeans were not so nearly affected by the local improvements and local conservancy department as the Natives were. It was the Native members that felt the hardship of the proposed change, which would involve the loss to them of the influence and dignity which, in their estimation, attached to the office of a Justice of the Peace. He thought it would be extremely unwise to diminish the influence which the Bench of Justices had hitherto possessed. They had hitherto exercised it entirely for good. He did not know one single instance in which the power had been exercised except for the good of the town and of the community. There was a feeling amongst the Native Justices that they formed part and parcel of the Government by reason of their holding a Commission of the Peace; and very often, in times of difficulty, particularly in the riots between Parsees and Mahommedans, some few years since, they had interposed, and exerted an unseen influence to put down the disturbances. He thought, therefore, that in remodelling the Municipal Commission, and in imposing new taxes upon the community to the extent of five lacs of Rupees a year, which the scheme provided in this Bill contemplated, the Council should not offend the feelings which had hitherto been usefully and loyally employed for the common good. He felt no inclination to give any undue importance to the political status of the Justices; but it was undeniable that they were a most useful body of men; and if the community of Bombay were to be deprived of their presence, he was convinced that many months would not elapse before their loss would be felt and deplored. He must also say that he did feel that there was a compact between the Government and the Justices on this subject, which ought not to be disregarded. The Government had distinctly consented that the Justices should have control over the municipal funds; and he thought it would not be right for this Council to come between them and the Justices, and place the Bench on a scale lower than that which it had hitherto occupied, by depriving it of the influence and power at present vested in it. He, therefore, begged to move that Section IX of the Bill be left out, and that the following new Section be substituted for it:—

"In execution of this Act and of Act XIV of 1856, and in administering the Municipal Fund, the Commissioners, in all matters other than such as are by the said Act expressly mentioned to be subject to control by the Government or its Officers, shall be under the supervision, direction, and control of the said Justices in Sessions assembled, or of such other persons as the Governor in Council may appoint to supervise and control the Fund. Provided that, in the event of the said Justices or such other persons as aforesaid rejecting any measure submitted for their sanction by the Commissioners, it shall be lawful for the Commissioners, if they see fit, to refer the matter to the Governor in Council, whose decision thereon shall be final."

MR. CURRIE said, he had been under the impression that the vote which the Council had just come to upon Section IV carried with it the whole of the alterations made by the Select Committee with respect to the constitution of the Municipal Body. Of course, it was open to the Hon'ble Member to move his amendment; but it seemed to him that the amendment was hardly consistent with the vote which the Council had just given on the last Motion.

With regard to the objection urged by the Honorable Member against this Section, that it seemed to him to set aside the Justices, and to cast a slight upon them—he (Mr. Currie) was certainly of opinion that the Justices ought not to be set aside; and it had been the endeavor of the Select Committee to reserve to them all the authority which they could properly reserve, and which the Justices could usefully exercise. It was impossible that so large and uncertain a body as a Bench of seventy Justices could exercise a beneficial control over all the details of the proceedings of the Executive Board. The Bill reserved to the Justices the election of the majority of the Municipal Commissioners. It also provided that no increase should be made in the house-rate except upon their representation; that the accounts of the Municipal Fund should be laid before them periodically, in order to enable them to perform this duty; and that no new work involving large expenditure should be submitted to the Government for sanction without having been first laid before them for their approval; and it further gave them control over the salaries of the establishments which might be appointed by the Commissioners. In all this, he thought the Council had reserved to the Justices all the powers which they could exercise with advantage.

The Honorable Member had said that the Native Justices would feel very strongly the change made by the amended Bill in their power of control and superintendence; but judging from the Report he (Mr. Currie) had read of the proceedings at the Meeting of Justices at which the constitution of the Municipal Body was taken into consideration, he thought that there could hardly be any strong feeling on the subject, since only twelve out of some seventy Justices attended the Meeting, and out of them, five at least must have been Europeans.

MR. LEGEYT'S Motion was then put. The Council divided:—

Aye 1.	*Noes* 7.
Mr. LeGeyt.	Mr. Forbes.
	Mr. Harington.
	Mr. Currie.
	Mr. Peacock.
	Mr. Ricketts.
	Mr. Grant.
	The Chairman.

Section X provided an annual rate of five per cent. on houses, buildings, and lands, subject to the proviso that the local Government might, on the representation of the Justices, fix any higher annual rate not exceeding 7½ per cent. It further provided that, "any rate so fixed shall be published in the Government Gazette before the commencement of the year in which such rate is to have effect"

MR. LEGEYT moved that this last provision be left out of the Section.

MR. CURRIE said, he had to apologize to the Council for troubling it so often; but it fell to him, as the only remaining Member of the Select Committee on the Bill, to answer the Motions which were being brought forward.

He confessed he did not see the object of the Motion just made. He did not understand upon what grounds the Honorable Member proposed to omit the last part of the Section. The Section provided that the five per cent. rate on houses should be an annual rate; the proviso provided that the rate which might be imposed in lieu of it, should be an annual rate; and the incorporated Act XXV of 1856 provided for an annual valuation and assessment. Every thing shewed that the rate was to be an annual one; and surely, if the Government determined to fix for any year a rate in excess of the ordinary rate prescribed, they ought to give notice of it before the commencement of the year in which it was to have effect. It, therefore, appeared to him that the words which the Honorable Member proposed to omit from the Section, were necessary. The Government said, in their letter to the Justices, that they would wish them to consider the provision in the 10th Section of the Bill—

"that extraordinary rates of assessment must be published in the Government Gazette before the commencement of the year in which the assessment is to be levied, which would possibly be before the necessity of the enhancement of the rate could be apparent."

But surely, if an extraordinary rate was to be levied in any year, the necessity for levying it must be apparent before the commencement of the year.

After some discussion, Mr. LeGeyt, with the leave of the Council, withdrew his Motion.

Section XIII provided that—

"The Commissioners may exempt from assessment any house, building, or land, the annual value whereof is less than twelve Rupees, if the same be the sole rateable property of the owner."

MR. LEGEYT moved two amendments in the Section;—first, that the word "may" after the word "Commissioners" in the first line of the Section be left out, and the word "shall" be substituted for it; and secondly, that the word "twelve" before the word "Rupees" be left out, and the word "twenty-four" be substituted for it. The reasons, he said, given by the Government of Bombay for these amendments, were to be found in paragraphs 2 and 3 of their Resolution dated the 17th of March 1858. The Justices stated in paragraph 7 of their letter to the Government as follows:—

"With reference to Section XIII, the Bench agree with Government that the sum justifying exemption from the rate on houses and lands should be at least double the amount proposed by the Legislative Council; but they are still of opinion that the annual value of forty-eight Rupees originally proposed would be the proper amount, and that the exemption should be absolute by law."

He had always understood that the practice in Bombay was not to assess any building of which the annual value was less than forty-eight Rupees; but in some of the annexures to the Bill, he saw it stated that twenty Rupees had been adopted as the limit. He was not certain which of these two figures was the correct one; but the reason advanced for not levying an assessment on these small tenements was that the proceeds of the tax were extremely small, and while the payment of it would be very inconvenient to the poorest class of the inhabitants, the expense and trouble of collecting it would never be repaid. He quite concurred with the Government of Bombay and the Justices that all buildings of which the annual rent was under twenty-four Rupees should be exempted from the assessment.

MR. CURRIE said, he had no objection to urge against the first amendment proposed. With respect to the second, he would merely say that the Select Committee, finding no reason alleged for so high a minimum as forty-eight Rupees, had thought it right to substitute for it twelve Rupees, which was the minimum already approved of for Calcutta and Madras. In Calcutta, it did not seem from the Report of the

Municipal Commissioners for last year that twelve Rupees had been found to be an inconvenient limit. It appeared, however, that heretofore the limit in Bombay had been twenty Rupees; and with reference to that circumstance, and to the reasons which had now been assigned by the Governor in Council, he should have no objection to adopt the limit of twenty-four Rupees proposed by the Government.

MR. RICKETTS said, it appeared to him that it should be the object of the Council that the houses in Bombay and in the other Presidency Towns should be improved; but if the Council were to substitute "shall" for "may" in the Section, any person who made his tenement a little worse than it now was, so as to depreciate its annual value below twenty-four Rupees, would be entitled to claim exemption from the assessment as a matter of right, whereas, in its present form, the Section would leave it to the discretion of the Commissioners to make the exemption or not.

THE CHAIRMAN said, his doubt about the proposed amendments did not arise from the fear expressed by the Honorable Member who had spoken last that the owners of small tenements in Bombay would, as it were, cut off their noses to spite their faces, by living in bad houses in order to escape the tax. That risk the Council must run whether they made the exemption imperative or discretionary. The consideration suggested by his Honorable Friend was no doubt in favor of the second amendment. But on the first amendment, he (the Chairman) greatly doubted, notwithstanding what was said by the Governor of Bombay in Council, whether it was expedient to substitute "shall" for "may" in this Clause. If the exemption were made imperative, you must needs give to every person who was not exempted from assessment, the means of questioning the decision of the Commissioners. He did not know what means the Bill as it stood would give; whether it would give a regular appeal to the Board of Justices, or leave the party aggrieved to contest the validity of the assessment in an ordinary Court of Justice. He would, however, observe that no one who had had any experience in assessing the value of small tenements—and, as he had once acted as a revising Barrister, he had some slight experience that way—but must be aware that on no kind of issue were you more apt to encounter a mass of contradictory evidence upon which it was extremely difficult to come to a conclusion. If, therefore, there was to be an appeal from the decision of the Commissioners, as there must be if it were obligatory upon them to exempt from assessment tenements of which the value was below a given sum, the Act would open a door to a great deal of litigation, and might subject the Commissioners and the Municipal Fund to much inconvenience and expense. All exemptions from a general tax on the ground of poverty were matters of favor rather than matters of right; and on the whole, he thought that it was preferable to leave this exemption from assessment to the discretion of the Commissioners, trusting to them for a fair and judicious exercise of the power.

He fully concurred in the proposal to raise the value of the tenements to be exempted from twelve to twenty-four Rupees.

MR. GRANT said, the word "may" was used in the corresponding Section of the Act for Calcutta, and he was pretty sure that it was used there advisedly, for the very reason mentioned by the Honorable Chairman. The question of the property assessed being "the sole rateable property of the owner" was one likely to lead to litigation, as well as the question of value. Therefore, in every point of view, it appeared to him that it would be better to leave exemption from assessment under the Act to the discretion of the Commissioners.

MR. PEACOCK said, he certainly thought it better, for the reasons suggested by the Honorable Chairman and the Honorable Member who had spoken last, to retain the word "may" in preference to the word "shall."

With respect to the maximum sum which should justify exemption from assessment, he would observe that the tax would be a tax, not on occupiers, but on owners. The reason given by the Bombay Government for making the maximum sum forty-eight Rupees instead of twenty-four Rupees per annum, was as follows:—

"In Bombay, where the cost of living is so much greater than in Calcutta or Madras, it seems scarcely equitable to tax the property of persons whose only means of livelihood may be a shed let for a rent barely sufficient for their subsistence."

But it was scarcely probable that any owner who let his house or shed either for twenty-four Rupees or forty-eight Rupees a year, lived upon the rent alone. If any such case existed, the Commissioners could exempt it under the word "may."

MR. LEGEYT said, the occupier would be the owner generally, though he perceived that the Government stated the contrary. He did not think that they were right. He would, with the leave of the Council, withdraw his first amendment; but he must press the second.

The first Motion was by leave withdrawn.

The second Motion was then put, and agreed to.

Section XVII provided that—

"Every person who may have owned or had charge of any vehicle or animal kept within the said town for any number of days in any quarter, shall be liable to the whole tax for that quarter."

MR. LEGEYT said that the Government of Bombay had written as follows in reference to this Section :—

"The Governor in Council considers that in Section XVII the substitution of the words "any number of" for the words "a period exceeding thirty," in Section XIX of the Original Bill, is not an improvement. His Lordship in Council has no reason for believing that the frauds which, in the Select Committee's observations on this Section, are stated to occur in Calcutta, prevail in Bombay. Government do not, however, object to the alteration which will be effected by Section XVIII of the new Bill."

The Select Committee in their Report said that the Section corresponded with Section V of the Suburban Roads Bill as settled in Committee of the whole Council, and that the alterations were intended to prevent the frauds, by fictitious transfers of vehicles, &c., which had been found to occur under the Calcutta Act XXVIII of 1856. As, however, the Authorities in Bombay stated that such frauds were not practised in that Presidency, and they preferred the more liberal provision contained in the draft Bill which they had sent up, and which did now stand in the Calcutta and Madras Bills, he hoped that the Council would see no objection to restoring the Section to the form in which it originally stood. He, therefore, moved that the words "any number of days in any quarter shall be liable to the whole tax for that quarter," at the end of the Section, be left out, and the following words substituted for them :—

"A period exceeding thirty days in any quarter, shall be liable to the whole tax for that quarter. If the period do not exceed thirty days, no tax shall be chargeable for that quarter. Provided that, when any person owning or having charge of any vehicle or animal, shall transfer the same to another person, he shall give notice thereof to the Commissioners within one week of the date of such transfer; or, if he fail to give such notice, shall be liable to the whole tax for the quarter, although the period during which he may have owned or had charge of such vehicle or animal, shall not have exceeded thirty days."

MR. CURRIE said, if the Section were restored to its original form, the Commissioners appointed under the Act would not thank the Honorable Member for it. The object of the change made in the Section by the Select Committee, was to obviate in Bombay an abuse which had actually arisen here under the Calcutta Act. In consequence of a representation made by the Municipal Commissioners on the subject, a similar alteration had been made in the Suburban Roads Bill. In England, if a person had possession of a horse for any portion of the period for which the tax was levied, he had to pay the tax for the whole of that period. It might be that, under this rule, the same horse might be paid for twice; but he saw no objection to that, as it amounted to but a small tax on the transfer.

MR. HARINGTON said, although the Council had the assurance of the Honorable the Governor in Council at Bombay that the frauds stated to be practised by certain classes in Calcutta in order to avoid payment of the tax upon their conveyances, to which they were liable under the Bengal Act, were not known at Bombay, he thought these frauds were likely to prove contagious, and he doubted not that, at no distant date, the infection would find its way into the Presidency; in which case, as remarked by the Honorable Member for

Mr. Peacock

Bengal, the Commissioners under the Act would not thank him for the alteration which he proposed to introduce into the Section. But as the Bill did not appear to contemplate that any vehicle or animal should pay the tax more than once for any quarter, he was of opinion that a provision to that effect should be added to the Section, and it was his intention to move such addition in the event of the amendment proposed by the Honorable Member for Bombay not being carried.

MR. PEACOCK said, he thought that the better way would be to make a person who had had possession of a horse or carriage during any portion of a quarter, pay the tax for that quarter. That was the principle adopted in England in regard to the assessed taxes, and it was a rule which appeared to him to rest on a sound principle. The provision in the Calcutta Act that no tax should be chargeable where a person had possession of a carriage or horse for less than thirty days, had led to frauds in many cases. The Commissioners, in their Report for the last year, stated that cases like this had occurred. A party of four gentlemen—if, indeed, persons who could be guilty of such devices could be called gentlemen—kept a carriage between them, and collusively transferred the property from one to another every month, and so avoided the tax. Now, he thought the Legislative Council ought not to allow itself to be laughed at in that way, and that it ought to provide that, if a person kept a horse or carriage for any part of a quarter, he should pay the tax, which was a very small one, for the whole quarter. The principle was that, if a person could keep a horse or carriage for his luxury or convenience, he should contribute towards the Municipal Fund. You judge of his capability to contribute by what he keeps. The Bill imposed taxes on what the poor actually consumed—such as rice, ghee, and even fire-wood; and he did think that a gentleman who kept a horse for his comfort for any portion of a quarter, ought to pay seven Rupees towards the Municipal Fund for that quarter.

MR. GRANT said, the Council had to choose between two principles—would it tax a carriage or horse once only every quarter?—or would it tax every owner of a carriage for what he had kept up within the quarter? If the Council resolved to tax a carriage or horse only once every quarter, perhaps the best way would be to make that person pay whose property the carriage or horse might be on quarter-day. The first thing, however, to be done was to determine which of the two principles should be adopted.

THE CHAIRMAN said, take it as one would, as there was to be no registration, the Commissioners must depend upon the returns which would be made by the tax payers; and therefore, the plan suggested by the Honorable Member who had spoken last, seemed to him the best mode of carrying out the object which the Honorable Member of the North Western Provinces had in view.

The question being put, the Council divided:—

Ayes 2	*Noes* 6
Mr. LeGeyt.	Mr. Forbes.
The Chairman.	Mr. Harington.
	Mr. Currie.
	Mr. Peacock.
	Mr. Ricketts.
	Mr. Grant.

MR. PEACOCK moved that the words "number of days in any" before the word "quarter" in the 5th line of the Section be left out, in order that the words "portion of a" might be substituted for them. In doing so, he said he had no objection to give the Commissioners power to exempt any person from the tax in respect of a horse and carriage which he kept for any portion of a quarter only for the purposes of business or trade.

MR. CURRIE said, he had no objection to a verbal alteration like the one proposed, except that it might throw some doubt on the interpretation of the wording of the Suburban Roads Act, which adopted the phrase "any number of days."

MR. PEACOCK said, "any number of days" would not mean one day; and it was better to make the amendment in the present Bill, leaving the Act relating to the Suburban Roads to be amended when necessary.

The Motion was put, and agreed to.

MR. HARINGTON moved that the following Proviso be added to the Section:—

"Provided that no more than one payment of the tax shall be required in any quarter on any such vehicle or animal; and that, where any change of ownership in respect of any vehicle or animal shall have taken place during any quarter, the person who may have owned or had charge of the vehicle or animal on the first day of the quarter shall pay the tax for the whole quarter."

MR. CURRIE said, he must beg to offer the most decided opposition to this amendment. If it was thought right that the tax on a particular carriage or animal should be paid only once a quarter, it was much better that the payment by each person who had been the owner, should be adjusted according to the portion of the quarter during which he had possessed it. The amendment now proposed, would be quite impracticable.

MR. PEACOCK said although the tax was called a tax on the carriage, it in reality was a tax on the owner in respect of the carriage. It was not the particular carriage that was taxed. Suppose a man kept a pie-bald horse: the tax imposed would be, not upon the piebald horse, but upon the owner for keeping it. If he sold the horse and purchased another during the same quarter, he would still be liable to the tax. If a man could afford to keep a horse for his luxury or convenience during any portion of a quarter, he could afford to pay seven Rupees for municipal purposes for that quarter. It would be impossible for the Commissioners, in every case where a horse might have changed hands, to discover in whose possession it was during particular portions of the quarter.

THE CHAIRMAN said, the fallacy of that argument was that, in most of these cases, the fact of keeping a horse or vehicle for a short time was not a test of the ability of the person keeping it to contribute in a larger degree to the Municipal Fund. Suppose the case of a man whose means enabled him to keep a horse and gig, and to keep no more. His horse broke down, and he had to get rid of that and buy another. Perhaps he bought the new horse before he could get rid of the old one, and for a few days both remained in his stable. His means, his presumable capacity to contribute to the Municipal Fund, remained the same; yet, if the Clause stood as the Honorable and learned Member would have it, he would be made to pay a double tax.

The Motion was then put, and negatived.

THE CHAIRMAN then moved that the following Proviso be added to the Section:—

"Provided that, in case any such person has kept or had charge of any vehicle or animal for a period less than thirty days, the Commissioners may remit any portion of the tax payable in respect of such vehicle or animal not exceeding two-thirds of the tax for the quarter."

MR. CURRIE said, this Proviso would be subject to the same sort of frauds which the Section in the Act for Calcutta had been found subject to.

THE CHAIRMAN said, if a man had kept two vehicles for say three weeks, but parted with one of them after that time, he would, under the Section as it now stood, have to pay a quarter's tax for both. His (the Chairman's) Proviso would make him liable for only one month's tax for the vehicle which he had kept only three weeks. He did not see that this provision was open to the Honorable Member's objection. The fraud of which he understood the Municipal Commissioners to complain was this. Two or three Baboos kept a carriage between them, each for only twenty-eight days, and so evaded the tax. Now, he would catch each of those three Baboos. He would not take a quarter's tax from each; but he would take at least a month's tax from each; and so the Fund would not lose by the change of ownership, whether it was colorable and fraudulent, or real and *boná fide*.

MR. PEACOCK said, he should prefer to leave the Section as it stood, except as to those horses and carriages which were kept for the purposes of business or trade.

MR. LEGEYT asked, what the words "business or trade" would include? By far the greater number of the vehicles kept in Bombay were kept by clerks and assistants who lived eight or nine miles distant from the Fort, and were consequently obliged to keep conveyances to bring them to their offices. Upon this class, the tax would press most heavily, and any relief that could properly be afforded to them ought not to be withheld. He, therefore, should with great pleasure vote in favor of the Honorable and learned Chairman's Proviso.

MR. CURRIE said, he thought that the Proviso would increase the difficulties experienced in collecting the tax. If a person returned a false schedule, shewing a less number of horses than he had actually had in his possession, it might not be very difficult to prove that it was false; but it would be utterly impossible to prove the exact number of days that he might have had possession of a particular horse. He thought that the simpler the provisions were, the better, and should vote against the amendment.

MR. GRANT said, if he thought that this Proviso would really make the collection of the tax difficult, he should vote against it; but it only gave a discretionary power to the Commissioners. It left it optional with them to remit a certain portion of a quarter's tax in respect of a horse or carriage kept for less than thirty days; and the proof that a carriage or horse had been kept for less than thirty days, would be on the person who claimed the remission. If he could not give such proof, he would not get the remission. And certainly, the Proviso was consistent with the principle of the carriage and horse-tax. This tax was not levied as an item of general revenue; its object was that every man should pay for the use which he makes of the roads. The Municipality repaired the roads; there were no turnpikes on them; and, therefore, all who used them with horses and vehicles ought to pay their fair share for the repairs. The strict principle would be to make a man pay so much a day; but that would be too complex in practice. The tax was made payable quarterly for the sake of convenience; but if a person used the roads only one day, it was hard to make him pay for ninety days. It appeared to him that the proposed Proviso sufficiently met in a rough way the justice of the case, and he should vote in support of it.

MR. PEACOCK said, with reference to what had fallen from the Honorable Member for Bombay, it appeared to him that there would not be one case in five hundred in which a person situated as the Honorable Member described, would keep a carriage for only a portion of a quarter, unless he gave up his business. The real objection which he saw against the Proviso was the difficulty in the collection of the tax to which the Honorable Member for Bengal had adverted. Under the Section as it stood, no such difficulty would arise.

The amendment being put, the Council divided:—

Ayes 4	*Noes* 4
Mr. Harington,	Mr. Forbes,
Mr. LeGeyt,	Mr. Currie,
Mr. Grant,	Mr. Peacock,
The Chairman.	Mr. Ricketts.

The numbers being equal, the Chairman gave a casting vote with the Ayes.

Section XXVI provided as follows:—

"All monies received by the Commissioners or paid to their credit by virtue of this Act, or of Act XIV of 1856, or of any other Act or Regulation, and all fines and penalties imposed and levied by the Court of Petty Sessions or by any Magistrate of Police or Justice of the Peace within the said Town, and all sums of money collected on account of fees for licenses granted under Act V of 1842, shall form a Fund which shall be called the Municipal Fund of Bombay."

MR. CURRIE said, in consequence of the alteration made to-day in Section I on the motion of the Honorable Member for Bombay, it would be necessary to amend this Section. The Council had acceded to the Honorable Member's wish to increase the Municipal Fund by the fees leviable under Section XIII Chapter II of Regulation XIX. 1827; but, as the Bill stood, the appropriation of those fees was not provided for. The fees were to be realized by the Collector. Act XI of 1845 had provided that they should go to the Municipal Fund; but that Act was repealed by the present Bill; and, therefore, there was now no provision for the appropriation of the fees. He had pointed this out to the Honorable Member, but the Honorable Member seemed to think that it was of no consequence, and that the Governor in Council might do what he pleased with the fees. He (Mr. Currie) thought that, if the fees were levied at all, they should go to the Municipal Fund; and as the Honorable Member would make no Motion on the subject, he (Mr. Currie) would move that the words and figures "or Section XIII Chapter II Regulation XIX. 1827 of the Bombay Code" be inserted after the figures "1842" in the 11th line of the Section, so that the fees collected under that provision should form an asset of the Municipal Fund.

Agreed to.

Section XXVIII placed the Municipal Fund under the management of the Commissioners, and directed that it should be applied "to the purposes of the Act, and the incorporated Act, and of Act XIV of 1856; and to the execution of any public works tending to the improvement of the said Town, which may be sanctioned by the Governor in Council, although not expressly mentioned in the Acts."

MR. LEGEYT moved that the words "or any measures connected with the comfort and health of the inhabitants" be inserted after the word "Town" in the 14th line of the Section. The Justices had recommended the insertion of these words in their letter to the Government of Bombay.

MR. CURRIE said, he thought the words proposed, were quite unnece sary. The Section had been framed by the Select Committee; and when they framed it, they had before them Section XIII of Act XI of 1845, which empowered the Justices to construct any "public works, tending to the improvement of the Town, connected with the comfort and health of the inhabitants thereof." The Select Committee thought that, in taking the general words which they did, in lieu of those used in the Section, they would provide for all that was necessary. Any measures of a public nature connected with the comfort and health of the inhabitants of a town, must be included in the terms "public works tending to the improvement of the town." He, therefore, thought the amendment quite unnecessary; and as no alteration should be made in a Bill already settled in a Committee of the whole Council without good and sufficient reason, he should vote against it.

The Motion was put, and negatived.

Section XXXI provided as follows:—

"The Commissioners shall carry out, with as little delay as possible, such a complete system of sewerage and drainage within the said Town as shall be directed by the Governor in Council; and until such system of sewerage and drainage has been completed, and all the expenses thereof defrayed, and all monies bor[rowed] for the payment of such expenses and interest thereon have been repaid, shall set [apart] for the purposes above-mentioned, out [of the] Municipal Fund, an annual sum not less than two hundred and fifty thousand Rupees. If such system of sewerage and drainage has been completed, and all the expenses thereof defrayed, and all monies borrowed for the payment of such expenses and interest thereon have been repaid, before the expenses incurred by Government for the construction of the said Vehar Water-works shall have been repaid, the said annual sum of two hundred and fifty thousand Rupees shall be added to the sum of one hundred and seventy-five thousand Rupees directed by the preceding Section to be appropriated annually to the repayment of the expenses of the said works."

MR. LEGEYT moved that the words—

"carry out, with as little delay as possible, such a complete system of sewerage and drainage within the said Town as shall be directed by the Governor in Council; and until such system of sewerage and drainage has been completed, and all the expenses thereof defrayed, and all monies borrowed for the payment of such expenses and interest thereon have been repaid, shall"—

after the word "shall" in the 1st line of Section XXXI, be left out, and the following words substituted for them, namely:—

"Until such a complete system of sewerage and drainage within the said Town, as shall be agreed upon between the Governor in Council and the Bench of Justices, shall have been completed and all the expenses thereof defrayed, and all monies borrowed for the payment of such expenses and interest thereon shall have been repaid,"

He said, this alteration was necessary, for there had been a sort of an agreement between the Government of Bombay and the Justices that the system of sewerage and drainage should be carried out by the former. It was at the suggestion of the Government of Bombay that he moved his amendment. The Government thought that the amendment would meet the difficulty of the case. He himself believed that it would, and hoped that the Council would see no objection to its adoption.

MR. CURRIE said, this Bill gave the Municipal Commissioners of Bombay a very large increase of revenue, and one of the principal objects for which that increase had been proposed and acceded to, was a complete reform of the sewerage and drainage of the Town. The Select Committee had thought it right that the Bill should contain a specific provision that such a system of sewerage and drainage should be carried out as speedily as possible, and that a certain portion of the Municipal Fund should be appropriated to that object. Accordingly, they had inserted Section XXXI. The amendment proposed by the Honorable Member was open to the objection that it did not provide expressly that such a system of sewerage and drainage should be carried out. It only provided that a certain sum should be reserved for the purpose. It was very important that there should be an express provision in the Bill requiring that the work, for which a large portion of the Municipal Fund was to be raised, should be carried out with all practicable speed; and if such a work was to be carried out, the proper persons to superintend it were, he thought, the Board of Commissioners. They would be able to do this more efficiently and satisfactorily than any Officers appointed by Government. He did not know whether the manner in which the Vehar Water-works had been carried out under the superintendence of Government had been such as to give satisfaction. But however that might be, the Municipal Commissioners were certainly the proper persons for carrying out a system of sewerage and drainage within the town. In Calcutta, the subject of improving the drainage of the town had been before the Government for more than twenty years. Reports on schemes of sewerage and drainage had been called for and laid aside; and the question was at last brought to a practical issue by the Municipal Commissioners. The Secretary to the Municipal Commissioners had proposed a plan of drainage which had been submitted to the Commissioners, and by them laid before the Government. It had been examined by Officers of Government, and approved by them in all material points. To the Municipal Commissioners, then, was due the praise of having brought the long-conceived project of reforming the drainage of Calcutta to a practical issue. He understood that the Bombay Government proposed to contribute from the Abkaree duties a large portion of the amount necessary for draining the Town, and it might perhaps impose as a condition of such contribution that the execution of the work should be left in its own hands. If such were the case, he should be unwilling to offer any opposition to the amendment; but unless it were so, he should prefer to leave the Section unaltered. At any rate, the amendment moved by the Honorable Member would require some alteration; because, in its present form, it pledged no one to the carrying out of that which was so necessary—a complete system of sewerage and drainage for Bombay.

Mr. LeGeyt said, the Honorable Member had re-opened a very large question, and one which, at this distance from Bombay, was more or less involved in obscurity. It was difficult to see exactly how the question lay at this moment. He believed that the Government, in paragraph 5 of their letter, had exactly hit upon the best course which could possibly be pursued in the case; and he did think that it would be most injudicious in the Council by any vote to tie up the hands of the Government, or to insist on any duty being performed by the Commissioners which the Government, after full consideration, had engaged, with the consent of the Municipality, to take into its own hands. If the Council did this, it would be doing Bombay a grievous and serious injury. He could not see the least reason to object to the proposition of the Government that this part of the Act should be a sort of declaration as to the existing state of things between the Government and the Municipality. The question relative to the Vehar Works was still an open one between them. A final reference on the subject was now before the Court of Directors. The Municipality hoped for a satisfactory result from that reference, and the Government had recommended that a compromise on the points of contention should be allowed. The state of the drainage question stands thus at the present moment. The Municipality had come forward, and done their part. They had agreed to contribute two and a half lacs a year towards the drainage. The Government, in their letter to the Justices dated the 19th March 1857, proposed, subject to the orders of the Government of India—

"That Government should undertake to expend in the construction of the works requisite for the introduction of a reformed system of drains and sewers in Bombay, in addition to a sum to be contributed (estimated at two lacs and fifty thousand Rupees) from the Municipal Fund for the like purpose, such amount as may be realized by Government over and above the present Abkaree and Customs Revenue from country spirits manufactured in or imported into Bombay by increasing the duty on such spirits so as to raise the same to one Rupee per gallon, the rate in force at Calcutta. It is roughly estimated that the increase of Revenue from the additional duty will amount to about two lacs and fifty thousand Rupees."

The Municipality accepted this proposal, and were perfectly willing to hand over the sum of two and a half lacs a year towards the carrying out of an efficient system of sewerage and drainage. The Government also proposed to take the work into their own hands, because they considered that they could do it better than the Municipality.

With respect to the Honorable Member's question regarding the Vehar Waterworks, he was prepared to say that those works *had* given satisfaction. No public work in India of the same magnitude had been so speedily and so efficiently carried out as they had been. Of course, as happened in the case of all public works of a similar nature, the actual outlay for the works had exceeded the estimate; but it was to be observed that these important works had been commenced upon and carried out in the short space of three years, and that they might have been used this year in supplying Bombay with water if there had been any pressing need for it. He was by no means persuaded that, if the system of sewerage and drainage were not left with the Government of Bombay, the Government would not say—"If we cannot carry out the work in our own way, we will take no further trouble in the matter." If the Government were allowed to carry out the sewerage and drainage, no difficulty would occur; and it would be a thousand pities if this Council were, by its vote, to let a work of so much importance to the Town of Bombay—of importance second in degree only to that of the introduction of water into Bombay—remain unexecuted, or be executed in an inefficient manner. He should, therefore, press his Motion.

THE CHAIRMAN said, he thought it would be better to adopt the suggestion of the Government of Bombay, which seemed to have been fully considered, and to be approved of by the community as represented by the Board of Justices. The only argument of the Honorable Member for Bengal which at all moved his mind was that the Section, as proposed to be amended, would not make the duty of carrying out a system of sewerage and drainage quite so imperative on the Commissioners as the Section in its present form made it; but on the other hand, although this was now declared to be their duty, it was so expressed as to leave it a duty of imperfect obligation. The words were—"The Commissioners shall carry out with as little delay as possible, such a complete system of sewerage and drainage within the said town as shall be directed by the Governor in Council." There was, therefore, something which the Governor in Council must first determine; and then, there would remain the very wide issue—"What was 'as little delay as possible?'" The real stringency of the existing Sections consisted in the provision which required a certain portion of the Municipal Fund to be set apart until a system of sewerage and drainage was carried out, and which forbade its application to any other purposes. That provision would remain if the Section were amended in the way proposed.

MR. GRANT asked if the Council was to understand that both the Government of Bombay and the Public of Bombay as represented by the Justices, were in favor of the change advocated by the Honorable Mover of the amendment?

MR. LEGEYT replied, entirely.

MR. PEACOCK said, he did not understand the question to be whether the Government or the Commissioners should carry out a system of sewerage and drainage, but whether there was any thing in the Act to compel the Government to carry out such a system. He thought that the Council might safely rely on the Government of Bombay, and that the system would be carried out efficiently as soon as the plan of operations should have been determined on, and the necessary funds were available.

MR. LEGEYT'S Motion was then put and agreed to, and the Section passed.

The Council having resumed its sitting, the Bill was reported.

MR. LEGEYT moved that the Bill be read a third time and passed.

The Motion was carried, and the Bill read a third time.

STATE OFFENCES.

MR. PEACOCK moved that the Council do resolve itself into a Committee on the Bill "to make further provision for the trial and punishment of offences against the State."

Agreed to.

The Bill passed through Committee with the addition of a Section limiting its duration until the end of the year 1859, and was reported.

MR. PEACOCK moved that the Bill be read a third time and passed.

The Motion was carried, and the Bill read a third time.

MR. PEACOCK moved that Mr. Ricketts be requested to take the above Bill to the President in Council in order that it may be submitted to the Governor General for his assent.

Agreed to.

MUNICIPAL ASSESSMENT (BOMBAY).

MR. LEGEYT moved that Mr. Ricketts be requested to take the Bill "for appointing Municipal Commissioners and for raising a Fund for Municipal purposes in the Town of Bombay" to the President in Council in order that it may be submitted to the Governor-General for his assent.

Agreed to.

ESTATE OF THE LATE NABOB OF THE CARNATIC.

MR. FORBES moved that a communication received by him from the Madras Government be laid upon the table and referred to the Select Committee on the Bill "to provide for the administration of the Estate and for the payment of the debts of the late Nabob of the Carnatic."

Agreed to.

MADRAS MARINE POLICE.

MR. FORBES moved that a communication received by him from the Madras Government be laid upon the table and referred to the Select Committee on the Bill "for the maintenance of a Police Force for the Port of Madras."

Agreed to.

The Council adjourned.

Saturday, July 3, 1858.

PRESENT:

The Honorable the Chief Justice, *Vice-President*, in the Chair.

Hon'ble J. P. Grant,	Hon. Sir A. W. Buller,
Hon'ble H. Ricketts,	H. B. Harington, Esq.
Hon'ble B. Peacock,	
P. W. LeGeyt, Esq.,	and
E. Currie, Esq.,	H. Forbes, Esq.

SUSPENSION OF SUITS AGAINST THE FAMILY &c. OF THE LATE NABOB OF THE CARNATIC.

THE VICE-PRESIDENT read a Message informing the Legislative Council that the Governor General had assented to the Bill "to continue for six months the privileges granted by Act I of 1844 to certain members of the family, household, and retinue of his late Highness the Nabob of the Carnatic."

ESTATE OF THE LATE NABOB OF THE CARNATIC.

THE CLERK presented to the Council a Petition from Mr. Alexander Orr, as Attorney of His Highness Prince Azeem Jah Bahadoor, praying the Council to delay further proceedings with the Bill "to provide for the administration of the estate and for the payment of the debts of the late Nabob of the Carnatic" until Saturday the 17th of July, to allow time for the arrival of an amended Petition from Prince Azeem Jah; or that His Highness be at once allowed to be heard by Counsel against the Bill, either before the Select Committee on the Bill, or before a Committee of the whole Council.

MR. PEACOCK said, it would be in the recollection of the Council that the Bill to which the Petition referred was read a first and second time on the 17th of March last. Afterwards, a communication was received from the Madras Government requesting that the Bill might be passed as quickly as possible. In consequence of that communication, he moved the suspension of the Standing Orders, in order that the Select Committee to whom the Bill had been referred might report upon it at the end of two months, instead of three, the period prescribed by the Standing Orders. On the 12th of June, Prince Azeem Jah presented a Petition to the Council describing himself as the Nabob of the Carnatic, and Subahdar of Arcot; and because he gave himself that title, the Council thought it could not receive his Petition. The Petition was accordingly rejected; and, on the 17th of June, the Clerk of the Council wrote a letter to the Prince stating that it had been rejected, and the grounds of the rejection. The Council had lately received a letter from the Government of Madras stating that the principal creditors of the late Nabob approved of the Bill, and urged that it should be passed as quickly as possible. On Saturday last, he was about to present the Report of the Select Committee upon the Bill; but he had postponed doing so for reasons which he stated at the time. To-day, the Council had heard the Petition of Mr. Orr, requesting that progress with the Bill should be delayed until the 17th of July. Under the circumstances of the case, he thought it was but reasonable that this should be granted. But it must be distinctly understood that on the 17th July the Report of the Select Committee would be presented, unless some fresh Petition should that day come before the Council which would induce it to refer it to the Select Committee for consideration.

He should, therefore, move that the Select Committee be instructed to delay the presentation of their Report until the 17th Instant.

Agreed to.

TRANSPORTATION OF CONVICTS.

Mr. LeGeyt moved that the Select Committee appointed to consider and report on the existing Law in the Straits Settlement regarding the transportation of convicts, be discharged. Since the appointment of the Committee, cases had occurred to show that any further proceeding on the subject referred to the Committee was unnecessary.

Agreed to.

The Council adjourned.

Mr. Peacock

Saturday, July 10, 1858.

PRESENT:

The Hon'ble the Chief Justice, *Vice-President*, in the Chair;

Hon'ble J. P. Grant,
Hon'ble B. Peacock,
Hon'ble H. Ricketts,
P. W. LeGeyt, Esq.,
E. Currie, Esq.,
Hon'ble Sir Arthur Buller,
H. B. Harington, Esq. and
H. Forbes, Esq.

NABOB OF SURAT.

The Clerk presented a Petition of Meer Jafur Alee Khan Bahadoor of Surat, on the part of himself and the widow and grand-daughters of the late Nabob of Surat, praying for the passing of an Act to amend Act XVIII of 1848 (for the administration of the Estate of the late Nabob of Surat, and to continue privileges to his Family) in conformity with the draft of an Act forwarded with the Petition.

Mr. Peacock moved that the Petition be printed.

Agreed to.

MASTERS AND SERVANTS.

The Clerk also presented a Petition from the Master, Wardens, and Members of the Calcutta Trade Association, praying for the introduction of a legislative measure to check wilful breaches of contract or desertion of service by workmen or servants by a system of summary punishments and summary remedies to be enforced by a Magistrate.

Mr. Currie moved that the Petition be printed.

Agreed to.

MADRAS MARINE POLICE.

Mr. Forbes presented the Report of the Select Committee on the Bill "for the maintenance of a Police Force for the Port of Madras." In doing so, he said he should have occasion for a very few minutes to trespass on the attention of the Council. Honorable Members were aware that the Police Force for the Towns of Calcutta, Madras, and Bombay exercised their powers under Act XIII of 1856. By Section XXIV of that Act, the Police had authority within the towns and suburbs of Calcutta, Madras, and Bombay; and by one of the Clauses of Section II, the word "Town" was defined to "include all places within the local limits of the jurisdiction of Her Majesty's Supreme Courts of Judicature at Calcutta, Madras, and Bombay." At Madras, the jurisdiction of Her Majesty's Supreme Court extended only to low-water mark; and in Calcutta and Bombay, only parts of the Ports were within the jurisdiction of Her Majesty's Supreme Courts. The draft of the present Bill sent up from Madras, contained a Section, inserted on the advice of the Company's Advocate General, providing that the Marine Police Force should have authority within the limits of the Port, which it was considered it would not have if it were constituted under Act XIII of 1856. But Mr. Eliott, in introducing the Bill, held a different opinion. He found that by Section XXVI of that Act the Magistrates of Police had authority to punish offences committed within the limits of the Port; and he argued that, if the Magistrates of Police had authority to punish offences committed within those limits, *ipso facto* the Police Force must have authority to bring the offenders before them for punishment; and that therefore the jurisdiction of the Police and the jurisdiction of the Magistrate must be co-ordinate. Accordingly, in the Bill which he brought in, he omitted that Section, and stated his reasons for so doing in a Minute which he transmitted to the Government of Madras, and which was by them referred to the Advocate General. That learned Gentleman gave every consideration to Mr. Eliott's reasoning, but was unable to agree with it. He maintained that, however much it might have been the intention of the Legislature that the jurisdiction of the Magistrates and of the Police should be co-ordinate, the Act of 1856, by some omission, made no such provision; that the Act must be construed strictly and literally; and that, as the jurisdiction which it gave to the Police was restricted to the Town, and the Town of Madras was comprised within the local limits of the jurisdiction of Her Majesty's Supreme Court of Judicature, the Police could not have authority within that part of the Port of Madras which was beyond that jurisdiction. The subject had been taken into consideration by the Select Committee on the Bill, who thought that it was one of considerable importance. Had it related to Madras only, they would have felt it incumbent on them to introduce such amendments into this Bill as would provide for the case in question; but it appeared to them that the question concerned Calcutta and Bombay just as much as it concerned Madras; and that, therefore, it ought to be considered in connexion, not with the present Bill which related only to Madras, but with Act XIII of 1856 which was applicable to the whole of India. The Select Committee had not the advantage of being associated with any Member of the Council who belonged to the profession of the Law; and they considered the question of sufficient importance to warrant their recommending that a Select Committee should be appointed to report upon it, of whom the Honorable and learned Chief Justice and the Honorable Mr. Peacock should be Members, in order that it might receive an authoritative and final decision. He should move for the appointment of such a Committee; and in doing so, he should propose that they be directed to submit their Report within one week; because, as the Bill for the maintenance of a Police Force for the Port of Madras would go before a Committee of the whole Council on Saturday next, and as, if it passed through the Committee, he should move that it be read a third time and passed, it was necessary that any amendment which might be desirable in Act XIII of 1856, should be made at the same time, in order that the Madras Marine Force might not find itself, directly it was constituted, unable to act within the Port within which its functions were to be exercised. He should therefore move that the Report of the Select Committee on the Madras Marine Police Bill, a Minute upon the Bill by the late Member for Madras, and the opinion of the Advocate General at Madras upon the question raised in that Minute, be referred to a Select Committee, consisting of the Vice-President, Mr. Peacock, and the Mover, with instructions to consider and report, at the next Meeting of the Council, whether, in their opinion, any amendment of Act XIII of 1856 was necessary.

Agreed to.

INSTITUTION OF SUITS AND APPEALS (N. W. PROVINCES).

MR. HARINGTON presented the Report of the Select Committee on the Bill "for the relief of persons who, in consequence of the recent disturbances, may have been prevented from instituting or prosecuting suits or appeals in the Courts of the North-Western Provinces within the period allowed by law."

SETTLEMENT OF ALLUVIAL LANDS (BENGAL).

MR. CURRIE presented the Report of the Select Committee on the Bill "to make further provision for the settlement of land gained by alluvion in the Presidency of Fort William in Bengal."

NOTICE OF MOTION.

MR. HARINGTON gave notice that he would, on Saturday the 17th instant, move the first reading of a Bill for conferring Civil jurisdiction in certain cases upon Cantonment Joint-Magistrates, and for constituting those Officers Registers of Deeds within the limits of their respective jurisdictions.

The Council adjourned.

Saturday, July 17, 1858.

PRESENT:

The Hon. the Chief Justice, *Vice-President*, in the Chair.

Hon'ble J. P. Grant,	P. W. LeGeyt, Esq.,
Hon'ble MajorGeneral Sir James Outram,	E. Currie, Esq.,
Hon'ble H. Ricketts,	H. B. Harington, Esq., and
Hon'ble B. Peacock,	H. Forbes, Esq.

BOMBAY MUNICIPAL ASSESSMENT: OFFENCES AGAINST THE STATE.

THE VICE-PRESIDENT read Messages informing the Legislative Council that the Governor General had assented to the Bill "for appointing Municipal Commissioners and for raising a Fund for Municipal purposes in the Town of Bombay,"—and the Bill "to make further provision for the trial and punishment of offences against the State."

ESTATE OF THE LATE NABOB OF THE CARNATIC.

MR. PEACOCK presented the Report of the Select Committee on the Bill "to provide for the administration of the Estate and for the payment of the debts of the late Nabob of the Carnatic."

POLICE OF THE PORTS OF THE PRESIDENCY TOWNS.

MR. FORBES presented the Report of the Select Committee on the jurisdiction of the Commissioner of Police and of the Police Force within the Ports of the Presidency Towns.

LUNATIC ASYLUMS.

MR. CURRIE presented the Report of the Select Committee on the Bill "relating to Lunatic Asylums."

PROCEEDINGS IN LUNACY IN THE SUPREME COURTS.

MR. CURRIE postponed the presentation of the Report of the Select Committee on the Bill "to regulate proceedings in Lunacy in Her Majesty's Courts of Judicature."

CANTONMENT JOINT MAGISTRATES.

MR. HARINGTON moved the first reading of a Bill "for conferring civil jurisdiction in certain cases upon Cantonment Joint Magistrates, and for constituting those Officers Registers of Deeds within the limits of their respective jurisdictions."

In doing so, he said, the proposition to invest Cantonment Joint Magistrates with civil jurisdiction in certain cases, and to appoint those Officers Registers of Deeds within the limits of their respective jurisdictions, was not now submitted to the consideration of the Legislature for the first time. From a correspondence which had been handed to him by the Clerk of the Council, he found that, so far back as the year 1847, Brigadier Steel, who at that period held the appointment of Superintendent of Cantonment Police, brought to the notice of the Commander-in-Chief certain objections which appeared to him to exist as respected the working of Act XI of 1841, the 2d Section of which declared that, in the Territories of the East India Company, subject to the proviso contained in the 1st Section,

"actions of debt and other personal actions against native officers, soldiers, and other persons amenable to the Articles of War for the Native Forces in the Military services of the East India Company, or residing within any station or Cantonment, and carrying on any trade or business in a Military bazar, shall be cognizable before a Military Court, and not elsewhere, provided the value in question shall not exceed two hundred Rupees, and the defendant was a person of the description mentioned when the cause of action arose, and when the suit was instituted, and provided also that no suit shall be brought before any Military Court under the Act to determine any dispute of caste, or concerning any right to real property."

Brigadier Steel's objections to this Act were that the temporary constitution of the Courts held under it would not admit of their making any investigation into the character of the parties who came before them; and that the consequence was that these Military Courts were a source of as much injustice as justice;—that the Members, including the European President, being changed every month, anything that occurred before one Court to establish the false swearing of an individual as prosecutor or witness, was entirely unknown to any other Court sitting subsequently, which Brigadier Steel considered a great disadvantage; —that it was not an uncommon thing for the Native Members of the Court, when they could not get over the affirmative evidence of the Plaintiff, to decree half the claim, and dismiss the rest;—and that, owing very much to these causes, a class of men had been raised up in almost every Military Cantonment who gained their livelihood by constantly appearing as Plaintiffs or witnesses in fictitious cases of debt. In a subsequent communication, Brigadier Steel gave the population of the Military Cantonment at Meerut, not including fighting men, at 45,480, and of Cawnpore at 49,975; and he annexed a statement of the claims submitted to the Military Courts of Requests at those two stations for six months ending with October 1847. From this statement, it appeared that from the 1st May to the 31st October 1847, 1,204 cases were instituted at Meerut, and 817 at Cawnpore; and as the Courts which heard and determined this large number of cases sat for only a few days in each month, Brigadier Steel pointed out how impossible it was for those Courts properly to have sifted the evidence brought before them in each case. To remedy what appeared to him to be the evils of the existing law, Brigadier Steel proposed that all actions of debt and other personal actions cognizable by Military Courts of Requests under the provisions of Act XI of 1841 should ordinarily be tried at stations where there was a Cantonment Joint Magistrate by that Officer, on a reference from the Commanding Officer of the station, except when the Defendant should be a native officer or soldier, or a mustered camp follower; and he submitted the draft of an Act, framed in accordance with these views, to be in force in all three Presidencies. The opinion of the Judge Advocate General having been called for on this proposition, it not only met with his entire approval, but he went farther, and, instead of excepting mustered camp followers from the Civil jurisdiction of the Cantonment Joint Magistrate's Court, as suggested by Brigadier Steel, he recommended that the exception should extend only to native officers and soldiers, and that, with these exceptions, all classes of persons liable to be sued before a Military Court of Requests under the provisions of Act XI of 1841, should be made amenable to the Civil jurisdiction of the Military Joint Magistrate's Court, from the operation of which he anticipated such beneficial results, that he thought it very probable that at no distant date it would be found expedient to extend the jurisdiction of that Officer's Court to native officers and soldiers likewise. With regard to Madras and Bombay, the Judge Advocate General observed that no new Act was necessary for those Presidencies, inasmuch as Section 1 Act XI of 1841 expressly provided that nothing contained in that Act should be held to alter or affect the jurisdiction of a single officer duly appointed under the rules in force in the Madras and Bombay Presidencies, for the trial of small suits in Military Bazars at Cantonments and stations occupied by the troops of those Presidencies respectively, or the trial by Punchayet of suits against Military persons according to the rules in force under the Madras Presidency. In submitting the correspondence for the consideration of the Supreme Government, the Adjutant General of the Army was instructed to state that the Commander-in-Chief entirely concurred in the suggestions of the Judge Advocate General, and there was every reason to believe, from notes contained in the correspondence to which he (Mr. Harington) had referred, that those suggestions would have been adopted and made the subject of a new enactment, had it not appeared to the Supreme Government that the wording of the 3 and 4 Vic. c. 37, s. 54 commonly called the East India Mutiny Act, presented an obstacle to the passing of a law in this country of the nature proposed. The Section referred to, enacted that—

"in all places where the forces of the East India Company now are or may be employed, or where any body of Her Majesty's forces may be serving with the forces of the said Company, situate beyond the jurisdiction of the Court of Requests established at the cities of Calcutta, Madras, and Bombay respectively, actions of debt and all personal actions against officers, all persons licensed to act as suttlers to any corps or detachment, or at any station or cantonment, all persons resident within the limits of a Military cantonment, or other persons amenable to the provisions of this Act, shall be cognizable before a Court of Requests and not elsewhere, provided the value in question shall not exceed four hundred Rupees, and that the defendant was a person of the description mentioned when the cause of action arose;"—

and in the face of this provision the President in Council remarked that he did not see how a single Officer could act as a Court of Requests without contravening the Act of Parliament. The decision of the Supreme Government having been communicated to Brigadier Steel, he addressed a letter to the Commander-in-Chief through the Adjutant General of the Army, in which he said:—

"Had I proposed any interference with the European Courts of Requests, I am aware that I should have found the Act of Parliament an obstacle. But Native Courts of Requests were first established by Regulation XX. 1810, and since amended by Act XI of 1841, whilst the 12 and 13 Victoria c. 43, s. 1, (and a similar if not a stronger Clause exists in the 3 and 4 Victoria), reserves to the local Government the right of making laws and regulations for the Native Army and followers in the same way as they have always exercised that power for their native subjects generally. I have stated in my former letters on this subject the total inadequacy of Courts of Requests, as at present constituted, to deal with the pecuniary differences of a population of upwards 45,000 people, exclusive of Military, who reside in the Cantonments of Meerut and Cawnpore severally. Under these circumstances, should Sir Charles Napier concur in my opinion, I hope he will see no objection to bringing the question again under the consideration of Government, more especially as the 1st Section of Act XI of 1841 adverts to the existence of the tribunal of a single Officer at the other Presidencies; and if considered legal there, I presume they cannot be deemed otherwise here."

This letter was also submitted, though without comment, for the consideration of the Supreme Government; but as the President in Council continued of opinion that the Act of Parliament precluded the proposed alteration in the law, he considered it sufficient to direct that a communication to that effect should be made to Brigadier Steel; and here the matter was allowed to rest.

The question of conferring upon Cantonment Joint-Magistrates the power of adjudicating petty Civil cases arising within their jurisdiction, had now been revived by Major Williams, the present able and energetic Superintendent of Cantonment Police; and the Right Honorable the Governor General considering it very desirable that Cantonment Joint-Magistrates should be empowered to dispose of Civil cases of a limited amount arising within Military Cantonments, provided that a simple and speedy mode of procedure for the trial of such cases should be at the same time introduced by the Legislative Council, he (Mr. Harington) had been desired to take the necessary steps to obtain legal sanction to such a measure, and he had accordingly prepared the Bill of which he was now about to move the first reading.

In drawing up this Bill, he had had to consider first the reason assigned by the Honorable the President in Council for declining to accede to a similar proposition when formerly made by the Military authorities; and secondly, whether the obstacle which was at that time stated to preclude the passing of an Act of the nature now contemplated, had been intermediately removed. Though this Council had no power to alter the Statutes which regulated Military Courts of Requests for the Queen's and Company's European troops, there could be no doubt of its competency to legislate for Courts of the same description for Native troops. This power was indeed expressly given to the Council by the 3 and 4 William IV, c. 85, s. 73, the 43rd Section of which contained the prohibition against any interference on the part of the Governor General in Council with the Acts for punishing mutiny and desertion of Officers and Soldiers, whether in the service of the Crown or of the East India Company; and taking these two Sections together, there could be no doubt, he thought, that the East India Mutiny Acts passed from time to time at home applied exclusively to the Queen's and Company's European troops serving in India, and had no application to the Native Army. The term "camp-followers" was certainly not to be found in the Section of the Act first quoted; but that the provisions of that Section were intended to apply and did apply to all persons amenable to the Indian Articles of War as described in Section 157 of Act XIX of 1847, was, he thought, clear from the proviso contained in the 20 and 21 Victoria, c. 66, s. 1, and the corresponding Section of the 13 and 14 Victoria, c. 43, which, though it had passed, had probably not reached India at the date of the order of the Supreme Government on Brigadier Steel's original reference. That proviso declared that

> "nothing contained in the Act should in any manner prejudice or affect any Articles of War or other matters made, enacted, or in force, or which may afterwards be made, enacted or in force, under the authority of the Government of India respecting Officers, or or Soldiers, or followers, being natives of the East Indies or other places within the limits of the Company's Charter; and that in the trial of all offences committed by any native Officer, or soldier, or follower, reference shall be had to the Articles of War framed by the Government of India for such native Officers, Soldiers, or followers, and to the established usages of the service."

It was, he presumed, under the authority of this Section and of the corresponding Sections in previous enactments, as well as of the Charter Act, that Act XI of 1841 was passed, and the Superintendents of Military Bazaars in the Presidencies of Madras and Bombay, were invested with Civil jurisdiction to try petty suits; and he confessed he could discover nothing in any Act of Parliament existing at the time, to have prevented the Government of this country from passing a law of the nature proposed by the Judge Advocate General of Bengal, in so far as the persons amenable to the Indian Articles of War, and therefore to Acts XI of 1841 and XII of 1842, were concerned. But while the Judge Advocate General and Brigadier Steel would have excluded Native Officers and soldiers from the operation of any such law, and Brigadier Steel would have extended the exemption to mustered camp-followers, both Officers would have made the law applicable to mere residents of Military Cantonments, though holding no Military post, and though not amenable to the Articles of War for the Native Army; and he apprehended that it was in respect of persons of this description that the Supreme Government considered itself to be precluded from adopting the suggestion of the Military authorities by the wording of the 3 and 4 Victoria, c. 37, s. 54, which expressly made all persons resident within the limits of a Military Cantonment amenable, in personal actions up to four hundred Rupees, to the Courts of Requests held under that Section, and to no other tribunal. The same provision was also to be found in the corresponding Section of the 13 and 14 Victoria c. 43; but as it had been omitted, he presumed designedly, from the last Mutiny Act passed for the Queen's and Company's European troops in India, the obstacle which formerly existed to the passing of a law of the nature proposed, as regarded non-Military residents of Cantonments, would seem to have been removed; in which case, so far as he could perceive, there was nothing now to prevent this Council from legislating for those persons in respect of Civil matters as well as for all persons of the description mentioned in Section II Act XI of 1841 as extended by Act XII of 1842; and he had framed the Bill in accordance with these views.

It proposed to give the Governor General in Council and the local Government of any Presidency or place, power to invest the Military Joint Magistrate of any Cantonment or Military Bazaar or Station, within the limits of their respective Governments, with Civil jurisdiction to hear and determine actions of debt or other personal actions against all persons of the description mentioned in Section 157 Act XIX of 1847, and other persons who, though not amenable to the Articles of War for the Queen's and Company's European Troops serving in India, or for the Native Army, were nevertheless resident within the limits of a Military Cantonment, provided that the value in question should not exceed the sum of two hundred Rupees and the defendant was a person of the description mentioned when the cause of action arose and when the suit was instituted. The procedure to be observed in the trial of such cases would be the same as that prescribed for Military Courts of Requests in Act XI of 1841. This procedure seemed sufficient for all useful purposes, and was, he thought, as simple and speedy as could be desired. It was not intended that there should be any appeal from the decisions of the Cantonment Joint Magistrate in cases cognizable by them, and those Officers would be at liberty at once to execute their decisions on the application of the decree holders, under the rules applicable to the execution of awards of Military Courts of Requests. No appeal was now allowed from the decrees of the Courts of Requests; and, considering that Cantonment Joint Magistrates were required to pass the same examination as Junior Civilians, and as it might be presumed that they would always be chosen for their general fitness for the duties which would be entrusted to them, he thought that we might anticipate that their decisions would be at least as good as those of the Native Military Courts of Requests; while he had no doubt that they would generally give much greater satisfaction. Under these circumstances, and looking to the limited amount of the Civil jurisdiction which it was proposed to give to the Officers in question, it did not appear to him to be necessary to render their decisions open to appeal. As regarded Madras and Bombay, in which Presidencies, as already noticed, the Superintendents of Military Bazaars had authority to hear Civil cases of small amount, the Bill would in no way affect the laws under which that jurisdiction was exercised unless the Governors in Council of those Presidencies should think proper to extend its provisions to them, which, as the amount of Civil jurisdiction exercised by the Superintendents of Military Bazaars in Madras and Bombay was exceedingly small, extending at Madras to only twenty, and at Bombay to only thirty Rupees, they might find it convenient to do.

These were the principal provisions of those Sections of the Bill which related to the Civil jurisdiction to be exercised by Cantonment Joint Magistrates in certain cases. It remained for him to notice the part which provided that these Officers might also be appointed Registers of Deeds within the limits of their respective jurisdictions; and on this portion of the Bill, it would not be necessary for him to occupy much of the time of the Council—on which, he feared, he had already trespassed too largely.

From papers which he had also received from the Clerk of the Council, he found that in the year 1845, the Officer commanding the Hyderabad Subsidiary Force brought to the notice of the Madras Government that a fraudulent practice had become prevalent at Secunderabad of executing fictitious mortgages for the purpose of evading the awards passed by Courts of Requests under Act XI of 1841, and he recommended that a law should be passed declaring that no Deed of Mortgage executed by native merchants or others, being British subjects, should be valid unless registered at or shortly after the date of execution in the office of the Superintendent of Police. Subsequently, in March 1850, Sir Charles Napier recommended a proposition made by Sir George Parker, Cantonment Joint-Magistrate at Meerut, and concurred in by the Advocate General of the Army and the Superintendent of Cantonment Police, for a similar law in respect of deeds of sale of houses within Cantonment Bazaars, the registry to be made in the office of the Cantonment Joint Magistrate. The matter having been referred to the Legislative Council, the Judge Advocate Generals of Bengal, Madras, and Bombay were called upon to furnish a draft of rules for registering the sale of houses within Military Cantonments, such as, in their opinion, should be embodied in a legislative Act, shewing how and where and with what fees and formalities registration should be made, what power of investigation should be adopted by registering Officers, and what should be the penalties for non-registration. Draft rules were framed in accordance with these instructions by each of the Judge Advocate Generals of the three Presidencies, which were referred to the Legislative Council to be taken into consideration with the amended general Law of Registration then before the Council, since which no further steps had been taken in the matter. He believed, however, that at no distant date a new Law of Registration applicable to all India would be proposed to the Council, probably by the Honorable Member on his right (Mr Forbes); but this was no reason why, in the meantime, the proposition made so long ago for constituting Cantonment Joint Magistrates Registers of Deeds within the limits of the Cantonments to which they stood appointed, should not be carried into effect; and as it was now proposed to give these officers Civil jurisdiction in certain cases, it seemed desirable that the opportunity should be taken of extending their powers to the registration of Deeds also within the same limits. From the position which they occupied, and from the knowledge which they must possess of the people residing in the Cantonments subject to their jurisdiction, it might, he thought, fairly be assumed that Cantonment Joint Magistrates were better qualified for the office of Register of Deeds within the Cantonments than the Native Judges living outside, by whom the appointment was generally held; and he anticipated that by appointing them to this post, much fraud and chicanery would be prevented. He did not consider it necessary that any special rules should be laid down at this time for the guidance of the Cantonment Joint Magistrates in the discharge of their duties as Registers of Deeds, particularly as it was probable, as already mentioned, that a general law would soon be introduced which would apply to all offices of Register of Deeds, by whomsoever held; and all that the Bill prepared by him proposed, was to give the Governor General in Council and the local Government of any Presidency or place, power to appoint any Military Joint Magistrate Register of Deeds within the limits of the Cantonments or Military station to which his jurisdiction extended, and to declare that, when such appointment was made, all rules now in force applicable to Registers of Deeds, should be applicable to the Military Joint Magistrate so appointed, and to the Deeds registered by him, or brought to him for registry. With these observations, he begged to move that the Bill be read a first time.

The Bill was read a first time.

STAMPS (BENGAL PRESIDENCY).

THE CLERK presented to the Council a Petition from Rammohun Bannerjee and Guddadhur Bannerjee, Zemindars of West Burdwan, praying that the Council may exempt from the operation of the Bill "to amend Regulation X. 1829 of the Bengal Code," cases instituted and pending in any of the Courts at the time of its passing.

MR. CURRIE moved that the Petition be referred to the Select Committee on the Bill.

Agreed to.

POLICE OF THE PORTS OF THE PRESIDENCY TOWNS.

MR. FORBES moved that the Report of the Select Committee on the jurisdiction of the Commissioners of Police and of the Police Force within the Ports of the Presidency Towns presented this day, be adopted.

Agreed to.

MADRAS MARINE POLICE.

MR. FORBES moved that the Council resolve itself into a Committee on the Bill "for the maintenance of a Police Force for the Port of Madras;" and that the Committee be instructed to consider the Bill in the amended form in which it had been recommended by the Select Committee to be passed.

Agreed to.

Section I provided that, to meet the expense of a Marine Police, the sum of three annas should be taken by the owner of every boat employed to convey cargo or goods to or from any ship or vessel in the Port of Madras, in addition to the hire payable under Act IV of 1842.

MR. PEACOCK said, he did not propose to move any amendment in this Section; but he had an amendment to move in Section II; and if that should be carried, it might be necessary to add some words to Section I. Section II provided that "no cargo or goods of any description shall be conveyed in any boat to or from any ship or vessel in the Port of Madras, unless accompanied by an Officer of Police." He thought it quite right that every boat which was hired for the purpose of carrying cargo, should pay the tax required by Section I; but it appeared to him objectionable that every boat carrying cargo should be accompanied by an Officer of Police, whether it was a private boat, or a boat engaged for hire, or whether the person or persons hiring it wished it to be accompanied by an Officer of Police or not. He could not see why he, for instance, if he chose to put himself and his luggage on board a catamaran at Madras to go off to a ship, should be bound to take a Police Officer with him; nor could he see why one or more merchants, if they employed a boat to convey cargo belonging to them, should be bound to send a Police Officer on board whether they wished it or not. The object of this Bill was to prevent depredations being committed in the boats employed in the conveyance of cargo in the Madras Roads; and if a merchant desired to send his own clerk or supercargo in charge of his goods, he saw no reason why he should not be permitted to do so, but should be bound to send a Police Officer instead. It appeared to him—and he had mentioned it on the motion for the second reading—that the obligation imposed by the Section to take a Police Officer in every case, might throw great impediment in the way of trade. Police Officers might not always be at hand to accompany boats, and the owner of the cargo might prefer to send his own clerk in charge to waiting for a Police Officer.

He (Mr. Peacock) proposed, therefore, when Section II came under consideration, to move the addition to it of words which would enable the owner or owners of cargo employing a boat for the conveyance of cargo, to dispense with the attendance of a Police Officer by giving a consent in writing that the boat should not be accompanied by such an Officer. If that amendment should be adopted, it might be necessary to insert words in Section I to the effect that whether a boat employed to convey cargo carried a Police Officer or not, the owner of the boat should be bound to receive and account for the tax prescribed by the Section. The Madras Government themselves did not press for the adoption of Section II in its present form. They said:—

"The present scheme, including the attaching of a Police Officer to each cargo boat, has, it must be observed, the full concurrence of the Merchants of Madras, by whom the fees are to be paid, and who may be presumed to be well acquainted with the local circumstances and requirements of the Port. If, however, it should, in the judgment of the Legislative Council, be deemed objectionable that the taking a Police Officer in every cargo boat should be rendered compulsory, it might be made optional. It might be left to the discretion of the party shipping or landing goods to have a Police Officer in the boat or not, as he thought fit."

He should move that the consideration of Section I should be postponed until the question as to Section II was determined.

Agreed to.

Section II being read by the Chairman—

Mr. PEACOCK said, for the reasons he had just stated, he should move that the following words be added to the Section:—

"unless the person by whom the boat shall be hired or employed to convey such cargo or goods, shall consent in writing that the boat shall not be accompanied by an Officer of the Police Force; or if such boat shall be hired or employed as aforesaid by several persons not jointly interested in such cargo or goods, unless all such persons shall give such consent in writing as aforesaid."

Mr. FORBES said, when this Bill was introduced by his Honorable friend Mr. Eliott, the Honorable and learned mover of the amendment and the Honorable Member for Bombay took the same exception to it which had just been so ably put. The objections urged on that occasion had been communicated by Mr. Eliott to the Government of Madras, and had been laid by the Government before the mercantile community of the place as represented by the Chamber of Commerce. That Body had considered all the arguments which had been advanced in support of them, and they stated that, in their opinion, it was to the interest of the mercantile community which they represented that no boat should convey cargo to or from any ship in the Port unless it was accompanied by an Officer of the Police Force. British Merchants were not in the habit of pressing upon the Legislature the enactment of a Law which, when passed, would operate injuriously against their interests by throwing obstacles in the way of business, and being a hindrance to trade. But this was the course which the Honorable and learned mover of the amendment assumed the mercantile community of Madras to have taken in the present instance. It was to be observed that the entire expense of the proposed Marine Police Force was to be met by contributions from that community. No part of it whatever would be provided by the Government. The whole would come from those whose property was to be guarded by the Force; and it did appear to him that, when the mercantile community of the Port had proposed a particular guard for their goods, and had offered to pay for the maintenance of that guard out of their own pockets, it was somewhat hard to deny them the privilege which they sought.

He had another objection to the amendment proposed. He thought that it was the duty of the Government to guard the property of every individual of the community, whether he desired it or not. We did not on shore find that any resident applied to have his house guarded by Policemen. Every man's property or land was guarded by the Police whether he wished it or not; and he (Mr. Forbes) was unable to see why the same principle should not be extended to property on the sea. Successful pilfering on boats might lead to petty larceny on shore; successful larceny on shore might lead to burglary; and burglary might lead to dacoity and all the evils that usually attend that crime. In a moral point of view, therefore, it was the duty of the Government to put an end to the commencement of the minor evil, and so to prevent the greater evil from falling on the community.

Moreover, it should be remembered that the circumstances of the Port of Madras were different from those of the Port of Calcutta. Here, a Captain or Merchant might employ any kind of boat to convey him or his cargo to or from a ship; but at Madras, where there was always a heavy surf, it was only masoolah boats, which were manned by crews trained to the particular duty, that could be employed for the purpose. It was impossible for any Captain or Merchant to communicate with the shore or with his ship except by means of those boats. If, then, the Merchants of Madras must employ masoolah boats for the conveyance of cargo between the beach and the shipping, he could not see any reason to suppose, as the Honorable and learned Member did, that the Peons of a Force established for the express purpose of accompanying these boats, would not be found when they were wanted. If thirteen boatmen could be had to convey cargo in a boat, one Peon could certainly be had to accompany the boat. Besides, the Marine Force was not to be an independent body acting without control, but it was to be under the superintendence of a European Officer, who would be subject to the Commissioner of Police; and there really was no more reason to suppose that a Marine Police so superintended, would be absent from their duty than that the Land Police would always be absent from theirs.

The Honorable and learned Member said he thought it quite right that owners of cargo carried in boats to or from vessels should pay the tax imposed by Section I, even though no Peons of the Marine Force were placed on board the boats to protect the cargo. But he (Mr. Forbes) thought that the owners might, in such cases, reasonably object to being charged with a tax which was to be levied merely for remunerating the Government for maintaining a Force from which, under the circumstances supposed, they would derive no benefit.

It was true that the Government of Madras said that "if, in the judgment of the Legislative Council, it should be deemed objectionable that the taking a Police Officer in every cargo boat should be rendered compulsory, it might be made optional;" but on the other hand, they expressly stated that

"the present scheme, including the attaching of a Police Officer to each cargo boat, has the full concurrence of the Merchants of Madras, by whom the fees are to be paid, and who may be presumed to be well acquainted with the local circumstances and requirements of the Port;"

and it was obvious that, although the Government did not press the present scheme contrary to the wishes of the Council, they, together with the Merchants of Madras, having given full consideration to that scheme, which had been before them since the year 1854, were of opinion that it was the one best adapted to the wishes and wants of the community.

For these reasons, he should vote against the amendment, and in support of the Section as it stood.

THE CHAIRMAN said, he did not think he could rest his objection to the amendment on the high moral ground taken by the Honorable Member for Madras; because the same train of reasoning might lead each of us to walk arm in arm with a Policeman in order to prevent some possible pick-pocket from taking the first step on that "facilis descensus Averni," which might conduct him to the gallows. A far stronger argument, to his mind, against the amendment was that which the Honorable Member had also urged, namely, that after this question had been mooted here on the second reading of the Bill, it had been considered at Madras; and that those who were to be subjected to the tax for the maintenance of a Marine Police Force there, and for the protection of whose interests that Force was designed, had expressed a strong preference of the Section as it now stood. He thought that, in matters of local legislation, it was always desirable to meet as far as possible the wishes of the class for whom the enactment was intended. The Sections in question, if examined, would, he thought, be found to apply only to boats employed in the conveyance of cargo or goods for the trade of the Port. They would hardly apply to a boat carrying a passenger with his baggage; and if one could conceive any thing so unlikely to present itself as his Honorable and learned friend (Mr. Peacock), a Member of the Supreme Government of India, and his portmanteau on a catamaran, he (the Chairman) believed that he would not be within the purvieu of this Law.

He thought, therefore, that it would be better to leave the Section as it stood; though he admitted that, to his mind, there was nothing really objectionable in the proposed amendment.

MR. GRANT said, he saw no provision in the Bill for the supply of these Peons. The effect of the Bill as it now stood would be that no masoolah boat could convey cargo without a Police Officer being on board. It should, therefore, be obligatory on some one to supply Police Officers for the duty.

MR. FORBES said, the calculation was that the Police Force would cost one thousand Rupees a month, and that, according to the present trade of the Port, three annas on each cargo boat would provide that sum. If the trade increased so that new Peons would be wanted, the aggregate sum collected would, of course, increase in the same proportion; and there was, therefore, no reason to anticipate that the Force would be insufficient.

MR. GRANT said, the provision for funds for the maintenance of the Force was quite ample enough. He had no doubt of that; but the point to which he would draw attention was that there was no provision making it the duty of any person to provide Police Officers for boats conveying cargo. He should suggest that a Clause be inserted requiring some Authority to provide a Police Officer for every such boat.

MR. FORBES said, he could not have the slightest objection to the insertion of such a Clause. He would impose the duty on the Commissioner of Police.

MR. CURRIE said, as a Member of the Select Committee to which this Bill had been referred, he wished merely to state that the point raised by the Honorable and learned mover of the amendment had been considered by the Select Committee, and that, for the reasons suggested by the Honorable and learned Chief Justice, they had come to the conclusion that it would be better to leave the Section as it stood. They thought that the merchants of Madras were quite able to determine what was best for their own interests and convenience; and, as that body had determined, after full consideration of the arguments urged by the Honorable and learned Member on the motion for the second reading, that it would not be expedient to make the taking of Police Officers on board cargo boats optional with the owners of cargoes, they had made no alteration in the Section.

The Honorable and learned Member proposed that when a boat conveying cargo was not to be accompanied by a Police Officer, the person or persons hiring it must consent in writing that it should not be so accompanied. But it did not appear to whom the written consent was to be delivered. He (Mr. Currie) should think that the formality of each person giving a consent in writing would be at least as troublesome a matter as placing a Peon on board.

MR. HARINGTON said, he did not understand the amendment to go to the length of refusing any boon or privilege that was asked or was necessary. On the contrary, the Honorable and learned Member agreed to give all the money that was required for the maintenance of a Marine Police at Madras, but would only make it optional with merchants to send Police Officers in charge of their cargoes or not. So long as they paid the fee required by Section I, he (Mr. Harington) could not see why they should not have this option.

MR. PEACOCK said, he would offer but a very few words in reply to what had been urged against his amendment.

If he were quite sure that Police Officers would always be ready on the beach to accompany boats for the protection of cargo, he should have no objection to the Section as it stood; but they might not always be at hand, and a merchant might much rather send off his cargo in charge of a supercargo of his own, than be subjected to the delay of waiting until a Police Officer arrived.

Besides this, the Section applied, not only to cargo, but to "goods of any description," and not only to cargo boats, but he believed to the classes of boats which were mentioned in Act IV of 1842; for Section I referred to that Act. There was a distinction made in the Act of 1842 between private boats and cargo boats.

The Honorable Mover of the Bill had said that the Council, if it adopted the amendment, would be denying the Chamber of Commerce their request; but he (Mr. Peacock) did not know that the Chamber of Commerce could bind every one in Madras. The Section did not say that no merchant or no Member of the Chamber of Commerce should send cargo in a boat except under the charge of a Police Officer, but that no person whatever, whether he resided within or without the Presidency, should send goods of any description except under such charge. Was it that these Police Officers were to prevent goods from being taken out of the boats,—or that they were to prevent goods from other boats being transferred to them? If they were to prevent goods from being taken out of the boats, he conceived that a merchant had a right to commit his property to the guardianship of his own clerk or supercargo, if he wished it. What he (Mr. Peacock) objected to was, the making it imperative on persons to take a Police Officer in every case. Why should not a merchant have the option of keeping his own boat to land or ship his own cargo under the care of his own clerk or supercargo? The Honorable Member had not said that this provision was intended for the purpose of preventing stolen goods being received into the boats. He had said that every man's property on land was guarded by the Police whether he wished it or not, and that he was unable to see why the same principle should not be extended to property on the sea; but every man was not bound to have a Police Officer in his house for the purpose of seeing that stolen goods were not taken into it. If the Chamber of Commerce at Madras chose to say that no goods belonging to any Member of the Chamber should be carried in boats except in the charge of a Police Officer, he should have no objection to make; but he did object to their saying that goods belonging to every person whatever should be subject to the same prohibition. The Honorable Member had said that if thirteen boatmen could be had to convey cargo in a boat, one Peon could certainly be had to accompany the boat. But boatmen must always be on the beach to obtain hire, whereas it would not be the interest of the Police Peons to be always there, since they would get their wages whether they were present or not. If a merchant should sustain damage in consequence of a delay in obtaining a Peon to go with his cargo, would the Chamber of Commerce indemnify him? He believed that the Chamber of Commerce did not include the whole of the mercantile community of Madras; and he thought that the Council ought to be careful not to pass this Bill as it stood, merely because the Chamber approved of it, if it considered that it would be a hindrance to the trade of the Port.

MR. FORBES said, the Honorable and learned Member had remarked that, while it would be the pecuniary interest of the boatmen aways to be at hand, it would not be the interest of the peons to be always on the beach, and that, therefore, they might not be at hand when they were wanted; and he had laid some stress on this point. But it appeared to him that it would be just as much the interest of the Peons to be always on the beach as it would be that of the boatmen; for they would be paid for performing a certain duty; and if they did not perform that duty, they would of course lose their situations.

MR. LEGEYT asked if the words "goods of any description" included passengers' baggage? If they did, the Section would be most vexatious. There could be no doubt that the Bill was designed only for the protection of mercantile cargo. That being its object, it was extremely probable that there would be great hesitation on the part of the Police Authorities in giving a man who was going off to a ship, a Peon to see that his great coat and portmanteau were not stolen; and yet, under this Section as it stood, no owner of a boat would carry him to the ship without a Peon. The point had escaped him and his colleagues in Select Committee; but he thought that some words ought to be introduced into the Section stating that "goods of any description" did not include light baggage.

He had the same objections to the Section itself as the Honorable and learned Member opposite (Mr. Peacock), and had stated them on the motion for the second reading; but they had been received at Madras in a spirit so different from that in which he had brought them forward, that he had not thought it necessary to follow them up in Select Committee. To his mind, none of those objections had been removed; and he still thought that the Bill, if passed as it stood, would be found to be very cumbrous, and in fact inoperative. As, however, the mercantile community of Madras appeared to wish to have it so, and as they would pay all expenses, it was their own affair. But the question whether the Section extended to passengers' baggage or not, affected the public convenience. He did not suppose that the Chamber of Commerce at Madras contemplated that a Police Officer should accompany a boat to protect a gentleman's umbrella and portmanteau; and he should suggest that light baggage be expressly excluded from the operation of the Section.

MR. FORBES said, he was quite willing to admit the objection taken by the Honorable Member for Bombay. It was very undesirable that mere passengers' baggage should be held to be subject to the provisions of the Bill; and if, when Section IX, which exempted boats conveying mails from its operation, came to be proposed, he would move that such baggage be included in it, he (Mr. Forbes) would be prepared to agree to the amendment.

With regard to the remark of the Honorable and learned Member on his left (Mr. Peacock) that the Chamber of Commerce at Madras did not represent every body, he would observe that this question had not originated with the Chamber, but was first brought to notice in a presentment from a Grand Jury in 1846, and a Grand Jury was selected, not from the mercantile body exclusively, but from all sections of the community.

MR. PEACOCK said, the words used were "cargo or goods of any description," and it was quite clear that the Section as it stood included every thing, —a gentleman's umbrella and portmanteau, just as much as mercantile cargo.

As to the value of the protection which the Section proposed to give to goods, it appeared from one of the printed papers annexed to the Bill that the Chamber of Commerce themselves had no great confidence in the Peons who were to be employed; for the Chairman suggested that "a European Constable should always be on duty in working hours on the top of the Master Attendant's Office, provided with a powerful telescope to watch both boatmen and Peons!" Now, if the Peons on board required watching with a powerful telescope from the shore, it was clear that

Mr. Peacock

much confidence could not be placed in them.

THE CHAIRMAN said, he would put it to the Honorable Member for Madras whether it might not be better to meet the wishes of the Honorable and learned Member, and to consent to the amendment. The feeling at Madras, no doubt, was that it was expedient that Peons should accompany all boats carrying cargo to or from vessels in the Port. The amendment, however, would not force any one to send his boat unaccompanied by a Peon; and there might be cases not contemplated, in which Peons might not be at hand, and in which it would be for the interest of the parties employing the boat, to exercise the option which the amendment would give them.

He himself did not believe that such cases, or even the difficulties regarding passengers' luggage which had been suggested, were very likely to arise. The Council was not dealing with an ordinary Port, in which there was an unlimited supply of boats. Nature had taken the matter into her own hands. There was but one class of boats which could be employed in the conveyance of goods across the surf. The number of them, he believed, was not so great but that, when this Act came into operation, each of them would easily have a Peon attached to it.

As to catamarans, he had never seen any person except a naked savage in one; and he was certain that no one would think of taking on board of such craft goods of whatever description.

MR. FORBES said, the amendment would give rise to the very evil which it was the object of the Honorable and learned Member who had moved it to guard against. If it were obligatory on the owner of every boat carrying cargo to take a Peon on board, Peons would always be ready on the beach to be taken; but if it were left to the option of owners of such boats to take Peons or not, the Peons, not being always wanted, would not always be at hand.

With respect to catamarans, the Honorable and learned Mover of the amendment was doubtless aware that a catamaran never went over the surf, but through it; and that, therefore, there was very little likelihood of any man putting either himself or his goods on board of one!

MR. GRANT moved that the words "or goods of any description" be omitted from the Section. That would leave the Act applicable only to cargo which was really the intention of the Chamber of Commerce and the Government of Madras.

THE CHAIRMAN said, he had, from the first, had a very clear opinion that if this Section was passed as the Honorable Member for Madras wished it, it would be necessary to introduce a new Section such as that which had been suggested by the Honorable Member on his right (Mr. Grant), to throw on the Commissioner of Police the duty of providing Peons for the boats; because if it were made compulsory on owners of boats to take Peons, and it should not be obligatory on the Commissioner of Police to provide Peons, it would be possible for that Officer, in the arbitrary exercise of his discretion, to prevent any particular owner of cargo boats from employing them profitably.

MR. PEACOCK said, the amendment proposed by the Honorable Member on his left (Mr. Grant) would require consideration with reference to Section I. If "goods" were not to be taxed, the question would arise whether the property to be carried was "cargo" or "goods?"

MR. GRANT said, he doubted whether there would be any difficulty on that point, because "cargo" always passed through the Custom House.

MR. CURRIE said, it would be safer to leave the words in the Section as they stood, and specially to exempt baggage of passengers in Section IX. That would be much more to the convenience of the public than the course which the Honorable and learned Member proposed; because if the Section were passed in the form in which he desired to amend it, every Passenger with a portmanteau who did not wish to take a Peon would have to go through the form of giving his consent in writing.

MR. GRANT, with the leave of the Council, withdrew his amendment.

MR. PEACOCK'S amendment was then put. The Council divided:—

Ayes, 4.	*Noes*, 5.
Mr. Harington.	Mr. Forbes.
Mr. Peacock.	Mr. Currie.
Mr. Ricketts.	Mr. LeGeyt.
Sir James Outram.	Mr. Grant.
	The Chairman.

MR. GRANT then moved that the following words be added to the Section:—"and it shall be the duty of the Commissioner of Police to provide every such boat with an Officer of the Police Force for this purpose."

The motion was carried, and the Section then passed

The postponed Section I was then put and agreed to.

Sections III to VIII were passed as they stood.

Section IX provided as follows:—

"None of the foregoing provisions of this Act shall be taken or deemed to extend or apply to any boat which shall convey Mails to or from any ship or vessel in the Madras Roads."

MR LEGEYT moved that the word "only" be inserted after the word "convey" in the fourth line of the Section.

Agreed to.

MR. LEGEYT moved that the word "only" after the word "mails" in the fifth line of the Section be left out, and that the words "or the baggage or private property of a passenger accompanied by such passenger or some other person in charge thereof" be substituted for it.

The question that the word proposed to be left out be left out, was put and agreed to.

The question that the words proposed to be substituted be substituted, being proposed:—

MR. FORBES moved by way of amendment that the words "or private property" be left out of the question. Those terms, he said, had a very large acceptation, and might be taken to include a carriage, for instance, which could hardly be said to be baggage.

After some discussion, the amendment was by leave withdrawn.

MR. GRANT moved by way of amendment that the words "or passengers with their baggage" be substituted for the words proposed to be substituted.

The motion was agreed to, and the Section as amended then carried.

MR. FORBES said, at the last Meeting of the Council, he had obtained the nomination of a Select Committee to consider whether any amendment was necessary in Act XIII of 1856, in consequence of a doubt having arisen whether the authority of the Commissioners of Police and the Police Forces of Calcutta, Madras, and Bombay extended under that Act to the Ports of those Presidencies respectively. The Report of that Select Committee he had presented this day. The Committee stated that they did not consider any amendment in the Act necessary, but that they were of opinion that the peculiar circumstances of Madras required that some Section should be inserted in this Bill to give the Police of that town the same authority within the limits of the Port which they already had within the limits of the town. In accordance with the recommendation of the Committee, he should move that the following new Section be inserted after Section IX:—

"From and after the passing of this Act, it shall be lawful for the Commissioner of Police and the Members of the Police Force at Madras to exercise within the limits of the Port of Madras, as defined under the provisions of Act XXII of 1855, all powers given to them respectively by Act XIII of 1856; and all provisions of the last mentioned Act applicable to the said Commissioner and Police Force at Madras, shall apply to them respectively in the execution of the powers hereby given."

MR. PEACOCK said, he did not think that the words "all powers given to them respectively by Act XIII of 1856" would be quite sufficient. Act XIII of 1856 gave the Magistrate jurisdiction to try cases of larceny under fifty Rupees. If a man stole property above the value of fifty Rupees, the Magistrate could not try him. But it appeared to him (Mr. Peacock) that, under this Bill, Police Officers ought to have the power of apprehending persons who stole goods in transit even though the value should exceed fifty Rupees. He should, therefore, move, as an amendment, that the words "or which may be lawfully exercised by constables within the local limits of the jurisdiction of the Supreme Court" be inserted after the words and figures "Act XIII of 1856."

The amendment was agreed to, and the Section then passed.

Section X, the Preamble, and the Title were passed as they stood.

The Council having resumed its sitting, the Bill was reported.

INSTITUTION OF SUITS AND APPEALS.—(N. W. PROVINCES.)

MR. HARINGTON moved that the Council resolve itself into a Committee on the Bill "for the relief of persons who, in consequence of the recent disturbances, may have been prevented from instituting or prosecuting suits or appeals in the Courts of the North-Western Provinces within the period allowed by law;" and that the Committee be instructed to consider the Bill in the amended form in which it had been recommended by the Select Committee to be passed.

Agreed to.

The Bill passed through Committee without amendment.

The Council having resumed its sitting, the Bill was reported.

ADJOURNMENT.

MR. GRANT moved that the Council adjourn till Wednesday next, the 21st instant, at 10 O'Clock, to enable him to introduce a Bill to extend Act IV of 1858 (for providing for the exercise of certain powers by the Governor General during his absence from the Council of India.)

Agreed to.

Wednesday, July 21, 1858.

PRESENT:

The Hon'ble the Chief Justice, *Vice-President*, in the Chair.

Hon. J. P. Grant,
Hon. Major Gen. Sir J. Outram,
Hon. H. Ricketts,
Hon. B. Peacock,
P. W. LeGeyt, Esq.
E. Currie, Esq.
Hon. Sir A. W. Buller,
H. B. Harington, Esq. and
H. Forbes, Esq.

ABSENCE OF GOVERNOR GENERAL.

THE VICE PRESIDENT read the following Message from the President in Council to the Legislative Council:—

"MESSAGE No. 148.

"The President in Council informs the Legislative Council that the Governor General has represented that it is expedient that he should be enabled to prolong his absence from the Presidency for a further period of six months.

"By order of the Honorable the President in Council.

"CECIL BEADON,
"*Secy. to the Govt. of India.*

"FORT WILLIAM,
"*July 17th*, 1858."

MR. GRANT said, in pursuance of the notice which he had given at the last Meeting of the Council, he now moved the first reading of a Bill to continue in force for a further period of six months Act IV of 1858, for providing for the exercise of certain powers by the Governor-General during his absence from the Council of India. When these Acts were first introduced into the system of Indian Government, the practice was not to limit their duration to a fixed time, but to make them cease on the return of the Governor General to the Presidency, whenever that should be. But in the administration of Lord Dalhousie, it was thought by that Nobleman right that, as such Acts provided for an abnormal state of affairs, and were in their nature temporary, they should bear that appearance on the face of them; and accordingly, they had since been passed only for a certain fixed period, it being always in the power of the Legislative Council to prolong them if the circumstances in which they originated continued to be the same. When Act IV of 1858 was passed, the same course was followed; and though the operation of the Law was limited to the short time of six months, he thought he might say that this was done rather on the possibility that events might so fall out that the country might be restored to its usual state of tranquillity in the course of that time, than in the expectation that this would be the case. That this had not been the case was manifest. Progress, and great progress had been made; but every Honorable Member was aware that the work had not yet been completed. He did not, of course, speak of the work of reorganization and reconstruction. That most arduous duty, which the Government had still before it, required deliberation and consultation. He did not speak in consequence of that work not having been yet done; but he spoke of the prompt daily action rendered necessary by the occurrence of daily events in the North-Western Provinces. One point which alone required the continued presence of Supreme Authority in the Upper Provinces, Honorable Members must be well aware of. In the Province of Oude, much remained to be done. It must be manifest to every body that for Military operations to be renewed in Oude, the commencement of the dry season was all that was awaited. These operations, he hoped, would, in one sense, be very different from those which occurred last year. He hoped that we had seen the last of our great and bloody struggles in the field. But a great Military demonstration was very obviously necessary in Oude—a demonstration which would have probably as much a political as a military character. For that, and for many other reasons, it was quite as requisite still that the Head of the Supreme Government should be on the spot, vested with the powers of the Governor General in Council which Act IV of 1858 had given him temporarily, as it was when that Act was passed; and it was necessary therefore for the Council, unless it wished to go backwards, to extend the operation of the Act.

With these observations, he moved the first reading of the Bill. It was very short, as also was the Statement of Objects and Reasons which he had annexed to it; and he suggested that both might be read in full by the Clerk at the table.

The Statement of Objects and Reasons and the Bill were read by the Clerk.

Mr. GRANT moved that the Standing Orders be suspended, in order that he might carry the Bill through its remaining stages forthwith.

Sir JAMES OUTRAM seconded the Motion, which was then carried.

Mr. GRANT moved that the Bill be now read a second time.

The Motion was carried, and the Bill read a second time.

Mr. GRANT moved that the Council resolve itself into a Committee on the Bill.

Agreed to.

The Bill passed through Committee without amendment, and was reported.

Mr. GRANT moved that the Bill be now read a third time and passed.

The Motion was carried, and the Bill read a third time.

Mr. RICKETTS was requested to take the Bill to the President in Council, in order that it may be transmitted to the Governor General for his assent.

The Council adjourned.

Mr. Grant.

Saturday, July 24, 1858.

PRESENT:

The Hon'ble the Chief Justice, Vice-President, in the Chair.

Hon. Major Genl. Sir Jas. Outram,	E. Currie, Esq.,
Hon. H. Ricketts,	Hon. Sir A. W. Buller,
Hon. B. Peacock,	H. B. Harington, Esq., and
P. W. LeGeyt, Esq.,	H. Forbes, Esq.

PROCEEDINGS IN LUNACY IN THE SUPREME COURTS.

Mr. CURRIE presented the Report of the Select Committee on the Bill "to regulate proceedings in Lunacy in Her Majesty's Courts of Judicature."

INSOLVENT DEBTORS (MOFUSSIL).

Mr. LeGEYT presented the Report of the Select Committee on the subject of a Law for the relief of Insolvent Debtors in the Mofussil.

MADRAS MARINE POLICE.

Mr. FORBES moved that the Bill "for the maintenance of a Police Force for the Port of Madras" be read a third time and passed.

The Motion was carried, and the Bill read a third time.

INSTITUTION OF SUITS AND APPEALS (NORTH-WESTERN PROVINCES).

Mr. HARINGTON moved that the Bill "for the relief of persons who, in consequence of the recent disturbances, may have been prevented from instituting or prosecuting suits or appeals in the Courts of the North-Western Provinces within the period allowed by Law" be read a third time and passed.

The Motion was carried, and the Bill read a third time.

ESTATE OF THE LATE NABOB OF THE CARNATIC.

Mr. PEACOCK moved that the Council resolve itself into a Committee on the Bill "to provide for the administration of the estate and for the payment of the debts of the late Nabob of the Carnatic;" and that the Committee be instructed to consider the

Bill in the amended form in which the Select Committee had recommended it to be passed.

Agreed to.

The Bill passed through Committee without amendment, and was reported.

SETTLEMENT OF ALLUVIAL LANDS (BENGAL).

MR. CURRIE moved that the Council resolve itself into a Committee on the Bill "to make further provision for the settlement of land gained by alluvion in the Presidency of Fort William in Bengal;" and that the Committee be instructed to consider the Bill in the amended form in which the Select Committee had recommended it to be passed.

Agreed to.

Section I provided as follows:—

"When land is added by alluvial accession to an estate paying Revenue to Government. if it be so agreed on between the Revenue Authorities and the proprietor or proprietors, the Revenue assessed upon the alluvial land may be added to the jumma of the original estate; and in such case a new engagement shall be executed for the payment of the aggregate amount, and that amount shall be substituted in the Collector's rent-roll for the former jumma of the original estate. If the proprietor or proprietors object to such an arrangement, or if the Revenue Authorities are of opinion that a settlement of the alluvial land cannot properly be made for the same term as the existing settlement of the original estate, the alluvial land shall be assessed and settled as a separate estate with a separate jumma, and shall thenceforward be regarded and treated as in all respects separate from, and independent of, the original estate."

MR. PEACOCK said, when this Bill was before the Council on the motion for the second reading, he took the opportunity of mentioning that he should not consider himself bound to the principle upon which it was prepared. It appeared to him that Section I altered the rights of private persons as they at present existed. By Regulation XI 1825, Section IV, Clause 1, it was enacted as follows:—

"When land may be gained by gradual accession, whether from the recess of a river or of the sea, it shall be considered an increment to the tenure of the person to whose land or estate it is thus annexed, whether such land or estate be held immediately from Government by a zemindar or other superior landholder, or as a subordinate tenure by any description of under-tenant whatever."

Regulation II. 1819 enacted that land gained by alluvion should be liable to assessment. Regulation XI. 1825 declared, for the first time, what were to be the rights of claimants to land gained by alluvion. It was merely a declaratory Act. Prior to its being passed, the Sudder Court had decided that all alluvion became a part of, and an increment to, the estate to which it accrued. Now if alluvion became a part of, and an increment to, the estate to which it accrued, he apprehended that the owner of the original estate had the same rights and interests in it as he had in the original estate. This Regulation declared that the increment "shall not entitle the person in possession of the estate or tenure to which the land may be annexed, to a right of property or permanent interest therein beyond that possessed by him in the estate or tenure to which the land may be annexed," and it reserved the rights of all under-tenants. When the Regulation said that the owner of the original estate was to have no right of property or permanent interest in the alluvion beyond that possessed by him in the original estate, it evidently implied that he was to have a right of property and an interest in it to that extent. As he (Mr. Peacock) understood the matter, the Courts had decided that, when an alluvion took place, it became a part of the original estate. Becoming a part of the original estate, the Regulation provided that it should be assessed with Government Revenue; and the question was—how was it to be assessed? In 1833, the Board of Revenue, by a Circular Order, declared:

"That all proprietors have a right to admission to terms of permanent engagement whenever they may think fit to demand it, unless indeed the alluvion has been let out in farm for a specified term, in consequence of their recusance."

In 1838, the Board issued another Circular Order, in which they said:—

"If the zemindar agrees to the terms of settlement, the jumma of the chur shall be added to, and included in, the original *tahood*, and the parent estate with its increment shall be considered a single mehal, charged with the aggregate increased jumma. But on the other hand, should the zemindar either refuse to accede to the terms of the settlement, or object to include it in his *tahood*, the land is to be let in farm for a period not exceeding ten years, the proprietor receiving malikana at the usual rate. Should, however, the parent estate be brought to sale for arrear of Revenue, the right of property in the churs will necessarily pass to the auction-purchaser."

By the terms of that Circular Order, the proprietor of an estate, if the estate was permanently settled, was entitled to have the alluvion, which became an increment to his estate, settled as a permanent tenure also. He had a right to have a fair assessment put upon the alluvion, to have the amount of that assessment added to the jumma of the original estate, and to hold both lands as one estate, charged with one consolidated jumma. But in 1841, the Board of Revenue issued another Circular Order, by which it was declared:—

"1st.—That the Commissioner of Revenue shall be the party to determine whether the settlement of a chur shall be permanent or temporary. 2ndly.—That if the party entitled to settlement object to the consolidation of the jumma of the chur with that of the parent estate, the increment shall be settled as a distinct mehal, and be henceforth held separately liable to the jumma assessed upon it."

By this Circular Order, the owner of a permanently settled estate to which alluvion had become annexed was entitled to have the alluvion settled as part of the original estate, and on a permanent footing, only in the event of the Commissioner of Revenue consenting to such a settlement. On the other hand, if the proprietor of the original estate objected to take the alluvion as part of that estate, the alluvion would be settled as a separate tenure, and would be separately liable for its own jumma. In 1857, the Board of Revenue applied to the Government of Bengal to rescind the Circular Order of 1841, and suggested that the proper mode of settling alluvial lands was that laid down in the Circular Order of 1838, to which, accordingly, they proposed that the Revenue Authorities should be permitted to revert. This Bill had been introduced in consequence of that recommendation, and of a decision passed by the Sudder Court. The Council would recollect that, as originally drawn, it appeared in a very different form. It was opposed on the motion for the second reading, and was referred to a Select Committee with instructions to submit a preliminary Report suggesting any alterations in it which they might deem expedient previously to its publication. The Committee recommended certain alterations, but left the Bill very much as before with regard to the rights of under-tenants in alluvial lands. The Bill had since been further amended by them, and it now provided for those rights; but he still considered that it was objectionable. The first objection he had to it was that it still followed the principle of the Circular Order of 1841. Section I did not allow the owner of a permanently settled estate, when it was increased by alluvion, to require the Revenue Authorities to settle it as part of the original estate, if he pleased to add the amount assessed upon it to the jumma of the original estate, and to treat both estates as one tenure. It required the assent of the Revenue Authorities to the settlement of alluvion as a permanently settled estate; and if the Council passed it as it stood, it would deprive proprietors of permanently settled estates of the right which, as he understood the law, they now possessed to insist upon such settlements being made independently of the assent of the Revenue Authorities. By Regulation VII. 1822, which provided that alluvion should be assessed to the Government Revenue, lands, exceeding one hundred Biggahs, held upon invalid tenures were also liable to assessment. Such lands, he apprehended, would be settled permanently if within the limits of a permanently settled estate. But however that might be, Regulation XI. 1825, enacted that an alluvion should be considered a part of the estate to which it became annexed, and that the Zemindar or under-tenant should have in it no right or interest beyond that possessed by him in the original estate; in other words, that he should have in it the same right and interest that he had in the original estate; if, therefore, the original estate were permanently settled, he thought that the proprietor was entitled to have the alluvion settled permanently if he pleased. The Honorable Member for Bengal had communicated with Mr. Trevor, one of the Judges of the Sudder Court on this

Mr. Peacock

subject, and Mr. Trevor had sent a reply, in which he stated the same objection against the Bill which he (Mr. Peacock) was taking to it. He said :—

"The two objections to the Bill as I have seen it are, first, that though you in Section I. in accordance with Regulation XI. of 1825 acknowledge the ownership of the chur to be in the proprietor of the estate to which it accreted, you do not consider him entitled, if he so wishes, to have the chur incorporated with the estate: but you leave it with the Revenue authorities to determine whether the new property which belongs to a man by reason of its having become annexed to other property of his shall be held under the same engagement with the old property or not. Now as laws of settlement are subordinate to and acknowledge rights of property, it seems to me that this should not be, but that the wishes of the owner to have the chur incorporated with the parent estate should entitle him to have that done."

It appeared to him (Mr. Peacock) that, when the Legislative Council was called upon to lay down such a rule as was contained in Section I of this Bill, it ought to consider whether or not it was a rule which affected private rights. An alluvion might be of very great importance to the estate which it adjoined. The value of the estate might greatly depend on its having a frontage on the river; but if an alluvion formed between it and the river, were to be treated as a separate estate, the original estate might be entirely cut off from its river-frontage, and its value consequently be materially diminished. He could see no necessity for the rule laid down in Section 1, by which the Revenue Authorities might refuse to settle alluvion permanently, though annexed to a permanently settled estate. The Board of Revenue saw no necessity for it. On the contrary, they considered it right, and had recommended that the Revenue Authorities should be permitted to return to the original rule of 1838, which gave the owner of a permanently settled estate the right of having land added to it by alluvion settled on the same terms as the original estate, and as part of such estate, without the consent of the Revenue Authorities. The Bill itself shewed no very good grounds for altering this private right. It purported to be designed for the removal, not of doubts as to the existence of the right, but of "doubts respecting the course proper to be followed in the settlement of land added by alluvial accession to estates paying revenue to Government." To him, it appeared that, unless some very good reason was shewn to the contrary, which in his opinion there was not, the course proper to be followed was to respect the private rights, which individuals interested in original estates now possessed by law, of insisting on alluvial accretions being incorporated with their estates if they pleased, and not to alter that right by making such incorporation subject to the consent of the Revenue Authorities.

He should move as an amendment that the words "it be so agreed on between the Revenue Authorities and" be omitted from the Section, in order that the following words, "is or are desirous that the alluvial land shall be assessed as part of the original estate," might be introduced after the word "proprietors." He had other objections to the Section, to which he would presently advert; but he thought it better that this point should be separately considered first. He would not pledge himself to support the Bill on the motion for the third reading, even if the amendment which he had proposed were carried; but the amendment would remove much of the objection which he now felt to the Bill, and, as he might be out-voted in his opposition to the motion for the third reading, he desired to avail himself of this opportunity of rendering it as little open to objection as possible.

MR. RICKETTS said, before remarking on the objections which had been brought forward by the Honorable and learned Member, he desired to remove an impression which apparently existed in the Council, and certainly prevailed out of doors, that the resumption and settlement of alluvial lands was still going on in Bengal. This was not the case. Resumption, and consequently settlement of such lands had been stopped in Bengal since the enactment of Act IX of 1847. Previous to the passing of that Act, it was usual for the Revenue Authorities, whenever they heard of alluvion having annexed itself to an estate, to depute persons to measure it, and, having measured it, to institute a suit for its resumption, and then to settle it. But that system had been found to be mischievous in many ways. It led to all sorts of abuses. If, for instance, a man had a spite against another, he accused him of being guilty of a chur; and corruption, perjury, forgery, and chicanery, followed as a matter of course. Act IX of 1847 was passed for the prevention of these abuses. It enacted that all investigations then pending regarding the liability to assessment of alluvial lands, should be discontinued forthwith, and that no suits for the resumption of such lands in any district should be instituted until ten years after the approval by Government of the revenue survey. It was necessary he should explain what had been the effect of that Law. For many years past, the whole of the Bengal Presidency had been under survey. This survey had not been completed yet. However much alluvion might now be found annexed to a zemindary, it must, as a matter of course, be measured as part of the original estate. In the Eastern parts of Bengal, there might be a case in which an estate originally consisting of perhaps only one thousand acres, now comprised ten thousand acres. All this increase must now be measured as part of the original estate; but ten years after the approval of the survey now in hand, should another survey take place, then, any land which might be found in excess of the land now measured, would be liable to assessment. There could be no resumption suit instituted now, and therefore there could be no settlement made now; and as the present survey could not be completed for four or five years, there would not be a second survey for some years to come. It appeared to him that this Bill, if passed, would probably be a dead letter for at least fifteen years to come.

He would now come to the objections urged by the Honorable and learned Member opposite (Mr. Peacock) against the Section.

It was quite true that the Revenue Authorities held one opinion as to the meaning of the Law in 1838, and another in 1841. As there was a difference of opinion then, so was there a difference of opinion now; and he would leave it to those learned Members who were better versed in construing law to decide which of these opinions was the correct one. He would apply himself to consider what the practical effect of altering the Section as the Honorable and learned Mover of the amendment desired, would be. These alluvial lands, when first surveyed and settled, were oftentimes nearly entirely waste. There might be one or two squatters; but with such exception, the land was generally entirely waste. The land being entirely waste, there were no legitimate assets on which to assess revenue; there were no rents. But the Revenue Authorities could not give up tens of thousands of acres of alluvion in perpetuity to the zemindars to whose estates the alluvion had attached itself without any revenue at all; and the only alternative would be to settle them subject to a *russuddee* assessment, which, being interpreted, meant an assessment progressively increasing. That must be, at best, mere guess work. But no one could well guess the suitable progressive assessment which should be fixed on many square miles; and the consequence would be that, when the Revenue Authorities came to assess this gradually increasing jumma on alluvial formations, the owners of the original estates would be frightened and unwilling to engage. The engagement might make their fortunes, or it might ruin them, and they would not incur the risk. The necessary result must be that the alluvial formations would be let out in farm, the Revenue Authorities of the day interpreting the Law as it was interpreted by the present Board of Revenue, and the owners of the original estates would lose possession. The settlement which was formerly made with farmers, had been made with the proprietors of original estates for the last twenty years; this was equally advantageous to the proprietors and the Government; and, whatever the intention of the old Laws might be, he certainly thought it advisable to let the existing ruling stand as it was, giving the Revenue Authorities discretion to settle alluvial formations on fair terms with the proprietors of original estates. He should, therefore, oppose the amendment.

MR. HARINGTON said, he concurred generally in the remarks of the Honorable and learned member of Council on his left (Mr. Peacock), and it was his intention to support the amendment moved by him. In the few observations which he had ventured to address to the Council in the debate which took place on the motion of the Honorable Member for Bengal for the second reading of the Bill now before the Committee, he had stated that he had no doubt that the framers of Regulation XI. 1825 fully intended that alluvial accretions should be incorporated with, and form part of, the estate to which they might annex themselves, and should share its fate, whatever that might be; and that such accretions could not be considered an estate within the meaning of Regulation VIII. 1800, though leased out to a farmer with a separate jumma, so long as they were not formally and absolutely severed from the parent estate with the consent and by the act of the proprietor; and notwithstanding the able arguments which had been adduced in support of a different construction of the law from that placed upon it by himself and others, he adhered to the opinion which he had formerly expressed. The subject had already been so fully discussed that he would not occupy the time of the Council with any lengthened remarks on the present occasion; but he must repeat that the phraseology made use of by the framers of Regulation XI. 1825, as well as by the framers of Act IX. of 1847, clearly shewed that they contemplated and intended the union or incorporation of alluvial formations of land with the estate to which they might become attached, not their separation therefrom, or that they should constitute a separate and distinct holding. In the one Law, we had the words "increment" and "annexed" used more than once: in the other, the word "added"; but in neither Law did we find any words of an opposite tendency, from which it might be inferred that separation was intended to be the rule just as much as addition—disjunction just as much as annexation. The Council had no right to assume that the words which he had quoted, had found their way by accident into the Laws of 1825 and 1847, or that they were made use of by the framers of those Laws merely because they were the most convenient terms they could employ. No doubt, they were introduced designedly, and with the intent which he had already mentioned; and so long as we retained the Law of 1825, which enacted that, "when land may be gained by gradual accession, whether from the recess of a river or the sea, it shall be considered an increment to the tenure of the person to whose land or estate it is thus annexed"—and the present Bill did not propose to abrogate this Law—he did not see how we could consistently pass an Act declaring the right of the Collector or Settlement Officer to sever such land from the estate to which it had accreted, and to form it into a separate estate with the usual liability to sale for any arrear of revenue that might accrue thereon, notwithstanding that the proprietor of the parent estate might desire the incorporation of the alluvial accretion with that estate, and might be quite willing to pay the additional revenue assessed upon it. The two Laws appeared to him to be incompatible. The one said, the alluvion shall be an increment—that was, something added; the other said, if the Collector pleases, it shall not be an increment, but something separate; and if the Council passed the proposed Law in its present form, he certainly thought it would go contrary to the spirit of the existing Regulations, and to the intention of those who had framed them.

But this was not the only objection that he had to the Section under discussion, as now worded. The object of the Bill, as stated in the title, was to make further provision for the settlement of land gained by alluvion in the Presidency of Fort William in Bengal; and this object the Bill proposed to accomplish by enacting in Section 1 that—

> "When land is added by alluvial accession to an estate paying revenue to Government, if it be so agreed upon between the Revenue Authorities and the proprietor or proprietors, the revenue assessed upon the alluvial land may be added to the jumma of the original estate, and in such case a new engagement shall be executed for the payment of the aggregate amount, and that amount shall be substituted in the Collector's rent roll for the former jumma of the original estate."

In the case, therefore, of permanently settled estates, in which there was this agreement between the two contracting parties—namely, the Government on the one side, and the proprietor of the alluvion on the other—the assessment of the alluvion became a permanent assessment, just as much as the assessment of the original estate had been a permanent assessment from the date of the decennial settlement, and the entire estate, composed partly of the original lands and partly of lands gained by alluvion, was a permanently settled estate within the meaning of the Law. So far, good; and in such cases, it was obvious that no injustice was done to the proprietors of alluvial lands, if willing to engage for the revenue assessed upon them. But the Section went on to say—

"If the proprietor or proprietors object to such an arrangement, or if the Revenue Authorities are of opinion that a settlement of the alluvial land cannot properly be made for the same term as the existing settlement of the original estate, the alluvial land shall be assessed and settled as a separate estate with a separate jumma, and shall thenceforward be regarded and treated as in all respects separate from, and independent of, the original estate."

Under this part of the Section, therefore, the right of determining whether the settlement of the alluvion should be a permanent or only a temporary settlement—whether it should be in perpetuity or for a term of years only—virtually rested with the Collector or Settlement Officer, subject to the control of the superior Revenue Authorities. But he knew of no Law which conferred this power, or this large discretion on the Revenue Officers. Section III Regulation II. 1819, according to which the settlement of alluvial lands was required to be made, certainly did not give it; and he would ask—from whence was it derived? It appeared to him that the owner of the alluvion in a permanently settled estate either had a right to have the revenue assessed thereon fixed in perpetuity, supposing him to be willing to pay the same, or that he had not that right. If he had a right to a permanent settlement, he (Mr. Harington) was not aware of any law under which the Collector could deprive him of it. If he had no such right, he (Mr. Harington) was equally ignorant of any law under the authority of which the Collector could confer it upon him. The question, then, resolved itself into one of right or no right; and he thought that this question should be carefully considered, and that a decision should be come to upon it by the Committee before passing the Section under discussion in its present form. After much consideration, the conclusion at which he had arrived was that the right existed; and he found himself borne out in this view by a Circular Order issued by the Sudder Board of Revenue under date the 24th August 1830, to which was appended a letter from Government dated the 27th July preceding, in which the Government said:—

"On the other hand, in cases of alluvion, land of wastes reclaimed, of jagheers resumed, of which there are no proprietors, and in all similar cases where the proprietary right is vested immediately in Government, the prohibition of the Honorable Court against the alienation of that right" (referring to permanent settlements) "applies in full force; but it does not apply to cases in which the Regulations have expressly declared the proprietary right to be vested in individuals. Of such lands, the proprietors are entitled to obtain perpetual settlements in those districts in which the revenue has been settled in perpetuity on their conforming to the conditions of the Regulations. The principle, indeed, has been distinctly recognized by the Honorable Court in reply to a letter from this Government dated the 1st August 1822, citing a former letter which contained the reasons for the conclusion that the zemindars in Behar are entitled, under the rules of 1793, to have the settlement of their lands made perpetual. The Honorable Court, in their Despatch dated the 10th November 1824, observed as follows:—'When the Law gives, as here you say it does, a right to the settlement in perpetuity, there is no doubt with respect to the proceeding which ought to be adopted; and even where the case may appear somewhat doubtful, Government should afford to individuals the benefit of a liberal construction.'"

The right of the proprietor of all alluvial lands to a permanent settlement of such lands when annexed to an estate settled in perpetuity, was further declared in the Sudder Board of Revenue's Circular dated 30th April 1833, and in the letter to the address of the Commissioner of Chittagong which was annexed thereto. In the concluding paragraph of that letter, the Board expressly said:—

"Whenever there is a right of property or permanent interest, as there must always be, in alluvial increments to permanently assessed estates, the zemindars of such permanently settled estates are entitled to engage for the revenue assessed upon the new land in perpetuity; and whenever there exists not this right of property or permanent interest, the orders of the Honorable the Court of Directors forbid a perpetual assessment."

Now, assuming this to be a correct interpretation of the law as respected the settlement of alluvial lands in per-

Mr. Harington

manently settled estates—and as, at the date of these Circulars, serious objections were entertained to permanent settlements, it could scarcely be conceived that the Government would have conceded the right of the owner of alluvial lands in permanently settled estates to a settlement thereof in perpetuity, had the law not clearly recognized such right—the Section of the Bill before the Committee appeared to him to violate the right of the proprietors of alluvial formations of land in permanently settled estates in this respect just as much as it infringed what he considered to be the right of the owner of the estate to insist upon the incorporation of the alluvion therewith upon the sole condition of his agreeing to pay the revenue assessed upon it. The two rights appeared to him to go together.

With regard to the observations which the Honorable Member of Council opposite (Mr. Ricketts) had based upon Act IX of 1847, he deemed it sufficient to remark that that law made no alteration in the rules existing at the date of its promulgation for the settlement of alluvial lands. On the contrary, Section VI expressly declared that—"whenever land has been added to any estate paying revenue directly to Government, the local Revenue Authorities shall without delay assess the same with a revenue payable to Government according to the rules in force for assessing alluvial increments, and shall report their proceedings to the Sudder Board of Revenue, whose orders thereupon shall be final." The rules here alluded to were those contained in Section III Regulation II. 1819 and Regulation XI. 1825; and Act IX of 1847 had, therefore, no bearing on this part of the question. No doubt, as remarked by the Honorable Member of Council, there was a difficulty in making a permanent settlement of alluvial lands immediately after their formation; but the difficulty in carrying a law into effect was no reason for acting contrary to it so long as it existed. The Collector must do his best, leaving to proprietors of alluvial lands either to accept or to decline the settlement of them on the terms proposed, according as they might consider most for their own interest.

THE CHAIRMAN said, the difficulties of this Revenue question (and the difficulties of most Revenue questions were neither few nor inconsiderable to those who had not, like the Honorable Member on his left, Mr. Ricketts, been conversant with such subjects from their youth upwards) were, he thought, greatly increased by the somewhat singular conduct which Honorable Members had thought it proper to adopt with respect to the Bill. The question which he had had the honor to put from the Chair was that the Council should resolve itself into a Committee upon the Bill, and should consider it in the form in which it had been recommended by the Select Committee to be passed. Among the names of the Members who composed that Select Committee, he found that of the Honorable Member for the North-Western Provinces; and yet, as far as he could follow the Honorable Member's speech, the Honorable Member seemed to have serious objections to the Bill itself, and he certainly had very considerable objections to the form in which it was recommended by the Select Committee to be passed. Then, the Honorable and learned Member who had moved the amendment, appeared to treat this Bill as if it were designed for the invasion of private rights, and in the observations which he had made, had not confined himself to the subject matter of his amendment or of the Section, but had gone largely into reasons tending to shew that no such Bill ought to be passed at all. He (the Chairman) must emphatically deny, for himself and for the other Members of the Council who were connected with the Bill, that they had the slightest intention to interfere with any private right whatever. He must also say that it was not exactly correct that the Select Committee which amended the Bill before publication, had made no provision for the rights of under-tenants. He admitted that the Select Committee to which the Bill had been referred after publication, had made ampler and clearer provision for them; but the Bill, as amended by the first Select Committee, fully reserved to under-tenants the rights conferred upon them by Section IV of Regulation XI. 1825. There had been considerable difference of opinion in the Council as to what the actual law was, and as to another point, which was perhaps not properly a matter for discussion here, namely, the correctness of a decision passed by the Sudder Court; but he had understood all in the Council—with, perhaps, the exception of the Honorable and learned Member—to be agreed in the propriety of a Bill which should provide, in some way or another, for the legalization and recognition of the separate settlement of these churs; and he understood the intention of the Act was rather to benefit than to invade the rights of the zemindar or the under-tenant, by protecting them from the disadvantages which, it was admitted, would result from the incorporation of an alluvial formation with the original estate. No one desired to do anything in derogation of the rights of zemindars or under-tenants. The main difficulty of the question arose from this. There were two distinct subjects, and distinct laws relating to each subject. On the one hand was the proprietary right in alluvial accretions, and the law declaring and defining that; on the other hand there was the superior right of the Government to the revenue to be assessed on these accretions, and the laws declaring that, and defining the mode in which the right should be asserted. All that was designed by this Section was to enable the Government to assert that right in a way which, while it would protect the public revenue, would, at the same time, be beneficial to the landholder. He admitted that it was a fair and legitimate question to raise whether the Section did not go too far in requiring the assent of the Revenue Authorities as well as the consent of the proprietor to the incorporation of the alluvial land with the original estate. The reasons for this provision had been stated by the Honorable Member on his left (Mr. Ricketts); and it appeared to him that, whether the Council thought it right or not to affirm the principle as this Section affirmed it, it must practically come to the same thing; because these churs were, in many cases, incapable of permanent assessment on any just principle; and if the Revenue Authorities were driven to incorporate them with the estates to which they accrued, subject to a permanent jumma, this must follow—that, to protect the public revenue, they must fix some arbitrary sum which would represent the right of the Government in the chur not as it existed then, but as it might be presumed to exist at some future time. The zemindar would say—" I shall not agree to such an arrangement. I prefer a settlement for a certain term, or to have the land let on lease;"—and if the chur were settled for a certain term, it must be settled as a separate holding. Therefore, whether the Section required the assent of the Revenue Authorities or not, the result would be the same.

On principle, he had no great objection to the amendment, but from all he had heard from the Revenue Authorities, he thought it would be better for all parties to leave the Section as it stood.

Mr. CURRIE said, he should first say a few words in reference to the prefatory observations of the Honorable Member on his right (Mr. Ricketts). The Honorable Member had said that this Bill, if passed, would be a dead letter for at least fifteen years to come. If he (Mr. Currie) thought so, he certainly would not have introduced it so prematurely, or, having introduced it, he would not have continued to press it upon the attention of the Council after the strong opposition which had been raised against it upon the Motion for the second reading. But he considered it a very necessary and important Law. It was very true, as stated by the Honorable Member, that resumption operations had been discontinued since the passing of Act IX of 1847; but the churs which had been resumed before that period had, for the most part, been settled on temporary engagements. These settlements were continually falling in; re-settlements had to be made; and the Settlement Officers required some Law for their guidance. Again, the new Law was enacted in 1847. The Survey of the Behar Province was pretty well finished when that Law came into operation. The Act provided that at any time after the expiry of ten years from the approval of a revenue survey in any district, the Government of Bengal might direct "a new survey of lands on the banks of rivers and on the shores of the sea, in order to ascertain the changes that may have taken place since the date of the last previous survey;" and that if, on such re-survey, land should appear

The Chairman

to have been added to any estate, it should be assessed with a revenue payable to Government. The Act also declared the approval of the revenue survey of Chittagong to have taken place on the 6th September 1842; of Behar, on the 9th November 1844; of Patna, on the 22nd June 1844; of Shahabad, on the 28th November 1846; of Sarun, on the 18th February 1847; and so on. The Government, therefore, if it chose, might now order a re-survey of the estates situate on the banks of rivers in those districts, and the present Bill, if passed, would at once come into operation. It would be necessary to settle the newly-formed lands, and they would be settled according to the Law and the practice which might be in force. He, therefore, thought that it was a very pressing and important measure.

With regard to the objection taken by the Honorable and learned Mover of the amendment, he had very little to say in addition to what had already been so justly urged by the Honorable Member on his right (Mr. Ricketts) and the Honorable and learned Chairman. The Honorable and learned Member, as had been remarked already, had not confined himself merely to his amendment, but had entered into arguments which went to the whole principle of the Bill. The principle of the Bill had already been determined by the vote of the Council on the Motion for the second reading. That vote recognized the expediency and justice of the separate settlement of alluvial lands. He should, therefore, on this occasion, confine himself to the objection that the Section as it stood deprived the owners of estates, to which alluvion had accrued, of the right of claiming that the alluvion should be incorporated with those estates. Now, the only ground on which the Revenue Authorities could ever object to incorporate alluvial land with the original estate, would be that the land was not fit for permanent settlement. Indeed, that was the ground expressly indicated in the Bill. If an alluvion was fit to be settled permanently, there could be no possible objection on the part of the Revenue Authorities to incorporate it with the original estate. The question therefore resolved itself into this:—Was the zemindar entitled to claim that, in all cases, he should have a permanent settlement? He (Mr. Currie) admitted at once that in permanently-settled districts, the general principle was that any settlement that was made, should be permanent; but cases might arise in which a permanent settlement would be obviously inexpedient; and where that was the case, permanent settlement should not be made, unless there was a legal necessity for it. No such legal necessity existed here. The pledge given at the decennial settlement applied only to estates which were at that time settled with the proprietors, or held khas, or let in farm. It was not necessarily applicable to lands which had formed since that period, or to lands which were waste, and not included in any estate at the time of the settlement. With respect to both these descriptions of land, the practice had been to make temporary settlements whenever the condition of the land was such as to be unfit for settlement in perpetuity.

The Honorable Member for the North-Western Provinces had relied especially on the terms of Regulation XI. 1825. He (Mr. Currie) had always contended, and he maintained still, that Regulation XI. 1825 had nothing whatever to do with the arrangements between the Government and the proprietor of the estate. Its object and effect were to determine the proprietary right in the alluvion as between individuals. The arrangements between the Government and the proprietor were expressly reserved to be dealt with under other Laws.

The Honorable Member had also referred in support of his argument to the wording of Act IX of 1847. But Act IX of 1847, so far as it bore on the question at all, was rather in favor of the view which he (Mr. Currie) took. Section V of the Act said:—

"And it is hereby enacted that whenever, on inspection of any such new map, it shall appear to the Local Revenue Authorities that land has been washed away from, or lost to any estate paying revenue directly to Government, they shall, without loss of time, make a deduction from the Sudder jumma of the said estate equal to so much of the whole Sudder jumma of the estate as bears to the whole the same proportion as the Mofussil jumma of the land lost bears to the Mofussil jumma of the whole estate."

And Section VI said :—

"And it is hereby enacted that whenever, on inspection of any such new map, it shall appear to the Local Revenue Authorities that land has been added to any estate paying revenue directly to Government, they shall without delay"—

do what? Not add the revenue payable upon it to the Sudder jumma of the estate, which would be the correlative of the previous Section, but—

"assess the same with a revenue payable to Government according to the rules in force for assessing alluvial increments."

Therefore, he maintained that, whether we looked at the pledge given at the time of the decennial settlement, or at the law now in force with respect to the settlement of alluvial lands, there was no legal right in a Zemindar to claim a permanent settlement of such lands. It was very true that, as the Honorable Member had said, the Board of Revenue did, in 1833 and 1838, recognize this right as attaching to proprietors of alluvial lands; but he doubted whether that construction had ever been acted upon; certainly, it had not been acted upon to any great extent; and the very same Authority interpreted the law differently in 1841. It then held that the Revenue Authorities should determine whether the assessment of alluvial formations should be permanent or temporary. The rule which was laid down in 1841, with the sanction of Government, and circulated to all Revenue Officers, and which had regulated the practice ever since, was this:—

"The Local Commissioner shall determine, with reference to the circumstances of each alluvial formation, whether a temporary lease for any number of years, or a permanent settlement shall be made. Should the party entitled to a settlement object to the consolidation of the jumma assessed on the increment with that of the original estate, the increment shall be settled as a distinct Muhal, and shall thenceforth be held separately liable for the jumma assessed upon it."

That was the rule now in force; and, as had been shewn already by the Honorable Member on his right and the Honorable and learned Chief Justice, it was highly expedient that such should continue to be the rule. The Honorable Member on his right had explained that, unless the Revenue Authorities were allowed to make temporary settlements when the land was not fit for settlement in perpetuity, the only alternative open to them would be to offer terms to proprietors which the proprietors could not, with any prudence, accept. Perhaps, it might not be out of place here to read the view which was taken by the Government regarding settlements of this nature. In a letter addressed by the Government to the Commissioner of Chittagong in the year 1842, occurred the following:—

"The objection taken by the Government to a russudee settlement is this,—that it is an assessment upon a contingency, and not upon a reality, and upon a contingency the occurrence of which is very likely to be prevented by the imposition of an assessment in anticipation. This objection, you will observe, applies as forcibly to a settlement in which the new jumma is suddenly imposed in full at the end of six years, as to one in which the enhancement is more gradual.

"The Government jumma, which is a tax upon rent, cannot properly be assessed until rent has begun to exist. A zemindar or farmer will often agree to a russud; and it may seem possible to argue that what one party willingly offers in a contract, the other may fairly take. But the consent of owners or speculators to given terms of contract in land revenue settlements in the country, is found by experience to rest very frequently upon no well-considered reasons; to be often occasioned by rivalry or spite; to be hasty, capricious, and improvident.

"Even if it were otherwise, as doubtless may sometimes be the case, it would seldom be right, upon the agreement of even a very careful party, to tax himself many years in anticipation of his resources, to hazard, not only the stability of the whole settlement, but what is of more consequence, the happiness of his under-tenants and cultivators, which must inevitably be affected by every change of settlement, farm, or ownership." * * * *

"Therefore, when a Mehal is to be settled of which more than a due proportion is out of cultivation, the settlement, if the Law allows an option, should be only temporary; the Mehal, under such circumstances, not being fit for permanent settlement. The assessment should be laid on the cultivated land, and during the term of the settlement, the uncultivated land should be left free of assessment."

He thought it had been clearly shewn that it would be for the interest of all parties—of the proprietor as well as of the Government—indeed, of the proprietor much more than of the

Mr. Currie

Government—that the Revenue Authorities should have the power of saying, in the first instance, whether the settlement should be permanent or temporary. The amendment proposed by the Honorable and learned Member opposite, though, as stated by the Honorable and learned Chief Justice, not objectionable in point of principle, was unpractical, unnecessary, and inexpedient; and he should, therefore, resist it.

MR. PEACOCK said if, in the course of his argument, he had said anything which could be interpreted into the assertion that this Bill was *intended* to interfere with private rights, he must ask to be forgiven. But he believed that he had said nothing which would admit of such a construction, and that he had been misunderstood. He had not said that the Bill was *designed* to interfere with private rights, but that it *did* interfere with private rights; and in order to shew that it did, it had been necessary for him to go into arguments proving that the Zemindar or owner of an estate to which alluvion had accrued, was, as the law now stood, entitled to have the alluvion settled as a permanently settled estate without the consent of the Revenue Authorities. He had taken no new ground to-day. When the Report of the Select Committee who amended the Bill before publication was presented to the Council, he urged against Section I the same objection which he was urging now. He said on that occasion:

"In assenting to the adoption of the Report, and the publication of the Bill in the form in which it was now presented, he must not be considered as binding himself to the alterations made in the Bill by the Select Committee. The first part of Section I authorized the assessment of alluvion as part of the estate, provided the Government should agree to that arrangement; whereas it appeared to him that the Zemindar had a right to insist upon such an assessment. The second part withheld from the Government the right of dissent in cases in which he thought it ought to have that right. * * * It appeared to him, therefore, that the Section was wrong—first in requiring the assent of Government to settlements to which Zemindars were entitled of right; and secondly, in not giving the Government a right of dissent in cases in which it might be necessary to exercise it—a right which he believed was now vested in them by law."

These were the two principal objections which he had to the Bill; and if he had trespassed on the time of the Council in advancing arguments in support of them which were unnecessary, he could only beg pardon; but he was not aware that he had brought forward any argument that had no bearing on the question. He wished to show that the owner of a permanently settled estate to which an alluvion had attached, had a right, as the law stood, to insist on the alluvion being likewise permanently settled, without the consent of the Revenue Authorities. The Honorable Member opposite (Mr. Ricketts) wished that the law should remain as it was; that was exactly what he (Mr. Peacock) wished. He wished the law to remain as it was; but the question was, what *was* the law? As he understood it, it was that which the Board of Revenue had interpreted it to be. The Board of Revenue said that the Circular Order of 1841 was not according to law, but that the Circular Order of 1838 was; and they asked permission to revert to the rule laid down in the latter Order. If the Circular of 1841 was law, where was the *necessity* for Section III of this Bill, which provided that "every separate settlement of alluvial land heretofore made shall be held as good and effectual for the purposes specified in Section I as it would have been if made subsequently to the passing of this Act?" If there was no doubt that the Circular Order of 1841 was law, there could be no necessity for declaring that all separate settlements of alluvion hitherto made under it, should be valid.

The Honorable Member opposite (Mr. Ricketts) had referred to Act IX of 1847. He (Mr. Peacock) had not alluded to that Act because he thought it bore more directly upon the objection which he had to the second branch of the first Section of the Bill than upon the point now under discussion; but it appeared to him that, taking the whole of the first Section together, it was directly at variance with that Act, and that, according to all the laws of construction, it would be a repeal of it *pro tanto*. According to the Act, as the Honorable Member opposite had shewn, ten years after the completion and approval of a revenue survey in any district, the Government of Bengal must direct a second survey.

MR. CURRIE—*not must*, but may.

MR. PEACOCK said, the intention was obviously that there should be a second survey ten years after the completion and approval of the first, and that a new map should be made in accordance with such survey: but, even if it were not compulsory, no settlement of alluvial land could be made until such a map was prepared. Section V of the Act said:—

"And it is hereby enacted that whenever, on inspection of any such new map, it shall appear to the Local Revenue Authorities that land has been washed away from or lost to any estate paying revenue directly to Government, they shall, without loss of time, make a deduction from the Sudder jumma of the said estate equal to so much of the whole Sudder jumma of the estate as bears to the whole the same proportion as the Mofussil jumma of the land lost bears to the Mofussil jumma of the whole estate."

Section VI of the Act said:—

"And it is hereby enacted that whenever, on inspection of any such new map, it shall appear to the Local Revenue Authorities that land has been added to any estate paying revenue directly to Government, they shall without delay assess the same with a revenue payable to Government according to the rules in force for assessing alluvial increments, and shall report their proceedings forthwith to the Sudder Board of Revenue, whose orders thereupon shall be final."

The object of these provisions was to make an allowance to the Zemindar in respect of land which might have been washed away from his estate, and at the same time to secure revenue to Government in respect of land which might have been added to his estate by alluvial accession. But Section I of this Bill said that, *whenever* land was added by alluvial accession to an estate, the increment should be assessed. Now a Zemindar might lose as much or more land on one side of his estate by encroachment of a river than he might gain on the other by recess of the river. Under Act IX of 1847, the revenue authorities could make no deduction in the sudder jumma of the estate for his loss and no increase with jumma for the gain until a new map was framed according to a re survey; but under Section I of this Bill, they could fix an assessment on the land gained whenever it accrued. He contended, therefore, that this Bill was inconsistent with Act IX of 1847, and it appeared to him that it was wholly unnecessary. It appeared to him unnecessary to say that a Zemindar should not be entitled to have an accretion to his estate settled permanently, like the original estate. When the Board of Revenue proposed that the Circular Order of 1841 should be rescinded, and that the Circular Order of 1838 should be reverted to, it consisted of three Members, Messrs. Dampier, Stainforth, and Allen. They observed:—

"Little need be said, the Board imagine, to prove to his Honor that the Circular Order of 1841, in so far as it differs essentially from that of 1838, must be, if not contrary to the law, at any rate at least defective in acting up to the requirements of it. The Board that recommended the rule of 1841 allowed the legality of the practice enjoined in 1838. This gave the zemindar the power of insisting upon a permanent settlement when engaging for the chur; that leaves it entirely with the Commissioner to determine the nature of the settlement. This lays it down that, if the zemindar refuses to have the jumma of the chur incorporated with that of the parent mehal, the chur is to be farmed out and the zemindar is only to receive malikana; that (in the event of a like refusal) he may engage for the chur as a separate estate."

He could see no greater difficulty in carrying out the rule laid down in the Circular Order of 1838, than there was in carrying out the rule laid down in the Circular Order of 1841. If the Zemindar wished to have an alluvion adjoining his estate, incorporated with the estate, and was by law entitled to have it so incorporated, let not the right be taken from him. It was idle to say that there would be difficulty in settling the alluvion as a permanently settled estate; because that difficulty applied, not only to this, but to other cases, and the Honorable Mover of the Bill did not propose to remove it with respect to any case except this. The difficulty must be got over. The law had pledged the Government to a permanent settlement of alluvial lands adjoining permamently settled estates. He contended that this was the true construction of the law: the Sudder Court had adopted the same view: the Board of Revenue in 1838 and in 1857 had adopted it: and of the present Board, one Member, Mr. Dampier, had recorded the following Minute:—

"I think that the proposed Law will complicate settlements of such alluvial lands much, and, where these lands are increments on under-tenures, will cause serious inconvenience to the holders of such tenures, to whom it is an object to have such lands, valuable from their river-frontage, incorporated with, and to be a part of these tenures. I also think that the wording of the proposed Law in Section I is obscure and confused. The alluvial land is to be assessed and settled as a separate estate with a separate jumma, subject to all provisions respecting the rights of property thereon which are contained in Section IV Regulation XI. 1825, and it is thenceforward to be treated as independent of the original estate—this is so far as the *estate* is concerned; but by Section IV Regulation XI. 1825, the proprietor of the under-tenure has the same right in the increment as he has on his tenure of which it is part. Is the estate to be separate, and the tenure not? or, if both are to be separate, and the tenure is a Putnee, how is the Zemindar to proceed for the recovery of his rents when due under Section VIII Regulation VIII. 1819? Is he to take a fresh pottah for the increment? and what course is he to pursue when he has, in the pottah of the original tenure, expressly relinquished any demands for rent on an increment of alluvion? whilst the alluvial lands formed part of the parent estate, this was easily arranged, but the new Law will embarrass the under-tenants and lead to much litigation.

"Again, why is the Zemindar to have the right of objecting to the alluvial lands being added to the parent estate, and the Revenue Authorities have no power to insist on such an arrangement? and why should the Revenue Authorities have the option of not assessing them as part of the estate, where the proprietors are willing? These rules interfere with the old customs and laws of the country supported by the decisions of the highest Courts, and are uncalled for. Section V Act IX of 1847 secures to the proprietors of estates deductions from their assessment whenever any proceedings under that Law are taken. Sections V and VI must be put in force simultaneously. Under all circumstances, and particularly with reference to Act IX of 1847 which secures to the Zemindars indemnity for losses, and to the Government its Revenue, from alluvial increments by periodical surveys, I can see no object to be gained for the Government, the proprietors of estates, or the holders of under-tenures, by the adoption of the proposed Law."

Another Member, Mr. Stainforth, wrote thus:—

"I object to the Preamble of the Bill, and approve of that part of it which legalizes past errors in making separate settlements of alluviated land.

"As to future settlements, they will mainly be those made under Act IX of 1847, and there would, I think, be little need of the Bill in respect to them if Officers were placed at our disposal to survey gains and losses of land. We should then be enabled to relieve landholders losing land, and take away all substantial ground of objection to adding the jumma assessed on new lands to that of the estate to which they are added."

On the whole, then, considering that all the Members of the Board of Revenue were against this Bill at the outset; that they held that the Circular Order of 1841 could not be enforced according to law; that they recommended that the Circular Order of 1838 should be followed; and that there would be no difficulty in following it;—considering, too, that this Bill interfered with private rights, he felt bound to oppose the first part of Section I as it stood, and to press his amendment.

THE CHAIRMAN said, the argument urged by the Honorable and learned Member that the Bill would interfere with Act IX of 1847, was a new one. He (the Chairman) could not follow the Honorable and learned Member on that point, because Section VI of Act IX of 1847 said:—

"And it is hereby enacted that whenever, on inspection of any such new map, it shall appear to the Local Revenue Authorities that land has been added to any estate paying revenue directly to Government, they shall without delay assess the same with a revenue payable to Government according to the rules in force for assessing alluvial increments."

As he understood this Section, "the rules in force" after the passing of this Bill, would be the rules laid down in the Bill. He would not conceive that the Legislature which passed Act IX of 1847 imagined that it had the power of tying up the hands of future Legislatures so as to provide that the rules which were in force then should continue to be in force for all time to come.

The diminution of the jumma of an original estate for land washed away from the estate was altogether a distinct question. If the proprietor lost any land by encroachment of the river, he had a right to have the jumma originally assessed on the estate diminished *pro tanto*. The sum which he should pay for land which had accrued to his estate by alluvion, could not be ascertained until the new land were assessed according to the rules in force, of which this Act would form part. He apprehended that this Bill was not intended to subject any land to assessment which was not now so liable by the existing law.

The Honorable and learned Member had laid stress on the fact that the Board of Revenue were opposed to this Bill. With all possible respect for the gentlemen composing the present Board of Revenue, he must remind the Honorable and learned Member that there were in this Council, and in favor of the Bill, two gentlemen who had been Members of the Board, and whose experience of Revenue questions, in the estimation of all who were conversant with such questions, ranked as high as that of any one in the Service.

MR. CURRIE said, the words of the Section were:—"When land is added by alluvial accession to an estate paying revenue to Government, if it be so agreed on between the Revenue Authorities and the proprietor or proprietors"—then, what was to be done? Not that the Revenue Authorities should immediately assess the revenue upon it, but that—"the revenue assessed upon the alluvial land"—that was to say, the revenue which might be assessed upon it when the time for assessment came—"may be added to the jumma of the original estate." This did not give the Revenue Authorities any power of bringing the land under assessment which they did not possess under the present law. It had never been intended that the Section should interfere with Act IX of 1847, nor, as far as he could see, did it interfere with it; but if it did, a verbal amendment might be introduced to save the operation of the Act.

THE CHAIRMAN suggested that this object would be gained by making the first part of the Section run thus:—

"When land added by alluvial accession becomes liable to assessment," &c.

MR. PEACOCK said, he had endeavored to shew that, under Act IX of 1847, alluvion which accrued to an estate could not be assessed with revenue except on inspection of a new map, framed in accordance with a re-survey; and that, when the Revenue Authorities referred to this map for the purpose of ascertaining how much land had been added to the estate by the river, they must also refer to it for the purpose of ascertaining how much land had been washed away from it by the river, in order that, as they would assess new revenue for Government in respect of the gain, so they might make a deduction from the original jumma for the benefit of the proprietor in respect of the loss. By the same Act, the re-survey according to which the new map must be framed, could not be held until ten years after the completion and approval of the previous survey. The Government could not assess a district *de novo* nine years after such survey. But Section I of this Bill said—first that, whenever land was added by alluvial accession to an estate, it might be assessed as a permanent estate, if both the Revenue Authorities and the proprietor of the estate so agreed; and secondly, that—

"if the proprietor or proprietors object to such an arrangement, or if the Revenue Authorities are of opinion that a settlement of the alluvial land cannot properly be made for the same term as the existing settlement of the original estate, the alluvial land shall be assessed and settled as a separate estate with a separate jumma and shall thenceforward be regarded and treated as in all respects separate from and independent of the original estate."

Under this Clause, therefore, if land should be added to an estate by alluvion five years after a survey, the Revenue Authorities would have the power of at once calling on the proprietor, without any map shewing what his loss by encroachment of the river might have been, to consent to a permanent settlement of the accretion. If the proprietor should refuse his consent, and should claim to have a settlement according to the provisions of Act IX of 1847, the Collector would say—"Since you will not take the land as a permanently settled estate, as I offer, I am bound by this Bill to assess it as a separate estate," and he would proceed to assess it accordingly. Or the Collector might be of opinion that a settlement of the land could not properly be made for the same term as the settlement of the original estate; and in that case, he would feel himself bound at once to assess and settle it as a separate estate. This was contrary to the provisions of Act IX of 1847, and it was not fair. No assessment of land gained by alluvion ought to take place until the Government was in a position to make a deduction from the sudder jumma for land which had been washed away.

The Chairman

MR. CURRIE asked if the Honorable and learned Member would have the goodness to point out the words in the Section which required the Collector to proceed to make a settlement before a new survey. He (Mr. Currie) contended that there was nothing in the Section which required the Collector to do any thing of the kind; but if the Honorable and learned Member could shew that there was, or that such was the effect of the wording of the Section, he would most readily insert words making it clear that the alluvion was not to be assessed until it became liable to assessment under the Law of 1847.

THE CHAIRMAN asked, did the Honorable and learned Member contend that no change could take place by law in the rules in force for the assessment of land which came to be assessed under Act IX of 1847?

MR. PEACOCK replied, he had never contended anything of the sort. If this Bill had proposed to repeal Act IX of 1847 in so many words, he should not have said that the Council had no power to repeal that Act; but he should have argued against the expediency of repealing it.

THE CHAIRMAN asked, if the Honorable and learned Member contended that there ought to be no change in the rules which were in force for the assessment of alluvial lands in 1847? If not, then the objection which arose on Act IX of 1847 would be only as to the occasion on which the rules would come into force, and not as to the provisions of this Bill. He would willingly agree to any amendment which would make it more clear that this Bill was not intended to interfere with Act IX of 1847, or define when land gained by accretions was to be assessed for revenue.

MR. PEACOCK said, what he contended was, that to alter the rules as they now existed would be an unjust interference with the rights of proprietors. He had endeavored to shew that the Section as it stood would alter the existing rules, inasmuch as it would authorize the assessment of land within ten years after a survey, and before a new map could be made. In the first place, he would lay down this position: the word "shall" was compulsory; the word "may" gave an option. He would now proceed to shew how the Bill was inconsistent with Act IX of 1847, and how the Revenue Authorities might assess lands before a new map was made out. Section I said:—"When land" by which, he understood "Whenever land" "is added by alluvial accession to an estate paying revenue to Government, if it be so agreed on between the Revenue Authorities and the proprieter or proprietors, the revenue assessed upon the alluvial land, may be added to the jumma of the original estate." He would suppose a case in which it was not so agreed upon;—a case in which the proprietor objected to such an arrangement—and the Honorable Mover of the Bill had shewn some very strong reasons why proprietors might in some cases object to such arrangements—what would follow in such a case? Under the second branch of the Section, "the alluvial land *shall* be assessed and settled as a separate estate with a separate jumma, and it *shall* thenceforward be regarded and treated as in all respects separate from and independent of the original estate." Or if the Revenue Authorities refused to settle it as part of the original estate, the same rule would follow. In either of the cases supposed, it would be the duty of the Collector to assess the land as a separate estate with a separate jumma, and it must thenceforward be treated as absolutely distinct from the original estate, and if a new map should not be made, the proprietor would still have to pay the jumma under the separate assessment though he could not have the benefit of a reduction of his original jumma in respect of the land which he had lost. That, he (Mr. Peacock) thought, was objectionable and unfair. The rule laid down in Act IX of 1847 appeared to him a just rule; namely, that the Government should wait for ten years after each survey and then re-assess, on the one hand charging additional revenue upon land gained, and on the other allowing a deduction for land lost, during that period.

[MR. RICKETTS remarked that that was the intention of the Act.]

Would the Council, then, alter the rule laid down by Act IX of 1847? He, for his own part, would not. He saw no reason for such alteration; and the Board of Revenue saw none. He would let the law remain as it stood, applying the principles of the Circular Order of 1838. If there was any doubt as to that Circular Order being law, he would make it law.

MR. CURRIE said, as the discussion had been already a great deal too much prolonged, he should say but a few words in reply. He had listened to the Honorable and learned Member's remarks with the greatest attention, but they failed to satisfy him that the Bill as it stood gave the Revenue Authorities any power which they did not now possess for assessing alluvial land. The Bill did not say that, when land is added by alluvial accession to an estate paying Revenue to Government, the Revenue Authorities *shall assess* revenue upon it; but that, when that event occurred, "*the revenue assessed* upon the alluvial land may be added to the jumma of the original estate;"—that was to say, the land, having become liable to assessment under other Laws, the mode in which it should be assessed was to be that which was provided by this Bill, and the second branch of the Section was merely a continuation of the first. He would not dwell on the objection taken, because it was a mere question of words; but he must say, in his own defence, and in that of his colleagues in the Select Committee, that neither they, nor any of the Officers who had commented on the Bill—the Board of Revenue and the Sudder Court Judges—had understood it as affecting the operation of Act IX of 1847. As he had said before, however, he had no objection to insert some additional words in it to save, beyond all question, the operation of that Act.

The Honorable and learned Member had read the remarks made by Mr. Dampier on the Bill, and had laid great stress upon them, and upon the opinions expressed by the Board of Revenue. No doubt, upon a Revenue question, the opinions of the Board of Revenue were entitled to great respect; but, as the Honorable and learned Chief Justice had observed, the Council should have regard not only to the present Members of the Board, but also to those who had gone before them. From some papers which he had obtained from the Board, he found that, on the 27th of February 1839, or only seven months after the Circular Order of 1838, which was so much insisted on, a note was written by the Secretary to the Board, shewing that the rules prescribed in the Circular were not generally acted on, and recommending some modification of them. With the permission of the Council, he would read some extracts:—

"Recent references from Jessore and Patna show that some more distinct construction of the Law is necessary, no uniformity of practice being observed in the mode of settling alluvial formations, and enforcing payment of the revenue assessed upon them. * * *

In the great majority of cases, it is not considered expedient or equitable to make a permanent settlement of the accretion. The interests alike of the State and of the proprietor are opposed to such a measure. In such cases, then, it is impossible to double up the accretion with the original estate. Whether the former be engaged for by the proprietor on a temporary lease, or let in farm to a stranger, the accretion and the settled estate must be borne upon the Collector's books as two distinct Mehals, and the inconvenience of being compelled to regard and treat them as a single property is abundantly evident. In such cases, they must, I conceive, almost of necessity, be allowed to become separate estates, each being held separately responsible for the revenue assessed upon it. * * * * *

I submit that it is expedient to modify in some measure the Circular Order of August 1838, and that the consolidation of the accretion with the parent estate as a single property, be insisted on only when a permanent settlement of the former be made and consummated. It might unobjectionably be made a condition of the proprietor being admitted to permanent engagements that he consent to the union of the accretion with his settled estate. But in all cases of temporary settlement and farming lease, the alluvion being necessarily borne on the Towjee as a separate and substantive Mehal, it will be convenient, if not absolutely necessary, to recognize it as a distinct property."

He read this to shew that, almost immediately after the issue of the Circular Order of 1838, the impracticability of carrying out that Order had become apparent. Notwithstanding that Circular Order, he believed that the practice which had existed from the first had been very nearly that which was prescribed in the Circular Order of 1841; and he would take it upon himself to say that the statement of Mr. Dampier, that the rules laid down in this Bill (following as they did the rules of 1841) were opposed to the old customs of the country, was not borne out by the fact. He had in his hand a Memorandum which shewed that in the single

District of Nuddea, there were no less than a hundred and eighty-three churs on the Collector's rent-roll. Of these, sixteen were farmed to strangers; five were said to be pending settlement; ten were settled permanently; and all the rest were settled temporarily with the proprietors. That was conclusive proof of the existing custom, and he could see no reason for departing from it. Subject to any amendment for saving the operation of Act IX of 1847, he hoped the Council would allow the Section to stand in its present form.

THE CHAIRMAN said, there was no intention whatever to interfere with Act IX of 1847; but to obviate all possible doubt on the point, he would move the insertion in the Section of the words which he had suggested before, if the Honorable and learned Member on his right (Mr. Peacock) would allow his amendments to take precedence of the one proposed by himself.

MR. PEACOCK withdrew his amendment.

THE CHAIRMAN then moved his amendments, which made the first lines of the Section run thus:—

"When land added by alluvial accession to an estate paying Revenue to Government, becomes liable to assessment," &c.

The amendments were severally agreed to.

MR. PEACOCK moved that the words "it be so agreed on between the Revenue Authorities and" be left out of the Section.

The amendment having been put, the Council divided:—

Ayes 3.	*Noes* 5.
Mr. Harington.	Mr. Forbes.
Sir Arthur Buller.	Mr. Currie.
Mr. Peacock.	Mr. LeGeyt.
	Mr. Ricketts.
	The Chairman.

So the amendment was negatived.

MR. PEACOCK said, he should now move to amend the second branch of the Section. By that part of the Section, if the owner of an estate to which alluvion had attached, refused to incorporate the alluvion with the estate, he would be entitled to insist on its being settled as a separate estate, in opposition to Government. He (Mr. Peacock) thought that the owner ought not to have that right, but that the separate settlement should be subject to the consent of Government, because the position of the alluvion might be such that the separation might depreciate the value of the original estate; and the security of the Government for the public revenue assessed upon it. Suppose the original estate to be a dock or a wharf, and alluvion to have formed between it and the river. It was obvious that, if the alluvion were made a separate estate, the dock or the wharf, from being cut off from its river-frontage, would become valueless, and the security of Government for the revenue payable in respect of it, might be destroyed.

Then, there was another difficulty. He did not quite see what was meant by the phrase "settled as a separate estate," as used in the Section. Was it intended that the alluvion should be so settled permanently, or that it should be so settled for a term? If the latter, the meaning ought to be clearly expressed.

MR. CURRIE said, the Bill as drawn, allowed the alluvion to be settled permanently or temporarily. He did not see any objection to that. At the same time, it might perhaps be unobjectionable to allow the claim of the proprietor to permanent settlement only on condition of his incorporating the alluvion with the original estate.

After some conversation, in the course of which Mr. Peacock read a proposed amendment, which however he said required some modification—

MR. CURRIE said, it was very difficult to see all the bearings and effects of an amendment on a question of this nature at the moment; and he should therefore move that the further consideration of the Bill be postponed until next Saturday, if the Honorable and learned Member would give previous notice of the alterations which he intended to move.

The motion was agreed to, and the Council resumed its sitting.

MR. PEACOCK gave notice that he would on Saturday the 31st instant, move to leave out all the words after the word "estate" in the 18th line of Section I of the above Bill, and to substitute the following for them:—

"If it be not agreed as aforesaid, and the Revenue Authorities and the proprietor or proprietors agree that the alluvial land shall be assessed and settled as a separate estate, it may be settled accordingly, and such separate settlement shall be permanent if the settlement of the original estate is permanent. Whenever alluvial land is assessed separately, it shall thenceforward be regarded and treated as in all respects separate from and independent of the original estate. If the Revenue Authorities and the proprietor or proprietors cannot agree that the revenue assessed shall be added to the original jumma, or that the alluvial land shall be assessed and settled as a separate estate, the land shall be let in farm for a period not exceeding years, reserving Malikana at the usual rate to the proprietor or proprietors for the time being of the original estate."

Mr. PEACOCK also gave notice that he would on the same day move to introduce the following new Section after Section II of the above Bill:—

"Whenever a settlement of alluvial land is made, the Revenue Officer shall determine whether any and what additional rent shall be payable in respect of the alluvial land by the person or persons entitled to any under-tenure in the original estate, to the proprietor or proprietors or to the farmer or farmers of the original estate; and if the alluvial land be let on lease under this Act, whether any and what rent shall be payable by the person or persons holding such under-tenures, to the farmer or farmers of the alluvial land."

MADRAS MARINE POLICE.

Mr. FORBES moved that Mr. Ricketts be requested to take the Bill "for the maintenance of a Police Force for the Port of Madras" to the President in Council in order that it may be submitted to the Governor General for his assent.

Agreed to.

INSTITUTION OF SUITS AND APPEALS (N. W. PROVINCES).

Mr. HARINGTON moved that Mr. Ricketts be requested to take the Bill "for the relief of persons who, in consequence of the recent disturbances, may have been prevented from instituting or prosecuting suits or appeals in the Courts of the North-Western Provinces within the period allowed by law" to the President in Council in order that it may be submitted to the Governor General for his assent.

Agreed to.

INSOLVENT DEBTORS (MOFUSSIL.)

Mr. LeGEYT gave notice that he would on Saturday the 31st instant move that the Report of the Select Committee on the subject of a Law for the relief of Insolvent Debtors in the Mofussil be adopted.

NABOB OF SURAT.

Mr. PEACOCK gave notice that he would on the same day move that Meer Jaffeer Alee Khan be informed that the Legislative Council have considered his Petition and that they see no sufficient ground for complying with the prayer thereof or for amending Act XVIII of 1848.

The Council adjourned.

Saturday, July 31, 1858.

PRESENT:

The Hon'ble the Chief Justice, *Vice-President*, in the Chair.

Hon. H. Ricketts,	H. B. Harington, Esq.
Hon. B. Peacock,	and
P. W. LeGeyt, Esq.	H. Forbes Esq.
E. Currie, Esq.	

GOVERNOR-GENERAL'S ABSENCE.

The VICE-PRESIDENT read a Message informing the Legislative Council that the Governor-General had given his assent to the Bill "to continue in force for a further period of six months Act IV of 1858 for providing for the exercise of certain powers by the Governor-General during his absence from the Council of India."

STAMP DUTIES (BENGAL).

The CLERK presented a Petition from the Rajah of Burdwan stating that the Petitioner's pecuniary interests were very largely involved in the success of the proposed Bill "to amend Regulation X. 1829 of the Bengal Code" for the

Mr. Peacock.

collection of Stamp Duties), and praying (with reference to the Petition of Zemindars of West Burdwan presented on the 6th Instant) that the Petitioner might be permitted to be heard by his Counsel in support of his interests at any time previous to the final consideration of the Bill.

MR. CURRIE said, the Bill had been introduced at the instance of an Agent of the Rajah himself, and its object was to carry out what the Rajah desired. There could, therefore, be no possible reason for his being heard by Counsel. He (Mr. Currie) should move that the Petition be printed and referred to the Select Committee on the Bill.

MR. PEACOCK said, this was a case entirely out of the rule under which parties could be heard by Counsel. The Bill was one affecting, not the Rajah's private rights, but the Stamp Laws generally. He should, therefore, oppose the Motion for referring the Petition to the Select Committee, if the Petition contained nothing else than a prayer to be heard by Counsel.

THE VICE-PRESIDENT suggested that the Petition should be read in full at the table.

The Petition having been read—

THE VICE-PRESIDENT said, although the Standing Orders admitted of persons being heard by Counsel in support of a Bill, it was obvious that, if the Council acceded to the prayer of this Petition, they could not refuse to hear Counsel on behalf of the promoters of the Petition to which it took exception, and this would lead to an indefinite litigation of the question.

MR. PEACOCK said, any reasons which the Rajah of Burdwan might have to urge in support of the Bill, further than those which he had already advanced, he should urge by Petition. This was not a case in which he should be heard by Counsel merely because others had come forward to object to the Bill. As the Honorable and learned Vice-President had very justly remarked, if the privilege were conceded to him, it must also be conceded to those who objected to the Bill; and the result might be an indefinite number of Petitions from other persons to be heard by Counsel. The Rajah was not the only person interested in the Bill. It was a Bill which affected the general Stamp Law; and though, by reason of his large estates, he might be interested in an amendment of the Law to a greater extent than others, yet he was not so peculiarly interested as to entitle him to be heard by Counsel in support of the Bill.

MR. CURRIE said, when he moved that the Petition be referred to the Select Committee on the Bill, he was not acquainted with its contents, and supposed that there may be something in it which might be advantageously considered by the Select Committee. Having now heard the Petition read, however, he begged, with the leave of the Council, to withdraw his Motion.

MR. PEACOCK then moved that the Clerk be requested to inform the Maha Rajah of Burdwan, that this was not a case in which he was entitled to be heard by Counsel in support of the Bill.

Agreed to.

EXCLUSIVE PRIVILEGES TO INVENTORS.

THE CLERK presented a Petition from Mr. George Rogers, Solicitor, praying that Section XXXV of the Bill "for granting exclusive privileges to Inventors," might be so amended as not to revive so much of Act VI of 1856 as provided that exclusive privileges obtained under that Act should cease, unless put into practice in India within two years after the passing of the proposed Act.

MR. PEACOCK moved that the above Petition be referred to the Select Committee on the Bill.

Agreed to.

SETTLEMENT OF ALLUVIAL LANDS (BENGAL).

THE CLERK presented a Petition from the British Indian Association against the enactment of any Law which might disturb or alter the existing Law as to the proprietary right to lands composed of alluvial formations, and praying that, for the protection of such right, a Clause be inserted in the Bill "to make further provision for the settlement of land gained by alluvion in the Presidency of Fort William in Bengal" in the terms of the amendment of which notice had been given by the Honorable Mr. Peacock.

ESTATE OF THE LATE NABOB OF THE CARNATIC.

THE CLERK presented a Petition from Prince Azeem Jah Bahadoor praying to be heard by Counsel against th Bill "to provide for the administration of the Estate and for the payment of the debts of the late Nabob of the Carnatic."

THE VICE-PRESIDENT said, he thought it his duty to bring to the notice of the Council that this Petition mus be taken as presented to-day, whereas under the Standing Orders, it should have been sent in before the Report of the Select Committee on the Bill. He did not wish to throw any technical difficulty in the way of the Petitioner, but to observe that any motion for the reception of this Petition should be accompanied by one for the suspension of the Standing Orders if they were not already suspended. He thought, however, that the Standing Orders had already been suspended in regard to this Bill.

MR PEACOCK said, they had been suspended only with one object, namely, to enable the Select Committee to present their Report on an earlier day than they would otherwise have done. In consequence of the several Petitions which had been submitted by Prince Azeem Jah, however, the full term of twelve weeks had now elapsed since the Bill had been referred to the Select Committee. If, therefore, the prayer of the Petition presented to-day was to be granted, it would be necessary to suspend the Standing Orders. To him, it appeared that this was a case in which it would be very proper to allow Prince Azeem Jah to be heard by Counsel. He thought, however, it should be distinctly understood that Counsel was to be heard only on the subject of the Bill, and not upon the construction of Treaties, or upon the question whether Prince Azeem Jah was entitled to be recognized as Nabob of the Carnatic or not. The question as to the effect of the Treaty had already been determined by the Government of Madras, by the late Governor-General, and by the Home Authorities. He should now move that the Standing Orders be suspended in order that Counsel on behalf of Prince Azeem Jah Bahadoor be heard on Saturday next at 11 o'clock upon the above Bill.

MR. HARINGTON seconded the motion.

MR. FORBES said, the Honorable and learned Member had said that Counsel should be restricted to advocate the private interests of Prince Azeem Jah, and should not enter upon the construction of Treaties. This, it appeared to him (Mr. Forbes), was a very proper restriction. But he hoped that the Honorable and learned Member would give a distinct engagement that he would move the third reading of the Bill on Saturday next either if Counsel should not appear, or if, appearing, Counsel should fail to satisfy the Council that Prince Azeem Jah's rights were injuriously affected by the Bill. The Bill had been introduced in the latter part of March, and read a second time and published for general information in April. It had therefore now been before the Council upwards of four months. Prince Azeem Jah had had all April, all May, all June, and all July to appear by Counsel against it, but either from a sense of his supposed dignity as uncle of the late Nabob, or for some other reason not explained, he had taken no steps whatever in the matter until the end of June. There were other parties besides Azeem Jah who were affected by the Bill There were many creditors of the late Nabob whose money had been locked up for a great number of years, and who would receive interest at only six per cent. from the date of the Nabob's death. Not a few of these were mercantile men, who could lay their money out to better advantage. He was the last person to oppose any obstacle to any claimant of the estate being heard in support of his just rights; but in doing full justice to Prince Azeem Jah, he thought that the Council should see that it did not do less than justice to the other parties. As four months had already elapsed since the Bill was brought in, he hoped the Honorable and learned Member would not object to give a distinct intimation that if Counsel should not appear on Saturday next in behalf of the Prince or, appearing, should fail to shew that this Bill injuriously affected the interests of his client, he (Mr. Peacock) would move the third reading.

MR. PEACOCK said, he did not understand why he should be called upon to give any such pledge as that proposed by the Honorable Member for Madras. If the delay in the progress of the Bill had been in any way owing to himself, there would have been good reason for requiring it of him; but he thought that the Council would acquit him of any share whatever in the delay, and would trust to him for the performance of his duty at the proper time. He had never shrunk from performing his duty, and he hoped that he never should. There was no reason why the pledge suggested by the Honorable Member, should be demanded of him. He should therefore decline to give it, and would reserve to himself the right of moving the third reading of the Bill whenever he should think fit, so that he might be free to act as circumstances might require. If he should not do so in proper time, there was nothing to prevent the Honorable Member for Madras from moving the third reading.

MR. FORBES said, he had no intention whatever, in his previous remarks, to invade the rights and privileges of the Honorable and learned Member. When on the 3rd Instant the presentation of the Report of the Select Committee on the Bill was postponed for a fortnight, so as to allow time for the arrival of an amended Petition from Prince Azeem Jah, the Honorable and learned Member had himself intimated that

> "it must be distinctly understood that on the 17th July the Report of the Select Committee would be presented, unless some fresh Petition should that day come before the Council which would induce it to refer it to the Select Committee for consideration;"

and he (Mr. Forbes) had meant nothing more by his observations than to request that the Honorable and learned Member would see whether it would not be expedient for him to give to-day a similar intimation to that which he had given of his own accord on a former occasion.

MR. PEACOCK'S motion was put and agreed to.

DESPATCH FROM THE COURT OF DIRECTORS.

THE CLERK reported to the Council that the had received from the Under Secretary to the Government of India in the Home Department, a copy of a Despatch from the Court of Directors reviewing the Acts of the Legislative Council for 1857.

SETTLEMENT OF ALLUVIAL LANDS (BENGAL).

THE CLERK stated that he had received a communication from the Acting Secretary to the Indigo Planters' Association applying, on behalf of the Central Committee of the Association, that the consideration of the Bill "to make further provision for the settlement of land gained by alluvion in the Presidency of Fort William in Bengal," be postponed for at least three months.

MR. CURRIE observed that he must say this was a very unreasonable request.

THE VICE-PRESIDENT said, he did not think that the communication which had been read by the Clerk was such a communication as was admissible under the Standing Orders.

MR. PEACOCK said, if the application to postpone the further consideration of the Bill was one which the Council thought should be entertained, the circumstance that it was made in an informal mode ought not to prevent it from being considered; but it appeared to him that there was no reason for staying the progress of the Bill through the Council.

MR. CURRIE said, he had not given any heed to the form in which the paper was drawn up. When he rose to address the Council, he was under the impression that it was in the usual form, and therefore he was proceeding to explain why the request which it contained, should not be granted. The feeling of the Council seemed to be that the request should not be complied with; but it might be as well to remark that ample time had been given to the Association and others to bring forward any objections which they might have to make to the Bill. The Bill had now been before the Council very nearly five months. Its subject had been fully discussed on the motion for the second reading, and, as was stated at the Meeting of the Association at which this application for delay was resolved on, full reports of the discussion were published in the newspapers of the 31st March and 8th April. Therefore, it was quite clear that the Association had had full warning and ample opportunity to bring forward whatever it had to say regarding the measure. Now that the Bill was about to be disposed of, the application was most unreasonable.

MR. RICKETTS said, if he thought that the interests of those whom the Association represented, would be injured by the Bill as it stood, he should have been disposed, however informal the nature of the communication presented, to give the time applied for; but he had before him a newspaper report of the proceedings of the Meeting at which the Bill was taken into consideration, and he did not see from it that the Bill would at all injuriously affect the interests of the applicants.

THE VICE-PRESIDENT said, at all events, it was desirable to pass the Bill through Committee to-day. The Association would then have an opportunity of seeing how the Bill was settled, and, if so advised, might object to the third reading of the Bill by a Petition properly framed, and containing such reasons as it might think proper to advance.

FORT OF TANJORE (MADRAS).

MR. FORBES presented the Report of the Select Committee on the Bill "for bringing the Fort of Tanjore and the adjacent territory under the Laws of the Presidency of Fort St. George."

ESTATE OF THE LATE NABOB OF THE CARNATIC.

MR. PEACOCK postponed the motion, which stood in the Orders of the Day, for the third reading of the Bill "to provide for the administration of the Estate and for the payment of the debts of the late Nabob of the Carnatic."

SETTLEMENT OF ALLUVIAL LANDS (BENGAL).

On the Order of the Day for the adjourned Committee on the Bill "to make further provision for the settlement of land gained by alluvion in the Presidency of Fort William in Bengal" being read, the Council resolved itself into a Committee for the further consideration of the Bill.

Mr. Currie

MR. PEACOCK said, the Council had determined, by its vote last Saturday, in reference to the first branch of Section I, that the Revenue Authorities should have power to say whether alluvial formations in estates should be settled as part of such estates or not. But the second branch of the Section provided as follows :—

"If the proprietor or proprietors object to such an arrangement, or if the Revenue Authorities are of opinion that a settlement of the alluvial land cannot properly be made for the same term as the existing settlement of the original estate, the alluvial land shall be assessed and settled as a separate estate with a separate jumma, and shall thenceforward be regarded and treated as in all respects separate from, and independent of, the original estate."

He proposed that all these words should be left out of the Section, in order that the following might be substituted for them :—

"If it be not agreed as aforesaid, and the Revenue Authorities and the proprietor or proprietors agree that the alluvial land shall be assessed and settled as a separate estate, it may be settled accordingly, and such separate settlement may be permanent if the settlement of the original estate is permanent. Whenever alluvial land is assessed separately, it shall thenceforward be regarded and treated as in all respects separate from, and independent of the original estate. If the Revenue Authorities and the proprietor or proprietors cannot agree that the revenue assessed shall be added to the original jumma, or that the alluvial land shall be assessed and settled as a separate estate, the land shall be let in farm for a period not exceeding twenty-one years, reserving malikana at the usual rate to the proprietor or proprietors for the time being of the original estate."

After the debate of last Saturday, it was unnecessary to enter into any further discussion of these questions. He would simply mention that the only particular in which the amendment he now moved differed from the amendment of which he had given notice was that it substituted the word "may" for the word "shall" between the words "such separate settlement" and "be permanent." The amendment as it originally stood gave the Revenue Authorities the option of settling alluvial lands as a separate estate or not; but it required that, when such settlements were made, they should be permanent if the settlement of the original estate was permanent. It might be that, in the absence of any knowledge of the nature of the soil, and of other particulars, the Revenue Authorities might find it inconvenient to make separate settlements of alluvion permanent; and consequently, having no power to make a separate settlement for a term, they might object to make a separate settlement at all. Thus, the proprietors might be injured. The substitution of the word "may" for the word "shall" would enable them to exercise a discretion in the matter.

He had also filled up the blank reserved in the amendment for the number of years during which alluvial land might be let in farm, with the figures 21. He thought a 21-years' lease would give the lessee such an interest in the land as would induce him to improve it. If, however, the Honorable Member for Bengal, who was more conversant with these details, preferred any other number, he (Mr. Peacock) should have no objection to substitute it for that which he had adopted.

MR. CURRIE said, he had two objections to the amendment. The first was that it militated against the principle of the Bill, inasmuch as it gave the Revenue Authorities the option of objecting to a separate settlement of the chur with the proprietor. The principle of the Bill was that the proprietor of alluvial land had in all cases the right to a separate settlement of such land. His second objection to the amendment was that it left untouched the doctrine laid down by the late decision of the Sudder Court, which was to the effect that, when alluvial land was let in farm, it remained attached to the original estate, although it was assessed with a separate jumma, and was entered in the Collector's rent-roll as a separate estate. Both these points had been already so fully discussed, and the vote which the Council had given upon them had so clearly affirmed the contrary principle, that he thought it would be impertinent in him to occupy their time and attention by further argument on the subject. The Honorable and learned Mover of the amendment still maintained that the Revenue Authorities should have authority to object to the separation of the alluvial land from the original estate. But even he did not say that the proprietor should be compelled to incorporate the alluvion with the original estate;—in fact, such compulsion would be impossible; and if the alluvion was not so incorporated, whether it were engaged for by the proprietor, or whether it were farmed, it became *de facto* a separate estate, as had been shewn at the adjourned debate on the motion for the second reading of the Bill by the Honorable Member (Mr. Grant) who, he regretted, was not present to-day. The argument in which the Honorable Member had made this appear, had been so clearly and ably put, that he (Mr. Currie) thought it unnecessary now to detain the Council by going over the same ground again.

It did not occur to him that he need say anything more than to remind the Council of what had transpired on that occasion, and to urge upon them that to adopt this amendment would be to reverse the vote which they had come to then, and to defeat the object of the Bill.

MR. RICKETTS said, as the Honorable and learned Member had substituted the word "may" for the word "shall" in his amendment, his chief objection to the amendment as it previously stood had been removed, because the substitution left it discretionary with the Revenue Authorities whether the settlement of the alluvion should be made for a term or in perpetuity. He had been told by many that what he had said on this subject on Saturday last was in several respects extremely obscure; and he had also been told that, when he modestly said that he would leave it to those learned Members who were better versed in construing Law, to decide which of the two varying opinions held by the Revenue Authorities in 1833 and in 1841 as to the meaning of the Law in question was the correct one—he had, in a manner, neglected his duty;—that, having been so long connected with the Revenue Department himself, he ought to have expressed his own opinion on the question, if he had one. He certainly had an opinion on the question; but as the point then under discussion was strictly a legal one, it had appeared to him that it was desirable to relieve the Council from a dissertation on a legal point by one who was not a Lawyer. That he had an opinion upon it, however, and that, in former days, he had been bold enough to avow that opinion, he would shew. In the year 1850, when in the Board of Revenue, he, with the concurrence of his colleagues, drew up a paper of instructions for Settlement Officers from which he would read one or two very short extracts :—

"The settlement of the alluvial lands should also be made with the occupant owner. Such lands belong to the proprietor of the estate to which a change in the channel of the river had added it, and his right to it is exactly co-equal with that by which he holds the estate to which the alluvion has attached itself. The proprietors have a right to admission to terms of permanent engagement, whenever they may think fit to demand it, unless the alluvion have been let out in farm for a specified term in consequence of their recusance, and unless the increment be not in a state for permanent settlement; in which cases, the local Commissioner will determine whether a temporary or permanent settlement shall be made, and should the party entitled to settlement object to the consolidation of the jumma with that of the original estate, the increment shall be assessed as a distinct mehal."

He contended in 1850 for the point for which he was prepared to contend now; but the substitution of the word "may" for the word "shall" in the amendment before the Council, would, if that amendment were adopted, leave the Section very much as it was originally drafted. As originally drafted, the second branch of Section I provided as follows :—

"In cases in which such union is not agreed on, the alluvial land shall be assessed and settled as a separate estate with a separate jumma, and shall thenceforward be regarded and treated as in all respects separate from, and independent of, the original estate."

The substitution of the amendment now before the Council for the second branch of Section I of the Bill as amended by the Select Committee, would have exactly the same effect as the words he had just read would have had—that was to say, the permanent or temporary settlement of alluvial formations when settled separately from the original estate, would be at the discretion of the Revenue Authorities. He had nothing more to urge upon that point.

Mr. Ricketts

But there was one point remaining on which he felt bound to occupy the attention of the Council for a few minutes. There would, he thought, be some uneasiness out of doors as to the effect of the words "unless the increment be not in a state for permanent settlement." The Revenue Authorities, in determining whether a separate settlement of alluvion should be made in perpetuity or for a term, were to take into consideration the condition of the land. Then would come the question—In what state must the land be to warrant a permanent settlement? That allowedly must be a question of great difficulty, and the words might be differently understood by different Settlement Officers. At the Meeting of the Indigo Planters' Association at which this Bill was considered, he observed that Mr. F. A. Goodenough put

"the case of the old bed of a river whose course has been changed;"—and said :—" the chur land formed in the old bed not being subject to increase or diminution, it should be the right of the Zemindar of the parent estate to be able to claim a permanent settlement with himself of the old chur land; for, the chur in question not being subject to change, it seems unfair that the Zemindar and his ryots should be subjected to the extortions of the subordinates in the employ of the Revenue Authorities in the periodical visits for the purposes of re-measurement and re-assessment, &c."

In a case like that, he (Mr. Ricketts) could not imagine that any Settlement Officer would, under the discretion which the amendment before the Council would give him, refuse to grant a settlement of the chur in perpetuity. On the contrary, he thought that he certainly would grant such a settlement; and therefore, if that was all that the Association had to ask, there was no occasion to delay the passing of this Bill. But, as it had been put to him a few days ago, supposing that one half only of alluvial land was under cultivation, should a permanent settlement be refused? Probably, it should not. Then, it might be asked if one-half, or one-fourth, or one-tenth were cultivated, should perpetual settlement be refused? It was utterly impossible to lay down any fixed rule for such cases; and he thought that the duration of the settlement must be left to the discretion of the Revenue Authorities.

MR. HARINGTON said, he had nothing to add to the observations which he had already made on the subject of the present Bill, and he should not have trespassed further upon the time of the Council to-day, but should have contented himself with giving a silent vote in favor of the amendment of the Honorable and learned Member of Council, though he should have preferred the use of the word "shall" to that of the word "may" in the sixth line, were it not that he was anxious to take advantage of the opportunity which the continuance of the debate afforded him, to say a few words in reference to a remark which fell from the Chair on Saturday last, and which imputed to him inconsistency of conduct in that, after having, as a Member of the Select Committee, signed the Report which recommended the passing of the Bill in its present form, he had joined the Honorable and learned Member of Council in proposing a material alteration in Section I. He could not deny that he had done both these things; and in appearance, therefore, at least, he must admit that his conduct was open to the charge brought against it. But what were the real circumstances? These, with the permission of the Council, he would briefly explain, and the result would, he trusted, be his acquittal of the charge. Previously to the introduction of the present Bill, which had given rise to so much discussion, he had never had occasion carefully to look into the Law of alluvion as existing in this country. He knew, of course, that there was such a Law, and he was not ignorant of its general features; but he could call to mind only a single case in which, during a not very short official career, he had been required to administer its provisions; and the point for determination in the case to which he referred was, not whether the proprietor of an estate to which some alluvial land had become attached, had or had not the right to insist upon that land being incorporated and settled with the original or parent estate, but to which of two contiguous estates, in reference to their peculiar formation, a narrow strip of land belonging to the one being found to intervene between some portion of the other estate and a part of the newly-formed land, the alluvion must be held to have accreted. The consequence was that, when the Honorable Member for Bengal introduced his Bill, he had a very imperfect knowledge of the subject to which it related. He lost no time, however, in endeavoring to make himself master of the Laws bearing on the question; and the result of his investigation of them was a doubt as to the correctness of the construction placed by the Honorable Member upon Regulation XI. 1825, and upon the intention of the framers of that Regulation. This doubt, which was shared in by others, including the Honorable and learned Member of Council on his left (Mr. Peacock), he communicated to the Honorable Member for Bengal; but the Honorable Member did not concur with him. It so happened that, on the day fixed for the second reading of the Bill, he was prevented by indisposition from attending the Meeting of the Council; and the Honorable Member for Bengal, on being made aware of this circumstance, with that courtesy and love of fair play which characterized his every act in which those qualities could be displayed, at once proposed the postponement of his Motion for the second reading of the Bill until the following Saturday. The Motion came on upon that day, and it would be in the recollection of the Council that he (Mr. Harington) opposed the Motion conjointly with the Honorable and learned Member of Council on his left and the Honorable Member for Bombay, but they were in a minority. Subsequently he was appointed a Member of the Select Committee which was directed, in the first instance, to make a preliminary Report, and to suggest any alterations that might be deemed proper in the Bill before it was published, and afterwards to submit the usual Report; and he thought the other Members of the Committee would recollect that at both Meetings of the Committee, he strongly advocated what he still contended for—namely, the right of the proprietor of an estate to which land might become annexed by alluvion, to insist upon the incorporation of that land with the parent estate on the sole condition of his agreeing to pay the revenue assessed upon it; and that he recommended that the Bill should be altered accordingly. The other Members of the Committee, however, did not agree with him; and finding that he stood alone, he consented to sign the Reports presented to the Council; and he submitted that those Reports would still have been the Reports of the Select Committee, even though he had refused to sign them, and had recorded his dissent, which, properly speaking, he ought to have done, and which he regretted now that he had not done. The next stage in the Bill was the presentation of the Reports of the Select Committee; and on the day on which the second Report was presented, he intimated to the Honorable Member for Bengal that, although he did not intend to propose any amendment of the Bill to make it accord with his views, yet, in the event of the Honorable and learned Member of Council on his left moving such amendment, which he fully expected he would do, he should consider it his duty to support him; and that was what he had done on Saturday last. He would only further observe that the conduct pursued by him in respect to the present Bill, was not altogether without precedent; in proof of which he need only refer to what had taken place during the passage through the Council of the Bombay Municipal Assessment Bill, which had been lately read a third time, and had now become Law. The Honorable Member for Bombay, who had charge of that Bill, candidly told the Council that he was opposed to some of the amendments proposed and adopted by the Select Committee, but that as he had found himself in a minority, he had signed the Report of the Select Committe without making any objection to it, and he afterwards allowed the Bill to pass through a Committee of the whole Council without any opposition on his part. Subsequently, in consequence of the receipt of a representation from Bombay, he himself moved several amendments in the Bill, to which, he (Mr. Harington) understood from what had fallen from him, he had all along been favorable, and some of these amendments were adopted by the Council, notwithstanding that they had previously passed the Bill in the form recommended by the Select Committee, and the Bill had been reported accordingly. Now, he did not recollect that any charge of inconsistency had been brought against the Council at large or against the Honorable Member for Bombay for their conduct in this instance, and he did not consider that they had laid themselves open to such charge.

He had to thank the Council for the indulgent hearing they had accorded to him, and had to apologize for occupying so much of their time in a matter in a great degree personal to himself.

THE CHAIRMAN said, he did not know whether his Honorable friend would be strictly in order in the House of Commons in taking notice of what had taken place a previous day; but he was the last person to oppose any technical objection to an Honorable Member offering any explanation regarding himself, and he was glad of the opportunity which his Honorable friend had now afforded him of withdrawing what he had said last Saturday respecting the consistency of the course which he had adopted with reference to this Bill. He ought to have remembered that his Honorable friend had expressed opinions in the Select Committee on this Bill similar to those which he expressed at the last debate; but he had no recollection of the fact when he spoke, nor indeed could he recall it to mind even now; though he willingly and unhesitatingly accepted the statement of his Honorable friend.

He could not think that it was necessary for his Honorable friend to quote a particular precedent for the course which he had taken in regard to this Bill. It seemed to be part of the normal state of the Select Committees of that Council. It continually happened to him before he came there to read the Report of a Select Committee which, being signed by all the Members of that Committee, and containing no indications of a difference of opinion, might be taken to imply that they were unanimous. Yet, when the Bill got into a Committee of the whole Council, one very soon discovered that this apparent "unanimity was wonderful," in the sense of its being no unanimity at all. For no sooner was the Bill in Committee, than an important debate might arise on an amendment moved by one of the Members of the Select Committee who had joined in signing a Report, recommending that the Bill should be passed as reported. These surprises were inconvenient; and he would venture to suggest that, where any Member of a Select Committee did not agree in opinion with his colleagues, his dissent should be specified on the face of the Report, so that the Council might come prepared to hear the question raised in Committee of the whole Council, and to discuss it. This, however, was beside the question then before the Council, and he would only repeat his apology to his Honorable friend for the observations imputing inconsistency to him on the last occasion.

With reference to the question raised by the amendment, it seemed to him that the whole difficulty, as indeed the difficulties of the Bill generally, had arisen from the various senses in which the word "settlement" was understood. When he first saw the Bill as it now stood, he confessed he was struck by the latter Clause, because he understood the word "settlement" to import a settlement, whether of a temporary or of a permanent character, between the Revenue Authorities and the proprietor of the land; but he was afterwards assured by the Honorable Mover of the Bill that every Revenue Officer would understand the term as comprehending a lease of the land for a time on the failure of the proprietor to engage for it; and believing this to be the case, he did not see any objection to the Clause as it stood. He wished further to observe that, if it was proposed so to amend the Clause as to distinguish between a temporary settlement and a settlement which would be permanent or would extend to the same period as the settlement of the original estate, he should have no objection to the amendment discussed at the last Meeting, and would prefer that the proprietor of an estate should have the option, on such a settlement, of incorporating an alluvial formation with the estate, and holding both subject to one consolidated jumma. His reason for supporting on the last occasion the Clause as it stood was that it made no distinction between permanent settlements and settlements of a temporary character, and he considered it would be better for all parties to leave it to the discretion of the Revenue Authorities whether the settlement of an alluvion should be in perpetuity or for a term. That question appeared to have now been settled by the Council, and he had no desire to re-open it, especially as the Petition of the British Indian Association, which complained that the Council had not adopted the views urged by the Honorable and learned Member on his right (Mr. Peacock) with respect to the amendment negatived last Saturday, gave one also to understand that the Association would be satisfied if the amendments now proposed by him, were adopted. That Clause, as it now stood, left it to the discretion of the Revenue Authorities whether the separate settlement of alluvial lands should be permanent or temporary, and that seemed to satisfy the Honorable Member on his left (Mr. Ricketts). He thought that the Clause was better than the words in substitution of which it was proposed, because it shewed more clearly that the settlements intended were settlements to be made with the proprietors themselves, and that leases to third parties would be a distinct thing. The only remaining objection made to the amendment was that it would still leave the right to malikana in the alluvion subject to be treated as passing to the auction-purchaser in the event of a sale of the original estate for arrears of revenue. If an alluvion was let on lease, there could be no default which would result in a Government sale of the alluvion.

MR. RICKETTS said, if the alluvion should be settled separately with the proprietors, and arrears of revenue should accrue upon it, it might be sold separately for such arrears.

THE CHAIRMAN said, any settlement made with the proprietor, would come under the first branch of the amendment proposed :—" If it be not agreed as aforesaid," (that was to say, that the alluvion should be incorporated with the original estate) :—

" and the proprietor or proprietors agree that the alluvial lands shall be assessed and settled as a separate estate, it may be settled accordingly, and such separate settlement may be permanent, or it may be temporary."

If the settlement was separate, the alluvion might be sold for arrears of revenue; but it could only be sold as distinct from the original estate; for the amendment provided that—

" Whenever alluvial land is assessed separately, it shall thenceforward be regarded and treated as in all respects separate from, and independent of, the original estate."

In any settlement made with the proprietor, whether temporary or permanent, the proprietor must take the alluvion subject to its liability to sale for arrears of revenue. But if the alluvion was let in farm, the only consequence, he apprehended, of a default in the payment of the rent would be the forfeiture of the existing lease, and the grant of a new lease still reserving malikana to the proprietor of the soil. But the objection suggested by the Honorable Member for Bengal was the liability of the proprietor to forfeit this right of malikana on a sale of the parent estate for the arrears of revenue assessed on that estate. He (the Chairman) was not so struck with the magnitude of this grievance, and considering that malikana was simply an incident to the right of the proprietor; that he enjoyed the right of malikana because he was proprietor of the parent estate, he did not greatly care whether it passed to the auction-purchaser or not. What he wished was, to give the proprietor the power of having a separate settlement made of the alluvion if he chose to engage for it, so that the original estate and the alluvion might be two distinct mehals, and neither be liable for the revenue assessed upon the other.

On the whole, and finding that it seemed to be viewed with favor by Zemindars and landholders, he was inclined to support the amendment.

Mr. CURRIE said, when he first addressed the Council, from the great anxiety which he felt to avoid saying more than was absolutely necessary on a subject which had been so very fully discussed, and on which he had repeatedly trespassed on the indulgence of the Council, he was afraid he had said less than he ought to have done. The Honorable Member on his right (Mr. Ricketts) and the Honorable Member for Madras were not in the Council when the discussion on the Motion for the second reading took place; and he would therefore explain very briefly on what grounds it was that he objected to the amendment now proposed. He objected to the words "and the Revenue Authorities and proprietor or proprietors agree that the alluvial lands shall be assessed and settled as a separate estate." He contended that if the proprietor was, from any cause, unwilling to incorporate the alluvion with the original estate, he was entitled to claim the separate settlement of the alluvion; and, to his apprehension, the amendment ought to run thus:—

"If it be not so agreed, the alluvial land shall be assessed and settled as a separate estate."

He thought that this was the right of the proprietor. Where alluvion had accrued, the proprietor was entitled to incorporate it with the original estate; but if he did not do that, he did not lose his right to the alluvion. If he was willing to pay the jumma assessed, he was entitled to a separate settlement of the chur, and the Revenue Authorities had no right whatever to say that he should not have it. But the amendment gave them that right.

Then the amendment said, that, the Revenue Authorities and the proprietor agreeing, the alluvion "may be settled accordingly," (that was to say, as a separate estate) "and such separate settlement may be permanent, if the settlement of the original estate is permanent." And then came the following.—

"If the Revenue Authorities and the proprietor or proprietors cannot agree that the revenue assessed shall be added to the original jumma, or that the alluvial land shall be assessed and settled as a separate estate, the land shall be let in farm for a period not exceeding twenty-one years, reserving malikana at the usual rate to the proprietor or proprietors for the time being of the original estate."

If the amendment were passed, the effect of this Clause would be that to which the Honorable and learned Chief Justice had alluded; namely, that, in accordance with the doctrine laid down by the Sudder Court, the rights of the proprietor in the chur would pass with the conveyance of the original estate, should the original estate be sold for arrears of revenue. Honorable Members talked of the proprietor's right to malikana; but it was to be remembered that the rights of the proprietor in an alluvion let in farm were not only the right to malikana during the continuance of the lease, but also the recurring right of engaging for the alluvion after a certain period, which period was limited by Regulation VII. 1822 to twelve

The Chairman

years. That was a substantive and valuable right. The Honorable and learned Mover of the amendment had objected on Saturday last to this Bill, on the ground that, in his opinion, it was an invasion of private rights. Now, he (Mr. Currie) maintained that this was a very serious and flagrant invasion of private rights, to say that the proprietary right in the chur should pass out of the owner's hands on account of a default under a distinct contract, for which default a specific penalty was provided by Law. Then he supposed that the amendment would go the whole length of the doctrine laid down in the decree of the Sudder Court, and that the proprietary right in the alluvion would pass to the auction-purchaser at a revenue sale of the original estate, although the proprietor of the original estate might have sold such right to another person. Every proprietor had unquestionably a full right to sell either the whole or a portion of his estate. If that was so, why had he not a right to sell the alluvion? The alluvion was not only a portion of his estate, but a distinct and separate portion, subject to a distinct and separate jumma,—or rather it was itself a separate estate; and why should the proprietor's right of disposing of it be controlled or nullified by declaring that it must of necessity follow the fortunes of the original estate?

If the intermediate Clause in the amendment, beginning—"Whenever alluvial land is assessed separately"—were transferred to the end of the amendment, it would be an improvement, because it would then provide that the alluvion when let in farm should be separate from and independent of the original estate; but the amendment would still be objectionable, because it would take from the proprietor his inalienable right of having a separate settlement of the chur, if he was willing to pay the jumma assessed upon it.

For these reasons, he would oppose the amendment. To accept it, would, it appeared to him, be entirely to defeat the object of the Bill.

With respect to the remarks of the Honorable and learned Chief Justice as to what the term "settlement" as used in the Bill implied, he (Mr. Currie) had no doubt that the assessment of the revenue and the definition and record of the rights of tenants and proprietors constituted the settlement. Whether the proprietor accepted the terms offered by the Revenue Officers, or whether he refused them, and the land was let in farm, the arrangement made was equally a settlement. But still, as so much doubt had been suggested as to the import of the term, he should propose, at the proper time, to add the following words to the Section:—

"Whether the separate settlement be made with the proprietor or proprietors, or the land be left in farm in consequence of the refusal of the proprietor or proprietors to accept the terms of settlement."

MR. RICKETTS said, should the amendment before the Council be negatived, he should propose to introduce some words into the Section as it stood, which, he thought, would meet the views both of the Honorable and learned Member opposite (Mr. Peacock) and of the Indigo Planters' Association. If the amendment was lost, he should move the insertion of words in the latter branch of the Section which would make it run thus:—

"If the proprietor or proprietors object to such an arrangement, or if the Revenue Authorities are of opinion *that special reasons exist why a separate* settlement of the alluvial land *should not* be made for the same term as the existing settlement of the original estate, the alluvial land shall be assessed and settled as a separate estate with a separate jumma, and shall thenceforward be regarded and treated as in all respects separate from, and independent of, the original estate."

Under that provision, the general rule all over Bengal would be to settle alluvial lands in perpetuity, except where special reasons should exist which rendered such settlement inexpedient.

MR. HARINGTON said, he had to express his acknowledgments to the Honorable and learned Chairman for the manner in which he had met the observations which he had ventured to address to the Council in reference to what had fallen from the Honorable and learned Chairman on Saturday last in connection with his conduct on the present Bill, and to say that he was quite satisfied. He agreed with the Honorable and learned Chairman that the present practice of all Members of

Select Committees signing the Reports on Bills referred for their consideration, notwithstanding that one or more of their number might be dissentient as respected the whole or some portion of the Report to be made, was inconvenient. The Report agreed to by the majority of the Select Committee, should still be the Report of the Committee; but any Member dissenting from his colleagues should record the grounds of his dissent; and he proposed to adopt this course in future.

And now as regarded the Section of the Bill under discussion. The Honorable Member for Bengal had stated that the proprietor of alluvial lands attached to the main land, had a right to demand a separate settlement of these lands; but he had not pointed out any Law as conferring that right upon him, and he (Mr. Harington) knew of no such Law. Regulation XI. of 1825 certainly did not give it; for that enactment declared that the alluvion should be an increment to the tenure of the person to whose land or estate it was annexed,—not that it should be held separately therefrom. The Government, had it pleased, might have declared its own right to all alluvial lands not existing at the time of settlement; and had it done so, he did not think that the proprietors of estates to which such lands might have subsequently attached themselves, or might hereafter become attached, would have had, or would have any just cause to complain; but instead of asserting this right, the Government consented to the alluvial formation becoming the property of the owner of the adjoining estate, intending, he thought, that, for all future time, it should belong to, and should be included within the limits of that estate. No doubt that, as stated by the Honorable Member for Bengal, the owner of an estate with which alluvial lands might have been incorporated and settled, had the power at any time to dispose of them by sale, gift, or otherwise, and by so doing, to constitute them a separate property; but in such case, he could not allot the revenue to be paid by the alluvion. That could be done by the Collector only; and in apportioning the revenue between the original estate and the alluvion, the Collector would of course take care so to distribute the amount that, in the event of the original estate being injured by the loss of its river-frontage, it should have no difficulty in paying the revenue assessed upon it such loss notwithstanding. He agreed with the Honorable and learned Chairman that it was a matter of comparatively little importance whether in the case of the alluvion being let in farm, and of the parent estate being sold for arrears of Government revenue, the sale should include the alluvion subject to the farming lease or should be exclusive thereof, provided that due intimation was given beforehand of what was to be sold, in order that intending purchasers might know what they were buying, and that there might be no ground for dispute on this point after the sale. The only objection that he had to the decree of the Sudder Court, so often referred to, was that, in the particular case in which that decree was passed, the Collector, whether rightly or wrongly, would seem purposely to have excluded the alluvion from the sale, and not to have sold it with the parent estate; in which case, the right of the purchaser of the latter to take the former also was at least doubtful.

Mr. PEACOCK said, he thought that the Honorable Member for Bengal had not clearly drawn a distinction between two material points. An alluvial formation might be added to an original estate as part of that estate in perpetuity, or it might be settled as a separate estate either permanently or for a term. If it was settled as a separate estate, whether permanently or for a term, the original estate was not liable for the jumma assessed upon it. The Honorable Member for Bengal said that the proprietors of estates to which alluvion accreted, had a right to the separate settlement of the alluvion; but he had not shewn under what Law they had that right. When the Law said that land added to an estate by alluvion should be considered an increment to the estate, he (Mr. Peacock) apprehended it meant that the land should be considered a parcel of the estate, and that one consolidated jumma should be reserved to Government in respect of both. But he (Mr. Peacock) knew of no Law which entitled the owner of an alluvion to have it settled as a separate estate if he pleased. Supposing, however, that the Honorable Member for Bengal was correct, the

Honorable Member had not said what sort of a separate settlement the owner was entitled to have,—whether a separate settlement in perpetuity, or a separate settlement for a term. The second branch of Section I. as it stood, gave no information on the point. If the alluvion were settled as a separate estate, notwithstanding the decision of the Sudder Court, it would be sold as a separate estate; but if it were incorporated with the original estate, it would, of course, be sold subject to its liability for the consolidated jumma. The Sudder Court's decision appeared to him to be perfectly correct. When the alluvion was let in farm, malikana allowance being reserved, the malikana ought to go to the owner of the original estate for the time being, since it was only an incident to the right of property in the original estate, and the amendment which he proposed would provide for that.

With respect to what had fallen from the Honorable Member opposite (Mr. Ricketts), he had no objection that the general rule should be that, if the Revenue Authorities were willing to settle an alluvial formation as a separate estate, and the original estate to which it had become annexed was permanently settled, the settlement of the alluvion should likewise be permanent. If the Honorable Member should propose to add a provision to that effect to his amendment, he should not object to such addition being made; but he did not think that it was necessary; because, as he had left it to the option of the Revenue Authorities whether the separate assessment of alluvion should be in perpetuity or for a term, he apprehended that they always would make such settlements permanent, if the settlement of the original estate was permanent, unless they should see special reasons to the contrary. He thought his amendment sufficient as it stood, and should press it.

MR. CURRIE said, he would not be drawn into an argument on the interpretation of Regulation XI. 1825, a subject which had been discussed *usque ad nauseam*. He would merely repeat, what he had said before, that Regulation XI. 1825 had nothing whatever to do with arrangements between the Government and the proprietor. Its object and effect were simply to determine questions of proprietary right between individuals.

The Honorable and learned Member had said that it was quite right that, if there was a sale of the original estate, the right to Malikana in respect of the alluvion should go to the auction-purchaser, inasmuch as it was a right which belonged to the proprietor of the original estate. [Mr. Peacock explained that he spoke of a private sale.] Well, if the proprietor of the original estate sold the estate with the chur, then of course the right to malikana for the chur would pass to the purchaser; but he understood the Honorable and learned Member to argue that the malikana was incident to the right of property in the original estate. Such was not the case. Malikana was an allowance to proprietors who did not engage for the revenue of their estates. In the case supposed, Malikana was given to the proprietor, not because he was the proprietor of the original estate, but because he was the proprietor of the chur, which alone was the subject of settlement.

The Honorable and learned Member had further said that there was nothing to shew that the proprietor had a right to a separate settlement of the alluvion. He had contended that the Regulations gave the proprietor only a right to incorporate it with the original estate, and had asked him to shew under what Law he was entitled to insist on its being separately settled. He replied, under that Law which declared proprietors of land to have a preferential right to engage for the revenue assessed upon the land. If the proprietor was willing to pay the revenue which the Revenue Authorities thought should be assessed upon the alluvion, he had an absolute and indefeasible right to have it settled with him. That was the Law upon which he stood.

MR. PEACOCK said, what he wanted to know was, whether the separate settlement was to be permanent or temporary.

MR. CURRIE said, it was in the option of the Revenue Authorities to make it either one or the other. He was quite prepared to shew that the proprietors of churs had not a right to have them settled in perpetuity. The ownership gave them a right of settlement, but it did not give them a right of settlement in perpetuity. But as the amendment before the Council did not raise that question, he declined to go into an argument upon it.

He was quite willing to assent to the amendment which the Honorable Member on his right proposed to move. His main objection, after all, was to the latter part of the amendment under discussion, which contemplated the alluvion continuing attached to the original estate, although it should have been separately settled.

THE CHAIRMAN remarked that after what had been just said, he doubted whether it would not be better to introduce a provision preventing the proprietary rights of the Zemindar in alluvion let out in farm, from necessarily passing under a revenue sale of the original estate. According to the construction of the existing Sale Law which the Sudder Court had adopted in the case of Koelwar, supposing that a Zemindar and the Revenue Authorities failed to come to an agreement as to the settlement of the chur, and that the Revenue Authorities let out the chur in farm for twenty-one years, reserving Malikana to the Zemindar; and supposing that, during the existence of the lease, arrears of revenue accrued on the original estate, and the original estate was put up for sale,—then, the right to the Malikana reserved in respect of the chur, and the right to engage for a settlement of the chur after the expiration of the lease, would necessarily pass to the auction-purchaser, even though the defaulting Zemindar had already sold or assigned those rights. [Mr. Currie—No doubt.] As he was one of those who thought that the Sale Law was far more stringent than it ought to be, he would gladly insert words which would prevent such consequences.

MR. PEACOCK'S Motion was then put that the second branch of Section I. be omitted.

The Council divided :—

Ayes. 3.	*Noes.* 4.
Mr. Harington.	Mr. Forbes.
Mr. Peacock.	Mr. Currie.
The Chairman.	Mr. LeGeyt.
	Mr. Ricketts.

The Motion was therefore negatived.

MR. CURRIE moved that the following words be added to the Section :—"Whether the separate settlement be made with the proprietor or proprietors, or the land be let in farm in consequence of the refusal of the proprietor or proprietors to accept the terms of settlement."

Agreed to.

MR. RICKETTS moved that the following words be inserted after Section I :—"The separate settlement may be permanent if the settlement of the original estate is permanent."

Agreed to.

Section II was passed after the insertion of the following words in the 11th line :—"To determine whether any and what additional rent shall be payable in respect of the alluvial land by the person or persons entitled to any under-tenure in the original estate."

Section III, the Preamble, and the Title were passed without amendment.

The Council having resumed its sitting, the Bill was reported.

INSOLVENT DEBTORS (MOFUSSIL.)

MR. LEGEYT postponed the motion, which stood in the Orders of the Day that the Report of the Select Committee on the subject of a Law for the relief of Insolvent Debtors in the Mofussil be adopted.

ABSENCE OF THE GOVERNOR GENERAL.

The Vice-President read a Message informing the Legislative Council that the Governor General had given his assent to the Bill "to continue in force for a further period of six months Act IV of 1858 for providing for the exercise of certain powers by the Governor General during his absence from the Council of India."

NABOB OF SURAT.

MR. PEACOCK moved, pursuant to notice, that Meer Jafur Alee Khan be informed that the Legislative Council have considered his Petition, and that they see no sufficient ground for complying with the prayer thereof, or for amending Act XVIII of 1848. In doing so, he said it would be right that he should state briefly the grounds upon which he thought that the Council ought not to comply with the prayer contained in the Petition. The Petitioner asked

Mr. Currie

that the Council should take his Petition into consideration, and pass an Act to amend Act XVIII of 1848, in conformity with the Draft Act submitted by him. The Draft Act submitted by him proposed—

"that so much of Act XVIII of 1848 as provides that no act of the Governor of Bombay in Council in respect to the administration to, and distribution of, such property from the date of the death of the said late Nabob shall be liable to be questioned in any Court of law, may be repealed;"

and—

"that it shall be lawful for the East India Company, or any person deeming himself aggrieved by any decision, order, or proceeding heretofore made or taken respecting the estate of Meer Ufzoloodeen Khan, the late Nabob of Surat, under the said recited Act, or hereafter to be made or taken under the said recited Act respecting the said estate, to appeal therefrom to Her Majesty in Council, in order that such appeal may be referred to and be heard by the Judicial Committee of the said Council pursuant to the provisions of an Act of Parliament passed in the Sessions of the third and fourth years of the reign of His late Majesty King William the Fourth, intituled 'An Act for the better administration of Justice in Her Majesty's Privy Council.' But any appeal against an order already made by the Governor in Council of Bombay shall be preferred within six months after the passing of this Act."

Section II of the Draft Act had been taken very nearly verbatim from a Bill which had been introduced into the House of Commons and passed there, but which was afterwards thrown out by the House of Lords, on the ground that it was not a private Bill.

The late Nabob died on the 8th of August 1842. At that time, he was not subject to the jurisdiction of the ordinary Civil Courts of the Government, and he had a certain jurisdiction over his relations and dependants. It appeared that upon his death the Government of Bombay took possession of his property, and sanctioned the payment of certain sums of money out of the proceeds of the estate for the maintenance of his family and the liquidation of his debts. In the year 1845, Sir Robert Arbuthnot, then Agent for the Governor at Surat, reported upon certain specific claims which had been preferred to property belonging to the estate of the late Nabob, and also upon the claims of the Nabob's creditors. In August 1846, Mr. Willoughby, then a Member of the Council of Bombay, suggested that an Act should be passed conferring power on the Government to arrange the affairs of the late Nabob. On the 8th September following, the Governor of Bombay recorded a Minute upon this suggestion, in which he said:—

"I certainly think, with Mr. Willoughby, that we ought to have an Act to legalize our proceedings in taking possession of and distributing, according to Mahomedan Law, the property of the late Nabob. Strictly speaking, perhaps, the Government should, on his demise, have interfered in no way whatever with any matter unconnected with the question of the continuance of the dignity, and the stipend paid by Government; but this course would evidently have given rise to endless disputes, and to the greatest injustice; and although our interference might not have been justifiable in the case of a private party, however wealthy or however high in consideration, yet it may have been so when we consider that His Highness had been recognised by us as a Sovereign Prince, while all the claimants to his property were at his demise, only ordinary subjects of the British Government."

The draft of an Act was framed and published in February 1848, Section I of which empowered the Governor of Bombay in Council to exempt from the jurisdiction of the Civil and Criminal Courts, the widows and such of the surviving relatives of the late Nabob as he should think proper, and to declare them amenable to the authority of an Agent appointed for the purpose. Section II enacted as follows:—

"And it is hereby enacted that it shall be competent to the Governor in Council of Bombay to act in the administration of the property of whatever nature left by the late Nabob of Surat, in regard to the settlement and payment of the debts and claims standing against the estate of the said late Nabob at the time of his demise, and to make distribution of the remaining property among his family; and that all acts of the said Governor in Council of Bombay, in respect to such property, from the date of the demise of the said late Nabob, shall be held to be valid, and not liable to be questioned in any Court of Law."

On the 11th of March 1848, Meer Jafur Alee Khan addressed a letter to the Governor in Council at Bombay, in which he said:—

"Having observed in the public papers that an Act for the administration of the estate of the late Nabob of Surat has been laid before the Legislative Council, I beg to call the attention of your Honor in Council to the second Clause of the Act, which I am advised is so framed as to prevent the Agent at Surat investigating and deciding upon several very important subjects relating to the Nabob's estate, which I am desirous of submitting to him for decision.

"Being satisfied that it cannot be the intention either of your Honor in Council or of the Legislative Council, to pass a Law for the purpose of debarring me from asserting what I believe to be my undoubted rights, and denying me even an appeal to the authority specially constituted under the Act to dispense Justice, I beg to submit, for the consideration of your Honor in Council, the accompanying Clause in lieu of Clause II of the Act; and I trust that your Honor will be pleased to recommend its adoption to the Legislative Council."

His complaint, as here stated, was that the proposed Act would prevent the Agent of the Government at Surat from investigating and deciding upon several questions relating to the Nabob's estate which he desired to submit to him for decision. The Clause which he proposed in lieu of Clause II of the Draft Act, was as follows:—

"That the estate and effects of the late Nabob, and the administration thereof, shall be exempt from the jurisdiction of the Civil Courts of Justice, and shall be under the authority of the Agent, to be appointed as aforesaid, but subject to the control of Government; and that no action or suit shall be brought in any Court of Law for any act done by the Agent or other Officer of the Governor in Council at Surat since the decease of the late Nabob respecting his estate or effects."

Thus it appeared that the object of Meer Jafur Alee Khan at that time was to exempt the administration of the estate and effects of the late Nabob from the jurisdiction of the Civil Courts of Justice, and to vest it in the Agent at Surat subject to the control of Government.

The letter was sent up by the Chief Secretary to the Government of Bombay to the Secretary to the Government of India on the 10th of April 1848, with the following communication:—

"With reference to the draft Act for the administration of the estate of the late Nabob of Surat, now before the Legislative Council of India, I am directed by the Honorable the Governor in Council to transmit to you, for submission to the Right Honorable the Governor General of India in Council, copy of a letter from Meer Jafur Alee Khan, dated the 11th Ultimo, soliciting a modification of Clause II in the draft Act in question.

"In forwarding this letter, I am directed to explain that it is the intention of this Government, on the passing of the above Act, to empower the Agent for the Honorable the Governor at Surat to summon all parties who claim to participate in the late Nabob's estate, and, after full inquiry, to adjudicate their respective claims, consulting on all points of law the Mahomedan Law Officers of the greatest repute.

"The Agent's decisions will be subject to the confirmation of, and all appeals against those decisions will be entertained and finally decided by Government.

"After the proceeds of the estate have been thus distributed, all future cases of dispute, with the exemptions noticed in the Act, will be subject to the jurisdiction of the ordinary tribunals of the country.

"Under the above explanations, the Governor in Council does not consider any change necessary in the draft Act as now framed."

In 1848, then, as he understood it, Meer Jafur Alee Khan's request was that claims relating to the estate and effects of the late Nabob should be investigated and determined by the Agent at Surat, subject to the control of the Government of Bombay. The Act was eventually passed, Section II being substantially the same as Section II of the draft as published for general information; and Meer Jafur Alee Khan and the widows and grand-daughters and two other distant relatives of the deceased Nabob were exempted from being sued in the Civil Courts unless with the consent of the Governor of Bombay. After the passing of the Act, instructions were sent by the Government of Bombay to the Agent for the Governor at Surat, and, amongst other things, he was instructed to issue a notification calling upon all persons having claims upon the Nabob to submit them to him; that, on claims being preferred, he was to enter upon their investigation, summoning parties and witnesses before him in the same manner as he would do as a Judge in a civil case; and on the conclusion of each case, he was to submit his proceedings to the Government, accompanied by his opinion upon the validity or otherwise of the claim; and he was authorized, in all his investigations, to consult any of the Government Mahomedan Law Officers. Mr. W. E. Frere, the Agent at Surat, proceeded upon the investigation; and, as regards the general property, he reported that the succession to the inheritance should be in the following shares, according to

Mr. Peacock

the Mahomedan Law of Inheritance; namely, The Nabob's two grand-daughters, Ruheem Ool Nissa Begum and Zeea Ool Nissa Begum, 8-16ths.
The Nabob's two widows, Padsha Begum,...................... 1-16th.
And Ameer Ool Nissa Begum, 1-16th.
Two greatgrandsons of the Nabob's great grandfather's brother in the male line, Meer Moyenoodeen, ... 3-16ths.
And Meer Kumroodeen, ... 3-16ths.

That Report was approved by the Governor of Bombay in Council, after having determined the several questions submitted to them by Meer Jafur Alee for decision; and the case was determined by that Government accordingly.

He (Mr. Peacock) thought it right here to call attention to two preliminary objections made by Meer Jafur Alee.—1stly. That it was the Governor in Council who, by the Act, was empowered to administer to the estate of the late Nabob, and that that authority could not be delegated to the Agent at Surat. 2ndly. That the Nabob having died, and the Nabobship having been declared extinct, the Petitioner and his wife immediately became subject to the jurisdiction of the Zillah Court, and could only be deprived of the Nabob's estate by the course laid down in the Regulations. He did not think that such objections came with a very good grace from Meer Jafur Alee, who, as he had already shown, had proposed that Section 11 of the Draft Act of 1848 should be so altered as to exempt the administrator of the Nabob's estate from the jurisdiction of the Civil Courts of Justice, and to vest it in the Agent, subject to the control of the Government; nor were they consistent with the statement in the Petition preferred to this Council by Meer Jafur Alee, in which he stated that

"Your Petitioner remained under the impression he had always entertained that the proceedings of the Agent and the Government were to be of the same judicial character as those in regard to the Sirdars of the Deccan, which entitled them to appeal from the Agent to the Governor in Council and from the latter, as of right, to Her Majesty in Council."

The objections were, however, overruled for the reasons given by the Governor of Bombay in paragraphs 2 to 8 of his Minute dated 3rd June 1853:—

"Before entering on the merits of the case, I would remove an objection made in the 143rd paragraph of Meer Jafur Alee's letter. This objection did not escape my observation, as will be seen in my Minute of the 25th of September last, and was anticipated by my Honorable colleague Mr. Bell, who, in his Minute of the 2nd of October, pointed out that it is the Governor in Council who, by the Act, is empowered to administer to the estate of the late Nabob of Surat, and that that authority could not be delegated to the Agent.

"The Act, however, does not prescribe what course the Governor in Council is to pursue in the discharge of this duty, and the course we have adopted appears to me not only perfectly unobjectionable, but the most fair and convenient for all parties.

"It would have been impossible for us to have prosecuted the inquiry into all these conflicting claims ourselves; the Agent for the Governor, who was the medium of communication between the Government and the late Nabob, was therefore (as the fittest person for that purpose) directed to make the necessary preliminary investigation. This was done; and we received Mr. W. E. Frere's Report on these claims. This Report we were at liberty to have adopted as our decision, and to have acted on at once, or we might have decided and acted in any way we pleased; but instead of adopting any arbitrary mode of proceeding, having generally approved of the Report, we desired Mr. Frere to draw it up in the form of a decree, and to furnish each of the parties concerned with a copy of it, directing them to prefer any appeal they might have to make within ninety days. We now have their objections before us, and can pass any decision in the case that appears to us just and proper, and this will be our decision as the Act requires it should be, and not the decision of the Agent, or of any subordinate Officer.

"There is also another plea which, though like the above objection, not brought forward till the close of Meer Jafur Alee's letter (vide para. 138), may be deemed preliminary, and one that should be disposed of before entering on the merits of the case.

"It is that the Nabob having died, and the Nabobship having been declared extinct, the petitioner and his wife immedietely became subject to the jurisdiction of the Zillah Court, and could only be legally deprived of the Nabob's estate by the course laid down in the Regulations, which he (Meer Jafur Alee) contends would have had the effect of placing him in the strong position of a defendant, with nothing to do but to defend his possession against the claims of others, instead of having the disadvantage of being forced to prove his own title to the estate.

"The Nabob died in 1842, and it was only in October 1846 that it was finally decided that on his death his relations and dependants ceased to be exempt from the jurisdiction of the Zillah Courts.

"It is impossible at this distance of time to say what the Zillah Judge might have done had he been aware of his authority, or what the Sudder Adawlut, who would have heard the appeal, might have decided; but I find that Chapter II of Regulation VIII provides for the appointment of an administrator both when the heir is present and undetermined, and when the heir is unknown; and from the intricate nature of this case, as shown in Mr. Frere's Report, it would, I think, have been judicious in the Zillah Judge had he, under existing circumstances, appointed an administrator when the Nabob died, and in such case, Meer Jafur Alee would have been in no better position than he is at present, nor would he have been entitled to the greater consideration he now claims at our hands, in virtue of the asserted hardship of his position."

Eventually, Meer Jafur Alee appealed to Her Majesty in Council; but the Judicial Committee held that an appeal would not lie. The judgment was delivered by the Lord Justice Knight Bruce. His Lordship said:—

"The Governor of Bombay, in execution of the power or duty, or both, thus conferred upon him, has exercised that power or duty in a manner unsatisfactory to members of the family of the Nabob, and, in consequence, the present Petitioners seek to have the case re-heard, or the distribution, thought right by the Governor of Bombay in Council, brought under the review of the Judicial Committee, as a matter of right, and in the exercise of its ordinary jurisdiction; and the question before their Lordships is whether that is a course authorized by the Statutes under which they, as members of the Privy Council, exercising the particular functions of the Judicial Committee, are now sitting.

"The question is not whether this may hereafter be a case which their Lordships may have to hear, if it shall so seem fit to Her Majesty, under the 4th Section of the Statute, 3 and 4 Will. IV., c. 41, to refer it to them. The question is entirely confined to the 3rd Section of that Statute. Their Lordships desire that nothing which is said on the present occasion shall be understood as referring, directly or indirectly, to anything that may be thought right to be done under the 4th Section. That is, in point of fact, a matter with which they have nothing to do. The 4th Section provides 'That it shall be lawful for His Majesty to refer to the said Judicial Committee, for hearing or consideration, any such other matters whatsoever, as His Majesty shall think fit; and such Committee shall thereupon hear and consider the same.' If, therefore, it shall hereafter be the pleasure of Her Majesty to refer the present petition, or any similar petition to their Lordships, their Lordships will of course hear it, and report to Her Majesty upon it. At present no such case is before us. The only question is whether, without a reference, and as a matter of right, a petition complaining of what has been done by the Governor of Bombay in Council, under the particular power that I have mentioned, shall be brought here in ordinary course; and that depends upon the question whether, within the true meaning of the 3rd Section of the Statute 3 and 4 Will. IV., c. 41, establishing the Judicial Committee, the act of which complaint is now made, is the act of a judge or judicial officer; the language of the 3rd Section being 'that all appeals, or complaints in the nature of appeals whatever, which, either by virtue of this Act, or any Law, Statute, or custom may be brought before His Majesty or His Majesty in Council, from or in respect of the determination sentence, rule, or order of any Court, Judge, or judicial officer, and all such appeals as are now pending,' shall be heard in the way that is there mentioned.

"Now, the 2nd Section of the Indian Act of 1848 I have already read; and it will be requisite, in considering it more particularly, to look at the two portions of it separately. The first is that 'the Governor of Bombay in Council is empowered to act in the administration of the property, of whatever nature, left by the late Nabob of Surat, in regard of the settlement and payment of the debts and claims standing against the estate of the late Nabob at the time of his death, and to make distribution of the remaining property among his family.' Now, whether, if the Section had stopped there, the discretion of the Governor in Council was one which could have been regulated or interfered with judicially, or was absolute, their Lordships do not mean to intimate any opinion. Let it be assumed for a moment that it was not absolute, but that it was a discretion bound to be exercised, according to some law, some custom, some state of rights. The mode of complaining of that must have been to the ordinary Courts of the country, either in one branch of the local jurisdiction or in another, from which it might have been brought in regular course of appeal before Her Majesty in Council. No such course has taken place in the present instance, nor could it, for the obvious reason that I am about to mention. It is plain, therefore, that the Petitioners would not be right here, upon the supposition that the enactment that I am reading had ended at the point to which I have read. But the Section proceeds—

"'And no Act of the said Governor of Bombay in Council, in respect to the administration to and distribution of such property, from the date of the death of the said late Nabob, shall be liable to be questioned in any Court of Law or Equity.' It is perfectly plain, therefore, that no local Court could have entered into the question of the propriety of the administration or distribution of that right by the Governor of Bombay in the exercise of this power. But the argument is that, though the ordinary Courts are excluded from interference, the Queen in Council is not; and perhaps (though their Lordships do not mean to pronounce any opinion upon it) the argument may well be founded, that if the Governor in Council was here constituted a Court, it might have exceeded the limits of the Indian Legislature—the limits of their power—to exclude the judicial functions (if I may use the expression) of Her Majesty in Council. Their

Lordships are of opinion, however, that the intention of this Act was not to create a Court; that the intention of the Act was to delegate, either arbitrarily, or subject to certain limitations of discretion, the administration and distribution of the Nabob's property, but in such a way that the administration and distribution should not be judicially questioned. The expression, it will be observed, is not, 'shall be liable to be questioned in any other Court of Law or Equity,' but, 'shall be liable to be questioned in any Court of Law or Equity.' * * * * * * * * * *

"Their Lordships, therefore, consider that, in the ordinary exercise of their functions, they are without jurisdiction to interfere. They are of opinion that the proceeding of the Governor of Bombay in Council has not been an act of a Court, Judge, or judicial officer, within the meaning of the 3rd Section of the Statute 3 and 4 Will. IV., c. 41, but has been the act of a person or body not in any sense judicial; delegated and authorized to perform a particular function as to the responsibility for the exercise of which, or as to any appeal from that exercise, they were exempted by the Legislature which created them. * * * * * * * * * * *

"The petitioners, therefore, will take such course as they may be advised, with reference to an application to the Crown, through the Board of Control, or otherwise. By possibility, in consequence of such application, if made, the matter may come here again; and their Lordships will readily do their duty in hearing it. At present they consider it not to be within their ordinary functions to do so."

What Meer Jafur Alee Khan now wished this Council to do was to repeal so much of Act XVIII of 1848 as provided that no act of the Governor of Bombay in respect to the administration to, and distribution of, property of whatever nature left by the late Nabob, from the date of his death, should be liable to be questioned in any Court of Law. If the Council were to repeal that part of the Act, the question would still remain whether, under the first part of the Section, the decision in question was a judicial decision. The Act provided that no act of the Governor of Bombay in Council in relation to the property left by the Nabob should be liable to be questioned in any Court of Law. If the decision at which the Government of Bombay had arrived with respect to the estate was a judicial decision, it was, he considered, out of the power of the Indian Legislature to take away the right of appeal to the Privy Council;—it was out of its power to affect any prerogative of the Crown. He considered it was equally out of the power of the Legislative Council to give a right of appeal to the Privy Council, where it did not exist. So far as he could judge, the decision to which the Agent of the Governor of Bombay in Council had come, and which the Governor of Bombay in Council had confirmed, after a full investigation of the claims preferred, was a very fair one. Supposing that this Council had the power to give a right of appeal to the Privy Council, and that it exercised that power, he thought it very probable that the case would have to be remitted for further evidence before it could be finally decided by the Judicial Committee. It appeared to him that there was one question which, on appeal, the Privy Council might have to determine,—namely whether the wife of Meer Jafur Alee Khan was the legitimate daughter of the late Nabob. That question had been brought before the Governor of Bombay in Council in a Petition dated 19th December 1853, from the Padsha Begum. The Governor of Bombay, in a Minute dated 11th April 1854, remarked on the Petition as follows:—

"The Petition of the Padsha Begum asserts the illegitimacy of Bukhtiar Ool Nissa Begum on the ground that her mother, Ameer Ool Nissa Begum, was neither the wife nor the slave, but the concubine of the late Nabob. Throughout the investigation of the various claims to the disputed property, it has been assumed—and the fact appears to be almost conceded by Meer Jafur Alee—that the marriage of Ameer Ool Nissa Begum, and consequently the legitimacy of Bukhtiar Ool Nissa Begum, could not be proved according to the strict provisions of the Mahomedan Law; but it was one of the few facts clearly established in this difficult case, that the late Nabob, to the day of his death, always recognised Ameer Ool Nissa Begum as his legal wife, and her daughter, Bukhtiar Ool Nissa Begum, as his legitimate child. His will on this subject was unequivocally expressed by a series of acts, and operating within his palace as the Supreme Law, it legitimated his daughter. It is not therefore material to the question at issue relative to Meer Jafur Alee's claims, whether his mother-in-law's marriage received all the sanctions of Mahomedan Law. Those claims rest upon different grounds, and are sustained by distinct, but sufficient, authority."

In a dissent recorded on the 12th November 1856, by Mr. Willoughby, then one of the Directors of the East India Company, and concurred in by Mr. Smith and Mr. Astell, Mr. Willoughby said:—

"In the event, moreover, of the Court being forced by further proceedings in Parliament into a Court of Law, I feel the strongest conviction that, however much others might be benefited, Jafur Allee and his daughters would not only take nothing, but would lose the handsome provision which has been assigned to them. Reserve now would be misplaced. In such an event the matter must be judged by the strict rules and principles of Courts of Justice; and hence, the question, which has never yet been fairly raised, of the legitimacy of the party through whom Jafur Allee claims, must and will be raised. The Select Committee of the House of Commons have expressly stated that it is their intention, and that it is only right and proper, that it should be investigated. It is only owing to the false delicacy of the Bombay Government, in originally waiving this question out of consideration to the Nabob's family, that an opportunity has been afforded to attack with plausibility the Court's decisions in this matter. Now, however, as was formerly remarked by Sir George Clerk when he filled the high office of Governor of Bombay, 'In the discussion of the late Nawab's affairs, the question of the legitimacy of the daughter through whom the Memorialist (Jafur Allee) claims was very properly though generously waived. The case, however, now assumes a different aspect when the Memorialist appears in the character of an aggrieved person. The Honorable Court should therefore, I am of opinion, be referred to the 65th to 85th paragraphs of the Honorable Sir G. Arthur's elaborate Minute, dated the 28th April 1843, on the demise of the late Nabob, in which the point is slightly touched upon, and more particularly to Sir G. Arthur's Minute dated the 19th March 1844, in the 3rd and 5th paragraphs of which the question of her legitimacy was specially touched upon. On the supposition that the daughters who were married to the sons of Meer Surafraz Allee were legitimate, the connexion thus formed would have been regarded as far below the Nabob's rank and family, since the Meer, I am told, is of no family or note whatever, having been the architect of his own fortune; and I am told by the Political Secretary that this want of respectable ancestry frustrated the Meer's endeavors to obtain for his two sons, wives from a family at Baroda, which, though of high rank, is, in point of wealth, far inferior to that of the late Nabob of Surat. The Memorialist, therefore, speculated in matrimony, and, notwithstanding his present complaint, may be considered fortunate. I am of opinion that he has been most liberally dealt with, and that the settlements made by the late Government ought not to be disturbed.'

"When this question is investigated, I can scarcely entertain any doubt but that the result will be adverse to the promoters of the Bill in Parliament. For the evidence in regard to the origin and birth of Ameer-ool-Nissa, the mother of Buktiyar-ool-Nissa, the wife of Jafur Allee, and daughter of the late Nabob, does not depend upon any interested party, but was obtained from her own lips by Mr. Elliot, the Governor's Agent, as follows. After having given some particulars derived from less trustworthy sources, Mr. Elliot reports:

"'With her sanction, I repaired to the Palace; and with every deference demanded by her retired habits and peculiar circumstances, I obtained from her own lips the following history of her early life.

"'She belonged to the Rajpoot caste, and resided at Bhownuggur. When about the age of twelve or thirteen, a stranger came there and purchased her, for what sum she knows not. He conveyed her to the town of Randier, and afterwards to the residence of the old Nabob, father of his late Excellency. The latter informed his mother that a young girl had been brought to the Palace, whom he wished to live with him. His proposals having been acceded to by his parents, she was given into his keeping. She recollects having heard that the person who brought her, in consideration of the purchase, received two hundred Rupees and a pair of shawls. Three children were the offspring of this connexion, of whom one alone, Buktiyar-ool-Nissa survives (that is, Jafur Alee's wife). After the bismillar of this child, four years, four months, and four days subsequent to its birth, she was married to the Nabob, who passed to her a deed of emancipation.'"

If an appeal were given from the decision of the Government of Bombay to the Privy Council, it must be borne in mind that the question of the legitimacy of Meer Jafur Alee Khan's wife might be raised by the other heirs general of the late Nabob for the purpose of depriving his two grand-daughters of the 8-16ths. adjudged to them.

The Judicial Committee might possibly hold that the recognition by the late Nabob of Ameer-ool-Nissa as his lawful wife and of Buktiar-ool-Nissa as his legitimate child did not necessarily legitimate the daughter. If so, it might be necessary to remit the case for further evidence upon that point. That would cause considerable delay in the distribution of the estate. The Nabob having died in 1842, he thought it was not advisable in 1858 to pass any Act which would delay the distribution of the estate, which was still in the hands of Government. If that part of Act XVIII of 1848, which declared that no act of the Governor of Bombay in Council in respect to the distribution of the property of the Nabob should be liable to be questioned in any Court of Law or Equity, were repealed, the Council would deprive the Bombay Government of that protection which it was intended to afford to them. That, he thought, was out of the question.

He thought that it was not competent to this Council to pass an Act to give jurisdiction to the Judicial Committee of the Privy Council. The only alternative, as it appeared to him, was either to give an appeal to the Supreme Court of Judicature from the decision of the Governor in Council of Bombay, or to vest the Supreme Court with original jurisdiction to determine how the property should be administered; in either of which cases, an appeal would lie to the Privy Council without any express enactment on the subject. Either of these courses would necessarily cause great delay, and he thought that it would be very inexpedient to pass any Law of the kind. He thought it would be better to leave the Petitioner to renew his application to the Privy Council or to Parliament, if he should be advised to do so. Parliament had the power, which he thought this Council had not, to give an appeal to Her Majesty in Council from the decision of the Government of Bombay, although it had been decided not to be a judicial decision. He doubted very much whether the Judicial Committee would give any effect to an enactment of this Council authorizing them to determine upon appeal a case in which, without such enactment, they considered that they had no jurisdiction. The application to this Council was an after-thought.

On the 7th July 1857, Meer Jafur Alee wrote to the Honorable Court of Directors a letter in the following terms:—

"In compliance with the intimation made to me by the Right Honorable the President of the Board of Control, I have the honor to request that the distribution of the property of the late Nabob of Surat may be suspended for a year from this time, as I am in great hopes, that, by personal conference at Surat with the parties interested against me, I shall be able to effect a voluntary settlement of this harassing litigation."

"If I should not succeed in this endeavor of mine, I shall return to England, and prosecute my appeal to the Privy Council or to Parliament."

He (Mr. Peacock) understood from this letter that Meer Jafur Alee, in the event of his being unable to effect an amicable settlement, intended to apply to Her Majesty to refer the question to the Judicial Committee under the 4th Section of the 3 and 4 Wm. IV c. 41, to which the Lord Justice Knight Bruce had referred in his Judgment, and that if he found he was not entitled to relief under that Section, it was his intention to apply to Parliament. He never intimated to the Honorable Court of Directors that he intended to apply to this Council to repeal any portion of Act XVIII of 1848, or to amend that Act. The Secretary to the Court of Directors wrote in reply as follows:—

"I am commanded by the Court of Directors of the East India Company to acknowledge the receipt of your letter of the 7th Ultimo; and I am instructed to inform you in reply, that the Court, with due consideration for the rights of others, are unable to comply with your request for the suspension, for one year from the present time, of the distribution of the private property of the late Nabob of Surat."

When that letter was laid before the Board of Control, it was altered, and sent back, in order that it might be forwarded as altered. In its altered form, the letter ran thus:—

"I am commanded by the Court of Directors of the East India Company to acknowledge the receipt of your letter of the 7th Ultimo, and I am instructed to inform you in reply that the Court will comply with your request for the suspension, for one year from the present time, of the distribution of the private property of the late Nabob of Surat."

The Honorable Court of Directors, in consequence of the alteration made by the Board of Control, caused their Secretary to write to the Secretary to that Board the following letter:—

"With reference to the alterations made by the Board of Commissioners for the Affairs of India in the draft of a letter to Meer Jafur Ali Khan, I am commanded by the Court of Directors of the East India Company to observe that, whilst these alterations entirely reverse the decision of the Court, the Board have furnished no reasons for the same.

"2. I am commanded further to observe that the distribution of the private property of the late Nabob of Surat under the decree of a Court of competent jurisdiction has already been suspended for nearly five years; and that they have reason to believe that many of the members of the family are, consequently, in distressed circumstances. The Court, therefore, entertain the strongest conviction that they cannot without great injustice to these persons, consent to any further delay at the request of Meer Jafur Ali, whose apparent object in making that request is to enable himself to return to India, and there to induce the other members of the family to waive in his favor a portion of their just right, as decreed to them by a competent authority.

"3. For these reasons, the Court earnestly deprecate the alterations of the Board, and request that they may be permitted to revert to the decision contained in the original draft of their letter."

To that letter the following reply was sent:—

"I am desired by the Commissioners for the Affairs of India to acknowledge the receipt of your letter of the 20th Instant, conveying the representation of the Court of Directors of the East India Company against the alteration made by the Board, in the letter which the Court proposed to address to Meer Jafur Ali Khan, as to the distribution of the property of the late Nabob of Surat.

"2. The Board regret that the reason for making the alteration was not communicated to the Court on the 7th Instant: but it is simply this; the Board do not see that injury will be done to any individual interested in the property, if the distribution, which has already been postponed for a long time, be delayed for a short time longer; and therefore they are not unwilling to grant the request made by Meer Jafur Ali."

On the 27th of the same month, Meer Jafur Alee was informed that the Court would comply with his request.

"I am commanded by the Court of Directors of the East India Company, to acknowledge the receipt of your letter of the 7th Ultimo; and I am instructed to inform you in reply that the Court will comply with your request for the suspension for one year from the present time of the distribution of the private property of the late Nabob of Surat."

It appeared, therefore, that the Board of Control were not unwilling to grant the request of Meer Jafur Alee Khan for a year's delay to enable him, if he could, to effect an amicable settlement; but it did not appear that they intended to give him a year to enable him to get Act XVIII of 1848 amended, and to obtain a right of appeal to the Privy Council, which might possibly occupy three or four years before it was finally decided, thus occasioning a delay which must be injurious to the rights of the other claimants. He (Mr. Peacock) did not think that it was the intention either of the Court of Directors or of the Board of Control to give Meer Jafur Alee more than one year's further delay, and that was in consequence of his request for the express purpose of enabling him to effect an amicable settlement—certainly not for the purpose of enabling him to obtain the means of protracting litigation. On the 14th April 1858, the Court of Directors, with the sanction of course of the Board of Control, wrote to the Government of Bombay as follows:—

"You have received an intimation that Meer Jafur Alee is engaged in taking steps for obtaining a repeal of Act No. XVIII of 1848 with the view of prosecuting his appeal against the decision of Mr. Frere in respect to the decision of the private property left by the late Nabob; and you solicit our instructions as to the course to be followed in the matter.

"You will subsequently have received our letter of 23rd September (No. 31) 1857, informing you that we had, at the request of Meer Jafur Alee, agreed to suspend the distribution of the private property for one year from the 27th August 1857. At the expiration of that year, should the amicable adjustment which Meer Jafur Alee professed to have in view, not have been effected, the distribution must, in justice to the other parties interested, take place without further delay."

He thought, therefore, that the Government of Bombay had no power to suspend the distribution of the property beyond the term allowed. The President in Council considered himself bound by the order of the Home Authorities, and had refused to extend the term for the distribution of the estate. If, therefore, the Draft Act proposed by Meer Jafur Alee were now to be read a first time in this Council, and to be passed subsequently, it would not stop the distribution of the property, but would only give Meer Jafur Alee a right to restitution even should his appeal to the Privy Council be successful. This would involve very extensive litigation. Issues might arise of such a nature that it was impossible to say when they would be determined. Now, the question was—should the Legislative Council, sixteen years after the Nabob's death, and ten years after the passing of the Act XVIII of 1848, alter the Law so as to enable the Petitioner to commence such litigation. It appeared to him that it should not, and that it should refuse his Petition. It should be borne in mind that the Petitioner's daughters, according to the decision of the Bombay Government, were entitled to one-half of the property, and the widows and the other heirs of the Nabob, according to the Mahomedan Law of inheritance, to the other half in certain specified shares. These persons, who had so long been kept out of the shares awarded to them, were, he believed, in distressed circumstances, and were unable to bear the expense of litigation. He therefore thought that, at the expiration of the year during which, according to the direction of the Home Authorities, the distribution had been suspended, the property ought to be distributed according to the decision of the Bombay Government, if in the mean time Meer Jafur Alee should be unable to effect an amicable settlement with the other claimants, and that Meer Jafur Alee should be left to take the course which, in his letter of the 7th July 1857, he stated it was his intention to adopt;—namely, "to prosecute his appeal to the Privy Council or to Parliament."

The Motion was agreed to.

The Council adjourned.

Saturday, August 7, 1858.

PRESENT:

The Hon. the Chief Justice, *Vice-President*, in the Chair.

Hon'ble J. P. Grant,	E. Currie, Esq.,
Hon'ble Major General Sir James Outram,	Hon. Sir A. W. Buller,
Hon'ble H. Ricketts,	H. B. Harington, Esq.,
Hon'ble B. Peacock,	and
P. W. LeGeyt, Esq.,	H. Forbes, Esq.

MADRAS MARINE POLICE: AND INSTITUTION OF SUITS AND APPEALS (N. W. PROVINCES).

THE VICE-PRESIDENT read Messages informing the Legislative Council that the Governor General had assented to the Bill "for the maintenance of a Police Force for the Port of Madras," and the Bill "for the relief of persons who, in consequence of the recent disturbances, have been prevented from instituting or prosecuting suits or appeals in the Civil Courts of the North-Western Provinces within the time allowed by law."

STAMP DUTIES (BENGAL).

THE CLERK presented to the Council a Petition of the Rajah of Burdwan concerning the Bill "to amend Regulation X. 1829 of the Bengal Code" (relating to the collection of Stamp Duties.)

MR. PEACOCK moved that the above Petition be referred to the Select Committee on the Bill.

Agreed to.

LITERARY, SCIENTIFIC, AND CHARITABLE INSTITUTIONS.

THE CLERK also presented a Petition of the British Indian Association praying for the passing of an Act for the incorporation of Literary, Scientific, and Charitable Institutions conformably with the recommendation of the Select Committee on the Bill "for the incorporation and Regulation of Joint-Stock Companies and other Associations, either with or without limited liability of the Members thereof."

MR. PEACOCK moved that the above Petition be printed.

Agreed to.

ESTATE OF THE LATE NABOB OF THE CARNATIC.

MR. PEACOCK moved that Counsel be now heard upon the subject of the Bill "to provide for the administration of the Estate and for the payment of the debts of the late Nabob of the Carnatic."

Agreed to.

Counsel on behalf of Prince Azeem Jah were heard accordingly.

MR. PEACOCK said, he was very glad that Counsel had been heard on this Bill. A good deal had been said in the course of their argument upon the subject of private Bills and of Estate Bills: but he apprehended that the material point was not whether this Bill was a public Bill or private Bill, but whether it was a fair and just Bill. If it did injustice to any person, the Council ought not to pass it; for the Council had no more right to do injustice by means of a public Bill than by means of a private or of an Estate Bill. It must be clear, he thought, that Prince Azeem Jah could not reasonably contend that the Council was disposed to ignore his rights and interests, seeing that it had just heard a learned and ingenious argument in support of them, addressed to it by his Counsel.

He would not go into the question relating to the Treaties between the East India Company and the Nabobs of the Carnatic, because the Council had stopped the learned Advocates on behalf of the Prince from entering into it. The construction of those Treaties was not a subject for argument here. It had been decided by the Government of Madras in 1856; that decision had been affirmed by the late Governor-General and subsequently confirmed by the Honorable Court of Directors with the sanction of the Board of Control. It was not for this Council to re-open the question, and to discuss whether that decision, so confirmed, was correct or erroneous. In their Despatch of the 19th March 1856, the Honorable Court said:—

"In the opinion both of the Governor-General and of the Madras Government, the dignity of the Nabob of the Carnatic has expired; the Treaties between the British Government and the successive heads of the family of Walajah are at an end; the British Government are under no obligation to recognize any person as successor to the rights hitherto enjoyed under those Treaties; and expediency being wholly against such recognitions, those authorities are unanimously of opinion that it ought not to take place.

"We have carefully examined the past history of the relations of the British Government with this family, and have bestowed on the important question referred to us the earnest deliberation due to all questions which can be supposed to involve considerations of public faith."

As the learned Counsel had been prevented from entering into any discussion as to the effect of the Treaty, he (Mr. Peacock) would not refer to the arguments of the Honorable Court upon the subject. It was sufficient for him to say that the Honorable Court declared "that they fully adopted the opinion of the Governor General and of the Madras Government that the title and dignity of Nabob and all the advantages annexed to it by the Treaty of 1801 were an end."

The Council must, therefore, determine the question affecting the claims of Prince Azeem Jah upon the assumption

Mr. Peacock

that the decision arrived at by the Home Authorities was correct, and that the Nabobship of the Carnatic never did descend to the Prince.

The learned Counsel had said that there was a variance between the Preamble of the Bill and its enacting Clauses. He said that the Preamble of the Bill provided that, after appropriating to the payment of the late Nabob's debts such portion of the property left by him as was liable for them, the surplus assets should be applied towards making provision for his family; but that the Bill itself contained no Clause by which any such surplus assets could be divided among the next of kin or any members of the family. To him (Mr. Peacock), however, it seemed perfectly clear that Section VIII of the Bill did make full provision for that purpose, and he had called the learned Counsel's attention to it whilst he was addressing the Council, in order that he might not be taken by surprise. Section VIII provided as follows:—

"It shall be lawful for any creditor *or person interested in the proper administration of the estate and effects of the said Nabob*, to apply for and obtain in a summary way, in the manner provided by Act VI of 1854, upon a summons to be served upon the said Receiver, an order for the administration of the estate and effects of the said Nabob."

This provision gave to any person interested in the proper administration of the estate, the right to institute an administration suit, not as in an ordinary case against the Administrator or Executor of the estate, because there was none—but against a Receiver to be appointed under the Bill. If the property left by the late Nabob had come within the provisions of the Administrator General's Act, the Administrator General would have taken possession of it for the benefit of all persons interested, and, in the event of any surplus remaining after the payment of the Nabob's debts, he would have divided such surplus amongst the next of kin or heirs, according to their legal rights. As, however, the property did not come within the jurisdiction of the Administrator General, a Receiver was to be appointed to collect and take possession of it. But he was not to take any property out of the possession of any member of the Nabob's Family, without the permission of the Government of Madras. Act I of 1844 exempted the person and property of the late Nabob from any writ or process of any Court, unless such writ or process were sued forth or prosecuted with the consent of the Government of Madras, and it also provided that the same privilege should extend to the persons belonging to the Family and household of His Highness whose names were contained in lists to be published by that Government from time to time. The last Section of this Bill, accordingly, provided that—

"No property shall be taken by the said Receiver out of the possession of any person mentioned in the list last published in the Government Gazette at Madras of persons entitled to privileges under the provisions of Act I of 1844, without the previous order of the said Governor in Council."

The object of this Section was to prevent the Receiver from interfering unnecessarily with any property that might be in the actual possession of any member of the Family of the late Nabob. The learned Counsel had stated expressly that he did not object to the appointment of a Receiver, but he objected to the Receiver's being authorized to realize or sell the property pending the decision of Parliament upon the appeal which his client had preferred against the ruling of the Home Authorities regarding his claims. The Receiver being appointed, the first question would be, how was the property left by the late Nabob to be got in for the purpose of distribution amongst his creditors? The Bill would enable him to take possession of it as if he were the Administrator or Executor dealing with an ordinary estate, and then any creditor or other person interested in the due administration of the property might proceed by the summary mode indicated in Section VIII to have the property duly distributed by him. In an ordinary case, any creditor or next of kin of a deceased person might apply for an order upon his Executor or Administrator for the administration of his estate and effects, and the Court would either refer it to the Master to take an account of the assets and liabilities, or under Act VI of 1854 the Court might itself investigate and decide upon the claims against the estate. In either case proper notices would be given by the Court and all persons interested either as creditors or next of kin might come in and be heard. In the present case similar proceedings would be taken against the Receiver. He would here refer to the objection taken by the learned Counsel that the Bill did not provide sufficiently for giving notice to his client or to any member of the late Nabob's Family to come in and prove their claims, but only provided for giving such notice to the creditors. But such was not the case. The latter part of Section VIII did make provision for notice to the Family of the late Nabob; for it said the Court "shall also by the said order give such directions as to the notices to be issued to such creditors (many of the creditors holding mortgages) *and otherwise*, and shall direct such enquiries, as to the Court shall seem fit." Under that provision, the Court would issue notice to all persons having claims, whether as creditors or as heirs or next of kin of the late Nabob, to appear before it and establish their claims. The learned Counsel had looked indignant and had said that it struck him with astonishment that the words "private property" were not expressly made use of in the Bill, as if the Legislative Council had some improper object in omitting these words. The learned Counsel acquitted them of any intention of that kind, but still he looked as if he thought it. Well, now, what did the Bill do? By Section V it appointed a Receiver, who, it said—

"shall have full power to collect, take possession of, and get in all property, moveable or immoveable, and whether of the nature of State or public property or *not*, to which the said late Nabob, at the time of his death, was entitled either at law or in equity, or which is liable either at law or in equity to satisfy the debts of the said Nabob."

The learned Counsel admitted that this included the whole of the property left by the Nabob; but it struck him with astonishment, and as most remarkable, that, while the Section mentioned "State or public property" it did not speak of "private property" in express terms. Now, the words "State or public property" were used for a particular purpose. It was considered that some doubt might arise whether certain property which was in the possession of the late Nabob when the Treaty of 1801 was entered into and which might be considered of the nature of State property, vested in the East India Company on the lapse of the titular sovereignty, or whether it was so far the property of the late Nabob as to be applicable to the payment of his debts in the first instance, and to be the subject of distribution amongst his family on the event of there being a surplus. When the Rajah of Tanjore died, his widow claimed all the private property left by him; she claimed only the private, and not the State property; and a question arose what was private and what was in the nature of State property. In the present case the Government relinquished all claim to any part of the property whether strictly private, or in the nature of State or public property left by the late Nabob, and in order to remove all doubt as to whether property of the nature of State or public property left by the late Nabob could be appropriated to the payment of his debts in the first instance, or would be distributable amongst his heirs in the event of a surplus remaining after payment of his debts, the words "whether of the nature of State or public property or not" were inserted in the Section. All property strictly private clearly came under the words "*or not*," and the learned Counsel had no difficulty whatever in discovering that the whole of the property of the late Nabob was included. Now the Government having relinquished all claim to any part of the Nabob's property, it was necessary to provide some mode by which the legal distribution of it could be enforced. Act I of 1844 enacted that no writ or process should be issued against the person or property of the late Nabob without the consent of the Madras Government. If the exemption from process given by that Act extended to the late Nabob's property after his death, the Courts had no right to seize such property in satisfaction of the demands of a creditor. It was, therefore, considered necessary to provide some means by which the property might be collected and properly distributed amongst the creditors of the Nabob, and the surplus, if any, amongst his heirs according to their respective rights. Accordingly, the Preamble of the Bill recited that

"whereas it is doubtful whether the creditors of the Nabob have, without the consent of the Governor in Council of Fort St. George, any remedy for enforcing their claims against the goods or property which belonged to the said Nabob at the time of his death; and especially whether any part of the property left by the said late Nabob, which was of the nature of State or public property, is liable for the payment of such claims: and whereas the East India Company is willing to give up any right which it has to any part of such property which is in the nature of State or public property, and to allow the whole property, moveable and immoveable, of whatever kind, left by the late Nabob, after appropriating to the payment of his debts such portion thereof as is liable to the payment thereof, to be applied towards making provision for the family and dependents of the late Nabob;"

and then, Section V empowered the Receiver to collect

"all property, moveable or immoveable, and whether of the nature of State property *or not*, to which the said late Nabob, at the time of his death, was entitled either at Law or in Equity, or which was liable either at Law or in Equity to satisfy the debts of the said Nabob."

And Section VIII gave power to any creditor or other person interested in the proper administration of the property to institute a suit in the Supreme Court in the summary mode provided by Act VI of 1854, in ordinary cases, for the due administration of such property. Provision was also made for the payment in full of all creditors who would consent to receive in full discharge of their debts such sums as should be found to be due to them according to certain just and equitable principles laid down by the Honorable Court. This had called forth from the learned Counsel the remark that the only ground upon which he could imagine that the East India Company would have undertaken to pay the late Nabob's debts, was that it knew that the Treaty had not been carried out in the way in which it was believed it would be carried out.

In strictness, the East India Company were not bound to provide either for the family or servants of the late Nabob or for the payment of his debts. But it would have been quite inconsistent with the liberal principles upon which they have always acted in similar cases to leave the Members of his family or his servants or followers without a suitable provision. Accordingly the Madras Government proposed to make provision for the Members of the Nabob's family, to pay the debts contracted by Prince Azeem Jah as Naib-i-Mooktear or Nabob Regent, during the late Nabob's minority; and also the debts contracted by the late Nabob himself. In sanctioning that proposal, the Honorable Court remarked:—

"We entirely agree in the liberal intentions of the Madras Government in favor of the family. We approve the proposals that 'a handsome allowance should be given to the Prince Azeem Jah Bahadoor,' that the debts incurred by him as Naib-i-Mooktear should be investigated by a commission, and such of them as are deemed legitimate paid by Government, that the same course should be pursued respecting the debts of the late Nabob, his personal property being first appropriated towards their liquidation."

The Honorable Court were aware that many persons had availed themselves of the necessities of the late Nabob, and had probably charged him more than they were fairly entitled to receive, and had contracted for exorbitant rates of interest. They therefore added

"that the salaries of the principal officers of the Nabob's household should be continued for their lives, and that all the servants, attendants, troops, and followers should be discharged, pensions or gratuities being granted to such as may have an equitable claim to such consideration.

"We shall only add that, in the adjustment of debts, the utmost care should be used to exclude fictitious or improper claims, that only sums should be admitted which can be proved to have been advanced; that in regard to articles sold, only the fair market price of the day should be allowed, and that our standing order limiting the interest in such cases to a maximum of six per cent. simple interest must be scrupulously observed."

Now, it having been determined, upon the construction of the Treaty, that the Nabobship did not descend to Prince Azeem Jah, it appeared to him that that was a very fair and liberal arrangement. The learned Counsel was, however, a little inconsistent in his argument. He said, if the Treaty had been carried out in the manner in which it was supposed it would be carried out, then all the creditors of the late Nabob would have been paid out of the one-fifth part of the revenues of the Carnatic which would have been continued to Prince Azeem Jah. How was this consistent with that part of his argument in which he contended that the late Nabob had merely a life-estate in his property, and that all his property, including the one-fifth of the revenues secured to him by the Treaty, was entailed upon his heirs and was not liable to the payment of his debts. The learned Counsel said—"Act upon the principles of Justice. Let right be done to every man to whom right is due." He (Mr. Peacock) contended that this was precisely what the Bill did. It provided that the late Nabob's property should be appropriated to the payment of his debts. The learned Counsel, however, thought that that was not right: he ignored the creditors altogether and contended that his client Prince Azeem Jah ought to take all the property of the late Nabob whether public or private as an entailed estate, and should not be bound to pay the debts. He argued that the late Nabob had only a life-interest in his property, and that that life-interest was all that the creditors looked to at the time when their debts were contracted, and all that they had a right to look to now; and as an illustration, he had referred to the case of the late Duke of Buckingham and the Marquis of Chandos, arguing that Prince Azeem Jah, whom he represented as in the position of the Marquis of Chandos, was not bound to surrender the property of the deceased Nabob, whom he compared to the Duke of Buckingham, for the payment of his debts. The learned Counsel's reasoning might have been perfectly correct as to the State or public property, though probably not as to the private property, if he had shewn that Prince Azeem Jah had become Nabob of the Carnatic. But, he was not allowed to argue upon that assumption. The learned Counsel had said that the Government of this Empire had passed from the East India Company which issued the order, to the Crown. Whether this assertion were correct or not he could not say; but he would remark that the learned Counsel had not adverted to the fact that the Despatch of the Honorable

Court could not have been written without reference to the advisers of the Crown. Probably, the learned Counsel was not aware that the Honorable Court's Despatches, before they were sent out to this country, were submitted to the Board of Control, and received the sanction of the President of that Board.

The learned Counsel proposed that this Bill should be modified and that the property should be retained in the hands of the Receiver until Parliament should have decided upon the Petition of his client. But the decision of the Court of Directors was passed on the 19th of March 1856. Two years and more had elapsed, and, according to the learned Counsel himself, the Petition to Parliament had only recently been forwarded. [Mr. Money—it was forwarded in the latter part of June.] Having been forwarded in the latter part of June, it would not arrive in time for Parliament to deal with it this Session, and therefore it would be nearly three years after the decision of the Honorable Court was passed before Prince Azeem Jah's Petition to Parliament could be presented. Prince Azeem Jah had allowed more than two years to elapse without presenting any Petition to Parliament. He had taken no steps with reference to the Petition until long after this Bill had been published. He (Mr. Peacock) did not think that the Council would do him any injustice by allowing the late Nabob's property to be sold for payment of his debts without waiting to ascertain what might be the result of the Petition. What property was it that was to be taken possession of by the Receiver, and of which the sale according to the argument would cause an irreparable injury to the Prince if Parliament should recognize his claims? The learned Counsel had talked about emblems of ancestorial dignity, and time-honored elements of pride and greatness; but the greater part of the property left by the late Nabob consisted of houses which he himself had purchased out of the allowance which he received from Government. There was one Palace, the Chepauk Palace, which he believed was the property of his ancestors in 1801 when the Treaty was entered into; but he (Mr. Peacock) knew of no other emblem of ancestorial dignity that the Nabob had left behind him. The learned Counsel had not specified any particular property which he wished to remain unsold in the hands of the Receiver. He insisted that the whole property should await the decision of Parliament on his client's appeal, and that it should not be sold and distributed amongst the creditors of the late Nabob, until it should be known that the decision of Parliament was unfavorable to his client, and he proposed that the East India Company should, in the mean time, pay the Nabob's debts. He (Mr. Peacock) saw no reason for coming to such a decision. Even as regarded the Chepauk Palace, he believed there was a question whether it was in the nature of State property, or whether it was merely private property. The Honorable the Court of Directors said in their Despatch :—

"We perceive that in the contemplations of the Madras Government the Palace at Chepauk will at once be at the disposal of the State as public property. Sir Henry Montgomery says that it was mortgaged, which might imply that it was considered to be private property. You will institute further enquiries upon this point, but whatever may be the correct view of the subject, we do not wish to see the ladies of the Nabob's immediate family deprived, against their inclination, of the privilege of residing in that edifice, and the most liberal consideration should be given to any claims they may prefer to portions of the personal property contained in the building."

A provision was originally inserted in the Bill that the Government of Madras should have power to purchase the Palace in order that the ladies of the late Nabob's family might be permitted to reside in it. He was at that time under the impression that the ladies continued to reside in the Palace after the death of the Nabob; but it appeared that they did not reside there, and he believed they never did; and therefore there was no occasion to purchase it for the purpose of carrying out the considerate and liberal intentions of the Honorable Court. If, however, there were any particular articles in the possession of the ladies or of any other member of the family which they desired to retain, he had no wish that they should be sold. The Bill provided that the Receiver should take no property out of the possession of the Nabob's family without the consent of the Government of Madras, and if there was any particular article of property which any member of the family desired to retain, he had no doubt that, on a proper representation being made, the Government of Madras would be most anxious to attend to their wishes. He thought that every protection that could fairly be claimed in this respect consistently with the rights of the creditors, was thrown around the family by the Bill.

The learned Counsel had objected to Section V as requiring the Receiver to realize the property with all convenient speed immediately after the passing of this Act. The Receiver would have power to realize the property, but he must act under the direction of the Supreme Court. Section I enacted that

"the Governor in Council of Fort St. George shall, immediately after the passing of this Act, appoint such person as he may think fit to act, *under the orders* of the Supreme Court of Judicature at Madras, in the administration of the property of whatever nature left by the said late Nabob."

Thus, the Receiver was not to proceed immediately to sell all the property he collected, moveable and immoveable, at his discretion; but he was to be subject, like any other Receiver, to the control of the Supreme Court. He (Mr. Peacock) did not think that the words "and realize," in Section V, coming after the words "he shall proceed to collect, take possession of," necessarily meant that the Receiver was to be bound to sell all the property he collected; but to avoid all possible doubt on the point, he had no objection to recommit the Bill for the purpose of striking out the words "and realize." That would still make it obligatory on the Receiver to collect the property with all convenient speed immediately after the passing of the Act, and would leave him with power to sell it subject to the orders of the Supreme Court.

The learned Counsel had also remarked upon Sections XXIV, XXV, and XXVI. There had been some difficulty in providing a tribunal for ascertaining the amount due to such of the creditors as should come in to have their claims adjusted in the manner prescribed by the Court of Directors. The Bill would not prevent any creditor from getting his full pound of flesh; but all who should insist upon their strict rights, must look to the assets of the estate, and to those assets alone. If they should be insufficient to pay the debts in full, the creditors who insisted upon their strict rights would recover only so much as a rateable division of the assets among the general body of creditors would provide for their shares. But to those who were willing to come in and have their claims estimated on the fair and equitable principle which the Despatch laid down—namely, in the case of loans, at the sums actually advanced, and in the case of goods sold, at the fair marketable value thereof at the time of sale with interest at six per cent., the Government offered to guarantee payment in full, and the assenting creditors would be paid immediately, without waiting for the termination of the administration suit. Then arose the question, by what tribunal the claims of such creditors could be best adjusted. It was at first suggested that they should be adjusted by Commissioners, and the Madras Government actually appointed Commissioners for the purpose; but that Government afterwards considered that the decisions of Commissioners appointed by Government would not be so satisfactory as the decision of the Supreme Court, and in order that there might be no room for dissatisfaction or for any suspicion of partiality, provision was made in this Bill that the Supreme Court should be the tribunal to investigate the claims, and adjust them on the principle he had just stated.

On the Bill being published, some of the creditors petitioned the Council representing that the principle laid down of allowing six per cent. interest might be held by the Court to require that the interest was to be calculated at that rate from the day on which the loans had been advanced or the goods delivered, and that a decision to that effect would not be fair to the creditors, since its effect would be, in cases where a higher rate of interest than six per cent. had been specifically paid, to cut down the principal by the excess of interest received over that rate, whereas the intention of the East India Company was to pay in full all such debts as should be proved to have been fairly and justly contracted. The Select Committee, acquiescing in the objection, amended the Bill providing that the calculation of interest at the rate of six per cent. should be made from the last specific payment of interest, at whatever rate, made on the Nabob's account. But, under Section XIV, the principal must be adjusted in the manner he had mentioned already. In all probability, the amount of claims adjusted in that manner, would be much less than the amount which would appear due according to the actual contracts, for the creditors, aware of the circumstances of the Nabob, and of the exemption from process provided by Act I of 1844, might have stipulated for interest at thirty per cent. or for double the fair market value of goods supplied. In an ordinary estate every creditor would have a right to appear before the Master; in this case, every creditor who consented to have his debt estimated according to the principle laid down, would have a right to go before the Court itself. The learned Counsel had said that, as Section XXV of the Bill stood, Prince Azeem Jah or any other Member of the late Nabob's Family would have no right to appear at this investigation before the Court, and contest the claims of the creditors; and that the finding of the Court as to the amount due would be conclusive against the estate, although the Family of the Nabob, who were interested in the estate, might have been able to shew that the claims should not be admitted. But that was not the case as he (Mr. Peacock) understood Section XXV; the finding of the Court on the summary investigation, although it would fix the amount which the creditor was entitled to be paid by the East India Company, would only be *primâ facie* evidence of the amount chargeable against the assets of the late Nabob in the administration suit. If the assets in the hands of the Receiver were sufficient, the amount found to be due on the summary investigation would be paid at once; if they were not sufficient, the creditor, having come in and established his claim on the principle of the Bill, was not to wait until the end of the regular administration suit, but was to be paid immediately out of the General Treasury. In the event of any amount paid under this provision out of the assets of the estate being larger than the amount chargeable against the assets in the regular administration suit, Section XXVI provided that the excess should be made good to the estate by the East India Company. It was possible, however, that some doubts might arise upon the wording of the Sections as they stood; and as the learned Counsel had taken exception to them, he (Mr. Peacock) was willing to insert amendments in them which would place their real meaning beyond all dispute.

Section XXIV provided as follows:—

"Upon every investigation under Section XXII of this Act (that was to say upon every summary investigation of a claim) the East India Company may appear and be heard by Counsel; and any creditor may appear in person or by Counsel or, if the Court shall think fit to allow the same, by Attorney or any other agent."

The learned Counsel proposed that the Section should be so altered as to enable Prince Azeem Jah and other members of the Family to appear at these investigations to contest claims. But the Section was only intended to enable the creditor whose claim was to be investigated, to appear either by Counsel or by Attorney or by other agent. Originally, it provided that the claimant might appear and be heard by Counsel. Some of the creditors presented a Petition praying that they might have the option of appearing to prove their claims either in person, or by Counsel or by Attorney or Vakeel of the Sudder Court, and the Select Committee had altered the Section; but he did not think that, if a creditor said—"I claim 500£ against the estate, and apply to have the amount of my claim summarily investigated by the Court"—all the creditors and other persons interested in the administration of the estate should have a right to appear at that investigation and be heard against the claim. They would have a right to appear and be heard in the regular administration suit, and might show if they could that the debt had been estimated at too high an amount, and that consequently the assets of the estate could not be debited with the full amount. That would be the proper time for hearing the creditors or heirs of the deceased upon the subject.

On the whole, then, he could not agree that injustice would be done by this Bill to any person whatever. He thought that the arrangement which it provided was a very fair and liberal one; and though he did not consider that any very great doubts could arise as to the meaning of Sections XXIV, XXV, and XXVI, yet, as objections had been taken, he should conclude by moving that the Bill be recommitted, in order that he might move amendments in them, to remove any doubts which might exist.

THE VICE-PRESIDENT, in proposing the question, remarked that he would say a few words, and but very few words—since, after the long and able speech of the Honorable and learned Member who had just spoken, but very few words seemed necessary upon the inculpation of the justice of this Bill. With the introduction of this measure, he had had nothing to do. When the Bill had been read a second time, he had made some observations upon certain of its Clauses which seemed to press hardly on mortgagees. He had then been asked to be one of the Members of the Select Committee to which the Bill was to be referred, and having consented to that, and acted on the Committee, he was no doubt responsible for presenting the Bill to the Council in its present shape. In considering the justice of this measure, we must consider the question with regard to the circumstances in which the Bill had been introduced. A resolution to which the Council had come had shut the mouths of the learned Counsel who had been heard against the Bill, upon the construction of the Treaties entered into between the East India Company and the Nabobs of the Carnatic. But it had always appeared to him that the mouths of this Council were also shut upon that question. When this Bill was introduced, it had already been determined by an authority which nothing short of the authority of Parliament could over-ride, that, on the death of the late Nabob of the Carnatic, the dignity should cease. With the merits of the question, he (the Vice-President) had nothing to do. The Government of Madras and the late Governor-General had decided it two years before this Bill came before the Council; the Court of Directors, with the sanction of the Board of Control, had approved and confirmed the decision; and, therefore, the rejection of the claims set up by the present Petitioner to the title of Nabob of the Carnatic—to a share in the revenues of the Carnatic—and, consequently, to that portion of the property left by the late Nabob which was of the nature of State property, or incidental to the dignity of Nabob—was, so far as this Council was concerned, "*un fait accompli.*" He freely allowed that it would be more consistent with the general law and usage to deal with the private estate of the late Nabob in an ordinary administration suit; but then, the Council found that certain members of His Highness's Family, including all his nearest heirs, certainly including the present Petitioner, were exempted from the jurisdiction of the Courts of Justice. The Council had to-day heard that this exemption was considered in the light of a hardship by the Petitioner; but the Council had certainly also heard, at the time when the Supreme Court at Madras ruled that the exemption had expired with the late Nabob, that a considerable sense of hardship was felt by the persons who had enjoyed the privilege, when it was thus suddenly taken away from them. The Council would recollect that, either at the instance of these persons, or because the Government of Madras had deemed that, for political reasons, the privilege should be continued, the Council had been called upon to pass an Act allowing the period of one year to those whom the decision of the Supreme Court affected, for the purpose of appealing to the Privy Council against it. No appeal was instituted within the time given for that purpose; and a Bill was then introduced into the Council in May last absolutely continuing the privilege to the Family and retainers of the late Nabob. If the privilege was considered a hardship by the family, it was certainly remarkable that no objection had come up to the Council from any of them against either Bill. In the absence of any such objection, he must take leave to believe that they were with their own assent exempted from the jurisdiction of the Supreme Court at Madras, which was, he believed, the only Court that could entertain a suit for the administration of the estate of the late Nabob.

The learned Counsel for the Petitioner, however, whilst he repudiated the exemption given by Act I of 1844, seemed to think that his client could support a claim to freedom from the jurisdiction of the Courts upon some pretext founded on the Law of Nations. He (the Vice-President) must confess that to him this seemed a wild and untenable proposition. It was notorious that, in what related to private claims, the very Princes of Europe had been held subject to the jurisdiction of the Municipal Courts of England. Therefore, there was no pretence for saying that anything in the Law of Nations gave the Petitioner exemption from the jurisdiction of the Courts at Madras. Such a proposition could not be supported for one moment, and had certainly never once been put forward when the question whether the privilege did not expire with the late Nabob, was argued in the Supreme Court.

Then, at the time when this Bill was introduced, the Council had these two facts before it—first, that it had been determined by an authority which the Council was bound to respect, that the payment of the fifth part of the revenues of the Carnatic which had theretofore been paid to the Nabob of the Carnatic, should not be continued to the Petitioner; and that he should not inherit the title of Nabob, or the State property that passed with that dignity; —and secondly, that he and the other members of the Family who, subject to the payment of his just debts, were entitled as heirs to the private property of the late Nabob, were exempt from the jurisdiction of the Supreme Court. That circumstance did not prevent them from placing themselves voluntarily under the jurisdiction if they wished; but so long as they did not so place themselves, the creditors of the late Nabob were remediless, unless some such Act as this were passed.

The Honorable and learned Member who had preceded him, had so well answered the objection taken as to the absence of the words "private property" from the Bill, that he (the Vice-President) considered it unnecessary to say more on the point than merely this—that it had struck him, whilst the learned Counsel was speaking, that he might as well quarrel with a man for calling him an Advocate of the Supreme Court, because he did not also call him Barrister-at-Law, as with this Bill, which mentioned everything of which "private property" could consist, because it did not speak of "private property" in so many words. The Bill dealt with property in the nature of State property —with the property which would have passed to the new Nabob, if there had been one, as Nabob; and which, therefore, in existing circumstances, passed to the East India Company. This the East India Company was willing to give up for the purposes of this Act. It also dealt with the private property of the late Nabob, but only, as he read the Bill, with that part of it which was liable to be applied in payment of his debts. If, as was suggested by the learned Counsel, there was property of a third class— property which was not State property, property which, being private property, was not subject to the payment of debts, but by some special custom of descent passed, on the death of one Nabob, to his heirs, unfettered by the obligation to pay his debts—if there was indeed property of this anomalous character— there was nothing in this Bill to prevent the Petitioner from establishing a title to it by proof of the alleged custom of descent.

Such property, if it existed, must be either in the possession of the Petitioner or out of it. If it were in his possession, what would be the consequence? The Receiver who was to be appointed under the Bill, would have no power to take any property out of the possession of any member of the Family without the consent of the Government of Madras. He would have no higher powers than a Receiver generally had; and if his title were resisted, he would have to enforce it by suit. If, then, he should seek to obtain possession of this property whilst in the hands of the Petitioner, he could not institute a suit for that purpose without the consent of the Government of Madras; and even if he did obtain the consent of the Government of Madras to institute such a suit, he could not prevent the Petitioner, as heir, from raising the question of his right to it by virtue of the custom alleged, if he chose to raise it. Again, supposing that the property eventually found its way into the hands of the Receiver, then, under the general power to institute an administration suit, the Petitioner, waiving his exemption, might come in and contest the right of the Receiver to apply the particular property to the payment of debts. Clearly, then, it seemed to him, with respect to the State property—with respect to that property which was supposed to be of a public nature—that the Bill could not be said to interfere in any degree with the rights of Prince Azeem Jah, because it had been determined by an authority which this Council was bound to respect—and the decision must be taken to be final until it was reversed by Parliament—that he had no title to it. And in the private property which was subject to the debts of the late Nabob, his rights as heir must be subject to the paramount rights of the creditors, and there must be some means for administering it. The Bill before the Council provided those means, and did so in almost the only mode which, in the peculiar circumstances in which the Family was placed, was feasible. Beyond getting in and distributing the property which was subject to the payment of the debts of the late Nabob, this Council had no desire to interfere with the rights of the heir; and to the introduction into the Bill of any words which would make that clear, he had no objection. The Honorable and learned Member who had charge of the Bill proposed to recommit the Bill now for the purpose of inserting amendments in it with that view. It was entirely for his consideration whether he would do so now, or let the Bill go back to the Select Committee for a week, in order that they might frame the amendments with a little more deliberation. If the Honorable and learned Member proposed to recommit it to day, he (the Vice-President) was ready to go into Committee at once.

MR. PEACOCK moved that the Bill be recommitted, in order that certain proposed amendments might be considered.

Agreed to.

The amendments proposed by Mr. Peacock were adopted, and, the Council having resumed its sitting, the Bill was reported.

GUARDIANSHIP OF MINORS; AND COURT OF WARDS.

MR. CURRIE presented the Report of the Select Committee on the Bill "for making better provision for the care of the persons and property of Minors, Lunatics, and other disqualified persons in the Presidency of Fort William in Bengal" and the Bill "to explain and amend Regulation X of 1793 and Regulation LII of 1803."

CARE OF ESTATES OF LUNATICS NOT SUBJECT TO THE SUPREME COURTS.

MR. CURRIE also presented the Report of the Select Committee, on the Bill "to make better provision for the care of the Estates of Lunatics not subject to the jurisdiction of Her Majesty's Courts of Judicature."

RYOTWAR ARREARS (MADRAS).

MR. FORBES moved the first reading of a Bill "for the better recovery of arrears of Revenue under Ryotwar settlements in the Madras Presidency." He said, when the Regulations of 1802, which provided for the collection of the Government revenue and for the realization of arrears, were passed in the Presidency of Madras, it was done under the impression that the permanent settlement, then in course of introduction, would be introduced throughout the Presidency. It was, however, soon decided to abandon a proceeding which would have revolutionized the tenure under which land had been held in Southern India for ages, and it was determined to maintain the ryots in the enjoyment of the rights and privileges the origin of which is far too remote to be traced.

The Regulations of 1802, therefore, passed to suit the permanent settlement, were never very well adapted to the Ryotwar system of revenue administration. Regulation XXV was enacted to define the rights conferred by the permanent settlement. Regulation XXVI regulated the sale and sub-division of estates. Regulation XXVII prescribed the mode of recovering arrears of public revenue from actual proprietors or farmers of land paying the assessment on their estates direct to Government; and Regulation XXVIII was passed to enable proprietors to collect their rents from their tenants.

Regulation XXVII declares in its 6th Section that the land shall be responsible for the revenue, and that it shall only be at the option of the defaulter that his personal property shall be first distrained for arrears; but the difficulty under which this law placed the revenue officers was avoided by their always having recourse to Regulation XXVIII, the 38th Section of which declared that its provisions, which allowed of the prior sale of personalty, were to be considered applicable to all cases in which a Khas collection was made on account of Government. This expression was, for very many years, understood to refer to Ryotwar collections; but the Sudder Court of Adawlut having decided that this interpretation was erroneous, and that Collectors could legally proceed only under Regulation XXVII which, as I have already said, renders the prior sale of land imperative unless the defaulter voluntarily surrenders his personalty, the greatest embarrassment resulted, and the revenue remained heavily in arrear.

To remedy the evil, Act XXIII of 1856 was brought in, but it had failed of effecting the desired end in consequence of having been worded so as to declare that the collection of the Government revenue, due on lands under settlement direct with the ryots, should be deemed Khas collection within the meaning of Section XXXVIII Regulation XXVIII, and the consequence of this had been as follows:

The Section of Regulation XXVIII which was then made applicable to the collection of Ryotwar arrears, declared that all Khas collections should be made under the rules laid down in the preceding Sections, and one of those Rules was that land should not be sold until after the end of the Revenue year, and then only through the intervention of the Zillah Court.

The Act which was intended to free the Revenue Officers from inconvenience, in effect had served only to substitute one inconvenience for another, and whereas before its enactment it was imperative first to sell land, by its enactment it has become no less imperative first to sell personalty, and should such sale not liquidate the arrear, the sale of land could be effected only through the intervention of the Court, and then only after the revenue year had closed.

It was from these embarrassments that it was proposed by the present Bill to free the Revenue Officers, and to give them that option to sell either land or personalty at their discretion, which, under similar circumstances, the Collectors in Bengal have had ever since 1799; and when they elected to sell land, to give them authority to do so as soon as an arrear had accrued.

The Bill was mainly based on Regulation XXVIII. 1802; and it was proposed to re-enact its provisions rather than to refer to them partly because some only are retained while others have become obsolete or were inexpedient, and partly in deference to the Despatch from the Honorable Court of Directors lately communicated to this Council by the Government of India, in which such a course was recommended.

The Bill was read a first time.

CANTONMENT JOINT MAGISTRATES.

MR. HARINGTON moved that the Bill "for conferring Civil jurisdiction in certain cases upon Cantonment Joint Magistrates, and for constituting those Officers Registers of Deeds within the limits of their respective jurisdictions" be now read a second time.

MR. LEGEYT rose merely to ask a question or two relative to the intended effect of part of Section I of the proposed Bill. He wished to know if it was the intention of the Honorable Mover of the Bill, that the jurisdiction of Cantonment Joint Magistrates should extend to all residents within a Cantonment not of the classes specified in the existing laws, and also to Europeans who might be so resident? He wished to know this because, in the Military Cantonments in the Presidency of Bombay, the present Superintendent of Bazars who exercises a limited jurisdiction in civil claims, did not take cognizance of claims for small debts against persons who were not strictly Military or registered followers of the Camp. This Bill, therefore, if adopted in the Presidency of Bombay, would materially alter the law as at present administered under Regulation XXII. 1827 of the Bombay Code as interpreted by the Sudder Dewanny Adawlut.

He had no objection whatever to offer to this change if it were intended. He approved of the principle of the Bill in Military Cantonments and hoped it would be generally adopted; but he thought it would be desirable that all its objects should be perfectly understood in places in which it would be published for general information previous to its being passed into law.

MR HARINGTON, in reply to the first question of the Honorable Member for Bombay, begged to observe that the Bill, as drawn, would include all residents within the limits of Military Cantonments, Bazaars, or Stations, whether belonging to the Army or not, who were not amenable to the Articles of War for the Queen's and Company's troops serving in India; and in reply to the second question, that the Bill would extend to European residents of Cantonments, Bazaars, and Stations not amenable to the Articles of War mentioned in the answer to the first question.

The question was put and agreed to.

The Bill was read a second time accordingly.

ESTATE OF THE LATE NABOB OF THE CARNATIC.

MR. PEACOCK postponed the motion (which stood in the Orders of the Day) for the third reading of the Bill "to provide for the administration of the Estate and for the payment of the debts of the late Nabob of the Carnatic."

SETTLEMENT OF ALLUVIAL LANDS (BENGAL).

MR. CURRIE postponed the motion (which stood in the Orders of the Day) for the third reading of the Bill "to make further provision for the settlement of land gained by alluvion in the Presidency of Fort William in Bengal."

LUNATIC ASYLUMS.

MR. CURRIE postponed the motion (which stood in the Orders of the Day) for a Committee of the whole Council on the Bill "relating to Lunatic Asylums."

PROCEEDINGS IN LUNACY (SUPREME COURTS.)

MR. CURRIE postponed the motion (which stood in the Orders of the Day) for a Committee of the whole Council on the Bill "to regulate proceedings in Lunacy in Her Majesty's Courts of Judicature."

FORT OF TANJORE.

MR. FORBES moved that the Council resolve itself into a Committee on the Bill "for bringing the Fort of Tanjore and the adjacent territory under the Laws of the Presidency of Fort Saint George;" and that the Committee be instructed to consider the Bill in the amended form in which the Select Committee had recommended it to be passed.

Agreed to.

The Bill passed through Committee without amendment, and was reported.

CANTONMENT JOINT MAGISTRATES.

MR. HARINGTON moved that the Bill "for conferring Civil jurisdiction in certain cases upon Cantonment Joint Magistrates, and for constituting those Officers Registers of Deeds within the limits of their respective jurisdictions" be referred to a Select Committee consisting of Mr. Peacock, Mr. LeGeyt, Mr. Forbes, and Mr. Harington.

Agreed to.

The Council adjourned.

Saturday, August 14, 1858.

PRESENT:

The Hon'ble the Chief Justice, *Vice-President*, in the Chair.

Hon. J. P. Grant,	P. W. LeGeyt, Esq.,
Hon. Major Gen. Sir J. Outram,	E. Currie, Esq.,
Hon. H. Ricketts,	H. B. Harington, Esq. and
Hon. B. Peacock,	H. Forbes, Esq.

THE CLERK presented to the Council a Petition signed by Damoodur Mohapattro on behalf of certain principal Sabaiths or Ministers of the Temple of Juggernath praying for a construction of Section I Clause 3, Regulation XXVII. 1814, of the Bengal Code, with reference to an order passed in appeal by the Sudder Court at Calcutta, whereby the Petitioners were obliged to pay the costs of several defendants against whom they brought a suit in which it is alleged their defences were the same, and one defence would have been sufficient.

THE VICE-PRESIDENT apprehended that the Petition could not be received—first, because the subject-matter of it properly belonged to a Court of Law, inasmuch as it prayed the Council to put a construction on a particular Regulation, and a construction contrary to that which had been put on that Regulation by a competent Court; secondly, because the Petition purported to be signed only by a Vakeel on behalf of the Petitioners.

INDIAN NAVY.

MR. PEACOCK presented the Report of the Select Committee on the Bill "to amend Act XII of 1844" (for better securing the observance of an exact discipline in the Indian Navy.)

ESTATE OF THE LATE NABOB OF THE CARNATIC.

MR. PEACOCK moved that the Bill "to provide for the administration of the Estate and for the payment of the debts of the late Nabob of the Carnatic" be read a third time and passed.

The Motion was carried, and the Bill read a third time.

SETTLEMENT OF ALLUVIAL LANDS (BENGAL).

MR. CURRIE moved that the Bill "to make further provision for the settlement of land gained by alluvion in the Presidency of Fort William in Bengal" be read a third time and passed.

MR. PEACOCK said, he could not give a silent vote upon the occasion. It appeared to him that the Bill altered the law as it at present stood, without any sufficient reason for such alteration. First, it altered the rights of proprietors of land; secondly, it altered the rights of Government; and thirdly, it contained a provision (to which he would hereafter advert) of which he could not foresee the effect. He saw no sufficient reason why they should be called upon to pass a law altering the existing rights of parties, a law which would possibly not only cause many difficulties in carrying out its provisions, but by which considerable litigation might be occasioned.

It appeared to him perfectly clear that a proprietor having an estate on the banks of a river became entitled to any alluvion which formed upon it, as an increment to his original tenure.

Section IV Regulation XI. 1825 enacted that

"when land may be gained by general accession, whether from the recess of a river or of the sea, it shall be considered an increment to the tenure of the person to whose land or estate it is thus annexed, whether such land or estate be held immediately from Government by a Zemindar or other superior landholder, or as a subordinate tenure by any description of under-tenant whatever. Provided that the increment of land thus obtained shall not entitle the person in possession of the estate or tenure to which the land may be annexed, to a right of property or permanent interest therein beyond that possessed by him in the estate or tenure to which the land may be annexed, and shall not in any case be understood to exempt the holder of it from the payment to Government of any assessment for the public revenue to which it may be liable under the provisions of Regulation II. 1819, or of any other Regulation in force."

He could not understand the words "shall be considered an increment to the tenure of the person to whose land or estate it is thus annexed" in any other sense than that the alluvion became a part of the estate paying Revenue to Government. The Circular Order No. 12 of 30th April 1833, which he would read from Marshman's Compilation relative to the Resumption and Settlement of estates, laid down the rule clearly. It said—

"In the permanently settled provinces, all land of alluvial formation appertains to the proprietor of the estate to which a change in the channel of the river has added it—except when, as contemplated in Clause 3, Section IV of the Regulation in question, it may be an island separated from the main land by a channel not fordable 'at any season of the year'—or when it may have accrued to an estate or waste tract, the Zemindary title of which is vested in Government. And the Sudder Board request your special attention, and that of your subordinates, to that part of Clause 1 of the Section above cited, which lays down, that the right of the party, thereby recognized as proprietor, is exactly co-equal, as regards the land of new formation, with that by which he holds the estate to which the alluvion has attached itself, whilst, at the same time, the concurrent lien of the State upon its share of the produce of all land formed subsequently to the date of the permanent settlement is declared with equal distinctness.

"It follows, therefore, that all proprietors—circumstanced as above stated—whether they have, or have not, disputed the claim of the Revenue Authorities to fix an assessment upon newly formed lands of the description contemplated by Clause 1 Section IV, Regulation XI. 1825—have a right to admission to terms of permanent engagement, whenever they may think fit to demand it, unless, indeed, the alluvion have been let out in farm, for a specified term, in consequence of their recusance, in which case, as well as while the lands may be held khas, they are, of course, entitled to Malikana. It is only necessary to add that the injunctions of the Honorable the Court of Directors against permanent settlements of lands at the disposal of Government, refer exclusively to cases where no party may possess a legal claim to such immunity; and that the Right Honorable the Governor General in Council has expressed himself strongly averse to the conclusion of temporary arrangements with persons upon whom the law has conferred the unqualified right above alluded to."

Thus it appeared that the proprietor had a right in the alluvion exactly coequal with the rights which he possessed in the original tenure—that he had a right to be admitted to a permanent engagement when the original estate was permanently settled—and that the Government had a lien upon the alluvion for the Revenue. Now, this Bill proposed to do away with both the right of the proprietor and the right of Government. It proposed to deprive the owner of a permanently settled estate which had been increased by alluvion, of the right of insisting upon the alluvion being permanently settled and added to the original estate as one tenure; and it compelled the Revenue Authorities without their consent to settle the alluvion separately and thereby to give up their lien thereon for the Revenue of the original estate. He (Mr. Peacock) confessed that he argued theoretically rather than practically, for he had had no practical knowledge whatever on the subject of these alluvions. But since he had last addressed the Council, a letter received from Mr. Samuells, the Commissioner of Patna, who was practically acquainted with the subject, had been printed, in which that gentleman took precisely the same view as he did. Mr. Samuells said:—

"When the proprietor of a parent estate engages with Government for the alluvion which has accreted thereto, he and the Government, being the only parties interested, may unquestionably make any arrangement as to the estate upon which they can agree, and the alluvion may in that case be settled as one separate estate, or half a dozen separate estates as may be determined. I know of no Law or decision which in any way militates against this. The law, it is true, declares the alluvion an increment of the original estate, and its tenure co-extensive with the tenure of the original estate; but as the Government and the proprietor, acting in concert, may carve the original estate into as many separate estates as they think fit, there is no reason why they should not do the same by the increment. Accordingly, alluvial lands have very frequently been settled as separate estates with the proprietors of parent estates, and such estates are never sold along with the parent estate at Revenue Sales for arrears due upon the former."

Then he went on to show that the decision in the Koilwar case was perfectly correct. He said:—

"The decision in the Koilwar case is, as I have said before, in strict conformity with the usual practice of the Revenue authorities. That practice is shortly this. If the proprietor of the parent estate agree to the additional assessment, *he can demand that it shall be consolidated in perpetuity with his original jumma.* If he prefers that the alluvion should be formed into a distinct estate, he represents his wish to the collector, who, *if he sees no objection*, makes a separate settlement with him in perpetuity and the two estates, the old and the new, cease to have any necessary connection with each other. In the generality of cases, however, the proprietor of the parent estate is unwilling to run the risk attendant on accepting the settlement himself, for even when the alluvion is settled as a separate estate, the risk is considerable."

Now the Board said that the proprietors have a right to admission to terms of permanent engagement whenever they may think fit to demand it, unless indeed the alluvion has been let out in farm for a specified term in consequence of their recusance.

This was the law as it was then understood, and according to that interpretation, the owner of an estate had an unqualified right to land that accrued to it by alluvion, and to demand that the assessment of the alluvion should be made on the same principle as that of his original estate.

One great object of the permanent settlement was that proprietors of land might lay out capital in improving their estates. A proprietor not only was entitled to demand that his alluvial formation should be treated as part of the estate to which it accrued, but he also had an unqualified right, if he chose, to have it settled on the same principles as the settlement of the original estate. He might, if the original estate were permanently settled, with safety expend his capital on the improvement of the alluvion; but, as proposed by the Bill, if the Revenue Authorities should refuse to settle the alluvion permanently, they might do so, and then there would be no security that any money laid out on the alluvion might not add to the assessment at a future time. He (Mr. Peacock) found that it was expressly stipulated in the engagement between the proprietor and the Government, that the proprietor was not entitled to any diminution of Revenue, if any portion of his estate were washed away. Under the old law his liability to pay the Government Revenue remained, although one half of his estate should be washed away. Under Act IX of 1847, until a new survey took place, the assessment could not be increased in consequence of alluvion, and he was entitled to a diminution if any part of his estate were washed away. But words had been inserted in this Bill which would deprive the proprietor of the right to a permanent assessment of the alluvion without the consent of the Revenue Authorities, and by depriving him of this right you deprive him of the power which was one of the great objects of the permanent settlement, namely, the power to lay out his capital in improving his estate, without becoming liable to an increase of the assessment in consequence of the improvements.

Mr. Peacock proceeded to show the evils which were occasioned by the system of tithes in England, and to obviate which the tithes-commutation was passed.

If it were left optional with the Collector (as this Bill proposed to leave it), to refuse to settle the estate permanently, the owner would have no security that, if he improved the alluvion by laying out his capital upon it, the Government might not come down upon him at a future time and subject him to additional taxation in consequence of the improvements.

This Bill then (he said) would act unfairly by the proprietor by depriving him of the right (as laid down in the books up to the time of the Circular Order of 1841) of taking alluvion as an increment of the parent estate and of having it settled as a permanent assessment. It would next act unfairly towards the Government, for Government had a lien upon the alluvion, and if you compel the Revenue Authorities to grant it out as a separate estate, without their consent, you deprive the Government of its lien. He (Mr. Peacock) spoke theoretically, but he must say that, if an original estate were cut off from its river-frontage, it might be greatly diminished in value; and it might so happen that it might not sell for a sufficient sum to pay the Revenue due to Government. Now, in the letter to which he had referred, Mr. Samuells took up that very point. He says—

"A case came before me the other day in which a proprietor, who had obtained a separate settlement for an alluvial formation, had gone on paying the assessment for five years after the alluvion was entirely washed away. He let it go at last and the Mehal was instantly purchased by a speculator on the chance of the re-appearance of the alluvion, an event which will be the ruin of the original estate, as it owed its value almost entirely to its river-frontage and the valuable churs which from time to time formed against it."

Again, Mr. Samuells said—

"An estate, for instance which has become little less than a bed of sand, continues to pay a high Revenue, because it possesses a valuable bazar on the banks of the river; a deara forms in front of this bazar, and a separate settlement is made with the malik of the original estate. He immediately allows the original estate to be sold for arrears of Revenue, and then constructs a new bazar on the banks of the deara which shuts up the old one, and the original estate must be resettled at a pepper-corn rent. For the time the Government may gain on the deara what they have lost on the permanent estate, but these dearas may be, and frequently are, washed away in a night, and then the Government find that what I cannot but term the crotchet of treating accidental and temporary increments in all cases as separate estates has resulted in a serious diminution of their Revenue."

Mr. Peacock

Now if any case could be put, and if a gentleman so practically acquainted with the subject as Mr. Samuells had put such a case, he (Mr. Peacock) apprehended that it was quite possible that such cases might arise in practice. He therefore proposed to leave it optional with the Collector to r fuse to grant the alluvion as a separate estate. The zemindar had a right to insist that it should not be separated from the original estate, and should be settled as a permanent estate; it was only in the event of his agreeing that it should be settled as a separate estate, that it could be so settled: but in that case Government should not be bound to forego its right to the alluvion as a security for the Revenue of the original estate. If the proprietor should refuse to have the jumma of the alluvion incorporated with that of the original estate, the Government ought to have the power of refusing to assess it as a separate estate, and in that case it would be let in farm reserving Malikana.

Another point was, whether it was expedient to make the alluvion a separate estate for all purposes when it was let out reserving Malikana. The Bill said that in such a case it should

"thenceforward be regarded and treated as in all respects separate from and independent of the original estate."

He did not know whether any great importance was attached to the word "estate." It would no doubt be said that that word was used in the sense explained by Regulation VIII. 1800, namely:

"Any land subject to the payment of Revenue, for which a separate engagement may have been executed to Government by the proprietor or by a farmer; or which may have been separately assessed with the public Revenue, although no engagement shall have been executed to Government."

He understood the word "estate" in the sense given to it by that Regulation But the Bill said that the *alluvial land* should be regarded and treated as in all respects separate from and independent of the original estate.

It was a rule that estates should be named, that is, estates in the Regulation sense of the term. Suppose, then, the owner of an estate called A. should make a will leaving it to his natural son, and that a large alluvion should be formed. By Regulation XI. 1825, the alluvion would be an increment to the tenure and would pass under the will. But by this Bill as it now stood, if the owner should refuse to enter into an engagement for the Revenue to be assessed upon it, and in consequence of his recusance it should be let in farm, the alluvion must thenceforward be regarded and treated as in all respects separate from and independent of the original estate Now suppose the owner should die without making a new will, and upon his death his heir-at-law should claim the alluvial land, a very important question would arise, namely, whether the alluvial land would pass as part of the estate A. He apprehended that under this Bill it would not pass, and the son to whom the estate was left would lose his river-frontage.

It might so happen that the owner of the estate might become lunatic or incompetent to make a new will after the formation of the alluvion, or he might not understand the effect of this Bill, and his son to whom the estate was devised, might thus lose the alluvion and be deprived of his river-frontage. He thought that the Legislature should be careful not to do injustice or to create doubts as to the rights of individuals by the use of such general words, and if the Bill were to be passed at all, he thought that the alluvial lands should be declared separate from the original estate only for Revenue purposes.

Again, the 2nd Section saved the rights of under-tenants, but the rights of mortgagees were not provided for, though the mortgager of the whole interest was not an under-tenant.

Again, suppose an estate were granted by the proprietor to a Putnee Talookdar and his heirs for ever reserving only a small rent. According to the law of 1825, any subsequent alluvion would be an increment to the tenure of the Talookdar. Suppose also that it should be stipulated that the rent reserved should not be diminished in consequence of any part of the estate being washed away, nor increased in consequence of the formation of any alluvion. The Talookdar might have paid a high premium in consideration of having to pay a low rent, or he might have paid a high price because he was aware that he would be benefited by all accretions. But if the alluvion must be settled as a separate estate, if the proprietor refused to have it assessed permanently as part of the original estate, and must thenceforward be treated as in all respects separate from the original estate, the Putneedar might be injured. The word "proprietor" was used in the first Section, and according to the definition of that word in Section VII Regulation VIII. 1793 a Putneedar was not included. If the Government let the estate to farm reserving Malikana to the Zemindar or proprietor, the Putnee Talookdar would not receive any additional rent from the ryots, but would be deprived of the benefits to which he would have been entitled, had the accretion been made a part of the original estate.

THE VICE-PRESIDENT said, he was interested in this part of the case which related to Putneedars, and he would wish the Honorable and learned Member to explain what difference there was in this respect between the proposed Bill and the law as now existing? He (the Vice-President) thought that in both cases the rights of the Putneedars were equally protected.

MR. PEACOCK resumed.—If you were to assess it permanently as part of the original estate, the right of the Putneedar would be confirmed. According to the present law the proprietor had a right to have the estate settled as part of the original estate, but he had no right to have it settled as a separate estate without the consent of the Revenue Authorities. But by this Bill, if he refused to take it as part of the original estate, he had a right to have it assessed as a separate estate. Thus Government might have to forego their Revenue, or do great injustice to the Putneedar. He had bought the estate for better and for worse. He was entitled to the benefit of all alluvion which might be formed. He was consequently the person to receive any additional rent which might be paid in consequence of the alluvion. Whereas, if the alluvion were let to farm reserving Malikana to the proprietor, the farmer would be entitled to the rents paid for the alluvion, whilst the Malik or proprietor of the estate would receive the Malikana. He (Mr. Peacock) would ask, how many separate and distinct estates were to be made? Alluvion might form upon alluvion; and if each formation must be granted as a separate estate, you might have three or four new, distinct, and separate estates between the original estate and the river, whilst the original estate might be deprived of its river-frontage and irreparably injured.

Now, this was not merely a theoretical argument. He had before him the opinions of practical men. He had the opinions of two of the Members of the Board of Revenue. All the Members of the Board of Revenue were in favor of returning to the rule laid down in 1838. With regard to the present Bill which altered that rule, Mr. Dampier, one of the Members, said :—

"In my opinion the Preamble is wrong; the proposed Bill enacts new rules for the settlement of land gained by alluvial accession to estates paying Revenue to the Government, and I think it is clear that such is the intent of the Law, where by Section II it legalizes the separate settlements of alluvial lands, heretofore made under the Circular Orders of the Board and Government contrary to the existing law.

I think that the proposed Law will complicate settlements of such alluvial lands much, and, where these lands are increments on under-tenures, will cause serious inconvenience to the holders of such tenures, to whom it is an object to have such lands, valuable from their river-frontage, incorporated with, and to be a part of these tenures. I also think that the wording of the proposed Law in Section I is obscure and confused. The alluvial land is to be assessed and settled as a separate estate with a separate jumma, subject to all provisions respecting the rights of property thereon which are contained in Section IV Regulation XI. 1825, and it is thenceforward to be treated as independent of the original estate—this is so far as the *estate* is concerned; but by Section IV Regulation XI 1825, the proprietor of the under-tenure has the same right in the increment as he has on his tenure of which it is part. Is the estate to be separate, and the tenure not? or if both are to be separate, and the tenure is a Putnee, how is the zemindar to proceed for the recovery of his rents when due under Section VIII Regulation VIII. 1819? Is he to take a fresh pottah for the increment? and what course is he to pursue when he has, in the pottah of the original tenure, expressly relinquished any demands for rent on an increment of alluvion? whilst the alluvial lands formed part of the parent estate this was easily arranged, but the new Law will embarrass the under-tenants and lead to much litigation.

Again, why is the zemindar to have the right of objecting to the alluvial lands being added to the parent estate, and the Revenue Authorities have no power to insist on such an arrangement? and why should the Revenue Authorities have the option of not assessing them as part of the estate, where the proprietors are willing? These rules interfere with the old customs and laws of the country supported by the decisions of the highest Courts, and are uncalled for. Section V Act IX of 1847 secures to the proprietors of estates deductions from their assessment whenever any proceedings under that Law are taken. Sections V and VI must be put in force simultaneously. Under all circumstances, and particularly with reference to Act IX of 1847 which secures to the zemindars indemnity for losses, and to the Government its Revenue; from alluvial increments by periodical surveys; I can see no object to be gained for the Government, the proprietors of estates, or the holders of under-tenures, by the adoption of the proposed Law."

Mr. Stainforth, the other Member, said:—

"I object to the Preamble of the Bill, and approve of that part of it which legalizes past errors in making separate settlements of alluviated land. As to the future settlements, they will mainly be those made under Act IX of 1847, and there would, I think, be little need of the Bill in respect to them if officers were placed at our disposal to survey gains and losses of land. We should then be enabled to relieve land holders losing land, and take away all substantial ground of objection to adding the jumma assessed on new lands to that of the estate to which they are added."

He (Mr. Peacock) entirely concurred in the above opinion. By all means set right all that has been done wrong, but do not do wrong for the future. According to the Bill, if the Collector and proprietor disagree, a Malikana was to be given. The proprietor gains by this course, for it would be his interest to disagree. If this Bill should be passed, it would injuriously affect private rights, and it might so affect the rights of Government also.

Mr. Samuells, who was a practical man, also said:—

"*The present practice is well understood and satisfies every one, why then should it be changed?* Would it be an improvement to render it compulsory on the Collector to form the alluvion into a separate estate in every instance in which the proprietor did not wish the jumma consolidated with that of the parent estate? I should think that the measure was likely to be distasteful to proprietors, *and I believe that it will effect a great change in the value of landed property on the banks of rivers and consequently endanger the stability of the Revenue assessed on these estates.* At present, while the proprietor avoids the risk of a settlement, he receives a fair share of the rent, and the right to all accretions of alluvion remains with his ancestral estate and greatly enhances its value."

Again he said:—

"Then as respects the interests of Government, the Law (Regulation XIX. 1814) which has been enacted for the division of estates, does not permit zemindars to make this division themselves. The Government having the paramount interest in the estate, carries out the partition through its own officers and apportions the jumma to each share so partitioned. The aim and object of the Collector in these partitions always is to give each share its due proportion of advantages whether of water, road, or river-communication. As a general rule, when two shares applied for a division of an estate having a deara attached to it, the Collector would divide the estate at right-angles to the river, so as to give to each share its proper proportion of alluvial lands and river frontage."

Then again he said:—

"I would respectfully deprecate any change in the present law of alluvion, which appears to me to be working on the whole, satisfactorily. Nothing can be fairer for all parties than the present practice. If the proprietor wishes to make a separate estate of his deara and the Collector is satisfied that the Government interests will not suffer thereby, his wish is acceded to."

Thus we had one Member of the Board of Revenue deprecating any alteration of the existing law and saying that it would cause confusion and increase litigation. We next had the opinion of another gentleman practically acquainted with the subject, who said that the Bill would injuriously affect existing private rights, and we had a Petition of the British Indian Association objecting to the Bill as it now stood.

He (Mr. Peacock) therefore wished to know why the law should be altered. If no sufficient reasons could be given (and certainly the Preamble of the Bill set forth no such reasons) why alter it? If we were to be constantly altering laws without sufficient reason, no one would know what the law was or what his rights were. He thought some better reason should be given than that set forth in the Preamble—and that, in altering existing rights, we should be satisfied that we were not injuring private parties. This Bill, it appeared to him, materially altered the law in two respects, both as affected private rights and those of the Government.

For these reasons he should vote against the third reading of this Bill.

MR. RICKETTS said, they had now been floundering in the mud for three months, and his Honorable and learned friend seemed inclined to keep them still in the same position, fighting these slimy Sections over again. He desired to leave points of law to others, but he would not shrink from endeavoring to explain his views. His Honorable and learned friend said that legislation was not necessary, but legislation only could settle the law. The Revenue Authorities of 1838 had taken one view, and those of 1841 another; and was not this Council divided?

His Honorable and learned friend had based his argument regarding the right to a settlement in perpetuity on Clause 1 Section IV Regulation XI. 1825. He maintained that, as the law declared that the person in possession of the original estate should not have a right in the chur beyond that possessed by him in the original estate, it followed that he must have an equal right. Whether that was the necessary logical sequence, he would not pretend to say; but, admitting that it was, it appeared to him that the interest which the law gave was only to right of property. Whatever right of property he possessed in the parent estate, he was to have the same right in the chur. If owner, then owner; if mortgagee, then mortgagee; if lease-holder, lease-holder. But, as regards settlement and assessment, he was not to be exempted from the payment to Government of any assessment for the public revenue to which he might be liable under the provisions of Regulation II. 1819 or any other Regulation. Regulation II. 1819 provided for resumption, but was silent as to assessment and settlement. You might go back, but you would find no mention of alluvion between 1793 and 1819. The proclamation of 1793 regarding permanent settlement might perhaps be twisted to apply to alluvion, but there was no mention of it, and in the absence of any legal provision, the Revenue Authorities necessarily used their discretion in settling these lands, either temporarily or in perpetuity. Government was much interested in these lands, for to the eastward, alluvial formations now stretched for miles and miles to the southward, and he (Mr. Ricketts) should not be at all surprised if they were called upon at some future time to survey chur Antipodespoor far beyond the line in the latitude of the Cape of Good Hope. He would leave his Honorable friend the Member for Bengal to speak on the propriety of making it compulsory upon the Collector to settle the alluvion as a separate estate in every instance in which the proprietor did not wish the jumma consolidated with that of the parent estate. His (Mr. Ricketts') opinion on this part of the subject was not so decided; he was prepared to be guided by the judgment of the Honorable Member for Bengal.

Now for a few words regarding the Putneedar. He (Mr. Ricketts) did not think that this part of the subject was so difficult as his Honorable and learned friend would make it out to be. A party having a Putnee right of property in the alluvion, was liable to an increase of rent for land which might annex to his property, whether alluvion was settled together or divided into two or ten parts. The Putnee right still existed on the part of the Putneedar. For all the new lands accruing to his tenure, he would be separately assessed, and he would have to pay whatever rent might be assessed to the superior holder, whether farmer or proprietor of the original estate. He could not be dispossessed by any party whether farmer or proprietor; and as his rent must be adjusted by the revenue officer and not by the farmer or proprietor, he could not see what difference it would or could make to him whether he paid his Putnee rents to one or to more persons.

MR. CURRIE said, he would not detain the Council more than a few minutes. He would endeavor to avoid the topics which had been so fully discussed at previous meetings of the Council, and should confine himself to the two points of objection urged by the Honorable and learned Member; namely, that the Bill interfered with the rights of proprietors, and that it interfered with the rights of Government.

The Honorable and learned Member

contended that a proprietor of alluvial land had an absolute right to incorporate the alluvion with the estate to which it annexed, and to have the jumma assessed on the alluvion added to the original jumma. It had been shewn in the debate in Committee that the only ground upon which the Revenue Authorities could object to this arrangement would be that the land was not fit for settlement in perpetuity. It was stated that, when such was the case, it would be the duty of the Revenue Authorities, in order to protect the interest of the Government (if a permanent settlement were insisted on), to assess a jumma in anticipation which the proprietor could not with prudence agree to pay, and therefore that the practical effect would be that the alluvion must be let in farm. It was more convenient for all parties that the Revenue Authorities should determine whether the settlement should be permanent or temporary. The question involved in the learned Member's objection amounted in fact to this. Is the proprietor of alluvial land in all cases entitled to claim a permanent settlement? He (Mr. Currie) contended that he was not. The common law of the country was, temporary settlements for periods optional with the ruling power. Before the British Government, settlements for long periods were never heard of, and even now settlements in perpetuity were unknown, except in the Provinces of Bengal, Behar, and Benares. The right to permanent settlement in those Provinces, therefore, must depend upon the pledge given to proprietors at the time of the settlement; it could not extend to any lands not expressly included in that pledge. Thus it did not extend to lands which were waste and not included within the limits of any estate at the time of the settlement; and temporary settlements of such lands had frequently been made. Nor did it extend to alluvial lands which were not in existence at the time of the settlement. Indeed, the case of alluvion was altogether exceptional, and no inference respecting it could be drawn from the principles of the permanent settlement. The application of those principles would have required that no remission should be claimed by proprietors for loss of land, and no increase should be demanded by Government for accession of land. But this would have been a one-sided arrangement; the Government might of course abstain from demanding any increase, but it could not avoid loss of revenue when estates were washed away, or so much reduced in area as to be unequal to the payment of the assessed Revenue. Accordingly, so far back as the year 1798, it was found necessary to grant remissions for loss of land, and a few years later in 1804 the Government asserted its right to assess alluvial formations. As the terms in which the Government order were expressed might be thought to bear upon some questions which had been raised in this discussion, he would ask permission to read an extract from it :—

"From the reports of the Canoongoes and Sherishtadars the right of property in lands gained by alluvion in the Province of Benares, appears still to be left indeterminate. On a consideration, however, of all the circumstances of the case, it does not appear to the Governor-General in Council to be necessary for Government to have recourse to the Courts of justice, or to proceed to an immediate attachment of the lands. In all cases of that nature, the assessment which Government is entitled to demand from the lands under the general laws and regulations of the country, is the primary object to which the attention of the public officers should be directed. If that object be secured, the right of property in the soil, even supposing Government could establish such a right (which at present appears to be very uncertain), is comparatively of little importance. Under these circumstances the Governor-General is of opinion that, whenever lands may be formed by alluvion, the Collector should call upon the person in actual possession of the property to enter into engagements for the revenue of the lands in question, *as a new estate*; and in the event of a refusal on the part of such person to execute the necessary engagements (after the jumma shall have been approved by your Board and confirmed by Government), that the Collector should take charge of the lands, and provide for the management of them, *in the manner observed with regard to other unsettled Mehals*, either in Benares or in any other part of the country."

"By an adherence to the foregoing rule, it is presumable that the increase in the jumma which may be obtained from lands gained by alluvion, will be nearly equal to the remissions which it may be necessary to grant, from time to time, in consequence of losses sustained by any of the Zemindars whose estates lie contiguous to the course of the Ganges."

This order established that all lands gained by alluvion should be liable to assessment, and fifteen years later the declaration was sanctioned by legal enactment. But why should it be assumed that the assessment must necessarily be permanent? The lands lying on the banks or in the shifting channels of the rivers of Bengal had no conditions of permanency, and this had been recognised by the last enactment on the subject which made the jummas of estates so situated subject to periodical adjustment. He thought, therefore, that it could not be made out that the proprietors of alluvial land had legally any absolute right to permanent settlement.

The Honorable and learned Member, however, said that this absolute right had never been questioned until the issue of the Circular Order of 1841. It was quite true that there were earlier Circulars which recognized such a right, and the one which had been most frequently alluded to in this discussion was the Circular of the 7th August 1838. Now, he had in his hand a paper which shewed that the Board which passed that order intended that its operation should be restricted to cases in which the alluvial land was fit for permanent settlement. A very few months after the issue of the Circular, on the 15th February 1839, they instructed the Commissioner of Dacca in the following terms:—

"Nevertheless, when, from the character of the accretion, *it may be deemed more proper to form a temporary settlement*, it will not be advisable to consolidate the jumma with that of the permanently settled estate; and in such cases, as the proprietor has a primary right to be admitted to engagement, the settlement made with him for the accretion must of necessity be distinct from that of the parent mehal."

It would be seen, therefore, that the views of the Revenue Authorities of those days with regard to the right of permanent settlement and also as to the necessity of keeping the chur attached to the old estate, were not very definite or consistent.

With regard to the learned Member's second point that the Bill alters the rights of Government, the learned Member contended that, when the proprietor refused to incorporate the alluvion with the original estate, the Government should have the right of refusing to give him a separate settlement of the alluvion and of keeping it attached to the old estate. But it had been fully shown in the debate on the second reading that, when a Zemindar refused or was not permitted to engage and the lands were let in farm, the arrangement was as much a settlement and the land became as much a separate estate for all revenue purposes, as if a separate engagement had been taken from the proprietor, and he thought that there was nothing in the letter from the Commissioner of Patna to shake the position so established. The learned Member said that Government had a lien on the alluvion for the revenue of the old estate. This was not in accordance with the first principle of revenue law: that principle was that all land was answerable for the revenue assessed upon it, and no land could be held liable for any arrears, except those which had accrued upon itself.

Then as to the risk of loss which it was said would be entailed on Government, by allowing alluvial lands to be treated in all cases as separate estates. The learned Member had referred to the case supposed in Mr. Samuells' 14th paragraph. He (Mr. Currie) had a right to assume that it was the strongest that could be put. It was certainly a very improbable, though not an absolutely impossible one. Mr. Samuells supposed the case of a highly assessed estate, the value of which consisted principally in its having a bazar on the bank of the river; a chur forms opposite the bazar, and a separate settlement of the chur is made with the proprietor: he establishes a new bazar on the chur, and allows the old estate to be sold for arrears; it is purchased by Government and re-settled at a reduced jumma. Now, what would be the result if, according to the Commissioner's principle, the chur were let in farm notwithstanding the proprietor's wish to engage for it. The damage to the old estate would be the same, for the farmer might establish a new bazar, or if restrained from this by special condition, the intervention of the chur would prevent access to the old bazar. Then why should the proprietor, whose old estate was endamaged by the formation of the chur, not be allowed all the compensatory benefit which the chur was calculated to afford? Why should he be deprived of the possession of the land and put off with a malikana allowance which might or might not be sufficient to meet the deficiency on the old estate? It did appear to him (Mr. Currie) that, in the attempt to do justice to Government, very great injustice might be done to the individual. Then, to follow out the case put by the Commissioner, suppose the chur with the new bazar to be washed away, and Government to lose the jumma which had been assessed on the new land. What was to prevent the Government farmer of the old estate from re-establishing the bazar on its former site? and then at the end of the lease, the estate would be again equal to the payment of the former revenue. It did appear to him that, on the Commissioner's own showing, the risk of loss to Government from the admission of what he contended to be the proprietor's right of separate settlement, was very remote and visionary.

In his opinion the Bill was not open to the objections brought against it, whether as regarded its affecting the rights of private individuals or the rights of Government.

The Honorable and learned Member had also taken objection to the wording of the latter part of Section I which declared that the alluvial land when separately settled should become a separate estate, in all respects independent of the original estate. Now, with respect to the meaning to be attached to the word "estate," of course it must from the context be taken in a revenue sense, and be held to mean a portion of land assessed with a specific jumma; and in that sense he (Mr. Currie) could see no difficulty in regarding the alluvial land as a separate estate.

As to the case put of a person who made a will and named in the will only the original estate, he (Mr. Currie) supposed that, if the chur and the old estate had become distinct properties at the time of the testator's death, the will could be of effect only with respect to the property named therein. But he did not see why that should be an objection to the separation.

Then with regard to the case of the mortgagee. If an estate on the bank of the river were mortgaged and a chur formed subsequently, the mortgagee would have the same lien on the chur, as he had on the original estate; and his rights would be recognized at the time of settlement.

After what had fallen from his Honorable friend (Mr. Ricketts) on the Putnee question, he thought he was not called upon to say much. But it did seem to him that the learned Member had not put the case of the Putneedar with his usual clearness. He had not shown how the position of the Putneedar would be affected by declaring the chur to be a separate estate. If the proprietor refused or was not permitted to engage, the chur must, of necessity, be let in farm; then, whether it were considered a separate estate, or whether according to the learned Member's doctrine it were held to be attached to the old estate, there would equally in either case be a stranger farmer representing the rights of Government, which rights were paramount to all others.

The Honorable and learned Member had asked how many separate estates would be created. It did not appear to him (Mr. Currie) that the effect of the Bill would be to increase the number of entries on the Collector's rent-roll. But he could tell the Honorable and learned Member what was the actual number of chur estates now existent in the four Districts of the Nuddea Division. From a Statement furnished to him by the Commissioner, it appeared that the total number of churs brought under settlement was three hundred and ninety-seven, of these only thirteen had been incorporated with the old estates, sixty-one had been settled with farmers, and for all the rest separate settlements had been made with the proprietors—eighty-five in perpetuity, and two-hundred and thirty-eight for terms of years. The practice of this Division, therefore, was separate settlement with the proprietors. From Mr. Samuells' letter, it would appear that the practice was different in the Patna Division. But the Bill, which followed the Circular Order of 1841, was in accordance with the practice generally in force, and he was quite satisfied that, while it affirmed that practice, it would in no respect injure any existent rights, whether of private individuals or of Government. He would therefore press his motion for the third reading.

MR. HARINGTON, said that, in rising to address the Council on this occasion, it was not his intention again to go over the whole of the ground over which they had already travelled so frequently, but before they proceeded to a division on the motion of the Honorable Member for Bengal, he was anxious to assert once more and for the last time the right which, according to the law as it at present stood, he concurred with the Honorable and learned Member of Council in considering to be vested in the proprietors of estates to which land might become annexed by alluvion, to insist upon the incorporation and settlement of that land with the parent estate upon the single condition of their engaging to pay the Government Revenue assessed upon it; and he made this assertion with the greater confidence to-day, not only in reference to the paper which had recently been printed and circulated to Honorable Members, but because he believed he could now cite the Honorable Member of Council opposite (Mr. Ricketts) as a witness in support of the view taken by him. In a former debate on the present Bill, the Honorable Member of Council mentioned that he had been charged with obscurity in the observations which he had made at a previous meeting of the Council, and with having held back from expressing his own opinion upon the questions of law raised in the course of the discussions on the Bill which he had left to be determined by others whom he considered better qualified than himself to deal with those questions; and in order to show not only that he had made up his mind as to the legal rights of the owners of alluvial formations, but that the opinion entertained by him upon this point was of some standing, and had not been formed subsequently to the introduction of the Bill before the Council, he read some instructions which, in concurrence with his colleagues in the Sudder Board, he had issued to the subordinate Revenue Authorities so far back, he (Mr. Harington) believed, as the year 1850. These instructions commenced by enunciating the very doctrine as to the rights of the proprietors of alluvial lands for which he had all along contended; but when he expressed his assent to what the Honorable Member had read, he checked him, and putting a comma or semicolon where he thought there had been a full stop, he went on to read what certainly looked like a qualification of that which had gone before, and seemed to recognize a discretionary power in the Revenue Authorities, scarcely compatible with the absolute right of the proprietors of alluvial formations which had just previously been declared. He came now to the testimony of the Honorable Member of Council which he considered to support the opinion held by him. This was contained in a little work of which the Honorable Member was generally considered to have been the author, and a copy of which he held in his hand. It was entitled "The Assistant's Cutchery Companion and help to the Revenue Examinations." He did not know when this work first appeared, as the preface to the first edition was without date and signature; but the title page to the second edition, the preface to which had the initials of the Honorable Member of Council attached to it, shewed that it was published in 1853. The preface to the first edition set out by saying—

> "The object of this little book is to enable an Assistant in the shortest period possible to make himself acquainted with the Regulations, Acts, and Circular Orders of the Revenue Department, and to conduct with some confidence and efficiency the duties entrusted to him."

But although the work was thus declared to have been published for the instruction in Revenue matters of the Junior Civilians as a class, he had been informed that the Honorable Member of Council was induced to write it chiefly to assist a young relative of his own in qualifying himself for the examinations which had shortly before been introduced into the Civil Service in Bengal. The relative alluded to was, he believed, the Honorable Member's son, whose gallant deeds on the banks of the Sutlej in the early part of the mutiny were probably fresh in the recollection of all who heard him. At page 91 of this Book, he found the following question and answer; (the book was written in the form of question and answer, which shape, the Author stated in the introductory Chapter, he considered had its advantages)—

Question.

"What parties have a right to demand that the settlement of alluvial accretions should be made with them?"

Answer.

"Such lands belong to the proprietor of the estate to which a change in the channel of the river has added them, and such proprietors are entitled to terms of permanent engagement whenever they may think fit to demand it. The increment may be added to the estate, to which it is attached, or settled as a separate Mehal as the owner may desire."

Not, it would be observed, as the Revenue Authorities might think proper, but as the owner might desire; and after the word "desire" there was no comma or semicolon, but a full stop, and the next question related to quite a different matter. The Author then proceeded to give the authority upon which he had thus declared the right of the owner of alluvial lands to demand a permanent settlement of such lands and to have them either incorporated with the original estate or settled as a separate Mehal, and that authority was Section IV Regulation XI. 1825, though the Honorable Member of Council had told them to-day that Regulation XI. 1825 related only to the right of property in alluvial lands, and was in no way connected with the settlement of lands of that description. Then again at page 129 of the Book, the following question was asked—

"To whom do lands gained from the sea or rivers belong?"

Answer.

"Such lands are to be assessed as an increment to the tenure of the person to whose land or estate they may have been annexed, whether such lands be held immediately from Government by a Zemindar or as a subordinate tenure by any description of under tenant."

And here also the authority given for the answer to the question was Clause 1 Section IV Regulation XI. 1825. Once more, at the page first mentioned it was asked—

"When a party is entitled by law to a settlement in perpetuity, must such settlement be made whatever the state of the Mehal?"

Answer.

"Yes, the settlement must be in perpetuity. The question in such cases will be a perpetual settlement at an increasing and a perpetual settlement at a fixed jumma. There cannot be a temporary settlement."

Authority—Section VIII Regulation XVIII. 1793. The Honorable Member for Bengal declared that no pledge had ever been given to the proprietors of alluvial lands that a permanent settlement of such lands should be made with them, but the Court of Directors and the Government in this country had repeatedly recognized the right to a settlement in perpetuity of parties who have a right of property or a permanent interest in alluvial formations, and he need not tell the Council that, under the law as it now stood, the proprietor of a permanently settled estate had to all intents as permanent an interest in any alluvial land which might accrete to that estate, as he possessed in the original estate. With regard to Putneedars and under-tenants generally, he would observe that, as proprietors of estates were at liberty to grant leases of their lands on any conditions and for any term that they might think proper, provided that they did not go beyond the period of their own lease, there was nothing to prevent them from entering into an agreement which should give the Putneedar or other under-tenant the benefit of any alluvion that might be formed without paying any additional rent. Such a contract would, he apprehended, be binding on the proprietor. The concluding paragraph of Clause 1 Section IV Regulation XI. 1825 would seem to support this view. It said—

"Nor if annexed to a subordinate tenure held under a superior land-holder, shall the under-tenant, whether a khoodhasht ryot holding a mouroosee istemrarce at a fixed rate of rent per Beegah, or any other description of under-tenant, liable by his engagements, or by established usage, to an increase of rent for the land annexed to his tenure by alluvion, be considered exempt from the payment of any increase of rent to which he may be justly liable."

So that, conversely, if the engagement of the under-tenant expressly stipulated that he should not be liable for any increased rent in respect of any alluvion that might become annexed to his tenure, he did not see how any additional rent could be taken from him. He concluded these remarks, as he commenced them, by declaring his conviction as to the absolute right of the proprietors of estates to insist upon the incorporation and settlement with those estates of any alluvial lands that might accrete thereto, if prepared to pay the revenue assessed upon them; and considering this right to be infringed upon by the Bill as now drawn, he should vote with the Honorable and learned Member of Council against its third reading.

MR. CURRIE said, lest it should be supposed from the questions read by the Honorable Member, who had just sat down, that there was legal authority for the statement that a proprietor of alluvial land had a right to settlement in perpetuity, whatever might be the state of the land, he would just observe that the authority quoted by the Honorable Member for a right to settlement in perpetuity, Section VIII Regulation XVIII (or as it should have been printed Regulation XIX) 1793, had reference only to resumed lakhiraj tenures, and did not bear at all on the question of alluvial formations.

THE VICE-PRESIDENT said that the Honorable and learned Member had stated that the Bill affected the under-tenants, but in his opinion the Bill made no alteration in the existing law, whatever that law might be. He might observe in passing, that he had once suggested to the Honorable Member for Bengal, that he thought it would be clearer if, instead of the phrase to which objection had been taken, the Bill had used the words "for all revenue purposes." However he thought that such would be the reasonable construction which any body, looking to the general scope and objects of the Act and taking its Clauses together, would put upon it. His Honorable and learned friend had contended that, if the chur were let in farm, this Bill would injuriously affect the rights of Putneedars or under-tenants in respect of the malikana. He was unable to follow his Honorable and learned friend's argument on that point. If the zemindar failed to engage for the land, the Putneedar might do so. If both refused to engage, then the farmer would come in and undertake to pay a revenue to Government and a malikana to somebody. The first Clause of the Bill did not mention the word "malikana." Malikana was originally payable to the zemindar. In Regulation VII. 1822, Section V, he found provisions modifying the rights to malikana and prescribing new rules on the subject. How far those enactments affected the relative rights of zemindars and under-tenants to malikana, or to what districts they extended, he was not prepared now to argue. But whatever those rights were, this Bill seemed to him to leave them as it found them. Clause 1 Section IV Regulation XI. 1825 clearly contemplated a possible liability on the part of the under-tenant to pay an increased rent in respect of alluvion, for it said—

"Nor if (land be) annexed to a subordinate tenure held under a superior land-holder, shall the under-tenant, whether a khoodkhast ryot, holding a mouroosee Istimraree tenure at a fixed rate of rent per Beegah or any other description of under-tenant liable by his engagements, or by established usage, to an increase of rent for the land annexed to his tenure by alluvion, be considered exempt from the payment of any increase of rent to which he may be justly liable."

But if any doubt touching the rights of the under-tenants could arise upon the 1st Section, it must be removed by the 2nd Section of the Bill, which said—

"Nothing contained in the preceding Section shall affect the rights of any under-tenant in any alluvial land under the provisions of Clause 1 Section IV Regulation XI. 1825."

It then provided that it should be the duty of the settlement officer to apply that law and to ascertain and record all such rights according to the rules prescribed in Regulation VII. 1822.

Whatever might be the effect of the existing law upon the question now under consideration, and whatever its merits or demerits, they remained very much what they now were. On the general question, whether this Bill should now be read a third time and passed, he must say that, with every respect for the very able paper from the Commissioner of Patna and for the arguments of his Honorable and learned friend, he continued to think that this Bill would effect a great improvement in the law of settlement. That some legislation was wanting, was clear. The Honorable Member for Bengal had

Mr. Harington

shown on a former occasion that, notwithstanding the Act of 1847, there continued to be frequent occasion for the settlement of alluvions on the expiration of farming leases or the like. That statement had oddly enough been confirmed during the past week by his (the Vice-President's) personal experience; for there had come before him, incidentally of course, in his judicial capacity, a revenue proceeding before the Commissioner of Nuddea for the settlement of a chur dated only a few months back. And as to the principles on which such settlements should be made, and even as to the existing law, there was obviously great diversity of opinion even amongst those most conversant with the revenue system.

On the whole, it appeared to him (the Vice-President) that proprietors of lands would be gainers by this Bill. If he were satisfied that, by practice or by any law, the proprietor was entitled to have his alluvion settled permanently when he chose and upon certain fixed terms, he (the Vice-President) would have supported the amendment of his Honorable and learned friend which gave the proprietor the right to insist on having the alluvion doubled up with the parent estate and assessed under one common jumma. It was the difficulty occasioned by the nature of the subject in saying when the settlement should be permanent, or in making a permanent settlement that would be just to both parties, that made him prefer the Bill as it stood. If we were to go back to the principles of the permanent settlement and follow them logically out, he must take leave to doubt whether the Government had any right to assess these alluvial increments at all. But that question had been settled by the Regulation of 1819; and the only question now was, how that right might most fairly be exercised. By this Bill the land must be assessed jointly with the parent estate, unless the Collector determined that the settlement ought to be temporary, or the proprietor desired a separate settlement.

The other objection was that the rights and interests of Government would be injuriously affected by giving the proprietor the right to insist on a separate settlement. He was not satisfied that this would be the case. The just principle seemed to be that each parcel of land should bear its own burden. And he thought the right would be a valuable one both to zemindars and to under-tenants. A great part of the Indigo cultivation of the country was carried on upon these churs. It would be a great advantage to the planter that he should be able to save his land from a sale for arrears of Revenue by depositing the sum assessed on the chur alone, instead of having to deposit the revenue assessed on both chur and the parent estate.

Upon the whole, therefore, he thought that the under-tenants would, as a general rule, be gainers: the proprietors would also be gainers; and not being satisfied that the public revenue would be endangered by it, he should vote for the third reading of the Bill with no more than that hesitation which every one ought to feel in dealing with a subject with which he is not conversant and on which those, who are conversant with it are greatly divided.

MR. RICKETTS said, he was sure the Council would permit him to say a few words in explanation of what had fallen from the Honorable Member of the North-Western Provinces. He could not admit that the Honorable Member had convicted him of inconsistency of opinion, but he must plead guilty to carelessness, although not quite so bad as the Honorable Member would make it out to be. He admitted the authorship of the book from which the Honorable Member had quoted. The answer which had been read was an incomplete answer, but the authority quoted was not the Regulation XI. 1825 only, but the Circular Order of the 26th November 1850 para. 74, written by himself, the provisions of which were entirely consistent with the opinions which he (Mr. Ricketts) now professed. The Honorable Member would have been more ingenuous had he pointed to the Circular Order as well as to the law.

The question being put, the Council divided.

Ayes, 7.	*Noes*, 2.
Mr. Forbes.	Mr. Harington.
Mr. Currie.	Mr. Peacock.
Mr. LeGeyt.	
Mr. Ricketts.	
Sir James Outram.	
Mr. Grant.	
The Vice-President.	

So the motion was carried, and the Bill read a third time.

FORT OF TANJORE.

Mr. FORBES moved that the Bill "for bringing the Fort of Tanjore and the adjacent territory under the Laws of the Presidency of Fort St. George" be read a third time and passed.

The motion was carried, and the Bill read a third time.

PROCEEDINGS IN LUNACY (SUPREME COURTS).

Mr. CURRIE moved that the Council do resolve itself into a Committee on the Bill "to regulate proceedings in Lunacy in Her Majesty's Courts of Judicature;" and that the Committee be instructed to consider the Bill in the amended form in which the Select Committee had recommended it to be passed.

Agreed to.

Section 1 being read by the Chairman—

Mr. PEACOCK said, this Section authorized the Court upon an application to make an order directing any Judge or the Master of the Court to enquire whether an alleged Lunatic, subject to the jurisdiction of the Court, was or was not of unsound mind and incapable of managing his affairs.

The Bill also empowered the Court, where the alleged Lunatic was not resident within the local limits of the jurisdiction of the Court, to appoint a Commission to make the enquiry.

He considered that this involved a most important question, namely, whether the power of deciding whether a man was of unsound mind and incapable of managing himself and his affairs, should be delegated to the Master of the Court either with or without the assistance of assessors. The result of such an enquiry was most important to the person to be affected by it; and it was necessary, in order to guard against abuse, that the evidence in such cases should be strictly scrutinized.

He had had some little experience in these matters; he knew the nature of the evidence brought forward on such occasions, and how easy it was to express an opinion that a man was of unsound mind.

He recollected a case which was tried before the late Chief Justice Tindal and a special Jury in which a Doctor was called as a witness to prove that a gentleman was of unsound mind. The witness, upon his cross-examination by the late Sir Thomas Wilde, afterwards Lord Truro, admitted that he entertained the theory that no man's mind was perfectly sound. He was asked what he thought of the Chief Justice's mind, whether he believed it to be perfectly sound. His answer was "No." A similar question was asked with reference to the minds of the foreman and gentlemen of the Jury, and a similar answer given. The witness was then asked whether he believed that his own mind was perfectly sound, to which he replied, "He could not say that it was." Whereupon he was told that he might stand down, and that that was probably the truest answer he had given during his evidence.

He also remembered another case in which the state of mind of a gentleman who was formerly in the service of the East India Company was the subject of enquiry. A lady, the matron of a Lunatic Asylum in which he had been confined, was called as a witness and swore that she had not the slightest doubt that he was a mad man. Upon cross-examination she was asked what grounds she had for her opinion; she answered, "Because he ate with a voracious appetite and did not sufficiently masticate his food."

He (Mr. Peacock) recollected the precise words, for they made a great impression upon him at the time. Enquiries of this nature were as important as any that could be submitted for trial; and he was in favor of having such questions tried openly by full Court before the three Judges.

The Advocate General had stated that the expense of an enquiry under a Commission of Lunacy, according to the present practice of the Supreme Court, varied from fifteen hundred to three thousand Rupees; and the Bill recited that it was expedient to lessen the cost. He (Mr. Peacock) had not seen the bills of costs, and therefore he could not say what were the principal items of expense. He did not believe that this Bill would much diminish them. It might save the fees of the Commissioner and of the Jury, which could be only a small part of the amount; but he could not see what other saving of expense would be effected by this Bill.

In the Statement of objects and reasons it was said that the object of the Bill was to assimilate the practice of the Supreme Courts in proceedings in Lunacy to that which prevailed in England under recent Acts of Parliament. But many of the provisions of the present Bill differed from those of the 16 and 17 Vic. c. 70 upon which it was supposed to be founded. He had not the same confidence in assessors as he had in a Jury, and he certainly thought that such enquiries should be made by the Court and not by the Master. He would therefore now move that the words "to make an order directing any Judge or the Master of the Court" be omitted from this Section.

THE CHAIRMAN remarked that this Bill had passed the second reading without any discussion. It was introduced at the instance of the learned Advocate-General who had proposed by it to assimilate proceedings in Lunacy in this country to the laws in force at home. Commissions of Lunacy were happily of very rare occurrence here. In the course of the twelve years during which he had been connected with the Supreme Court, he did not think there had been more than six. But in all cases of that nature, it was obvious that the enquiry might be very simple and it might be very intricate. The supposed Lunatic might be in a state in which there could be no rational doubt of his madness. And to subject the estate, which might be very small, to the cost of a Commission or even to that of a trial before the full bench of the Supreme Court, seemed unreasonable. He thought it would be better to follow the analogy of the English Statute, and to let the Master or a single Judge in Chambers (he had no desire to insist upon the Master, if the Honorable and learned Member objected to that tribunal) deal with such cases. Either might be presumed to be as capable of dealing with them as a single Master in Lunacy to whom they would be committed at home.

He might observe that the last Commission of Lunacy issued in the Supreme Court was in the case of a purdah lady. In such a case it was obviously necessary that those who made the enquiry, should go to the house and visit the supposed Lunatic. It seemed hardly necessary, if the case were one of a simple character, to carry the whole Court down to some family-house in the native quarter of the town. He made this objection, not on the score of dignity, but of convenience.

With respect to the more difficult cases, he had felt great doubt upon this Bill, whether it did not go too far in depriving the supposed Lunatic of a Jury if he saw fit to insist on one. And considering that the full Court would exercise that controlling power over the tribunal that made the enquiry, which was exercised at home by the Lord Chancellor—that there was no other authority which stood in the Chancellor's place—he felt doubtful whether a provision, that the more complex cases should be tried by a single Judge and a Jury, might not be preferable to the procedure proposed by the Honorable and learned Member.

On the whole, he should prefer that the question should be more deliberately considered, and he would move that the Bill be referred back to the former Select Committee with the addition of the Honorable and learned Member.

After some discussion, the Motion was put and agreed to.

CARE OF ESTATES OF LUNATICS NOT SUBJECT TO THE SUPREME COURTS.

MR. CURRIE moved that the Council resolve itself into a Committee on the Bill "to make better provision for the care of the estates of Lunatics not subject to the jurisdiction of Her Majesty's Courts of Judicature;" and that the Committee be instructed to consider the Bill in the amended form in which the Select Committee had recommended it to be passed.

After some conversation, the Motion was agreed to.

Sections I to III were passed as they stood.

Section IV provided as follows—

"When the Civil Court is about to institute any such enquiry as aforesaid, the Court shall appoint a Jury consisting of a Medical Officer of Government and two respectable inhabitants of the district; and the enquiry shall be conducted by the Court in the presence and with the assistance of the Jury so appointed."

THE CHAIRMAN said, this Section made it imperative to appoint a Medical Officer of Government. He thought, however, that, at the places where this Bill would be brought into operation, there would seldom be more than a single Medical Officer resident. He probably would have attended or examined the supposed Lunatic. He might obviously be able to give the most important testimony in the case; and it was better that he should do this as a witness in open Court and subject to cross-examination, rather than bring his knowledge to bear on the decision of the case whilst exercising the functions of a juror. Of course he assumed a paucity of Medical men to exist in the Mofussil. He therefore moved the omission of the words "a medical officer of Government and two," and the substitution for them of the words "at least three."

After some discussion, the Motion was agreed to, and the Section, as amended, was then passed.

MR. PEACOCK thought that the Act should contain some provision requiring notice of the intended enquiry to be given to the alleged Lunatic. He therefore moved that the following Section be introduced after Section IV namely :—

"Before the enquiry shall be held, the alleged Lunatic shall have sufficient notice of the time and place at which it is proposed to hold the enquiry."

Agreed to.

MR. PEACOCK suggested that the Bill should provide for the constitution of the jury, and also for compelling their attendance.

MR. HARINGTON drew attention to the provision on the subject of the constitution of Juries, which was contained in Section CCLX of the Code of Criminal Procedure proposed by Her Majesty's Commissioners.

After some further conversation—

MR. CURRIE moved that the Bill be referred back to the former Select Committee with the addition of Mr. Peacock, in order that the questions just raised might receive a more careful consideration.

Agreed to.

LUNATIC ASYLUMS.

MR. CURRIE postponed the Motion (which stood in the Orders of the Day) for a Committee of the whole Council on the Bill "relating to Lunatic Asylums."

ESTATE OF THE LATE NABOB OF THE CARNATIC.

MR. PEACOCK moved that Mr. Ricketts be requested to take the Bill "to provide for the administration of the estate and for the payment of the debts of the late Nabob of the Carnatic" to the President in Council, in order that it might be submitted to the Governor General for his assent.

Agreed to.

SETTLEMENT OF ALLUVIAL LANDS (BENGAL).

MR. CURRIE moved that Mr. Ricketts be requested to take the Bill "to make further provision for the settlement of land gained by alluvion in the Presidency of Fort William in Bengal" to the President in Council, in order that it might be submitted to the Governor General for his assent.

Agreed to.

FORT OF TANJORE.

MR. FORBES moved that Mr. Ricketts be requested to take the Bill "for bringing the Fort of Tanjore and the adjacent territory under the Laws of the Presidency of Fort St. George" to the President in Council, in order that it might be submitted to the Governor General for his assent.

Agreed to.

The Council adjourned.

Saturday, August 21, 1858.

PRESENT:

The Hon'ble the Chief Justice, *Vice-President*, in the Chair;

Hon'ble H. Ricketts,	H. B. Harington,
Hon'ble B. Peacock,	Esq.
P. W. LeGeyt, Esq.,	and
E. Currie, Esq.,	H. Forbes, Esq.
Hon. Sir A W. Buller,	

POLITICAL PENSIONS.

THE CLERK presented to the Council a Petition from Ramchunder Venkutesh Goona of Poona, praying to be informed to what pensions or allowances Act VI of 1849 (for securing Military and Naval pensions and superannuation allowances) was intended to apply, and whether it was applicable to pensions granted in commutation of Surinjams.

The VICE-PRESIDENT conceived that this Petition could hardly be received. It asked for a legal opinion from the Council.

INDIGO PLANTERS.

The CLERK also presented a Petition from the Indigo Planters' Association, praying, on behalf of Indigo Planters, for further protection and improved means of redress against Ryots to whom they had made advances and who broke their engagements; and also against persons, Zemindars or others, by whose inducement or interference such breaches of engagement were brought about, and against those who purchased or received Indigo Plant from Ryots, knowing that the Ryots were committing a breach of contract in selling or delivering it to them.

Mr. CURRIE moved that the above Petition be printed.

Agreed to.

STAMP DUTIES (BENGAL).

Mr. PEACOCK presented the Report of the Select Committee on the Bill "to amend Regulation X. 1829 of the Bengal Code" (for the collection of Stamp Duties.)

SIR JAMSETJEE JEJEEBHOY'S ESTATE.

Mr. LeGEYT begged to move the first reading of a Bill "for settling a sum of Company's Rupees twenty-five lacs Bengal Government four per centum Promissory Notes, and a Mansion-house and hereditaments called Mazagon Castle in the Island of Bombay, the property of Sir Jamsetjee Jejeebhoy, Baronet, so as to accompany and support the title and dignity of a Baronet lately conferred on him by Her present Majesty Queen Victoria, and for other purposes connected therewith."

He said, the object of this Bill was sufficiently set forth in the title which had just been recited. It would probably be in the recollection of the Honorable Members that the individual on whom the Sovereign had been pleased to confer the dignity of a Baronet was a Parsee gentleman of Bombay, distinguished alike for his success during a long and honorable commercial career, his consistent loyalty to the Government, and his unceasing efforts in promoting the welfare of his fellow-citizens and relieving the necessities of those standing in need of charitable aid.

He (Mr. LeGeyt) believed he was not wrong in saying that this distinguished gentleman had expended upwards of forty lacs of Rupees on works of charity and public utility in Bombay and its neighbourhood. His private charities also were unbounded, and he had attained the years usually allotted to man, beloved and respected by all classes. Two years ago, the community, European and Native, of Bombay, resolved to erect a statue in his honor. That statue had just been completed and was now on its way from England for the purpose of being placed in the Town Hall of Bombay in juxtaposition with those of Elphinstone, Malcolm, Sir Charles Forbes, and other worthies whose names lived in the recollection of the community of Western India.

Several years ago, the Queen was pleased to confer on this gentleman the honor of Knighthood; and last year, as a special mark of Her Majesty's sense of his merits, he was advanced to the dignity of a Baronet, and was the first native of India on whom a hereditary English title of distinction had ever been conferred. It was thought proper, in the uncertainty of the Parsee laws and customs of inheritance which unhappily prevailed in that tribe, to make some arrangements by which the hereditary dignity and title should not, at any future time, descend to a person unable to keep it up with honor and respectability. It was suggested to Sir Jamsetjee Jejeebhoy, and readily acquiesced in by him, that a certain sum of money should be vested in Trustees for the use of the person on whom the Baronetcy might descend, and that the income of the capital so vested should be paid to such holder. The sum of twenty-five lacs of Rupees in the four per cent. Company's Paper was agreed on, as a proper sum to be so invested; and to this, at Sir Jamsetjee Jejeebhoy's own request, a Mansion-house and estate near Bombay, which went by the name of the Mazagon Castle, had been subsequently added, with a condition that every future Baronet should assume the name of "Jamsetjee Jejeebhoy" in lieu of any other.

To give effect to this measure, a Bill was prepared by the legal Officers of the East India Company in communication with Sir Jamsetjee Jejeebhoy's friends in London, which it had been proposed to present to the Imperial Parliament. But it was afterwards ascertained that the settlement was a subject which could be more conveniently disposed of by the Indian Legislature. The Bill which he now had the honor to lay before the Council was prepared in exact conformity with the draft framed in England.

The Preamble enumerated the several purposes of the proposed Act.

Section I provided for the Governor in Council of Bombay being a Corporation for the execution of the trusts created by the Act. Now, with regard to this, a doubt had been started as to the power of this Council to create Corporations. But he did not think it worth while to await the opinion of the Company's Law Officers in England to whom the question had been referred. The Council had on several occasions legislated in the matter; and he had found on record a Despatch from the Honorable the Court of Directors, dated 3rd July 1839, in which the Court observed:—

"You will have the satisfaction of learning that, in the opinion of the Attorney and Solicitor General and the Company's Standing Counsel, the creation of a Corporation by an Act of the Governor General of India in Council is valid, and, moreover, that the same authority has the power of limiting the liability of members of a Trading Association to the same extent as the Crown may do under the Act of the 7th William IV and 1st Vic: Cap. 73."

This authority seemed to him a sufficient warrant for the introduction of the Bill; the propriety of its being further proceeded with could be discussed on its second reading.

Section II provided that the future Baronets should take the names of the first Baronet.

Section III related to the investment of twenty-five lacs of Rupees in trust for the use of the Baronet in possession.

Section IV provided for the settlement of the Mansion-house (called the Mazagon Castle) and its hereditaments in support of the Baronetcy.

Section V provided for the refusal or discontinuance to use the names of the first Baronet.

Section VI conferred the power of jointure on the Baronet in possession; and Section VII limited the aggregate of jointure payable contemporaneously.

Section VIII provided that the Mansion-house and hereditaments should not be subject to Dower. Section IX prohibited alienation during the Baronetcy. Section X provided indemnity for Trustee, and Section XI was a general saving Clause.

The Bill and papers would be printed as soon as possible, and circulated to the Honorable Members, whereupon he would give notice of a day for the second reading thereof. He would also, in consequence of a communication which he had received from Bombay, move for a suspension of the Standing Orders in order that the Bill might be forthwith passed through its remaining stages without the usual delay attending its publication. Sir Jamsetjee was at an advanced age, and it was his particular desire that all the necessary arrangements might be fully carried out in his life-time, and the Bombay Government as well as Sir Jamsetjee had expressed a wish that the Bill might be passed into law as speedily as possible.

The Bill was read a first time.

RYOTWAR SETTLEMENTS (MADRAS PRESIDENCY).

Mr. FORBES moved that the Bill "for the better recovery of arrears of Revenue under Ryotwar Settlements in the Madras Presidency" be now read a second time.

The motion was carried, and the Bill read a second time.

INDIAN NAVY.

Mr. PEACOCK moved that the Council do resolve itself into a Committee on the Bill "to amend Act XII of 1844" (for better securing the observance of an exact discipline in the

Indian Navy); and that the Committee be instructed to consider the Bill in the amended form in which the Select Committee had recommended it to be passed.

Agreed to.

The Bill passed through Committee without amendment, and was reported.

RYOTWAR SETTLEMENTS (MADRAS PRESIDENCY).

MR. FORBES moved that the Bill "for the better recovery of arrears of Revenue under Ryotwar Settlements in the Madras Presidency" be referred to a Select Committee consisting of Mr. LeGeyt, Mr. Currie, Mr. Harington, and the Mover.

Agreed to.

MR. FORBES moved that a communication received by him from the Madras Government be laid upon the table and referred to the above Committee.

Agreed to.

The Council adjourned.

Saturday, August 28, 1858.

PRESENT:

The Hon'ble the Chief Justice, *Vice-President*, in the Chair.

Hon. Lieut.-Genl. Sir J. Outram,	E. Currie, Esq.,
Hon. B. Peacock,	H. B. Harington, Esq.,
P. W. LeGeyt, Esq.,	and H. Forbes Esq.

CARE OF ESTATES OF LUNATICS NOT SUBJECT TO THE SUPREME COURTS.

MR. CURRIE presented the Report of the Select Committee on the Bill "to make better provision for the care of the Estates of Lunatics not subject to the jurisdiction of Her Majesty's Courts of Judicature."

MUNICIPAL ASSESSMENT (SCINDE).

MR. LEGEYT moved the first reading of a Bill "for enabling improvements to be made in certain districts and towns in the Province of Scinde."

He said, the object of this Bill was to enable the Chief Commissioner in Scinde to carry out certain Municipal and other improvements in that province, and to provide by taxation the necessary funds for those improvements. Its provisions, it would be seen, went far beyond the mere Municipal provisions of Act XXVI of 1850 which, it was found after trial, did not, in that Province at least, answer the purpose for which it was passed. Perhaps in no part of the British dominions in India had that Act received a fairer trial than in the Province of Scinde. Perhaps also there was a feeling among the inhabitants of that Province to promote local improvements and to foster institutions which were recognized in all civilized countries to be beneficial to the community. Though they, in common with all other Asiatics, were very averse to devise any scheme of self-taxation, they were yet willing (as would be found from the correspondence which would form the annexure to the Bill) to pay taxes, provided they were told what benefit they would derive therefrom.

Mr. Frere, with his accustomed philanthropy and zeal, had for some years laboured very much to introduce Municipal and local improvements into the towns of the Province subject to his control, and his success had been very great, particularly in Kurrachee. But the inhabitants of the smaller towns objected that, while the inhabitants of towns had to pay for improvements, the inhabitants of districts were not taxed. The object of this Bill was to extend taxation to the districts.

Mr. Frere had gone farther even than Act XXVI of 1850 provided. He (Mr. LeGeyt) had before him the fifth annual Report of the Proceedings of the Kurrachee Municipality for 1857-58, which contained a full account of what was now going on at Kurrachee. Besides the ordinary improvements of towns, the Municipality had been able to create a Charitable Dispensary which afforded great relief to the poorer portion of the population. Acting upon this, Mr Frere proposed to extend the operation of the Bill to Hospitals, Asylums, and Infirmaries for persons unable from mental or bodily ailments to provide for themselves, schools, district roads, and bridges.

He had printed in the annexure to this Bill a correspondence between the Government of Bombay and the Government of India. From this correspondence it would be seen that Mr. Frere had thus described the effect of Act XXVI of 1850 after several years' experience of its working:

"I am compelled to admit that, as applied to Scinde, any claim to the character of a voluntary system of Municipal taxation and management would be, with a few exceptions, in such communities as Kurrachee, a gigantic imposture."

He therefore applied to the Bombay Government to know whether he could not, within the limits of Scinde, so modify Act XXVI of 1850 as to embrace all the purposes which, in his opinion, were required there. The Bombay Government referred the matter for the consideration of the Government of India, enquiring whether any system of taxation for Municipal purposes, analogous to that proposed by the Commissioner of Scinde, had yet been introduced into any of the non-Regulation districts administered by the Supreme Government, and requesting an expression of opinion as to the expediency of permitting any such modification of the provisions of Act XXVI of 1850. In reply, the Government of India observed that no such scheme had been introduced into any of the non-Regulation districts under their direct administration. They also stated their opinion that the proposed law had no resemblance to the Municipal law, and that, as the general Regulations had not been extended to Scinde, Act XXVI of 1850 could not be applied in the manner proposed. The Government of India, however, saw no objection to the proposal of a local Municipal law applicable to the special circumstances of Scinde.

Accordingly, the Bill which he (Mr. LeGeyt) now had the honor to present to the Council, was prepared. He had had it in hand some little time, and he confessed he had felt some difficulty in bringing it forward, being aware that its principle was so much opposed to the sentiments enunciated by the Council in 1855 when a somewhat similar measure was introduced by the late Honorable Member for Bengal. However, after reading all that had been said on the subject, he did not see that there was any thing in the Bill which might not be conceded, if it were admitted that local improvements were desirable. The Bombay Government had certainly been able to introduce Act XXVI of 1850 into many of the towns and villages of that Presidency. But from the remarks of the Bombay Government which were contained in the papers which he had received, he found reason to believe that the working of the Act had not been more successful in the Regulation Provinces of that Presidency than Mr. Frere had found it to be in Scinde.

The funds which Mr. Frere proposed to raise for the purposes of this Act were—

1st. The application of an additional cess not exceeding 5 per cent. of the land-tax, to be levied in the same manner as the land-tax.

2nd. A tax on shops or stalls.

3rd. A tax on houses.

4th. A tax on Imports and Exports or such other town duties as might be considered advisable

5th. Tolls or taxes on carriages or beasts of burden.

6th. Such items of public Revenue as might be granted to the Municipality by Government for the purposes of this Act.

The last he supposed would be ferry tolls and the like.

The objects for which he proposed to provide were—

1st. The construction and repair of streets and roads, with bridges, drains, and all necessary appurtenances within the town or district.

2nd. The cleansing, watering, and lighting of streets and roads.

3rd. The construction of wells, tanks, and other works, for ensuring a proper supply of water.

4th. The erection and maintenance of schools and other educational expenditure.

5th. The erection and maintenance of Asylums for the support of those who were mentally and physically incapacitated from supporting themselves.

6th. The erection and maintenance of Hospitals, Infirmaries, and Dispensaries.

7th. The maintenance of a Municipal police.

This he (Mr. LeGeyt) understood to be a Village Police. In Scinde there was a very inefficient Village Police, for the abuses committed by which this Bill was intended to provide a remedy.

8th. The prevention of nuisances.

9th. The erection of market-places and any other works of public utility, or calculated to promote the public health, comfort, or convenience, which might be sanctioned by the Chief Commissioner.

These were the improvements which Mr. Frere hoped to introduce into Scinde by means of this Bill. He mentioned in his letter to the Bombay Government that the system now advocated was not new or experimental, and that the principle at least had been in force in the districts resumed from Meer Ali Moorad in 1851. He stated that, instead of abolishing the local taxes then levied, as had been done elsewhere on the introduction of our rule, the collection of them was placed in the hands of local Committees, which still exist to the great benefit of the country. He stated also that there was an attempt made by the tax-payers to get rid of them altogether as in our older districts. But by a little persuasion and by calling attention to the fact that the funds were faithfully expended for their improvement, the people became reconciled to the imposition and had since cheerfully submitted to it. There could be no doubt that, if Mr. Frere were enabled to carry out the improvements contemplated by this Bill, when the community for whose benefit they were intended were willing to be taxed to provide the necessary means for the purpose, a great and incalculable boon would be conferred.

The Council were aware that, after the discussion in 1855, a Committee was appointed to consider the subject of Municipalities in the Mofussil. The labors of that Committee, however, had been totally without any result, either in the shape of information or schemes for the attainment of the object in view. In some of the few places in Bengal, where Act XXVI of 1850 had been introduced, he believed it had been given up; and in Scinde, as Mr. Frere observed, experience had showed that the people of that Province were not, and could not be for several generations to come, fit to be entrusted with their own Municipal Government. He (Mr. LeGeyt) had no doubt that, if such an Act as was now proposed by Mr. Frere were extended to India generally, it would be of great benefit. He believed that, if local improvements of a Municipal or a more extended nature were postponed till the native community came forward on the voluntary principle and asked to be allowed to pay a tax for them, such improvements would not be introduced in India for the next hundred years. A man of Mr. Frere's ability and circumspection would recommend no Bill, if he were not tolerably sure of being able to carry out its provisions without offending any public prejudice. He had proposed a scheme which seemed practicable in itself and most promising in its effects. Even as an experiment, therefore, it could not be in better hands than his.

In conclusion, Mr. LeGeyt called serious attention to Mr. Frere's letter, and trusted that the Bill would receive a liberal consideration from the Council on its second reading.

The Bill was read a first time.

SIR JAMSETJEE JEEJEEBHOY'S ESTATE.

MR. LEGEYT moved the second reading of the Bill "for settling a sum of Company's Rupees Twenty-five Lacs, Bengal Government four per centum Promissory Notes, and a Mansion-house and hereditaments called Mazagon Castle in the Island of Bombay, the property of Sir Jamsetjee Jeejeebhoy, Baronet, so as to accompany and support the title and Dignity of a Baronet lately conferred on him by Her present Majesty, Queen Victoria, and for other purposes connected therewith."

The Motion was carried, and the Bill read a second time.

INDIAN NAVY.

MR. PEACOCK moved that the Bill "to amend Act XII of 1844 (for better securing the observance of an exact discipline in the Indian Navy)" be read a third time and passed.

The Motion was carried, and the Bill read a third time.

STAMP DUTIES (BENGAL).

MR. PEACOCK moved that the Council resolve itself into a Committee on the Bill "to amend Regulation X. 1829 of the Bengal Code" (for the collection of Stamp Duties); and that the Committee be instructed to consider the Bill in the amended form in which the Select Committee had recommended it to be passed.

Agreed to.

Section I was passed as it stood.

Section II provided as follows:—

"Every deed, instrument, or document specified in the said Schedule (that is Schedule A. Regulation X. 1829) which is or shall be contained in more than one sheet or piece of paper, or other material, shall be deemed to be sufficiently stamped if any one or more of such sheets or pieces of paper or other material shall bear the requisite stamp or stamps *of equal value*, whether the signatures or seals of the parties and witnesses shall or shall not be upon such sheet or sheets," &c.

MR. PEACOCK said that his attention had been called by the Honorable and learned Chairman to the words "of equal value" in the 10th line. Possibly some doubt might arise as to the true construction of those words. The meaning was that stamps equal in value to the requisite stamp would be sufficient. To prevent all doubt, therefore, he begged to move the substitution for those words of the words "equal in value to the requisite stamp."

The Motion was carried, and the Section as amended was agreed to.

The remaining Sections, with the Preamble and Title, were passed as they stood.

The Council having resumed its sitting, the Bill was reported.

PROCEEDINGS IN LUNACY (SUPREME COURTS).

MR. CURRIE moved that the Council resolve itself into a Committee on the Bill "to regulate proceedings in Lunacy in Her Majesty's Courts of Judicature"; and that the Committee be instructed to consider the Bill in the amended form in which it had been recommended by the Select Committee to be passed.

In making this motion, he remarked that the Select Committee had not thought it necessary to present a formal Report; the amendments proposed being in conformity with what seemed to be the opinion of the Council when the Bill was under discussion. An enquiry before the Court or a Judge had been substituted for the enquiry before a Judge or Master. Also when the alleged Lunatic was not within the local limits of the jurisdiction, the Court was empowered to direct an inquiry before a Mofussil Court instead of the enquiry by Commissioners.

The Motion was agreed to.

The Bill passed through Committee after some verbal amendments; and, the Council having resumed its sitting, was reported.

CARE OF ESTATES OF LUNATICS NOT SUBJECT TO THE SUPREME COURTS.

MR. CURRIE moved that the Council resolve itself into a Committee on the Bill "to make better provision for the care of the estates of Lunatics not subject to the jurisdiction of Her Majesty's Courts of Judicature;" and that the Committee be instructed to consider the Bill in the amended form in which the Select Committee had recommended it to be passed.

Agreed to.

Sections I and II were passed as they stood.

Section III provided that application for enquiry into an alleged lunacy might be made "by any relative of the alleged Lunatic or by any Public Curator appointed under Act XX of 1841," &c.

Mr. CURRIE moved that the figures "XIX" be substituted for the figures "XX."

Agreed to.

Mr. HARINGTON moved that the words "or by the Government Pleader" be inserted after the figures "1841" and before the word "or" in the 5th line of the Section. He said that his reason for making this motion was that, if no part of the property of an alleged Lunatic consisted of land or of any interest in land, it would not be competent to any Public Officer, as the Section was now framed, to make the application contemplated therein unless a Public Curator should have been appointed, under the provisions of Act XIX of 1841, to the district in which the property was situate. No such Officer had as yet been appointed in the North-Western Provinces or he believed elsewhere, and he did not anticipate that the appointment would ever become general, from the difficulty which existed in regard to the remuneration of the persons who might be appointed without encroaching upon the Revenues of the State, to which the Government was not likely to agree, and he did not think that it could be expected to do so. The Section certainly allowed any relative of an alleged Lunatic to make the application mentioned in Section I, but there was nothing in the Bill to render the making of such application obligatory upon any person, however nearly related he might be to the supposed Lunatic; and it would not unfrequently happen that the relatives of the alleged Lunatic, from interested motives, would rather that the Civil Court should not interfere,in which case the object of the Bill, which was "to make better provision for the care of the estates of Lunatics not subject to the jurisdiction of Her Majesty's Courts of Judicature," would not be attained. According to the Bill for regulating proceedings in Lunacy in the Courts of Judicature established by Royal Charter, which had just passed through a Committee of the whole Council, the Advocate General was empowered to make the application for enquiry contemplated in that Bill; and his motion, if carried, would give the same power to the Government Pleaders in the Mofussil Courts as the Bill just referred to conferred upon the Advocate General in the Queen's Courts.

The Motion was carried, and the Section as amended was agreed to.

Sections IV to XXIII, with the Preamble and Title, were passed as they stood.

The Council having resumed its sitting, the Bill was reported.

LUNATIC ASYLUMS.

Mr. CURRIE moved that the Council resolve itself into a Committee on the Bill "relating to Lunatic Asylums"; and that the Committee be instructed to consider the Bill in the amended form in which it had been recommended by the Select Committee to be passed.

Agreed to.

Section I was passed as it stood.

Section II provided, among other things, that "the executive Government shall appoint for every Asylum not less than three visitors, one of whom at least shall be a Medical Officer."

Mr. PEACOCK said, the local Government had no power to create a new office without the sanction of the Governor General in Council. He therefore moved that the words "with the sanction of the Governor General of India in Council" be inserted after the word "Government" and before the word "shall" in this Section.

Mr. CURRIE said, it was not contemplated that the visitors should be paid officers.

Mr. PEACOCK observed that the Charter Act mentioned new offices as well as paid officers; and he referred to Section LIX of the Act (3 and 4 Wm. IV c. 85) which provided

> "that no Governor or Governor in Council shall have the power of creating any *new office*, or granting any salary, gratuity, or allowance, without the previous sanction of the Governor General of India in Council."

Mr. CURRIE said, it seemed to him that a more complete and effective sanction could not be given than by an Act of this Council. Other offices had been created by Acts of the Legislature without the provision for which his learned friend contended.

Mr. PEACOCK said that, for the purpose of making a law, the present Council was the proper Council, but in executive matters it had no power. It appeared to him that what was proposed was an executive act. The question was whether it was legislative or executive.

Mr. CURRIE said, that the clause in the Charter Act just quoted, restricted the powers of the local Governments, but did not affect the powers of this Council.

Mr. PEACOCK said he apprehended that this Council was not competent to confer any power contrary to the Charter Act.

The Chairman said, that the argument resembled that which would arise upon another Bill respecting the Royal Prerogative. No doubt, the Governor General in Council in his executive capacity might authorize the creation of a new office. But he (the Chairman) would be sorry to admit the principle that the Legislature had not also that power. Might not the Legislature do the same thing by force of its legislative power, which the Government in its executive capacity could do? Referring to the words of the Section under consideration, he noticed that it provided that "the executive Government *shall* appoint," &c. If the law directed this, it would be obligatory on, and not discretionary with, the Government to appoint. The Statute restricted the powers of the local Governments, but not of this Council. Had the words been "may appoint," he should have had no doubt of the propriety of introducing the word proposed.

MR. PEACOCK said, he did not think that any question could arise as to the legality of any acts of the visitors, and, therefore, he would not press his motion.

The Motion was accordingly by leave withdrawn.

Section III was passed as it stood.

Section IV provided for wandering and dangerous Lunatics being sent to the Magistrate, who was empowered, after personal examination with the assistance of a Medical Officer, to order such Lunatics being detained in a Lunatic Asylum—

> "Provided that, if any friend or relative of any *such Lunatic* shall undertake in writing to the satisfaction of the Magistrate that such Lunatic shall be properly taken care of, and shall be prevented from doing injury to himself or others, the Magistrate, instead of sending him to an Asylum, may make him over to the care of such friend or relative," &c.

MR. CURRIE said, this Section provided for two classes of Lunatics, namely, "Lunatics wandering at large," and "dangerous Lunatics." As the proviso had reference to the latter only, he proposed two amendments by which the words "Lunatic who is believed to be dangerous" were substituted for the words "such Lunatic."

The motions were severally carried.

Sections V and VI were passed as they stood.

Section VII provided as follows:—

> "Except as otherwise hereinbefore provided, no person shall be received into a Lunatic Asylum in any Presidency town or in any Station of the Straits Settlement without an order under the hand of some person in the form B in the schedule to this Act, together with such statement of particulars as is contained in the said form B, nor without the Medical Certificate containing the particulars in form A in the schedule to this Act," &c.

THE CHAIRMAN said, the form B in the Schedule contemplated that the Lunatic to be received into the Asylum might have been found Lunatic by inquisition or by enquiry directed by the Court. It occurred to him that it would hardly be necessary in such cases to require a further Medical Certificate, which might be attended with some expense. He therefore moved the insertion of the words, "unless such person has been found Lunatic by inquisition or under an enquiry directed by an order of one of the Courts of Judicature established by Royal Charter" between the word "nor" and the word "without."

Agreed to.

The Section was passed with a verbal amendment in a subsequent part, which was rendered necessary by the foregoing amendment.

Section VIII Clause 1 provided by whom application should be made in the Mofussil for an order for the reception of a Lunatic in an Asylum when the "Lunatic is *possessed of property* and a guardian for such Lunatic has been appointed by *order of the Court of Wards or of the Civil Court.*"

MR. PEACOCK wished to ask the Honorable Member for Bengal whether he intended to allow Lunatics in the Mofussil to be received into a Lunatic Asylum without an order or a certificate of a Medical man. It appeared to him that this Bill, as it stood, did not contain any provision to prevent a man from being confined as a Lunatic without such an order or certificate except in a Presidency Town, or where a guardian was appointed for a Lunatic possessed of property; but suppose he had no property, and some one wished to put him into a Lunatic Asylum without an order or a certificate of a Medical man. The object of the certificate was to provide against an improper confinement. A Medical certificate might not always be obtainable in the Mofussil, otherwise Section VII might well extend to all cases.

MR. CURRIE said, it would be found on a careful perusal of the whole Section, that the object of preventing improper confinement was more effectually secured in the Mofussil than in the Presidency Towns where any person, by signing an order and getting a certificate, might cause a person to be confined. It was not thought proper to give such a power in the Mofussil.

Clause 1, to which the learned Member referred, provided for the case of a person who had been found Lunatic by judicial enquiry. In all other cases, by Clause 2, on application being made to the Court, a like enquiry was to be instituted, and the Judge might then, if the Lunacy were established, make an order for the Lunatic's admission into an Asylum.

MR. PEACOCK said, Clause 2 authorized a relative to make an application to a Judge. But it did not contain any negative words or make it illegal for the keeper of a Lunatic Asylum to confine such a person without the order of a Judge; he proposed to add some words to this Clause to the effect that a Lunatic should not be confined without an order. As the Clause stood, it only authorized a relative to make an application; but suppose he did not apply, there were no negative words to the effect that without an order no person should be admitted into an Asylum.

MR. CURRIE said, it would be more convenient to introduce a new Section for this purpose towards the end of the Bill.

MR. PEACOCK said, he was quite willing that the amendment he proposed should be made by a separate Section, and he would make a motion to that effect in a subsequent part of the Bill.

MR. CURRIE then said, that the words "appointed by order of the Court of Wards or of the Civil Court" in Clause 1, were not quite correct. The order was usually made not by the Court of Wards, but by the Collector; and the Court of Wards afterwards confirmed it. He therefore moved the substitution for those words of the words "appointed by the Court of Wards, or the Collector, or by the Civil Court."

The Motion was carried, and the Section was passed after a similar amendment in Clause 2.

Sections IX to XIV were passed as they stood.

Section XV provided that

"the Magistrate or Commissioner of Police by whom any Lunatic has been sent to a Lunatic Asylum, if it appear to such Magistrate or Commissioner that such Lunatic has an estate applicable to his maintenance and more than sufficient to maintain his family, or that any person is legally bound to maintain and has the means of maintaining such Lunatic, may apply to the Chief *Court of Civil Judicature within the local jurisdiction of which the said Asylum may be,*" *&c.*

MR. CURRIE said, the proper Court, it seemed to him, would be that within whose jurisdiction the property might be situate or where the person bound to maintain the Lunatic resided. He therefore moved the substitution for the words in italics of the words,—

"Civil Court of original jurisdiction within the local jurisdiction of which the estate of the Lunatic may be situate or the person legally bound to maintain him may reside."

The Motion was carried, and the Section as amended was then agreed to.

Section XVI was passed as it stood.

MR. PEACOCK moved that the following new Section be introduced after Section XVI:—

"No person shall be received into a Lunatic Asylum in any place not within a Presidency Town except under an order of a Judge or Magistrate made in pursuance of this Act."

Agreed to.

Section XVII provided as follows:—

"Nothing contained in this Act shall affect the provisions of Act IV of 1849, entitled 'An Act for the safe custody of Criminal Lunatics.'"

MR. PEACOCK said that, at the request of Sir Arthur Buller, he moved that the words, "be taken to interfere with the power of any of the Courts of Judicature established by Royal Charter over any person found to be Lunatic by inquisition or under the provisions of Act of 1858, or with the rights of any Committee of the person or estate of such Lunatic or to" be inserted between the word "shall" and the word "affect."

The motion was carried and the Section as amended was agreed to.

Section XVIII, Forms A and B, and the Preamble and Title were passed as they stood.

The Council having resumed its sitting, the Bill was reported.

SIR JAMSETJEE JEEJEEBHOY'S ESTATE.

MR. LEGEYT moved (in pursuance of notice) that the Standing Orders be suspended to enable him to proceed with the Bill "for settling a sum of Company's Rupees Twenty-five lacs, Bengal Government Four per Centum Promissory Notes, and a Mansion-house and hereditaments called Mazagon Castle, in the Island of Bombay, the property of Sir Jamsetjee Jejeebhoy, Baronet, so as to accompany and support the Title and Dignity of a Baronet lately conferred on him by Her present Majesty, Queen Victoria, and for other purposes connected therewith."

In doing so, he said that this Bill was peculiarly of a private nature, and had been framed in accordance with the wishes of the parties who were immediately concerned, and who, as he had stated last Saturday, were very anxious that it should be passed without delay.

SIR JAMES OUTRAM seconded the motion.

MR. PEACOCK said, he did not object to the suspension of the Standing Orders for the purpose of going into Committee on the Bill; but he thought it would be better not to read the Bill a third time until it had been sent home for Her Majesty's sanction.

It was stated by Sir Richard Bethell and Mr. Leith in their opinion:—

"Further, as an Act creating a Corporation may be considered to affect the Prerogative of the Crown, we advise an application to be made, under Section XXVI of Statute 16 and 17 Victoria c. 95, for the previous sanction of the Crown to such intended Act. The required sanction must be signified under the sign manual of Her Majesty, countersigned by the President of the Board of Commissioners for the affairs of India for the time being."

His own opinion was that the Council was fully competent to pass an Act like this. The Council also had an opinion expressed some time ago by the Law Officers of the Crown, which had been referred to, that it had the power to create a corporation. But inasmuch as a later opinion had been given that the Council had no power to pass an Act for granting exclusive privileges to Inventors and the Council had been directed to repeal that Act because it affected the royal prerogative, and as the present question appeared to him to stand upon the same principle, he thought that it would be safer that the Bill should be sent home for sanction. What was the meaning of the words "affect the prerogative of the Crown?" Was it meant that the Legislature could not do that which the Crown by its prerogative might do, or that it could do nothing which affected or took away the prerogative? He thought that, if there was any doubt, such a Bill as this ought not to be left subject to it. He made these observations now, because he wished not to be understood as assenting to the third reading of the Bill, if it should be moved before the sanction of the Crown should be obtained.

MR. CURRIE thought that the Council had repeatedly exercised the power of creating bodies corporate. The Assam Company's Act of Incorporation had been lately passed; and more recently the Council had created Municipal bodies corporate.

THE VICE-PRESIDENT said, he thought that Sir Jamsetjee Jeejeebhoy would add one more to his many public services if he procured an authoritative solution of this question. Notwithstanding the high authority of those who determined that the Patents Act was beyond the powers of the Council, he confessed that he continued to be of a contrary opinion. He agreed with his Honorable and learned friend (Mr. Peacock) that, according to the true construction of the restriction on its powers, the Legislative Council was competent to pass Acts which merely did, by the exercise of Legislative power, that which the Crown, by the exercise of its prerogative, could also do. Such an act was the creation of a corporation. The Legislative Council had undoubtedly exercised this power in the case of the Bank of Bengal, of the Assam Company, and in other instances. This power was, he believed, supported by the opinions of very eminent lawyers which had been taken at home. Doubt was now thrown upon it by the very eminent lawyers under whose advice the Patents Act had been disallowed. The question was a very grave one. He thought it would be better that the Act should be sent home with such a representation as would lead to some final and authoritative decision, so that the Council might no longer be in the dark respecting its power in this respect.

With respect to the principle of the Bill, he desired to say a few words. If the

Bill were simply intended to carry into effect Sir Jamsetjee Jeejeebhoy's wishes and create a perpetual entail of his property, he (the Vice-President) should have felt some difficulty in acceding to the wishes even of one who had established such claims on the public gratitude. He made this observation to guard against the supposition that a precedent had been established for passing such Bills on the application of private individuals. He supported this Bill on the ground which had been stated in the Preamble, namely, that it was an arrangement between the Crown which conferred the title and the recipient of the title, that some such provision as this should be made for its support. This, he thought, justified the creation of what was known to the Continental Jurists as a "*majorat.*"

Mr. LeGeyt's motion was put and carried.

Mr LeGeyt then moved that the Council resolve itself into a Committee on the Bill.

Agreed to.

Sections I to XI were passed as they stood.

The Preamble having been read from the Chair—

Mr. Peacock said, as this was in the nature of a private Bill with respect to which Sir Jamsetjee Jeejeebhoy had obtained legal advice, he thought it would hardly be right, if any doubt existed, to depart from the course which had been recommended by his legal advisers, and which, it appeared, Sir Jamsetjee Jeejeebhoy had desired should be followed In the Bill prepared by Sir Richard Bethell and Mr. Leith, the following words occurred :—

> "And whereas such Act hath received the previous sanction of the Crown signified under the royal sign manual of Her Majesty, countersigned by the President of the Board of Commissioners for the affairs of India for the time being, under the Statute 16 and 17 Vic. c. 95. s. 26."

This showed that it was intended that Her Majesty's sanction should be obtained.

If the Council were not competent to pass the Bill, the settlement of the twenty-five lacs would be invalid, and he could scarcely think that even Sir Jamsetjee Jeejeebhoy would desire to act in opposition to the opinion of his own legal advisers. The words, as they stood, would not quite suit the present altered circumstances, as probably there was now no President of the Board of Commissioners ; but he proposed to insert words to the like effect which were taken from Act XVIII of 1855 "to remove doubts relating to the power to grant Pardons and Reprieves and Remissions of Punishments in India." He accordingly moved that the words

> "The sanction of Her Majesty to the passing of this Act having been previously obtained and signified in pursuance of an Act passed in the 17th year of the reign of Her said Majesty entitled 'An Act to provide for the Government of India,'"

be added to the Preamble.

Mr. LeGeyt said, after what had fallen from the Honorable and learned Member, he should be endangering the Bill if he insisted in carrying it through in its present state. He would not therefore oppose the motion. But he mentioned that he believed the sanction of the Crown had been applied for ; and if it meanwhile should arrive, he wished to know whether the Bill, having been sent home, could be proceeded with ?

Mr. Peacock said that, if the Bill were exactly as it stood before, the sanction would apply to it ; but the Bill had been, in some respects, altered. He thought that probably some general sanction would be given.

Mr. LeGeyt said, he had been given to understand that the application had been made, though the sanction had not yet been received. But it was expected and, he believed, was now on its way to Bombay. When it arrived, it would be a great disappointment to those concerned to find that the Bill could not be passed into law merely because it had been sent home for the royal sanction which had since been received in a slightly different form.

The Chairman said, he conceived that the sanction would, in all probability, be a sanction to pass a Bill. It was only one particular provision that required this sanction. Perhaps it might be in terms a sanction to create a corporation.

Mr. LeGeyt thought it would be better to send the Bill home without the proposed alteration and to get the

Queen's sanction to it in that form. On receipt of the sanction, words similar to those now proposed might be inserted hereafter if necessary.

Mr. PEACOCK said he was not sure that the Council would be justified in altering the Bill after Her Majesty had given her sanction to it.

The CHAIRMAN said that, when the facts were more correctly known, the Council would be able more clearly to see what course should be pursued. It was in every respect desirable that there should be no doubt as to the power of the Council to pass the Bill. The question might hereafter be raised in a Court of Law by one of the descendants of Sir Jamsetjee Jeejeebhoy and decided adversely to the entail.

Mr. PEACOCK said, the better plan would be to put the Bill in a proper form for going home, so that, if sanctioned by Her Majesty, it might be passed at once in that form. The Council pledged itself, he thought, to pass it in the form in which it was submitted for sanction. If a sanction should be sent out before the Bill should arrive at home, there would be no objection to the Honorable Member moving the third reading, and on that Motion it might be also re-committed. There could be no objection to the introduction of the words proposed by him.

The CHAIRMAN said, if the sanction should be different, though it might vary somewhat in form from the terms of the Bill, the Bill might be re-committed and its provisions made to correspond to the sanction sent.

Mr. PEACOCK'S motion was carried.

The Bill passed through Committee after a further verbal amendment in the Preamble, and a similar amendment in Section III and the Title.

The Council having resumed its sitting, the Bill was reported.

Mr. LeGEYT moved that Mr. Peacock be requested to take the Bill to the President in Council in order that it might be transmitted to England for the sanction of Her Majesty.

Agreed to.

INDIAN NAVY.

Mr. PEACOCK moved that Sir James Outram be requested to take the Bill "to amend Act XII of 1844 (for better securing the observance of an exact discipline in the Indian Navy)" to the President in Council in order that it might be submitted to the Governor General for his assent.

Agreed to.

The Council adjourned.

Saturday, September 4, 1858.

PRESENT:

The Hon. the Chief Justice, *Vice-President*, in the Chair.

Hon'ble H. Ricketts,	H. B. Harington, Esq.,
Hon'ble B. Peacock,	and
P. W. LeGeyt, Esq.,	H. Forbes, Esq.
E. Currie, Esq.,	

ESTATE OF THE LATE NABOB OF THE CARNATIC—SETTLEMENT OF ALLUVIAL LANDS (BENGAL)—AND FORT OF TANJORE.

The VICE-PRESIDENT read Messages informing the Legislative Council that the Governor General had assented to the Bill "to provide for the administration of the Estate and for the payment of the debts of the late Nabob of the Carnatic;" the Bill "to make further provision for the settlement of land gained by alluvion in the Presidency of Fort William in Bengal;" and the Bill "for bringing the Fort of Tanjore and the adjacent territory under the Laws of the Presidency of Fort Saint George."

PENSIONS.

The CLERK reported to the Council that he had received from the Home Department a copy of a communication from the Secretary to the Government of India with the Governor General on the policy of applying the provisions of the Government Order of 1st December 1857, which affect Military pensioners, to pensioners in the Civil Department, and to the holders of rent-free lands.

CIVIL PROCEDURE.

Mr. PEACOCK had the honor to present a Joint Report from the Select Committees on the Bills for simplifying the Procedure of the Courts of Civil Judicature of the East India Company.

He said, there were several Bills on the subject—one for the Lower Provinces of Bengal, another for the North-Western Provinces, a third for Madras, and a fourth for Bombay. The Bills were all separately published in the manner in which they had been prepared by Her Majesty's Commissioners. The Select Committees had sat together and had found it convenient and proper that they should prepare one Bill and present one Joint Report applicable to all the Presidencies.

ARTICLES OF WAR (NATIVE ARMY).

MR. PEACOCK begged to move the first reading of a Bill to amend Act XIX of 1847, which contained the Articles of War for the Native Army.

He said, there were several points which had been suggested by the Commander-in-Chief and the Governor General with reference to these Articles. He thought it might be necessary hereafter that the whole of the Articles should be revised, and an Act passed to amend them and to consolidate all the alterations which had recently been made. But this was a work which would require much consideration, and many Officers would have to be consulted. He now only proposed to amend the Articles in a few particulars, some of which had been suggested by the Commander-in-Chief and approved by the Governor General.

The first object was to give Commanding Officers larger powers than they now possessed. Under the law as it now stood, Commanding Officers had no power to dismiss or to reduce to the ranks any Native Officer or Soldier, except by the sentence of a Court Martial or by order of the Commander-in-Chief at the Presidency to which he might belong.

Article 2 provided—

"No Commissioned Officer shall be dismissed except by the sentence of a General Court Martial. No Non-Commissioned Officer or Soldier shall be discharged as a punishment except by the sentence of a Court Martial, or by order of the Commander-in-Chief at the Presidency to which he may belong. Every such dismissal or discharge shall include forfeiture of all claim to pension. Provided also, that the Governor General in Council in his Executive capacity, and the Governor in Council of any Presidency to which a Commissioned or Non-Commissioned Officer or Soldier may belong, shall have power to order his dismissal or discharge."

By Article 110—

"No Non-Commissioned Officer shall be reduced to the ranks but by the sentence of a Court Martial, or by order of the Commander-in-Chief of the Presidency to which the offender shall belong. Provided that no Non-Commissioned Officer shall be reduced to the ranks for any limited period; nor suspended from his rank, nor reduced from higher to a lower grade of Non-Commissioned Officer; nor sentenced to suffer Corporal Punishment, or imprisonment, without being first reduced to the ranks."

The proposal now was to allow Commanding Officers to dismiss or reduce to the ranks Native Non-Commissioned Officers, and to dismiss Soldiers, without the sentence of a Court Martial. He therefore proposed to repeal so much of Article 2 as required that no Non-Commissioned Officer or Soldier should be discharged except by the sentence of a Court Martial, and so much of Article 110 as required that no Non-Commissioned Officer or Soldier should be reduced to the ranks but by the sentence of a Court Martial, and also to authorize Commanding Officers to dismiss or reduce to the ranks.

The next amendment related to transportation. By the present law, whenever the punishment of transportation was awarded, it must be for life. The Council had recently before it a law which provided that, in any case where there might be a sentence of imprisonment for not less than three years, the prisoner might be transported. He now proposed, with reference to the Clauses which required that sentences of transportation must be for life, to authorize the Court, whenever it might think it necessary to award transportation for a limited period, to award transportation for any term not less than three years. There had been some sentences of Courts Martial which had acted upon the principle of awarding transportation for less than life. He apprehended, however, that these sentences were illegal. Though the sentences were beneficial to the prisoners, still they were not legal. He recollected a case in England, where a Court of Quarter Sessions sentenced a prisoner to transportation for life when the legal sentence was death.

The prisoner brought a writ of error, and the Court of Queen's Bench reversed the judgment on the ground that death was the legal sentence, and transportation for life could not be given, and discharged the prisoner. It would be very mischievous to act upon that principle in the cases to which he had adverted. He, therefore, proposed to render those sentences valid, and to provide that, whenever a prisoner had been sentenced to transportation for a less period than life for an offence punishable with transportation for life, the sentence should be as effectual and valid as if it had been for life. What he proposed was merely to render such sentences legal. It was an advantage to the prisoner to have received sentence of transportation for a term of years instead of for the whole term of his life. He (Mr. Peacock) had no doubt that, if a sentence passed by a Court were illegal, and the conviction were reversed, the prisoner might be tried again and receive the legal sentence. It was no hardship on him, therefore, to render legal the sentence of transportation for the term of years which had been passed upon him.

There was another class of cases in which prisoners had been sentenced to imprisonment with hard labor instead of simple imprisonment, and it had been stated by the Judge Advocate General that, in the opinion of the Commander-in-Chief, the only way in which the cases could be disposed of by him was to direct the prisoners' release from jail when they might be summarily discharged. The Commander-in-Chief proposed that, in order to guard against the ends of justice being defeated, it would be desirable, in all cases in which simple imprisonment might be awarded, that it should be lawful to add hard labor. The Governor General did not quite agree in this view of the Commander-in-Chief, but proposed that in a certain class of cases imprisonment with hard labor should be substituted for simple imprisonment; and His Lordship proposed that the Act should give validity to the sentences of imprisonment with hard labor which had been passed. There were some cases in which simple imprisonment or corporal punishment or both might be inflicted. In such cases there could be no objection, in his (Mr. Peacock's) opinion, to adding hard labor to imprisonment. It might be going too far if imprisonment with hard labor were authorized in all cases of imprisonment for purely Military offences. He proposed only to add it in certain classes of cases, which would include cases of absence without leave, and cases of the nature suggested by the Governor General. He thought it would be advisable to consider the expediency of providing that, whenever corporal punishment might be inflicted, imprisonment with hard labor might be given. It appeared to him that it was not more degrading to be punished by imprisonment with hard labor than by corporal punishment.

He also proposed to legalize the sentences in which imprisonment with hard labor had been given instead of simple imprisonment. In one case, a Soldier in one of the disarmed Regiments had been found in possession of arms which he had concealed. He was tried and found guilty and sentenced to imprisonment with hard labor. The Judge Advocate thought that the sentence was not legal. The Governor General had recommended that validity should be given to the sentences of imprisonment with hard labor which had been passed, and he (Mr. Peacock) saw no objection to the addition of a provision to this effect.

There was another Article of War (Article 112) which provided—

> "In case of light offences, a Commanding Officer may, without the intervention of a Court Martial, award extra drill, with or without pack, for a period not exceeding fifteen days; restriction to Barrack limits not exceeding fifteen days; confinement in the Quarter Guard or Defaulter's Room, not exceeding seven or eight days; removal from staff situations or acting appointments; or may order Soldiers to be employed in piling and unpiling shot and in cleaning accoutrements of men in Hospital; but none of these descriptions of punishment shall be awardable by sentence of a Court Martial. And a Commanding Officer may award solitary confinement not exceeding seven days."

It had been suggested by the Officiating Military Secretary that this Article should be amended, and that the Commanding Officer should not be restricted to awarding extra drill for fifteen days only. It was a matter of Military discipline, and he thought that so much of this Article as contained any restriction should be repealed, and that Commanding Officers should have power to order extra drill or any other Military duty without restriction, provided it was not contrary to any General Order of the Commander-in-Chief. He (Mr. Peacock) therefore proposed that the Article should be so modified. The Bill would be published and sent to the Commander-in-Chief. This provision had not been suggested by His Excellency but by the Officiating Military Secretary; and the Commander-in-Chief would have an opportunity of stating whether he saw any objection to it.

Another suggestion by the Judge Advocate General and recommended by the Commander-in-Chief was to make the Articles of War for the Native Army correspond in a certain particular with the Articles of War for the Queen's and Company's European Troops. By Article 147 of the Articles of War for the European Troops, it was provided that—

> "If any Soldier shall have been illegally absent from his duty for the space of two months, a Regimental Court of Enquiry of three Officers shall forthwith assemble and, having received proof on oath of the fact, declare such absence and the period thereof, and the Officer Commanding the Corps shall enter a record of such absence, and of the declaration of such Court of Enquiry thereon in the Regimental books: and if such Soldier should not afterwards surrender or be apprehended, such record shall have the legal effect of a conviction for desertion;—and if such Soldier should surrender or be apprehended after such record shall have been so entered, such record, or a copy thereof purporting to bear the signature of the Officer having the custody of the Regimental books, shall, on the trial of such Soldier on a charge for desertion, be admissible in evidence of the fact therein recorded, and on proof of the identity of the prisoner with the Soldier therein mentioned, he may be found guilty of desertion;—and if he be convicted, the sentence of any such Court shall be inserted in the Soldier's discharge;—provided nevertheless, that such trial may be dispensed with in any case in which it shall appear to the Commander-in-Chief that there are special circumstances to justify the exception."

There had been considerable difficulty in regard to Soldiers in the Native Army absent without leave. In some cases they had been found guilty of desertion. It had been thought that the Courts Martial had overstrained the evidence by finding such persons guilty of desertion when their offence was absence without leave. The object of the provision just quoted was to ascertain whether a Soldier was absent, the length of such absence, and whether he was absent without leave or not. The finding of the Court of Enquiry would be evidence in other Courts; and if a Soldier should be found at a distance from his own Regiment, it would be evidence of his absence without leave; and until he surrendered, it would be tantamount to a conviction for desertion. He (Mr. Peacock) had adopted that Section and introduced it into the present Bill.

There was another provision which the Judge Advocate General had recommended to be inserted in a General Order, but it was considered to be one requiring legislative sanction. The substance of it was that, if you prove a Soldier absent for two months, that absence should be *primâ facie* evidence of desertion, and would warrant a conviction for desertion, unless it appeared that he was detained in his village whether by sickness or other cause, or unless he could show clearly that he was not guilty of desertion. It also provided that, if a Soldier, to show that he was not guilty of desertion, should refer to a Civil or Military Officer of Government for the purpose of proving sickness or some good excuse for not returning to his duty, the Civil or Military Officer to whom the reference was made should certify to the fact, and that certificate should be made evidence in the Soldier's favor, and should have the same effect as if the Government Officer certifying was present. It appeared to him (Mr. Peacock) that this would be found very convenient. It could not be supposed that any Government Officer would give a wrong certificate, and he would be saved the inconvenience of being compelled to attend.

These were the principal alterations which he proposed to make; and he begged to move that the Bill be read a first time.

The Bill was read a first time.

PROCEEDINGS IN LUNACY (SUPREME COURTS).

MR. CURRIE moved that the Bill "to regulate proceedings in Lunacy in the Courts of Judicature established by Royal Charter" be now read a third time and passed.

The motion was carried, and the Bill read a third time.

CARE OF ESTATES OF LUNATICS NOT SUBJECT TO THE SUPREME COURTS.

MR. CURRIE moved that the Bill "to make better provision for the care of the Estates of Lunatics not subject to the jurisdiction of the Supreme Courts of Judicature" be now read a third time and passed.

The motion was carried, and the Bill read a third time.

LUNATIC ASYLUMS.

On the Order of the Day being read for the third reading of the Bill "relating to Lunatic Asylums"—

MR. CURRIE said, before moving the third reading of this Bill, he would ask leave to re-commit it for the purpose of making an amendment therein.

Agreed to.

MR. CURRIE said, the Section which required alteration was a new Section which stood after Section XVI. The Bill applied not merely to the several Presidencies but also to the Straits Settlement; and the Section as it stood, excepting only the Presidency Towns, would preventany one,without the order of a Judge or Magistrate made in pursuance of the Act, from being received into a Lunatic Asylum in any Station of the Straits Settlement. This was inconsistent with Section VII, which allowed a person to be received into a Lunatic Asylum in any Presidency Town or in any Station of the Straits Settlement under the order of an individual accompanied by the prescribed Medical Certificate.

Instead of altering the wording of this Section as it stood, he proposed to introduce the restrictive provision in Section VIII so as to make it correspond with Section VII, and to omit the new Section altogether. Section VII was for the Presidency Towns and Straits Settlement; and Section VIII was for places other than the Presidency Towns and Straits Settlement. He therefore moved that the words "when a Lunatic is possessed of property" after the word "Section" in the 3rd line of Clause 1, Section VIII be left out, and the following words substituted for them, namely:

"no person shall be received into a Lunatic Asylum, except as otherwise hereinbefore provided, without an order of the Civil Court.

Clause 2. When any person has been adjudged to be a Lunatic"—

The motion was carried, and the Section as amended was agreed to.

MR. CURRIE then moved that the new Section after Section XVI be left out.

Agreed to.

The Council having resumed its sitting, the Bill was reported.

MR. CURRIE moved that the Bill be read a third time and passed.

The motion was carried, and the Bill read a third time.

STAMP DUTIES (BENGAL).

MR. PEACOCK said that a very important alteration had been introduced in the Bill "to amend Regulation X. 1829 of the Bengal Code (for the collection of Stamp Duties)," after its publication, making it applicable to suits previously tried. He should therefore move that the Bill, as settled in Committee of the whole Council, be published for general information, and that it be re-considered after a month.

Agreed to.

CIVIL PROCEDURE.

MR. LEGEYT gave notice that he would, either on Saturday the 11th Instant or before the Council should resolve itself into a Committee on the Bill "for simplifying the Procedure of the Courts of Civil Judicature not established by Royal Charter," move that the Bill be republished for general information.

LIMITATION OF SUITS.

MR. CURRIE moved that a communication received by him from the Bengal Government, on the subject of amending Act XIII of 1848 (for limiting the time within which a suit may be brought to contest the awards of the Revenue authorities in the Presidency of Bengal), be laid upon the table and referred to the Select Committee on the Bill "to provide for the acquirement and extinction of rights by prescription, and for the limitation of suits."

Agreed to.

GUARDIANSHIP OF MINORS.

MR. CURRIE gave notice that he would, on Saturday next, move for a Committee of the whole Council on the Bill "for making better provision for the care of the persons and property of Minors in the Presidency of Fort William in Bengal."

PROCEEDINGS IN LUNACY (SUPREME COURTS); LUNATICS (MOFUSSIL); AND LUNATIC ASYLUMS.

MR. CURRIE moved that Mr. Ricketts be requested to take the Bill "to regulate proceedings in Lunacy in the Courts of Judicature established by Royal Charter;" the Bill "to make better provision for the care of the Estates of Lunatics not subject to the jurisdiction of the Supreme Courts of Judicature;" and the Bill "relating to Lunatic Asylums"—to the President in Council in order that they might be submitted to the Governor General for his assent.

Agreed to.

PENSIONS.

MR. PEACOCK moved that the communication from the Home Department reported this day be referred to a Select Committee consisting of the President of the Executive Council, Mr. LeGeyt, Mr. Currie, Mr. Harington, and the Mover.

Agreed to.

The Council adjouned.

Saturday, September 11, 1858.

PRESENT:

The Hon'ble the Chief Justice, *Vice-President*, in the Chair.

Hon. Lieut.-Genl. Sir J. Outram,	E. Currie, Esq.,
Hon. H. Ricketts.	Hon. Sir A.W. Buller,
Hon. B. Peacock,	H. B. Harington, Esq., and
P. W. LeGeyt, Esq.,	H. Forbes, Esq.

NABOB OF THE CARNATIC.

THE CLERK reported to the Council that he had received from the Foreign Department a copy of a Despatch from the Court of Directors to the Government of Madras on the subject of the affairs of the late Nabob of the Carnatic.

EMIGRATION TO ST. VINCENT.

THE CLERK also reported to the Council that he had received from the Home Department a copy of a Despatch from the Court of Directors and of its enclosures, regarding the proposed Emigration of Indian Laborers to the Colony of St. Vincent.

MR. PEACOCK moved that the above communication be printed.

Agreed to.

CONTINUANCE OF CERTAIN PRIVILEGES TO THE FAMILY, &c OF THE LATE NABOB OF THE CARNATIC.

MR. FORBES presented the Report of the Select Committee on the Bill "to continue certain privileges and immunities to the family and retainers of His late Highness the Nabob of the Carnatic."

EXCLUSIVE PRIVILEGES TO INVENTORS.

MR. PEACOCK presented the Report of the Select Committee on the Bill "for granting exclusive privileges to Inventors."

BREACHES OF CONTRACT BY WORKMEN, &c.

MR. CURRIE moved the first reading of a Bill "to provide for the punishment of Breaches of Contract by Artificers, Workmen, and Laborers in certain cases." He said, the preparation of this Bill was suggested to him by a Petition of the Calcutta Trade Association praying for a law to prevent Breaches of Contract by workmen and others, which was presented to the Council some weeks ago.

The Petitioners complained of the loss to which they were subjected by the fraudulent conduct of their workmen in wilfully failing to perform work for which they had received advances. The Petitioners represented the utter inefficacy of a civil action to afford redress in cases of this nature, and they prayed for a summary remedy by application to a Magistrate.

Now it seemed to him that taking

money in advance for the performance of any specified work, and then wilfully neglecting or refusing to perform the work for which payment had been received beforehand, was a fraud, the commission of which ought to be followed by penal consequences. He understood that all the work of the manufacturing Tradesmen in this City, Coachmakers, Cabinet-makers and others, was done by the piece—and he need not tell the Council that no piece-work was done in this country without an advance. It was the universal custom—and any manufacturer who attempted to break through it would find it impossible to obtain workmen. But if the workmen insisted on the preservation of this custom, it was but reasonable that their employers should be protected against its abuse.

He had seen some of the Petitioners on this subject, and he had a memorandum given to him shewing that five Firms alone had advances out-standing to the aggregate amount of one and a half lac. One Firm gave him a list of sums which they despaired of recovering, with the names of the defaulters, showing a loss within a year or two of Rupees 3,527.

He thought, therefore, that a case was made out for the interference of the Legislature, and he had accordingly prepared a Bill which proposed to authorize a Magistrate on complaint of the employer, and on proof of the receipt of an advance and wilful neglect on the part of the workman to fulfil his contract, to order the workman either to return the money advanced or to perform the work contracted for, as the employer should require, and, on default, to sentence him to imprisonment with hard labor for a term not exceeding three months. If the workmen were ordered to perform the work, security might also be required of him for its due performance.

These were the principal provisions of the Bill, which he had framed in great measure upon a Draft Act which was submitted by the Trades' Association to the Supreme Government in 1846. That Draft Act was intended to amend the then existing Calcutta Bye-laws bearing on the subject, and embraced a good deal more than the single offence which he had thought necessary to provide for in this Bill.

Mr. Currie

Some Members of Council would probably recollect that a somewhat similar measure was brought before the Council in 1855; and that the Select Committee on the Penal Code to whom it was referred, recommended that it should not be entertained. But the object of the Draft Act to which he alluded and which was sent up by the Madras Government, was not identical with that of the present Bill. It proposed to render liable to punishment any Clerk, workman, or servant who should desert his service without due warning or before the expiration of any specific period for which he had contracted to serve. Now it was scarcely necessary to remark that the mere abandonment of service without warning, by which the servant probably lost some arrear of wages due to him, was a very different offence from the wilful and fraudulent refusal to perform work for which payment had been made beforehand, and this latter only was the offence for which the present Bill was intended to provide.

It remained only to observe that the Bill, as he had drawn it, was limited in its operation to the Presidency Towns. Two or three considerations had influenced him in thus limiting it. The cry for relief came from a Presidency Town; the European manufacturers who were the persons that suffered from the practices which he had described resided chiefly in the Presidency Towns, and in Calcutta at least the Bill would merely restore to employers in a more effective shape the remedy which they formerly possessed under the old Calcutta Bye-laws which were repealed by the Police Act of 1852. The Mofussil law of Bengal, Regulation VII. 1819, punished the refusal to fulfil a contract of service by imprisonment, and this law he understood had been found to be effective for the prevention of fraud of the description alluded to. On the whole, therefore, he had thought it advisable to restrict the Bill to the Presidency Towns. If it should be thought that its provisions or some similar provisions might advantageously have general operation, the Select Committee on the Penal Code would doubtless consider the point in connexion with the Chapter on Criminal breaches of contract of service, but in the mean time there seemed to be no sufficient reason why the remedy, which had been so urgently called for by the manufacturers of Calcutta, should not be at once extended to the Presidency Towns.

The Bill was read a first time.

MUNICIPAL ASSESSMENT (SCINDE).

MR. LEGEYT moved the second reading of the Bill "for enabling improvements to be made in certain districts and towns in the Province of Scinde." In doing so, he begged to call the attention of the Honorable Members to Section III of the Bill. This Section was not in the original draft sent up by the Bombay Government. The Bill, as originally prepared, was so indefinitely worded that he could not venture, after what had passed on a former occasion, in March 1855, to bring it before the Council. In order, therefore, to establish the principle which this Section advocated, he had imported into the Bill some of the provisions of the Bombay Municipal Act and the Calcutta Suburbs Act. He had done so with the intention, if the Bill should be read a second time and referred to a Select Committee, that the authorities at Bombay and in Scinde might be able to propose such modifications of this Section as might be locally necessary, bearing in mind what seemed to be the established rule of the Council with regard to refusing to delegate powers of taxation to any other authority. The rest of the Bill was almost entirely as drawn up by Mr. Frere and approved of by the Bombay Government.

MR. RICKETTS said, he must say he had sundry misgivings connected with this Bill. He must allow that we were bound to receive with the greatest respect every thing that came with the authority of Mr. Frere, whose character stood equally high for ability and circumspection. The Bill also had the high authority of the Bombay Government. But still he did not see the necessity of flooding the people with such taxation as that now proposed.

We were told that the people of Scinde were altogether unlike any other people. He found it stated in paragraph 2 of Mr. Frere's letter of 13th May 1858, that the people of Scinde "are quite willing to pay any thing the Government might demand" (he wished we had fifty millions of such subjects on this side of India). In another place (paragraph 6) he observed that it was actually stated, with reference to the Land-tax and the Shop and Stall-tax, "that the facility with which these taxes are collected in Scinde is remarkable." It would therefore appear that the people of Scinde were unlike other people, for they delighted in being taxed. Supposing this to be the case, it might be very sweet, still we all know that even sweets too long indulged in became very bitter.

Section III of the Bill provided the Funds to be levied. It first proposed to increase the land-tax by five per cent.; and on this matter he should have a word to say presently. Then came a tax on houses not exceeding five per cent. on the annual rental—then, a tax on Imports and Exports, and besides them, such additional town-duties as might be considered advisable. This tax on Imports and Exports applied to cows, calves, buffaloes, goats, kids, and other animals; but he could not understand from the Bill in what case they were to be taxed, whether on entry into the town or district, or otherwise. As the Bill stood, if these animals were carried to one town, they would pay the tax; and so also if to another. Then the Bill would not only tax people's houses, but their houses before they became houses—their timber, chunam, and other materials for building houses. Then, as to rental, the houses to be taxed were not all the large houses in towns, but every hamlet; and there could be no rental because every man owned the house in which he lived. If a house-tax be imposed, he would recommend the Council to refer to the mode in which the tax was imposed at Akyab. There the tax was assessed, not on the rental, but on each square foot occupied by the house; and he found that this plan had worked exceedingly well in Akyab.

We were told that the people of Scinde were so very willing to be taxed. But he thought he found from the correspondence that they had shown some symptoms of impatience under taxation. The inhabitants of the principal towns and hamlets forming the Mehur division of the Shikarpore Collectorate presented a petition for the introduction of Act XXVI of 1850. They no sooner had it than they were very discontented with it, and applied to the authorities for the suspension of the Act almost as soon as it was carried into effect. Farther on, he found it represented in the correspondence that,

"instead of preparing the statistics and other information required by Government, the headmen were reported by the Deputy Magistrate to be raising all possible obstacles in the way of the Officials and to be urgent in their request that the provisions of the Act may not be carried out."

These objections, it was said, were only against the provisions of Act XXVI of 1850; but this Bill did not so much differ from that Act that we could suppose that those who were so discontented with it would be very well satisfied with the Bill.

Again, we were told "that there is still a strong inclination on the part of the inhabitants of the Mehur Deputy Collectorate for the more extended system of local taxation and Municipal management formerly proposed:" and that the purport of the petition presented in 1856 was to show that the people were only discontented with that Act, but were quite willing that such a provision as this should be introduced. It rather appeared to him that the people of the towns wished to get rid of the taxes imposed on them and throw them on the country people, and not that they were ready and willing that taxation of this nature should be imposed on them.

But suppose the Bill were allowed to go to a second reading, he would point out that the additional cess of five per cent. of the Land tax was in fact an increase of Land Revenue to the extent of five per cent. As things stood in Scinde, the limit was only what the people could pay. If additional Revenue were required, it should be demanded not for Municipal purposes but for Government. If it were given up, let it be given up as a "donation from Government," but let it be called by its right name.

It was stated that this donation would amount to six thousand two hundred and fifty Rupees per mensem. He found on calculation that that was in fact seventy-five thousand Rupees per annum, which was five per cent. on the fifteen lacs paid by Scinde.

Mr. Ricketts

He would suggest to his Honorable friend on his left (Mr. LeGeyt) that it might be advisable, instead of taxing all these separate articles and animals, to try and see if the Government would not give up a portion of the Land Revenue for Municipal purposes. It was stated that, in Scinde, the people were naturally so dirty in their habits, and their dwelling-houses so wretchedly constructed, that miasma and disease were generated with unusual rapidity, and that a widely spreading river-inundation gave rise to so many local forms of sickness and discomfort that the advantages of Municipal arrangement would be greater in Scinde than in any part of the world.

Now with such reasons as these, he thought it possible that Government might consent to give up five per cent. for Municipal purposes or, if not, to give two Rupees for every one that the people would contribute. If so, let us follow the example of the Punjab where heavy town duties were levied in every town without objection on the part of any class. These duties, with the addition from the Land Revenue, would yield a sum of not less than two hundred and twelve thousand Rupees for Municipal purposes, and this plan would be far preferable to imposing so many new taxes.

He would not say he would vote against his Honorable friend if he should attempt to carry the Bill to a second reading and to appoint a Select Committee. But he (Mr. Ricketts) thought it might be advisable to make enquiry whether the authorities at Bombay and Scinde were disposed to attend to the suggestions which he had made.

Mr. PEACOCK said, he must go farther than the Honorable Member opposite (Mr. Ricketts) in saying that he had misgivings with regard to this Bill. He had strong and grave objections to it, and he could not therefore vote in favor of the second reading.

His chief objection was to Section VI. Section I authorized the Chief Commissioner in Scinde to declare any district or town within the Province to be subject to the Act, and Section II provided that, when any town or district was declared so subject,

"the Chief Commissioner shall appoint a local Board, which shall be superintended by, and shall assist the Magistrate or any Officer subordinate to the Magistrate and especially appointed by him as Superintendent of the Board, in the Municipal administration of the district or town subject to the control hereinafter provided."

It was not stated of what kind of persons the Board was to consist: but having got that body, Section VI gave them certain powers. It provided that

"the Superintendent of the Municipal Board, acting with the consent of the Board, shall, under the general control of the Chief Commissioner, have the same powers for carrying out the provisions of this Act as are granted under Act XXVI of 1850 to the Commissioners appointed by that Act."

Now it appeared that the chief alteration of the law which this Bill proposed to make was to take away the necessity, which existed under Act XXVI of 1850, of showing that the Inhabitants were desirous of its introduction; and to limit the rates to the four kinds mentioned. It was expressly enacted by Section VI that the Superintendent might make any rules which the Commissioners were authorized to make under the Act of 1850. Now what were those rules? It appeared to him that they amounted in substance and in fact to laws, and this power we ought not to depute to a Magistrate or his Assistant even though he had the sanction of the Commissioner. To do so would be in effect to substitute the Magistrate or Assistant Magistrate for the Legislative Council, and the Commissioner for the Governor General who alone had the power to sanction laws.

The Bill did not say that the tax was to be paid by every one, but it said—

"The Funds required for the purposes of this Act shall be raised by any or all of the following methods as may be approved by the Chief Commissioner; and the Magisterial Officers in the district shall have the charge of collecting and disposing of these Funds with the advice and assistance of the Board."

It did not say upon whom the rates were to be imposed. That would be provided for by the rules. The rules to be prepared by the Commissioners under Act XXVI of 1850 were required to provide, among other things,

"the definition of the persons or property within the Town or Suburb to be taxed for raising the monies necessary for the purpose of this Act, whether by house assessment or town duties, or otherwise; the amount or rate of the taxes to be imposed; the manner of raising and collecting them, and ensuring the safety and due application of them when collected."

They were to lay down which of the landholders and which of the householders and which of the other inhabitants were to be taxed.

Then, although the amount of the rate was to be limited to five per cent., the rules as to the manner of recovery were to be left to the Magistrate. It would be in his power to say whether there should be an appeal against his decision or not. When the Legislative Council lately legislated for Municipal purposes, they laid down rules. They first passed an Act (XXV of 1856) by which general rules were fixed. Having passed that Act, they then passed the particular Acts for each Town. It might be that Act XXV of 1856 (or some of the rules which it prescribed) were not applicable to Scinde. But the authorities in Scinde might prepare such rules as they might deem fit, and submit them to the Legislative Council, who would pass them, if reasonable.

Section IV of Act XXV of 1856 defined how the annual value was to be ascertained, and then it provided for appeals. But this Bill defined nothing. Here it was left to the Magistrate's discretion whether he would levy the whole or any of the taxes. If he liked, he might impose a land-tax, a house-tax, an import and export-tax on animals and other articles, and a tax on carriages and horses. It appeared to him (Mr. Peacock) that he should not have these powers.

Then again with regard to the collection of the rates, there was a rule laid down, but he thought it a very objectionable one. The provisions of Act II of 1839, which were applied to the non-payment of fines imposed by way of punishment for offences, were made applicable to the non-payment of taxes. Accordingly, if a man could not pay a tax and no distress could be found, he might be imprisoned for two months if the amount did not exceed fifty Rupees, and for four months if it did not exceed one hundred Rupees, and for six months in any other case. The late Municipal Acts referred to by him provided for this. They gave no power to imprison;

they merely authorized distress and sale. The Bombay Municipal Act laid down no such power, then why should such a law be passed for Scinde?

Then let us see what the taxes were. The Honorable Member opposite (Mr. Ricketts) had made some very important observations on the first, the land-tax.

Then there was "a tax on houses not exceeding five per cent. on the annual rental." Act XXVI of 1850, which authorized a similar tax, could not be imposed without the consent of the inhabitants. He recollected an instance in which that Act had been put in force with the consent of two-thirds of the inhabitants, and afterwards the feeling against it was so strong that the Government withdrew it. At Vellore a very zealous Magistrate got more than two-thirds of the inhabitants to consent to the introduction of the Act. On the introduction of the Act, every man shut up his shop, and the feeling was so strong against it that the Government thought it right to withdraw it. The Court of Directors had made some very strong remarks on the subject of Act XXVI of 1850, even when introduced with the consent of the inhabitants. But it was proposed that this Act might be introduced without any consent of the inhabitants. The Court of Directors, speaking of Act XXVI of 1850, said—

"We are most anxious that the Act should not be put in force in any place where the bulk of the population has not, after full acquaintance with its object, declared unequivocally in its favor."

Again they said—

"It should be considered whether the measure should be persevered in if after experience the feeling against it be found to continue unabated."

If such were the directions which the Government had received with regard to the introduction of Act XXVI of 1850, were we to authorize the introduction of a more stringent Bill in Scinde against the wish of the Inhabitants? It was said in the annexures that the people were against the introduction of the Act of 1850. They were not better off under this than under the other law. Under this Bill there was to be, besides a land-tax and a house-tax, a tax on imports and exports, with the addition of such other town duties as might be considered advisable; what they were we did not know. That was to be left to the Magistrate or his Assistant with the consent of the Board under the general control of the Commissioner. The Honorable Member opposite (Mr. Ricketts) had asked where the tax on imports and exports was to be paid. It was difficult to say. According to the Bill the tax proposed was not merely a town duty, but a transit duty. Transit duties had been generally abolished. Whether intended or not, the proposed tax was nothing less than a transit duty, for it was to be charged on articles imported into or exported from the town or district. The Bill did not even say that it was to be levied on the inhabitants only or upon articles intended for consumption within the town or district. The Honorable Member for Bombay had had the Bombay Municipal Act before him, which provided that

"duties at the rates specified in the Schedule annexed to the Act, shall be levied in respect of the several things therein mentioned when imported from any place into the Town of Bombay *and intended for consumption or use therein.*"

It was only in respect of those articles which were imported into the town for consumption therein that the inhabitants of Bombay were to pay that tax: there was no export duty. But by this Bill there might be not only import duties but duties upon exports. If a man living in a district had a cow and sent it to a market out of the district for sale, he would have to pay export duty; or if he sent it out to graze, as was suggested by the Honorable Member on his right (Sir Arthur Buller), he would be compelled to pay a tax. He might have to sell it in a district which had not been made subject to this duty. In such case he could not compete with persons who were not subject to similar duties. It was not a fair or just tax, and yet it was left to the Magistrate or his Assistant with the consent of the Board to impose it if he pleased.

He (Mr. Peacock) apprehended that town duties on articles might, in some cases, be a legitimate tax in this country, but export duty had never been proposed even for Bombay where the inhabitants were much richer than the people in Scinde. At Bombay only articles imported for consumption were subjected to import duty, but the unfortunate people in Scinde were to be subjected to pay duty on all things which might be imported, and export duty also. He did not know if this was intended, but he spoke of the Bill as it stood. The Bill also used the general words "with the addition of such other town duties as may be considered advisable," thus leaving it to the Magistrate to impose any other duties. Now, if a tax were to be imposed, he (Mr. Peacock) thought that the Legislative Council was the authority to determine whether it was a proper tax. There might be peculiarities in Scinde which did not exist elsewhere. If so, let those who were entrusted with the administration of Scinde prepare rules adapted to such peculiarities and submit them to the Council. They must do this at some time before the law could come into operation. But why postpone to a future day what must be done at some time or another? Let the authorities in Scinde propose what taxes they pleased and make what rules they pleased, but let them be sent to the Legislative Council for approval before they become obligatory. If there were any special reasons applicable to Scinde, let them be pointed out. This, he thought, was the duty of those who had the administration of a Province. They were not vested with any legislative power and the Council were not justified in deputing such powers to them. He would read an Extract from an excellent Despatch from the Honorable Court of Directors on this subject. He had cited it once before when a somewhat similar measure was proposed by the Government of Bengal. The Bill on that occasion was thrown out, only one vote having been given in support of it. The Despatch to which he referred was sent out soon after the passing of the Charter Act of 1833, almost immediately after the powers of legislation under which this Council acted were conferred, and it was addressed to the Government of India. Referring to the Governor General in Council, they said:—

"Heretofore you have been invested with extensive powers of superintendence over the legislation of the subordinate Presidencies. But as these Presidencies have had the right of legislating for themselves, your superintendence has been exercised only on rare and particular occasions. Now, their legislative functions, with a reserve for certain excepted cases, are to be subordinate to those of the Supreme Government. The whole responsibility rests upon you; and every law which has an especial reference to the local interests of any of those Presidencies, and every general law in respect of its particular bearing and operation on such local interests, ought to be pre-considered by you with as deep and as anxious attention as if it affected only the welfare of the Presidency in which you reside. You may indeed, as we have already observed, receive from the subordinate Presidencies suggestions or drafts of laws, and these it may frequently be expedient to invite.

"But in no instance will this exempt you from the obligation of so considering every provision of the law as to make it really your own, the offspring of your own minds, after obtaining an adequate knowledge of the case. We say this, knowing as we do how easily the power of delegating a duty degenerates into the habit of neglecting it; and dreading lest, at some future period, under the form of offering projects of law, the subordinate Presidencies should be left to legislate for themselves with as little aid from the wisdom of the Supreme Government as when the power of legislating was ostensibly in their own hands.

"There are two sets of occasions, on one of which the suggestions of the subordinate Presidencies are more, on the other, less necessary.

"When provision is to be made for local peculiarities, the information of local observers is of peculiar importance, and when the law wholly or mainly relates to such peculiarities, the first draft of it will be most advantageously prepared by those who are best acquainted with them.

"The greater number of laws, however, are not of this description. They relate to general matters in which local peculiarities have subordinate concern, and in which, therefore, such peculiarities need not otherwise be consulted than by prescribing some modification of the general provisions of the law in applying them to particular cases."

It appeared to him that we were now asked to give the Magistrate the power of making rules which were in effect laws. It was in fact giving the local authorities power to make a law. As he had said before, the Magistrate must make the rules at some time or another. There could be no more difficulty in making them now than at any future period, and in his opinion they ought to be made and submitted to the Legislative Council who were the proper authority to see if they should be passed into a law.

Again, the disposal of the rates was to be left entirely to the Superintendent and the Board. The approval of the Chief

Commissioner was requisite, but still it was left to the local authorities. There was considerable discussion in the Council on a former occasion, and had it not been for that discussion, a very large sum would have been applied for lighting Calcutta with gas; and cleansing and draining would probably have been neglected for want of funds. According to this Bill, the whole might be applied to any purpose. Cleansing might be more important than lighting in some districts, wells and tanks in others, embankments in others, and market-places in others. No distinction was made between houses and lands. In England, by the Health of Towns Act a very great distinction was made in this matter. By this Bill, land in a district might be taxed five per cent. for lighting a town in the same district, and houses might be taxed for works of irrigation from which they might not receive any benefit. All property in the same district might be taxed, and the taxes applied indiscriminately, according to the discretion of the Magistrate and the Board, to any of the purposes mentioned in the Act. One of the purposes was education. If the inhabitants were to be taxed for education against their will, they might wish to have their own religion taught in their Schools. They might say let us have our own Schools and let our religion be taught there. Would the Government superintend a School of that sort? This was a very important matter. If there was any peculiar reason for taxing the people of Scinde for education, let the reasons be assigned. In Bengal the inhabitants were not taxed for education, but the Government gave up a certain portion of the general Revenues for the purpose of education, and they laid down rules for its application. The people in Scinde contributed to the general Revenues of the country, and there appeared to be no sufficient reason for taxing the people in Scinde separately for the purposes of education when the inhabitants of Calcutta and other places were not obliged to do so. If it was right, let such a tax be imposed generally throughout the whole country. But it was a grave and serious question for consideration, whether a Municipality should be compelled to pay rates for the purposes of education. The Bill was silent as to the persons to be educated. Were they to be the children of the inhabitants of the district? All this was to be left to the Magistrate and the Board.

Then there was some thing bordering on a Poor Law—"the erection and maintenance of Asylums for the support of those who are mentally or physically incapacitated from supporting themselves." Who were to be introduced into these Asylums—any wandering lunatic found in the district? Such persons should be supported at the expense of the State and not by the district. The people in Scinde were no more bound to provide for such persons than the people of Calcutta. According to the English Poor Laws (God forbid that they should be applied here), the parish had to pay for its own parishioners.

In conclusion, he observed that, whatever rules were prepared should be submitted to the Council, who, if they saw no objection, would pass them as part of the law. But he could not consent to depute to others the power of making these rules.

For these reasons he should vote against the second reading.

Mr. Currie said, the Bill was open to some but not, he thought, to all the objections taken by the Honorable and learned Member opposite (Mr. Peacock). There was also much force in the remark made by the Honorable Member on his right (Mr. Ricketts) as to the percentage on the Government Revenue. But these were matters which a Select Committee might deal with. His own objection to the Bill arose from what had been stated by the Honorable Mover, that the taxation was imaginary and not that which had been recommended by the Chief Commissioner in Scinde; that it was merely something which the Honorable Member had thought it necessary to specify to avoid submitting an indefinite proposition for taxation.

He therefore thought it hardly advisable to entertain the Bill in its present shape; and he would suggest that it be withdrawn, and that another Bill be introduced in its stead, containing the real items of taxation which might be considered proper to be imposed, and stating definitely what powers were intended to be conferred on the Board in lieu of those so indefinitely mentioned in Section VI of the present Bill.

For these reasons he should feel some difficulty in voting for the second reading; he should be better pleased if the Bill were withdrawn.

MR. LEGEYT said, he was prepared for this Bill encountering some objection and opposition; and, as he had stated on the first reading, he had doubts himself as to the propriety of introducing it in the form in which it was sent from Bombay. He had therefore felt forced to introduce the details of taxation in Section III in order to obviate the manifest objection to the Draft Act on account of the indefinite powers of taxation which it conferred. They were not, as had been said, wholly imaginary, because the draft contained provision for raising the following funds:—

1st. The application of an additional cess not exceeding 5 per cent. of the land-tax, to be levied in the same manner as the land-tax.

2nd. A tax on shops or stalls.

3rd. A tax on houses.

4th. A tax on Imports and Exports or such other town duties as might be considered advisable.

5th. Tolls or taxes on carriages or beasts of burden.

6th. Such items of public Revenue as might be granted to the Municipality by Government for the purposes of this Act.

He would not go through the objections in detail, because it would be necessary for that purpose to make a reference to Scinde. But he should be glad to say a few words with regard to what fell from his Honorable friend on the right (Mr. Ricketts) regarding the land-tax.

If we were to wait until the Government came forward and said, "Here is five per cent. of the land-tax; take it and spend it on Municipal improvement," the time devoted to this subject would be wasted, and we might just as well be totally without Municipal improvement. The Government of this country for the last thirty or forty years had done nothing at all towards Municipal improvement to warrant the expectation that such would be the result, if application were now made to them for such an addition as was referred to. The records of Government teemed with most positive and absolute refusals to expend for Municipal purposes the general Revenues of the country. They had declared over and over again that what was spent on local purposes must be raised by local taxation. We were at one time better off in the Bombay Presidency in the shape of Municipal taxes. We had the Moortuffa and Vera cesses which were no doubt intended to provide for Municipal purposes, but which, before our Government had taken possession of the Peshwa's territories, had fallen into the general Revenue. These had been abolished in 1844, and ever since then attempts had been made in the Presidency of Bombay to establish Municipalities. Act XXVI of 1850 had been put in force in many towns, but did not make satisfactory progress. It had had a fair trial in Scinde, and Mr. Frere had declared his opinion to that effect and had called it "a gigantic imposture."

Some blame seemed to have been thrown upon Mr. Frere, which he did not deserve. It would appear as if he had stated that the people in Scinde delighted in taxation, and yet they were averse from it. Now this was not a fair way of interpreting Mr. Frere's statement. What Mr. Frere meant to say was, as he (Mr. LeGeyt) understood it, that the town people objected to be taxed when the country people were untaxed. They said,—"If you tax us, tax them too." They would not come forward and say, "Tax us in this particular or that particular way," but were willing to try what might be suggested to them; and in this respect they were by no means singular. In the Districts in which he had had local experience about Municipal taxes, they did not object to pay a tax; but their answer to him was, "Don't ask us: let the Government say what is required, and we will try to comply." If asked what tax they would pay, one section of the people would perhaps suggest something that would not fall on them—another section would suggest another, and this was the sort of difficulty which had been experienced wherever Act XXVI of 1850 had been tried. He could understand how they had proceeded in Scinde. The men of influence got the people not to object to the introduction of the law, and the silence of a vast number was interpreted into consent. No absolute objection had been made, but when touched by the tax, there came mutterings of discontent which would equally happen in the case of every new tax. Moreover they were apt to doubt whether the money raised would really be spent among them for local purposes: such had been the general feeling among the people, and he believed that all the authorities in the Bombay Presidency had come to the conclusion that, unless the Government was empowered to declare that local taxation should be levied whenever the local authorities had made out a case for the necessity of local improvements, any progress in that direction was out of the question. As far as he had understood, and he hoped he was right, the principle of local taxation was not disputed by the Council. That being so, he would gladly act on the suggestion of his Honorable friend on his left (Mr. Currie) and withdraw the Bill as it now stood, and introduce another Bill with the same principles of local taxation. With this understanding, he would ask leave to withdraw this Bill.

The Bill was accordingly withdrawn.

GUARDIANSHIP OF MINORS (BENGAL).

MR. CURRIE moved that the Council resolve itself into a Committee on the Bill "for making better provision for the care of the persons and property of Minors in the Presidency of Fort William in Bengal;" and that the Committee be instructed to consider the Bill in the amended form in which the Select Committee had recommended it to be passed.

Agreed to.

Sections I to III were severally passed as they stood.

Section IV provided as follows:—

"Any *near* relative or *creditor* of a Minor in respect of whose property such certificate has not been granted or, if the property consist in whole or in part of land or any *interest in land*, the Collector of the district may apply to the Civil Court to appoint a fit person to take charge of the property and person of such Minor."

MR. CURRIE proposed to omit the word "near" before relative, and to substitute the word "friend" for the word "creditor" in the beginning of the Section.

Agreed to.

MR. PEACOCK proposed to insert the words "not paying Revenue to Government" after the words "interest in land." Section II said that the Civil Court should not have power over estates paying Revenue to Government, and taken under the protection of the Court of Wards. Was the Collector to interfere in cases where the land paid Revenue to Government but was not in fact under the charge of the Court of Wards?

MR. CURRIE said, that was intended. Section II excepted only the estates of proprietors, "*who have been or shall be* taken under the protection of the Court of Wards." If the Court of Wards could not or did not interfere, the Civil Court would have jurisdiction; and if it were desirable that the Minor's property should be provided for, application might be made to the Civil Court. It was optional with the Court of Wards to interfere or not, as it thought proper.

MR. PEACOCK asked, would that Court have the power to take charge, after other provision had been made?

THE CHAIRMAN said, he apprehended that the intention was as the Honorable Member for Bengal had stated. The Collector was only to apply to the Court in those cases in which there was land and that land paying Revenue to Government. It was left general, no doubt, but what had the Collector to do with the matter except in respect of land paying Government Revenue? There would be no conflict of authority, because the Court of Wards was in fact the Commissioner who acted invariably through the Collector.

MR. CURRIE said, it was but a very small portion of the land paying Revenue to Government in the possession of Minors that could come under the jurisdiction of the Court of Wards. The Court of Wards had jurisdiction only where the Minor was the sole proprietor, or where all the proprietors were Minors. If one or more of the sharers were Minors, and there were other qualified sharers, the property could not be taken charge of by the Court of Wards. This Section was intended to provide for all cases, whether the land were land paying Revenue immediately to Government or not. It was not imperative on the Collector to apply, but he might apply if he thought it proper to do so from his

Mr. LeGeyt

knowledge of the circumstances of the proprietors. It appeared to him (Mr. Currie) that the Section was right as it stood.

MR. PEACOCK would not press his motion.

The Section, as before amended, was then agreed to.

MR. CURRIE moved the introduction of the following new Section after Section IV:—

> "If the property be situate in more than one district, any such application as aforesaid shall be made to the Civil Court of the district in which the Minor has his residence."

Agreed to.

Section V provided for the Court, on application, making a summary enquiry and granting Certificate to the executor of the deceased or the near relative of the Minor.

After the insertion, on Mr. Currie's motion, of words similar to those in the Curator's Act, providing for notice of application, and fixing a day for the hearing—

MR. PEACOCK said, it appeared to him that this Section gave too great power to executors. He thought there was a wide difference between the appointment of an executor and of a Guardian for a child. Now, the executor may be a very proper person, or he may be a very improper person to act as Guardian. But, according to this Section, the executor must be appointed Guardian whether he was or not a fit person for that office. If the child had a large independent estate over which the father had no control, and the father appointed an executor for his own estate, it was not proper that he should have the guardianship. This would give the executor a preference over a relative or friend. If there were an executor, then, whether it was right or not that heshould have the guardianship, the Court would appoint him guardian; but if a relative or friend, then the Court was required to enquire whether or not he was a fit person. The executor might be a very unfit person for the office. He might be a very proper person to manage the estate, but he might be a very improper person to take charge of the child. The child might have an estate wholly unconnected with the father's; or the father might not have wished the executor to be entrusted with his child's education. Let the executor be appointed guardian if there was no objection, or if nominated guardian by the father. He (Mr. Peacock) thought that the Section must be altered or perhaps omitted altogether.

MR. CURRIE said, the fact was that in this country wills were very rare. He admitted, however, that the Section was open to the objection which had been taken to it.

MR. PEACOCK said, suppose the father was converted to Christianity, but the child was not converted, would he be put under the guardianship of the father's executor?

THE CHAIRMAN did not agree that wills were so unfrequent an occurrence. In and about Calcutta, he thought, they were on the increase. Often the *factum* of the will was open to suspicion; but even if there was no doubt thrown upon the *factum*, as far as his experience of Hindoo executors went, it was desirable that there should be some person to see that they did their duty. The guardian would be this person. Therefore he could not assent to the general proposition that, because a man was executor, he should also be the guardian of the child. Even with reference to the property, he thought it would be better to leave the discretion of the appointment of a guardian with the Court, controlling it only in cases, where the father by will appointed certain persons *eo nomine* to be guardians.

The further consideration of this Section was postponed, on the motion of Mr. Currie.

Section VI provided that, if a Minor's estate consisted in whole or in part of land, the Court might call upon the Collector for a report on the character and qualification of a relative desirous or willing to be entrusted with the charge of the Minor's property and person.

MR. PEACOCK said, he did not know that the Collector would have a better opportunity of judging of the character and qualification of the relative, because the Minor's estate consisted in whole or in part of land. He did not see how the Collector would know more of the relative because the father had land. It seemed to him a *non-sequitur.* He proposed to allow the Court *in any case* to call for a report from the Collector.

MR. CURRIE said, he did not think it a *non-sequitur.* The Section had reference specially to the proprietary villages of the North-Western Provinces. In Bengal, the Collector knew little more of the Zemindars than the Judge. In the North-Western Provinces, every proprietor was well known to the Collector or to his local officer the Tehsildar, and the case was very different.

MR. HARINGTON said, the Act did not make it obligatory, but only permissive, where the Court saw it necessary or thought it desirable, to call for a report from the Collector, who had opportunities of knowing the character and qualification of the proprietors.

MR. PEACOCK said, he did not object to the Court having power to refer to the Collector, but he only objected to the power being confined to a particular case. He would leave it to the Court's discretion to exercise this power in all cases. By this Section, the Judge could not ask the Collector's opinion unless where the testator left land. He moved to omit the words "when the estate of the Minor consists in whole or in part of land or any interest in land."

MR. CURRIE objected to the proposed amendment, because then the Section would involve a palpable *non-sequitur.* The reason why the Collector might be called upon was that, where there was land, the Collector would have some knowledge of the parties. If the Minor was a proprietor of land, his relatives, it might be presumed, would be proprietors likewise.

MR. HARINGTON said that the Collector had an interest generally in *all* lands in his District.

THE CHAIRMAN said, it seemed to him that, if the amendment was carried, it would leave the power to the Court in every case where it was now given, and it would give it power in other cases. No doubt the Collector in the North-Western Provinces might often be a very proper person to guide the discretion of the Courts as to the character and qualifications of a relative. But he agreed with the Honorable and learned Member (Mr. Peacock) that he would not necessarily be able to do this because the deceased person, or the Minor as his heir, was possessed of land. It might be that, if the estate of the proposed Guardian consisted of land, the Collector would be able to report on his qualifications to the Judge. For these reasons, he would support the amendment.

The question having been put, the Council divided:—

Ayes, 5.	*Noes*, 4.
Mr. Forbes.	Mr. Harington.
Sir Arthur Buller.	Mr. Currie.
Mr. Peacock.	Mr. LeGeyt.
Sir James Outram.	Mr. Ricketts.
The Chairman.	

So the Motion was carried.

MR. CURRIE moved that the words "or Magistrate" be added after Collector. The mention of land having been struck out, there was no longer any special reason for a reference to the Collector.

The Motion was agreed to and the Section passed.

The consideration of Section VII was postponed on the Motion of Mr. Currie.

Section VIII was passed after verbal amendments.

Section IX was passed as it stood.

MR. CURRIE moved that the words "and of the duties to be performed by the Manager and the Guardian respectively, so far as the same may be applicable," be inserted after the word "appointments" in the 10th line of Section X.

The motion was agreed to and the Section passed.

MR. CURRIE moved the introduction of the following new Section after Section X namely:—

"In all enquiries held by the Civil Court under this Act, the Court may make such order as to the payment of costs by the person on whose application the enquiry was made, or out of the estate of the Minor or otherwise, as it may think proper."

Agreed to.

Section XI was passed after verbal amendments.

Section XII was passed as it stood.

Section XIII was passed after verbal amendments.

Sections XIV to XIX were passed as they stood.

Section XX provided as follows:—

Mr. Peacock

"The Public Curator and every other Administrator to whom a Certificate shall have been granted under Section VIII, shall be entitled to receive such Commission on the sums received and disbursed by him, or such other allowance, to be paid out of the Minor's Estate, as the Civil Court shall think fit."

MR. PEACOCK said, he thought there should be a limit to the amount of Commission. The Administrator General's Act and the Curator's Act allowed five per cent. Perhaps the words "not exceeding five per centum" had better be inserted after the word "Commission."

MR. CURRIE said, that a limit could not conveniently be fixed, because in some cases, where a person was appointed to take charge of a single estate, five per cent. might not be sufficient. The Section had no application, if the relative of a Minor had the administration, but only to the Public Curator or an Administrator to whom a certificate was granted under Section VIII.

THE CHAIRMAN said, the principle of commission had been abolished in the case of Executors or Administrator properly so called. Why adopt it for the Mofussil?

MR. HARINGTON said that, in the Mofussil, if persons refused to undertake the office of administrator, there was not, as in the Presidency Town, any officer to discharge the duty.

The Motion was carried, and the Section as amended was agreed to.

Section XXI was passed as it stood.

Mr. CURRIE moved the introduction of the following new Section:—

"For the purposes of this Act, every person shall be held to be a Minor, who has not attained the age of eighteen years."

In doing so, he said that eighteen years was the limit of minority fixed by the Court of Wards' Regulation and might also be properly adopted in this Bill.

THE CHAIRMAN said, he entertained some doubts as to whether it was advisable, as it were by a side-wind, to make a change in the law of the country. As it now stood, eighteen was by construction the time when Mohamedans attained majority. It was left in the Hedaya very vague and dependent on the physical and mental development of each person; but, he believed, the Courts had generally adopted eighteen as the age. In the case of Hindoos, it was equally clear that sixteen was the age of majority, except in the case of a Minor entitled to a Zemindary when the Court of Wards' Regulation made eighteen the age when he should be emancipated and considered to have attained majority. But he apprehended that any contract executed not relating to the Zemindary would be valid: eighteen might be a better age than sixteen; but, if altered, it would be better to do so by a law directed to that end than by a Section in a law relating to Guardians. The Section had not been published, and had therefore not elicited observations. He thought it would be better not to introduce this Section.

MR. CURRIE said that the proposed introduction of this Section was his main reason for circulating a notice of amendments. The Bill, as originally prepared, had no such provision. It was introduced at the recommendation of a Hindoo gentleman who thought it was desirable to fix the limit of Minority and who considered that the present Hindoo limit was too short. He had suggested that the limit fixed by the Court of Wards' Regulation should be adopted. He (Mr. Currie) was quite sensible of the force of the objection stated by the learned Chief Justice; and he felt that, if the Section were introduced, it would be necessary to republish the Bill. The question was an important one, and he suggested that, as the Bill would again come under consideration next Saturday, the consideration of this Section be postponed.

The further consideration of this Section was postponed accordingly.

MR. CURRIE moved that the words "It shall be lawful for the Civil Court to refer to any of the subordinate Courts of the District, any investigation or enquiry which the Civil Court is required or authorized to hold under this Act, and" at the beginning of Section XXII be left out.

The motion was agreed to and the Section passed.

Section XXIII was passed after verbal amendments.

The Preamble and Title were severally passed as they stood.

The Council resumed its sitting.

CIVIL PROCEDURE.

MR. LEGEYT said that, on further consideration, he would not make the motion (which stood in the Orders of the Day) for the republication of the Bill "for simplifying the Procedure of the Courts of Civil Judicature not established by Royal Charter."

MR. PEACOCK gave notice that he would, on Saturday the 18th Instant, move for a Committee of the whole Council on the above Bill. He thought that some limit should be fixed up to which the consideration of the Bill in Committee should proceed next Saturday. His idea was that it should be divided into three parts, and he was about to propose as far as "appearance of the parties." But his Honorable friend on his right (Mr. Harington) suggested as far as "Written Statements" which was only two pages further on. There were so many points to be considered in the Bill that he thought Honorable Members would prefer to have notice as to how far the consideration of the Bill would probably extend.

After some conversation, it was agreed that the Committee of the whole Council should not proceed further than the head "Written Statements" on Saturday.

EXCLUSIVE PRIVILEGES TO INVENTORS.

MR. PEACOCK also gave notice that he would, on Saturday next, move for a Committee of the whole Council on the Bill "for granting exclusive privileges to inventors."

The Council adjourned at half-past one o'clock on the motion of Mr. Ricketts.

Saturday, September 18, 1858.

PRESENT:

The Hon'ble the Chief Justice, *Vice-President*, in the Chair;

Hon. Lieut.-Genl. Sir J. Outram,	E. Currie, Esq.,
Hon'ble H. Ricketts,	Hon. Sir A. W. Buller,
Hon'ble B. Peacock,	H. B. Harington, Esq., and
P. W. LeGeyt, Esq.,	H. Forbes, Esq.

INDIAN NAVY.

THE VICE-PRESIDENT read a message informing the Legislative Council that the Governor-General had assented to the Bill "to amend Act XII of 1844 (for better securing the observance of an exact discipline in the Indian Navy)."

ARTICLES OF WAR (NATIVE ARMY).

MR. PEACOCK moved the second reading of the Bill "to amend Act XIX of 1847 (Articles of War for the government of the Native Officers and Soldiers in the Military Service of the East India Company)."

The motion was carried, and the Bill read a second time.

GUARDIANSHIP OF MINORS (BENGAL).

On the Order of the Day for the adjourned Committee of the whole Council on the Bill "for making better provision for the care of the persons and property of Minors in the Presidency of Fort William in Bengal" being read, the Council resolved itself into a Committee for the further consideration of the Bill.

The postponed Section V provided as follows:—

"When application shall have been made to the Civil Court either by a person claiming a right to have charge of the property of a Minor, or by any relative or friend of a Minor, or by the Collector, the Court shall issue notice of the application, and fix a day for hearing the same. On the day so fixed, or as soon after as may be convenient, the Court shall enquire summarily into the circumstances, and *if it shall appear that the deceased has left a will, and that the executor or executors named therein is or are willing to undertake the trust, or, when the deceased has not left a will or the executor or executors named in any will is or are unwilling to undertake the trust, if any near relative of the Minor shall desire or be willing to administer to the estate, and the Court shall be of opinion that such relative is a fit person to be entrusted with the charge of the property and person of the Minor, the Court shall grant a certificate to such executor or executors or near relative as the case may be.*"

MR. CURRIE said, the objection taken to this Section, he believed, was that it appeared to make it imperative on the Court to make the executor guardian of the minor when the deceased left a will and the executor named therein was willing to undertake the trust. It was not so expressed, but certainly the Section might be so understood. He had, therefore, prepared two amended Sections in which he had separated the case of an executor from the case of a relative who might be willing and qualified to take charge of the estate. It was to be borne in mind that under Section III every person claiming a right to have charge of property in trust for a minor under a will or other deed, or by reason of nearness of kin or otherwise, might apply to the Civil Court for a certificate of administration, without which he would not be competent to institute or defend any suit connected with the estate of which he claimed the charge, or to give any legal discharge to the debtors of such estate. He would now propose that all the words in italics be omitted from the Section, and the following substituted for them: —

"pass such order as it may deem proper.

"If it shall appear that the deceased has left a will, and that the executor named therein is willing to undertake the trust, the Court shall grant a certificate to such executor. If no guardian is named in the will, or if the guardian named in the will is unwilling to act, the Court may appoint the executor, or any relative or friend of the minor to be guardian of the person of the minor.

"When the deceased has not left a will, or the executor named in any will is unwilling to undertake the trust, if any near relative of the minor shall desire or be willing to administer to the estate, and the Court shall be of opinion that such relative is a fit person to be entrusted with the charge of the same, the Court shall grant a certificate to such near relative, and may also appoint such near relative or any other relative or friend to be guardian of the person of the minor."

MR. PEACOCK said, he thought it very desirable that this matter should be postponed until next Saturday. He was not sure that he clearly understood the bearing of the proposed amendments; it would be desirable to print and circulate them.

MR. CURRIE said, he had no objection to postpone the amendments with a view to bringing them forward next Saturday. The matter having been discussed last Saturday, and the point to be provided for, as he thought, settled, he had not thought it necessary to print the amendments. He had shown them to the Honorable Member for the North-Western Provinces who had concurred in them.

The consideration of this Section and of Section VII was again postponed.

The new Section after Section XXI provided as follows :—

"For the purposes of this Act, every person shall be held to be a minor who has not attained the age of eighteen years."

MR. CURRIE said, this Section also had been reserved for further consideration. He had given his best attention to this subject, and the conclusion at which he had arrived was that the Section should form part of the Bill, otherwise there would be two periods of minority for different sorts of property.

The law as it stood was as follows. By the Court of Wards Regulation (X of 1793) the term of minority for proprietors of estates paying Revenue to Government was fixed at fifteen years. But it was soon seen that this was too low a limit, and it was extended in the same year to eighteen years by Section II Regulation XXVI, Section III of which declared that the rule was to be considered to extend to proprietors of joint undivided estates. Therefore, with respect not only to landed property paying Revenue to Government which was under the Court of Wards, but also to all landed property directly paying Revenue to Government, the age of minority was extended to eighteen. Except in the case of sole proprietors of estates, the Court of Wards did not interfere. Regulation I. 1800 gave the Civil Courts jurisdiction in the case of minor proprietors in joint undivided estates. By the present Bill the Civil Courts would as heretofore have jurisdiction in such cases, and also with respect to other property. It therefore embraced two descriptions of property, namely, land paying Revenue to Government for which the period of minority was eighteen years, and all other property, whether moveable or immoveable, for which the period would be the common law term of sixteen years.

In Bombay it did not appear that there were any distinct provisions regarding minors. But in the Regulation relating to the limitation of suits

(Regulation V. 1827) it was provided in Section VII Clause 3 that in cases of minority "no limitation shall bar the recovery of a claim sued for within six years of the minor attaining the age of eighteen years." Therefore it was to be inferred that in Bombay the recognized period of minority was eighteen years.

In Madras, however, the case was different. In 1804 a Regulation (V) was passed establishing a Court of Wards. That Regulation, unlike the Bengal Regulation, was not limited to proprietors of whole estates paying Revenue to Government and subject to the Court of Wards. The Preamble of the Regulation was general and spoke of the injuries which might accrue to persons who were incapacitated from taking charge of their property, without specifying any particular description of property. And Section IV was to the following effect :—

"Where minors may succeed to inheritable property, they shall not, in any case, be competent to take charge of or to administer their own affairs during the period of their minority; and for the better understanding thereof, the duration of minority shall, without exception, continue until the completion of the eighteenth year of age.

That Section, therefore, was as general in its terms as it could be; and that it was not applicable only to Court of Wards' property was evident from Sections XX and XXI of the same Regulation. Section XX gave jurisdiction to the Civil Court in the case of minor proprietors in joint undivided estates. Section XXI contained rules for the conduct of guardians appointed either by the Court of Wards or the Civil Court, and Clause 5 of the Section provided that "the duration of the office of guardian shall not continue longer than the eighteenth year of the age of the wards being minors." Those Sections (XX and XXI) were extended by Regulation X. 1831 to property of all descriptions, real and personal; so that in Madras there could be no doubt that, with respect to all property, the proprietor was disqualified until he attained the age of eighteen. He (Mr. Currie) could see no reason why the same rule should not be adopted here.

The learned Chairman was reported to have said last Saturday :—

"In the case of Hindoos, it was equally clear that sixteen was the age of majority, except in the case of a minor entitled to a Zemindary when the Court of Wards' Regulation made eighteen the age when he should be emancipated and considered to have attained majority. But he apprehended that any contract executed not relating to the Zemindary would be valid."

It seemed to him (Mr. Currie) that this could hardly be the case as to a proprietor under the Court of Wards, for the law expressly gave the manager appointed by the Court of Wards the charge of all the property of a minor, real and personal, and authorized him to continue in charge until the minor attained the age of eighteen. Possibly it might apply with regard to sharers in joint undivided estates, and if so, when the minor sharer in a joint estate was possessed also of personal property, the term of his minority would be different in respect of the different descriptions of property. He thought it inadvisable that such a state of things should exist and equally so that there should be any doubt on such a subject. Therefore it was in every way desirable that the Section should be allowed to stand. Its effect was merely to assimilate the law in Bengal to the law as it actually existed at Madras.

THE CHAIRMAN said that his objection was not so much, according to his personal opinion, to an extension of the age of minority to eighteen instead of sixteen, as it was to the particular provision and the mode in which the thing proposed, whatever were its merits, was proposed to be done. The Clause submitted to the Council was this. (He here read it.) If the Common-Law age of minority was sixteen, the Statutory alteration in that age proposed by this Section would be only for the purposes of this Act. He conceived that there might be many minors who would not necessarily be brought under this Act, and that it would be extending, what he had always regarded as very inconvenient, the existence in the same country and presidency of two different ages of minority depending on the accident whether the minor had property within the jurisdiction of the Court of Wards or not. If the Section stood, then a minor under the Act would not be of age until eighteen. But he might not be brought under it until he was seventeen,

Mr. Currie

and what would be the effect of all contracts executed between sixteen and seventeen. He had not looked closely or with attention at the Regulations on this subject since the question was mooted. But, according to his general recollection of them, it seemed to him very questionable whether, supposing any one of those minors who were brought for their education into Calcutta, being within the ages of sixteen and eighteen years, were to run up a bill at Messrs. Allan and Hayes and were afterwards sued for the recovery of the amount in the Supreme Court, he would not be held in that Court and for the purposes of that action responsible. That there should be any doubt upon such a matter was a great inconvenience. As to the age of sixteen, he had been reminded that Sir H. Seton had expressed a strong opinion that it was too early. If persons of that age were considered of too tender years and of too immature understanding to be pronounced *sui juris*, the open and reasonable way of dealing with the question was to bring in a Bill providing that, for all purposes and in all Courts and jurisdictions, minority should terminate at eighteen. Possibly such a Bill might be favorably received by the Hindoo community; possibly not. That seemed to be the mode of dealing with the question rather than inserting in that Bill a Clause which might make it incumbent on a person dealing with one who was between the age of sixteen and eighteen to enquire whether he had been brought under this Act or not.

MR. HARINGTON said, that to the observations which had been made by the Honorable Member for Bengal in support of the new Section which he wished to introduce into the part of the Bill now before the Committee, he would only add that, as respected the full age of Infants, he believed the English law prescribed different periods for different purposes.

THE CHAIRMAN said that, by the Scotch law which was founded on the Civil law, it was so; but that the English law, according to which a person attaining the age of fourteen might have made a will of personalty, had been repealed.

MR. HARINGTON continued. He was not aware that the English law to which he referred had been repealed; but according to the Scotch law, then, there were different periods. At fourteen a male might appoint a guardian or dispose of his personal property by Will, and at seventeen he might be an Executor. The Bengal Regulations, for wise purposes, had declared that persons brought under the superintendence of the Court of Wards should continue subject to that superintendence until they had completed their eighteenth year, though according to the Hindoo and Mahomedan Laws they had attained their majority two years before; and, as noticed by the Honorable Member for Bengal, the Bombay Regulations contained a similar provision in respect to the limitation of actions; while the Madras Code went even farther. In providing, therefore, a different period of minority for the purposes of the Bill before the Committee from that fixed by the existing law, they were introducing no new principle. He need not tell the Council that the object of the special laws to which he had referred was to protect young persons who, though of age according to the law of the land, had nevertheless scarcely sufficient experience and discretion to enable them to manage their own affairs with prudence, and who, if left to themselves, would fall an easy prey to the numerous greedy attendants and companions by whom the native gentry, and particularly young men of property in this country, were almost invariably surrounded, and who frequently caused the ruin of youths of this class before they had arrived at a period of life when they could be safely entrusted with the management of their property. The new Section proposed by the Honorable Member for Bengal was framed with the same object, and as it would merely assimilate the Bill before the Committee, as respected the persons who would be affected by it, to what was already the law in regard to minors subject to the jurisdiction of the Court of Wards, and, as already noticed by him, would introduce no new principle, he should vote in favor of the Section. With regard to what had fallen from the Honorable and learned Chairman on the subject of shop-debts incurred by young persons while under the protection of guardians appointed under this Bill, notwithstanding that they were already of full age according to the Hindoo or Mahomedan Law, he did not understand that the Bill would exempt such persons from liability on account of any purchases made by them of the nature referred to. He observed that under the Bill it would not be competent to the Civil Courts to act of their own motion, and, when applied to, their action would be confined to the care of the property and person of the minor in whose behalf the application was made.

MR. PEACOCK thought it very inconvenient that a Clause of this sort should be added almost at the last moment. It altered entirely the law as to majority. If introduced, it would certainly be necessary to republish the Bill, because the Bill had been published as a Bill "for making better provision for the care of the persons and property of Minors, Lunatics, and other disqualified persons, in the Presidency of Fort William in Bengal." It was now proposed to alter the whole principle of this law which he observed would apply to all minors. A guardian would have the care of the person even of a married woman up to eighteen. Was it intended that a Hindoo or Mahomedan married lady under the age of eighteen was to be held a Minor, and was her guardian to have the charge of her person and maintenance? The preceding Section (XXI) applied only to male Minors. A guardian was not bound by this Bill to educate a female minor, but still the charge of her person might be taken out of her husband's hands. If it were necessary to alter the law as to the age at which persons were to cease to be Minors, it would be better to do so by a separate Bill applicable to that particular subject. Then, whenever a person was a Minor under that law, he would fall within the provisions of the present Bill. For these reasons, he (Mr. Peacock) should vote against the introduction of the proposed Section.

MR. CURRIE said, he thought it very desirable that a general Act should be passed fixing the age of majority for all purposes and all places. But that did not appear a sufficient reason for striking out the Section from this Bill which would be incomplete without it. Property under the Court of Wards was not the only property in respect of which eighteen years was the legal term of the proprietor's minority. All landed property paying Revenue direct to Government was in that predicament. If the Bill passed without this provision, there would be different periods of minority according to the different kinds of property. In passing this Section, the Council would only do what had been done many years ago with regard to Minor proprietors in the Madras Presidency. He would therefore press his motion.

THE CHAIRMAN, before putting the question, begged to say, by way of explanation, that he would have had less objection to what was proposed, if it laid down definite rules that all infants should be capable of certain acts at one age, and of certain others at another age; but the Clause left the class to which the infant would belong, and therefore his powers, open to doubt. It was uncertain whether he would or would not be brought within this law.

MR. CURRIE said, he had omitted to mention that he would republish the Bill if the Section passed.

The question being put, the Council divided.

Ayes, 6.	*Noes*, 3.
Mr. Forbes.	Sir Arthur Buller.
Mr. Harington.	Mr. Peacock.
Mr. Currie.	The Chairman.
Mr. LeGeyt.	
Mr. Ricketts.	
Sir James Outram.	

So the Section was carried.

THE CHAIRMAN wished to ask to what places the Bill would apply. He understood it was not intended to have operation in the Presidency town. It was in terms a Bill "for making better provision for the care of the persons and property of minors in the Presidency of Fort William in Bengal;" and he thought that, to limit its operation to the Mofussil, a Clause should be inserted to the effect that the Act was not to affect the powers of the Courts established by Royal Charter over the persons or properties of minors. As the further consideration of the Bill was postponed, perhaps something to that effect might be introduced in the manner most convenient to the Honorable mover of the Bill.

MR. CURRIE signified his assent.

The Council resumed its sitting.

CIVIL PROCEDURE.

The Order of the Day for a Committee of the whole Council on the Bill "for simplifying the Procedure of the Courts of Civil Judicature not established by Royal Charter" being read—

MR. PEACOCK moved that the consideration of this Bill be postponed until after the consideration of the other Bills.

Agreed to.

EXCLUSIVE PRIVILEGES TO INVENTORS.

MR. PEACOCK then moved that the Council resolve itself into a Committee on the Bill "for granting exclusive privileges to Inventors;" and that the Committee be instructed to consider the Bill in the amended form in which the Select Committee had recommended it to be passed.

Agreed to.

Sections I to XIII were passed as they stood.

Section XIV provided in what cases a petitioner might apply for leave to file an amended specification.

MR. PEACOCK said, this was a new Section which was proposed to be introduced by the Select Committee. It only authorized an application to the Governor-General in Council to amend a specification in which through inadvertence or mistake there was a mis-statement. That Clause was not in the original Bill; but he recollected a case which had occurred under the former Act,and in which an inventor was advised that his specification was not sufficient. He presented a petition to Government for leave to file an amended one. But the Governor-General in Council had no power to authorize him to do so, and he was told that in any action which might be brought against him or which he might bring against any party, he would have an opportunity of applying to the Court for an amendment. He (Mr Peacock) thought it would be well to permit such an amendment also on a petition to Government, where there was an error arising from mistake or inadvertence, otherwise the exclusive privilege might be wholly lost; for if the inventor applied for a new exclusive privilege, it might not be valid, because the invention would then have become publicly known. The Clause at the end of the new Section provided that such amendment should not extend or enlarge any exclusive privilege before acquired; the inventor could therefore add nothing to his original claim in respect of any subsequent improvement, because that would be enlarging the invention for which the exclusive privilege had been obtained. He mentioned this because a letter had been recently received by the Clerk of the Council, in which a suggestion that a Section to that effect should be introduced into the Bill, was made. The discovery of a new use for an old invention could not be deemed a new invention in respect of which an exclusive privilege could be granted.

He then referred to the last Clause of the Section, which provided as follows :—

> "An amended specification filed under the provisions of this Act shall, except as to suits or proceedings relating to the exclusive privilege, have the same effect as if it had been the specification first filed, provided that nothing contained in an amended specification shall extend or enlarge any exclusive privilege before acquired."

The meaning of that Clause was that the effect of the amended specification would be the same as that of the original specification, except as to suits or proceedings relating to the exclusive privilege "which shall be pending at the time of the filing of such specification."

But, as the Section was worded, it was not very clear. He would therefore move that those words be introduced after the word "privilege."

Agreed to.

Section XV provided among other things that no person was entitled to an exclusive privilege "*if the petition contains any wilful or fraudulent mis-statement.*"

MR. CURRIE suggested that this Section should provide against wilful or fraudulent mis-statements in specifications also.

MR. PEACOCK referred to Section XXIV, and moved that the following words taken from that Section be substituted for the words in italics :—

> "If the original or any subsequent petition relating to the invention or the original or any amended specification contain a wilful or fraudulent mis-statement."

Agreed to.

Sections XVI to XVIII were passed as they stood.

Section XIX declared that an invention not publicly used or known in the United Kingdom or in India, before the application for leave to file a specification, should be deemed a new invention within the meaning of this Act.

Mr. CURRIE said, he was glad to see that the Select Committee by whom the Bill had been prepared had ultimately come to the conclusion that an importer of an invention should have no exclusive privilege. But in this Section the words "actual inventor" occurred. Every inventor within the meaning of the Bill, as it now stood, was an actual inventor. In the Interpretation Section of the former Act it was provided that "the word 'inventor,' when not used in conjunction with the word 'actual,' shall include the importer of an invention not publicly known or used in India." That Clause was of course omitted from the present Bill. Then came the following Clause:

> "The words 'inventor' and 'actual inventor' shall include the executors, administrators, or assigns of an inventor or actual inventor as the case may be."

This last Clause was still in the Bill, and would seem to indicate that the "inventor" and "actual inventor" were not identical. He therefore moved to omit the word "actual" wherever it occurred before the word "inventor" in this Section.

Mr. PEACOCK agreed that the word ought to be omitted.

The motion was carried, and the Section as amended was agreed to.

Section XX was passed after a similar verbal amendment

Sections XXI and XXII were passed as they stood.

Section XXIII provided as follows:—

> "No such action shall be defended upon the ground of any defect or insufficiency of the specification of the invention, nor upon the ground *that the petition contains any wilful or fraudulent mis statement*; nor shall any such action be defended upon the ground that the plaintiff was not the inventor, unless the defendant shall show that he is the actual inventor or has obtained a right from him to use the invention either wholly or in part. Any such action may be defended upon the ground that the invention was not new, if the person making the defence, or some persons through whom he claims, shall, before the date of the petition for leave to file the specification, have publicly or actually used in India or in some part of the United Kingdom, the invention, or that part of it of which the infringement shall be proved; but not otherwise."

Mr. CURRIE asked whether the Section should not make mention of all the contingencies mentioned in Section XV. It seemed to him that the words omitted from the Section relative to a misdescription of the invention should be retained, and also that it should provide that the plea of the invention not being useful, should not be a ground of defence.

Mr. PEACOCK said, the Bill drew a distinction between a defence to an action and an application to set aside an exclusive privilege. The principle was to allow an action to be defended only on grounds specially applicable to the defendant which did not extend equally to the public; if the defendant were not peculiarly interested, there should be an application to set aside the exclusive privilege. In England the inventor bringing an action would be the plaintiff; on the other hand in proceeding by *scire facias* for a repeal of the Letters Patent, he would be a defendant. According to his experience the plaintiff in an action for infringement generally succeeded; while, in the other proceeding, the person moving to set aside the patent, being the plaintiff and having the last word with the jury, generally prevailed. Cases had occurred in which the patentee as plaintiff had succeeded, and afterwards, as defendant in the proceeding to repeal the Letters Patent, had been unsuccessful. As to the present question, which was whether a misdescription of the invention in the petition should be a ground for defending the action, it seemed to him that this was a matter in which the defendant had no special ground of defence beyond those which extended equally to the public in general, and that it ought not to be set up as a bar to an action; it was rather a ground for applying to get rid of the whole exclusive privilege. He referred to Section XXXI, which had been altered, and which provided that a mis-statement in the petition not wilful or fraudulent should not defeat the exclusive privilege.

THE CHAIRMAN said, the object of the Select Committee was to limit the matters of defence in the action. Certain grounds of objection were to be asserted in a particular form so that the whole public might get the benefit of a decision respecting them.

MR. CURRIE said, suppose the defendant in the action pleaded that there was a misdescription of the invention in the petition (those words having now been omitted from the Section), would not his plea be a good defence?

MR. PEACOCK replied that it would not. According to English law any misdescription, such as a wrong title to the invention, would avoid the patent, and this was a cause of much expense and litigation to patentees. If a defendant in an action showed that the petition contained a mis-statement, the action failed; but the next day the patentee might bring actions against other persons. A fraudulent misdescription was a proper ground for applying to set aside the exclusive privilege, but it ought not to be put forward as a defence to an action, and a misdescription not fraudulent should, in no case, be a defence.

Utility was not mentioned in this Section. An invention might be useless in the shape for which an exclusive privilege had been obtained, still the privilege until set aside would exclude others from using it. He thought this should be introduced here; it ought not to be a ground of defence in the action, but should be the subject of an application to set aside the privilege.

After some conversation, MR. PEACOCK moved that the word "petition" in the 6th line of the Section be omitted, and the following words substituted for it:—'original or any subsequent petition relating to the invention, or the original or any amended specification."

Agreed to.

MR. PEACOCK moved the introduction of the words "nor upon the ground that the invention is not useful."

Agreed to.

Sections XXIV to XXX were passed as they stood.

Section XXXI provided as follows:—

"An exclusive privilege shall not be defeated upon the ground that, *the petition contains a mis-statement*, unless such *mis-statement* was *wilful* or fraudulent."

MR. CURRIE enquired whether, with reference to the provisions of Section XV and Section XXIV, this Section was necessary.

THE CHAIRMAN referred to the new Section XIV, and asked why the word "petition" only was mentioned in Section XXXI.

MR. PEACOCK said, that a mis-statement in the specification, if it caused the invention not to be properly described, would be injurious to the public, inasmuch as they would not derive from it that knowledge to which they were entitled as the condition upon which the exclusive privilege was to be obtained, and at the expiration of the exclusive privilege they would not be able to avail themselves of the invention. The misdescription in the specification therefore, though not fraudulent, might be equally injurious to the public. That was not the case with the petition, for the public acquired their knowledge from the specification; a misdescription in the specification should therefore be a ground for setting aside the exclusive privilege, unless it could be amended. As to Section XXXI it was a negative Section. It declared that advantage was not to be taken of a mis-statement in a petition, *unless* it was wilful or fraudulent. Strictly, perhaps, the Section was not required, but it would be better to leave it, as Sections XXIV and XXV were merely affirmative. The object was to prevent an inventor from being defeated by a technicality. The inventor ought not to be told, when the petition contained some accidental mis-statement—"Your invention is not claimed for this, but for something different, therefore your petition misdescribes it"

The case supposed (he could not at that moment think of an illustration) was where an inventor in his petition did not quite describe what he had invented. He ought not to lose his privilege because what he asked for by his petition did not quite correspond with what he subsequently described in the specification.

The Section was agreed to.

Sections XXXII to XXXVII were passed as they stood.

Section XXXVIII was the Interpretation Clause, and provided among other things that "the word 'India' shall mean the *British Territories in India.*"

Mr. PEACOCK moved that the following words be substituted for the words in italics:—

"territories which are or may become vested in Her Majesty by the Statute 21 and 22 Victoria c. 106, entitled 'An Act for the better Government of India.'"

The motion was carried, and the Section as amended agreed to.

The Schedule, Preamble, and Title were passed as they stood.

The Council having resumed its sitting, the Bill was reported.

CONTINUANCE OF CERTAIN PRIVILEGES TO THE FAMILY, &c, OF THE LATE NABOB OF THE CARNATIC.

Mr FORBES moved that the Council resolve itself into a Committee on the Bill "to continue certain privileges and immunities to the family and retainers of His late Highness the Nabob of the Carnatic;" and that the Committee be instructed to consider the Bill in the amended form in which the Select Committee had recommended it to be passed.

Agreed to.

The Bill passed through Committee without amendment, and was reported.

CIVIL PROCEDURE.

Mr. PEACOCK moved that the Council resolve itself into a Committee on the Bill "for simplifying the Procedure of the Courts of Civil Judicature not established by Royal Charter;" and that the Committee be instructed to consider the Bill in the amended form in which the Select Committee had recommended it to be passed.

Agreed to.

Sections I to III of Chapter I were passed as they stood.

Section IV related to the jurisdiction of the Civil Courts.

The Chairman would ask, whether the words "work for gain" were intended to mean a personal work for gain and distinct from carrying on business?

Mr. HARINGTON said that such was the intention of the words.

Mr. PEACOCK said, perhaps the word "personally" should be introduced to show that a constructive working was not intended; and he made a motion to that effect.

Agreed to.

Section V was passed after a verbal amendment.

Sections VI to XI were passed as they stood.

Chapter II Section I provided that parties might appear in person or by recognized agent or by pleader.

Sir ARTHUR BULLER asked, whether it might not possibly be very inconvenient in some of the smaller Courts to compel a person resident within the jurisdiction (an Indigo Planter for instance) to appear in person or by a pleader. He could not appoint a recognized agent for he was actually residing within the jurisdiction. According to Section XXV, however, besides recognized agents, any person residing within the jurisdiction might be appointed an agent to receive service of summonses and other process. He wished to know if it would not be advisable to allow persons so situated the power to appoint agents other than these recognized agents.

Mr. HARINGTON said that, formerly, parties were permitted to employ agents, not being authorized pleaders, to conduct their suits; but the Regulation (XII of 1833) under which this was allowed, being found inconvenient in practice, it was rescinded; and as authorized pleaders were now attached to all the Civil Courts in the Regulation districts in Bengal, and he believed in Madras and Bombay also, he saw no reason why parties should not appear by them, if they found it inconvenient to conduct their suits in person.

The Section was carried.

Sections II to VIII of Chapter II, and Section I of Chapter III were passed as they stood.

Section II prescribed the particulars to be given in the plaint.

Sir ARTHUR BULLER, referring to the words "as per account at foot" in line 34 of Clause 3 said, he presumed that an account was always to be added, as without it there would be no particulars of the demand.

The CHAIRMAN said, he thought that was implied.

Mr. LeGEYT moved the omission of the words "Company's Rupees" wherever they occurred in this Section.

The motions were carried, and the Section as amended was agreed to.

Sections III to VII were passed as they stood.

Section VIII provided as follows :—

"If, upon the face of the plaint and after questioning the plaintiff if necessary, it appear to the Court that the plaintiff has no cause of action, the Court shall reject the plaint. If it appear to the Court that the cause of action did not arise, or that the defendant is not dwelling or carrying on business or working for gain within the limits of the jurisdiction of the Court, or, if the claim relate to land or other immoveable property, that such land or other property is not situate within such limits, the Court shall return the plaint to the plaintiff in order to its being presented in the proper Court."

THE CHAIRMAN asked, whether it would not be better, instead of repeating the several causes of jurisdiction, to say briefly "or if the Court has no jurisdiction to entertain the suit ?" He also wished to observe, with reference to the present Section, that, as he understood it, it would not be for the Court to take the objection that the suit was barred by lapse of time; that would be left for the defendant. Considering that Statutes of limitation did not furnish a very conscientious defence, and that defendants might not wish to avail themselves of such a defence, and further that there were many limitations and exceptions to the operation of such laws, he thought the Judge should not have power to reject a plaint on any such ground, especially if the law were understood to bar the right as well as the remedy. He should think the Court could not, under this Clause, reject a plaint on the ground that the cause of action was barred by lapse of time.

MR. HARINGTON said that, as the Section was originally framed by the Select Committee, it gave the Court power to reject a suit, if the cognizance of it appeared upon the face of the plaint to be barred by lapse of time; but this part of the Section was afterwards struck out as it was considered to go beyond the proper province of the Court at this stage of the suit. He agreed with the Honorable and learned Chairman that, as the Section now stood, no Court would reject a plaint on the ground that the cause of action was barred by lapse of time. The cause of action might have arisen within the Court's jurisdiction, though the period for bringing a suit upon it might have expired. It was not a question of jurisdiction. There might be a good cause of action still existing notwithstanding the lapse of time.

MR. PEACOCK proposed to substitute "or" for "and" after the word "plaint" in the beginning of the Section.

As it now stood, it declared that "if, upon the face of the plaint, and after questioning the plaintiff if necessary, it appear to the Court that the plaintiff has no cause of action, the Court shall reject the plaint." It should be to this effect. If the facts stated in the plaint gave no cause of action, the plaint should be rejected, if the plaint was in that respect sufficient, still if the Court upon questioning the plaintiff as to the facts should ascertain that in point of fact there was no cause of action, the plaint should be rejected, so that the Court would be at liberty to reject the plaint, if the facts which it stated were not true.

THE CHAIRMAN said he rather thought that other provisions of the Code gave the Court sufficient power to enable the plaintiff to amend or add to his case. If so, he should prefer the word "and" to "or" in the Clause under consideration. The plaintiff might go to the Court in person in this first stage without employing a pleader. Often an ignorant man would fail to state his cause of action, though he really had one, and a Judge anxious only to get rid of suitors would reject his plaint. This would be a hardship to such persons, for, when the plaint had been rejected, they would have again to provide themselves with stamps in order to renew the suit. It seemed limiting too much the right of suit and giving too great a power to the Court. Would it be proper to impose upon the Court the duty of setting the plaintiff right ?

MR. PEACOCK said, he ought to have before stated that he proposed introducing in a later part of the Section a power to amend the plaint. Suppose the Judge, on questioning the plaintiff, should see that, if the whole case were stated, there would be a sufficient cause of action, this should be made to appear on the face of the plaint itself.

MR. HARINGTON said, he did not understand it to be intended that the examination of the plaintiff at this stage of the case should go to the extent proposed by the Honorable and learned Member of Council. All that the Court would have to consider was whether the plaintiff had a cause of action against the defendant, and this the Court should ascertain either from the plaint or by questioning the plaintiff if necessary.

MR. PEACOCK said, suppose the examination should show something differing from the plaint, the defendant would be called upon to answer the plaint and not what had been disclosed upon the plaintiff's examination. He thought it would be better to substitute "or" and then given a power of amendment

THE CHAIRMAN said, he would not encourage the Judge entering into the merits of the case. He had always thought there was great force in Sir Lawrence Peel's objection to Mr. Cameron's system of getting the party to the suit into the presence of the Judge and eliciting from him the points in dispute, that it gave the Judge a prejudice, but the advantages of the system might outweigh that. He feared, if the Judge were allowed to examine and cross-examine a suitor who came to him to obtain the process of the Court, it might lead to great abuse. It should be considered that this Code was intended for the subordinate Courts as well as for others. Doubtless many of the Judges of those Courts were men of strict integrity. Still all of them were not above suspicion in the general estimation. It was possible that a crafty and ingenious Judge might cross-examine an ignorant plaintiff and reject his plaint in such a form that there would be no remedy by appeal. He would prefer to limit the duty of the Court to ascertaining that there was a sufficient cause of action and that the facts were true.

MR. PEACOCK said, he would give a power to amend the plaint if the examination of the plaintiff or of any other person showed that an amendment was proper, his object being that the defendant should be called upon to answer the plaint and not the examination which he might never see.

MR. PEACOCK'S motion was put and carried.

MR. PEACOCK then moved that the words "if necessary" before the word "it" in the 3rd line of the Section be omitted.

Agreed to.

MR. HARINGTON, with reference to doubts which had been expressed, moved that the words "plaintiff has no" before the word "cause" in the 5th line of the Section be omitted in order that the words "subject-matter of the plaint does not constitute a" might be substituted for them.

Agreed to.

MR. PEACOCK proposed to move the introduction of the words "or other person" after the word "plaintiff" in the 2nd line of the Section The plaintiff might not himself know the facts; in that case he should be at liberty to produce other evidence.

MR. HARINGTON objected to the examination at this stage of the case of any person but the plaintiff or his pleader or authorized agent. He thought that this was not the proper stage of the suit for going into the merits of the claim, or for receiving evidence as to the facts.

THE CHAIRMAN observed that the verification was only that the plaintiff's statement was true according to his information and belief.

MR. PEACOCK moved that the following Proviso be inserted after the word "plaint" in the 6th line of the Section:—

"Provided that the Court may, in any case, allow the plaint to be amended, if it appear proper to do so."

Agreed to.

MR. PEACOCK then moved that the word "personally" be inserted before the word "working" in the 10th line of the Section.

Agreed to.

SIR ARTHUR BULLER moved that all the words from and after the word "If" in the 6th line of the Section stand as a new Section.

The motion was carried and the Section as amended was passed.

SIR ARTHUR BULLER said he would now propose a Clause to set at rest the question respecting the Statute of Limitation. He apprehended that now the Court would be able to entertain a suit although barred by lapse of time. Why bring a defendant into Court, if the result must be that the suit fails because thus barred. If it appeared that the action was barred, let the Court call upon the plaintiff to explain under what exception he fell. What was the use of calling upon the defendant to answer a suit which could not be maintained? He would therefore move the introduction of the following new Section:—

"If it shall appear on the face of the plaint that the right of action is barred by lapse of time, the Court may call upon the plaintiff to explain the grounds upon which he maintains his right to sue; and if he cannot satisfy the Court that he has such right, the Court shall reject the plaint. If such grounds appear sufficient, the Court shall direct the plaint to be amended by inserting them."

THE CHAIRMAN suggested that the plaint should be amended so as to state the exception upon which the plaintiff relied as preventing the bar.

MR. HARINGTON said, he doubted whether it was advisable to put the result of the examination into the plaint, having a due regard to the particulars to which it was the object of the Code to confine that paper, so that it might not become a lengthened pleading.

THE CHAIRMAN said, it appeared to him that, if the first part of his Honorable and learned friend's amendment was right, the other was almost a logical consequence. The question for decision was whether the bar which appeared on the face of the plaint was a thing of which the Judge should take notice, and which he should require to be explained There was a defect patent on the face of the plaint which might be removed by showing that the party was within one of the exceptions of the law of limitation, as infancy or the like. If that apparent defect be removed, it ought to appear upon the face of the plaint, not only that there was a cause of action originally, but that it was still subsisting and capable of being maintained. He agreed that the question should be cleared up because, as the Section stood, one Honorable Member who had sat in a Sudder Court assured them that the Judges would invariably consider that the words would be understood to include the right of raising the question of a bar by statutes of limitation; while another Honorable Member. who had also been a Sudder Judge, took the opposite view in which he must say he concurred. If there was this great difference of opinion, it was right that the Legislature should clear it up. He would prefer to leave the statute to be brought forward by the defendant rather than give a power to the Court to reject the plaint on this ground. But if the Legislature determined to give the Judge the power of rejecting the plaint, it was only right that the grounds should appear and should be stated in the same manner as any other material statement in the plaint.

MR. CURRIE suggested that, instead of amending the plaint, the Court should have the power of noting such grounds on the face of the plaint, since the plaintiff could hardly go into a statement of the grounds of his right to sue under the restrictions prescribed by the Code respecting the particulars to be stated in the plaint.

MR. HARINGTON said that, on referring to the Code of Civil Procedure prepared by Mr. Mills and himself, he found that, when a suit was brought after the period ordinarily allowed by law for the institution of Civil actions, the plaintiff was required to state in the plaint the ground on which exemption from the law was claimed, and as, under the Section which had been proposed by the Honorable and learned Member on his left (Sir Arthur Buller), the Court would be competent to reject a plaint, if upon the face of it the suit appeared to be barred by lapse of time, he thought a similar provision should be added to Clause 3, Section II. He asked permission, therefore, to return to that Section, and moved that the words

"and if the cause of action accrued beyond the period ordinarily allowed by any law for commencing such a suit, the ground upon which exemption from the law is claimed"

be inserted after the word "accrued" in the 13th line.

Agreed to.

MR. PEACOCK moved that the following illustration be inserted after the words "Balance due" in the 26th line of the same Section:—

"If the plaintiff claim exemption from any law of limitation, say 'the plaintiff was an infant (or as the case may be) from the day of to the day of '."

The motion was carried and the Section as amended was passed.

SIR ARTHUR BULLER'S new Section was then put and carried.

Section IX (suit to be in name of party really interested: Court to reject plaint, if a substituted or fictitious name is given).

SIR ARTHUR BULLER said, he wished to know (if this Section was intended to apply to *benamee* transactions,) who would be the party really interested? The *benamee* person would be told "You have no actual existing interest in the matter." Then the real owner would come in and he also would be told the same thing.

MR. CURRIE said, the particular class of cases for which this Section was intended to provide was where a man of high rank (say the Nabob Nazim) sued in the name of a person having no interest whatever.

THE CHAIRMAN said, still the nominal plaintiff must somehow prove his interest.

MR. HARINGTON said, according to the Code, certain obligations were imposed on a plaintiff, thus, he might be required to attend the Court in person to answer any questions put to him by the Judge or to appear as a witness on the motion of the opposite party and he would be liable to be tried for perjury if he gave false evidence. He should not be allowed to escape from these liabilities by putting forward another person as plaintiff. This would be prevented in a great measure by the Section under discussion.

THE CHAIRMAN said, he confessed that the Clause appeared to him to be rather unintelligible. It would seem that the objection must be taken in the first or initiatory stage of the suit. Suppose a party sued upon a written document, and the written document gave a nominal interest in certain property, though in reality *benamee* for another? If it was advisable to strike at the *benamee* system,—which could hardly be effected by this Bill—it must be done by a substantive law. The Privy Council had treated it as a matter of inveterate presumption that a father purchasing in his son's name was purchasing *benamee*. He did not see how the Court could take upon itself to say that a person appearing on the face of documents to be the owner, was only a trustee. Again, he believed there were great facilities in the Mofussil Courts for allowing parties who were transferees of choses in action to sue. Was the Court to institute an enquiry as to whether the transferree was beneficially entitled to the thing sued for? It would be better to treat it as a matter for defence. Besides, did not the Section come in the wrong place here before summons issued?

SIR ARTHUR BULLER said, he would move the omission of the Section. If any Honorable Member should desire its introduction on any future occasion, he might make a motion for the purpose. But it was clear from what had been said that this was not the proper place for it.

The Section was negatived.

Section X authorized the Court to reject the plaint when security was not furnished by the plaintiff if residing out of the British territories in India.

THE CHAIRMAN said, it occurred to him upon this Section that it might be going a little too far. It seemed almost to throw upon the Court the duty of rejecting the plaint if the plaintiff did not come prepared with his security. He (the Chairman) should have thought it quite sufficient to provide that, if a plaintiff resided out of the British territories, the Court at the time of the plaint being presented might require security from him before filing the plaint. It seemed to him (the Chairman) that the plaintiff might be ignorant of the law on that point. The defendant was not prejudiced so long as the security was given before the summons issued.

MR. LEGEYT said, the law in Bombay now was as the Honorable and learned Chairman seemed to think it should be.

MR. PEACOCK moved that the words "or within such time as the Court shall order" be inserted after the word "plaint" in the 9th line of the Section.

The motion was carried and the Section as amended then passed.

Sections XI to XIII were passed as they stood.

Section XIV related to the production of written documents.

MR. HARINGTON said, it had been suggested to him that the words

"The plaintiff may, if he think proper, deliver the original document to be filed instead of the copy"

might be advantageously introduced in line 17 of this Section after the word "plaintiff." As the law now stood, the plaintiff was required to file with his plaint the original documents on which be relied in support of his claim; but as these might be tampered with before the day appointed for the first hearing of the suit, the Section provided that copies only should be retained, the originals being returned to the party filing them. As, however, the making of the copies would entail expense, there seemed no reason why the plaintiff, if he thought proper, should not be allowed to file the original documents. He therefore moved that the words "the plaintiff may, if he think proper, deliver the original document to be filed instead of the copy" be inserted after the word "plaintiff" in the 17th line of the Section.

The motion was carried, and the Section as amended was then passed.

Sections XV to XLIX were passed as they stood.

Section L provided how the Court should proceed on an application for arrest before judgment.

SIR ARTHUR BULLER thought that this Section required some addition for the defendant's protection. Suppose the Court arrived at the conclusion that there was probable cause and issued a warrant. The Section did not in terms give any opportunity to the defendant to show cause. He should have some opportunity of doing so as he might be able to show that he was not going to leave the jurisdiction. He (Sir Arthur Buller) should move that the words "show cause why he should not" be inserted after the word "may" in the 12th line of the Section.

The motion was carried.

THE CHAIRMAN moved that all the words of the Section after the word "appearance" in the 13th line be omitted.

The motion was carried and the Section as amended was agreed to.

MR. PEACOCK then moved that the following new Section be introduced after Section L:—

"If the defendant fail to show such cause, the Court shall order him to give bail for his appearance at any time when called upon whilst the suit is pending and until execution or satisfaction of any decree that may be passed against him in the suit; and the surety or sureties shall undertake in default of such appearance to pay any sum of money that may be adjudged against the defendant in the suit with costs."

Agreed to.

Sections LI and LII were passed as they stood.

Section LIII provided as follows:—

"If on the trial of the suit, it shall appear to the Court that the arrest of the defendant was applied for on insufficient grounds, or if the claim of the plaintiff is disallowed, the Court may (on the application of the defendant) award against the plaintiff in its decree such amount as it may deem a reasonable compensation to the defendant for any injury or loss which he may have sustained by reason of such arrest. Provided that the amount of compensation awarded under this Section shall not exceed one hundred Rupees if the decree be passed by a Court whose jurisdiction may not exceed the sum of one thousand Rupees, or five hundred Rupees if it be passed by any other Court. An award of compensation under this Section shall bar any suit for damages, in respect of such arrest."

MR RICKETTS called attention to the strict limitation contained in this Section. If a defendant were arrested on insufficient grounds, no Court could award a compensation exceeding five hundred Rupees. It appeared to him that there might be a case or many cases in which that compensation would barely be sufficient for a person unnecessarily committed to prison. Under Section LXIII (providing for grant of compensation for an attachment applied for on insufficient grounds) and Section LXIX (providing for grant of compensation for needless issue of injunction,) the Court had an unlimited discretion. Of course it must be admitted it was not easy in those cases to determine the compensation; still as such a wide discretion was there given, he could not see why, in this case, it should be so strict and limited. He would move to omit the Proviso. Should the Council not agree with him he would be inclined to propose to substitute five thousand Rupees for five hundred Rupees.

MR. HARINGTON said, the Honorable Member of Council opposite had stated that under this Section, as now framed, no Court could award a larger sum by way of compensation to a defendant who had been improperly arrested, than five hundred Rupees; but this was not strictly correct. No doubt under this particular Section a larger sum than that mentioned by the Honorable Member of Council could not be awarded. But the defendant, instead of applying for compensation in the suit in which he had been arrested, might bring a separate action for damages and lay the amount at any sum he pleased, in which case there was nothing to prevent the Court from awarding the whole or such portion of the amount claimed as it might consider a reasonable compensation for the injury sustained by the arrest. There might be no objection to increase the amount mentioned in the Section, but he would not take away the proviso altogether, for in that case a Moonsiff might award a lakh or even a crore of Rupees. There ought to be some restriction. As regarded the other Section referred to by the Honorable Member of Council, the attachment was required to be proportioned to the amount or value of the claim, and, ordinarily, he supposed that the award of compensation would be limited to that amount. There was not therefore the same reason for imposing any restriction upon the discretion of the Court in such cases, though, if considered necessary, he should not object.

THE CHAIRMAN observed that this Section was not the defendant's only remedy. It applied only where the defendant made application to the Court. The Section did not prevent a separate action.

MR. PEACOCK said, he would suggest that the Court should have power to award damages to the same amount which in a suit in the Court it might have awarded; there was such a provision, he thought, in the Evidence Act.

MR. RICKETTS said, as there was some difference of opinion about this Section, and as it was now past four o'clock, he would move that the further consideration of this Bill be postponed till next Saturday.

The motion was carried, and the Council resumed its sitting.

INSOLVENT DEBTORS (MOFUSSIL).

MR. LEGEYT moved that a communication received by him from the Bombay Government, connected with the subject of a Law for the relief of Insolvent Debtors in the Mofussil, be laid upon the table and printed. He said, when this communication was printed, it would be found to go considerably beyond that subject. Still it might be useful, when the Council came to the Sections in the Civil Procedure Bill relating to Insolvency, to have the opinions of certain high authorities in the Bombay Presidency contained in this communication, before them.

Agreed to.

ARTICLES OF WAR (NATIVE ARMY).

MR. PEACOCK moved that the Bill "to amend Act XIX of 1847 (Articles of War for the government of the Native officers and Soldiers in the Military Service of the East India Company)," be referred to a Select Committee consisting of the Vice-President, Sir James Outram, and the Mover.

Agreed to.

MR. PEACOCK then moved that the Standing Orders be suspended to enable the Select Committee on the above Bill to present their Report within six weeks.

SIR ARTHUR BULLER seconded the motion, which was then carried.

SIR JAMSETJEE JEJEEBHOY'S ESTATE.

MR. LEGEYT moved that a communication received by him from the Bombay Government, relative to the Bill "for settling a sum of Company's Rupees twenty-five Lacs, Government four per centum Promissory Notes, and a Mansion-house and hereditaments called Mazagon Castle, in the Island of Bombay, the property of Sir Jamsetjee Jejeebhoy, Baronet, so as to accompany and support the title and dignity of a Baronet lately conferred on him by Her present Majesty Queen Victoria, and for other purposes connected therewith," be laid upon the table and printed. Sir Jamsetjee Jejeebhoy wished the Bill to be slightly modified, so that, instead of specifically settling twenty-five Lacs of Rupees in four per cent. Government Promissory Notes, it might provide that such an amount of Government Promissory Notes be settled as would yield an income of not less than one Lac of Rupees per annum. This modification would leave it optional with Sir Jamsetjee Jejeebhoy to invest, for the purposes of the Act, either four or five per cent. Notes or both, and in such proportions as might be most convenient to him. But the Bill having been transmitted to England, he (Mr. LeGeyt) apprehended that there might be some difficulty in altering it now.

MR. PEACOCK said, if the Bill was to be amended, the Council should go into Committee and settle it. Perhaps, the better course now would be to amend the Bill, and to send the amended Bill home. The Bill, as it stood, had already been transmitted to England; but there would probably be no objection to the course he proposed. He supposed that the mere fact of having sent the former Bill for sanction would form no objection to this course. The Bill had been settled in Committee of the whole Council, but had not been passed, and the Council therefore had power to amend it.

The motion was carried.

MR. LEGEYT then gave notice that he would, on Saturday next, move for a Committee of the whole Council on the Bill.

CIVIL PROCEDURE.

MR. PEACOCK gave notice that the consideration of the Bill "for simplifying the Procedure of the Courts of Civil Judicature not established by Royal Charter" would be proceeded with next Saturday to the end of Chapter IV if possible.

The Council adjourned.

Saturday, September 25, 1858.

PRESENT:

The Hon. the Chief Justice, *Vice-President*, in the Chair.

Hon. Lieut.-General Sir James Outram,	E. Currie, Esq.,
Hon'ble H. Ricketts,	Hon. Sir A. W. Buller,
Hon'ble B. Peacock,	H. B. Harington, Esq., and
P. W. LeGeyt, Esq.,	H. Forbes, Esq.

LUNACY.

THE VICE-PRESIDENT read Messages informing the Legislative Council that the Governor General had assented to the Bill "to regulate proceedings in Lunacy in the Courts of Judicature established by Royal Charter," the Bill "to make better provision for the care of the estates of Lunatics not subject to the jurisdiction of the Supreme Courts of Judicature," and the Bill "relating to Lunatic Asylums."

GUARDIANSHIP OF MINORS (BENGAL).

THE CLERK presented to the Council a Petition of the British Indian Association praying for such a modification of the Clause introduced at the last meeting of the Council into the Bill "for making better provision for the care of the persons and property of Minors in the Presidency of Fort William in Bengal," as would extend the age of Minority of Wards to twenty-one years.

MR. CURRIE moved that the above Petition be printed.

Agreed to.

AHMEDABAD MAGISTRACY.

MR. LEGEYT moved the first reading of a Bill "to empower the Governor in Council of Bombay to appoint a Magistrate for certain Districts within the Zillah Ahmedabad." He said, the Rajah of Bhownuggur was a dependent Chief on the Western Coast of the Gulf of Cambay, some of whose estates were included in the Zillah of Ahmedabad, and were subject to the British Laws. Certain of these estates he held independently, being within the Province of Kattywar, in respect to which he was under the control of the Political Agent of that country. The Magisterial and Police duties of these districts in the Ahmedabad Zillah, had, for some time past, been the subject of discussion and difficulty; and some time ago, the Government of Bombay resolved to relieve the Magistrate of Ahmedabad of the charge of the districts, and place them under the Political Agent of Kattywar. A legal difficulty soon presented itself, as the Appellate Courts had no jurisdiction over the Political Agent, and the returns of crime in those districts were no longer furnished to the Sudder Fouzdaree Adawlut by the Magistrate of Ahmedabad. The Sudder

Court at Bombay was required to frame the draft of an enactment empowering the Government of Bombay in Council to appoint the Political Agent of Kattywar, the Magistrate of certain villages in the Bhownuggur estate; and the Bill which he had now the honor to present, had been prepared accordingly, together with a Schedule containing the names of one hundred and seventeen villages, which had hitherto been under the jurisdiction of the Magistrate of Ahmedabad, but which would, under the Bill, be exempt from that jurisdiction in future. The proposed new arrangement was a mere matter of convenience; and as long as it was carried out properly, and a proper appeal was provided, it appeared to him there could be no objection to the measure.

The Bill was read a first time.

BREACHES OF CONTRACT BY ARTIFICERS, &c.

MR. CURRIE moved that the Bill "to provide for the punishment of breaches of contract by artificers, workmen, and laborers in certain cases" be now read a second time.

The motion was carried and the Bill read a second time.

CONTINUANCE OF CERTAIN PRIVILEGES TO THE FAMILY &c. OF THE LATE NABOB OF THE CARNATIC.

MR. FORBES moved that the Bill "to continue certain privileges and immunities to the family and retainers of His late Highness the Nabob of the Carnatic" be now read a third time and passed.

The motion was carried and the Bill read a third time.

GUARDIANSHIP OF MINORS (BENGAL).

On the Order of the Day for the adjourned Committee of the whole Council on the Bill "for making better provision for the care of the persons and property of Minors in the Presidency of Fort William in Bengal," being read, the Council resolved itself into a Committee for the further consideration of the Bill.

Section V (the further consideration of which had been reserved) provided as follows:—

Mr. Le Geyt.

"When application shall have been made to the Civil Court either by a person claiming a right to have charge of the property of a Minor, or by any relative or friend of a Minor, or by the Collector, the Court shall inquire summarily into the circumstances, and if it shall appear that the deceased has left a Will, and that the Executor or Executors named therein is or are willing to undertake the trust, or when the deceased has not left a Will or the Executor or Executors named in any Will is or are unwilling to undertake the trust, if any near relative of the Minor shall desire or be willing to administer to the estate, and the Court shall be of opinion that such relative is a fit person to be entrusted with the charge of the property and person of the Minor; the Court shall grant a Certificate to such Executor or Executors, or near relative as the case may be."

MR. CURRIE said, he begged to move the amendment in this Section of which he had given notice last Saturday, and which had since been printed. The objection taken to the Section as it originally stood was that it seemed to require that the person who should have the administration of the estate of a Minor, should also have charge of the person of the Minor. In that respect, the Section was defective; and he had moved that its consideration be postponed, in order that he might frame an amendment. The amendment which he had framed was intended to cure that defect. It corresponded with the previous Sections of the Bill, and also with the subsequent Sections; and he believed that it met the object which was desired. He now begged to move its adoption.

The amendment was as follows:—

"That all the words after the word 'circumstances' in the 8th line of the Section be omitted, and the following be substituted for them:—

'And pass orders in the case.

'If it shall appear that any person is entitled to have charge of the property of a Minor as Executor under a Will, and is willing to undertake the trust, the Court shall grant a Certificate of administration to such Executor. If there is no Will, or the Executor named in any Will is unwilling to undertake the trust, and there is any near relative of the Minor who is willing and fit to be entrusted with the charge of his property, the Court may grant a Certificate to such relative. The Court may also, if it think fit, (unless a Guardian have been appointed by the father) appoint such Executor or such relative, or any other relative or friend of the Minor to be the Guardian of the person of the Minor.'"

MR. PEACOCK said, it appeared to him that the new Clause was also objectionable. He did not thoroughly understand what was meant by the term "Executor." He did not know whether it was used here in the sense which the English Law gave to it, or whether it was intended to mean a trustee or devisee. There was a great distinction in England between an Executor and a trustee or devisee. The duty of an Executor was to dispose of the property he received according to the terms of the Will—to apply it to the payment of the debts of the deceased, and to hand over the surplus to the devisee. In a case arising under this Section, an Executor would cease to hold the surplus property in trust for the infant, but would hand it over to the person who was intended to be the trustee. It appeared to him, therefore, that the word "devisee" should be substituted in the proposed amendment for the word "Executor." He was not aware whether there was such a term known in the Mofussil; but it struck him that it would be better to substitute it.

But suppose that this amendment should be made, still he did not quite understand what was intended to be the effect of the Clause. We must read it in connexion with Section III. That Section said:—

"Every person who shall claim a right to have charge of property in trust for a Minor under a Will or other Deed, or by reason of nearness of kin, or otherwise, may apply to the Civil Court for a Certificate of administration, and no person shall be competent to institute or defend any suit connected with the estate of which he claims the charge, or to give any legal discharge to the debtors of such estate, until he shall have obtained such certificate."

If a person who did not claim to have such right under the Will, held nevertheless a large property in trust for a Minor, and applied for a Certificate of administration, another person who was the Executor of a small property in trust for that Minor, might come forward, and he, under the proposed amendment, would become manager of the estate, and, as such, would manage the whole of the property, including the property in the hands of the person applying for the Certificate of administration. Because the amendment said:—

"If it shall appear that any person is entitled to have charge of the property of a Minor as Executor under a Will, and is willing to undertake the trust, the Court shall grant a Certificate of administration to such Executor. If there is no Will, or the Executor named in any Will is unwilling to undertake the trust, and there is any near relative of the Minor, and fit to be entrusted with the charge, the Court may grant a Certificate to such relative."

But supposing that the person making the application was not an Executor under a Will, but only a Trustee for the infant by a Deed, was the relative of the infant to supersede him who had been appointed by the donor of the property, and to take all that property out of his hands?

Then, the proposed amendment provided that

"the Court may also, if it think fit, (unless a guardian have been appointed by the father) appoint such Executor or such relative, or any other relative or friend of the Minor to be the guardian of the person of the Minor.

If the Court should appoint an Executor, the Executor would hold the property in trust for the Minor. He (Mr. Peacock) took a distinction between a man appointed an Executor, and a man appointed guardian by the father. The term "Executor" in the proposed amendment clearly meant, not an Executor appointed by the father, or intended by him to be the guardian of the Minor. The amendment supposed first, the case of an Executor, and then the case of a Guardian appointed by the father. If that was so, there seemed to him to be no reason why, because a person who had charge of a Minor's property merely as an Executor, he should also have the guardianship of his person and the control of his education. Why should not a person who held the property in trust, do the same? The question was not, how the property came. By this amendment, the guardianship of a Minor would depend, not upon the fact of a person holding the property of the Minor, but on the question how he had come to hold it, irrespectively of the consideration whether he had or had not been appointed guardian of the Minor by the donor.

Then, with reference to the words "unless a guardian have been appointed by the father"—supposing that the father of a child was living, was the

Executor or anybody else who might have left property to the child, to supersede him, and to assume the guardianship of the child's person and the management of his education? He (Mr. Peacock) apprehended that the father, whilst living, was the lawful guardian of his child during its minority, and that he ought never to be superseded in such guardianship, unless it could be proved that he was unfit to be entrusted with it. The duty was vested in him by law; and except upon proof of some disqualifying cause, it ought to remain with him.

Then, suppose that a Hindoo lady under age, was married to an adult husband who was competent to take care of his own and his wife's property. If any one should happen to be an Executor under a Will, and, as such, should claim to hold property in trust for the wife, he might, under the proposed amendment, claim also to be the guardian of the wife. The husband was the legal guardian of his wife, and the father was the legal guardian of his child; and the power and duty of such guardianship ought not to be taken away from them, unless it could be satisfactorily shown that they were persons in whom the duty could not properly be reposed. The principles of the Hindoo law relating to this subject were thus laid down in Macnaghten's work, Vol. I. Chap. VII.:—

"A father is recognized as the legal guardian of his children, when he exists; and when the father is dead, the mother may assume the guardianship; but where the duties of manager and guardian are united, she is, in the exercise of the former capacity, necessarily subject to the control of her husband's relations: and with respect to the Minor's person likewise, there are some acts to which she is incompetent; such as, the performance of the several initiatory rites, the management of which rests with the paternal kindred. In default of her, an elder brother of a Minor is competent to assume the guardianship of him. In default of such brother, the paternal relations generally are entitled to hold the office of guardian; and failing such relatives, the office devolves on the maternal kinsmen, according to their degree of proximity; but the appointment of guardians universally rests with the ruling power."

The father, therefore, was recognized as the legal guardian of his children while he existed. It might happen that a child might have property left to him while his father was living. An uncle might leave property to him, or he might succeed to property in preference to his father. If he should gain property by virtue of any of these means, the father ought not to be deprived of the guardianship of his person. Then, it was further laid down in Macnaghten's Hindoo Law—

"that the guardianship of a female, whether she be a Minor or adult, until she be disposed of in marriage, rests with her father: if he be dead, with her nearest paternal relations. After her marriage, a woman is subjected to the control of her husband's family. In the first instance, her husband is her guardian: in default of him, her sons, grandsons, and great grandsons are competent to assume the guardianship, and in default of them, her husband's heirs generally, or those who are entitled to inherit his estate after her death, are competent to exercise the duties of guardian over herself and her property. On failure of her husband's heirs, her paternal relations are her guardians; and failing them, her maternal kindred. In point of fact, females are kept in a continual state of pupilage."

He thought, therefore, that the proposed amendment was wrong in being so framed as to admit of an Executor being appointed guardian in supersession of a father or a husband.

Again, it was provided by Section IX that:—

"Whenever the Court shall grant a certificate of administration to the estate of a Minor to the Public Curator or other person as aforesaid, it shall at the same time appoint a guardian to take charge of the person and maintenance of the Minor. The person to whom a certificate of administration has been granted, unless he be the Public Curator, may be appointed guardian. Provided always that the legal heir of a Minor shall not be appointed guardian of his person."

There might be many cases in which a father might be the legal heir of his child, and there might be cases in which a husband might be the legal heir of his wife. For instance, a man might marry a girl who had arrived at the age of puberty, but was still a Minor; she might have a *streedhun*; she might bear no children, and consequently would have no grandson. It was laid down that, in such a case, the husband might inherit the *streedhun*. But by Section IX of this Bill, because he thus was his wife's legal heir, he was not to have the guardianship of her person.

Then, again, this Bill made no special provision with respect to the guardianship of female Minors, which the Court of Wards Regulation (X. 1793) did. Section XXI of that Regulation said :—

"The rules contained in Section VIII for the election of managers are to be applied also to the choice of guardians : with these differences, that the guardianship shall, in no instance be entrusted to the legal heir or other person interested in outliving the ward."

That would exclude the husband. The Section then proceeded :—"And that female Minors shall have guardians of their own sex." When he found such a provision made in the Court of Wards Regulation, he thought that a similar provision should be made in this Bill.

Then, some provision ought to be made for the education of a Minor. If male, he should be sent to a College ; if female, the control of her education should be committed to her husband, provided he was not an improper person. The Court of Wards Regulation made provision for this object. It said :—

"The guardians of female Minors, who, agreeably to Section XXI, are to be of the same sex, are also to take care that their wards, when arrived at the age of tuition, receive an education suitable to their condition."

There was no such provision in this Bill. The Bill provided that Minors ought to be educated, if their estates paid revenue to Government.

Section VI of the Court of Wards Regulation said :—

"The trusts of manager for disqualified landholders, and guardian to them, are to be considered altogether distinct, but, as hereafter specified, they may, in some instances, be vested in the same person ; and the rules contained in the following Sections relative to managers and guardians respectively are founded on this distinction."

And then, Section XV provided—

"Agreeably to the distinction laid down in Section VII, the manager is to have the entire care of the estate, real and personal. He will therefore have the exclusive charge of all lands, Malgoozaree or lakhiraj, as well as all houses, tenements, goods, money, and moveables, of whatever nature belonging to the Proprietor whose estate may be committed to his charge, excepting only the house wherein such Proprietor may reside, the moveables wanted for his or her use, and the money allowed for the support of the Proprietor, and his or her family, entitled to a provision, which are to be left to the care of the guardian, where distinct guardians may be appointed. Both managers and guardians, on their receiving charge of any property, are to sign an exact inventory of the same, which is to be deposited in the treasury of the Collectorship."

All these provisions were made by the Court of Wards Regulation. This Bill certainly did not contain them. If the amendment now proposed in Section V were to be adopted, by which the guardianship of a Minor might be given to an Executor, some provision ought to be made that the Executor should not supersede the natural and legal right of a father to be the guardian of his own children ;—and again, that the guardianship of a female Minor who was married to an adult husband, should be left to her husband.

In accordance with these views, he should move that the following Proviso be added to Section V :—

"Provided that nothing in this Act shall authorize the appointment of a guardian of the person of a female, whose husband is not a Minor, or the appointment of a guardian of the person of any Minor whose father is living and is not a Minor; and provided also that nothing in this Act shall authorize the appointment of any person other than a female as the guardian of the person of a female."

The object of this Proviso was that the fact of property coming to a Minor or an infant wife, should not deprive the father or the husband of their respective rights of guardianship. In England, if the Court saw that a father was an improper person to have the guardianship of the person of his child, or a husband of the person of his wife, it might remove him from such guardianship. He (Mr. Peacock) did not know what the Law on that subject might be in the Mofussil. If it was intended now to provide a Law in respect either to fathers or to husbands, then there ought to be some distinct Clause to the effect of the Proviso proposed by him. The Proviso only said that an Executor ought not to be appointed in supersession of a father or a husband. He supposed that this Bill was really intended to provide for the case of orphans—children without fathers; but nevertheless, as its scope was general, and as it would comprehend the case of all Minors, it appeared to him that there ought to be some provision like that contained in the Proviso which he submitted. This Act dealt with every one living out of the jurisdiction of the Supreme Court, except a British subject; and when so dealing, it ought not to deprive fathers and husbands of their natural and legal right to the guardianship of their children and wives.

THE CHAIRMAN said, he wished to say a few words about the term "devisee" before the amendment was put to the vote. Probably the best mode of taking the sense of the Committee on the points raised would be to put the question that the amendment moved by the Honorable Member for Bengal be adopted; and if that were decided in the affirmative, to put the further question that the Proviso moved by the Honorable and learned Member who had spoken last, be added to the Section.

With respect to the proposed change of phraseology in the amendment moved by the Honorable Member for Bengal, he spoke under correction as not familiar with the practice in the Mofussil, but he thought that it would be very inexpedient to introduce such a word as "devisee" or any word which implied a distinction between gifts by will of immoveable property, and gifts by will of moveable property. The wills that would most frequently be the subject of enquiry under this Act were the wills of Hindoos. In nine out of ten of these cases, the word used was "turney" or "attorney." In the Supreme Court, that term was considered as implying a person to whom the whole of the property passed upon the trusts of the Will; and he imagined that the same was the case in the Mofussil. Looking back to the former Section of the Bill to which the Honorable and learned Member had drawn attention, it appeared to him that (though he believed the case would be of very rare occurrence) the Bill did contemplate the right of a trustee appointed by a Deed to have charge of the property of a Minor; and, therefore, he thought it would be better if the Honorable Member for Bengal would alter his amendment so that it should run thus :—

"and pass orders in the case.

"If it shall appear that any person claiming the right to have charge of the property of a Minor is entitled to such right by virtue of a Will or Deed, and is willing to undertake the trust, the Court shall grant a Certificate of administration to such person. If there is no person so entitled, or if such person is unwilling to undertake the trust, and there is any near relative of the Minor who is willing and fit to be entrusted with the charge of his property, the Court may grant a Certificate to such relative. The Court may also, if it think fit, (unless a guardian have been appointed by the father), appoint such person as aforesaid or such relative, or any other relative or friend of the Minor to be the guardian of the person of the Minor."

MR. PEACOCK said, the alteration suggested by the Honorable and learned Chairman would meet both the objections he had taken to the proposed amendment. He thought that the party appointed ought to have the guardianship of the person of the Minor whether his appointment was by Will or by Deed.

THE CHAIRMAN said, he had no objection whatever to make it incumbent on the Court to recognize the natural and legal right of a father to the guardianship of his infant child, or that of a husband to the guardianship of his wife, unless he were personally unfit to be entrusted with the charge; but he should have thought that the words of the amendment which recognized the right of the father to appoint a guardian seemed to imply that he, if living, was the proper person to be appointed guardian, in the rare cases in which the appointment of a guardian in his lifetime might become necessary. The 9th Section, however, as it stood, might prevent such an appointment, inasmuch as the father would often be the presumptive heir of his infant son.

He felt a very strong objection to the provision inserted by the Select Committee in that Section which would, in many cases, exclude persons having a preferential right to guardianship, on the ground that they would also be entitled to property on the death of their wards. A Hindoo father might leave a widow and a son. If the son died during his minority, of course the property inherited by him from his father would pass to his mother; but that was no reason why the mother should be deprived of the guardianship of her child while he lived. He had no objection to the amendment proposed, if it were altered as he had suggested; and at the proper stage, he would move that the provision in Section IX to which he had referred, be omitted.

MR. CURRIE said, he was much obliged to the Honorable and learned Chairman for the alteration he had suggested in his amendment. It would certainly make Section V more complete. The only case contemplated by the earlier Regulations of a person holding property in trust for a Minor, was that of an Executor; and it was following these earlier Regulations that he had made mention of an Executor only in this Section.

The amendment was then altered as suggested by the Chairman and agreed to.

MR. PEACOCK, with the leave of the Council, withdrew his Proviso, stating that he should move it as a substantive Section after Section XXII.

Sections VI and VII were passed after verbal alterations rendered necessary by the amendments made in Section V.

THE CHAIRMAN moved that the Proviso in Section IX (which excluded the legal heir of a Minor from the guardianship of his person) be omitted.

The Motion was carried, and the Section then passed.

MR. PEACOCK then moved that the following be inserted as a new Section after Section XXII :—

"Nothing in this Act shall authorize the appointment of a guardian of the person of a female whose husband is not a Minor, or the appointment of a guardian of the person of any Minor whose father is living and is not a Minor; and nothing in this Act shall authorize the appointment of any person other than a female as the guardian of the person of a female. If a guardian of the person of a Minor be appointed during the minority of the father or husband of the Minor, the guardianship shall cease as soon as the father or husband (as the case may be) shall attain the age of majority."

MR. CURRIE said, he had no objection to that part of the proposed Section which referred to married females and to females generally; but he thought it would be better to leave out all mention of the father, because almost the only case in which property would come to a Minor whose father was living, would be the case of adoption. In a case of adoption, the father ceased to have any interest in the child, and probably would not be the most suitable person to be appointed his guardian. Then, the Bill left it entirely in the discretion of the Court to appoint the most suitable person. Unless the child should have left his family altogether by adoption, the father would generally be the most suitable person to be his guardian, and it might be safely left to the Court to appoint him. He (Mr. Currie) did not mean to offer any opposition to the proposed Section, especially as the Bill would be published, and the Section might be further considered hereafter; but he should wish it to be restricted to females.

The Section was put and agreed to.

Section XXIII (the interpretation clause) provided that

"the expression 'Civil Court' as used in this Act shall be held to mean the principal Court of original jurisdiction in the District."

MR. CURRIE moved that after the word "District," the following should be inserted :—

"and shall not include the Supreme Court; and nothing contained in this Act shall be held to affect the powers of the Supreme Court over the person or property of any Minor subject to its jurisdiction."

The Motion was carried, and the Section then passed.

The Council then resumed its sitting, and the Bill was reported.

CIVIL PROCEDURE.

On the Order of the Day being read for the adjourned Committee of the whole Council on the Bill "for simplifying the Procedure of the Courts of Civil Judicature not established by Royal Charter"—

MR. LEGEYT moved that the consideration of the Bill be postponed until after the consideration of the next Bill.

Agreed to.

SIR JAMSETJEE JEEJEEBHOY'S ESTATE.

MR. LEGEYT moved that the Bill "for settling a sum of Company's Rupees twenty-five lacs, Government four per centum Promissory Notes, and a Mansion-house and hereditaments called Mazagon Castle, in the Island of Bombay, the property of Sir Jamsetjee Jeejeebhoy, Baronet, so as to accompany and support the title and dignity of a Baronet lately conferred on him by her present Majesty Queen Victoria, and for other purposes connected therewith" be re-committed to a Committee of the whole Council for the purpose of considering proposed amendments therein.

Agreed to.

MR. LEGEYT said, the Council would have learnt from the paper from the Secretary to the Government of Bombay which had been circulated last week, that a wish had been expressed by Sir Jamsetjee Jeejeebhoy and concurred in by the Government, that a slight modification should be made in the Bill as passed by a Committee of the whole Council and transmitted to Her Majesty for assent. Last Saturday, it was suggested to him that the Bill might be recommitted, and the new provision recommended by the Government of Bombay considered. The provision was contained in the 3rd paragraph of Sir Jamsetjee's letter to the Government of Bombay. Sir Jamsetjee said :—

"I take this opportunity of intimating my wish that the Draft Act which I forwarded to you on the 28th Ultimo, should be slightly modified as follows, namely, instead of specially settling 'twenty-five lacs of Rupees in *four per cent.* Bengal Government Promissory Notes,' I would wish it provided in the Act that such an amount of Government Promissory Notes be settled, as will yield an income of not less than one hundred thousand Rupees per annum.

On going back to the original correspondence in England between the friends of Sir Jamsetjee Jeejeebhoy and the President of the Board of Control, he found that in pursuance of that correspondence, a Bill was drafted, and forwarded to the Legislative Council; and, as the Council was aware, it was passed in that form in Committee of the whole Council. The alteration now proposed was that, in Section III, after the word "Notes" in the sixth line, the following words should be introduced :—"or such amount of Government Promissory Notes as will yield an income of not less than one lac of Rupees per annum." He did not propose to make any specific mention of five per cent. Promissory Notes. He thought it sufficient to say such amount of Government Promissory Notes as would yield an annual income of not less than one lac of Rupees.

MR. PEACOCK said, it was not his intention to oppose the proposed alteration. Sir Jamsetjee Jeejeebhoy said :—

"As the proposed change is in itself trivial, so far as the Act is concerned ; as it involves no departure from the spirit or intention of the Act; and as the originally proposed amount of annual income derivable from the settlement will remain unaffected thereby—I feel confident that Government will consider my proposal a very reasonable one."

He (Mr. Peacock) could not say that the income derivable from the settlement would remain unaffected by the change proposed. What Sir Jamsetjee Jeejeebhoy proposed was to substitute twenty lacs of five per cent. Promissory Notes for twenty-five lacs of four per cent. Promissory Notes. The interest of five per cent. had been guaranteed for a certain period only. If after that period it should be reduced to four per cent. the investment now proposed would yield only eighty thousand Rupees a year, or produce only twenty lacs of money in the event of the trustees refusing to a diminution of the rate of interest, so that the income of this Baronetcy might be reduced from one lac to eighty thousand Rupees a year. Therefore, the settlement would be materially affected by the alteration desired. If Sir Jamsetjee Jejeebhoy wished to secure an investment which would yield eighty thousand Rupees a year, he (Mr. Peacock) had no objection to his so doing if it were in conformity with the understanding on which the Baronetcy had been granted. If the modification proposed were adopted, it could not be said that Sir Jamsetjee Jejeebhoy was securing a lac a year for the Baronetcy.

MR. LEGEYT said, there was no denying the force of the objection taken by the Honorable and learned Member;

but did it not equally apply to the four per cent. loan? There was no guarantee that the four per cent. Promissory notes would always yield four per cent. The interest payable upon them might be reduced to three and a half per cent. The nature of the guarantee did not appear to be such as to ensure beyond all possible chance of a change an income of a lac a year for the Baronetry. The income must be subject to certain changes of which no one could now say that they would take place or not.

The motion was then put, and agreed to, and the Section then passed.

The Preamble and Title were next re-considered and amended.

The Council resumed its sitting, and the Bill was reported.

CIVIL PROCEDURE.

On the Order of the Day for the adjourned Committee of the whole Council on the Bill "for simplifying the Procedure of the Courts of Civil Judicature not established by Royal Charter," being read—the Council resolved itself into a Committee for the further consideration of the Bill.

Section 49 of Chapter III provided that in suits for moveable property, when the Defendant is about to leave the jurisdiction "with intent to avoid or delay the Plaintiff," the Plaintiff may apply that security be taken for his appearance.

Sir ARTHUR BULLER moved that the words "or to obstruct or delay the execution of any decree that may be passed against him" be inserted after the words "with intent to avoid or delay the Plaintiff."

Agreed to.

Sir ARTHUR BULLER moved that the words "or that he has disposed of or removed from the jurisdiction of the Court his property or any part thereof" be inserted after the words "is about to leave the jurisdiction of the Court."

The motion was carried, and the Section then passed.

Section 50 prescribed the mode in which the Court should proceed on such application.

Sir ARTHUR BULLER moved that the words "or that he has disposed of or removed from the jurisdiction of the Court, his property or any part thereof with intent to obstruct or delay the execution of any decree" be inserted before the word "it" in the 9th line of the Section.

The motion was carried, and the Section as amended passed.

The postponed Section 53 provided that "if, on trial of the suit, it shall appear to the Court that the arrest of the Defendant was applied for on insufficient grounds, or if the claim of the Plaintiff is disallowed," the Court may award compensation to the Defendant;

"Provided that the amount of compensation awarded under this Section shall not exceed one hundred Rupees if the decree be passed by a Court whose jurisdiction may not exceed the sum of one thousand Rupees, or five hundred Rupees if it be passed by any other Court."

Mr. HARINGTON moved that the words "on the trial of the suit" be omitted from the Section.

Agreed to.

Mr. PEACOCK moved that the words "and it shall appear to the Court that there was no probable ground for instituting the suit" be inserted after the word "disallowed" in the 5th line of the Section.

Agreed to.

Mr. RICKETTS, with the leave of the Council, withdrew the Motion which he had made at the last Meeting for the omission of all the words after the word "arrest" in the 10th line of the Section, observing that the amendment just made entirely met his views.

Mr. HARINGTON moved that the words "not exceeding the sum of one thousand Rupees" be inserted after the word "amount" in the 7th line of the Section.

Agreed to.

Mr. HARINGTON moved that the words "amount of compensation awarded under this Section, shall not exceed one hundred Rupees if the decree be passed by a Court whose jurisdiction may not exceed the sum of one thousand Rupees, or five hundred Rupees if it be passed by any other Court" be left out, and the words "Court shall not award a larger amount of compensation under this Section, than it is competent to such Court to decree in an action for damages" substituted for them.

The motion was carried, and the Section as amended passed.

Sections 54 to 56 were severally passed as they stood.

The consideration of Sections 57 to 59 was postponed.

Sections 60 to 62 were severally passed as they stood.

Section 63 provided as follows:—

"If on the trial of the suit, it shall appear to the Court that the attachment was applied for on insufficient grounds, or if the claim of the plaintiff is disallowed either wholly or in part, the Court may (on the application of the defendant) award against the plaintiff in its decree such amount as it may deem a reasonable compensation to the defendant for the expense or injury occasioned to him by the attachment of his property. An award of compensation under this Section shall bar any suit for damages in respect of such attachment."

MR. HARINGTON moved that the words "on the trial of the suit" after the word "If" in the first line of the Section, be left out.

Agreed to.

MR. PEACOCK moved that the words "or if the claim of the plaintiff is disallowed either wholly or in part" after the word "grounds" in the fifth line of the Section, be left out, and that the words "if the suit of the plaintiff is dismissed, or judgment is given against him by default or otherwise, and it shall appear to the Court that there was no probable ground for instituting the suit" be substituted for them.

Agreed to.

MR. HARINGTON moved that the words "not exceeding the sum of one thousand Rupees" be inserted after the word "amount" in the ninth line of the Section.

Agreed to.

MR. HARINGTON moved that the words "provided that the Court shall not award a larger amount of compensation under this Section, than it is competent to such Court to decree in an action for damages" be inserted after the word "property" in the 12th line of the Section.

The motion was carried, and the Section, as amended, passed.

MR. PEACOCK moved that the Standing Orders be suspended to enable him to move an amendment in Section 53.

Agreed to.

MR. PEACOCK moved that the words "if the claim of the plaintiff is disallowed" after the word "or" in the 4th line of the Section, be left out, and that the words "if the suit of the plaintiff is dismissed, or judgment is given against him by default or otherwise," be substituted for them.

The motion was carried and the Section then agreed to.

Section 64 provided as follows:—

"Attachments before judgment shall not affect the rights of persons not parties to the suit, nor bar any person holding a decree against the defendant from applying for the sale of the property under attachment in execution of such decree. Provided that, in the case of a person holding a decree, he shall satisfy the Court that he has used due diligence in endeavoring to enforce the decree; but any neglect on the part of the person holding the decree shall not prevent the sale of the property in execution, if such person can show that the attachment before judgment was obtained for a fraudulent purpose."

THE CHAIRMAN said the Proviso was a sort of Proviso on a Proviso. The object of the first part of the Section was good; it provided that an attachment obtained before judgment should not over-ride the claim of any creditor holding a decree against the defendant to sell the property in satisfaction of his decree; but the Proviso appeared to him objectionable and likely to cause unnecessary litigation, and he should move that it be omitted.

THE CHAIRMAN moved that the proviso above quoted be omitted.

The motion was carried and the Section then passed.

Section 65 was passed as it stood.

Section 66 provided as follows:—

"Whenever lands paying revenue to Government form the subject of a suit, if the party in possession of such lands shall neglect to pay the Government revenue, and a public sale shall in consequence be ordered to take place, the party not in possession shall, upon payment of the revenue due previously to the sale (and with or without security at the discretion of the Court) be put in immediate possession of the lands, and the Court in its decree *shall* award against the defendant the amount so paid, with interest thereupon at such rate as to the Court may seem fit."

THE CHAIRMAN moved that the word "shall" in the 13th line of the Section be struck out, in order that the word "may" might be substituted for it.

Agreed to.

MR. PEACOCK moved that the words "or may charge the amount so paid, with interest thereupon, at such rate as the Court may order, in any adjustment of accounts which may be directed in the final decree upon the cause" be added to the Section.

The motion was carried, and the Section then passed.

Section 67 provided for the issue of injunctions to stay waste or alienation of property in dispute in any suit, and for the appointment of a receiver or manager if necessary. It further provided that

"if the property be land paying revenue to Government, the Court shall appoint the Collector to be receiver and manager of such land, if the Government by a general order in that behalf shall so direct."

MR. RICKETTS moved the substitution of the words "and it is considered that the interest of those concerned will be promoted by the management of the Collector" for the words "the Court shall" in the 34th line.

Agreed to.

MR. RICKETTS moved the omission of the words "if the Government, by a general order in that behalf shall so direct" at the end of the Section.

MR. PEACOCK said the management of an estate for the prevention of waste was a duty as between private persons. The Government had no interest in it. The Collector received a high salary from Government for the performance of his public duties, and his time ought not to be given to such additional duties as were contemplated by the proposed amendment. In many districts, the Collectors would be also Magistrates; and if the duties were cast upon them, they would be prevented from discharging the legitimate functions of their office. He did not mean to oppose the amendment; but it did appear to him that it had better not be inserted.

MR. RICKETT'S motion was then put and carried.

MR. PEACOCK moved the addition of the following words to the Section:—

"unless the Government shall, by any general order, prohibit the appointment of Collectors for such purpose, or shall in any particular case prohibit the appointment of the Collector to be such receiver."

MR. RICKETTS said, he could not say he thought it desirable that these words should be added to the Section. It was not likely that the Government would take advantage of them, but still he would *not* give it so large a power as they would confer. It had been the practice for Collectors to manage lands paying revenue to Government in these cases; the practice had proved to be very much to the advantage of the persons concerned, and he would leave the Section as it now stood. He believed that the discretion of appointing Collectors or not, was much better in the hands of the Court than in those of the Government.

The motion being put—

The Council divided.

Ayes, 5.	*Noes*, 3.
Mr. Forbes.	Mr. Currie.
Mr. Harington.	Mr. LeGeyt.
Sir Arthur Buller.	Mr. Ricketts.
Mr. Peacock.	
The Chairman.	

So the motion was carried and the amended Section passed.

Section 68 was passed as it stood.

THE CHAIRMAN moved that the following new Section be introduced after Section 68 namely—

"The Court may in every case before granting an injunction require such reasonable notice of the application for the same to be given to the opposite party as to it shall seem fit."

Agreed to.

Section 69 was passed after amendments similar to those in Section 63.

The further consideration of the Bill was postponed, and the Council resumed its sitting.

SIR JAMSETJEE JEJEEBHOY'S ESTATE.

MR. LEGEYT moved that the Bill "for settling a sum of money and a mansion-house and hereditaments called Mazagon Castle, in the Island of Bombay, the property of Sir Jamsetjee Jejeebhoy, Baronet, so as to accompany and support the title and dignity of a baronet lately conferred on him by her present Majesty Queen Victoria, and for other purposes connected therewith," as now amended, be forwarded to the President in Council for transmission to the Secretary of State for India with the request that he will obtain Her Majesty's sanction to the same, but with an intimation that, if any objection should exist to the Bill in its present form, the Council will be prepared to pass the Bill as it was settled on the 28th of August last.

Agreed to.

CONTINUANCE OF CERTAIN PRIVILEGES TO THE FAMILY &c. OF THE LATE NABOB OF THE CARNATIC.

MR. FORBES moved that Mr. Ricketts be requested to take the Bill "to continue certain privileges and immunities to the family and retainers of his late Highness the Nabob of the Carnatic" to the President in Council in order that it may be submitted to the Governor General for his assent.

Agreed to.

STATE OFFENCES.

MR. LEGEYT moved that a communication received by him from the Bombay Government relative to an amendment of Act XI of 1857, regarding State offences, be laid upon the table and referred to the Select Committee on the Indian Penal Code. It would be in the recollection of the Council that, when that Act was passed, the Presidency of Bombay was specially excluded from its provisions. The Government of Bombay now complained that the enactment still in force in that Presidency—Regulation XIV. 1827, did not suit them so well as Act XI of 1857 would do. A Commission Court was held at Ahmednuggur on the 21st of August last for the trial of certain prisoners charged with Treason and Rebellion. The Commissioner, in submitting the Proceedings, stated that, under Section VII of Regulation XIV. 1827, the Court had no alterative but to pass the *only* sentence therein set forth, which was sentence of "Death and confiscation of property." He added—

"The Bombay Code admits of no intermediate punishment between Death and ten years' imprisonment for Treason and Rebellion. The first punishment is in all ordinary cases too severe; the second is frequently inadequate. I think, therefore, it would be expedient to cancel the Proviso in Section I of Act XI of 1857, which renders that Act not applicable to the Regulation Provinces of the Bombay Presidency."

Mr. LeGeyt

The Government of Bombay fully concurred in this suggestion, and desired a rescission of the Proviso referred to. He Mr. (LeGeyt) felt considerable difficulty in dealing with the subject; but as he understood that the Acts in question would go before the Select Committee on the Penal Code for consideration in connexion with the Chapter relating to State offences, he thought that the best course would be to refer the communication he had received, to that Committee.

THE CHAIRMAN said, he certainly had no recollection that he was responsible for the alterations by which the Presidency of Bombay had been excluded from the provisions of Act XI of 1857 to which the Honorable Member had alluded. But referring the present communication to the Select Committee on the Penal Code would hardly meet the wish of the Government of Bombay, because there was no doubt that that Code would provide a general law relating to the offences against the State for all India. That, however, was not the present object of the Government of Bombay. They wished for the immediate application of a temporary Act to their Presidency. The better plan would be to bring in a short Bill for the purpose.

MR. LEGEYT, with the leave of the Council, withdrew his motion.

BREACHES OF CONTRACT BY ARTIFICERS, &c.

MR. CURRIE moved that the Bill "to provide for the punishment of breaches of contract by artificers, workmen, and laborers in certain cases" be referred to a Select Committee consisting of the Vice-President, Mr. LeGeyt, Mr. Forbes, and Mr. Currie.

Agreed to.

GUARDIANSHIP OF MINORS (BENGAL).

MR. CURRIE moved that the Bill "for making better provision for the care of the persons and property of Minors in the Presidency of Fort William in Bengal," as settled in Committee of the whole Council be published for general information.

Agreed to.

FRAUDS ON INSURERS.

Mr. LeGeyt moved that a communication received by him from the Bombay Government relative to a certain class of frauds practised in Guzerat on Insurers, be laid upon the table and referred to the Select Committee on the Indian Penal Code.

Agreed to.

CONSERVANCY OF MILITARY CANTONMENTS (BENGAL).

Mr. Peacock moved that the Select Committee on the Bill "for the Conservancy of Military Cantonments in the Presidency of Bengal" be discharged.

Agreed to.

CIVIL PROCEDURE.

Mr Ricketts gave notice that he would propose an amendment in Section 72 Chapter IV of the Bill "for simplifying the Procedure of the Courts of Civil Judicature not established by Royal Charter" to the effect that no party shall be imprisoned under a decree for less than fifty Rupees for any period exceeding one month, and under a decree for less than five hundred Rupees for any period exceeding six months.

Also an amendment in Section 76 of the same Chapter to the effect that, when a defendant shall have been imprisoned and having delivered up all his property shall have been discharged by the Court, if the amount of the decree under execution shall not exceed five hundred Rupees, it shall be competent to the Court to declare the defendant absolved from all further liability under such decree.

Mr. LeGeyt gave notice that he would propose to omit so much of Section 143 Chapter III of the above Bill as requires that depositions of witnesses shall be taken and that the notes by the Judges shall form the record.

The Council adjourned.

Saturday October 9, 1858.

PRESENT :

The Honorable the Chief Justice, *Vice-President*, in the Chair.

Hon'ble Lieut. Genl. Sir J. Outram,	E. Currie, Esq.,
Hon'ble B Peacock,	H. B. Harington, Esq., and
P. W. LeGeyt, Esq.,	H. Forbes, Esq.

The Clerk presented a Petition of Inhabitants of the 24-Pergunnahs praying, with reference to the Bill "for making better provision for the care of the persons and property of Minors in the Presidency of Fort William in Bengal," that the age of majority be not fixed at twenty-one years.

Mr Currie said, the Petitioners had misunderstood the Bill altogether. The age of majority was fixed at eighteen, as in the Court of Wards Regulation, and not at the age of twenty-one years. As, however, there was a Petition before the Council from the British Indian Association suggesting the extension of the age of majority to the twenty-first year, he would move that the Petition now presented, be printed.

Agreed to.

CIVIL PROCEDURE.

On the Order of the Day being read for the adjourned Committee of the whole Council on the Bill "for simplifying the Procedure of the Courts of Civil Judicature not established by Royal Charter," the Council resolved itself into a Committee for the further consideration of the Bill.

Sections 57, 58, and 59 of Chapter III related to the sale of property in execution of decrees.

Mr. Harington said, that the consideration of these Sections had been postponed on his motion at the last meeting of the Committee, on the understanding that, in the course of the week, he would print and circulate the amendments in them which appeared to him to be necessary. This he had done, and he should now move the omission of the Sections as they stood, and the substitution for them of the amended Sections prepared by him. A few remarks would suffice to explain the alterations which he considered desirable. The first amendment proposed in Section 57, would give a defendant, for the attachment of whose property, *pendente lite*, the plaintiff might apply, and who might in consequence be called upon to furnish security to save his property from attachment, an opportunity of shewing cause why the order should not be enforced. A similar provision had been introduced, at a previous meeting of the Committee, on the motion of the Honorable and learned Judge who usually sat on his left (Sir Arthur Buller), in Section 50, which related to applications for the arrest of the defendant on mesne process, and there seemed no reason why a defendant called upon to furnish security, or, in default, to submit to the attachment of his property, *pendente lite*, should not be accorded the same privilege of being heard against the order. The amended Section also gave the Court power to order the attachment of the whole or any part of the defendant's property specified in the plaintiff's application, at the same time that it called upon the defendant for security. This power was given in Section 59 as it was originally framed, but in the Select Committee words had been introduced which would restrict the exercise of it to moveable property. The application of the plaintiff, however, frequently related to immoveable as well as to moveable property, and as some time would be allowed to the defendant to enable him to furnish the security required of him, the failure to furnish which alone would, as the Section now stood, subject his immoveable property to attachment; and as the only use which a fraudulent debtor would probably make of the interval would be to alienate the property indicated by the plaintiff, which there would be nothing to prevent him from doing, it seemed to him that the power should again be made general, and should be capable of being exercised in respect to both descriptions of property.

With regard to Section 58, he deemed it sufficient to remark that the alterations which he had made in that Section ... necessarily the amendment proposed in Section 57.

Harington

He should therefore move that Section 57 be omitted, in order that the following new Section might be substituted for it :—

"If the Court, after examining the applicant, and making such further investigation as it may consider necessary, shall be satisfied that the defendant is about to dispose of or remove his property with intent to obstruct or delay the execution of the decree it shall be lawful for the Court to issue a warrant to the proper Officer, commanding him to call upon the defendant, within a time to be fixed by the Court, either to furnish security in such sum as may be specified in the order to produce and place at the disposal of the Court, when required, the said property or the value of the same or such portion thereof as may be sufficient to fulfil the decree, or to appear and show cause why he should not furnish security. The Court may also in the warrant direct the attachment until further order of the whole or any portion of the property specified in the application."

Agreed to.

MR. HARINGTON next moved that Section 58 be omitted, and the following new Section be substituted for it; namely :—

"If the defendant fail to show such cause, or to furnish the required security within the time fixed by the Court, the Court may direct that the property specified in the application, if not already attached, or such portion thereof as shall be sufficient to fulfil the decree, shall be attached until further order. If the defendant show such cause or furnish the required security and the property specified in the application or any portion of it shall have been attached, the Court shall order the attachment to be withdrawn."

MR. HARINGTON further moved that Section 59 be left out.

Agreed to.

Sections 70 to 73 were passed as they stood.

Section 74 prescribed the proceeding in case of the death of one of several plaintiffs where the cause of action accrued to the survivor and the representative of the deceased.

THE CHAIRMAN said, he had some little doubt as to the last part of the Section, which said :—

"If no application shall be made to the Court by any person claiming to be the legal representative of the deceased plaintiff, the suit shall proceed at the instance of the surviving plaintiff or plaintiffs; and the legal representative of the deceased plaintiff shall be interested in, and shall be bound by the judgment given in the suit in the same manner as if the suit had proceeded at his instance conjointly with the surviving plaintiff or plaintiffs."

The original scheme or project of law had provided that something like a notice should be given to the legal representative of the deceased plaintiff to come in and proceed with the suit. The Section as amended in Select Committee made no provision for any such notice whatever, and yet said that, unless the legal representative did come forward and have his name entered in the register of the suit in the place of the deceased plaintiff, the suit should proceed at the instance of the surviving plaintiff, and he should not only be bound by the judgment given if it were in favor of the defendant, but also be interested in the judgment if it were in favor of the plaintiff. It might so happen that the representative might not know that the suit was pending. Such a thing was not very likely, but still, it *might* happen; and he thought it would be better to give the Court a discretion in the matter. To do this, he had prepared the following proviso, which he moved should be added to the Section:—

"Provided that the Court, if it shall see fit, may direct notice of the suit to be served on the legal representative of the deceased plaintiff."

The original project of law had provided that if, even after a proclamation calling on the legal representative to appear, the representative should fail to appear, the judgment should be binding upon him equally with the surviving plaintiff if it was given in favor of the defendant, but that if it was given against the defendant, it should be only to the extent of the share or shares of the surviving plaintiff, and with a reservation of the rights of the legal representative. As the Section stood now, he (the Chairman) was only afraid of possible collusion between the surviving plaintiffs and the defendants in fraud of the representatives of the deceased plaintiff. Perhaps the question had been considered by the Select Committee, but by way of raising it now, he would move that the proviso he had read be added to the Section.

Mr. HARINGTON said, the Section as framed by Her Majesty's Commissioners, contained a provision for the issue and publication of a proclamation calling upon the representatives of a deceased plaintiff to appear on a day to be fixed therein, and to proceed with the suit; but looking to the fact that a proclamation stuck up in the Court-house was not likely to come to the knowledge of the family of the deceased plaintiff, the Select Committee had struck out this provision as useless. The objection to requiring the Court to issue a notice to the representatives of the deceased was that there would be nobody to pay the peon's fees for serving the same. The co-plaintiff, or co-plaintiffs could not be required to pay them; and as no notice could be issued without the previous deposit of the necessary fee for serving it, he did not see how this difficulty could be got over. He thought it would generally happen that the family or representatives of a plaintiff, who might die during the pendency of a suit, would be the first to hear of his death, and it would be their duty to lose no time in taking the necessary steps for carrying on the case in his stead. If they failed to do this, they must abide the consequences of their neglect. As to the other part of the Section, he considered that, as it had been amended by the Select Committee, it was really more favorable to the family of a deceased plaintiff than the original Section, seeing that it gave them an interest in any judgment that might be passed in favor of the surviving plaintiff or plaintiffs.

The CHAIRMAN asked how the plaintiff would enforce his decree.

Mr. HARINGTON said, he supposed in the same manner as any other decree-holder. He presumed that the representative or reprentatives of the deceased plaintiff would be at liberty to unite with the surviving plaintiff or plaintiffs in applying to the Court for execution of the decree passed in their joint favor, and that the Court would be bound to grant execution in the same manner as if such representative or representatives had been originally parties to the suit.

The CHAIRMAN said, he would not press his motion if there was any difficulty about it. He should have thought, however, that in such cases the plaintiff who had the conduct of the case would pay the fees for the notice in the first instance, and add them to the costs.

With the leave of the Council, the amendment was withdrawn, and the Section was passed as it stood.

Sections 75 and 76 were severally passed as they stood.

Section 77 prescribed the proceeding to be adopted in case of the death of one of several defendants, or of a sole or sole surviving defendant.

THE CHAIRMAN said, the Select Committee had in this Section put two Sections of the original project of law together. He presumed it was intended, not that the suit should begin *de novo* when the legal representative of a deceased defendant was made a party to the suit, but that he should be bound by all the former proceedings in the suit. To make this clear he (the Chairman) should move that the words "and had been a party to the former proceedings in the suit" be added to the Section.

The amendment was agreed to, and the Section then passed.

Sections 78 to 82 were severally passed as they stood.

Section 83 provided as follows:—

"If, on the day fixed for the defendant to appear and answer or any other day subsequent thereto, to which the hearing of the suit may be adjourned, neither party shall appear, either in person or by a pleader, when duly called upon by the Court, the suit shall be dismissed, with liberty to the plaintiff to bring a fresh suit, unless precluded by the rules for the limitation of actions."

MR. PEACOCK (for Sir Arthur Buller) moved that all the words after the word "dismissed" in the 9th line of the Section be left out, and that the following words be substituted for them:—

"Whenever a suit is dismissed under the provisions of this Section, the plaintiff shall be at liberty to bring a fresh suit, unless precluded by the rules for the limitation of actions; or if he shall, within the period of thirty days, satisfy the Court that there was a sufficient excuse for his non-appearance, the Court may issue a fresh summons upon the plaint already filed."

The motion was agreed to, and the Section then passed.

Section 84 provided as follows:—

"If the plaintiff shall appear in person or by a pleader, and the defendant shall not appear in person or by a pleader, and it shall be proved to the satisfaction of the Court that the summons was duly served, the Court shall proceed to hear the suit *ex parte*. If the defendant appear on any subsequent day to which the hearing of the suit is adjourned, and shall assign good and sufficient cause for his previous non-appearance, he may be heard in answer to the suit in like manner as if he had appeared on the day fixed for his appearance.

MR. LEGEYT moved that after the word "may," and before the words "be heard" in the 15th line of the Section, the words "on his undertaking to pay all expenses occasioned by his so appearing and being heard" might be inserted. He said he should further move that all the words after the words "*ex parte*" in the 11th line of the Section should be omitted. With respect to the first motion, it appeared to him that such a provision was only reasonable. The second was of more importance. He thought that a defendant might be inclined to hold off until the end of the suit before he thought it worth his while to come in and make his defence, and then, when once admitted, he would be at liberty to call back any witness who had been examined in chief for the purpose of cross-examination. This would be a great hardship upon witnesses, some of whom might be living at a distance of twenty or thirty miles from the Court. Three-fourths of the cases now decided, were decided *ex parte*, in consequence of the defendants not appearing The defaulters had no intention of resisting the claims preferred; but they would not pay unless there were decrees against them.

MR. HARINGTON said, the addition proposed by the Honorable Member for Bombay would not in his opinion be any improvement. The Honorable Member appeared to have overlooked the fact that a defendant could not be allowed to be heard after the time fixed for his first appearance, unless he shewed good and sufficient cause for his previous non-appearance. Now it might and frequently would happen that a defendant, in a case ordered to be tried *ex parte* by reason of his non-appearance within the time allowed, taking advantage of the opportunity which would be afforded to him under the Section as at present worded, of showing cause against the order previously to the decision of the suit, might satisfy the Court that the summons had not been duly served upon him in any of the prescribed modes, or when the summons had been returned as served, he might be able to show that the return was a false one, and that the plaintiff had himself been a party to and had actually contrived the fraud practised on the Court. In such a case he did not think that the Honorable Member for Bombay would contend that the defendant was not entitled to be placed on the same footing as if he had appeared and answered on the day fixed for the first hearing of the suit, or that, if willing to bear the expense, he would deny him the right of re-summoning any of the plaintiff's witnesses who had been examined in his absence, if he thought that by cross-examining them he should be able to elicit any thing in his favor, or to shake their previous testimony. The Section did not require that the plaintiff should reproduce his witnesses, or that they should be recalled at his expense, but that the defendant, having excused his previous non-attendance, should be heard in answer to the suit in the same manner as if he had appeared on the day fixed for his appearance. This seemed to him (Mr. Harington) only fair and proper, even though it should involve the re-appearance of the plaintiff's witnesses on the application of the defendant for the purposes of cross-examination, the defendant as already noticed, bearing the costs of the fresh summonses, which in that case would require to issue. By Section 90 a defendant against whom an *ex parte* decision might be passed, might apply, at any time not exceeding thirty days after any process for enforcing the judgment had been executed, for an order to set aside the decision, and if he should satisfy the Court that his previous default had not been wilful, it would be the duty of the Court to restore the case to the file and to grant a new trial. Now, when a new trial might be allowed under the Section just referred to, the defendant's right to demand that the witnesses for the prosecution, who had been examined in the original trial, should again be required to attend at his expense, in order that he might be confronted with, and have an opportunity of cross-examining them, appeared to him quite clear, and, considering that the defendant should have the same power in cases falling under the concluding clause of the Section under discussion, he should vote against the Honorable Member's amendment.

MR. LEGEYT asked what the difference was between the re-hearing provided for by Section 84, and that provided for by Section 90.

MR. HARINGTON replied that in the one case the defendant appeared and showed cause before judgment, in the other, he appeared and showed cause after judgment.

MR. LEGEYT said, in that case he thought the best course would be to omit Section 90 altogether. It would be generally found that defendants would prefer to come in under Section 84. If a defendant did not choose to appear during any stage of the trial, he (Mr. LeGeyt) did not see why, with the ample grace allowed to him by Section 84, he should have unrestricted liberty to come in and lengthen out the proceedings after judgment given. After the observations made by the Honorable Member for the North-Western Provinces, he should be very glad, with the leave of the Council, to withdraw the amendment which he had moved; but he should move that all the words after the word "*ex parte*" in the 9th line of the Section be omitted.

The original Motion was accordingly withdrawn.

The second Motion being proposed—

MR. HARINGTON said, the Bill as originally drawn having allowed a defendant against whom an *ex parte* judgment had been given, to obtain a new trial if he applied within a certain time, and satisfied the Court that his failure to appear on the day fixed for the first hearing of the suit was not wilful—it became the duty of the Select Committee to consider whether, if a defendant, in a case ordered to be tried *ex parte* owing to his omission to attend within the time allowed, appeared before judgment was pronounced and showed cause for his previous default, the Court should be compelled to wait until after judgment had been given against him, and process for enforcing the same taken out, and then, in the event of the defendant applying for a new trial and excusing his non-attendance when the suit was called on for hearing, set aside the judgment, and replace the case on the file; or whether the Court, having the defendant before it, should not at once go into his reasons for not having appeared within the time fixed in the summons, and if satisfied of their sufficiency, permit him to be heard in answer to the suit in like manner as if he had appeared on the day fixed for his appearance. The question was fully discussed, and the conclusion arrived at was that the latter was not only the proper course, but that it would be scarcely less beneficial to the plaintiff than to the defendant, inasmuch as it would materially expedite the final settlement of the matters in dispute between the parties, and might save them both much expense. The Committee accordingly introduced the words objected to by the Honorable Member for Bombay, and which he proposed to omit. The present practice was in accordance with the Section as amended by the Select Committee, and he (Mr. Harington) had tried numerous cases in which the great convenience and advantage of that practice had been apparent He could not therefore support the Honorable Member's motion.

The motion was then put, and negatived.

MR. PEACOCK moved that the words "upon such terms as the Court may direct as to the payment of costs or otherwise" be inserted after the word "may" in the 15th line of the Section.

The motion was carried, and the Section then passed.

Sections 85 to 89 were severally passed as they stood.

Section 89*a* provided that if either the plaintiff or the defendant in a suit, who was summoned or ordered to appear personally, should fail to do so without lawful excuse or showing sufficient cause, the Court might either pass judgment against him, or make such other order in relation to the suit as he might deem proper in the circumstances of the case.

MR. CURRIE moved that all the words of this Section be left out, and that the following new Section be substituted for them, namely:—

"If any plaintiff or defendant, who shall have been ordered or summoned to appear personally under the provisions of Section 17 of this Chapter, shall not appear in person or show sufficient cause to the satisfaction of the Court for failing so to appear, such plaintiff or defendant shall be subject to all the provisions of the foregoing Sections applicable to plaintiffs and defendants, respectively, who do not appear either in person or by pleader."

Agreed to.

Section 89 being read by the Chairman, it was moved by Mr. Currie that all the words of this Section be left out, and that the following new Section be substituted for them, namely:—

"In support of the cause shown by a plaintiff or defendant for failure to appear in person, the Court shall receive any declaration in writing on unstamped paper, if signed by such plaintiff or defendant and verified in the manner hereinbefore provided for the verification of plaints."

Agreed to.

Sections 90 and 91 were severally passed as they stood.

Section 92 provided as follows:—

"If the defendant desire to set-off against the claim of the plaintiff any demand for which he might have sued the plaintiff in the same Court, he shall tender a written statement containing the particulars of such demand, and the Court shall investigate the claim of the defendant in the suit before it, along with the claim of the plaintiff, if it shall consider it reasonable so to do. If the demand proposed to be set-off exceed the sum to which the jurisdiction of the Court extends, the defendant shall not be allowed to set-off the same unless he abandon the excess."

MR. HARINGTON said it had been suggested to him that it might be hard upon a defendant who had a counter-claim against a plaintiff exceeding the amount of the plaintiff's claim, to compel him, as was required by the last part of this Section, to abandon the excess before he could be allowed to plead a set-off to the claim of the plaintiff, and considering that there was some force in the objection, he proposed to meet it by striking out all the words after the word "extends" in the 10th line, and substituting the following words:—

"The Court shall forward the case to the principal Civil Court of original jurisdiction in the district, and it shall be competent to such Court either to decide the case itself or to refer it for trial and decision to any Court subordinate to its authority, and competent in respect of the value of the suit."

At the same time he thought that, if these words were introduced, the counter-claim of the defendant should be chargeable with the same stamp duty as a petition of plaint, and he would therefore move, in the first instance, that the words "which shall be engrossed on a stamp paper of the value prescribed for plaints" be inserted after the word "demand" in the 6th line of the Section.

Mr. CURRIE said he had some doubts as to the insertion of the words proposed. The Section had been very fully considered by the Select Committee, and they thought that, where a defendant did not go into Court of his own free will, it was fair that he should be allowed to have his set-off without paying the Stamp fee which he would have had to pay if he had sued the plaintiff of his own free will.

Mr. HARINGTON, with the leave of the Council, withdrew his motion and the further consideration of the Section was postponed.

Sections 93 to 95 were severally passed as they stood.

Section 96 provided as follows:—

"At the first hearing of the suit, and if necessary at any subsequent hearing, any party who appears in person, or the pleader of any party who appears by a pleader, may be examined orally by the Court. Previously to the examination of a party to the suit, he shall be admonished in the manner hereinafter provided for the admonition of witnesses."

Mr. FORBES moved that the consideration of this Section be postponed until after the consideration of Section 145, which provided that witnesses should be examined without oath or affirmation, and in which he proposed to move an amendment.

Agreed to.

Section 97 provided as follows:-

"If any party who appears in person shall refuse to answer any material question relating to the suit which the Court may think proper to put to such party, the Court may pass judgment against him, or make such other order in relation to the suit as it may deem proper in the circumstances of the case."

The CHAIRMAN said, he had some doubts about this Section. It seemed to him rather unsafe to give a Court the power of "passing judgment against" a party who might refuse to answer any question which it might happen to think material. The duty of the Court would be to decide the case under investigation upon the evidence before it. In doing so, it would couple the other evidence in the case with the refusal of the recusant party, and come to such a conclusion as that might appear to it to justify. But this Section said, in effect, that the Court might punish a suitor who, foolishly perhaps, refused to answer any particular question, by "passing judgment against him," whatever the evidence in the case might be. It was, as he had said before, an unsafe power to give to a Court, and he saw no necessity for the Section at all.

Mr. HARINGTON said, the Section was almost word for word the same as Section 141, which provided as follows:—

"If any person, being a party to the suit, who shall be ordered to attend to give evidence or produce a document, shall, without lawful excuse, fail to comply with such order, or attending or being present in Court, shall, without lawful excuse, refuse to give evidence, or to produce any document in his custody or possession named in such summons as aforesaid, upon being required by the Court so to do, the Court may either pass judgment against the party so failing or refusing, or make such other order in relation to the suit as the Court may deem proper in the circumstances of the case."

That Section had been taken from the present Law of Evidence, which had been found to work well, and as he could see no reason why, when the parties to a suit attended in person, and were examined at the first hearing, they should not be subject to the same penalty in the event of their refusing to answer any material questions put to them, as they would be, under the Section just quoted, for a similar refusal in cases falling under that Section, or why the powers of the Court should not be the same in the one case as in the other, he hoped that the Committee would allow the Section to stand. The object in view was to elicit the truth, and by compelling the parties to tell all that they knew, to enable the Court to dispose of the case, if possible, at the first hearing.

Mr. PEACOCK said, this Section would meet the case of a party to a suit, who, though not summoned to appear, was present at the hearing of the case, but refused to answer any question put to him under Section 141, which provided that if any person, being a party to the suit, who should be ordered to attend to give evidence, or produce a document, should, without lawful excuse, fail to comply with such order, or, attending or being present in Court, should, without lawful excuse, refuse to give evidence, or to produce any document in his custody or possession, upon being required by the Court so to do, the Court might either pass judgment against him, or make such other order in relation to the suit as it might deem proper in the circumstances of the case. But if the party was in Court without having been summoned, and should refuse to give his evidence, though the whole case might hinge upon it, he would not come under Section 141. Section 97 would place him in the same position as that of a party who had been summoned, but failed to appear, or, appearing, refused to answer any question put to him.

MR. CURRIE said, he was inclined to agree with the Chief Justice's opinion. The examination contemplated by this Section was a mere conversational examination. It was hardly in the nature of a formal examination such as that contemplated in Section 141. When the Code was in preparation, he had doubted whether the provision respecting previous admonition in Section 96 should be inserted. The principle of the Code in this respect was that the Court should endeavor to elicit the facts of the case by the questioning of the parties. Then, the question was, whether, not having been formally summoned, the case should be decided against a party for refusing to answer.

MR. PEACOCK said, if Section 97 were omitted, and a party to a suit who was present in Court without having been summoned should refuse to give his evidence, the Court would only postpone the examination, and then summon him to attened. If he failed to appear, or, appearing, persisted in his refusal to give evidence, the Court would then have the power, under Section 141, either to decide the case against him if he was the defendant, or to dismiss the suit if he was the plaintiff. What was the use of this double proceeding? Why should not the Court have the power of decreeing or dismissing in the first instance?

THE CHAIRMAN said it seemed unwise to refuse the only support tendered to him, but he felt bound to say that he did not object to place a party examined under this Section on the same footing with a party examined at some other stage of the case. The best part of the Code framed by Her Majesty's Commissioners was that which was intended to put a stop to vexatious litigation at the outset, and therefore, it appeared to him that whatever examination was held in the first stage of a case, ought to be subject to the penalties of perjury, and to any other consequences which would fairly affect the witness if he were under examination at the trial of the case. His (the Chairman's) doubt with respect to the Section was whether it did not go too far in giving the Court the power of deciding against a party to the suit, merely because he refused to answer a particular question.

The question might touch his notions of honor, and yet, if he refused to answer it, the Court, under this Section, would have the power of passing judgment against him simply because of the refusal. For instance, a Hindoo would never tell the name of his wife. The Judge should come to his decision by looking at the whole evidence in the case.

The Section was then passed, after verbal amendments.

Section 98 was passed after similar amendments.

Section 99 was passed after an amendment.

Section 100 provided as follows:—

"all exhibits produced by the parties shall be received and inspected by the Court; but it shall be competent to the Court, after inspection, to reject any exhibit which it may consider irrelevant or otherwise inadmissible."

MR. HARINGTON moved that the words "recording the grounds of such rejection" be added to the Section.

The motion was carried, and the Section then passed.

Sections 101 and 102 were severally passed as they stood.

Section 103 enacted that admitted exhibits should be marked and filed, "provided that, if the exhibit be an entry in any shop-book or other book, a copy of the entry endorsed as aforesaid shall be filed as part of the record, and the book shall be returned to the party producing it."

MR. LEGEYT moved that the words "by the party producing it" be inserted after the word "filed" in the 11th line of the Section.

After some discussion, the Motion was by leave withdrawn.

MR. LEGEYT moved that the words "a copy of the entry endorsed as aforesaid" after the word "book" in the 9th line of the Section be left out, and that the words "the party on whose behalf such book is produced, shall furnish a copy of the entry, which copy shall be endorsed as aforesaid and" be substituted for them.

The Motion was carried, and the Section then passed.

Sections 104 to 107 were severally passed as they stood.

The consideration of Section 108 was postponed.

Sections 109 to 111 were severally passed as they stood.

Section 112 was passed after an amendment.

MR. LEGEYT moved that the following new Section be introduced after Section 112; namely:—

"But if, after such amendments, either party should be still dissatisfied with the issues as framed, the Court may, on the dissatisfied party paying all expenses and furnishing such securities as are hereinafter provided for appellants in regular appeals, certify to the next higher Court a special appeal to try whether the issues directed are the proper issues; and pending such enquiry, the proceedings in the lower Court shall be stayed.

THE CHAIRMAN remarked he could not help saying that it was very inexpedient to admit these interlocutory appeals, since they would occasion very great delay.

After some conversation, Mr. LeGeyt, with the leave of the Council, withdrew his motion.

Sections 113 to 116 were severally passed as they stood.

Section 117 empowered the Court to grant time to either of the parties, and to adjourn the hearing of the suit.

MR. LEGEYT moved that the following Proviso be added to the Section:—

"Provided that in all such cases, the party applying for time shall pay the costs occasioned by such adjournment, unless the Court shall otherwise direct."

The Motion was carried, and the Section then passed.

Sections 118 to 129 were severally passed as they stood.

Section 130 was passed after a verbal amendment.

Sections 131 to 142 were severally passed as they stood.

Section 143 provided as follows:—

"On the day appointed for the hearing of the suit or on some other day to which the hearing may be adjourned, the evidence of the witnesses in attendance shall be taken orally in open Court, in the presence and hearing, and under the personal direction and superintendence of the Judge. In cases in which an appeal may lie to a higher tribunal, the evidence of each witness given upon such examination shall be taken down in writing, in the language in ordinary use in proceedings before the Court, by or in the presence and under the personal direction and superintendence of the Judge, not ordinarily in the form of question and answer, but in that of a narrative, and, when completed, shall be read over in the presence of the Judge and of the witness, and also in the presence of the parties to the suit or their pleaders, or such of them as are in attendance, and shall be signed by the Judge. It shall be in the discretion of the Court to take down, or cause to be taken down, any particular question and answer, if there shall appear any special reason for so doing, or any party or his pleader shall require it. If any question put to a witness be objected to by either of the parties or their pleaders, and the Court shall allow the same to be put, the question and answer shall be taken down, and the objection, and the name of the party making it, shall be noticed in taking down the depositions, together with the decision of the Court upon the objection. The Court shall record such remarks as it may think material respecting the demeanor of the witness while under examination. In cases where an appeal does not lie to a higher tribunal, it shall not be necessary to take down the depositions of the witnesses in writing at length; but the Judge shall make a short memorandum of the substance of what each witness may have deposed, and such memorandum shall be written and signed with his own hand, and shall form part of the record."

MR. LEGEYT said, he had to move an amendment of this Section. The question which it involved had been very much discussed in Select Committee. He had been unable to concur in the decision to which they had come, and he had not yet given up all hope of what he considered ought to be the mode of recording evidence in the Criminal Courts at least, if not also in the Civil. What he proposed to have done was that the witness should be brought into Court and examined, that he should orally depose what he knew of the case, and that the Judge should immediately write with his own hand, or, if he should be unable, from sickness or any other cause, to do so, cause to be written, a careful note of what the witness did say. That note should be carefully explained to the witness in his vernacular language and signed by him; and it would then, as he (Mr. LeGeyt) contended, form a much better record than the kind of deposition that was now taken. It had been for many years the practice, he would not say of every Court, but certainly of several Courts in Bombay at least, to take down the evidence of witnesses in a most slovenly manner. When Commissioners went round on their tours of inspection, the subordinate Courts were careful to do everything according to proper form and order; but there was too much reason to believe that, not only in the subordinate but also in the higher Courts, when a witness had a long statement to make, a very imperfect and hasty outline of it was taken down by some sheristadar. He was then asked whether he had stated what appeared on the paper, and in almost every case, his answer was —"Yes," his chief wish being to get away from the irksome state in which he had been during the whole time that his statement was being extracted from him. On such a record, it was impossible that any confidence could be placed by any Court of Justice. He (Mr. LeGeyt) contended that, if the appellate Courts had the Judge's own notes before them, they would be a more trust-worthy record of what had been said by the witnesses than any which they now had. They would also have the advantage of getting a record written in their own language, and would be able to determine what each witness really had meant to say. The principle of the amendment he proposed, was admitted in that part of the present Section which said—

"In cases where an appeal does not lie to a higher tribunal, it shall not be necessary to take down the depositions of the witnesses in writing at length; but the Judge shall make a short memorandum of the substance of what each witness may have deposed, and such memorandum shall be written and signed with his own hand, and shall form part of the record."

The record in appealable cases would be much shortened by this being done with the addition which he proposed of a full note being taken of each deposition as it was given. He believed he was right in saying that in the Supreme Court at Madras, only the notes of the English Judges went up to the appellate Courts.

MR. FORBES said, a translation of the whole proceedings went up.

MR. LEGEYT, in continuation, said, he knew that in the Bombay Courts, in both Criminal and Civil proceedings, the Judges kept very full notes of the depositions, and the record was much fuller, and a most decided improvement on the mode of taking depositions which obtained elsewhere In all Civil cases, the Judge's notes formed the only record. He should conclude by moving the following amendment:—

[The Honorable Member read an amendment to the effect he had stated.]

MR. HARINGTON said it appeared to him that this Section, which corresponded almost word for word with the Section as prepared by Her Majesty's Commissioners, very properly made a wide distinction between cases which were open to appeal, and cases which were not open to appeal. In cases of the latter class, if the Judge was intelligent, honest, and industrious, and went carefully into all the proofs which were exhibited before him, it was a matter of comparatively little importance how much or how little of those proofs he placed upon record; but it was different when an appeal was allowed to a higher tribunal. In such cases, the Judges of the appellate Court were not only deprived of the advantage enjoyed by the lower Court of questioning the witnesses and of observing their demeanor, but the amendment of the Honorable Member for Bombay, if carried, would place them under the further disadvantage of not even hearing what the witnesses had said, substituting for their evidence in detail a brief memorandum

Mr. LeGeyt.

[Mr. LeGeyt said—Careful.]

Mr. HARINGTON continued, it came pretty much to the same thing whether the memorandum was to be a brief or careful one; it was left to the Judge in the Court below to confine it to what he considered sufficient or necessary. Now, it certainly appeared to him that the appellate Court was entitled to have before it the whole of the evidence of each witness in the very words in which the evidence was given, in order that it might compare the statements of the several witnesses one with another, and judge how far the evidence of each witness was deserving of credit. The Honorable Member for Bombay had said that in that Presidency the practice was to record evidence in a most careless and slovenly manner. Of that, of course, the Honorable Member for Bombay had had better opportunities of judging than he (Mr Harington) had had; but if such was the practice among the Judges of Bombay, he certainly had no reason to think that it was so amongst the Judges on this side of India.

Mr. LeGeyt said, he did not mean to limit his remarks on this point to the Presidency of Bombay. He believed it to be applicable to the Company's Courts all over India.

Mr. HARINGTON said, his own experience did not confirm what had been stated by the Honorable Member for Bombay, but if the case was as had been represented, all he could say was that the Judges who were in the habit of taking evidence in the loose and slovenly manner described by the Honorable Member, were guilty of a gross dereliction of duty. But, supposing the practice to be general, how would the course proposed by the Honorable Member remedy it? What reason had they for expecting that Judges who deliberately violated the present law, which in its terms was as clear and express as any law could be, would be more scrupulous or at all more conscientious under the rule proposed by the Honorable Member for Bombay? He could not believe that such would be the case, and he should therefore oppose the amendment.

Mr. PEACOCK said, where a case was appealable, there ought to be some record of the depositions of the witnesses; whether the record should be taken down by the Judge or by an Officer, was another matter. Formerly, a Judge was allowed to make over the task to an Officer, and certainly great abuses were committed under that system; but this Section provided that "in cases in which an appeal may lie to a higher tribunal, the evidence of each witness shall be taken down in writing by, or in the presence, and under the personal direction and superintendence of the Judge, and, when completed, shall be read over in the presence of the Judge and of the witness, and also in the presence of the parties to the suit or their pleaders, or such of them as are in attendance, and shall be signed by the Judge."

If, in the face of this provision, any Judge should allow several witnesses to be examined at once in different parts of the Court, or to be examined in his absence, he would be guilty of a great dereliction of duty, and would be liable to be brought to account by the Government under whom he was placed. He (Mr Peacock) should object to the motion to omit all the words from line 9 to line 45 of the Section; but he thought it would be right to say that, if the evidence was not written down by the Judge at the time it was given, he should make a memorandum in his own vernacular language of the substance of it during the examination, and make that memorandum a part of the record. In appealable cases, however, it was preferable that everything should be taken down.

The CHAIRMAN said, he was quite clear that, in appealable cases, the depositions of the witnesses should be taken down in full by some body or other. He believed that the experiment had been tried in the Sonthal districts—of the Judge taking down the evidence (as we understood the phrase) in his own language, and that the system had been found to be in many respects an improvement upon the course of the regular Courts; all the Judges, however, in those districts were European Officers, and the whole system of administering justice to that barbarous people was made as simple as possible. This was to be a Code for the whole of India, it might be unreasonable to pass a Section by which a Mahommedan Judge, for example, would be bound to take down the evidence as given in Bengali; for many Mahommedans would be unable to write Bengali rapidly; and on the other hand it might be unsafe to let him send up only his own version of it in Oordoo. In the Supreme Court, generally speaking, the evidence was delivered by the witness in the vernacular, and taken down by the Judges in all cases, and by an Officer also in appealable cases, in English; but it was so taken down from the interpretation of skilled Interpreters, who were sworn to interpret truly, and whose sole occupation it was to interpret. Considering the various classes and races from which Judges were taken in this country, he thought the Council could hardly call on them to take down the evidence in the vernacular language of the witnesses, but the memorandum which the Honorable Member for Bombay proposed the Judge should record, would be a very great improvement on the existing practice, because it would give the appellate Court an opportunity of testing the value of the depositions sent up, and, at all events, it would be extremely valuable as showing how the evidence had struck the Judge's mind, at the same time that it would be a check on the omlah who was writing down the depositions. He (the Chairman) was not prepared to vote for the motion of the Honorable Member for Bombay. He did not think that the Honorable Member would get by the machinery he proposed, those materials which the appellate Court ought to have; but at the same time, he was disposed to vote for the motion of the Honorable and learned Member on his right (Mr. Peacock) as it provided for that which would be useful in addition to the system proposed by the Section as it stood.

MR. LEGEYT said, after what had passed, he saw that there was no chance of his amendment being carried. The object of it was to secure a more trustworthy record than now existed, and as that would be met if

The Chairman

the course suggested by the Honorable and learned Member opposite (Mr. Peacock) were adopted, he would not press his amendment to a division, if the Honorable and learned Member would frame an amendment and bring it forward at the next meeting of the Council.

THE CHAIRMAN said, he would suggest the insertion of a clause in the amendment to be framed for the purpose of correcting what seemed to him to be a most ridiculous state of things. Suppose that the Judge who tried a case was an English Judge, and that an English witness went before him. The witness would be allowed to give his evidence in English. Ought not that evidence to be taken down in the language in which it was given? Nothing could be more absurd than to translate that witness's good English into bad Bengalee, in order that it might go up to the appellate Court, which also consisted of English Judges, to be read out with the nasal twang of the Native Omlah. It appeared to him that a clause should be inserted in the intended amendment, which would prevent such an absurdity.

MR. CURRIE said, he had some doubt as to the utility of the memorandum. The reason of the Honorable Member for Bombay for urging that it should be written with the Judge's own hand, was that it was the only way to ensure his attending to the examination. But if a Judge was disposed to do what was contrary to the law, he might just as well make the memorandum while the deposition was being read to him, or he might take the deposition home, and write out the memorandum from it there.

Then he did not think that the memorandum would be of any advantage to the appellate Court, and it would considerably enlarge the record. If an English Judge was trying the case, and the case went up in appeal, the memorandum would doubtless be useful; but even then, there would be the risk of the appellate Court deciding on the memorandum and not looking into the evidence. In Bengalee cases, which formed nine-tenths of the cases tried, the memorandum would be of no advantage in addition to the detailed deposition. So that, in any point of view, he very much doubted whether the making of the memorandum ought to be required.

Mr. LeGeyt's amendment was accordingly withdrawn and the further consideration of the Section postponed.

Section 144 was passed after an amendment.

Sections 145 and 146 were postponed.

Sections 147 to 149 were severally passed as they stood.

Sections 150 and 151 were severally passed after amendments.

Sections 152 to 166 were severally passed as they stood.

Section 167 was postponed.

Sections 168 to 170 were severally passed as they stood.

The consideration of Chapter IV was postponed.

Sections 1 to 15 of Chapter V, Sections 1 to 16 of Chapter VI, and Sections 1 to 4 of Chapter VII, were severally passed as they stood.

The further consideration of the Bill was postponed, and the Council resumed its sitting.

NOTICE OF MOTION.

Mr. FORBES gave notice that he would, on Saturday the 9th Instant, move that Section 145 of Chapter III of the above Bill be omitted, in order that the following Section may be substituted for it; namely :—

"Before any witness is examined, the Court shall administer to such witness such oath as it may consider to be most binding on the conscience according to the religious persuasion of such witness, requiring him to speak the whole truth and nothing but the truth."

EXCLUSIVE PRIVILEGES TO INVENTORS.

Mr. PEACOCK moved that Sir James Outram be requested to take the Bill "for granting exclusive privileges to Inventors" to the President in Council, in order that it might be transmitted to England for the sanction of Her Majesty.

Agreed to.

AHMEDABAD MAGISTRACY.

Mr. LeGeyt gave notice that he would, on Saturday the 9th Instant, move the second reading of the Bill "to empower the Governor in Council of Bombay to appoint a Magistrate for certain districts within the Zillah Ahmedabad."

The Council adjourned.

Saturday, October 9, 1858.

Present :

The Honorable the Chief Justice, *Vice-President*, in the Chair.

Hon'ble J. P. Grant,	Hon'ble Sir A. W. Buller,
Hon'ble Lieut.-Genl. Sir J. Outram,	H. B. Harington Esq.,
Hon'ble H. Ricketts,	and
Hon'ble B. Peacock,	H. Forbes, Esq.
P. W. LeGeyt, Esq.,	
E. Currie Esq.,	

STAMP DUTIES (BENGAL.)

The CLERK presented to the Council a Petition of Rammohun Bannerjee and Guddadhur Bannerjee, Zemindars of West Burdwan, concerning the Bill "to amend Regulation X. 1829 of the Bengal Code (for the collection of Stamp Duties.)"

Mr. PEACOCK moved that the above Petition be printed.

Agreed to.

ENDOWMENT OF MOSQUES, HINDOO TEMPLES, AND COLLEGES.

The CLERK presented a Petition of Protestant Missionaries praying for the repeal of the Regulations of the Bengal and Madras Codes providing for the maintenance of endowments for the support of Mosques, Hindoo Temples, and Colleges.

Mr. CURRIE moved that the above Petition be printed.

Agreed to.

CHURRUCK POOJAH.

The Clerk also presented to the Council a Petition of Protestant Missionaries praying for a legislative enactment to suppress all those public practices at the Churruck Poojah, whether nominally religious practices or not, which are in themselves cruel and inhuman.

MR. CURRIE moved that the above Petition be printed.

He said that in making this motion he did not pledge himself to take any farther steps in the matter, for it appeared that the subject had already been considered by the Court of Directors, and the Honorable Court had expressed an opinion against the expediency of any direct interference on the part of Government. The Lieutenant-Governor of Bengal, after a careful review of the question, had also come to the same conclusion. With the permission of the Council, he would read a statement of what had been done in the matter from the general Administration Report of the several Presidencies for the year 1856-57:—

"The Honorable the Court of Directors having remarked that, if the practice of swinging on Churrucks was found to be attended with cruelty, and liable to be enforced without the free consent of parties submitting to it, they doubted not that the Government would consider what measures should be adopted with reference to it—the Commissioners of the South-Western Frontier and Assam, and the Superintendents of Police Lower Provinces, Chittagong and Cuttack, were requested to report on the subject, and to state whether the existing law was sufficient for preventing the crime, or whether, in their opinion, any special measures were required.

"Intermediately however, the order calling for the opinions of the Officers above-mentioned, was reviewed by the Honorable Court, who recorded the following remarks regarding it:—

"'We observe that enquiry has been instituted by the Lieutenant-Governor with a view to the authoritative suppression of the practice of swinging on the Churruck, as it is stated that it would be regarded with satisfaction by the sensible part of the Hindoo Community, and with indifference by the rest.

"'We should prefer, however, that your endeavors for the suppression of this practice should be based on the exertion of influence rather than upon any act of authority.'

"Subsequently also to the issue of the Circular to the Commissioners, a memorial regarding the Churruck Poojah was received from the Calcutta Missionary Conference."

Then followed the Memorial, which no doubt was much to the same effect as the Petition now presented.

"After careful consideration, the Lieutenant-Governor came to the conclusion that, as the case was one of pain voluntarily undergone, the remedy must be left to the Missionary and the School Master, and that, as stated by the Honorable Court, all such cruel ceremonies must be discouraged by influence rather than by authority."

Such were the opinions which had been recorded. It would however be for the Council to consider whether the Petitioners had now made out such a case as seemed to call for legislative interference.

The motion was carried.

FALSE WEIGHTS AND MEASURES.

THE CLERK reported to the Council that he had received a communication from the Chairman of the Madras Chamber of Commerce, representing that the provisions of the Police Act, XIII of 1856, were not a sufficient check against the fraudulent use of false weights and measures inasmuch as they restricted a Police Inspector entering a shop or premises to inspect the weights and measures used therein only upon complaint made to him.

MR. FORBES moved that the above communication be referred to the Select Committee on "the Indian Penal Code."

Agreed to.

MERCHANT SEAMEN.

MR. CURRIE presented the Report of the Select Committee on the Bill "for the amendment of the law relating to Merchant Seamen."

AHMEDABAD MAGISTRACY.

MR. LEGEYT moved the second reading of the Bill "to empower the Governor in Council of Bombay to appoint a Magistrate for certain Districts within the Zillah Ahmedabad."

MR. RICKETTS said, he would submit to the Council that, on the whole, it would be better, instead of legislating for the particular districts in question, to provide for all districts in the same position throughout the Bombay Presidency. The Zillah of Ahmedabad was a Regulation district. The neighbouring Province of Kattywar was a non-Regulation district under the control of a Political Agent. For some reason or another, not explained in the annexures to the Bill, the Magistrate of Ahmedabad had been unable to manage the people of a Pergunnah called Bhownugghur, which was on the confines of Kattywar; but the Political Agent of Kattywar was able to manage it. The Bombay Government, therefore, had appointed the Political Agent Magistrate of the districts in Bhownugghur, in lieu of the Magistrate of Ahmedabad; but shortly after, questions arose regarding appeals from the districts from the Magisterial decisions of the Political Agent, and the Sudder Adawlut discovered that the Rules of Bombay were so strict that there could be but one Magistrate in each Zillah, and therefore recommended alteration of the Law. Regulation XII. 1807 of the Bombay Code enacted that the duties of Police in each Zillah should be conducted by the Collector of that Zillah, and further, that the Collector of each Zillah should, under the denomination of Zillah Magistrate, perform the functions of Police. The Legislature had long ago provided for cases of that nature on this side of India. Regulation XVI. 1810 of the Bengal Code provided as follows :—

"The Governor General in Council, whenever he may deem it advisable, will invest the Magistrate of any Zillah with a general concurrent authority as Joint Magistrate in any contiguous or other jurisdiction, or in any part thereof."

An enactment of this kind would exactly meet the case which had induced the Honorable Member for Bombay to bring forward the present Bill. Under Regulation XVI. 1810, the Collector of a Zillah in Bengal could and did exercise the jurisdiction of a Magistrate.

But it appeared to him that there was another point to be provided for. It was the intention of the Bombay Government that the Political Agent of Kattywar should be Magistrate of Bhownugghur. It could not be intended that, if appointed such Magistrate, he should leave the district of Bhownugghur and go to Kattywar. Probably the intention might be that people should be brought from Bhownugghur to the office at Kattywar; and in that case, it would be necessary also to enact that it should be lawful for that Officer to exercise his Magisterial duties beyond the confines of his jurisdiction.

He should therefore move as an amendment that the second reading of the Bill before the Council be postponed until this day three months, and suggest to the Honorable Member to bring in a Bill to the following effect in the meantime :—

"It shall be lawful for the Government of Bombay to appoint a Joint or Assistant Magistrate, with the powers of a Magistrate, in any District subject to the Bombay Government, and to give such Joint or Assistant Magistrate concurrent jurisdiction with the Magistrate over any part or over the whole of the District, or to place any portion of the District exclusively under such Joint or Assistant Magistrate.

"A Joint or Assistant Magistrate so appointed shall be subject to the jurisdiction of the Sessions Judge of the Zillah within which the local jurisdiction assigned to him may be, and to the Sudder Court in like manner with the District Magistrate.

"It shall be lawful for the Governor in Council in Bombay to authorize any Magistrate or Joint or Assistant Magistrate to hold trials at a place beyond the confines of his jurisdiction."

THE VICE-PRESIDENT said, the more general course in this Council had been to vote against the second reading.

MR. LEGEYT said, he did not think the Honorable Member (Mr. Ricketts) had given quite a correct version of Regulation XII. 1807. If he had understood the Honorable Member aright, the Honorable Member had stated that, under the present law, the Governor in Council of Bombay had no power to allow any one but the Magistrate of a Zillah, as described in Section III of Regulation XII. 1807 of the Bombay Code, to perform the duties of a Magistrate within his Zillah; but if he would look farther on, he would see that the 3rd Clause of Section III of the same Regulation provided for the appointment of Assistant Magistrates, and that subsequent Sections provided for vesting Assistant Magistrates with the full powers of a Magistrate. Then there were other Acts for appointing Joint Magistrates in Zillahs. If the Governor in Council of Bombay had considered that either Assistant Magistrates with full powers, or Joint Magistrates, or Deputy Magistrates, appointed under the existing Regulations, would have answered for the Bhownugghur villages, he would doubtless not have sent up this Bill for the approval of the Legislative Council. But he (Mr. LeGeyt) thought the Governor in Council did not consider that such appointments would have answered, and considered that, for political reasons, the Political Agent of Kattywar should exercise Magisterial powers in the districts of Bhownugghur. It would hardly do to appoint the Political Agent of Kattywar, who was an officer of equal rank with, and perfectly independent of the Magistrate of Ahmedabad, Assistant to the Magistrate with full powers. Nor, he (Mr LeGeyt) apprehended, was it intended that he should be appointed Joint Magistrate; for although as Joint Magistrate he would exercise powers concurrently with the Magistrate, yet in some portions of his duties he would be subject to the control of the latter. He believed it was to avoid these inconveniences that the Governor in Council preferred to meet the exigency now felt by appointing the Political Agent of Kattywar Magistrate of Bhownugghur. If he (Mr. LeGeyt) had rightly understood the draft Act which the Honorable Member proposed to substitute for the present Bill, it would do no more than allow the Governor in Council to appoint a Joint or Assistant Magistrate That would entail an alteration of the whole procedure laid down in the Bombay Code. The object of the Bill he had introduced was that the Governor in Council should have power, without creating a new Zillah, of appointing an Officer with the full powers of a Zillah Magistrate. If the Political Agent of Kattywar should be appointed a Joint Magistrate or an Assistant Magistrate, he would, in a certain degree, according to the present Law, be subject to the Zillah Magistrate. He (Mr. LeGeyt) could not see how the arrangement proposed in this Bill was in any way calculated to lead to the inconvenience of the Public. The Bombay Government thought it calculated to further the administration of Justice. They had the power of appointing Assistant Magistrates with full powers, and Joint Magistrates, but had not thought it expedient to exercise that power in this instance, and he, for his own part, did not see why the Bill should not pass into Law.

Mr. CURRIE said, he thought it would be as well if the Honorable Member for Bombay would himself consider, and also consult the Bombay Government on the expediency of extending to that Presidency the general powers now conferred in Bengal by Regulation XVI. 1810. It was very convenient that the executive Government should have those powers, and as occasion had arisen for them in Bombay, he thought it would be better if the Regulation for Bengal were extended to it.

The question being put, the Council divided:—

Ayes 8.	*Noes* 2.
Mr. Forbes.	Mr. Currie.
Mr. Harington.	Mr. Ricketts.
Sir Arthur Buller.	
Mr. LeGeyt.	
Mr. Peacock.	
Sir James Outram.	
Mr. Grant.	
The Vice-President.	

The motion was accordingly carried, and the Bill read a second time.

CIVIL PROCEDURE.

On the Order of the Day being read for the adjourned Committee of the whole Council on the Bill "for simplifying the Procedure of the Courts of Civil Judicature not established by Royal Charter," the Council resolved itself into a Committee for the further consideration of the Bill.

The postponed Section 92 of Chapter III provided that a defendant desiring to set-off any demand against the plaintiff's claim must tender a written statement containing the particulars of such demand, the excess of set-off over claim being abandoned.

Mr. HARINGTON said, in consequence of a remark which fell from the Chair at the last Meeting of the Council, and which had reference to the law or practice of what was called a set-off as it obtained in the Courts in this country, whether established by Royal Charter or by the local Governments, he had been led, in the course of the week, to look into the English law on the subject, and to consider whether it might be acted upon with advantage in framing any amendment of the Section before the Committee. He observed that in Blackstone and other English law books it was stated that a set-off, when used as a mode of defence to a suit or action, was of that nature that it admitted the claim of the opposite party to be just, only insisting that the debtor was also a creditor in some other manner in respect of which the opposite debt was counter-balanced either wholly or in part. He did not know whether this was still the law in Her Majesty's Courts; but whether it was so or not, a rule which required that a defendant who desired to set-off against the claim of the plaintiff a demand for which he might sue the plaintiff separately, should first acknowledge the justice of the plaintiff's claim, appeared to him to be strictly equitable and reasonable, and to be consistent with the real meaning of the term "set-off;" and, accordingly, in the first of the two amended Sections prepared by him, he had proposed it for adoption. When a defendant in an action of debt, assumpsit, or the like, not only pleaded a set-off to, but also denied the justice of the plaintiff's claim either in the whole or in part, there would be two causes of action which might have accrued on different dates, and the proofs upon which they severally rested would often be found to be quite distinct. In such cases, so far as he could perceive, no advantage could result to either party from doubling up the two claims and treating them as a single suit, while in practice he thought that much inconvenience might ensue from such a proceeding. There could, of course, be no objection, but the contrary, to the two claims proceeding step by step together to a decision, and to the decision of the one following immediately upon the decision of the other, though in all other respects they should be dealt with as distinct actions which in reality they were. Such was indeed the present practice which was found to be very convenient, while it gave to either party the full benefit of any claim which he might succeed in establishing against the other. Under these circumstances it did not appear to him that any thing would be gained by allowing a defendant, who denied the justice of the plaintiff's claim, to meet that claim with a counter-demand by way of set-off, which he might make the subject of a separate action, unless the Committee should be of opinion that the counter-claim of the defendant should not be subject to the stamp duty imposed upon petitions of plaint, and which the defendant would have to pay if he appeared in the character of plaintiff. When, however, a defendant, acknowledging the justice of the plaintiff's claim, assigned as his only reason for not satisfying it that he had a counter-demand against the plaintiff, which, if proved, should be allowed to counter-balance the plaintiff's claim either wholly or in part, the case was very different. By such admission the matters in dispute between the parties were at once reduced to a single controversy, and the Court, instead of having to investigate and determine the claim of the plaintiff as well as the claim of the defendant, would be required to look to the claim of the latter only; and as by acknowledging the justice of the plaintiff's claim, the defendant would relieve the Court from the labor and responsibility of adjudicating upon it, he thought that the stamp duty paid upon the plaint might fairly be allowed to cover the counter-claim of the defendant, and that the Court should proceed to determine the single action remaining to be decided, provided, of course, it had jurisdiction over the demand of the defendant in respect of its value or amount. The first of the two amended Sections prepared by him had been framed in accordance with these views. The second amended Section, which he should not have occasion to bring forward should the Committee agree to the first Section, was nearly the same as the Section which he had proposed on Saturday last. To that Section it had been objected by the Honorable Member for Bengal that, when a suit was brought against a person who had a counter-demand against the plaintiff, which, but for the plaintiff's suit, might never come into Court, it would be hard to charge the defendant with a stamp duty on his demand, and the Honorable and learned Member of Council on his left (Mr. Peacock) had made a further objection to the latter part of the Section, which pointed out what was to be done in the event of the counter-demand of the defendant exceeding the jurisdiction of the Court in which the suit was brought. It appeared to the Honorable and learned Member that the provision contained in this part of the Section might encourage the defendant to increase any demand that he might have against the plaintiff beyond the jurisdiction of the Court in order to cause the removal of the suit to another Court, whereby the plaintiff might be harassed and subjected to heavy expense. He (Mr. Harington) was not prepared to say that this might not happen, but he thought such a case would be of very rare occurrence. It must be remembered that the counter-demand of the defendant would be chargeable with a stamp duty proportionate to its amount, which he would not recover from the plaintiff in the event of his failing in his proofs, while after all the suit would not be removed to a different district, but only from one Court to another Court of the same district, and that a superior Court. It was unnecessary, however, for him to notice these objections further at present, as the first of the two amended Sections prepared by him was free from them. He would only further remark that both Sections contained words to show that it was not every demand of a defendant which would constitute a valid or legal set-off to the claim of the plaintiff, and that, when a set-off was pleaded, it would be the duty of the Court to consider whether it was of such a nature that, if proved, it should be allowed to counter-balance the claim of the plaintiff. Her Majesty's Commissioners appeared to have taken it for granted that there was already some law of set-off in the Mofussil, and they had contented themselves with providing that, when a set-off was pleaded in a Moonsiff's Court, its character or amount should not be looked to, but that if the claim was considered to be established, the Moonsiff should decree for the amount. There was, however, no law of the kind, and as the rule proposed by Her Majesty's Commissioners was obviously open to serious objections, he thought that the Select Committee had acted wisely in refusing to adopt it. With these remarks he begged to move that Section 92 should be omitted, with a view to the substitution for it of the first of the two amended Sections prepared by him, which was as follows:—

"If the defendant admit the claim of the plaintiff but desire to set-off against it any demand for which he might sue the plaintiff in the same Court, he shall tender a written statement containing the particulars of such demand, and if the Court be of opinion that the demand of the defendant is of a nature which, if proved, should be allowed to counterbalance the claim of the plaintiff either wholly or in part, it shall proceed to investigate the demand of the defendant in the suit before it. When a defendant may be allowed under this Section to set-off a demand against the claim of the plaintiff, he shall be debarred from bringing a separate suit in respect of the same cause of action."

MR. CURRIE said, he had given notice of an amendment on this subject, having some objection to those proposed by the Honorable Member for the North-Western Provinces. The amendment before the Committee appeared to him to be open to two objections. He thought first that the defendant should not be required to admit the plaintiff's claim, at least in the whole; and secondly, if the counter-claim exceeded the amount cognizable by the Court, he thought the defendant should not on this ground be debarred from pleading it. He had prepared a Section which avoided these objections. He also proposed that the defendant should not be liable for stamp duty in respect of a set-off; but if he sought for judgment for a sum in excess of the plaintiff's claim, it seemed right that the written statement containing the particulars of his demand should be upon such stamp paper as would be required for a plaint for the amount of such excess.

THE CHAIRMAN thought that the Honorable Member for the North-Western Provinces went on a correct principle in requiring admission of plaintiff's claim to some extent; but he went too far. For instance, two persons having mutual dealings came into Court; the plaintiff said that a large sum was due to him; the defendant might be prepared to admit half, and to insist that he had a demand which ought to be set-off. The amendment seemed to require that he should admit the plaintiff's claim to the full extent. He begged to suggest the introduction of the words "either wholly or in part" after the words "if the defendant admit the claim of the plaintiff" He was not prepared, considering the preliminary examination of the parties, and the verification of the pleadings that were proposed, to give the defendant that latitude which he had in the English Courts, or to let him both deny the existence of any demand on the part of the plaintiff, and meet it, if proved, by a plea of set-off. He observed that the Honorable Member's amendment proposed to leave it in the discretion of the Judge to say whether the cross-demand was proper to be admitted by way of set-off. It might be better that the law should define the nature of the counter-claims which should be allowed to be set-off, rather than that the Court should have this power. He was clear, however, that there should be some limitation to the defence of "set-off." It would be very inconvenient to admit, besides money demands, claims founded on assault, slander, &c.; many false claims would thus be brought forward, by which plaintiffs would be harassed and the hearing of causes inconveniently protracted. The limitation of the English law of set-off might not be the best; but it was better than admitting all claims whatsoever as matter of set-off.

Sir ARTHUR BULLER said, he did not see why an admission of the plaintiff's claim should be the condition of the plea of set-off. Why might not the defendant say, "I don't admit that the plaintiff has any valid claim against me; but even if I am mistaken in my law, I have a set-off?" These two defences were certainly not incompatible according to English law. Technically speaking, the mere plea of set-off would, as the Honorable Member for the North-Western Provinces said, admit the plaintiff's claim, but then the defendant always fortified his case by another and perfectly admissible plea of denial of the plaintiff's claim altogether. But what he (Sir Arthur Buller) most objected to was the leaving it to the Judge to determine what sort of set-off he would allow. One Judge might have no hesitation in admitting a set-off for damages for assault, or libel, or criminal conversation. Another might make it a rule to admit of no set-off except for a fixed ascertained debt, and one Judge's practice would not be binding on another. It never would do to leave this, which should be settled by substantive law, to the caprice of individual Judges; and in his opinion the original Clause was far better than this or any other amendment which was before them; but he had no very strong opinion one way or another, as to whether the right of set-off should extend to all demands, or whether it should be in some degree limited.

Mr. PEACOCK preferred Section 92 as it stood, though it might require some amendment. The expression "along with the claim of the plaintiff if it shall consider it reasonable so to do" did not mean that the Judge had the option whether to try or not; it compelled him to try the question of set-off some time or other before the suit was determined, for that was provided by the Section relating to the decree (161). He preferred the present Section, because it did not oblige a defendant to admit the plaintiff's demand if he set up a counter-claim. A defendant might honestly deny that he owed any thing; he might state the facts truly, and submit whether he was indebted. He might say, "I contend I am not indebted; but if I am, I have a cross-demand." He ought not to be obliged to admit the whole claim which might depend on some difficult question of law which might be decided against the plaintiff. He thought that the Honorable Member for the North-Western Provinces had made a slight mistake as to the English law. The plea of set-off must admit the demand, but there might be a denial of liability in a separate plea. A defendant might say, "If you determine against me on this claim, then I ask you to investigate my case against him; he is insolvent—

do not compel me to pay his demand, when I have a larger claim against him." If the words "if it shall consider it reasonable so to do" were applicable to the whole Section, he would prefer to omit them. According to English law, a set-off was allowed only in cases of debts and liquidated damages. Vindictive damages, as for assault, &c., could not be matter of set-off. This Section went farther and provided that, if one man sued another and there was a counter-claim, the plaintiff should not issue execution until the counter-claim had been determined; therefore, if the subject of the counter-claim was within the jurisdiction of the Court, it ought to be investigated, whatever it might be. The principle adopted in Act IX of 1850 (for the more easy recovery of small debts and demands) was this. If there were cross-judgments between the same parties, execution was to be taken out by that party only who had judgment for the larger sum, and for so much only as should remain after deducting the smaller sum. It mattered not what were the nature of the claims. The defendant was not to be imprisoned, nor was his property to be seized if he held a decree against the plaintiff for an equal or larger amount. Suppose a suit for rent and a cross claim, not for a debt, but for unliquidated damages, say a sale of Indigo seed to the defendant, which, though warranted good, had turned out to be worthless; the Judge would decide that the rent was due. Was he to permit execution to issue before deciding upon the other question? It might be that the defendant had sustained damages by the loss of a crop far beyond the amount of the rent. It ought not to be discretionary with the Judge to investigate that: he should be bound to do so. If both cases were within his jurisdiction, he should try both before execution issued. Section 92 might easily be amended if his view were wrong. He referred to the latter part of the proposed Section:—

"When a defendant *may be* allowed under this Section to set-off a demand against the claim of the plaintiff, he shall be debarred from bringing a separate suit in respect of the same cause of action."

Mr. Peacock

It meant, if there should be a decree for or against the defendant or that the suit was pending. This was not sufficient, because plaintiff might abandon his suit; in that case the defendant should nevertheless have the benefit of his set-off.

MR. HARINGTON said that, when the jurisdiction was limited, it was necessary that the set-off should also be limited. The latter part of the amended Section had been introduced for this reason. He referred to Blackstone's Commentaries and said that there were various grades of Courts with different jurisdictions, and that they could not properly exceed their respective jurisdictions. The question must also be considered with reference to the stamp laws in which the Government had an interest. It occurred to him that, if the defendant admitted the justice of the plaintiff's claim, the Government might fairly forego the stamp duty on the defendant's counter-demand; but if the defendant disputed the plaintiff's claim, as already noticed by him, there was no advantage in doubling up the two claims. They had better be tried as separate suits.

MR. GRANT asked, if it was meant that a Judge must suspend judgment in one action because another was pending? If this were so, a plaintiff in a very simple case might never get a decree at all. Suppose, for example, the simple case of a ryot not paying his rent. The Zemindar must get his rent; if not, he cannot pay his revenue, and he loses his estate. An action is brought. the ryot has no defence to the claim, but states that last year the Zemindar slandered him, and that he has an action for damages which must be tried in the way of a set-off, it matters not whether in the same suit or not. He demands that judgment be stayed till both actions are determined. The slander case might require months to get up the proof. Should the other simple case, which might be decided in five minutes, be postponed until the tedious and complicated slander-suit, which had no connection with the other matter, should be settled? His own opinion was that the practice of the

Supreme Courts was better, which as he understood, restricted claims of set-off to cases of debt. If the dispute was all one matter of account, that might conveniently be decided at once, and the balance ascertained. But this would not be possible, if many claims, for various unascertained amounts, arising out of quite different transactions, were to be heard together. He was uncertain, from the terms of Section 92, what was actually the intention.

THE CHAIRMAN said, it would be better to abandon the whole principle than open a door to a flood of sets-off arising in respect of claims of all descriptions. He thought that his Honorable and learned friend (Mr. Peacock) proceeded on a greater presumption of fair dealing in litigation than existed in this country. Such a provision would be for the encouragement of false claims; and when it was found that execution could not be taken out while a counter-claim was in litigation, the plaintiff would be harassed by false claims. If the principle could be limited to cases of money and liquidated damages, convenience might require that it should be admitted. He could put no other construction on the Section than that it meant to give the Judge a discretion. "Along with the claim of the plaintiff" meant not of course that he was to hear simultaneously, but *in the same suit*, and that one decree would determine the whole. Such a discretion might be objectionable. If there were difficulties, the Section might be abandoned and provision made in the Chapter relating to execution of decrees for a set-off of cross-judgments. But such a provision should not go to the extent of suspending one judgment for an indefinite time until all possible questions should have been determined. It should be limited to judgments actually recovered. One party might push on his action while the other was pending; but there should be a strict limit of the time during which the judgment should be suspended.

MR. CURRIE suggested that the Section might be limited to such cases of debt &c. as had been referred to.

MR. PEACOCK said, the objection that false claims might be brought forward applied as much to a set-off on account of a debt as to a set-off of other matters. It was said that Zemindars might be delayed; but they should not legislate only for them. Every one (whether Zemindar or not) had to pay his just debts. A more probable case than that supposed, had been suggested to him. It was much more likely that a forged bond should be attempted to be set-off than a case of slander. The forged bond would fall within the rule, if a set-off for debt were allowed, for the validity of the claim must be tried before it could be rejected. But it was said that the case supposed was that of a good cause of suit as a trespass, slander, &c., but one requiring long proof. It might be inconvenient to admit such a case to be tried as a set-off. He should be content to confine the set-off to debts, and to introduce a Clause like Section LVII of Act IX of 1850:—

"If there be cross-judgments between the parties, execution shall be taken out by that party only who shall have obtained judgment for the larger, and for so much only as shall remain after deducting the smaller sum; and satisfaction for the remainder shall be entered, as well as satisfaction on the judgment for the smaller sum; and if both sums shall be equal, satisfaction shall be entered upon both judgments."

Where there was a counter-claim, it might be left to the Judge's discretion not to allow execution to issue on one decree if he thought it reasonable to delay it until another claim should be determined. If this should be the opinion of the Council, he would prepare a Section.

MR HARINGTON'S motion to omit Section 92 was then carried, and the motion to substitute the proposed Section was by leave withdrawn.

The postponed Section 107 of Chapter III being read by the Chairman—

MR. LEGEYT moved that the following words be added to the Section:—

"But in every such case, a copy, properly certified and made at the expense of the applicant, shall be substituted for the original in the record of the suit."

The motion was agreed to, and the Section then passed.

The postponed Section 108 of Chapter III being read by the Chairman—

MR. LEGEYT moved that the Section be left out, and the following new Section be substituted for it :—

"Whenever an exhibit once received by a Court of Justice and admitted in evidence is returned, a receipt shall be given by the party receiving it, in a receipt book kept for the purpose.

Agreed to.

The postponed Section 143 of Chapter III being read by the Chairman—

MR. PEACOCK moved that it be omitted, in order that the following new Section might be substituted for it :—

"On the day appointed for the hearing of the suit, or on some other day to which the hearing may be adjourned, the evidence of the witnesses in attendance shall be taken orally in open Court in the presence and hearing, and under the personal direction and superintendence of the Judge. In cases in which an appeal lies to a higher tribunal, the evidence of each witness given upon such examination shall be taken down in writing, in the language in ordinary use in proceedings before the Court by or in the presence and under the personal direction and superintendence of the Judge, not ordinarily in the form of question and answer but in that of a narrative, and when completed shall be read over in the presence of the Judge and of the witness and also in the presence of the parties to the suit or their pleaders, or such of them as are in attendance, and shall be signed by the Judge. If the evidence be taken down in a different language from that in which it has been given, and the witness does not understand the language in which it is taken down, the witness may require his deposition as taken down in writing to be interpreted to him in the language in which it was given. It shall be in the discretion of the Court to take down, or cause to be taken down, any particular question and answer if there shall appear any special reason for so doing, or any party or his pleader shall require it. If any question put to a witness be objected to by either of the parties or their pleaders, and the Court shall allow the same to be put, the question and answer shall be taken down, and the objection and the name of the party making it shall be noticed in taking down the depositions, together with the decision of the Court upon the objection. The Court shall record such remarks as it may think material respecting the demeanor of the witness while under examination. In cases in which the evidence is not taken down in writing by the Judge himself, he shall be bound, as the examination of each witness proceeds, to make a memorandum of the substance of what such witness deposes, and such memorandum shall be written and signed by the Judge with his own hand, and shall accompany the record. In cases in which an appeal does not lie to a higher tribunal, it shall not be necessary to take down the deposition of the witnesses at length, but the Judge, as the examination of each witness proceeds, shall make a memorandum of the substance of what such witness deposes, and such memorandum shall be written and signed by the Judge with his own hand, and shall form part of the record. If the Judge shall be prevented from making a memorandum as above required, he shall record the reason of his inability to do so, and in cases not appealable shall cause such memorandum to be made in writing from his dictation in open Court, and shall sign the same, and such memorandum shall form part of the record."

The question that the words proposed to be omitted be omitted was put, and agreed to.

The question that the words proposed to be substituted be substituted being proposed—

SIR ARTHUR BULLER moved, by way of amendment, that the words "if necessary be corrected, and shall" be inserted after the word "shall" in the 21st line of the proposed Section.

Agreed to.

SIR ARTHUR BULLER moved that the words "Where all the parties to the suit present and the pleaders of such as are absent, consent to have such evidence as is given in English taken down in English, the Judge may so take it down in his own hand" be inserted after the word "given" in the 28th line of the proposed Section.

Agreed to.

MR. HARINGTON moved that the words 'In cases in which the evidence is not taken down in writing by the Judge himself, he shall be bound, as the examination of each witness proceeds, to make a memorandum of the substance of what such witness deposes, and such memorandum shall be written and signed by the Judge with his own hand, and shall accompany the record" after the word "examination" in the 45th line of the proposed Section, be left out.

He said, the Honorable Member for Bombay had stated at the last meeting of the Council that some of the Judges, unmindful of the moral and legal obligation which the present law imposed upon them of requiring the evidence of every witness to be reduced into writing in their immediate presence and hearing, and under their personal direction and superintendence, allowed the evidence of witnesses to be taken in their Courts in a most careless and slovenly manner, it being not an uncommon practice for the Judge to engage in other business or duties while the examination of a witness was going on, whereby the intention of the law was entirely defeated; and in order to put a stop to this practice, and to insure the evidence of every witness being taken in the manner prescribed by law, the Honorable and learned Member proposed to insert the words which he had just read. The sole object of the rule proposed by the Honorable and learned Member was to compel the Judges to do that which, but for such a rule, it was thought probable that some of them might fail to do. But were they sure, or had they good reason, to believe that the rule proposed by the Honorable and learned Member would be more efficacious than that contained in the earlier part of the Section. What was there to prevent a Judge, if so disposed, from evading the duty prescribed in the proposed rule in the same manner and with the same ease as it was said that some Judges violated the obligation imposed upon them by the existing law; and if the proposed rule failed to produce the effect intended, he thought that the Honorable and learned Member would agree with him that it would not only be useless, but that it might be mischievous, inasmuch as the appellate Court, having the memorandum, which the Judge of the Court of first instance was to write with his own hand, before it, might be led to suppose that the evidence had been taken in the manner prescribed by law, that is, in the hearing and under the personal direction and superintendence, as well as in the presence of the Judge, and might be induced in consequence to place greater reliance upon it; whereas, in truth, at the time the witness was being examined, the Judge might have been engaged in some other business, or giving his attention to some other matter. It was not pretended that the memorandum which the rule required, would be in itself of any use to the Judge who was to write it, in deciding the case, or to the Judges of the appellate Court who might have to hear an appeal from that Judge's decision, as a means of testing the correctness of the record, which would still have to be made of the examination in full of each witness. The object aimed at was simply what had been already stated. As had been pointed out by the Honorable Member for Bengal, there would be nothing to prevent the Judge from preparing the memorandum required of him, not at the time that the evidence was being taken, but when it was being read over to the witness for the purpose of being attested, or, indeed as remarked by him, after the rising of the Court at the Judge's private residence; and when, as was too often the case, the Judge cared more for the number of cases disposed of by him within a given period, than for the manner in which they were decided, this would probably be the general practice. It had often been remarked that they ought not to distrust their Judges, and this was one of the reasons assigned for doing away with appeals in cases of a simple character, and of a small amount. He (Mr. Harington) thought that no Judge had a right to complain that his decision in every case was open to appeal; but whatever distrust might be involved in an appeal, it appeared to him that every Judge might fairly protest against the distrust which would be implied, and the slur which would be cast upon his judicial character if the rule proposed by the Honorable and learned Member should be adopted. There appeared to him to be other objections to the proposed rule, one of which was that it would have the obvious effect of greatly increasing the size of the record, but this was comparatively a trifling matter, and he should resist the introduction of the words in question on the broad ground that they would be ineffectual; and that, if they failed in their object, they would not only be ineffectual, but might be mischievous.

Mr. GRANT asked, if the objection felt by the Honorable Member to the Section was a substantial objection? Did the Honorable Member object to the process prescribed by it?

Mr. HARINGTON said, he objected to the proposed memorandum because it would be of no use either to the Court of first instance or to the appellate Court in deciding the suit, and was intended only to make the Judge do what the Section as it now stood required him to do.

MR. RICKETTS said, the Section directed the Judge to take the evidence, and the addition to which the Honorable Member for the North-Western Provinces objected, directed him how to do that.

MR. GRANT said, according to the first part of the Section, the evidence in appealable cases may be taken down either by the Judge or by some Officer of the Court. If it is not taken down by the Judge, the Section provided that the Judge "shall be bound, as the examination of each witness proceeds, to make a memorandum of the substance of what each witness deposes, and such memorandum shall be written and signed by the Judge with his own hand, and shall accompany the record." If the Judge took this record home to frame his memorandum, he certainly would do what the law told him not to do. His (Mr. Grant's) opinion was that the course prescribed by the provision in question was what every Judge ought to follow. He thought it a useful provision that every Judge, Civil or Criminal, should take a memorandum of the evidence as the examination proceeds. That being the proper course, he did not see why the law should not require it to be taken. If the law did require it, and a Judge violated the law, he did not see why the authorities who had dominion over Judges should not call him to account.

MR. HARINGTON said, the Honorable Member for Bombay had declared that in the Courts of the East India Company the evidence, instead of being taken as the law required, was generally taken in a loose manner, and he was bound to state that within the last few days he had been assured by a Judge of the Calcutta Sudder Court, and one of the ablest pleaders in that Court, that in the Moonsiffs' Courts two or three cases were usually tried at the same time, the excuse given being that, unless this was done, the prescribed number of cases could not be disposed of nor the file kept clear. No doubt, that was a serious violation of the law, but he did not think that the proposed amendment would correct it.

MR. GRANT said, it would add another provision of the law—another check.

THE CHAIRMAN said, he did not look on the proposed new Section as implying any distrust of the Judges who would administer the Code. A memorandum made by a Judge of the substance of the evidence taken before him might often be of material use to Judges of the appellate Courts, as a check on the fuller record taken down by his omlah (which it might be desirable to have done if the evidence was given in Bengali), and would also be valuable as showing to the appellate Court the mode in which the evidence had struck the mind of the Judge. Therefore, disclaiming any intention of implying distrust of the Judges for whose guidance the Section was designed, he thought the provision a useful provision, and should vote against the amendment.

MR. LEGEYT said, he thought the provision a most useful one. If it had been in force now, it never would have allowed a state of things which admitted of evidence being taken, in some Courts at least, in a careless and slovenly manner. In all Courts in Bombay, whether Civil or Criminal, which were presided over by Europeans, it had been for many years a rule that every Magistrate and Judge should decide cases upon evidence taken down in the Vernacular language, and that they should also note down the proceedings with their own hands. In cases of appeal these notes were always sent up to the appellate Courts as part of the record, and were looked at by the Judges in appeal. He observed that such a rule was contemplated, and indeed enjoined, so long ago as 1827. Regulation IV of that year, Section XXXVII, provided as follows:—

> "If both parties in a suit should express in writing such to be their wish, the recording of the evidence and proceedings at length shall be dispensed with, and the Court's notes alone shall be preserved; if a suit so tried be appealed, the said notes shall be held to be the record of the suit, and the fact therein recorded shall be deemed to be determined, the appeal being admitted only (so far as such facts are concerned) on the deductions drawn from them."

He did not think that in the Native Courts in Bombay, the practice here required was much resorted to; nor did he believe that it was the practice in Native Courts generally, to take these notes, which it would be under the Section before the Council, and which, he thought, would have the effect of making Judges hear cases with much greater care and attention than, it was to be feared, were now always bestowed.

MR. PEACOCK said, the Section required the Judges who would exercise jurisdiction under this Code, to do no more than the Lord Chancellor, and every other Judge in England who performed his duty, did. The Honorable Member for the North-Western Provinces said that the memorandum of the Judge would be of no use. To him (Mr Peacock), it appeared that it would be of very great use. If the Judge should take full notes of the evidence himself, it would doubtless be of no use; but if the notes were taken by an Officer, the memorandum by the Judge would be valuable in showing whether the record by the Officer had been taken correctly or not. If he (Mr. Peacock) thought that any Judge was capable of making his memorandum from the notes of the evidence at home, when the law expressly required him to make it independently of the notes as the examination proceeded, he should certainly insert a clause to guard against the abuse; but he could not conceive that any Judge could be guilty of such conduct, and it would be casting an unmerited slur upon an honorable body to make any provision on the subject. But the Council would cast no slur upon that body in pointing out its duty to it, and it merely did that when it provided that in all appealable cases, where the Judge did not take down the evidence of the witnesses himself, he should make a memorandum of the substance of each deposition as it was being given. The law required a Judge to take an oath of office. There was no slur implied in that. Whether an oath of office was a good thing or not, was not the question; but it cast no slur upon the person who took it; nor did he think it would be casting any slur upon the Judges who were to administer this Code to insert in it a Section which would prevent two or three witnesses in the same suit being examined at the same time.

MR. HARINGTON said the amendment was proposed to be inserted at the last Meeting of the Council simply and solely on the ground that some of the Judges did not do their duty, and that it was therefore necessary to impose this additional check upon them. It was quite true that Judges and Juries were sworn before they entered upon the duties of their respective offices, but they did not tell them that this was done because if they were not sworn it was believed that they would be corrupt or dishonest. Had the amendment proposed by the Honorable and learned Member formed part of the Section as it was originally framed, he (Mr. Harington) might not have had the same objection to it as he had now by reason of the ground upon which it was proposed to introduce it.

MR. HARINGTON'S motion was put and negatived.

MR. PEACOCK'S new Section as amended, was put, and carried.

THE postponed Section 145 of Chapter III provided that witnesses should be examined without oath or affirmation, and prescribed a form of admonition to be used preliminary to their giving evidence.

MR. FORBES moved that this Section be omitted, and that the following be substituted for it:—

"Before any witness is examined, the Court shall administer to such witness such oath as it may consider to be most binding on the conscience according to the religious persuasion of such witness, requiring him to speak the whole truth and nothing but the truth."

He said that, in rising to move an amendment to the Section, he must commence by an expression of the wish he so strongly felt, that some other Honorable Member more competent than he was to do justice to so important a subject had been willing to bring it forward for discussion; but as he stood alone among those Members of the Select Committee who usually attended its Meetings in protesting against the principle which it was now sought to introduce into our Courts of Justice, he felt that, unless he put himself forward on this occasion, the matter, important though it was, might not be discussed at all. He felt sure that he should not look in vain for the indulgence of the Council, and that he should not ask in vain that this question might be decided on its own merits only, and might not be prejudiced in the judgment of Honorable Members by the very imperfect treatment it would receive at his hands.

He did not intend on this occasion to enter on a discussion of the general abstract question of oaths. Whether or not it was ever right and expedient to demand an oath, was not now the question; but assuming that, in proper places and on proper occasions, an oath might properly be demanded, the question was, whether a Court of Justice was a proper place, and the delivery of evidence was a proper occasion on which an oath might be demanded?

All evidence was taken on oath prior to the passing of Act V of 1840. The Preamble to that Act stated that it was passed because obstruction to justice and other inconvenience had arisen in consequence of persons of the Hindoo and Mahomedan persuasions being compelled to swear by the water of the Ganges or upon the Koran, or according to other forms which are repugnant to their consciences or feelings.

Now, although the Act which abolished oaths was founded on the impression that it was the objection which they felt to an oath that made respectable men unwilling to appear in our Courts, it was, he believed, now very generally admitted that that impression was wholly and entirely erroneous. It was to appearance in our Courts at all, and not to being sworn when there, to which the native gentry objected, the objection being grounded on a feeling that exemption from attendance was the sign and mark of a particular position in society. But as some Honorable Members might take their stand on this Act, and be unwilling to repeal a law passed for the relief of conscientious scruples, it might be well to see what was on record by those most competent to form an opinion on the subject regarding the impression under which Act V of 1840 had been passed.

In his notes on the Code of Civil Procedure prepared by the Commissioners in England, the present Chief Justice of the Supreme Court had said:—

"I must beg to express my dissent from the proposal to abolish judicial oaths, and every sanction in the nature of one. I think the measure proposed in itself inexpedient, and the reasoning by which the Commissioners support it (*see* note at page 57 of the Report) seems to me to proceed, in part at least, upon an erroneous assumption of matters of fact. They determine to throw over every sanction because one class of suitors (the Hindoos) are supposed to object to a particular sanction. It is assumed that it is this objection which keeps what are called respectable natives out of Court. If this were so, one would expect them to be more ready to appear in the Courts of the East India Company, where the evidence is taken on solemn affirmation, than in the Supreme Court. Yet the contrary is, I believe, the fact. That an unwillingness to be sworn may occasionally keep a respectable native out of Court, I do not deny; but I believe that the repugnance of that class of persons to appear in Courts of Justice is far more frequently caused by a foolish notion of personal dignity more prevalent in the Provinces than in Calcutta, and an unwillingness (for which there is sometimes a more rational foundation) to submit themselves to cross-examination."

In their annual Report on the administration of Civil Justice for 1845, the Sudder Court at Agra remarked, with reference to Act V of 1840:—

"That there was no necessity for the Act in reference to its proposed end of removing the obstruction to justice, arising from persons of the Hindoo and Mahomedan persuasions being compelled to swear by forms repugnant to their feelings and consciences, because former Regulations provided for the exemption of those whom, according to the usages of the country, it would have been improper to subject to such compulsion, by simply prescribing a declaration or *halufnamah*."

"*2ndly.*—That, though repugnance to be sworn might be the ostensible reason of the unwillingness of certain persons to appear as deponents in our Courts, it is not the real one, which is connected with other and distinct considerations, not removed or removeable by the Act in question. The disinclination of certain classes to appear in Court was attributable rather to the ideal consequence attached by them to a position, which, they supposed, set them above the summons of a Magistrate or other Officer, the privilege of not appearing in Cutcherree being considered the distinguishing line between the higher and middle classes."

But this was not all that was on record regarding the impression under which Act V of 1840 was passed. In February 1847, the Government of the North-Western Provinces called upon the Sudder Court to obtain the opinions of the Native Judges on the operation of the Act, and in their reply dated in November of the same year, the Court submitted an abstract of the opinions they had received, to which he would again refer. It was now necessary only to quote so much of the Court's Report as stated that, in the opinion of the highest Native Judicial Officers,

"the educated and respectable classes were not, as it was once supposed, deterred from giving evidence by the necessity of submitting to the requisition of that oath, but by a repugnance to personal attendance in Court, which the substitution of the declaration for the oath has, of course, been ineffectual to remove."

And lastly, in a Minute recorded by Mr. H. Lushington, a Judge of the Agra Sudder Court, that Officer said—

"It has been supposed that respectable Natives formerly objected to appear in Courts as witnesses on account of aversion to swear upon the Koran or upon the Ganges water. The reports now before us show that this was an erroneous supposition. Respectable Natives are *not* more willing to attend now than they were prior to the passing of Act V of 1840: they object to attending the Courts, not to taking the oaths; and if they could be examined in their own houses, they would seldom object to give their evidence. The supposed aversion, then, of respectable Natives to the taking of an oath cannot be urged as a reason *against* the repeal of the Act."

We had, therefore, the testimony of the Sudder Court in 1845; we had the same testimony repeated after mature deliberation in 1847; and we had the concurrent testimony of all the Native Judges who must be admitted to be the best evidence on such a subject—that the grounds on which Act V of 1840 was passed had never had any real existence, and that the respectable classes were not, as was once supposed, deterred from giving evidence by the necessity of submitting to an oath, but by repugnance to personal attendance in our Courts—a repugnance which the abolition of oaths had, of course, been ineffectual to remove.

As, therefore, the grounds on which Act V of 1840 was passed, never had any real existence, they could not be brought forward as arguments against its repeal, and before the question was definitively settled by the enactment of the Section now before the Committee, it would be well to consider whether its repeal would or would not be a desirable and expedient measure.

For what purpose were Courts established? He apprehended that they were established in order that justice might be done between man and man—he apprehended further that truth and justice were inseparable, and that without the one, we could not hope to do the other. If this were so, the question arose whether all reason, experience, and the recorded evidence of those most competent to judge, did not lead to the conclusion that the requisition of an oath did, or did not, increase the probabilities of our obtaining the truth, and consequently improve our means of doing justice.

He maintained that it did; but as his opinion would carry no weight with the Council, he would, at the risk of being somewhat tedious, read to the Committee some extracts from the evidence that had been laid before the Council on the subject—evidence, let it be remembered, that was not of his collection, but which had been obtained from the records of the Government of India, and had been printed and referred to the Select Committee on the motion of the Honorable and learned Gentleman (Mr. Peacock).

The first extract which he would read was from the notes of the learned Chairman, who said—

"I admit that a really conscientious and intelligent witness will speak truth without being sworn, as he will speak truth after taking an oath. I admit that very many who do take an oath are foresworn. But I nevertheless believe, that there is a large class of men who are more likely to give their evidence truthfully and cautiously when they give it on oath, than they are when they give it without that sanction, and I am not prepared to abandon any innocent mode of getting at truth, however unphilosophical. With that object I would break a plate over the head of a Chinaman, or put a tiger's skin on the back of a Cole."

The Calcutta Supreme Court had said—

"It became speedily apparent from the increasing discrepancies between the statements of these witnesses in the Supreme Court and their statements before the Magistrates in the same cases, that some evil had resulted from the change. It has happened on several occasions that a witness, on being asked why his statement in Court varied from that before the Magistrate, gave as an explanation, which he seemed to consider as satisfactory, that he was not on his oath in the latter case; and experience leads us to think that some will speak truth under the influence of their oath, who will depose falsely if that restraint be moved. The general principle of the Draft Act substitutes in all judicial proceedings a solemn declaration for an oath. If the former be as high a security that truth will be spoken as an oath, it is on all accounts to be preferred. We think, however, that it is not so high a security: though, if all men reasoned or felt correctly, it would be. We cannot conscientiously recommend this substitution in the Supreme Court."

The Chief Justice of the Bombay Supreme Court had said—

"I have no doubt many a witness would be more deserving of belief if he were sworn than if he merely made the affirmation in question."

The Honorable Mr. Willoughby had said—

"But uncertainty in the administration of justice, the success of fraud, and impunity of crime by legal process are evils so grievous and demoralizing to society, and so encourage the disposition to commit the crimes which produce them, that I think we are justified in availing ourselves of every aid of passion or prejudice, however absurd it may appear to a higher intelligence and better knowledge, which may in any way or degree tend to prevent such evils. Many Native witnesses who will, without hesitation, and for a very little profit, perjure themselves in our Courts, acknowledge some form or ceremony of adjuration which would have restrained them from the offence; and I think our old Regulations very wisely directed a judicial admonition to the witness, and gave the Judge a discretion to adopt such form of oath as was known to be most binding on his conscience."

The Sudder Court at Madras had declared their belief

"that a mistake was made in abolishing the old form of oath which was often effectual where the present was not, and that the objectionable state of things described can be remedied only by a return to the former system of administering oaths, a course of proceeding which they also would support with their strong recommendation."

The Sudder Court at Bombay had said—

"The Court is of opinion that the oath was more binding than the affirmation, from the allusion to and connexion with, however slight, the religion of the witness, and from its being in conformity with usage; but that neither is effective, and that, to command truth, the placing of the hand on the Geeta, the Cow, the Child, or the Grain must be reverted to; and under this view, the Judges would strongly recommend a reversion to the former system of oaths as prescribed by the Bombay Code, to be administered in such manner as may appear to the trying authority desirable."

The Sudder Court at Agra had said—

"The Court having their attention particularly directed to this subject, have caused a comparative statement to be compiled from the records of their Office; and it appears that from 1836 to 1839, both inclusive, the commitments in all the districts of the North-Western Provinces amount to 332 during the four years extending from 1842 to 1845, the total number of commitments was 456, or 124 more than in the four years antecedent to the operation of Act V of 1840. These facts are of themselves sufficient to favor the presumption that perjury has been fostered by the new law; but when it is considered that a very large proportion of evidence is taken and recorded in the Native Courts, that the officers presiding in those Courts do not attach the same degree of moral turpitude to false swearing that it conveys to an educated and well ordered mind, and are slow to appreciate the importance and bear the opprobrium of exposing it, and that consequently not two-thirds of the perjuries actually committed are made the ground of a criminal prosecution, the comparative increase in the number of commitments for the offence in question carries with it an irresistible proof of its greater prevalence, and justifies the Court in proposing a reconsideration of the law's provisions. It seems clear, from all the evidence available, that the formula which the Act prescribes does not bind the conscience; and any observance that fails to procure this principal object of an oath, that fails to impose upon the deponent an obligation to depose truly, may be as well abandoned altogether. 'The present apology for an oath,' observes Mr. Thomas, 'is, to say the mildest of it, a failure; for three-fourths of the witnesses do not understand it, and so cannot feel its force, whilst those who can comprehend its meaning do not regard it as an oath, but treat it with contempt.' Mr. H. B. Harington, when officiating Judge of Jounpore, commenting on the operation of the Act, took occasion to lament the daily increase of perjury; and the Court are persuaded that, were the local officers generally consulted, it would be found that the experience of the last four or five years has not altered the unfavorable opinion formerly expressed of the law's provisions and effects."

The opinion of the Native Judges was given as follows in a letter from the Sudder Court at Agra, to the Government of the North-Western Provinces :—

"I am desired accordingly to submit an abstract of the replies received from the several Principal Sudder Ameens in the North-Western Provinces, and it will be observed that, with few exceptions, the highest Native Judicial Officers of the country declare that the oath on the Koran and Ganges water, was more binding on the consciences of their countrymen, than the present declaration; that though the educated classes regard this declaration with the respect which an invocation of the deity should command, the ignorant and superstitious, who mostly frequent our Courts as witnesses, do not understand or feel its sacred obligation; and that the crime of perjury is now more prevalent than it was under the system which Act V of 1840 abolished. It will likewise be observed that, with one exception, all the functionaries who have been consulted either advocate a return to the former practice of swearing deponents on the Koran and Ganges water, or deliver it as their opinion that, owing to the multitude of sects both among Mussulmans and Hindoos, no one form of attestation can be prescribed, and that consequently a discretion should be left to the Court to swear each witness in the manner that may be most binding upon his conscience."

Mr. H. Lushington, in a minute recorded at the same time, said :—

"If it be once indisputably established that witnesses now lie more than they used to do, and that, in the opinion of a vast majority of those most competent to judge, means may be found to make them lie less, these means ought to be employed; the unanimous declaration of the Principal Sudder Ameens, the opinion of nearly all the Judges, and the well-known verdict of all the Public, must be held to have established these two points. Why do we hesitate to apply the remedy? Of what use are Laws and Courts in a country where facts cannot be ascertained? Why require unceasing labor, why incur enormous expense, why accumulate and record the results of experience, if national falsehood defies the application of our principles! The wisdom of the wisest tribunal is laughed to scorn by the perjury of a single scoundrel. But it is superfluous to dwell upon the self-evident truth that the character of evidence is the most important consideration in all civilized societies; and we are therefore bound, if we value the happiness of the millions whom Providence has committed to our care in this country, to improve its character whenever we can discover how to accomplish so desirable an object. If we continue to administer injustice when we might administer justice; if we persist in doing wrong when we might do right—we incur a fearful responsibility, both in this world and in the next. The objection made to a return to the Koran and Ganges water is generally thus worded—'we cannot go back.' Why not? If we have taken a step in the wrong direction, it is the very best thing we can do. The act of retrogression is not objectionable *per se*; and, upon the data now before us, we are compelled to admit that we ought to retrograde. Should the Government ever make up their mind to yield so much to the peculiarities of their subjects, I should not hesitate to go even farther, and in conformity with Section VII Regulation III. 1803, to authorize the Courts to use any form of oath which they considered most binding upon the conscience of the witness about to be examined. I would purchase truth at any price; nor would I hesitate, if so I might obtain it, to place the koran in the hands of the first witness, the Ganges water in the palm of the second, a plate to a third, the name of some long departed sage to a fourth, the tail of a cow to a fifth, his son's head to a sixth, burnt ghee to a seventh, and so on. Let the natives be educated by all means, let their morals be improved, and let them be invited to walk in that path which we believe to be conducive to their future welfare; but let us in the mean time give security to their persons and to their property, and await the hour when these Pagan ceremonies may be more safely abandoned.'

The Sessions Judge of the Saugor and Nerbudda Territories had said—

"With the tangible oath in a witness's hand, especially among the lower classes in India, I have generally found that some adherence to veracity can be enforced. From two and a half years' experience of the working of Act V of 1840, I do not hesitate to record my conviction that the affirmation is not held to be so binding as the tangible oath by nine-tenths of the witnesses; and I will mention two inferential proofs. When a witness's veracity is questioned, the common answer is—'I would say the same even if you put Gunga-jul into my hand.' And in the decision of Civil claims in these territories, where an appeal to the opposite party's oath is very common, the request is now almost invariably accompanied with a condition that 'the affirmation be not substituted for a formal oath."

The Sessions Judge of Dharwar (Mr. W. E. Frere), now a Member of the Bombay Government, had said—

"The natives of this country generally are, as timid people are elsewhere, deficient in veracity; but that they still have, every one of them, oaths which they respect, is constantly apparent to all who have ever noticed the effect of referring a Civil suit for decision to the oath of the opposite party. Men who have urged or denied claims when pleading in Court and have consented to swear to the truth of their assertions, have, when taken to the temple to swear, quailed, and refused the oath which the other party then has readily taken. With several of these cases in my mind, I cannot join in the opinion that oaths are not binding upon the natives of this country; and I fear that it is by abolishing them in our Judicial proceedings that we have opened the door to perjury, and that we have thereby incurred an awful responsibility."

The Session Judge of Poona had said :—

"I do not believe that the Act in question has in any way added to the crime; though every Native that I have spoken to on the subject latterly, holds that it has."

And lastly there was a statement of the crime of perjury in the Magistracy of Candeish for the years prior and subsequent to the abolition of oaths, from which it appeared that, since their abolition, the crime had increased in the ratio of 148 to 18.

Now from these extracts which he had read, the Council would have learnt that the Supreme Courts were against the abolition of oaths, that the Sudder Courts were against it, that the Sessions Courts were against it, and that the Native Judges were unanimously against it. But the Council would have learnt something more, and a fact of the very first importance, namely, that the crime of perjury had increased in the ratio of 148 to 18 since oaths were abolished by the passing of Act V of 1840. It might be thought that this fact would have been alone sufficient to carry conviction to the minds of all, and to have led to an immediate recurrence to former practice, for Honorable Members would at once see that much more was implied in the statement than at first sight appeared. He asked the Council for one moment to reflect on the great injustice of which our Courts must have been the unconscious instruments when made the tools of such a mass of perjury as was implied in an increase of detected cases from 18 to 148. It was, he believed, generally admitted that certainty of punishment was one of the best preventives of crime; if, therefore, any crime increased greatly in extent, it was to be assumed that detection and punishment had become less certain. Let this principle be applied to the statement now in question, and he thought we must conclude that the vast increase in the number of detected cases of perjury proved beyond a doubt that a far greater number had remained altogether undetected.

If, however, these facts were not sufficient to decide the question, and if the evidence of all the Courts, whether established by Royal Charter or presided over in the Mofussil by Europeans or Natives, were insufficient to decide the question, by what should it be decided? These facts and this evidence could not be set aside; there were no facts and no evidence on the other side to show that good had resulted from the abolition of oaths; but he would anticipate the answer that would be made to the present motion. It would be admitted that it was to be regretted that Act V of 1840 had ever been passed; but having been passed, it would be said that it was inexpedient to go back, and that as the same oath was not equally binding on all, if oaths were admitted, a discretion must be allowed to the Courts to administer whatever oath it considered to be most binding upon each witness, that much trouble and inconvenience might arise, and that a Judge might here and there be found, who would resort to unbecoming means of testing the credibility of evidence.

If this were to be the defence of the Section as it now stands, he would take leave to say that it would be no defence at all, for in the first place he agreed with what Mr. Lushington had said in the Minute from which he had just now read an extract, that if a false step in legislation had been made, it was a plain and simple duty to retrace it; it was a false pride that induced us to be consistent in error. As regarded any fear that might be felt regarding the discretion of some one or two Judges, he submitted to the Council that they could not legislate for individual and exceptional cases, and that it would be doing a grievous wrong to the people of this great country, if they were deprived, as regards their persons and property, of the safeguard which evidence delivered on oath was admitted by all to afford, by a vague indefinite fear that, here or there, at sometime or other, a Judge might possibly arise whose zeal in the pursuit of truth would outrun his discretion. Such a case, if ever it did arise, should be dealt with at the time by whatever authority might have the supervision of our Courts, and the people should not be deprived of what was inexpressibly valuable to them from a vague apprehension of a very remote contingency. He would ask, if no discretion were used by the Judges now? Were all punishments so exactly defined that a Judge could exercise no discretion whether to recommend a capital punishment or a mitigated punishment of transportation? Was there no discretion as to length of imprisonment or amount of fine? There was a discretion in all these matters, and should it be said that we could trust our Courts with discretion in matters of life and death and liberty, and yet would not trust them with a discretion in the administration of an oath?

As regarded any trouble that might arise from administering different oaths to different people, it was not necessary to say much. Was trouble worth more consideration than truth? Ought we to allow a little trouble to weigh even as a dust in the balance in comparison with the immense benefit which that trouble was to gain? If it were the part of wisdom to select the less of two evils, could there be a moment's hesitation as to the choice that should be made between a little trouble on one hand and boundless perjury on the other?

But how stood opinions in this Council? He would ask the learned

Judges of the Court that was here established by Royal Charter, if they would consent to the abolition of oaths in the Court over which they so honorably and ably presided? if they said no, he would ask them if they could consistently refuse to the Mofussil what they believed to be of such value to the Metropolis? He would ask the Honorable and gallant gentleman—whose services, long and arduous though they had been, had not been longer than they had been brilliant, or more arduous than they had been chivalric—if from his experience of Courts-martial he was of opinion that unsworn testimony was as valuable as that which was declared on oath? and if he said no, he would ask him to vote on this motion accordingly.

[Sir Jas. Outram. Decidedly not.]

He would ask the Honorable and learned gentleman—whose distinguished career at the bar had fairly earned for him his present high and influential position—if his experience of Courts in England led him to believe that oaths might be safely abandoned there? and if he said no, he would ask him if the people of this country were more moral and more truthful than were the people of England? He would ask all those Honorable Members who, in their several careers, had presided in Courts and Cutcherries, if they really and seriously believed that oaths were of no value? He would ask the whole Council, of what use was this Code on which they were engaged, if, after all, its most elaborate simplicity was to end in our Courts deciding on perjured evidence? What was the use of our Courts, if they were to be only Courts of Law and not Courts of Justice? To what end would it be that the plaint was made out according to form, that the witnesses and defendant were summoned *secundum artem*, and that throughout the whole record every *t* were crossed and every *i* dotted according to strict rule, and then a wrong judgment were to be given? It was his firm conviction that the utmost confusion of procedure, if it ended in a right judgment, would be preferable to the most rigid uniformity, if perjury were allowed to run riot in our Courts and utterly to confound all right and wrong.

He would not resume his seat without apologizing for the length of time he had occupied, and without tendering his acknowledgments for the attention that had been accorded to him; and anxious to leave on the minds of Honorable Members a good impression upon the subject of this motion, he would, in place of concluding with any words of his own, read an extract from a report sent in by his Honorable friend on his left (Mr. Harington) when Judge of Gorruckpore. It was as follows:—

"Courts of Justice are established for the good of the public at large, and for the protection of the lives and properties of the people; but when it is found that they are made the instruments of oppression and injury by designing and dishonest men, the Government are surely justified, after having tried all ordinary means in vain, in having recourse to extraordinary measures, not inconsistent with a civilized Government, to render their Courts of Justice a blessing and not an evil to their subjects."

SIR ARTHUR BULLER said, if he were called on to give a vote on the present occasion, he should vote for some provision which would require that Native witnesses should be required to swear by some practicable binding oath rather than that they should give their evidence under no religious sanction at all, because it appeared to him, from the annexure in circulation, that beyond all question the preponderating weight of opinion was in favor of testimony upon oath rather than upon solemn affirmation, and therefore *à fortiori* in favor of such testimony rather than of testimony given under no sanction whatever. The Native Officers were unanimous in that view: no doubt all were also agreed as to this, that do what you will, invoke what sanction you please, neither the fear of Divine vengeance nor of temporal punishment would universally avail to check the fatal propensity to lying. Nevertheless, if it could be shown that one witness out of ten would tell the truth under the sanction of any oath who without that sanction would tell a lie, how, as guardians of public justice, would they be justified in dispensing with it? If called upon to vote now, he had said he should support the amendment, or at all events the principle of it;

but he trusted that he should not be driven, on the present occasion, to a final expression of opinion, but that his Honorable friend would consent to leave this great question to be considered at another time and on a more appropriate occasion. He thought that it should be made the subject of a separate Bill, which should deal generally with the subject in all its bearings. The provision under discussion was limited to the examination of witnesses in Civil cases in the Mofussil Courts. The same question would again arise when they were dealing with witnesses in the Code of Criminal Procedure and with Juries; and no doubt the principle adopted then in the Mofussil would, he presumed, be adopted in the Supreme Courts. It was, therefore, far better to consider in one separate Act the whole question. It might be said that the principle must be the same in all; therefore why not settle the question at once? His answer was that they were not in a proper position now to settle it. They had not before them all the information which they might have. The printed papers before them only contained the expression of opinions as to the working of the Act of 1840 from its passing up to about 1846. Since th latter date they were comparatively uninformed upon the point. But why throw away the experience of the last ten years, during which time opinions might have been modified or confirmed or possibly changed altogether? Why not enquire first what the most experienced persons thought now, and they must not forget that they had never collected opinions upon the broad question with which they were now dealing. They had never put it to any one—"What do you think of doing away with all oaths and affirmations and declarations alike"? He thought it could be hardly said that the publication of this Bill, with a provision to that effect in it, was tantamount to an invitation to the public to express their opinion upon it; for the provision, contained as it was in Section 145 of Chapter III and buried in such a heap of other Sections, was not likely to have attracted many eyes, and in fact the Council could form no idea as to the state of public opinion upon the precise question on which they proposed to legislate. He hoped and trusted, therefore, that they would not come to a conclusion now, but reserve for further and more solemn consideration the whole question—and he would suggest that, in place of the proposed amendment, they should adopt an amendment to the effect that witnesses be examined upon oath or affirmation or otherwise according to the law for the time being in force in relation to the examination of witnesses.

Mr. FORBES said, he would assent to what appeared to be the general wish on the subject, and withdraw his amendment upon the understanding that a separate Bill would be introduced at no very distant date.

Mr CURRIE said, a Select Committee was appointed for the express purpose of considering the project of Law relating to oaths and affirmations, but it had been discharged, and the papers had been referred to the Select Committees on the Civil Procedure Code.

Sir ARTHUR BULLER said, the Select Committee had expressed no very conclusive opinion one way or the other upon the point, and at all events they had before them no further evidence or communications by which a new light was thrown upon the subject.

Mr CURRIE said, he merely meant to observe that, in the event of the Honorable and learned Member's suggestion being adopted, it would be well to bring this controverted matter to a decision, either by appointing another Select Committee for its consideration, or in some other mode.

Mr. HARINGTON said, he agreed with the Honorable Member for Bengal. Some steps should be taken for obtaining the opinions of the local Officers since the date of the last communication; unless that was done, they would gain nothing by the postponement.

Sir ARTHUR BULLER said, he would undertake to bring in a Bill himself, or, what would be much better, he felt sure that his Honorable friend, the Member for Madras, would do so.

MR. FORBES said, upon that understanding he would withdraw his amendment.

THE CHAIRMAN said, he hoped that whoever undertook to frame the measure would provide for what appeared to have been an omission in the amendment proposed by the Honorable Member for Madras—the reception, upon affirmation or otherwise, of the evidence of those who conscientiously objected to take an oath. He had, as the Honorable Member for Madras had shown, expressed an opinion favorable to the retention of oaths in judicial proceedings generally. But he had never advocated a system whereby those who had a conscientious objection to take an oath, might be subjected to what they might fairly think persecution in the shape of penal consequences; and valuable testimony might be lost to the parties to the suit.

MR. FORBES explained that he had not thought such a provision necessary, with reference to the following remarks on the subject by the Chairman, which he had found in the printed papers:—

"To support their theory on this point, the Commissioners somewhat hastily assume that the discretion given to the Court by the 9 Geo. IV, c. 74 s. 36 has had considerable practical effect. On this point I can only say that I have sat nearly eight years on the Bench of the Supreme Court, and that I cannot call to mind that, during that space of time, the discretion in question has been exercised in the case of eight *different* witnesses."

On referring to the Report of the Municipal Commissioners for 1857, he found that the population of Calcutta was set down as 4,15,000, and it appeared, from what the learned Chairman had said in the remark just now quoted, that the exemption had not been claimed even so frequently as eight times in eight years. It certainly had appeared to him that a question that would affect only one man in 4,15,000, was one to which the legal maxim of *de minimis non curat lex* would apply. He was, however, sure that whoever undertook to prepare the Bill, would be careful to attend to the suggestion now made by the learned Chairman.

SIR ARTHUR BULLER then moved that the following new Section be substituted for Section 145:—

"All witnesses shall be examined upon oath or affirmation or otherwise according to the provisions of the law for the time being in force in relation to the examination of witnesses."

Agreed to.

The postponed Section 146 of Chapter III (providing punishment for false evidence) being read by the Chairman, it was moved by him that it be left out.

The Section was put and negatived.

The postponed Section 96 of Chapter III was passed after amendments.

The postponed Section 167 of Chap. III being read by the Chairman—

MR HARINGTON moved that it be left out.

Agreed to.

Sections 1 to 7 of Chapter IV were severally passed as they stood.

MR. LEGEYT said he had a new Section to propose after Section 7. Under the Bombay Code, it had been the law, in executing decrees, to exempt from attachment property of the defendant by which he gained his livelihood. Section 62, Clause 2, of Regulation IV. 1827 provided as follows:—

"But it is to be clearly understood that, if the defendant shall point out any of his property for sale in preference to that specified by the plaintiff, the property so pointed out shall be first sold, and that such implements of manual labor, and such cattle and implements of agriculture, as may, in the judgment of the Court from which the process issues, be indispensable for the defendant to earn a livelihood in his respective calling, or cultivate any land that he may hold for that purpose, shall be exempt from attachment."

This exemption had been in force in Bombay for the last thirty years, and he believed it had also been in force previous to the enactment of the existing Code. The Code now before the Council was a deviation from that law, for it rendered all property belonging to a defendant, including implements of trade, liable to attachment and sale. This would be considered as a very great hardship. It might be said that, when a man incurred debts, it was a just principle to make all the property he had in the world pay those debts; but when it came to be a question of utter ruin to the defendant, it had been held by the framers of the existing Code, and by the distinguished Statesman who presided over the Government of Bombay when it was under preparation, that he was entitled to some consideration. The Council would observe that, though it was not the law in Bengal to exempt implements of trade from attachment under decrees, it was the practice to exempt them from distraint.

Then, he thought there was another right which ought to be secured to a defendant. Suppose that, in the case of a small debt, execution was sued out, and the plaintiff went with an order for general attachment, or that he went with an order for especial attachment, and attached a horse belonging to the defendant. The horse might be worth a great deal more than the claim, and might be sold at a sacrifice at such a sale, but the defendant might have a bullock, which would fetch a price that would satisfy the decree. The defendant ought to have the power of compelling him to sell the bullock instead of the horse. He should, therefore, move that the following be inserted as a new Section after Section 7:—

"But if the defendant points out any of his property for sale in preference to that specified by the plaintiff, the property so pointed out shall be first sold. Such implements of manual labor and such cattle and implements of agriculture as may, in the judgment of the Court from which the process issues, be indispensable for the defendant to earn a livelihood in his calling or trade, shall be exempt from attachment."

If this Section should be adopted, he should move two others, which he had taken from Section LXIX of Regulation IV. 1827, which were as follows:—

"Land and its crop, of whatever kind, shal not be attached and sold separately until after the crop has been reaped or gathered.

Second. When corn or other production of khalsa land paying annual rent to Government is attached and sold, the Collector or his officers may prevent its being sold or carried off such lands, unless the purchaser shall pay the amount due on account of the revenue; but in no case shall the purchaser be liable for more than one year's revenue.

Third. The same right of detention for arrears of rent, similarly restricted, shall be exercised by a land-holder where his tenant's corn or other production of the soil is attached."

He brought forward these Sections with considerable diffidence; but it did appear to him that they ought to be inserted. They now stood in what was regarded at Bombay as the Civil Code of that Presidency; and if this Bill should pass, that Code would be repealed. He therefore threw out to the Council that, certainly with respect to Bombay at least, the three new Sections he proposed should be inserted. He did not know how far they would be applicable to the state of things in the other Presidencies. In Bombay, they would protect principally the Government, who, in these cases, was the direct landlord.

MR. CURRIE said the greater portion of the first Section proposed by the Honorable Member could hardly be inserted in this part of the Bill, supposing that the Section were inserted at all. The Bill in this place merely declared what property belonging to a defendant was liable to seizure and sale. The first part of the proposed Section might be a suitable provision; but it could only be inserted among the provisions relating to sale. It had nothing to do with this part of the Bill which declared what property should be liable to attachment and sale.

With respect to the second part of the Section, he thought it might be reasonable to insert some provision respecting implements of trade. In the Small Cause Courts Bill, the following Section was inserted on that subject:—

"In executing a writ of execution against the moveable property of a debtor liable under this Act, the Nazir shall except the tools and implements of the trade or business of such debtor and seed intended for the sowing of land cultivated by him."

At the end of Section 7 of Chapter IV of the present Code, a similar exception might be inserted.

That would probably meet the object which the Honorable Member had in view.

MR. HARINGTON asked, in reference to the first part of the first amendment proposed by the Honorable Member for Bombay, who was to answer any objection which might be made by a third party to the sale of any property which the defendant might, under the rule contained in that part of the amendment, require to be sold in preference to the property seized and attached by the judgment creditor. It would frequently happen that the defendant, to save his own property, would point out property not belonging to him, but to some other person, and as the owner of the property so pointed out would certainly object to the proceeding, who was to answer the objection? The judgment creditor could not be expected to do so. He might fairly say that he had not pointed out the property to which the objection referred, and he did not wish that property, but some other property which he knew to belong to the defendant, to be sold; and if the defendant was required to answer the objection, delay and further obstruction to the execution of the decree could only be looked for. However, taking the case of the horse and the cow put by the Honorable Member for Bombay, if the defendant thought that it was more for his interest that his cow should be sold than his horse, what was there to prevent him from selling the cow himself and appropriating the proceeds to the liquidation of the decree. He was not aware that there was any particular advantage in a forced sale; on the contrary, people generally went to auctions to get bargains. He should oppose the amendment.

After some further discussion, Mr. LeGeyt, with the leave of the Council, withdrew his motion.

Sections 8 to 13 were severally passed as they stood.

Section 14 was postponed.

Sections 15 to 22 were severally passed as they stood.

Section 23 provided as follows:—

"If the decree be for land or other immoveable property not in the occupancy of ryots or other persons entitled to occupy the same, delivery thereof shall be made by putting the party to whom the land or other immoveable property may have been adjudged, or any person whom he may appoint to receive delivery on his behalf, in possession thereof, and, if need be, by removing any person who may refuse to vacate the same."

MR. LEGEYT said, the Sudder Adawlut at Bombay had sent up a remark in relation to this Section which he desired to lay before the Council. Their remark was on Section 17 of the Bill as published for general information. They said they "would leave out the provision 'and if need be, by removing any person who may refuse to vacate the same' at the end of the Section, as giving too much power to the Bailiff or other proper Officer, and as, in some degree, opposed to the provisions of Section 19."

The provisions here alluded to as contained in Section 19 of the original Bill stood in the amended Bill as Section 26, which said:—

"If, in the execution of a decree for land or other immoveable property, the Officer executing the same shall be resisted or obstructed by any person, the person in whose favor such decree was made may apply to the Court at any time within one month from the time of such resistance or obstruction. The Court shall fix a day for investigating the complaint, and shall summon the party against whom the complaint is made to answer the same. If reasonable ground shall be shown to the satisfaction of the Court for believing that the obstruction or resistance in question was occasioned by the defendant or by some other person at his instigation, the Court shall also issue a summons to the defendant, calling upon him to appear on the day appointed for the investigation."

It appeared to him that Section 23 and Section 26 of the present Bill were inconsistent with each other, and he should move that the words "and, if need be, by removing any person who may refuse to vacate the same" be left out of the former.

MR. HARINGTON said, where the Court had adjudged property to the decree-holder, and the defendant refused to give possession, the Court would, under Section 26, have the right to put him out of the property, and give it to the decree-holder. If the party dispossessed thought that he was wrongly removed, he could come in and dispute the right of the decree-holder to remove him under Section 29, but in the meantime he thought the Court ought to have the power of removing the person in possession.

After some further discussion, Mr. LeGeyt, with the leave of the Council, withdrew his amendment.

THE CHAIRMAN moved that the word "land" after the word "for" in the 1st line of the Section be left out, and the words "a house" substituted for it.

Agreed to.

THE CHAIRMAN moved that the words "ryots or other persons entitled to occupy the same" after the word "of" in the 3rd line of the Section be left out, and the words "a defendant or of some person in his behalf" subsituted for them.

Agreed to.

THE CHAIRMAN moved that the word "land" before the word "or" in the 7th line of the Section be left out, and the word "house" substituted for it.

Agreed to.

The further consideration of the Section was postponed.

Section 24 was postponed.

Sections 25 to 27 were severally passed as they stood.

Section 28 provided as follows:—

"If it shall appear to the satisfaction of the Court that the resistance or obstruction to the execution of the decree has been occasioned by any person, whether a party to the suit or not, on the ground that the property is not included in the decree, or by any person claiming *bonâ fide* to be in possession of the property on his own account, or on account of some other person than the defendant, the Court shall, without prejudice to any proceedings to which the defendant or other person may be liable under any law for the time being in force for the punishment of such resistance or obstruction, proceed to investigate the claim in the same manner and with the like powers as if the claimant had been made originally a defendant to the suit, and shall pass such order for staying execution of the decree, or executing the same, as it may deem proper in the circumstances of the case."

THE CHAIRMAN said, on this and several other Sections, he wished to observe that they did not appear to him to give the Courts all the necessary power which he thought should be given to them. The Section now before the Committee gave a Court the power of investigating a claim made by any person claiming to be in possession of the property taken in execution, and "pass an order for staying execution of the decree, or executing the same, as it may deem proper in the circumstances of the case." Section 29 authorized the Court to investigate the claim of the party dispossessed although no resistance or opposition should have been offered, and "pass an order for restitution," "or such other order as it may deem proper in the circumstances of the case." Then Section 30 provided that "any order passed by the Court" under either of the last two preceding Sections, shall not be subject to appeal; but the party against whom the order may be pronounced shall be at liberty to bring a suit to establish his right at any time within one year from the date thereof. Here, the Code pre-supposed conflicting claims made by persons not parties to the suit. What he desired to know was the reason for making these orders not subject to appeal, but leaving the dispossessed party to bring a regular suit for the recovery of the property. He could not see why, under the procedure which the Code provided, the Court should not deal with all these claims very much as the Supreme Court deals with similar claims under the Inter-pleader Act. A Court acting under this Code, would, in this respect, be exactly in the same position as in an original suit if the question were one of title between the execution creditor and a person not a party to the suit in which the execution had been decreed. If that was so, why did not the Code give to the unsuccessful party the same right of appeal which he would have had if the question had been decided in an original suit, and to the successful party the same right which he would have had under the decree, confirmed on appeal, instead of leaving him uncertain during a whole year whether he might not have again to litigate his title in a regular suit. It was possible, however, that the Select Committee had been influenced, in dealing with the question, by reasons which were not present to his mind.

MR. HARINGTON said, the Code, as framed by Her Majesty's Commissioners, took away the right of appeal, and continued a right of suit only. Under the present practice, after the summary decision, there might be two appeals, a summary and a special appeal, in the miscellaneous department, and, subsequently thereto, the three stages of a regular suit, namely, the original suit, a regular appeal, and a special appeal, which certainly appeared to him to be more than the ends of justice required; and upon the whole, he was disposed to agree with the Honorable and learned Chairman.

THE CHAIRMAN then moved that the further consideration of Sections 28, 29, and 30 be postponed.

Agreed to.

Sections 31 to 34 were severally passed as they stood.

Section 35 was passed after an amendment.

Section 36 was postponed.

Sections 37 to 43 were severally passed as they stood.

The further consideration of the Bill was postponed, and the Council resumed its sitting.

CRIMINAL PROCEDURE.

MR. HARINGTON moved that a correspondence received by him from the Secretary to the Government of the North-Western-Provinces regarding the present system of investigation into Criminal offences by Darogahs and other subordinate Officers of Police be laid upon the table, and referred to the Select Committees on the Bills for extending the jurisdiction of the Courts of Criminal Judicature of the East India Company, for simplifying the Procedure thereof, and for investing other Courts with Criminal jurisdiction.

Agreed to.

MR. HARINGTON moved that certain correspondence relating to prosecutions for perjury and subornation of perjury and forgery, and knowingly issuing forged deeds in Civil proceedings, be laid upon the table and referred to the Select Committees on the above Bills.

Agreed to.

AHMEDABAD MAGISTRACY.

MR. LEGEYT moved that the Bill "to empower the Governor in Council of Bombay to appoint a Magistrate for certain Districts within the Zillah Ahmedabad" be referred to a Select Committee, consisting of Mr. Harington, Mr. Forbes, and the Mover.

Agreed to.

The Council adjourned.

Saturday, October 30, 1858.

PRESENT:

The Hon'ble the Chief Justice, *Vice-President*, in the Chair.

Hon'ble Lieut.-Genl. Sir J. Outram,	E. Currie, Esq.,
Hon'ble H. Ricketts,	Hon'ble Sir A. W. Buller,
Hon'ble B. Peacock,	H. B. Harington, Esq., and
P. W. LeGeyt Esq.,	H. Forbes, Esq.

CONTINUANCE OF CERTAIN PRIVILEGES TO THE FAMILY &c., OF THE LATE NABOB OF THE CARNATIC.

THE VICE-PRESIDENT read a message informing the Legislative Council that the Governor General had assented to the Bill "to continue certain privileges and immunities to the family and retainers of His late Highness the Nabob of the Carnatic."

DELHI TERRITORY.

THE CLERK reported to the Council that he had received from the Home Department a communication from the Secretary to the Government of India with the Governor General, suggesting that, as the greater part of the Delhi Territory is now administered by the Chief Commissioner of the Punjab, an Act be passed for the formal repeal of Regulation V. 1832 of the Bengal Code.

MR. PEACOCK moved that the above communication be referred to the Select Committee on the Bill "to remove from the operation of the General Laws and Regulations the Delhi Territory and Meerut Division, or such parts thereof as the Governor General in Council shall place under the administration of the Chief Commissioner of the Punjab."

Agreed to.

SMALL CAUSE COURTS (MOFUSSIL.)

MR. HARINGTON moved the first reading of a Bill "for the establishment of Courts of Small Causes beyond the local limits of the jurisdiction of the Supreme Courts of Judicature established by Royal Charter". He said, the title of the Bill of which he was now to move the first reading, would probably lead some Honorable Members to enquire why, instead of bringing in a new Bill for the establishment of Courts of Small Causes—which in the remarks that he was about to make, he should assume to be, by general admission, the great desideratum at the present time in the administration of Civil Justice in this Country beyond the local limits of the jurisdiction of the Supreme Courts—he had not rather gone to the Honorable and learned Member of Council on his left, and proposed to him to proceed with the Bill "for the more easy recovery of small debts and demands" which had been before the Council from the time it was established, being one of the Bills transferred to it from the former Legislature, and which, having passed first through the Select Committee appointed to report upon it, and afterwards through a Committee of the whole Council, now only awaited a third reading and the assent of the Right Honorable the Governor General to become law. Probably no legislative measure had ever occupied a larger amount of the time and attention of this Council, or had ever received from it more careful and anxious consideration than the Bill to which he had just alluded. To this fact, in so far as the labors of the Select Committee were concerned, ample testimony was borne by the Honorable and learned Vice-President in the debate which took place on the motion for the whole Council going into Committee upon the Bill. On that occasion the Honorable and learned Vice-President remarked that:

"Whatever difference of opinion there might be in the Council as regarded the merits of the measure, he thought there could be none on the point last touched upon by the Honorable and learned Member of Council on his left in the speech delivered by him in making the motion, namely, the extreme care, and he would add the great ability, which the Members composing the Committee had bestowed upon the Bill, and the degree to which this Council was indebted to them for their labors."

There were therefore strong reasons for his adopting the course, which, as already suggested, some Honorable Members might think was the proper course, and which, under other circumstances, he should certainly have considered himself bound to pursue. This would no doubt have been the simpler mode of proceeding, and it would have made his task a very easy one But the objections to the adoption of that course appeared to him so weighty, and to preponderate so greatly over any thing that could be advanced in favor of it, that he had determined not to shrink from the responsibility which the bringing in of a new Bill would impose upon him, and he trusted to be able presently to show that he had good ground for the determination to which he had come, and that he should not be considered by the Council to have been guilty of any want of courtesy towards the Honorable and learned Member of Council in respect to the Bill under his charge, much less of any wish to snatch from him the honor of passing that Bill, or to deprive him of the gratification which he would naturally feel in giving to the people of this country the great blessing of a cheap, simple, and speedy mode of obtaining redress as regarded the great mass of the disputes arising amongst them. Undoubtedly it must be a subject of deep and sincere regret that all the time which had been expended, and all the labor which had been bestowed on the Bill to which he had been referring, should have been spent in vain, and that a measure which exhibited so much care and ability in its preparation as to have called forth the encomium from the Honorable and learned Vice-President which he had quoted, and which, if passed into law, would probably cover nearly two-thirds of the suits instituted in our Courts, should never come to maturity, but such, he believed, must be the result of the labors of the Council in respect to this particular measure; under existing circumstances he did not think they could have any other termination, and such being the case he felt the less compunction in bringing in a Bill which, though it might, if carried, have the effect of hastening the fate which, according to his belief, awaited its predecessor, would not be chargeable with producing the result anticipated by him. Impressed with this belief he did go to the Honorable and learned Member of Council before giving notice of his intention to bring in a new Bill. The object, however, of his visit was not to ask the Honorable and learned Member to move the third reading of the Bill under his charge—that, after what he had just stated, he could not consistently do—but to explain why he thought that Bill should not be proceeded with, and his reasons for wishing, if the Honorable and learned Member saw no objection, to bring in a new Bill having the same end in view, though differing materially in one important respect, to which he should allude more particularly hereafter. He believed he was correct in stating that the Honorable and learned Member concurred with him that there were difficulties in the way of proceeding with his Bill, and he was good enough to say that he had no objection to his (Mr. Harington) bringing in a Bill of the character proposed by him. He was bound, however, to add that nothing that fell from the Honorable and learned Member during their interview would justify him in calculating with any degree of certainty upon his support, though he trusted that this would not be withheld, and that the Honorable and learned Member would allow his Bill to be read a second time. He could not of course ask the Honorable and learned Member to pledge himself to vote for the second reading, much less to adopt his (Mr. Harington's) Bill in lieu of the one so ably and indefatigably conducted by him to the stage which he had mentioned, because he knew that he entertained a very strong and decided opinion upon the point to which he had referred, directly opposed to the views of himself and others. Under these circumstances it seemed to him that he had no alternative, and that he must either himself bring in a Bill for the establishment of Courts of Small Causes, or leave matters in their present very unsatisfactory state, and that being the case, he could have no hesitation or doubt as to the course which it was his duty to pursue.

It would be in the recollection of some Honorable Members now present, that the Bill "for the more easy recovery of small debts and demands," after passing through a Committee of the whole Council, was ordered to be re-published for general information, and with a view to elicit the opinions of the public on the amendments introduced in Committee. Shortly after, the Code of Civil Procedure prepared in England by Her Majesty's Commissioners appointed for the purpose, reached this country, and, as the framers of that Code declared that it would apply to all ordinary Civil Courts with exception to the Courts of Small Causes at the Presidency Towns, it seemed undesirable to proceed with the Bill before the Council until there should have been sufficient time carefully to examine the Code sent out from England, with a view to ascertain whether its adoption would supersede the necessity of further and separate legislation in so far as the procedure of our Civil Courts was concerned, a single Code of procedure applicable to all classes of cases, if sufficiently summary for the simplest description of suits, and capable of being easily administered, being obviously preferable to two or more Codes applicable to different classes of cases, though to be administered by the same Courts. The Code received from England was formed into a Bill with some few modifications, and the Bill thus framed having been read a first and second time, was referred in the usual course to a Select Committee, before whom it remained for several months, and at whose hands it underwent a very careful revision. The greater part of the Code had now been considered and discussed by a Committee of the whole Council, and Honorable Members had therefore had ample opportunities of learning its character, and of judging for themselves whether it deserved what had been said of it by its framers, namely, that in the simpler classes of suits the procedure which it prescribed would be equally expeditious and economical with that of the Courts of Small Causes at Calcutta, Madras, and Bombay. Her Majesty's Commissioners had assigned this as a reason for not considering it necessary to extend the system of Courts of Small Causes to the other principal Stations in the country as had been sometimes proposed, and if the Code prepared by them should be adopted, and should be found to be of the simple and comprehensive character claimed for it, it was scarcely necessary for him to say that it would only complicate matters, and could answer no useful purpose to pass those provisions of the Bill "for the more easy recovery of small debts and demands" which related to procedure alone. This was his chief reason for considering that so much of that Bill should not be proceeded with. He had reason to know that the Honorable and learned Member of Council on his left, whose opinion on this as well as on all other matters coming before this Legislature, must always carry with it very great weight, considered the Code sent out from England to be altogether of too cumbrous a character for Courts of Small Causes. No doubt some of the provisions of that Code were not adapted to Courts exercising merely what was understood by Small Cause jurisdiction, but those provisions were evidently framed, not so much for simple actions of debt and the like, as for suits relating to real property an other su ts of difficulty and complexity, and he thought it w uld be found that they would rarely, if ever, be brought into operation in cases of the nature of those to which the Bill "for the more easy recovery of small debts and demands" was intended to apply. But whatever might be the character of the Code received from England, he believed he might say that the Select Committee, to whom it was referred for report, had carefully abstained from proposing the introduction of any amendments which would have the effect of detracting from its simplicity, and he thought there could be no doubt that some of the amendments recommended by the Committee would, if adopted, render the Code better fitted for Courts of the character of those which he was anxious to see established, than would be the case were it to be passed exactly in the form in which it was sent out from home. He alluded particularly to the power proposed to be given to all Courts, of requiring the personal attendance of the plaintiff and defendant, with a view to their being confronted, on the day fixed for the first hearing of a suit. This power should, he thought, be possessed and freely exercised by all Courts of Small Causes, whosoever established, and whosoever might preside in them. The position in life of the parties, who were usually concerned as plaintiff or defendant, in cases coming before Courts of that description, was clearly not such as to oppose any obstacle to their personal attendance, and it was only very recently that he was informed by the learned and excellent first Judge of the Court of Small Causes at Calcutta, that he attributed it very much to the extent to which the practice of requiring the personal attendance of the parties was carried in that Court that it was able to get through the large quantity of work which the annual returns showed to be disposed of by it. Mr. Wylie had kindly sent him a copy of the last official year's Report, from which he observed that between the 1st May 1857 and the 30th April 1858, or on two hundred and fifty sitting or working days, he and his two colleagues disposed of no less than thirty thousand, seven hundred, and twenty-four cases, giving a daily average of more than a hundred and twenty cases, and that the amount litigated in the suits instituted during the same period exceeded eight lacs of Rupees. He could not refrain from expressing his astonishment at the immense amount of business which was shown by this Report to have been dispatched by this very useful Court, and his admiration of the zeal and attention to their duties on the part of the Judges, of which it furnished such satisfactory proof.

He passed on to consider that part of the Bill "for the more easy recovery of small debts and demands" which related to the agency by which the object contemplated by the Bill was proposed to be effected. The original Bill, which was drawn up by Mr. Mills and himself, gave the Executive Governments of the Presidencies of Bengal, Madras, and Bombay power to invest any existing Courts under their respective Governments with Small Cause jurisdiction for the purpose of trying certain classes of suits, and, with the previous sanction of the Governor General of India, to constitute new Courts for the same purpose. It appeared to Mr. Mills and himself absolutely necessary to the success of the measure that on its first introduction, the caution enjoined by that distinguished Nobleman and eminent Statesman, Lord Dalhousie, who held the Office of Governor General at the time the Bill was laid before the Legislature, should be strictly observed, and that in those places in which, from the paucity of the Inhabitants, or from any other cause, it might not be considered necessary or advisable to establish separate Courts of Small Causes, only those Native Judges should be invested with Small Cause jurisdiction who were reported by the Sudder Courts competent to exercise, and otherwise fit to be entrusted with it. Such was also the opinion of the Honorable the Lieutenant-Governor of Bengal, than whom there was no Officer in India better qualified to give an opinion on the point. He said:—

"We know that Small Cause Courts are required. But we are far from knowing what existing functionaries among the Native Judges are fit to be Small Cause Judges. That knowledge will come in time and after experiment. The Commissioners do not contemplate giving such powers on this side of India to men paid and selected as the Moonsiffs now are. They contemplate a better class. (See Paragraphs 18 and 19.) They did therefore wisely, in my humble opinion, when they left the selection to the Local Governments, meaning that the Local Government would be likely, or rather would be directed, to select for such powers men adequately paid. The bulk of our Moonsiffs at a hundred Rupees a month are quite unfit to be trusted with such powers, and to give it to them would cause great discontent, and, as is not indistinctly intimated by the Commissioners, hazard the success of the whole plan."

The Select Committee, however, on the Bill refused to adopt the views entertained by Mr. Mills and himself, though supported by the high authority of the Lieutenant-Governor of Bengal, and, instead of the provision which he had quoted from the original Bill, they recommended, and the Committee of the whole Council concurred in the recommendation, that the Court of every Moonsiff in the three Presidencies should be a Court for the trial of summary actions up to fifty Rupees in amount and should exercise summary jurisdiction; while in a later part of the Bill a Section was introduced declaring it to be lawful for the Executive Government:—

"To invest any Civil Court of the East India Company now existing, or which might hereafter be established with the sanction of the Governor General in Council, with the summary jurisdiction of a Small Cause Court under the Act for the adjudication of claims to an amount not exceeding five hundred Rupees, and from time to time to determine the territorial limits within which such Court should exercise such summary jurisdiction. Provided that no Court should be invested with jurisdiction as a Small Cause Court beyond the amount of its ordinary jurisdiction."

An attempt was made in the Committee of the whole Council by his (Mr. Harington's) predecessor in the representation of the North-Western Provinces to restore the original Section, but it failed, two only out of the eight Members who attended the Meeting of the Committee having been found to vote for it. The question, therefore, as to whether, supposing a Bill of the nature of that under consideration to pass, the principle of gradual introduction proposed by Mr. Mills and himself, or of immediate extension to all parts of the country according to the recommendation of the Select Committee, should be acted upon, might be considered to have been definitively determined in favor of the latter course, and the steps which he was now taking, and which, if successful, would have the effect of disturbing that determination, might be regarded not only as an unnecessary occupation of the time of the Council, but as somewhat irregular. On looking, however, over the debates which took place during the progress of the Bill through the Committee of the whole Council, he had been led to believe that it was mainly in consequence of the introduction of the amendment to which he had alluded that the Bill was ordered to be re-published instead of proceeding at once to a third reading, the object being to elicit the opinions of the public, chiefly upon the particular Section in which that amendment was contained. The question might, therefore, be looked upon as still an open one. In support of what he had just stated he would again refer to the speech of the Honorable and learned Vice-President, from which he had already made one quotation. He remarked:—

"The first question of principle which arose upon this measure, was, whether it was desirable to make that change which the majority of the Select Committee proposed to make, namely, to constitute every Moonsiff's Court in the country a Small Cause Court at once with a jurisdiction limited to fifty Rupees;—or, whether it was desirable to leave it to the Executive Governments to confer such a jurisdiction upon certain Officers selected at their discretion, with power to enlarge it for any particular Court or district, and, with the sanction of the Governor General in Council, to erect new Courts. He must confess that the question was one upon which he found it extremely difficult to come to a conclusion very satisfactory to his own mind; and in whatever form the Bill might leave the Committee of this Council, supposing the changes which the Select Committee recommended should be introduced, he hoped that it would be published, in order to invite the opinions of the public upon its provisions."

And the Honorable and learned Vice-President concluded his speech by observing that:—

"He should certainly prefer going into Committee upon the Bill, and should do his best to suggest any improvements in its provisions which might appear to him expedient; but, at the same time, he did not wish to commit himself to any final opinion as to the policy of extending, in Bengal at least, the jurisdiction given by it to every Moonsiff's Court, until the different Governments and the public had had a further opportunity of expressing their opinions upon the subject."

Accordingly, as suggested by the Honorable and learned Vice-President, the Bill was re-published, and what had been the result? Why, an almost unanimous verdict in favor of the views entertained by Mr. Mills and himself, and against the amendment introduced by the Select Committee and adopted by a Committee of the whole Council. With the permission of the Council he would read some of the opinions elicited by the re-publication of the Bill, taking them in the order in which they had been printed. The first report was from the Sudder Court of Bombay:—

"They consider that the Act is not suited to the object for which it professes to legislate; that the indiscriminate extension of a Native Judge's jurisdiction to try suits up to fifty Rupees is unsafe, and that the delegation of the authority and the amount should be vested in the Executive Government."

This was followed by a letter written by order of the Chief Commissioner of the Punjab, whose opinion would, he was sure, be received with the utmost respect by every Member of this Council, and could not fail to command great attention. Opinions might differ as to the comparative advantages of what was called the Punjab system and the system in force in the older or Regulation Provinces. On this point the Honorable Member of Council opposite (Mr. Ricketts) might have one opinion; he (Mr. Harington) might have another opinion; but there could be no difference of opinion amongst them as to the distinguished merits of the great man who, for so many years, had administered the former system with an ability which could not be surpassed, and whose eminent services during the past year had laid his country under a debt of gratitude to him which no honors, no rank, no money, could adequately repay. Sir John Lawrence said:—

"In the event of the new Act being introduced in the Punjab, then he would at all events earnestly recommend that the Sections relative to appeals should be excepted. He believes that the rules contained in those Sections would not work well if applied to the Tehseeldaree Courts of the Punjab. Whether the entire absence of appeal, except under certain provisions, is generally desirable or not, is a point on which he does not presume to offer an opinion. He only submits that it is not desirable in the Province.

"The power of appealing is evidently a salutary one, giving satisfaction to suitors and to the public, and operating as a proper check upon the judiciary. In his (the Chief Commissioner's) opinion the Punjabees regard the power of appeal as a kind of palladium of their rights. If it were taken away, even in an inconsiderable proportion of cases, they would be led to think less well of the administration of Justice under British Rule. Again, he would urge that, in all cases, the right of appeal is requisite as a check on our Tehseeldars. He admits the merits of these Officers as a body. But they assuredly are not all that could be desired. Some are old employés of the Sikh Government, deficient in business habits. Some were hastily appointed after annexation, without sufficient scrutiny of antecedents. Few of them are really as yet trained to judicial duties. Many of them are stationed in isolated localities at a distance from European control. All of them have heavy and varied duties to perform, and must, therefore, be liable to error from inadvertence or haste as well as from ignorance or inefficiency. He thinks that they are not the men to be left without so useful a check as that imposed by the power of appeal. While this check remains, he gladly acknowledges that they satisfy the public generally, and dispense substantial justice tolerably well. If it were removed, their attention might relax, or their morale deteriorate. Throughout India it is well known that native agency is very efficient and tolerably trustworthy, provided that it be sufficiently controlled. Such control is especially required for our Tehseeldars, and is often materially dependent on the existence of appeal in all cases. By these means the conduct of every one of these Judges is periodically supervised. Without these means misconduct or incompetency on their part might never be discovered until much mischief had been done past remedy, and until general dissatisfaction had manifested itself in some marked manner. Then, indeed, the evils might with much trouble be partially cured, which might have been entirely prevented had the power of appeal existed."

Then came a letter from the Secretary to the Government of the North-Western Provinces, containing the sentiments of the Lieutenant-Governor of those Provinces, the late Mr. Colvin, whose opinions, so valuable while he was alive, would lose none of their weight now that he was no longer amongst them to enforce them. This letter said :—

"The Lieutenant-Governor strongly concurs in the view urged by the Court, which is held also by a very great majority of the Judicial Officers under this Government, that it would be as yet decidedly unsafe and inexpedient to vest the Moonsiffs indiscriminately with the very independent jurisdiction to be exercised under the new law, up to the limit of fifty Rupees' value. This limit would, as shown by the Court, include more than sixty per centum of the whole number of suits instituted, of the large class for the trial of which the Bill provides.

"The Judges who may be armed with the powers of this law, will, in a country where public observation is so inactive and public opinion so feeble, be the arbiters of the fortunes and happiness of the great mass of the residents in their neighbourhoods. The general and progressive improvement in the Moonsiffs as a body is fully admitted, and is a subject of much satisfaction to this Government. Some of the objections, which are pressed in the discussion respecting the Bill, to the employment of the Moonsiffs in the new scheme of summary Judicature, spring only from prejudiced, or perhaps selfish, feelings; and to yield to them would be inconsistent with the wise and just policy which would elevate the Natives of India to places of extensive and high trust in the public administration. But it is because he would warmly wish to forward the objects of the present important measure, and to raise and use the agency the aid of which is chiefly looked to in its execution, that the Lieutenant-Governor would recommend that the Legislature should proceed with a prudent caution, and not treat as light and worthless the local experience of the public Officers, who report their opinions as to its probable acceptance and effects in different parts of the empire. Such a measure is to be introduced within the Bengal and North Western districts for the first time. The Moonsiffs are not yet adequately paid. Nor have all the old class of Moonsiffs, inferior as it unquestionably was in character, self-respect, and public repute, yet ceased to hold office. The best of the grade will be quite new to the possession of so much authority. The right of an unrestricted appeal upon facts is one which has hitherto been fully open to all suitors. To give over at once, under such circumstances, more than half of the common litigation of the country to all the present Moonsiffs, subjected avowedly to but little practical check, is a hazard so great that the Legislative Council must, as the Lieutenant-Governor would persuade himself, hesitate to incur it. On the question whether the whole body of the Moonsiffs should be at once invested with these powers by a fixed rule in the law, the facts of the case appear to be simply these. The Moonsiffs now holding office have been appointed under a system which requires a minute verbal record of all the proceedings in their Courts, and subjects all their orders to an unlimited appeal. They have been considered fit to be retained in office under that system of close check. A majority of them would now, the Lieutenant-Governor believes, be qualified to exercise, within certain limits, the higher and more independent powers of the Small Cause jurisdiction. The remainder, chiefly older public servants placed in their posts when the standard of feeling was not what it at present is in their class, cannot be held to be so qualified. Is it right that these should be instantly removed from their employments, and, when near to the termination of their service, cut off by that means from the prospect of their retiring pension, because they have not the character and capacity required for a class of functions so novel and enlarged as entirely to alter the constitution of their Courts? Is it right, on the other hand, that they should be invested with an authority which experience does not warrant their superior Officers and the Government in recommending them for? Will it be a benefit to the people to clothe them with that authority whatever may be the feeling of the Government? The part of practical wisdom and equity seems surely to be in admitting of some little delay in the complete or universal introduction of the new judicature. The Government, anxious to forward the purposes of the Legislature, and to make justice every where more readily accessible, will lose no time in conferring the powers on all the Moonsiffs, as soon as a more trustworthy, and generally esteemed, set of Officers has been gradually substituted for those in regard to whom doubts may now exist."

The opinion of the Sudder Court at Agra followed. The Court remarked :—

"Approving, as they do, of the general scope and principle of the new Bill, they would notice, in the first place, the two material points in which it differs from the drafts originally framed, and regarding which particularly the opinions of the Zillah Judges have been sought, namely :—

"*First.*—The investiture of the Moonsiffs in general with the summary jurisdiction of a Court of Small Causes. Section I of the Bill.

"*Second.*—The omission of the special limitation clauses provided by Sections VI to X of the Bill as originally framed.

"With regard to the first point, His Honor will observe that one Judge alone (the Officiating Judge of Cawnpore, Mr. C. W. Fagan), and only three Principal Sudder Ameens, namely, those of Cawnpore, Allygurh, and Jounpore, have given an opinion in favor of investing the Moonsiffs generally with the powers of Small Cause Court Judges. All the other Zillah Judges and Principal Sudder Ameens are unanimous in considering this a most dangerous experiment, and as calculated most seriously to detract from, if not entirely to nullify, the beneficial effects of the proposed Bill; the enactment of the original draft, in which it was provided that the summary jurisdiction should be conferred, according to the discretion of the Executive Governments, on those Native Judges in whom they had full confidence, is, in the consideration of these Officers, preferable to the passing of the Bill as it stands.

"In this opinion of the majority, the Court fully concur. They remark that a measure, such as the present, which creates a most material change in the system of Civil Judicature, and practically invests the lowest class of Native Judges with irresponsible powers in suits up to fifty Rupees, must, to be successful, carry along with it the sense of the people whose interest it affects. That such is not the case with the present Bill is undoubted. As far as the Courts have been able to ascertain for themselves, and as is apparent from the answers of the Zillah Judges, it is clear that the Native

Community in these Provinces are strongly opposed to investing the Moonsiffs in general with these summary powers, and that they look forward with considerable distrust and apprehension to the passing of the Bill in its present shape. The Court readily acknowledge that, for some years past, the Moonsiffs, as a body, have considerably improved, and are still improving in character and capacity; but they are constrained to state (and this opinion is shared very generally by the Community) that there are some Moonsiffs who have not established that character for integrity and independence as to render it safe to invest them with the large powers provided by this Bill.

"That this is a question deeply affecting the interests of the people, and more particularly of the poorer classes, is apparent from the fact that out of 13,910 suits for money or other personal property, exclusive of suits relating to arrears or exactions of rent, instituted in the Civil Courts of these Provinces during the first three months of 1855, more than sixty per cent. (as will be seen from the accompanying return, marked B.) were for claims not exceeding fifty Rupees in value, which would, therefore, be cognizable by the proposed Small Cause Courts. It can consequently be no matter of surprise that the Native Community dislike the idea of entrusting more than half of their litigation touching pecuniary transactions to Judges in whom they have not perfect confidence, and whose decisions would be open to no appeal upon the facts."

In the Calcutta Sudder Court there was some difference of opinion, two of the Judges, Mr. Dick and Sir R. Barlow, approving of the Section as it now stood, by which every Moonsiff's Court would become a Court of Small Causes, while the other three Judges, Messrs. Raikes, Colvin, and Patton—

"would prefer to see the Act introduced gradually by the establishment of special Courts in particular Towns and Marts of importance, to be presided over by Officers selected for this duty on account of their judicial aptitude, the Executive Government having the power to extend the number and jurisdiction of these Courts as it might deem necessary."

The Court having thus given their own opinion went on to say :—

"The general feeling appears to be strong against the introduction of the Act into all the Moonsiffs' Courts unless an appeal on the merits is allowed in every case"

Last, though certainly not least in importance, they had a Minute by the Honorable the Lieutenant-Governor of Bengal, in which was embodied the opinion of the Sudder Court at Madras, and he believed the Honorable Member for Madras could tell them that the Sudder Court at that Presidency, as at present constituted, had recently given it as their opinion that the District Moonsiffs did not command the confidence of the people in point of either integrity or efficiency. Mr. Halliday said :—

"To set up my single opinion against any part of a Bill which has been approved by a majority of the Legislative Council, would be rash and presumptuous, and if I stood alone in my objections, I should be silent. But I find myself supported as to one or other of my reasons by very weighty authorities, and I may in this manner quote with assurance the opinions of the framers of the original Bill, of a majority of the Zillah Judges, and of the Sudder Court of this Presidency, of the Sudder Court and the Government of Bombay, of the Sudder Court of Madras, of the Sudder Court and the Lieutenant-Governor of the North-Western Provinces, and of the Governor General as Governor of Bengal.

"What our judicial system has appeared to me most urgently to require as an improvement upon our present dilatory and complicated methods, is a plan by which the smaller and simpler, but by far the most numerous suits, should be decided under a plain and easy procedure, and by trustworthy and competent tribunals, speedily, cheaply, and finally. Our Mofussil judicatories have heretofore been invariably constructed on the assumption (unavoidable in former days) that, either by reason of inexperience and want of training in some cases, or doubtful integrity in others, no firm reliance could be placed on any Judges of first instance, but that all their decisions and all acts and orders must necessarily be guarded by the security of constant appeal. Hence of necessity have arisen long, formal, expensive, and tedious systems of procedure and record, which, to say the least, have seriously impaired the utility of our judicatories, and hence have been engendered in the minds of the people a habit of continuous litigation, and a fondness for multiplied appeals, which, though they may have always lurked in the characters of the Natives of India, ought rather to have been checked than fostered, and had certainly no opportunity of development before the introduction of our judicial systems.

"But while we thus nourished and cultivated the litigious propensities of our subjects, we were avowedly very far from giving them satisfaction by any of our methods of judicature, and the first and only one of our multifarious experiments in this direction, which seems to have been attended with complete success, was the establishment of Small Cause Courts at the Presidencies; in which, reverting at last to the system most obviously in accordance with oriental notions and prejudices, we (practically) abolished appeal, and adopted a procedure simple, speedy, and final.

"The eminent success, and the great general popularity of this tribunal among the natives, could not fail to attract attention. For here at last appeared to be solved the question of the judicature best suited to the mass of Native litigants; and here at all events was a Court largely resorted to, giving constant satisfaction by its facile methods, and its speedy decisions, and in the judgments of which even Bengalee litigants were content to rest without further appeal.

"Accordingly, this Court was justly looked upon as the model upon which our experimental improvements in the Mofussil ought to be framed, and the first movement towards the large and difficult measure now before the Legislative Council was a proposition, which I still think wiser than the improvements since grafted upon it, and which I greatly wish had been adhered to, for introducing gradually into the large Towns and Marts, and thence step by step into other places in the interior, Small Cause Courts after the pattern of the successful Courts in Calcutta, thereby weaning the Natives from their attachment to judicial formalities and continuous appeal, and by little and little accustoming them to the use of simple, informal, and final Courts of Justice, just as the Natives of Calcutta have been gradually accustomed to the Calcutta Small Cause Court, until it has become with them an entirely favorite institution.

"It was no part of the scheme of the framers of the original Bill that every Moonsiff should be made a Small Cause Court Judge. On the contrary, they gave good reasons why this ought not to be done, and, as I have elsewhere remarked, they not indistinctly intimated that to do this would hazard the success of their whole plan.

"The Sudder Court at Madras, though they made on the 19th October 1854 a recommendation not easily reconcileable with such an opinion, had previously, that is, on the 14th July 1854, intimated in indirect, but unmistakeable terms, that the class of Judges to whom it is now proposed to give the functions of Small Cause Judges were not men whose honesty is unimpeachable, and in whose efficiency in the discharge of their duties every reasonable confidence may be reposed. And they argued that, if this course was persevered in, it would be absolutely necessary to give an appeal on the facts.

"The Natives, chiefly of Calcutta, represented by the "British Indian Association," considered that the success of the experiment, which they designated as an innovation of magnitude, would depend mainly upon the selection of the places at which it might be tried, as well as of the agency by which it might be worked, and they suggested the utmost discrimination in selecting the places where the new Courts are to be instituted, in appointing the Judges by whom they are to be presided over, and in regulating the maximum value of the suits to which their jurisdiction in particular places shall extend. It is evident that the Association had no notion of extending the jurisdiction suddenly to all Moonsiffs, or of spreading it over the face of the whole country.

"In the papers now submitted, it will be found that eighteen out of twenty-five Zillah Judges object to giving the jurisdiction generally to all Moonsiffs, three out of five Sudder Judges being of the same opinion. Regarding appeals, the prevailing opinion of the Sudder Court seems to be that, if the measure were gradually introduced by the appointment of well-selected Judges in a few places, appeals might well be omitted, but that, if all the Moonsiffs are to be made Small Cause Court Judges, a right of appeal must be allowed to an extent beyond what the present Bill proposes. And the Native Judges and Pleaders consulted are reported to be very generally against the introduction of the Act into all the Moonsiffs' Courts, unless an appeal on the merits is allowed in every case. The general view of the kind of measure required by the circumstances of the country which is taken by the Judges of the Sudder Court, may be inferred from the manner in which they quote the opinion of the English Commissioners, that in claims of small amount the evils caused by an occasional miscarriage are more than counterbalanced by the advantages presented by a local tribunal, the proceedings of which are simple, cheap, speedy, and final.

"It appears to me from all this that the Act, as now proposed to be passed, has been settled contrary to the general suggestions of experience in all parts of India, and that it may, therefore, be expected to fail of complete success. There are many large and important towns under the Bengal Government in which the introduction of a simple, informal, and final system of Small Cause Courts would have been a great and important measure. The people would have resorted to them as the people in Calcutta have done to their Small Cause Court, the system would gradually have been popularized, more of such Courts would have been from time to time called for in other places, and thus in the most safe and certain way the principle of such jurisdiction would have become established in the habits and feelings of our subjects, and afterwards, with their entire assent and concurrence, extended over the whole country. The Act now proposed will, I fear, have no such effect. The reform it introduces into the system of procedure might be looked upon as considerable were it not so likely (may I not say so sure) to be neutralized by the incompetency of the Judges to whom it is entrusted, by the unmanageable extent of their jurisdictions, and by the inevitable consequences of appeals which are invariably productive of formality and delay in the lower Courts. And whatever there may be in the proposed Act of novelty and improvement, being entrusted indiscriminately to a body of Judges who have not yet acquired the full confidence of the Government or the public, the changes made in the law, even if worked better than I anticipate, will be received with doubt and dislike, the principle on which they proceed will gain no hold on the inclinations of the people, and the result will, I apprehend, hardly be an advance, if indeed it do not end in retrogression."

Now, he submitted that the opinions which he had just read at the risk of being thought tedious, were conclusive in favor of the proposition of Mr. Mills and himself and against that of the Select Committee on the Bill "for the more easy recovery of small debts and demands", and as the object in view in republishing that Bill was to elicit the opinions of the public on this point, he apprehended that the verdict almost universally given against the amendment introduced by the Select Committee could consistently and properly be followed only by the abandonment of the principle on which that amendment was based, and it had been abandoned accordingly in the Bill which he was about to present. He (Mr. Harington) did not think that they could turn round upon all the high authorities whose opinions he had quoted, and say to them—"We are better acquainted with the character of the Native Judges than you are; we know more of the habits, feelings, wishes, and wants of the people of this country than you do; we value your opinion at *nil*; we hold our own opinion still, and you shall either take our Bill in all its integrity as settled by the Committee of the whole Council or you shall have no Bill at all; choose between these alternatives." It certainly did not app a to him that this would be a wise, prudent, or proper course for this Council to pursue, and he did not think that it would consist with its duty to the public.

On referring to the debate to which he had more than once alluded, he found that the Honorable and learned Member of Council on his left (Mr. Peacock) had put the following case; he said :—

"Suppose a summary jurisdiction under the provisions of this Act were conferred by the Executive Government upon the Moonsiff's Court in district A, but not upon the Moonsiff of the adjoining district B. Suppose, also, that an inhabitant of district B. were to petition the Executive Government to confer a similar procedure on district B, he would say :—

"'My friends and neighbours in district A. can sue for claims under fifty Rupees by paying a much smaller amount of stamp duty, and can recover their claims in much less time and with much less trouble than I can. I am forced, whenever I enter into a contract for a sum not exceeding fifty Rupees, to go into district A. in order to avoid the necessity of suing upon it in my own district. Do, pray, give district B., in which I live and carry on my business, a Small Cause Court also.'

"What would be the answer that the Executive Government could make to this petition? Why, if the argument against the general extension of this Act was to be used, they must say :—

"'We approve of the summary procedure which we have conferred upon the Moonsiff in district A. We would willingly give your district a Small Cause Court. It works well in district A; but the Moonsiff in your district is incompetent to exercise the jurisdiction, and we cannot trust him'

"Now could that be said? Ought it to be said? Ought it to be said that a Judge, who was trusted to decide claims to the amount of three hundred Rupees under a system which required a record such as that to which he had before alluded, was not competent or could not be trusted to decide cases under a system very much more simple? Would not such an answer tend to throw discredit upon the whole of that class of the civil institutions of the country? Would not the petitioner have a fair right to reply—

"'Then give us a competent Moonsiff?'"

Now the reason that had always operated in his mind against the extension at once to all parts of the country of a measure of the nature of that under consideration, instead of its gradual introduction as fitting instruments could be found for carrying it into effect, was not the possible incompetency of individual Judges or of any particular class of Courts to decide suits under the new system of procedure which would be introduced thereby, but the inexpediency of permitting all Courts, whatever might be the character of the Judges presiding in them, to decide suits up to a certain amount without the safeguard of an appeal and without any thing deserving of the name of a record, which could not be dispensed with if an appeal was allowed. He did not remember ever to have said that, in so far as the mere adjudication of the matter in dispute between the parties went, the present Moonsiffs or any of them would not be just as competent to decide simple suits of the nature of those to which the Bill "for the more easy recovery of small debts and demands" was intended to apply under the rules of procedure therein prescribed, as they were to decide suits of a higher amount and of a more difficult character under the present system. This was not his position. What he had all along contended for, and what he still contended for, was that it was not wise, safe, or proper to give a final jurisdiction in any case to the lowest class of Courts, seeing that it was notorious that the greater number of the Judges appointed to those Courts were, on their first appointment, totally devoid of judicial experience, many of them never having even seen a Civil suit tried, and their judgments were consequently not matured. He should perhaps be told that they were not justified in appointing new and untried men to the Bench, and that it was their duty to select older and more experienced instruments for first appointments to the Judicial branch of the public service. But he would ask where were such men to be got? The salary now drawn by the Moonsiffs was so small and so disproportionate to their duties, responsibilities, and position in life that a respectable Vakeel in moderate practice would not accept the appointment, and there was no other school in which the Natives of this country could be trained up for Judicial employment. What was the case at home? There, he believed, only Barristers of five years' standing were eligible to the office of Judge in the County Courts or Courts of Small Causes, and if Honorable Members would consider the birth of an English Barrister, the education which he received, his station in Society, and the experience and knowledge of the duties of a Judge which he might acquire during five years' practice in Courts presided over by some of the ablest and most distinguished men in England, with a bar unsurpassed in ability, intelligence, and integrity by any bar in the world, and then contrast all this with the antecedents of the class of men from which the Native Judges were from necessity drawn, their birth, their position in society, their means of education beyond the Presidency Towns, and their previous occupation if they had had any, and the vast superiority of the one class over the other would be painfully apparent. To the former class almost any amount of Judicial power might be safely entrusted, whereas any power given to the Native Judge would almost certainly be abused unless he was most vigilantly supervised and controlled by his European superior. Nor in making the comparison should the fact be lost sight of, that the duties of the two classes were precisely similar, the cases of the simplest description decided by the Native Judges in this country presenting the same difficulties as the cases tried by the Judges of the County or Small Cause Courts at home, or, if there was any difference, it was against the Native Judge arising out of the character of the people with whom he had to deal, and the vices inherent in almost all litigation in this country in which the Natives were concerned; so that he thought he was justified in saying that, if the right of appeal was taken away in cases up to a certain amount, and those cases were left to be decided by the lowest class of Courts without distinction, (many of the Judges presiding in those Courts being, as already noticed, young and inexperienced men) they would commence at the wrong end, and give large powers to those who were the least fit to be entrusted with them, and that, too, over the most indigent and most helpless classes of the people who could ill afford to lose the smallest sum and who were the most destitute of power to complain or make known their grievances.

From the letter from the Chief Commissioner of the Punjab, part of which he had already read, it would be seen that Sir John Lawrence was very decidedly of opinion that, even in the smallest causes, at least one appeal should be allowed either on law, procedure, or matter of fact on any point whatever regarding which either of the litigants might feel dissatisfied. He (Mr. Harington) observed also that, in a Code of Civil Procedure which Mr. George Campbell, the intelligent Judicial Commissioner in Oude, was engaged in preparing for the use of the Civil Courts about to be established in that Province, he proposed that in every case there should be one appeal as the right of a dissatisfied party, and that, when an order in favor of any party was reversed on the appeal of the other party, he in turn should have an appeal. Under this rule it was obvious that there might be two appeals in every case—one on the part of the unsuccessful party in the Court below, and should he succeed in appeal, one on the part of the party defeated in the Appellate Court. Mr. Campbell supported his proposition by saying that in India, with so little fixity of the law, and without a proper public opinion, they must have appeals; they could not be avoided. But the great thing was to have good and discreet appellate tribunals, which would not interfere unnecessarily. He had already quoted what Sir John Lawrence had said on this subject. He declared the power of appeal not only to be a salutary one, giving satisfaction to the suitors and the public, and operating as a proper check upon the Judiciary, but that it was looked upon by the Punjabees as a kind of palladium of their rights, and that, if it was taken away, even in an inconsiderable proportion of cases, they would be led to think less well of the administration of Public Justice in India. A somewhat similar opinion had been given by Mr. Mills and himself in laying the draft of the Bill "for the more easy recovery of small debts and demands" before the Government of India. They said—

"We are aware that our proposal to vest the Courts established under this Act with summary jurisdiction to try cases even of the smallest amount and of the most simple nature, without an appeal upon the facts, will be received with dissatisfaction by the Native Community."

Now he was very sensible that it might be retorted on him that, if these views were correct, instead of doing away with the right of appeal in any case, they should follow the recommendation of the Chief Commissioner of the Punjab, and give one appeal at least in every case, however small in amount, however simple in character, and however competent the Judge of the Court of first instance; and he was bound to say that such was the opinion of almost every Native to whom he had spoken on the subject, as well as of many old and experienced European Judges. Only a few days ago, he had been told by an intelligent Vakeel of the Calcutta Sudder Court, that, if a final jurisdiction was given to the Courts of first instance in cases up to a certain amount, every plaintiff would raise his claim above that amount, not in the expectation of getting a decree for the full sum claimed, but in order that he might preserve the right of appeal; that this right was so much prized, and so little confidence was felt in the Courts of first instance, that, if appeals were abolished in any cases, the people would prefer that the right of suit in the same class of actions should also be taken away. He might be asked whether he thought that this tenacity of purpose in Native litigation and this feeling of distrust as regarded the Courts of first instance, should be encouraged or humoured. That question he could have no hesitation in answering in the negative; but in order to overcome the tenaciousness of the Natives in this respect, or their litigiousness, if that was the proper term, and their want of confidence in the Courts entrusted with the adjudication of more than three-fourths of the entire Judicial business of the country, instead of hastily introducing what would certainly be regarded by many as a violent measure of reform, he would proceed cautiously, and, again, to quote the words of the Honorable the Lieutenant-Governor of Bengal—

"Introduce gradually into the large Towns and Marts, and thence step by step into other places in the interior, Small Cause Courts after the pattern of the successful Court in Calcutta, thereby weaning the Natives from their attachment to Judicial formalities and continuous appeal, and, by little and little, accustoming them to the use of simple, informal, and final Courts of Justice, just as the Natives of Calcutta had been gradually accustomed to the Calcutta Small Cause Court, until it had become with them an entirely favourite institution."

There could be no doubt that in some parts of the country Courts of Small Causes were more required than in other parts, and that, where they were most required, not only would the amount of litigation which would fall within the cognizance of Courts of that description furnish ample employment for the Judges appointed to them, but it might fairly be expected that the income derived from the sale of Judicial Stamps which would be used in their proceedings, would nearly, if not altogether, cover the salaries of the Judges and their establishments. It was well known that the cost of the greater part of the Moonsiffs' Courts was defrayed from this source; and from the returns of the Court of Small Causes at Calcutta, to which he had already referred, he found that, while the fees credited to Government during the last official year amounted to Rupees 1,12,624-6-9, the charges, including the salaries of the Judges and of their establishment, came to only one lac, three thousand, two hundred, and sixty-four Rupees leaving a balance in favor of Government of nearly ten thousand Rupees on the year. There was not the same demand for Courts of Small Causes in the rural districts, and should the Rent Bill brought in by the Honorable Member for Bengal pass into law, as he hoped it would, a large proportion of the small causes arising in those districts would be cognizable under that Bill, the Revenue Officers acting as Judges of first instance. It was at the Sudder Stations of the different districts and in the large towns and cities in the interior where the want of Courts of Small Causes was so much felt, and at those places, should his scheme be adopted, he hoped to see separate Courts of Small Causes with a jurisdiction extending over a radius of about twenty miles at once established wherever they might be shown to be required. The Judges appointed to these Courts should have no other duties to perform. He considered it to be essential to the successful working of a system of Courts of Small Causes, that the Officers who presided in them, when the amount of litigation was sufficient to keep them fully employed, should be able to devote their whole time and attention to the cases instituted in their Courts. Every case should, if possible, be taken up on the day fixed for a hearing, and the work of each day should, as far as practicable, be disposed of before the Court rose. But this could scarcely ever be done if the Judges of Courts of Small Causes were also Criminal Judges or Magistrates and had other Civil suits to decide. If Civil duties of different kinds as well as Criminal duties were combined in the same Officer, he could never command his time, and his attention was constantly liable to be diverted from work which should be performed at once, to other work which was or appeared to be of a more pressing character. Great care should be taken in selecting men for the Courts which he wished to see established, and in order that there might be a large field for selection, liberal salaries should be given to the Officers appointed; five hundred, seven hundred, or even one thousand Rupees a month would not, he thought, be too much, looking to the duties to be performed and the amount of trustworthiness required. As regarded the other parts of the country, where, owing to the scantiness of the population, or from any other cause, separate Courts of Small Causes could not conveniently be established, he would invest such of the existing Judges with Small Cause jurisdiction as might be reported by the Sudder Courts to be competent and otherwise qualified to exercise it. In this way he hoped at no distant date to see the whole country covered either with separate Courts of Small Causes or with Courts exercising small cause jurisdiction concurrently with their other jurisdiction. He could see no reason why, the want being admitted, though not capable, from causes already mentioned, of being immediately met in every place, they should not at once supply it where they could, and where the want was most felt, instead of waiting until they could do at one time all the good which it was their anxiety and wish to accomplish. Had the principle of not doing good here because they could not do good there at the same time, been always acted upon, the present Courts of Small Causes at Calcutta, Madras, and Bombay would not now be in existence, though he had never heard that the persons residing beyond the limits of those Courts had ever complained that similar Courts were not established for their benefit. They were willing to wait until the Government was in a position to extend the advantages of the system to them. At the same time it must be remembered that they were about to give a vastly improved Code of Civil Procedure to the whole country by which all cases would benefit, the only difference really made by this Code in the trial of different classes of suits being that, while in cases in which no appeal was allowed the evidence of the witnesses would be recorded in detail, in cases in which an appeal was not allowed, a brief memorandum only of what each witness deposed would be made by the Judge with his own hand. Whether the Natives would consider this latter mode of proceeding any advantage, was open to question. He observed that, under the Bombay Code, if both the parties to a suit expressed a wish in writing to that effect, the recording of the evidence and of the proceedings at length was dispensed with, and the Court's notes only were preserved. The Honorable Member for Bombay could tell them whether the option thus given was often taken advantage of—he (Mr. Harington) could only say that, so far as his own experience went, if a similar rule was introduced on this side of India, it would quickly become a dead letter, while, as regarded the right of appeal, he thought he might safely affirm that those to whom that right was continued while it was taken away from others, would not complain of the distinction, and that, if any complaint was made, it would be of the loss of the right, not of its retention.

He would proceed now briefly to notice the principal provisions of the

Bill of which he was about to move the first reading.

It proposed to give to the Executive Government of any Presidency or place, with the previous sanction of the Governor General in Council, power to constitute Courts of Small Causes at any places within the limits of their respective Governments with the required establishment of Officers, and, without such sanction, to invest any of the existing Courts under their Governments with small cause jurisdiction for the trial of cases under the Bill, and to fix and, from time to time, to alter the territorial limits of the jurisdiction of the Courts so constituted or invested.

The cases which would be cognizable by the Courts constituted or invested with small cause jurisdiction under the Bill would be the same as were described in Section II of the Bill "for the more easy recovery of small debts and demands"; but, instead of restricting the cognizance of those Courts to cases not exceeding in value or amount the sum of fifty Rupees, it was proposed that five hundred Rupees should be the limit of their pecuniary jurisdiction.

Whenever a Court was constituted in the manner provided, all suits cognizable under the provisions of the Bill, which might arise within the local limits of the jurisdiction of such Court, would be cognizable by it, and by no other Court, and in like manner all suits of the same description arising within the local limits of the jurisdiction of a Court invested with small cause jurisdiction, would be governed by the provisions of the Bill.

The Code of Procedure to be observed in the trial and decision of cases cognizable under the Bill, would be that now passing through a Committee of the whole Council under the title of a Bill "for simplifying the Procedure of the Courts of Civil Judicature not established by Royal Charter."

No appeal would be allowed in suits not exceeding in amount or value the sum of fifty Rupees, nor any special appeal in suits exceeding that amount; but it would be competent to every Court trying a case under the Bill, whether originally or in appeal, in which any question of law or usage having the force of law, or the construction of a document affecting the decision of the case, might arise in respect of which the Court might entertain reasonable doubt, to state a case for the opinion of the Sudder Court, either of its own motion, or upon the application of any of the parties to the suit, and every Court would also be at liberty to grant one new trial, on sufficient cause shown, if applied for within a reasonable time from the date of the decision objected to.

From this sketch of the Bill, the Honorable Members for Madras and Bombay would observe that the passing of the Bill would not necessarily be followed by the introduction of Courts of Small Causes into those Presidencies or by the investment of any of the existing Courts with small cause jurisdiction; but that it would rest with their respective Governments to extend the provisions of the Bill at such time and to such places as they might think proper.

He begged to apologize for having tresspassed so long upon the time of the Council, and thanking them for the hearing they had accorded him, he would now move that the Bill be read a first time.

The Bill was read a first time.

LEASES OF GHATWALEE LANDS (BEERBHOOM.)

Mr. CURRIE moved the first reading of a Bill "to empower the holders of Ghatwalee lands in the district of Beerbhoom to grant leases extending beyond the period of their own possession." He said, the principal object of this Bill was to remove an impediment to the development of the mineral resources of a portion of the district of Beerbhoom. A wild uncultivated tract in that district, supposed to be rich in minerals, was occupied by what are called the Ghatwalee mehals. These mehals were a kind of jageer, subject to a fixed rent, the holders of them being bound to the performance of certain Police services. By a special law (Regulation XXIX. 1814) the rents of the Ghatwalee lands, though included within the

Zemindaree of Beerbhoom, were made payable to Government, and certain rules were laid down explanatory of the terms on which the lands were to be held. It was declared by Section II thatthe Ghatwals

"and their descendants in perpetuity shall be maintained in possession of the land, so long as they shall respectively pay the revenue at present assessed upon them, and that they shall not be liable to any enhancement of rent so long as they shall punctually discharge the same and fulfil the other obligations of their tenure;"

and then Section V provided—

"Should any of the Ghatwals at any time fail to discharge their stipulated rents, it shall be competent for the Governor General in Council to cause the Ghatwalee tenure of such defaulter to be sold by public sale in satisfaction of the arrears due from him, in like manner and under the same rules as lands held immediately of Government, or to make over the tenure of such defaulter to any person whom the Governor General in Council may approve, on the condition of making good the arrear due; or to transfer it by grants assessed with the same revenue, or with an increased or reduced assessment, as to the Government may appear meet; or to dispose of it in such other form and manner as shall be judged by the Governor General in Council proper."

Such were the legal conditions of these tenures. They differed from the ordinary Zemindaree or Talookdaree tenure, inasmuch as they provided for other obligations besides the punctual payment of the revenue, and gave the Government the option of transferring the lands to any person it might think proper in case of default, instead of bringing them to auction sale. The nature and incidents of the Ghatwalee tenure had been more particularly defined by decisions of the Sudder Court. In a suit for a share of a Ghatwalee Talook, decided in June 1837, the Court ruled that

"the Ghatwalee lands are grants for particular purposes, especially of Police, and to divide them into small Portions amongst the heirs of the Ghatwalee, would be to defeat the very ends for which the grants were made."

The Judges of the Court, with one exception, were of opinion

"that a mehal of this nature cannot be divided, but should, on the death of an incumbent, devolve entire on the eldest son or the next Ghatwal."

This decision, therefore, established the point that the peculiar conditions of the Ghatwalee tenure are such as to remove it from the operation of the ordinary law of inheritance.

There was another decision bearing on the question. It arose out of the attachment of a Ghatwalee Mehal in execution of a decree for debt. The Judge held, with reference to the opinions expressed by Government and the Sudder Court in regard to the intent and object of Regulation XXIX. 1814,

"that a Ghatwalee tenure could not legally be held under attachment with a view to the liquidation from the profits of the debts of the Ghatwal."

The case being appealed to the Sudder Court, was referred to a full Bench, and the judgment was—

"that, under the law, the Ghatwalee tenures of Beerbhoom, being not the private property of the Ghatwals, but lands assigned by the State in remuneration for specific Police services, are not alienable or attachable for personal debts."

Such being the law and the ruling of the Courts in respect of these tenures, a question had lately arisen of the competency of a Ghatwal to grant a lease extending beyond the period of his own possession. It seemed that one of these mehals had come under the superintendence of the Court of Wards, and the Manager appointed by the Court was desirous of granting a lease of the mineral products of the mehal to an English gentleman on terms advantageous to the estate. But as the outlay for working the Mines would be considerable, it was necessary that the lease should be for a long term of years, and the Commissioner was of opinion that a Ghatwal, and by consequence the Court of Wards acting on his behalf, had not power to grant a lease which would be binding on his successor in the Ghatwalee. The Superintendent of Legal Affairs was of the same opinion, and it seemed to him (Mr. Currie), with reference to the precedents established by the Sudder decisions, that they were correct. The Sudder had ruled expressly that the Ghatwalee talooks were not alienable, and, as Mr. Beaufort said,

"to admit that the Ghatwal has the power to create an incumbrance which his successor is bound to respect, is to admit the power of alienation."

If, therefore, the mineral resources of this wild country were to be developed, the interference of the Legislature must be accorded. There could be no question of the advantages which would result to the estate, and to all the neighbouring country, from the Mines being worked. He had accordingly prepared a short Bill giving to the Beerbhoom Ghatwals the same power which was enjoyed by all other proprietors of granting leases for any term they might think desirable—with this proviso that the lease should be submitted to and have the sanction of the Commissioner. This restriction was necessary, with reference to the declared nature of the tenures, in order to prevent an improper alienation of their resources.

There was a second Section giving the same power to the Court of Wards and the revenue authorities in the event of any Ghatwalee mehal coming under the superintendence of the Court or being otherwise subjected to the direct control of the Officers of Government. This was necessary, because under the existing law a Manager under the Court of Wards could not grant a lease extending beyond the life of the proprietor, and the Court of Wards could not give a farm of any estate under the management of the Court for a longer period than ten years.

The Bill was read a first time.

CIVIL PROCEDURE.

On the Order of the Day being read for the adjourned Committee of the whole Council on the Bill "for simplifying the Procedure of the Courts of Civil Judicature not established by Royal Charter," the Council resolved itself into a Committee for the further consideration of the Bill.

The consideration of the postponed Section 14 of Chapter IV was again postponed on the motion of Mr. LeGeyt.

The postponed Section 23 provided as follows:—

"If the decree be for a house or other immoveable property not in the occupancy of a defendant or some person in his behalf, delivery thereof shall be made by putting the party to whom the house or other immoveable property may have been adjudged, or any person whom he may appoint to receive delivery on his behalf, in possession thereof, and, if need be, by removing any person who may refuse to vacate the same."

MR. PEACOCK moved that this Section be omitted and that the following be substituted for it:—

"If the decree be for a house, land, or other immoveable property in the occupancy of a

Mr. Currie

defendant or some person on his behalf, or of some person claiming under a title created by the defendant subsequently to the institution of the suit, the Court shall order delivery thereof to be made by putting the party to whom the house, land, or other immoveable property may have been adjudged, or any person whom he may appoint to receive delivery on his behalf, in possession thereof, and, if need be, by removing any person who may refuse to vacate the same."

Agreed to.

The postponed Section 24 provided as follows:—

"If the decree be for land or other immoveable property in the occupancy of ryots or other persons entitled to occupy the same, delivery thereof shall be made by erecting a pole upon some place within or adjacent to the land or other immoveable property, and proclaiming to the occupants of the property by beat of drum, or in such other mode as may be customary, at some convenient place or places, the substance of the decree in regard to the property."

MR. PEACOCK moved that this Section be omitted, and that the following be substituted for it:—

"If the decree be for land or other immoveable property in the occupancy of ryots or other persons entitled to occupy the same, the Court shall order delivery thereof to be made by affixing a copy of the warrant in some conspicuous place on the land or other immoveable property and proclaiming to the occupants of the property by beat of drum or in such other mode as may be customary, at some convenient place or places, the substance of the decree in regard to the property."

Agreed to.

The postponed Section 28 provided as follows:—

"If it shall appear to the satisfaction of the Court that the resistance or obstruction to the execution of the decree has been occasioned by any person, whether a party to the suit or not, on the ground that the property is not included in the decree, or by any person claiming *bonâ fide* to be in possession of the property on his own account or on account of some other person than the defendant, the Court shall, without prejudice to any proceedings to which the defendant or other person may be liable under any law for the time being in force for the punishment of such resistance or obstruction, proceed to investigate the claim in the same manner and with the like powers as if the claimant had been made originally a defendant to the suit, and shall pass such order for staying execution of the decree, or executing the same, as it may deem proper in the circumstances of the case."

MR. HARINGTON said that, when this Section and the following two Sections were last under the consideration of the Committee, it was suggested by the Honorable and learned Chairman that as, under Section 28 as it now stood, it would not only be competent to, but it would be the duty of the Court to investigate any claim which might be preferred under that Section in the same manner and with the like powers as if the claimant had been made originally a defendant to the suit, there seemed to be no good reason for allowing a new suit to contest the decision to which the Court might come in respect of such claim, and that it would be sufficient for the ends of justice if an appeal was allowed on the part of either party who might be dissatisfied with the decision. This suggestion was concurred in by the Honorable Member for Bengal and himself, and he undertook to prepare a new Section in conformity with the opinion expressed by the Honorable and learned Chairman. It had since occurred to him, and the Honorable Member for Bengal to whom he had spoken on the subject agreed with him, that the words in italics in lines 6, 7, and 8, and at the commencement of line 9, as well as the words "the defendant" in lines 13 and 14, which had been introduced by the Select Committee, had been wrongly inserted and that the framers of the Bill had properly restricted the application of the Section to parties other than the defendant. In cases in which the resistance or obstruction was occasioned by the defendant, there was no reason why a fresh suit should be allowed to contest the decision of the Court in respect of such resistance or obstruction. Any dispute arising between the decree-holder and the defendant should be disposed of by the Court charged with the execution of the decree in the miscellaneous Department. The Sections of which he had given notice had been framed in accordance with these views, and he begged now, therefore, to move that the following new Section be substituded for Section 28 :—

"If it shall appear to the satisfaction of the Court that the resistance or obstruction to the execution of the decree has been occasioned by any person other than the defendant claiming *bonâ fide* to be in possession of the property on his own account or on account of some other person than the defendant, the claim shall be numbered and registered as a suit between the decree-holder as plaintiff and the claimant as defendant; and the Court shall, without prejudice to any proceedings to which the claimant may be liable under any law for the time being in force for the punishment of such resistance or obstruction, proceed to investigate the claim in the same manner and with the like powers as if a suit for the property had been instituted by the decree-holder against the claimant under the provisions of this Act, and shall pass such order for staying execution of the decree, or executing the same, as it may deem proper in the circumstances of the case".

Agreed to.

The postponed Section 29 provided as follows :—

"If any person, whether a party to the suit or not, who shall be dispossessed of any land or other immoveable property in execution of a decree, shall dispute the right of the decree-holder to be put into possession of the property, on the plea that it was not included in the decree; or if any person, not being a party against whom the decree was passed, shall dispute the right of the decree-holder to dispossess him of such property under the decree; it shall be lawful for the Court, upon the application of the person so dispossessed, if the application be made within one month from the time of such dispossession, although no resistance or opposition shall have been offered, to summon the party who shall have been put into possession and proceed to investigate the claim of the applicant and pass an order for restitution if the Court shall be satisfied that the applicant ought not to have been dispossessed, or such other order as the Court may deem proper in the circumstances of the case."

Mr. HARINGTON moved that this Section be omitted and that the following be substituted for it :—

"If any person other than the defendant shall be dispossessed of any land or other immoveable property in execution of a decree and such person shall dispute the right of the decree-holder to dispossess him of such property under the decree, on the ground that the property was *bonâ fide* in his possession on his own account or on account of some other person than the defendant, and that it was not included in the decree, or, if included in the decree, that he was not a party to the suit in which the decree was passed, he may apply to the Court within one month from the date of such dispossession; and if, after examining the applicant, it shall appear to the Court that there is probable cause for making the application, the application shall be numbered and registered as a suit between the applicant as plaintiff and the decree-holder as defendant, and the Court shall proceed to investigate the matter in dispute in the same manner and with the like powers as if a suit for the property had been instituted by the applicant against the decree-holder."

Agreed to.

The postponed Section 30 provided as follows :—

"Any order passed by the Court under either of the last two preceding Sections shall not be subject to appeal, but the party against whom the order may be pronounced shall be at liberty to bring a suit to establish his right at any time within one year from the date thereof."

Mr. HARINGTON moved that this Section be omitted, and that the following be substituted for it :—

"The decision passed by the Court under either of the last two Sections, shall be of the same force as a decree in an ordinary suit, and shall be subject to appeal under the rules applicable to appeals from decrees; and no fresh sui shall be entertained in any Court between th same parties or parties claiming under them i respect of the same cause of action."

MR. LEGEYT said, he was opposed to the alteration. The published returns of the average duration of suits gave a very false idea of the rea length of time suits occupied from the commencement till the claim was satisfied, if the time when a decree-holder had to wait for execution was excluded. Sometimes for six or seven years he got nothing, that time being occupied by the disposal of suits to remove attachments. He considered the provision that there should be no appeal a decided improvement.

THE CHAIRMAN drew attention to this, that though the appeal was taken away by the original Section, it allowed what was perhaps a greater evil than an appeal, namely, a regular suit to try the question over again.

MR. LEGEYT was aware of that, but it did not involve the staying execution of the decree.

MR. HARINGTON said that the Section proposed to be substituted for Section 30 gave a right of appeal instead of the right of instituting a new suit. If a new suit was allowed, the unsuccessful party would have his regular appeal, and there might be a special appeal also; so that he did not see how the alteration proposed by him would be less beneficial to the decree-holder than the Section as it now stood. It appeared to him that the contrary would be the case. According to the existing practice a summary enquiry was made, and the order was not only open to a summary appeal, but from the order passed in appeal there might be a special appeal, which again might be followed by a regular suit and two more appeals, so that in every case there might be six stages instead of the two or at the most three stages now proposed. Under the new Code he trusted that the procedure in a regular suit would be nearly as summary as it was now in the Miscellaneous Department, in which case he did not think that the decree-holder would have much cause to complain, and he should therefore press his amendment.

The motion was carried.

Section 26, after providing for the investigation of complaints of obstruction or resistance to execution of decrees for immoveable property, proceeded as follows:—

"If reasonable ground shall be shown to the satisfaction of the Court for believing that the obstruction or resistance in question was occasioned by the defendant or by some other person at his instigation, the Court shall also issue a summons to the defendant calling upon him to appear on the day appointed for investigation."

MR. HARINGTON desired to go back to Section 26, in which some alteration had become necessary, in consequence of the amendments which had been adopted in Sections 28 to 30. The special provision, moreover, for summoning the defendant, contained in the latter part of Section 26, did not seem to him to be required. He should therefore move that all the words after the word "same" in line 12 be omitted.

The motion was carried, and the Section then passed.

MR. HARINGTON then moved hat the following new Section be introduced after Section 26:—

"If it shall appear to the satisfaction of the Court that the obstruction or resistance was occasioned by the defendant or by some person at his instigation on the ground that the land or other immoveable property is not included in the decree, or on any other ground, the Court shall enquire into the matter of the complaint and pass such order as may be proper under the circumstances of the case."

Agreed to.

Section 27 was passed after a verbal amendment on the motion of Mr. Harington.

MR. PEACOCK moved that the following new Section be introduced before Section 31:—

"If there be cross-decrees between the same parties for the payment of money, execution shall be taken out by that party only who shall have obtained a decree for the larger sum, and for so much only as shall remain after deducting the smaller sum; and satisfaction for the smaller sum shall be entered on the decree for the larger sum as well as satisfaction on the decree for the smaller sum; and if both sums shall be equal, satisfaction shall be entered upon both decrees.

"The above rules shall apply to decrees sent to a Court for execution as well as to decrees in the same Court.

"Whenever a suit shall be pending in any Court against the holder of a decree of such Court, by the person or persons against whom the decree was passed, the Court may, if it appear just and reasonable so to do, stay execution on the decree until a decree shall be passed in the pending suit."

THE CHAIRMAN said, the proposal of the Honorable and learned Member seemed to meet what was desired. He would only ask, with reference to the latter part of the proposed Section, if it would not be an improvement to insert words importing that the Court might do so either absolutely or on such terms as it might consider just. The Court staying execution might consider that there was such a degree of doubt respecting the merits of the pending suit as to make it proper to require security from the plaintiff.

MR. PEACOCK said, he quite agreed in the suggestion of the Honorable and learned Chairman, and thought that the Section would be greatly improved by the introduction of the proposed words.

MR. CURRIE said, he had no objection to the proposed Section, but he felt some doubt whether this Section was altogether effective as a substitute for set-off—probably on a reconsideration of the Bill some provision for a set-off in the case of actual debts might be made.

MR. PEACOCK assented. The present Section was prepared with reference to the discussion at the last Meeting. He thought that, where there were simple debts all being within the jurisdiction of the Court, a set-off should be allowed.

THE CHAIRMAN agreed. The difficulty seemed to be, in the absence of any substantive law of set-off, to say what limit should be laid down to the right. He had no objection to a further consideration of the question.

MR. PEACOCK'S motion with the Chairman's amendment, was then put and carried.

The postponed Section 36 provided as follows :—

"Where the property shall consist of money, or of any security standing in the name of the defendant or to his account and in deposit in any Court of Justice or Office of Government, the attachment shall be made by a notice to such Court or Office, requesting that the money or security may be held subject to the further orders of the Court by which the notice may be issued."

MR. HARINGTON moved that this Section be omitted, and that the following be substituted for it :—

"Where the property shall consist of money or of any security in deposit in any Court of Justice, or in the hands of any Officer of Government, which is or may become payable to the defendant or on his behalf, the attachment shall be made by a notice to such Court or Officer requesting that the money or security may be held subject to the further order of the Court by which the notice may be issued. Provided that, if such money or security is in deposit in any Court of Justice, any question of title or priority which may arise between the decree-holder and any other person, not being the defendant, claiming to be interested in such money or security by virtue of any assignment, attachment, or otherwise, shall be determined by the Court in which such money or security is in deposit.

He said it had been objected to this Section, as at present worded, that it gave larger powers to the Court ordering the attachment of any money or of any security in deposit in any other Court, over such money or security, than to the Court in which the same was deposited, which seemed to be reversing the natural order of things, and the Section proposed by him had been framed with a view to meet this objection.

Agreed to.

Sections 44 to 52 were passed as they stood.

Section 53 prescribed the period for making good the amount of the purchase money, and provided that—

"In default of payment within such period, *then and afterwards as often as such default shall occur*, the deposit, after defraying the expenses of the sale, shall be forfeited" &c.

MR. CURRIE moved that the words in italics be omitted. They were taken from the Revenue Sale Law, and were intended to provide for the contingency of a re-sale. But they were not absolutely necessary, and their meaning was not very clear.

The motion was carried, and the Section then passed.

Section 54 provided as follows :—

"If the proceeds of the sale which is eventually consummated be less than the price bid by such defaulting purchaser, the difference shall be leviable from him under the rules for enforcing the payment of money in satisfaction of a decree of Court."

MR. CURRIE moved that the words "and such difference shall be treated as part of the purchase money" be added to the Section.

THE CHAIRMAN thought the addition scarcely necessary, for the difference was in fact a part of the purchase money.

MR. CURRIE said, it was not expressed what was to be done with the money levied, and he had therefore moved the addition of the proposed words. But if it was thought that there could be no question as to the effect of the Section as it now stood, he would not press his motion.

The motion was by leave withdrawn, and the Section then passed.

Sections 55 to 59 were passed as they stood.

MR. CURRIE moved that the following new Section, taken from the Revenue Sale Law, be introduced before Section 60 :—

"The certificate shall state the name of the person who at the time of sale is declared to be the actual purchaser; and any suit brought against the certified purchaser on the ground that the purchase was made on behalf of another person not the certified purchaser, though by agreement the name of the certified purchaser was used, shall be dismissed with costs."

Agreed to.

Sections 60 and 61 were passed as they stood.

Sections 62 and 63 were amended so as to correspond with Sections 23 and 24.

Section 64 was passed after a sligh amendment on the motion of Mr. Currie.

Section 65 was divided into two separate Sections, which were severally passed, with slight alterations.

Section 66 provided as follows :—

"If the purchaser of any property sold in execution of a decree shall be resisted or obstructed in obtaining possession thereof, the provisions hereinbefore contained, relating to resistance or obstruction to the party in whose favor a suit has been decreed in obtaining possession of the property adjudged to him, shall be applicable in the case of such resistance or obstruction."

MR. HARINGTON moved that this Section be omitted, and that the following be substituted for it :—

"If the purchaser of any immoveable property sold in execution of a decree shall be resisted or obstructed in obtaining possession of the property, the provisions contained in Sections 26 and 27 of this Chapter, relating to resistance or obstruction to a party in whose favor a suit has been decreed in obtaining possession of the property adjudged to him, shall be applicable in the case of such resistance or obstruction."

Agreed to.

MR. HARINGTON moved that the following new Section be introduced after Section 66 :—

"If it shall appear that the resistance or obstruction to the delivery of possession was occasioned by any person other than the defendant claiming a right to the possession of the property sold as proprietor, mortgagee, lessee, or under any other title, or if in the delivery of possession to the purchaser any such person claiming as aforesaid shall be dispossessed, the Court, on the complaint of the purchaser or of such person claiming as aforesaid, if made within one month from the date of such resistance or obstruction or of such dispossession as the case may be, shall enquire into the matter of the complaint and pass such order as may be proper in the circumstances of the case. The order shall not be subject to appeal, but the party against whom it is given shall be at liberty to bring a suit to establish his right at any time within one month from the date thereof."

Agreed to.

Sections 67 to 69 were passed as they stood.

MR. HARINGTON said, the Sections which he was anxious to see introduced in the part of the Bill to which the Committee had now come, had been suggested to him in a great measure by the amendments to Sections 72 and 76 of the same Chapter, of which the Honorable Member of Council opposite (Mr. Ricketts) had given notice, and which they would have to consider presently. The first of these Sections appeared to him to raise the whole question of imprisonment for debt, and as to whether, if a judgment debtor, on being arrested, surrendered or placed at the disposal of the Court, whatever property he might be possessed of, or should be able to satisfy the Court of his inability from want of means to satisfy the decree, he should still be subjected to the disgrace of being sent to jail, and of being confined therein though only for a brief period. The amendments proposed by the Honorable Member of Council, if adopted, would not interfere with the power now possessed by a judgment creditor of causing the imprisonment of his judgment debtor in every case, but they seemed to regard that imprisonment rather as a punishment for indebtedness than as means of enforcing payment of the debt, while the maximum period of imprisonment fixed by the first of the Honorable Member's amendments, when the amount of the decree did not exceed the sum of fifty Rupees, was so short that he thought it would be found that the great majority of persons by whom that small sum would generally be owing, would elect to go to jail for thirty days rather than pay the amount. It was on this ground chiefly that he objected to the Honorable Member's amendments, which appeared to him to proceed on an erroneous principle. It must be remembered that, under the law as it now stood, and the Bill before the Committee did not propose to introduce any change in that respect, no judgment debtor could be imprisoned except at the instance of the judgment creditor and at his expense. If, therefore, imprisonment for debt was to be by way, not of coercion, but of punishment, of what benefit, it might be asked, would it be to the judgment creditor who, after the expiration of the time for which the judgment debtor could be detained in custody, would often find himself in a worse position than when he took out process of arrest against the person of his debtor, inasmuch as he would have had to feed him in the interval, so that, if it was considered correct in principle that imprisonment for debt should be of a punitive and not of a coercive character, he submitted that the judgment creditor should at least be relieved from the charge of maintaining the judgment debtor while in jail, which should be borne by the Government. No doubt imprisonment of every kind, whether under Civil or Criminal process, or whether undergone in the Civil or Criminal jail, carried with it some degree of punishment, the one being inseparable from the other; but that the punishment of the judgment debtor was not what was aimed at in his imprisonment, and that his confinement was intended merely as a process to compel payment of what he owed, was, he thought, clear from the fact that, as soon as the judgment debtor surrendered whatever property he possessed, and showed that he had not been guilty of any fraudulent conduct as regarded the means at his disposal for satisfying the decree passed against him, he became entitled to his release, which he could claim as of right, although the value of the property surrendered might fall far short of the amount of the judgment creditor's claim. It was this principle which he was anxious to see extended, and instead of confining the application of it to cases in which the judgment debtor was actually in jail, he would allow a judgment debtor, on being arrested, to obtain his discharge from custody without going to jail, on the same terms as he might claim his release after going to jail, namely, by surrendering whatever property he possessed and satisfying the Court that his inability to pay the claim in full arose from no dishonest conduct on his part. This was not a new idea. In the Code of Civil Procedure drawn up by Mr. Mills and himself, they proposed that no debtor should be imprisoned in execution, if he satisfied the Court that he had done his best to pay the debt, and had no property or effect remaining from which the debt could be discharged, and in their remarks on this Section they observed that—

"with the view of mitigating the law of arrest, in order that it might operate with less severity on the honest debtor, they had made provision that no debtor should be imprisoned if he could show to the satisfaction of the Court that he had done his best to pay the debt, and that the Court might at any time suspend execution of a decree upon proof of the inability of the debtor from any temporary cause to discharge the debt or damage awarded against him."

With these observations he would move that the following new Section be introduced before Section 70:—

"Any person arrested under a warrant in execution of a decree for money may, on being brought before the Court, apply for his discharge on the ground that he has no present means of paying the debt, either wholly or in part, or, if possessed of any property, that he is willing to place whatever property he possesses at the disposal of the Court. The application shall contain a full account of all property of whatever nature belonging to the applicant, whether in expectancy or in possession, and whether held exclusively by himself or jointly with others, or by others in trust for him (except the necessary wearing apparel of himself and his family, and the necessary implements of his trade,) and of the places respectively where such property is to be found, or shall state that, with the exception above-mentioned, the applicant is not possessed of any property, and the application shall be subscribed and verified by the applicant in the manner hereinbefore prescribed for subscribing and verifying plaints."

MR. RICKETTS had no objection to offer to the proposed Section. His object was to proportion a man's sufferings to his sins. As the 72nd Section then stood, it authorized imprisonment for two years for the smallest debt; according to the old law the principle which he supported was in some measure preserved. But as he had no objection to what was proposed, he would reserve what he had to say until Section 72 was brought forward.

The motion was then put and carried.

MR. HARINGTON moved that, after the above Section, the following new Section be introduced :—

"Upon such application being made, the Court shall examine the applicant in the presence of the plaintiff or his pleader as to his then circumstances, and as to his future means of payment, and shall call upon the plaintiff to show cause why he does not proceed against any property of which the defendant is possessed, and why the defendant should not be discharged; and should the plaintiff fail to show such cause, the Court may direct the discharge of the defendant from custody. Pending any enquiry which the Court may consider it necessary to make into the allegations of either party, the Court may leave the defendant in the custody of the Officer of the Court to whom the service of the warrant was entrusted, on the defendant making the necessary deposit for paying the fees of such Officer, or if the defendant furnish good and sufficient security for his appearance at any time when called upon while such enquiry is being made, his surety or sureties undertaking in default of such appearance to pay the amount mentioned in the warrant, the Court may release the defendant on such security."

Agreed to.

MR. HARINGTON moved that, after the above Section, the following new Section be introduced :—

"The discharge of the defendant under the last preceding Section shall not protect him from being arrested again and imprisoned, if it should be shown that, in the application made by him, he had been guilty of any concealment or of wilfully making any false statement respecting the property belonging to him, whether in possession or in expectancy or held for him in trust, or had fraudulently concealed, transferred, or removed any property, or had committed any other act of bad faith; nor shall such discharge exempt from attachment and sale any property then in the possession of the defendant, or of which he may afterwards become possessed."

THE CHAIRMAN said, he was not quite clear as to this Section. His doubt was that, although this was a sort of Insolvent law, there was no provision for distribution among all the creditors. On the other hand, the right of arrest was suspended without giving the particular decree-holder a preferable claim to the debtor's future property. It seemed unjust to take all his present and future property for the satisfaction of the particular decree-holder. It was much to be regretted that, in consequence, he supposed, of the difficulties of the machinery, the Code must be defective for want of provisions for the distribution of the assets of an Insolvent, and also for the administration of the estates of deceased persons.

The Section was then put and agreed to.

Sections 70 and 71 were passed as they stood.

Section 72 limited imprisonment for debt to two years.

MR. RICKETTS having enquired what would be the operation of the amendments just carried by Mr. Harington, said, he thought they might suffice without his amendment.

MR. HARINGTON explained that the effect of his amendment, if carried, would be that a judgment debtor who, on being arrested, could satisfy the Court of his inability to pay the debt, need never go to jail at all.

The Section was then put and carried.

Sections 73 and 74 were passed as they stood.

Section 75 provided for applications for discharge on a surrender of the whole of the debtor's property.

MR. PEACOCK asked, whether there should not be some power given to the Court to deal with cases in which debts had been fraudulently contracted. Supposing the debtor was willing to give up all his property, but the Court was satisfied that he had contracted the debt fraudulently or without having any prospect of paying it. In England the Court might commit him to custody. By the Statute 7 and 8 Vic. c. 96 s. 57, imprisonment for a debt below £20 was abolished, and all such debtors were authorized to be discharged out of custody. But there were many remonstrances by tradesmen against that law, and in consequence the Statute 8 and 9 Vic. c. 127 was passed. That Statute gave a power to summon a judgment debtor before a Commissioner of Bankruptcy or Court of Requests. The debtor appearing was examined, or failing to appear he might be committed to prison. If he had been guilty of fraud in contracting the debt, or having wilfully contracted it without reasonable prospect of being able to pay it, he might be committed to prison.

The English County Court Act, 9 and 10 Vic. c. 95, repealed this Act as to all places having Small Cause Courts established under the Act. The jurisdiction of such Courts (then limited to £20) had since been extended. The present law was that, if a man obtained credit under false pretences or by means of fraud, or wilfully contracted a debt without reasonable expectation of being able to pay it, he might be committed to the Common Jail or House of Correction. They could not extend that provision to India in consequence of the difficulties of knowing what persons to exempt from its operation, but he felt some doubt whether the present Clause should stand so as to apply to persons who had been guilty of fraud in contracting debts or who had contracted debts without any probable means of paying them. Under the Insolvent Act the Court could commit such a debtor to custody, or leave him to the mercy of his creditors; it did not absolutely discharge him. He should wish to propose some such words as those in the Insolvent Act.

MR. CURRIE said, it seemed to him that the legitimate object of a suit in the Civil Court was simply to recover money due. If the defendant satisfied the Court that he had not the means of paying it, and gave up all his property, it would seem that the Civil Court had discharged its duties, and that it was hardly its province to punish a man for having committed what might be considered a fraud in contracting a debt for which he had not probable means of payment. If there was any fraud in the transaction before the Court, the previous Section provided for the debtor being detained in custody, and he did not think it necessary to go farther.

THE CHAIRMAN said, the Code gave to the creditor who had been defrauded by an actual fraud, though perhaps one not within reach of the Criminal Law, the option of keeping his debtor in prison for any time less than two years. The proposal was to extend that option to a creditor who had been defrauded by that species of moral fraud which consisted in a man recklessly contracting debts which he knew he would be unable to pay. The object of the Clause now under discussion was to prevent the imprisonment of a man who was not guilty of fraud and who had done what he could to pay his debt.

There was nothing inconsistent in limiting the indulgence to really honest debtors: if a man recklessly, and therefore dishonestly, incurred the debt, let him be left to the general law of imprisonment.

MR. HARINGTON thought that the proposed provisions would be inoperative in the Mofussil.

MR. PEACOCK said, he would not press his amendment.

The Section was then passed as it stood.

Section 76 provided as follows:—

"A defendant once discharged shall not again be imprisoned on account of the same decree, except under the operation of the last preceding Section, but his property shall continue liable under the ordinary rules to attachment and sale until the decree shall be fully satisfied."

MR RICKETTS said, he had given notice of an addition to this Section, but since it had been printed he had seen occasion to alter the amendment which he proposed. It was true that, as the Section stood, it was in conformity with the laws of 1806 and 1850. His object was that the old man should not for ever sit on the shoulders of the debtor, but that he should be discharged from his debt. He could not think such a provision suitable to the state of things in this country. He had originally given notice of an amendment empowering the Court to give an absolute discharge to the extent of five hundred Rupees. Upon further advice, he was afraid to go so far. He believed that such a law would be a great blessing to all the poorer classes of natives. A man now got a decree and held it over his debtor for the remainder of his life. There were other Code Makers besides themselves. By Clause 28 of the Sonthal Code, it was provided that

"Imprisonment for debt is altogether abolished."

Clause 30 provided that—

"If a Sonthal appear before a Hakim and request to be released from his debts, his statement shall be taken on solemn affirmation as to the amount thereof and his means of discharging it, and a day shall be fixed for the appearance of his creditors, of which due notice will be given them. The Majee of applicant's village, and applicant himself, with all the male members of his household, shall be warned to appear on the same day, and the Hakim shall then make full enquiry, and if satisfied that the applicant's statement is true as to the number and names of his creditors, and the amount due to each, and the extent of his property, he shall take measures to sell or transfer the latter to the creditors, and give the applicant a release in full from all debts due to the creditors whom he has named and upon whom notice has been served,"

and then this Clause proceeded to provide—

"Release under this rule is absolute as regards all property acquired by the Insolvent after release. Property which he may not have surrendered at his release is always liable when discovered, and at the same time Insolvent may be punished as if for a false claim."

The Sonthal Pergunnah was thus in advance of all the rest of India, which had no Insolvent Code. He did not however go so far. He only proposed that, when the debt did not exceed a hundred Rupees, the Court should be allowed to give an absolute discharge.

Such a law, it was possible, might increase the interest demanded on small debts. It would not have that effect where the borrower was a man of substance and of character, but if it stopped altogether an advance to a person of a different class, this he thought would be no evil. He then moved that the following be added to the Section—

"Unless the decree shall be for a sum less than one hundred Rupees and on account of a transaction bearing date subsequent to the passing of this Act. When the decree shall be for a sum less than one hundred Rupees and on account of a transaction bearing date as above, the Court may declare a defendant who shall be discharged as aforesaid absolved from further liability under that decree."

MR. PEACOCK asked, if it ought to apply to every case. Suppose a man took away his neighbour's cow and sold it, and then told the owner—"I have only one Rupee; here it is—" should he be discharged. There were certain cases, for example criminal conversation, slander, &c., in which it would be wrong to give an absolute discharge. He had no wish to offer opposition, but he thought it should be confined to cases of contract.

MR. HARINGTON said, his objection to the amendment proposed by the Honorable Member of Council was, that it would put the vigilant or active judgment creditor, at whose instance the judgment debtor had been arrested and sent to jail, in a worse position than all other creditors of the same person. It was not proposed to release the judgment debtor from all his debts to whomsoever owing, but only from that particular debt the non-payment of which had led to his being imprisoned. The judgment creditor who took out process of arrest against the person of his debtor had committed no wrong; he had simply been active. Why then should he be placed upon a different footing from the other creditors? Again, if the amendment was carried, a judgment creditor might abstain from arresting the person of his judgment debtor lest the result of his imprisonment should be his discharge from further liability, but he would still hold his decree over him, and there would be nothing to prevent him from seizing and selling the property of his judgment debtor as fast as he acquired any; from that the amendment of the Honorable Member would not relieve the judgment debtor, so that he did not think that much would be gained by the adoption of the amendment, and he should prefer to leave the Section as it stood.

THE CHAIRMAN said, all the Sections were open to the objection that they provided a rude and imperfect Insolvent law. The judgment creditor got the fat as well as the lean, for, if his debtor was dicharged, the creditor on the other hand got all the property in preference to all other creditors, and not *pari passu*. So far he had the advantage: the disadvantage was that he alone was prevented from going against the future property when his debt was limited to a hundred Rupees. He was in favor of the principle of letting a man start fair again if he relinquished all his property.

Mr. PEACOCK thought that the first objection made by the Honorable Member for the North-Western Provinces was not so tenable as the second, for every creditor had the same power. As to the second objection, he should vote for the amendment of the Honorable Member (Mr. Ricketts), because, if the creditor chose to imprison his debtor, and the Court afterwards thought he should be discharged, it seemed reasonable that it should be an absolute discharge, the creditor choosing that remedy must be satisfied with the discharge of his debtor.

Mr. RICKETTS' motion was then carried, and the Section agreed to.

Section 77 was passed after a verbal amendment.

Sections 78 to 90 were passed as they stood.

Mr. PEACOCK said that, though it might be some what irregular, he would ask to return to Section 72. It had occured to him, when the Honorable Member (Mr. Ricketts) withdrew his amendment, that two years was too long a period of imprisonment, and he was about to suggest a shorter period. The Small Cause Court Act both here and in England provided a limit of six months when the debt was five hundred Rupees.

It was reasonable, especially as the Honorable Member for the North-Western Provinces proposed to extend that law, that there should be the same limit.

MR. CURRIE said, he entirely concurred so far as the limit of six months was concerned, but doubted whether they should go farther: the object was not to punish by imprisonment but to coerce; a poor man might think it better to go to jail for three months than to pay a debt of fifty Rupees.

MR. PEACOCK said, even in the case of a felony, a distinction was made.

Mr. HARINGTON—Yes, but in a case of felony imprisonment was intended as a punishment.

MR. PEACOCK continued—The object was to compel the debtor to give up his property; the Code gave the creditor power to take it, and to bring the debtor before the Court for examination; it was too severe also to give him the power to lock up his debtor for a long period.

THE CHAIRMAN said, admitting the principle (that the debtor was locked up to make him disclose his property), then, if six months was the presumable period of imprisonment, which, rather than undergo, he would pay five hundred Rupees, if he had the means of paying, it might be supposed that, given the same means, he would rather pay fifty Rupees than undergo three months' imprisonment. No doubt a ryot whose time was of no very high value might prefer imprisonment to payment, but that was not the class of people who had the means of concealing their property, which consisted perhaps of bullocks, or something not capable of concealment. If the debtor really possessed property, he would ordinarily be a person whose time would be of such value that he would gladly pay rather than undergo imprisonment. He thought that in principle there was nothing inconsistent in the proposed amendment.

MR. HARINGTON said, they had just adopted a Section which rendered imprisonment under certain circumstances payment in full of a debt, and it behoved them to be careful that they did not make the period of imprisonment so short as to hold out a strong inducement to judgment debtors generally to go to jail rather than make an effort to pay what was owing by them. The object in view in imprisoning a party against whom a judgment had been given, was not only to oblige him to disclose his property, but also to compel him to make some arrangement for satisfying the claim either by instalments, giving security for their payment, or in some other way, or to induce his friends to come forward to assist him.

THE CHAIRMAN said, the amendment which had been adopted only gave the Court power (if it thought fit to use it) to discharge the debt absolutely.

MR. PEACOCK'S amendment was put and carried, and Section 72 then passed.

Section I Chapter VIII was passed after verbal amendments.

Sections 2 to 10 were passed as they stood.

Section 11 provided as follows:—

"It shall be in the discretion of the Appellate Court to demand security for costs from the appellant or not as it shall see fit, before the respondent is called upon to appear and answer."

MR. CURRIE moved that the following proviso be added to the Section:—

"Provided that the Court shall demand such security in all cases in which the appellant is residing out of the British Territories in India, and is not possessed of any land or other immoveable property within those territories independent of the property to which the appeal relates; and in the event of such security not being furnished at the time of presenting the memorandum of appeal, or within such time as the Court shall order, the Court shall reject the appeal."

Agreed to.

Sections 12 to 27 were passed as they stood.

Section 28 was passed after an amendment.

Sections 29 to 35 Chapter VIII, Sections 1 to 5 Chapter IX, and Sections 1 to 3 Chapter X, were passed as they stood.

Section 4 Chapter X was passed after an amendment.

Sections 1 to 5 Chapter XI., and Sections 1 and 2 Chapter XII, were passed as they stood.

Sections 3 and 4 Chapter XII were passed after verbal amendments.

Sections 5 to 7 Chapter XII, and Schedules A, B, and C were passed as they stood.

The postponed Section 14 Chapter IV was passed as it stood.

MR. LEGEYT moved that the following new Sections be introduced after the above:—

"But if the defendant points out any of his property for sale in preference to that specified by the plaintiff, the property so pointed out shall be first sold. Such implements of manual labor and such cattle and implements of agriculture as may, in the judgment of the Court from which the process issues, be indispensable for the defendant to earn a livelihood in his calling or trade, shall be exempt from attachment.

Land and its crop, of whatever kind, shall not be attached and sold separately until after the crop has been reaped or gathered.

Second. When corn or other production of Khalsa land paying annul rent to Government is attached and sold, the Collector or his officers may prevent its being sold or carried off such lands, unless the purchaser shall pay the amount due on account of the revenue; but in no case shall the purchaser be liable for more than one year's revenue.

Third. The same right of detention for arrears of rent, similarly restricted, shall be exercised by a landholder where his tenant's corn or other production of the soil is attached."

MR. HARINGTON said, during the recess he had carefully considered the amendments which the Honorable Member for Bombay wished to see introduced in the part of the Bill now before the Committee, and the conclusion to which he had come in regard to them was that, with exception perhaps to the second clause of the first amendment, they would not benefit either the judgment creditor or the judgment debtor. It had often occurred to him to witness, and he had done so with surprise and regret, the different treatment received from our Courts by the same party in the successive characters of plaintiff and decree-holder. So long as he appeared in the former character only, he found the Court willing and anxious to afford him assistance and to expedite the decision of the suit as far as lay in its power. This was no doubt all very proper. But the scene changed; the second act of the drama commenced; the party who had hitherto appeared in the sober garments of a plaintiff, now came upon the stage in the gayer habiliments of a decree-holder, and in that character he fully expected, and not unreasonably, that he should speedily attain the end which he had in view in instituting the suit. But he quickly discovered his mistake; he now found that all the sympathies of the Court, of which, so long as he was only a suitor for redress, he was the object, were transferred to the defendant; he was deemed an inexorable creditor; the defendant was regarded with feelings of compassion; in fact, the treatment which he received was such that he was not sure that in getting a decree he had not committed some crime; at any rate he looked back with regret to those comparatively happy days when he was a plaintiff only. Now all this consideration for the defendant might be very benevolent, but the benevolence was of that character which was most fitly described by the epithet "speculative;" it was speculative benevolence, which was often more injurious to its object than a sterner line of conduct would be. He (Mr. Harington) had himself seen numerous instances in which, had the property seized by a judgment creditor in execution of his judgment been at once sold, and the proceeds applied to the liquidation of the claim, the debt would have been paid, and the debtor would have been a free man; but Mr. Speculative Benevolence intervened, pleaded for delay, and otherwise assisted the judgment debtor in throwing obstacles in the way of the decree-holder, and in the end, instead of a portion of the judgment debtor's property being found sufficient to satisfy the decree, it became necessary to sacrifice the whole of the property possessed by him, and still a balance remained. The amendments proposed by the Honorable Member for Bombay appeared to him to furnish an illustration of these remarks. In connection with the first amendment, he would take the case of the judgment debtor's horse and cow which had been put by the Honorable Member at the last meeting of the Committee. A party obtained a decree for two hundred Rupees, and in execution seized a horse belonging to the judgment debtor, worth about that sum, or it might be a little more, and requested that it might be sold; but the judgment debtor did not wish his horse to be sold; he had no idea of losing his evening ride, and he said to the Court, take my cow and sell that instead. Under the first amendment proposed by the Honorable Member for Bombay the Court would have no alternative but must sell the cow. Well, the cow was sold, and brought fifty Rupees; then the horse had to be sold and realized two hundred and fifty Rupees In this case he would ask how was the judgment debtor benefited; had the horse been sold first, in accordance with the request of the judgment creditor, the cow would have been saved, and the judgment debtor's family would have continued to enjoy its milk, whereas, in consequence of the option given by the first amendment, both horse and cow had been sacrificed. Then came the amendment which declared that land and its crop of whatever kind should not be attached and sold separately until after the crop had been reaped or gathered. Why not? If the judgment creditor was content to sell the standing crop alone in the expectation that the price of it would be sufficient to satisfy his demand, why compel him to sell the land also? why oblige him to deprive the judgment debtor of perhaps the only means that he possessed of supporting himself and family not only for a single year, but for all future time, which might be the consequence of selling his land as well as the crop standing upon it? and what interest would the judgment debtor have in looking after the crop after its attachment, or in watering and weeding it, and should it be destroyed by blight or drought, would not the loss fall upon him, and not upon the decree-holder? For these reasons he considered the amendments proposed by the Honorable Member for Bombay objectionable, and he should therefore vote against them.

MR. RICKETTS said according to his recollection the Honorable Member for Bombay had withdrawn a part of his proposed amendment.

[MR. LEGEYT signified dissent.]

MR. RICKETTS resumed.—He would prefer that the amendment should run thus—that standing crops should not be sold without the consent of the cultivator—he would not allow standing crops to be sold under any circumstances, in execution of a decree; no one was benefited by such a proceeding. Standing crops could now be sold for arrears of revenue, but it was seldom that any one applied for their sale, the expense was so great—when such an application was made, it was usually from some motive of revenge or desire to injure. What with the expense of reaping, carrying, storing, &c., nothing was left for the decree-holder. Moreover it might be argued that it was unfair to allow the decree-holder to deprive the debtor of food for himself and his family.

MR. HARINGTON said, the motion only proposed that the land and the crop standing thereon, should not be sold separately, not that standing crops should on no account be sold in execution of a decree. The present motion made no objection to the standing crop being sold with the land.

MR. CURRIE said, he quite agreed that it was very inexpedient that standing crops should be attached and sold in execution of decrees. He supposed they might according to the law be sold at any time after the land was sown, or as soon as the crop began to grow, in that case they would realize but little, whereas, if allowed to come to maturity, the case would be very different. Moreover, the crop was hypotheticated to the landlord for the rent, and the claim of the landlord would often conflict with that of the decree-holder. So long as this crop was in the ground, and until it had been reaped or gathered, he thought it could hardly be considered as property liable to attachment.

MR. PEACOCK said, he also had supposed that the amendment had been withdrawn. The debtor might say—"sell my cow," but when sold, a third person might come forward asserting that the cow was his property, whereas the debtor had a horse which was his undoubted property. Was the plaintiff to be involved in another suit because of this? One of the proposed exemptions was "cattle and implements of Agriculture"; why was Agriculture so much looked after? The hackeryman's hackery and bullocks were seized, though he might be prevented earning his livelihood by the loss of them, but if the bullocks were employed in Agriculture, they were to be privileged, the only assignable reason was that the interests of landlords were thereby protected. They might be sold for revenue, because there the Government was concerned, but if it was right to sell them for revenue, why should they not be sold for other claims? Again, implements of manual labor were exempted, but nevertheless the workman might be locked up in prison so that he could not use them. Again, as to land and crops; in most cases they belonged to different persons; if the crops belonged to the ryot, they could not be sold for the Zemindar's debt—but was not the crop to be sold for the ryot's debt? It might be ripe, yet the ryot was to be allowed to reap, and to have full opportunity of making away with it. Whatever property the execution debtor had, he would allow it to be sold. He would oppose the amendment.

MR. RICKETTS referred to Regulation V. 1812, Section XIV, which provided that—

> "ploughs and other implements of husbandry, bullocks and other cattle employed in Agriculture, shall not be subject to distress and sale on account of arrears of rent, although the tenant from whom such arrears may be demanded shall not possess other property sufficient to make good the arrear."

MR. PEACOCK said, in such cases there was no decree of a Court, but the landlord distrained by virtue of the authority which the law gave to him. It might be that no rent was really due to him. But it was very different allowing the execution creditor, whose claim had been investigated, to execute his decree against his debtors' property.

The question being put, the Council divided:—

Ayes 2.	*Noes 6.*
Mr. LeGeyt.	Mr. Forbes.
Mr. Ricketts.	Mr. Harington.
	Sir Arthur Buller.
	Mr. Currie.
	Mr. Peacock.
	The Chairman.

So the motion was negatived.

The Preamble and Title were passed as they stood, and the Council having resumed its sitting, the Bill was reported.

LITERARY, SCIENTIFIC, AND CHARITABLE SOCIETIES.

Mr. CURRIE gave notice that he would, on Saturday the 6th Instant, move the first reading of a Bill for the registration of Literary, Scientific, and Charitable Societies.

RYOTWAR SETTLEMENTS (MADRAS PRESIDENCY)

MR. FORBES moved that a communication received by him from the Madras Government be laid upon the table, and referred to the Select Committee on the Bill "for the better recovery of arrears of Revenue under Ryotwar Settlements in the Madras Presidency."

Agreed to.

PENAL CODE.

MR. CURRIE moved that two communications received by him from the Bengal Government be laid upon the table and referred to the Select Committee on "The Indian Penal Code."

Agreed to.

NABOB OF SURAT'S PROPERTY.

MR LEGEYT moved that a communication received by him from the Bombay Government regarding the distribution of the private property of the late Nabob of Surat, be laid upon the table and printed.

Agreed to.

OATHS.

MR. Forbes gave notice that at the next meeting of the Council he would move the first reading of a Bill to provide for the admission, in certain cases, of testimony on Oath.

CIVIL PROCEDURE.

MR. PEACOCK gave notice that he would, at the next meeting of the Council, move for the re-publication of the Bill "for simplifying the Procedure of the Courts of Civil Judicature not established by Royal Charter."

The Council adjourned.

Saturday, November 6, 1858.

PRESENT:

The Hon'ble the Chief Justice, *Vice-President*, in the Chair.

Hon'ble Lieut. Genl. Sir J. Outram,	Hon'ble Sir A. W. Buller.
Hon'ble B. Peacock,	H. B. Harington, Esq., and
P. W. LeGeyt, Esq.,	H. Forbes, Esq.
E. Currie, Esq.,	

POLICE CHOWKEYDARS (BENGAL.)

THE CLERK presented to the Council a Petition of Inhabitants of Dacca concerning defects in the administration of Act XX of 1856, "to make better provision for the appointment and maintenance of Police Chowkeydars in Cities, Towns, Stations, Suburbs, and Bazars in the Presidency of Fort William in Bengal."

MR. CURRIE moved that the above Petition be printed.

Agreed to.

NATIVE PASSENGER VESSELS (BAY OF BENGAL.)

THE CLERK reported to the Council that he had received from the Home Department, a copy of an Extract from Proceedings in the Foreign Department respecting the evasion of the provisions of Act I of 1857 (to prevent the over-crowding of vessels carrying Native Passengers in the Bay of Bengal) by vessels clearing out from Foreign Ports within the Coast limits of the Madras Presidency.

MR. FORBES moved that the above communication be referred to a Select Committee consisting of Mr. Peacock, Mr. LeGeyt, Mr. Currie, and the Mover.

Agreed to.

MERCHANT SHIPPING ACT 1854. (SINGAPORE.)

THE CLERK reported that he had received from the Home Department a copy of a Despatch from the Court of Directors regarding the Merchant Shipping Act 1854 as it affects Singapore.

MR. CURRIE moved that the above communication be printed.

Agreed to.

CIVIL PROCEDURE.

THE CLERK reported that he had received from the Home Department, for consideration in connection with the Code of Civil Procedure, an Extract of a communication from that Department to the Bengal Government on the subject of relieving the Bengal Sudder Court of a large mass of its least important business, in order to allow the regular number of Judges to dispose of the most important portion satisfactorily, and without falling into arrears.

MR. PEACOCK moved that the above communication be printed.

Agreed to.

DELHI AND MEERUT.

MR. PEACOCK presented the Report of the Select Committee on the Bill "to remove from the operation of the General Laws and Regulations the Delhi Territory and Meerut Division, or such parts thereof as the Governor General in Council shall place under the administration of the Chief Commissioner of the Punjab."

PENSIONS.

MR. PEACOCK postponed the presentation of the Report of the Select Committee on the Project of a Law for applying the provisions of the Government Order of the 1st December 1857, which affect Military Pensioners, to Pensioners in the Civil Department, and to holders of rent-free lands.

LITERARY, SCIENTIFIC, AND CHARITABLE SOCIETIES.

MR. CURRIE moved the first reading of a Bill "for the registration of Literary, Scientfic, and Charitable Societies." He said, in the Report of the Select Committee on the Bill "for the incorporation and regulation of Joint-Stock Companies" it was stated that—

"many of its provisions are unnecessary, if not inapplicable, to Associations not having gain or profit for their object. We think that a separate Bill should be introduced for the formation of such Societies of this class as may not desire to come under the provisions of this Bill."

The interference of the Legislature in behalf of those Societies was indeed the more necessary, inasmuch as the Joint-Stock Companies Act repealed a former law (Act XLIII of 1850) which, though in an ineffective and unsatisfactory manner, did provide expressly for the registration of such Societies, while the new Act was altogether unsuited to them. The necessity for fresh legislation on this subject had since been urged upon the Council, not only by the Petition of the British Indian Association presented on the 7th August last, but also by parties who had an immediate interest in the matter, the Managers and Secretary of the Military Orphan Society, who represented themselves as being subjected to heavy loss from their inability to empower any one to sue in their behalf. The British Indian Association remarked :—

"That the number of Associations established for the promotion of literature, science, education, charitable purposes, &c., will continue to increase, and they cannot well come under the operation of Act XIX of 1857, in consequence of many of its provisions 'being unnecessary if not inapplicable' to them. An enactment allowing Associations not established for gain or profit to sue and be sued and to hold property in their registered name is felt as a want and required to enable them to recover their just claims, and hold property without being subject to the inconveniences incidental to transfers in the event of the death of any of the parties in whose names the property may be held."

Agreeing in these views, and thinking the case to be one of some urgency, he determined, with the concurrence of his Honorable and learned friend opposite (Mr. Peacock) and the assistance of the learned Clerk of the Council, to bring in a Bill for the purpose of giving the relief required.

He believed that few, if any, of the numerous Societies existing in Calcutta and other parts of India ever availed themselves of the option of registration given by Act XLIII of 1850. The Managers of the Military Orphan Society remarked that many of its provisions "could not possibly be fulfilled by so large a body as the Officers of the Bengal Army, in which alterations occur daily by deaths, resignations, and additions;" and the Curators of the Calcutta Public Library pointed to several of the Sections and Clauses of the Act in question—such as those requiring the half yearly audit of accounts (Section VIII. cl. 6,) and the filing and verification of them by the oath of auditors half-yearly (Section VIII. cl. 7,) and the clauses requiring the filing of the memorials of the shareholders, directors, and registered Officers so soon and so often as they occurred—as being evidently intended more for banking and trading companies than for literary, scientific, and charitable institutions, and as causing needless trouble and expense to the latter. Upon this letter of the Curators, there was a Minute by Sir C. Jackson, then he believed Officiating as Legislative Member of the Council, and concurred in by the Governor General and other Members of Council to the following effect :—

"The machinery of Act XLIII of 1850 is much too cumbrous for Companies such as those referred to in Major Marshall's letter, and will no doubt operate as a discouragement to the registration of such Institutions. I think an Act might be framed conferring on Companies exclusively formed for literary, scientific, or charitable purposes, all the benefits of Act XLIII (such as the right to register by their style, and in the name of their Secretary or other ministerial Officers, as well as the power to sue and be sued in the name of such Officer) and declaring the other provisions of the Act, which are chiefly suited to trading Companies, inapplicable to literary, scientific, and charitable Institutions"

The Bill which he had the honor to introduce was prepared in accordance with these suggestions.

There was a late Act of the British Legislature (17 and 18 Vic. c. 112) which gave to Literary and Scientific Institutions all the legal facilities to which he had referred without even requiring the formality of registration. But it seemed to him that, if the means of registration were made sufficiently easy, there could be no objection to imposing on the Societies which might desire to avail themselves of the benefit of the Act the necessity of being registered, and it might be convenient to persons having claims against a Society that there should be a ready mode of ascertaining the person against whom the claims should be enforced. On the whole, therefore, he had thought it advisable to retain so much of the principle of the former law as required that Societies having the benefit of the Act should be registered.

The first four Sections of the Bill contained some simple provisions for registry: a memorandum of Association containing the name of the Society, its objects, and the names, addresses, and occupations of its governing body, together with a copy of the rules and regulations of the Society, was to be filed with the Registrar of Joint Stock Companies under Act XIX of 1857, and a list of the governing body showing any changes which might have taken place since the preparation of the previous list, was to be filed annually.

The next twelve Sections were taken almost *verbatim* from the Statute to which he had referred, and contained provisions for the Society suing or being sued in the name of the President, Secretary, or other Officer as determined by the rules—for the enforcement of judgment against the property of the Society—for enabling the Society to recover from the Members penalties imposed by the rules or byelaws, and arrears of subscription—for enabling the Society to alter, extend, or abridge the purposes for which it was established, and to dissolve itself. There were also provisions for enabling Societies existing at the time of the Act coming into force, to avail themselves of its provisions.

The last Section declared what Societies might be registered under the Bill. It was somewhat more comprehensive than the English Act which applied only to Literary and Scientific Institutions, including Institutions for the purpose of adult instruction. He proposed that the new law should be extended to all educational, and also to all charitable Societies. Indeed, he thought that even a wider application might probably be given to it, and that it might extend to such Associations as the Bengal and United Service Clubs, but the advisability of this might, if the Bill should be read a second time, be considered by the Select Committee after the Bill had been published.

The Bill was read a first time.

OATHS AND AFFIRMATIONS.

MR. FORBES moved the first reading of a Bill "concerning Oaths and Affirmations." He said that, after having trespassed so long on the time and patience of the Council very lately, on the occasion of moving an amendment on that Section of the Bill for simplifying Civil Procedure which provided for the reception of evidence without oath or affirmation, he felt that the best apology that he could offer on again rising to bring the same subject forward, was to promise on this occasion to be brief. Honorable Members would recollect that the amendment which he had moved on a former occasion was withdrawn at the suggestion of the Honorable and learned Judge on his left, a suggestion to which he believed the Council generally assented, that the question would be more satisfactorily dealt with by a separate Bill, than if it were the subject of one Section out of the many of which the Civil Procedure Bill was composed. In accordance with this suggestion, the Bill of which he was presently to move the first reading had been prepared, and he desired to acknowledge the great assistance which, in its preparation, he had received from the learned Judge. There were one or two points on which he had not felt able to adopt to the fullest extent the views of the learned Judge, and he referred to them now only that, in admitting his obligations to the learned gentleman, he might not be considered as attributing to him views which he did not hold; and that, while he ascribed to him all that was excellent in the Bill, he might be considered as taking all its deficiencies on himself. He had no intention of recapitulating all that he said on the subject of oaths when he last addressed the Council, nor of again reading all that had been recorded on the question. He was well content to leave that record to the candid consideration of Honorable Members, without weakening its effect by any comments of his own, but on one or two points he desired very briefly to occupy the attention of the Council.

In the objections which were felt to the re-introduction of oaths, he could not help thinking first, that one side of the question was too exclusively looked upon, and second, that, in considering the difficulties that will attend the proposed change, the imagination was drawn upon far more largely than the memory. That some evil might attend the re-introduction of oaths, was only saying that the system sought to be introduced was human—nothing human was perfect—and all that man could hope to do was to follow that line of action which as far as he could judge would be attended with the least amount of evil. It was admitted—he believed universally admitted—that evil attends the admission of unsworn evidence; it was feared that evil might attend the re-introduction of oaths—all that he asked Honorable Members to consider and to decide was, which of the two evils was the greater, the certain and admitted evil of unsworn testimony, or the anticipated and problemetical evil of again introducing oaths? He had no doubt in his own mind which was the greater evil, and he had also no doubt of this, that, whatever objection any man or any class of men might make to having the truth of their own evidence tested by an oath, there were none who would not wish that that test should be applied to all evidence brought against them. Honorable Members of this Council might have no reason to apprehend that they would ever be in a position to make it of any personal importance, whether evidence was taken on oath or not; but before they decided to vote against this Bill, they ought to endeavor to imagine themselves in the position of those to whom it might be of importance. What consolation would it be to a man who lost property or liberty through the means of false evidence, to be told that, although, had the evidence against him been on oath, a different result would have arisen, the administration of the oath which the Court would have prescribed, might possibly have been disagreeable to the witness? Let those who could see only the evil that might attend the re-introduction of oaths say, in the case supposed, which would have been the greater evil, that the man should have lost property or liberty, or perhaps life, from false testimony borne against him, or that the witness might have been inconvenienced by the form of oath demanded of him?

He now turned for one moment to say a few words on what he had previously adverted to, that it appeared to him from what he had in private heard urged against this measure, that the imagination was more drawn upon than the memory.

It was, he believed, supposed by some, that the discretion to administer whatever oath might be considered most binding on the conscience of each particular witness, was a discretion that could not safely be given to the Courts; that witnesses would be oppressed by being made subject to oaths prescribed only for the purpose of annoyance, and that the Courts might indulge in unbecoming methods of testing the credibility of a witness. Now, he said that these were imaginary, and not practical objections, because they were not founded on any thing that occurred during the time that intervened between 1793, when this very discretion was given to the Courts, and 1840, when proposed to do was nothing new, it was the law of the land for forty-seven years, and he for one had never heard that during all that time witnesses were bullied by the Courts, or that the Judges descended from their high position to perform fantastic tricks. It was possible that some one isolated case might be adduced, but, if there were such a case, it would be an exception to the general practice, and such an exception as would serve only to prove the general rule to have been the reverse; and if in an active career that had extended over more than twenty-seven years, he could say that he never even heard of such a case, he thought he was justified in assuming that they must have been most uncommon.

After the Council had risen on the last occasion of this subject being discussed, an Honorable Member told him an anecdote which had been communicated to him by the Officer immediately concerned. It was that, on an occasion of the crime of dacoity being proved against a prisoner by abundant but unsworn testimony, he made such an appeal to the Officer who tried him, and who himself narrated the anecdote, as to induce him to put the witnesses on their oath, when one and all withdrew all that they had said against the prisoner. Now he begged the Council to keep this anecdote in mind for one moment, while he referred to a circumstance that occurred when he had last the honor to address them. It might be recollected that the Honorable and learned Chief Justice noticed that the amendment which he then moved made no provision for exempting from oaths those who had conscientious scruples to taking an oath, and that, when he attempted to defend the omission by referring to the learned Judge's own admission in the notes which he had written on the Civil Procedure Code, that in eight years not eight cases of witnesses claiming exemption on account of conscientious scruples had come before him, that is, not so often as once a year, the learned Judge said that still, even for so small a fraction, it was necessary that the law should provide. Now, if it were necessary, and he was not at all intending to argue that it is not, but if it were necessary that the law should specially provide for the contingency of a conscientious scruple that did not occur in this city so often as once a year, was it not *a fortiori* necessary that it should provide for the preservation of liberty, and perhaps of life in such a case as that referred to in the anecdote he had just referred to? Was the law to make provision for the bare possibility of a conscientious scruple, and to make no provision for the great probability of life and liberty being in jeopardy from false testimony?

Before he sat down, he wished to be allowed to say a word on what fell from the Honorable and gallant gentleman on the last occasion of this subject being under discussion. On his expressing a hope that the Honorable and gallant gentleman's experience of Courts Martial would lead him to support the motion, the Honorable and gallant gentleman said that he would wish to see all oaths before Courts Martial at once abolished. Now, when, on a question connected with Military matters, he was so unfortunate as to hold an opinion that differed from that held by the Honorable and gallant gentleman, he could not but be anxious so far to justify himself as to give the grounds of his opinion. When in 1835 the question of abolishing oaths was under discussion, it was mentioned in papers then recorded by the Sudder Dewany Adawlut, that one ground of objection to their abolition was to be found in the statement of many Military men that Sepoys who would state matters as facts before a Court of enquiry when they were not sworn, would frequently refuse to abide by those statements when put upon their oath before a Court Martial. He hoped that the Honorable and gallant gentleman would be able to admit this statement which appeared in the records of the Sudder Dewany Adawlut as some justification of his maintaining an opinion upon a subject connected with Military matters, that was not in accordance with his.

He had little to say in explanation of the several Sections of this short Bill; it had been drawn so as to include all occasions on which an oath could ever be demanded, whether from a witness, or juror, a party making affidavit, or swearing to the correctness of accounts; and the authorities whom it would concern included, besides Courts of Justice, all persons empowered by law to administer oaths and affirmations.

In the third Clause provision had been made, in accordance with the suggestion of the Honorable and learned

Chief Justice, for exempting persons who had conscientious scruples to taking an oath, and with some doubt on his own part, because, contrary to the opinion of a high authority, the Section also contained the exemption made in the old law in favor of those whose rank would, according to the prejudices of the country, make it improper to compel them to take an oath. This was a point on which, if the Bill should pass a second reading, the Council would no doubt receive suggestions and opinions from various quarters, and it might remain an open question for decision in Committee.

He would only further say that, if this Bill should pass a second reading, he hoped that those Honorable Members who represent the several Presidencies in the Council, would request the particular attention of the local Governments to its provisions, so that before it went into the Committee the Council might have the benefit of knowing what all authorities and particularly the Native Judges, thought upon the subject, and he should not consider that an assent to the second reading would bind any Honorable Member to continued support to the measure if the preponderance of opinions should be adverse.

SIR JAMES OUTRAM begged to thank the Honorable Member for Madras for the opportunity which he had afforded him of rectifying the mistake which he had observed recorded in the Official Report of the Proceedings of the Council, with regard to his opinion on the question of administering oaths to Sepoys before Courts Martial. He had intended, however, to have pointed out the mistake himself. He would now only add that, upon the second reading of the Bill, he would do himself the honor to explain more fully his views on the subject, being informed that it was not customary to do so upon the first reading.

The Bill was read a first time.

CIVIL PROCEDURE.

Upon the Order of the Day for the motion to republish the Bill "for simplifying the Procedure of the Courts of Civil Judicature not established by Royal Charter" being read—

Mr. CURRIE moved that the Bill be re-committed to a Committee of the whole Council for the purpose of considering certain proposed amendments, and more especially with a view to his moving for the introduction of a new Section regarding set-off.

Agreed to.

SIR ARTHUR BULLER said that, after he had proposed a Section (which had been carried and now stood as Section 9 of Chapter II) providing for the rejection of a plaint if the plaintiff's right of action appeared upon the face of it to be barred by lapse of time, the Council went back to a preceding Section (2) which prescribed the particulars to be contained in the plaint. The latter Section had been amended so as to require the plaintiff to state in the particulars of his plaint the ground upon which he claimed exemption from the law of limitation if the cause of action accrued beyond the time ordinarily allowed for commencing the suit. That being the case, it appeared to him to render unnecessary almost all of the Section which he had proposed. He should therefore move for its withdrawal; but, before doing so, he would suggest that in Section 8 the words "or that the right of action is barred by lapse of time" be inserted after the words "cause of action" in the 5th line, otherwise the Court would not have power to reject a plaint which appeared upon the face of it to be barred by lapse of time. The Section, as it now stood, was insufficient, because there might be a cause of action notwithstanding that the right to sue was barred by lapse of time.

The motion was carried, and the Section as amended passed.

SIR ARTHUR BULLER then moved that Section 9 be omitted.

Agreed to.

Section 18 provided that, in issuing the summons, the Court might order the personal appearance of the defendant or of the plaintiff.

MR. CURRIE said, he thought it desirable to have a similar provision in this Section to that contained in Clause 4 Section XVII of the Small Cause Courts Bill. He should therefore move that the following proviso be added to the Section:—

"Provided that no plaintiff or defendant shall be ordered to attend in person, who at the time is *bonâ fide* residing at a distance of more than fifty miles from the place where the Court is held."

The motion was carried, and the amended Section then passed.

On the motion of Mr. Currie, a verbal amendment was made in Section 70.

MR. CURRIE said that, although the discussion which had taken place in the Section relating to set-off, had resulted in the omission of that Section, it seemed to be the general opinion of the Council that the right of set-off, if limited to debts, might unobjectionably be allowed. He therefore moved that the following new Section be inserted before Section 96:—

"If in a suit for debt the defendant desire to set off against the claim of the plaintiff the amount of any debt due to him from the plaintiff, he shall tender a written statement containing the particulars of his demand, and the Court shall thereupon enquire into the same. Provided that, if the sum claimed by the defendant exceed the amount cognizable by the Court, defendant shall not be allowed to set-off the same unless he abandon the excess."

Agreed to.

MR CURRIE then moved to restore the former Section 167, which prescribed what the decree should contain when a claim to set-off was allowed, with a few verbal alterations.

Agreed to.

MR. CURRIE also moved to transpose the new Section 32 of Chapter IV relating to cross-decrees, so that it might stand after Section 9 of the same Chapter.

Agreed to.

Verbal amendments were made in Sections 5 and 7 of Chapter V.

MR. PEACOCK said, when the Bill was before the Select Committee, it was thought that, if the Sections were numbered in order from Section 1 to the end of the final Chapter, it would be more convenient than the present mode of numbering the Sections under each Chapter separately. He therefore moved that the Sections be numbered consecutively.

Agreed to.

The Council having resumed its sitting, the Bill was reported.

MR. PEACOCK moved that the Bill, as settled in Committee of the whole Council, be published for general information, and that it be re-considered after two months.

Agreed to.

OATHS TO HINDOOS AND MAHOMEDANS.

MR. HARINGTON moved that an application be made to the Supreme Government that copies of any correspondence in the Office of the Home Secretary which might have taken place relative to the administration of Oaths to Hindoos and Mahomedans, and which might have led to the passing of Act V of 1840, be laid before the Council.

Agreed to.

PILOT COURTS (BENGAL.)

MR. CURRIE gave notice that he would, on Saturday the 13th Instant, move the first reading of a Bill to amend the law for the trial of Officers of the Bengal Pilot Service accused of breach of duty.

DELHI AND MEERUT.

MR. PEACOCK gave notice that he would on the same day move for a Committee of the whole Council on the Bill "to remove from the operation of the General Laws and Regulations the Delhi Territory and Meerut Division, or such parts thereof as the Governor General in Council shall place under the administration of the Chief Commissioner of the Punjab."

The Council adjourned.

Saturday, November 13, 1858.

PRESENT:

The Honorable the Chief Justice, *Vice-President,* in the Chair.

Hon'ble Lieut.-Genl. Sir J. Outram,	E. Currie, Esq.,
Hon'ble H. Ricketts,	H. B. Harington, Esq., and
Hon'ble B. Peacock,	H. Forbes, Esq.

CIVIL PROCEDURE.

THE CLERK reported to the Council that he had received from the Home

Department, copies of two Despatches from the Court of Directors suggesting the enactment of a law to render compulsory the institution of Civil Suits in the Courts of lowest jurisdiction competent to take cognizance of them.

MR. PEACOCK said, he did not think it necessary to move that this communication be printed, inasmuch as a new Section to the effect proposed had been introduced into the Code of Civil Procedure.

ELECTRIC TELEGRAPHS.

THE CLERK also reported that he had received from the Home Department a copy of a correspondence with the Superintendent of Electric Telegraphs relative to certain amendments in Act XXXIV of 1854, "for regulating the establishment and management of Electric Telegraphs in India."

MR. PEACOCK moved that the above communication be printed.

Agreed to.

PENSIONS.

MR. PEACOCK postponed the presentation of the Report of the Select Committee on the Project of a Law for applying the provisions of the Government Order of the 1st December 1857, which affect Military Pensioners, to Pensioners in the Civil Department, and to the holders of rent-free lands He said that the Report was not yet ready, as there was some difference of opinion among the Members of the Committee; besides which, one of them (the Honorable Member for Bombay) was absent.

PILOT COURTS (BENGAL).

MR. CURRIE postponed the motion (of which he had given notice for this day) for the first reading of a Bill to amend the law for the trial of Officers of the Bengal Pilot Service accused of breach of duty.

LEASES OF GHATWALEE LANDS (BEERBHOOM).

MR. CURRIE moved the second reading of the Bill "to empower the holders of Ghatwalee lands in the District of Beerbhoom to grant leases extending beyond the period of their own possession."

The motion was carried, and the Bill read a second time.

MEERUT AND DELHI.

MR. PEACOCK postponed the motion (of which he had given notice for this day) for a Committee of the whole Council on the Bill "to remove from the operation of the General Laws and Regulations the Delhi Territory and Meerut Division or such parts thereof as the Governor General in Council shall place under the administration of the Chief Commissioner of the Punjab." He said he understood that a communication on the subject of this Bill had recently been addressed by the Honorable Member for the North-Western Provinces to the Sudder Court at Agra, to which no reply had yet been received.

SMALL CAUSE COURTS (MOFUSSIL).

MR. HARINGTON gave notice that he would next Saturday move the second reading of the Bill "for the establishment of Courts of Small Causes beyond the local limits of the jurisdiction of the Supreme Courts of Judicature established by Royal Charter".

OATHS AND AFFIRMATIONS.

MR. FORBES gave notice that he would, on the same day, move the second reading of the Bill "concerning Oaths and Affirmations".

TRIALS FOR RAPE.

MR. CURRIE moved that the Select Committee on the Bill "to enable Session Judges to pass sentence on trials for Rape" be discharged, and that the Bill be referred to the Select Committees on the Bills for extending the jurisdiction of the Courts of Criminal Judicature of the East India Company, for simplifying the procedure thereof, and for investing other Courts with Criminal jurisdiction.

Agreed to.

PETTY OFFENDERS AND WITNESSES.

MR. CURRIE moved that the Select Committee on the Bill "for enforcing the attendance of petty offenders and witnesses" be discharged, and that the Bill be referred to the Select Committees on the same Bills.

Agreed to.

CRIMINAL JURISDICTION OF MOONSIFFS AND TUHSEELDARS (N. W. PROVINCES).

MR. CURRIE moved that the Select Committee on the Bill "for conferring Criminal jurisdiction upon Moonsiffs and Tuhseeldars in the North-Western Provinces" be discharged, and that the Bill be referred to the Select Committees on the same Bills.

Agreed to

The Council adjourned.

Saturday, November 20, 1858.

PRESENT:

The Honorable the Chief Justice, *Vice-President*, in the Chair.

Hon'ble Lieut.-Genl. Sir J. Outram,	E. Currie, Esq.,
Hon'ble H. Ricketts,	Hon'ble Sir A. W. Buller,
Hon'ble B. Peacock,	H. B. Harington, Esq., and
P. W. LeGeyt, Esq.,	H. Forbes, Esq.

NATIVE PASSENGER VESSELS (BAY OF BENGAL).

THE CLERK reported to the Council that he had received from the Home Department a copy of a further Extract from Proceedings in the Foreign Department respecting the evasion of the provisions of Act I of 1857 (to prevent the over-crowding of vessels carrying Native Passengers in the Bay of Bengal).

MR. FORBES moved that the above communication be referred to the Select Committee on the former communication.

Agreed to.

IMPROVEMENT OF COURTS (BOMBAY).

THE CLERK reported that he had received from the Home Department papers regarding certain suggestions made by Mr. H. B. E. Frere for improving the Courts in the Regulation Provinces of the Bombay Presidency.

MR. LEGEYT said, it was very much to be regretted that these papers had not been forwarded in time to receive the consideration of the Select Committee on the Code of Civil Procedure. They contained some very valuable suggestions which had been made so long ago as 1852. The opinions of Judicial and other Officers had been given on them, and he found that they were forwarded to the Government of India in September 1857. This still allowed sufficient time to lay them before the Select Committee.

He had looked over these papers, which appeared to embrace nine different topics.

1*st.* The want of Courts of Summary Jurisdiction and easy access for the disposal of Small Causes.

This would very properly be considered by the Select Committee to whom the Bill on the subject introduced by the Honorable Member for the North-Western Provinces would be referred, if it should pass a second reading.

2*nd.* The propriety of Judges making circuits and trying appeals from the decisions of Moonsiffs at the stations of the Moonsiffs.

3*rd.* The examination of Plaintiff and Defendant in a suit.

This had been provided for in the Code of Civil Procedure.

4*th.* The want of efficient Bankruptcy Laws.

5*th.* The amendment of the law relative to the raising of attachments imposed in execution of decrees.

This was a point which could hardly be said to be a closed question in connection with the Civil Procedure Bill. The present provisions in that Bill were as nearly as possible the same as those upon which this letter was a commentary, and he hoped that consideration would be given to those comments.

6th. The more frequent employment of Punchayets.

7th. The propriety of raising the salaries of Sheristadars.

This would more properly be considered in connection with the subject of the constitution of the Courts.

8th. The advantage of making the Establishments of Native Judges a portion of the regular stipendiary establishment of Government.

This was a matter which had never been before this Council. The Bombay Government had adopted the suggestion, and had stated that the result had proved satisfactory.

9th. The propriety of providing good Native Law Books.

This was not a subject requiring consideration here.

He thought that Mr. Frere's observations and the opinions of the various authorities on most of these topics, with the Minutes of the Bombay Government thereon, should be printed. What he proposed to print were in respect to the 1st, 2nd, 3rd, 4th, and 5th points. He should, therefore, move that so much of these papers as relate to those five points be printed.

Agreed to.

OATHS AND AFFIRMATIONS.

THE CLERK reported that he had received from the Home Department papers relating to Act V of 1840 (concerning the Oaths and Declarations of Hindoos and Mahomedans).

MR. HARINGTON moved that these papers be laid upon the table.

Agreed to.

PENSIONS.

MR. PEACOCK presented the Report of the Select Committee on the project of a law for applying the provisions of the Government Order of the 1st December 1857, which affect Military Pensioners, to Pensioners in the Civil Department, and to the holders of rent-free lands.

RYOTWAR SETTLEMENTS (MADRAS PRESIDENCY).

MR. FORBES presented the Report of the Select Committee on the Bill "for the better recovery of arrears of Revenue under Ryotwar Settlements in the Madras Presidency."

Mr. LeGeyt

PILOT COURTS (BENGAL).

MR. CURRIE moved the first reading of a Bill "to amend the law for the trial of Officers of the Bengal Pilot Service accused of breach of duty." He said, the Officers of the Bengal Pilot Service, when accused of breach of duty, had the privilege of being tried by a Court formed in some measure on the model of Courts Martial. By the Act XXIV of 1845, the Superintendent of Marine might, when he thought necessary, bring any Member of the Pilot Service to trial before a Court, consisting of a President, two Merchants, four Ship Captains, and two Branch or Master Pilots. The finding and sentence were to be according to the votes of the majority of the Court.

It was provided that, if the breach of duty charged against the accused was punishable "under a certain Code, called the Penal Code, for the better order and Government of the Members composing the Pilot Service, passed by order of the Right Honorable the Vice President in Council on the 21st December 1826," the punishment awarded by the Court was to be that prescribed by the Code.

Now it was obvious that the Code passed on the 21st December 1826, being specified in the Act as that, which was to regulate the sentences of the Court, no modification of the Code could be made otherwise than by Legislative enactment, or rather that, if the Code were modified, an alteration of Act XXIV of 1845 would be necessary to enable the Courts to act in accordance with it.

So far back as December 1845 the Code of 1826 was represented to be defective, and a revised Code, prepared by the then Marine Judge Advocate (Captain Clapperton), was laid before Government, and other versions of an amended Code were submitted by the late Marine Superintendent (Captain Rogers), and the President of Marine Courts (Mr. Piddington), in April 1846 and June 1848. In consequence of these representations, the Legislative Member of Council (Mr. Bethune) seemed to have contemplated the preparation of a new law, apparently intending to embrace in that law the provisions of a revised Code; but nothing was done in the matter.

In 1852, Mr. Piddington submitted to Government a paper on the operation of Act XXIV of 1845. He observed that—

"A brief experience of the working of this Court (meaning the Courts constituted according to the provisions of the Act) convinced me that, while it was a most necessary and useful institution, and one most essential to the safety of the Port, its utility was much limited from practical defects in its constitution, and this judgment has been confirmed by the many successive unsatisfactory findings and sentences which I have had to regret, and which have really been at times verdicts against evidence or sentences nullifying the verdicts when those were most justly given."

Mr. Piddington proceeded to comment at length upon the unsatisfactory operation of the existing Courts, and the reasons which had led to such a result. He recommended a total change in their constitution, and in lieu of a Court consisting of nine Members, and deciding according to the votes of the majority, proposed one consisting of—

"1. A President, whose sole decision would be the finding, and his award the sentence; this last to be regulated by a detailed Penal Code.

2. One Branch Pilot, one Merchant Captain, and one Mercantile Assessor, to sit with the President, having all the privileges of members of the present Courts; their separate findings and award of punishment to be stated with written grounds, if they think proper to submit them, but to be in no way binding upon the decision of the President."

This communication therefore raised another question altogether different from that of the alleged defectiveness of the Penal Code of 1826, and the Government had before it these two questions; first, the proposed revision of the Penal Code, for which three several recommendations had been submitted, and secondly, Mr. Piddington's suggestion for a change in the constitution of the Courts by which the Code was to be administered.

With regard to the first question he (Mr Currie) entirely concurred in the opinions expressed by Mr. Grant, then Secretary to the Government of India, in a Note dated 11th December 1852. He said:—

"What is called a Penal Code is, in fact, no more than a part of the regulations of the Pilot Service such as a master lays down for his servant's observance. The penalties involve nothing beyond what a Master can inflict of his own authority on those who choose to enter or remain in his service, such as dismissal, degradation, and suspension from pay. It does not appear what necessity there is for putting such instructions and penalties into a law. Indeed, from the nature of the relation of master and servant, the details of such regulations must be subject to frequent change. The regulations of the service might be left to be made, and amended from time to time, by the Executive Government; and the penalties for breach of regulation or other misconduct might be left to the same Government, as well in the case of Pilots as in that of any other class of servants in the Civil Department. All that a law is requisite for is to enable Government to ascertain facts, to the minutest particular."

On the grounds here set forth it was, he (Mr. Currie) thought, clear that the revision of the so-called Penal Code was not within the province of the Legislature, that it should be left to the Executive Government, and that all that the law should do in respect of the Code should be to require any Court constituted by law for the trial of offences contained in the Code to regulate its sentences in accordance with it.

The other question remained, namely, what was the best constitution for such a Court. Mr. Piddington described the existing Courts as consisting of:—

1st. "A President who is competent and perfectly unbiassed.

2ndly. Two Merchant Members, who are on some points but partially competent and rarely unbiassed by fears of delay or mischief to property in which they have directly or indirectly a stake either as Merchants or Under-writers, and who allow themselves at times to be a good deal led by the opinions of the Branch Pilots.

3rdly. Four Merchant Captains, of whom it may be said at once that, though quite competent, two if not three and sometimes all four of them are afraid of, or partial to the Pilots; and of whom some will not, as they express it, risk damage to their owner's interest and their own prospect by appearing to form part of a Court which has punished a Pilot, if they can avoid it.

4thly. Two Pilot Members who are as a general rule and naturally the advocates of their own service. To this, however, there are some few honorable exceptions, as there are also in what I have said above of the four nautical and other members; and it must be avowed that their fears of damage to their property and prospects, if exaggerated, are not wholly unfounded, when it is known that the Pilots have a club of which many are members for their mutual support in all cases of prosecution."

Mr. Piddington remarked that in Courts so constituted

"there is generally a preponderating majority most unwilling to convict; or who are afraid to punish when they cannot avoid convicting; or who compromise with their consciences by the quibble that if they are sworn to determine and administer justice according to the evidence,

&c., this does not oblige them to inflict any severe punishment."

The remedy which he proposed was, as had been stated, that the trial should be held by a President or Judge assisted by Assessors, the finding and sentence to rest entirely with the President.

Within the last few months another representation had been laid before the Bengal Government by the present President of Marine Courts, Mr. Graham. This gentleman said that, without at the time being aware of the recommendations of his predecessor Mr. Piddington, he had felt it his duty to record some remarks on the existing Courts. In these remarks he writes:—

"I would venture respectfully to bring again to the notice of Government the operation of the present system, of which even a limited experience convinced me that very material alterations were requisite to render these tribunals deserving of the confidence of Government or the respect of the mercantile community."

Mr. Graham's views of the defects of the existing Courts were precisely the same with those of Mr. Piddington. He observed—

"that there is almost invariably an undue bias (and occasionally a most unseemly partiality) on the part of the Pilots on the Court in favor of the accused. Added to this, the Commanders of Ships, whether from fear of injury, as concluded by Mr. Piddington, or other cause, generally follow the votes of the Pilots, even on questions other than nautical. The combination of these two classes is sufficient at any time to outvote the Merchants and the President (who of course are entirely disinterested) and has at times been productive of decisions manifestly contrary to the evidence."

Mr. Graham, however, did not altogether agree with Mr. Piddington in respect to the remedy. He was opposed to the system of Assessors, and recommended a Court of five persons composed of the President, two Merchants and two Captains of Ships, of whom three might be a quorum. The verdict to be according to the votes of the majority, and the President to vote only in case of the opinions of the other members being equally divided. The sentence in case of conviction to rest with the President. The Superintendent of Marine concurred generally with Mr. Graham, but proposed, instead of two Captains of Ships, one Captain and one Branch Pilot.

Considering what had been said of the general unfitness of the classes of persons (or at least two of the classes of persons) of which the Court was to be composed to sit as Judges, he must say that his own judgment inclined rather in favor of Mr. Piddington's plan, namely, a Judge with Assessors. But he found that the Lieutenant-Governor of Bengal, whose long experience of the business of the Bengal Office, had made him fully acquainted with all particulars connected with the Pilot Service, with the feelings of the Pilots, and the operation of the existing law, was strongly opposed to the plan of Assessors which he thought would be unpopular and distasteful, and that he would greatly prefer the Jury system. The testimony, too, of Mr. Grant, when Secretary to the Government of Bengal, in a Note upon Mr. Piddington's suggestion, supported this view of the question. He said:—

"The law, Act XXIV of 1845, Section XVIII, requires that every finding and sentence of a Marine Court shall be subject to the approval of the Governor of Bengal. The trials held under this law, therefore, always come under the revision of Government. The result of the experience of the three years and a half that I have been in this Office, has been to create the impression on my mind, that, generally, where these trials have been unsatisfactory, the fault has been rather in the penal sentence than in the verdict. My own belief is that, if these Courts were constituted upon the principles recognized in our ordinary Courts of Justice, the result would be generally satisfactory. If the President were to perform the functions of a Judge, and the other Members were restricted to the proper functions of a Jury, that is to say, to the decision of the single question of guilty or not guilty, free from all the difficulties attendant on the determination of questions of degree, there is nothing in what I have seen of the working of these Courts, to make me doubt that they would work well."

Influenced by these opinions expressed by persons best able from experience to form a sound judgment on the subject, and being informed also that the plan of Assessors, where it had had a practical trial, as in Ceylon, had not been found to work satisfactorily, he determined to provide for a Court constituted on the ordinary principle of a Judge and Jury. But it seemed to him that, from what had been said both by the former and the present Presidents of the bias of the Pilots in favor of the accused, and their influence on the other Members of the Court, it would not be right that any Members of the Pilot Service should sit on the Jury. He had thought, also, that there was no use in summoning more persons to sit as Jurors than were really necessary for the purpose, and that the number of Jurors should be as small as was consistent with the formation of an efficient Jury. For these reasons he proposed that the Jury should consist of three persons, namely, two Merchants and one Commander of a Merchant Vessel, the verdict to be according to the votes of the majority of the Jurors, and the sentence to be pronounced by the Judge.

He had made provision for a new trial in the event of the Judge certifying the verdict to be clearly contrary to the evidence. There were several other alterations of the existing law, most of them growing out of the change made in the constitution of the Court, but it was not necessary to occupy the time of the Council with any detailed explanation of them. With these observations he begged to move the first reading of the Bill.

The Bill was read a first time.

SMALL CAUSE COURTS (MOFUSSIL).

MR. HARINGTON postponed the motion (of which he had given notice for this day) for the second reading of the Bill "for the establishment of Courts of Small Causes beyond the local limits of the jurisdiction of the Supreme Courts of Judicature established by Royal Charter."

OATHS AND AFFIRMATIONS.

MR. FORBES moved the second reading of the Bill "concerning Oaths and Affirmations."

MR. CURRIE said, he was not disposed to concur in the proposal to read the Bill a second time. If read a second time, it would go forth to the public that the principle of the Bill had been approved of by the Council, and that it was their intention to pass it, or some similar measure. He was not at all prepared to agree to this. He would not then enter into his reasons, because he had reason to believe that the Council would consent to the course which he was about to propose. Otherwise he should wish to have an opportunity of stating his views on the measure proposed in the Bill.

But, besides the objection already stated, he had another objection to the publication of the Bill. The question raised by the Bill was, whether the present form of adjuration should be abandoned, and the old forms revived; whereas the question before the Council when in Committee on the Civil Procedure Bill, the question which gave occasion for the introduction of the present Bill, was one altogether different. That question was, whether, according to the recommendation of Her Majesty's Commissioners and the Select Committee on the Procedure Bill, the religious element should not be altogether dispensed with. That was the question on which the Council more particularly desired to have information. For these reasons, he thought it highly desirable that the second reading of the Bill should be deferred for three or four months, and that in the meantime measures should be adopted for procuring information through the several Governments, both on the point to which he had just referred, and on the question raised by this Bill. The representative Members would probably undertake to procure that information.

He therefore begged to move, as an amendment, that this Bill be read a second time this day four months.

MR. FORBES said, in introducing the Bill now before the Council, he had done so with the view of eliciting information; as it had been said by the Honorable and learned Judge (Sir Arthur Buller), at whose suggestion a separate Bill had been brought in, that the information before the Council did not extend over any period within the last ten years. He had also himself said at the first reading of the Bill, that he did not consider that a vote for the second reading would pledge Honorable Members to the principle of the Bill. But he was quite willing to assent to the amendment. He only hoped that those Members who represented the several local Governments in this Council, would press upon them the necessity of taking early and decisive measures to obtain the requisite information.

MR. LEGEYT said, he had no objection to the postponement, but he would prefer the adoption of a more decided course. They had had sufficient experience of the great difficulty of getting information from a distance on any subject, however important. It was extraordinary that it should be so, but so it was. They appointed Select Committees on various matters, which stood over for three, or six, or twelve months, or even for two years, waiting for information which had never come.

The question of Oaths, however, was one of paramount importance, which should be decided one way or the other. Her Majesty's Commissioners had proposed that the examination of witnesses should be taken without any oath, solemn affirmation, or warning. There had been a Select Committee of the Council on this very subject of Oaths and Affirmations which was discharged two years after it had been appointed, and he did not believe that a single communication had been received by this Committee to throw any light on the question. Instead of leaving the matter in the hands of four individual representative Members to act separately, he thought that a Select Committee should be appointed with instructions to take every means to obtain information from all parts of India. He would, therefore, propose as an amendment that a Select Committee be appointed to enquire and report on the matter.

SIR ARTHUR BULLER said, he thought that the moving an amendment on an amendment would somewhat embarrass the Council. Nor could he see the necessity for such a course, as the questions were entirely independent of each other. The question now before the Council was—"Shall we postpone this Bill for four months or not?" When that question was disposed of, the amendment of the Honorable Member for Bombay might be brought forward in the shape of a separate and substantive motion.

MR. LEGEYT assented, and said that he would defer his motion till afterwards.

THE VICE-PRESIDENT said, he supposed that the Honorable Member for Bengal had it in contemplation to move something in addition after his present motion had been disposed of, otherwise the course proposed would be open to this objection. The Bill, if not read a second time, would not be published, but this Bill was introduced upon an understanding that some distinct measure should be put forth on which the present opinion of the public with respect to judicial oaths could be taken. If this could be done without reading the Bill a second time, it might be well to adopt the suggestion of the Honorable Member for Bengal, and thus to avoid the inference generally drawn from a second reading, namely, that the Council had committed itself to the principle of the Bill. Most of them agreed, even those who like himself thought it a questionable policy to abolish oaths in the Mofussil Courts, that it was desirable to have information of a later date than that before the Council.

Whether the machinery by which they were to obtain information was to be that suggested by the Honorable Member for Bengal, or the Select Committee proposed by the Honorable Member for Bombay, he (the Vice-President) thought it would be equally necessary to publish the Bill.

MR. CURRIE said, he did not propose to move either for the publication of the Bill or for the appointment of a Select Committee. He did not see how the Bill could be published without pledging the Council to an intention to legislate in accordance with its spirit. He thought, too, that there was little use in publication. For more than a year a Bill "to amend the law relating to the recovery of Rent in the Presidency of Fort William in Bengal" had been before the public, and though it touched the interests of every Ryot and every Zemindar in the country, nothing had been elicited from them. The reference to a Select Committee was too often tantamount to shelving a question. Referring to the list of Select Committees, he found a Select Committee appointed "to take into consideration the Projects of Law connected with the Marine Department, and to prepare such Bill or Bills as may be necessary with reference thereto." He believed the Ports Bill had been prepared by that Select Committee, but it had done nothing more. He had himself, upon the urgent request of the Bengal Government, prepared and introduced the Merchant Seamen's Bill, and he had this day brought in a Bill for the reform of Marine Courts.

Next, there was a Select Committee "to consider and report upon the question of Municipal Law for the conservancy of Towns in the Territories under the Government of the East India Company." His predecessor had brought forward a Bill on this subject for the Bengal Presidency which was thrown out by the Council, and this Select Committee had been appointed, but he was not aware that it had ever done any thing.

Again, there was a Select Committee appointed "to consider and report on the question of enabling the Legislative Council to call for evidence." A Bill had been brought in, discussed, and withdrawn, and this Select Committee had been appointed to consider the general subject, possibly with the intention that the whole project should be shelved; at all events nothing had ever been done.

For these reasons he was of opinion that the most effective course would be for each representative Member to take upon himself to communicate with his own Government and to obtain information; and he had therefore limited his motion simply to deferring the second reading of the Bill.

MR. CURRIE'S amendment was then put and agreed to.

LITERARY, SCIENTIFIC, AND CHARITABLE SOCIETIES.

MR. CURRIE moved the second reading of the Bill "for the registration of Literary, Scientific, and Charitable Societies."

The motion was carried, and the Bill read a second time.

DELHI AND MEERUT.

MR. PEACOCK moved that the Council resolve itself into a Committee on the Bill "to remove from the operation of the General Laws and Regulations the Delhi Territory and Meerut Division, or such parts thereof as the Governor General in Council shall place under the administration of the Chief Commissioner of the Punjab"; and that the Committee be instructed to consider the Bill in the amended form in which the Select Committee had recommended it to be passed.

Agreed to.

Section I was passed as it stood.

Section II provided that all suits and proceedings which were pending at the time when the Delhi Territory was placed under the Chief Commissioner of the Punjab, and which had been or might be transferred to the Courts or Officers established or appointed therein, should be deemed to have been lawfully transferred to such Courts and Officers according to their respective jurisdictions.

MR. HARINGTON said that, since the Bill was reported upon by the Select Committee, it had occurred to the Honorable and learned Member on his left (Mr Peacock) and himself, that the Bill did not provide for suits and proceedings instituted subsequently to the Delhi Territory having been placed under the Chief Commissioner of the Punjab, but only for suits and proceedings pending at the date of the transfer. He therefore moved that the following words be added to the Section:—

"And any suits or proceedings which, subsequently to the time when the said Territory was so placed under such administration, shall have been instituted in any such Court or before any such Officer, shall be deemed to have been lawfully instituted."

The motion was carried, and the Section as amended then passed.

Section III was passed as it stood.

Section IV provided that "all appeals or proceedings pending" in the Sudder Court and Sudder Board of Revenue for the North-Western Provinces "at the time when the said Territory was so placed under the administration of the said Chief Commissioner," should be determined by such Court or Board in the same manner as if this Act had not been passed.

MR. HARINGTON said that, from a communication lately received by him from the Sudder Court at Agra, it appeared that, subsequently to the time when the Delhi Territory was placed under the Chief Commissioner of the Punjab, several applications for special appeal which, at the date of the transfer, were pending on the file of the Sudder Court, had been admitted by the Court, and as the Section, as at present worded, would not reach these cases, he begged to move the insertion of the word "now" between the words "all appeals or proceedings" and the word "pending" in line 1, and the omission of the words "at the time when the said Territory was so placed under the administration of the said Chief Commissioner" in lines 7 to 9.

The motions were severally carried, and the amended Section then passed.

Section V and the Schedule, Preamble, and Title were passed as they stood.

The Council having resumed its sitting, the Bill was reported.

LEASES OF GHATWALEE LANDS (BEERBHOOM).

Mr. CURRIE moved that the Bill "to empower the holders of Ghatwalee lands in the district of Beerbhoom to grant leases extending beyond the period of their own possession" be referred to a Select Committee consisting of Mr. Peacock, Mr. Harington, and the Mover.

Agreed to.

LITERARY, SCIENTIFIC, AND CHARITABLE SOCIETIES.

Mr. CURRIE moved that the Bill "for the registration of Literary, Scientific, and Charitable Societies" be referred to a Select Committee consisting of the Vice-President, Mr. LeGeyt, Mr. Forbes, and the Mover.

Agreed to.

OATHS AND AFFIRMATIONS.

Mr. FORBES moved that the Clerk of the Council be directed to address the Government of India and to express the wish of the Legislative Council that they would call upon the several local Governments to obtain and transmit the opinions of the several Judicial authorities, European and Native, upon the question of the re-introduction of Oaths, and also upon the proposition of Her Majesty's Commissioners that all Oaths and Affirmations be dispensed with, and generally to invite the opinions of the public upon the subject.

Mr. LeGEYT said, he could not agree to such a motion in its present shape. He did not think it was at all becoming for this Council to ask the Executive Government to do what was their (the Legislative Council's) own duty. Why should they not perform that duty themselves, either by a Select Committee or by the Clerk of the Council?

It was not unusual for the Supreme Government on matters of general interest to call for information. His own experience of the result of such enquiries was not favorable. A certain number of copies of the questions were struck off and sent every where, and in eight out of twelve instances they remained a dead letter. Then came a refresher, which was after long delay followed by a peremptory demand for replies, and then came apologies that press of work and various reasons had prevented time or attention being devoted to the subject, and one can easily judge of the value of the information so elicited. The time thus lost in collecting opinions generally defeated the object of the enquiry. He would much prefer to see a Select Committee appointed with stringent instructions and full powers to enquire into and report on what might appear to be the general feeling of the country on the proposed change in the existing law contained in the Bill, and also whether the examination of witnesses in Civil and Criminal trials without oath, affirmation, or warning, as proposed by the Commissioners in England, was advisable, and for this purpose that the Select Committee take such measures as might seem to them best calculated to elicit the fullest information on this important subject. That was the measure, the adoption of which he would strongly advocate in preference to an application from the Council to the Supreme Government to obtain information for them. He thought that a communication from a Select Committee of this Council calling for information, with an intimation that it was urgently required within four months, and that silence would be taken for assent, would be much more likely to attain the object.

Mr. Harington

Information also should be sought not only from the Official Authorities, but also from the people, so that the Council might acquire knowledge of the real feelings of the country on this subject. There were some oaths that carried terror to the native mind, and if they were imposed it was pretty certain that falsehood would not be told under their direct influence; but such oaths were of such a nature that they could hardly be conveniently administered in Courts of Justice. He believed that the affirmation prescribed by the Act of 1840 was not considered to convey any religious obligation; the Brahmins told the Hindoos "it is the Feringhee's oath," and the Mahomedans said "you have not been sworn on the Koran." He believed the only part of that Act which made any impression, was the warning given to the witness that if he spoke falsely he would be punished. He believed that the dread of punishment would alone deter persons whose moral sense was like that of most of the witnesses who appeared in Courts of Justice in India, and to preserve that dread the penalty ought to be immediate. He trusted he should yet see the Courts armed with power to punish for false swearing by a summary sentence—such as fine—which need not be irrevocable, but which, he believed, would check the wholesale false swearing which was said to disgrace our Courts.

Before this amendment was put, it was agreed that Mr. Forbes' motion and the amendment should be withdrawn, to enable Mr. LeGeyt to make the following motion.

MR. LEGEYT moved that the Bill "concerning Oaths and Affirmations" be published for general information.

He said that the Honorable Member for Bengal had objected to the publication of the Bill that it might commit the Council to an expression of approval of the principle of the Bill. But he thought that this would not be so, because the Bill had only been brought in by an individual Member whose opinions were entitled to great consideration, but nothing had passed to pledge the Council. The Bill was proposed to be published merely for information, and he therefore did not see how the publication would have such an effect as that apprehended by the Honorable Member for Bengal.

MR. CURRIE said, he had already stated his objection to publication. Notwithstanding any thing that might be said in that room, if the Bill were published, it would go forth as having received the sanction of the Council. The Proceedings of the Council were often not reported at all, or, if reported, the report was frequently unintelligible, and probably seldom read; therefore the public generally would not know what had passed there. The appearance of the Bill in the *Gazette* would be taken as an intimation of the intention of the Council to pass a measure of this sort.

THE VICE-PRESIDENT said, he could not see the slightest objection to the publication of the Bill. The object was to elicit opinions; it was surely desirable that the points on which their opinions were given should be stated as definitely as possible. If the representative Members sought for the information, it would require no very astute mind to discover that some proposition on this subject had been made, and that there was some intention to legislate. The Council now committed itself to nothing, and the Bill would be put forth as one which had been postponed for four months, because the Council was desirous to obtain further information on the subject matter of it before proceeding with or rejecting it.

MR. CURRIE said that, if this Bill were published with some such preface as that indicated by the Honorable and learned Vice-President, it would obviate his objection to the publication.

MR. LEGEYT'S motion was then put and agreed to.

MR. FORBES' motion and Mr. LeGeyt's amendment were then again brought forward.

The amendment having been proposed—

MR. RICKETTS said, it appeared that the Council were resolved that nothing should be done until further information had been obtained. The only question now was, how it could be obtained speedily and completely. It was objectionable to apply to the Executive Government, for by so doing the Council would acknowledge that they had not themselves the power of calling for information. If allowable under the Standing Orders, he suggested that the information required should be called for by the Clerk in the name of the whole Council, and not in the name of a Committee only.

MR. PEACOCK said that the Governor General in the Legislative Council had the same power of calling for information as the Governor General in his Executive Council had. Though the Governor General was absent, yet the Vice-President was appointed to supply his place. The Legislative Council might direct the Clerk of the Council to address the local Governments. He was not sure whether the Honorable Member for Bombay intended that the Clerk should write to the local Officers; the proper course would be to apply to the local Governments A request made by the Clerk of the Council by the direction of the Council would no doubt be complied with. He saw no objection to the appointment of a Select Committee who would determine upon what points information was required.

THE VICE-PRESIDENT said, he inclined to the proposition of the Honorable Member for Bombay. The Select Committee would be able to consider the sort of information required, and to classify it. He was not prepared to say whether they would have the same powers of addressing through the Clerk of the Council the local Governments and other authorities as the Council had. But if they had not, any Member of that Select Committee might on any Saturday move for and obtain the sanction of the Council to any address of that kind which it was desirable to make. The motion of the Honorable Member for Madras, that application should be made to the Government of India, he thought objectionable. Every additional body interposed between the Council and those whose information was sought, caused some delay. The Honorable and learned Member (Mr. Peacock) had suggested that the local Governments should be addressed. They would not in that case get the opinion of Officers in the Non-Regulation Provinces unless the expression was understood to include Chief Commissioners, &c. A Select Committee, when it met, might see other modes of obtaining information which did not at the present moment suggest themselves to the mind of any Member of the Council, and information of a kind which was not procurable through the local Governments.

MR. RICKETTS observed that a letter might be prepared by a Select Committee but the call should be in the name of the Council. Being unusual, it would for that reason be more immediately attended to than a letter from the Government of India. The opinions of Officers in the Non-Regulation Provinces should be obtained by addressing the Secretary to the Government of India. It might also be desirable to address questions to individual Europeans and Natives.

MR. LEGEYT would leave the Select Committee to act in an unrestricted manner. If they thought information could be elicited from individuals, they would forward the papers to them. He was sure Natives, to whom such communications would be sent by the Legislative Council, would receive them with great satisfaction, and feel honored by them. The person addressed would show the communication to his neighbours, and would discuss the subject with them. He felt sure that more attention would thus be bestowed on them than if the information were sought by a formal written letter from the Registrar of the Sudder addressed to the different Zillah Judges.

The question being then put that the words proposed to be omitted be omitted, the Council divided:—

Ayes 4.	*Noes* 5.
Sir Arthur Buller.	Mr. Forbes.
Mr. LeGeyt.	Mr. Harington.
Sir James Outram.	Mr. Currie.
The Vice-President.	Mr. Peacock.
	Mr. Ricketts.

So the motion was negatived.

MR. FORBES' motion being proposed—

SIR. JAMES OUTRAM said, he understood the proposition to be for an enquiry to be made through the Judicial Officers. His objection was that the enquiry should not be confined to Judicial Officers. He was not sure if the rules of the Council would permit his proposing such an amendment, but he thought that information should be sought from all classes, whether Europeans or Natives, and whether Government Servants or not. The object was to ascertain what were the true feelings of the Natives on this subject, and they were not so likely to attain that object if the enquiry were confined to official channels.

THE VICE-PRESIDENT said that the Honorable Member who last addressed the Council had anticipated him in the objection which he had intended to make to the proposition of the Honorable Member for Madras. The doubt in his (the Vice-President's) mind was as to the power of the local Governments to call for information from non-official persons. The amendment of the Honorable Member for Bombay was calculated to have that effect; but as it had been negatived, he did not see what amendment could be grafted upon the original question, which would have the same effect.

MR. FORBES then withdrew his motion, and made the following amended motion, namely, that the Clerk of the Council be directed to address the Government of India and the local Governments, and to request them to obtain and transmit the opinions of the several Judicial and Revenue Authorities, European and Native, and of such other persons as the local Governments might think fit, upon the question of the re-introduction of Oaths, and also upon the proposition of Her Majesty's Commissioners that all Oaths and Affirmations be dispensed with, and generally to invite the opinions of the public upon the subject.

Agreed to.

MR. LEGEYT said, he thought that, before dismissing the subject, they should come to a distinct understanding as to what was to be done, either that a Select Committee should be appointed for the purpose of considering and settling the letter to be addressed; or that the letter, when drawn up by the Clerk of the Council, should be circulated among the Members, and brought forward at the next Meeting, when it might be proposed that the following letter be sent to the Government of India and the local Governments. This would have the advantage of ensuring a wider circulation, for the letter would be read, and reported in the newspapers, and men's minds would be turned towards the matter, before the official communications reached them.

After some conversation—

MR. LEGEYT moved that the Clerk be directed to frame and circulate the letter among the Members of the Council, and that the letter be afterwards submitted to the Council for adoption.

Agreed to.

RYOTWAR ARREARS (MADRAS PRESIDENCY).

MR. FORBES gave notice that he would on Saturday next move for a Committee of the whole Council on the Bill "for the better recovery of Arrears of Revenue under Ryotwar Settlements in the Madras Presidency."

The Council adjourned.

Saturday, November 27, 1858.

PRESENT:

The Hon'ble the Chief Justice, *Vice-President*, in the Chair.

Hon'ble J. P. Grant,	E. Currie, Esq.,
Hon'ble Lieut.-Genl. Sir J. Outram,	Hon'ble Sir A. W. Buller,
Hon'ble H. Ricketts,	H. B. Harington, Esq., and
Hon'ble B. Peacock,	H. Forbes, Esq.
P. W. LeGeyt, Esq.,	

ACTS OF THE COUNCIL.

THE CLERK reported to the Council that he had received from the Home Department a Despatch from the Secretary of State for India reviewing Acts I to XIX of 1858.

LIMITS OF FORTS (PRESIDENCY TOWNS, &c.).

THE CLERK reported that he had received from the Home Department papers regarding the limits of the Forts at the Presidency Towns and in the Straits Settlement, which it was proposed to exclude from the jurisdiction of the Commissioners of Police and Municipal Commissioners.

OFFICE OF CORONER (STRAITS SETTLEMENT).

THE CLERK reported that he had received a communication from the Governor of the Straits Settlement on the subject of the abolition of the Office of Coroner in that Settlement, or its limitation to the precincts of the Towns only of the several Stations.

MR. PEACOCK moved that the above communication be printed.

Agreed to.

SMALL CAUSE COURTS (MOFUSSIL).

MR. HARINGTON moved the second reading of the Bill "for the establishment of Courts of Small Causes beyond the local limits of the jurisdiction of the Supreme Courts of Judicature established by Royal Charter."

SIR ARTHUR BULLER said, he hailed with great satisfaction the appearance of this Bill. He looked upon it as a move in the right direction, and peculiarly opportune and valuable at the present moment, as he thought the Council were in no slight danger of marring all its attempts at judicial reforms by beginning at the wrong end. They had disposed, he hoped satisfactorily, of the principal difficulties of Procedure, but they had still to deal with the more important question of the reform of our Courts. He thought he was not wrong in calling that the more important question, for surely the interests of justice were far more substantially secured by the trustworthiness and efficiency of the functionaries by which it was administered than by any simplicity or perfection of Procedure; and when he spoke of the danger of their beginning at the wrong end, his fear was that, instead of directing their best efforts so to purify and improve our Courts of first instance that they should be the least likely to go wrong, they might be induced to leave them too much as they were, and to expend their ingenuity and their resources in devising the best means of correcting their errors after they had been committed. This fear was the more natural, because the course he was deprecating not only offered a more inviting opportunity for the exercise of their legislative invention, but because it had the additional attraction of being essentially the course recommended by the high authority of the Royal Commissioners He welcomed this Bill, therefore, as boldly enunciating an opposite principle. He welcomed it because he saw in it a deliberate, and, as far as he could judge, a well considered plan to supplant, wherever it could be done, the existing Courts in which they had no faith, by better and more trustworthy tribunals. He fully felt the boldness of questioning any scheme which had the sanction of gentlemen of such experience and acknowledged ability as the Royal Commissioners. But nevertheless he would not shrink from declaring his strong conviction that the scheme, as developed in the Blue-Book, was open to many serious objections, but eminently to the objection of beginning at the wrong end. It elaborated with the greatest care a wide-embracing, though still, he believed, impracticable system of appeals. But it did nothing to elevate the character of the inferior Courts of original jurisdiction; and leaving them in their normal state of inefficiency, it multiplied their chances of doing mischief by on the one hand extending their jurisdiction, and on the other by taking away in the vast majority of cases the right of appeal, which was the only safeguard they possessed against the certainty of not unfrequent failure of justice.

The great merit of this Bill on the contrary was that it boldly enunciated the principle of prevention and not of cure, and struck at the root of the real mischief. It was useless disguising or hesitatingly admitting the fact that the Moonsiffs' Courts were utterly untrustworthy. Such was notoriously the case; and instead of taxing their ingenuity to discover the sort of superstructure that should sit most safely upon that rotten foundation, they had far better devote their best energies to the repairs of the foundation itself, for in his belief the cunningest scheme of appeals they could devise would do but very little towards defeating the organized and time-honored corruption of the existing Courts.

[Here Sir Arthur Buller was obliged to resume his seat; being prevented by indisposition from proceeding farther.]

THE VICE-PRESIDENT said, he entirely agreed with the Honorable and learned Member who had just spoken, and regretted that indisposition had prevented his saying more. The Bill might to some seem open to the objection, that it proposed but a partial remedy, and that it established Courts only in certain Districts. The Bill originally proposed by the Honorable and learned Member (Mr. Peacock) provided for the establishment in every village and in every locality of Small Cause Courts having final jurisdiction except in reserved cases, or on what was known as special appeals on points of law. It must, however, be admitted that the large body of evidence elicited by the re-publication of that Bill, showed a general opinion that Moonsiffs could not be trusted with that jurisdiction. He did not pretend to say whether that opinion was right or not, but he thought that the Honorable and learned Member and the Council had exercised a sound discretion in not attempting to force the Bill on the community in opposition to a feeling so generally entertained. On the other hand, the Council had the recommendations of Her Majesty's Commissioners, which would leave the jurisdiction of the Moonsiffs much as it was, with the old system of appeals.

This Bill was framed on a correct principle, but the measure was to be regarded as experimental. The new Courts would be introduced at first into certain places, and, when tested, he had no doubt that in a few years they would be extended. He therefore saw nothing in the objection that the Bill would favor certain localities, for other places would ultimately share in the benefits.

In addition to what had fallen from the Honorable and learned Member who preceded him, he must say that, not only as regards Courts of first instance, but also as regards all Courts, the Code of Civil Procedure was an imperfect remedy, and they must hope that a reform of the Courts would be among the measures of judicial reform to be introduced by their successors, if not by themselves.

The Select Committee on the Procedure Bill had considered several schemes for the re-constitution of the Courts, but feeling that financial and other considerations might retard the adoption of any one of their schemes, and the creation of new Courts which it involved, they had thought fit to present the Code of Procedure, as being, so far as it went, a remedial measure. He must repeat, however, that it was to be considered as an instalment only in the way of judicial reform. He would further say that, although his Honorable and learned friend had accurately described the Moonsiffs' Courts as the root of the evil, he thought that they must look higher also, and to the very top of the tree, and that no substantial good would be done until some measure was devised by which the Sudder Court was relieved from the great pressure of work which at present clogged its action.

Another most important consideration connected with the constitution of improved Courts of original jurisdiction was, that some solution, satisfactory to a large and increasing class of the community, might thereby be afforded of that question which, however shelved for a time, must ever recur, and must sooner or later be decided, namely, the provision of competent tribunals for the trial of Europeans at such a distance from the Presidency Towns as to make the wide Criminal jurisdiction of the Supreme Courts sometimes nugatory, and always most difficult and expensive.

Taking this Bill as far as it went, he thought that the Council was under great obligation to the Honorable Member for the North-Western Provinces for its introduction.

MR. LEGEYT said, no one felt more deeply than he did the weight of obligation under which the Council lay to the Honorable Member for the North-Western Provinces for the introduction of the present Bill. But he was sorry he could not support the Bill. In bringing it forward, he was sure that the Honorable Mover had felt that the Code of Civil Procedure, the rules contained in which were proposed to be followed for the disposal of cases under this Bill, was an imperfect and insufficient measure. He had no objection to the principle involved in this Bill, of conferring final jurisdiction on Courts of original jurisdiction. but he confessed he did not approve of the Bill as brought forward in its present shape, and he would have much preferred if the whole question of the re-constitution of the Courts had been first brought forward. He looked upon the Bill as a patchwork and piecemeal sort of legislation.

Probably this Bill would pass, but it would take some time before it came into operation, since the several local Governments would probably have different views as to how these Courts should be constituted, and by whom they should be presided over. If, therefore, instead of this Bill, a measure had been brought forward having the effect of forcing on the question of the constitution of the Courts, it would have been the first step in the right direction. That the judicial administration of this country required improvement, had never been denied. The question had been before the Legislature for several years past, and had been fully discussed. Very little, however, had proceeded as yet from that discussion. The Bill "for the more easy recovery of small debts and demands" which was suffered to drop still-born at an advanced period of gestation, and the present Bill, were the only practical attempts which had been made to amend the present course of the administration of Civil Justice; for the Civil Procedure Bill (he spoke particularly in reference to the Presidency of Bombay) would not alter it in any material point. The judicial administration required improvement, not from the untrustworthiness of the Native Judges, for he believed there was no great extent of corruption among them. In his opinion there were not more faithful or assiduous Officers of Government than the Native Judges; but they did not give satisfaction, and why so? The cause he thought was attributable solely to the Procedure. He observed that all persons—plaintiffs, defendants, and witnesses—united in condemnation of our Courts. Defendants complained probably because they were compelled to pay their debts, but plaintiffs had just cause of complaint. They complained of the tedious process of recovering what was their due, and of the still more tedious process of putting the decree (when they obtained one) into execution. Witnesses complained of being taken and detained from their homes at a very inadequate remuneration. All these classes of non-contents had united in the outcry against the present system, to which no sufficient answer had yet been given. But now the time had arrived when a remedy must be devised, and that remedy was a total re-organization of the Courts from the lowest to the highest. He would propose only two classes of Courts, namely, Small Cause Courts with original jurisdiction limited to a certain sum, and Courts in each district composed of three Judges having final jurisdiction. The Small Cause Courts should be presided over by Judges possessing the confidence of the people. But he would not give the present Courts final jurisdiction. The verdict of the country was against such a measure, and he could not see how the Council could force upon so large a population as that of India any thing short of what he had proposed.

This Bill however did not go far enough. It provided for final jurisdiction under fifty Rupees, and so far so good. But it did not meet the universal objection advanced to giving certain Judges that power. If it was intended that Natives should not preside over these Courts, then there must be European Judges only. He thought himself that Natives should not preside over these Courts, and that they should be presided over by Europeans. But such a general innovation would require the gravest deliberation before it was adopted.

If the Civil Procedure Bill was not sufficient to make the administration as perfect as it should be, and he took the very introduction of this Bill to be an admission to that effect, he would respectfully advocate the postponement of the present Bill till measures had been adopted for determining the question of a reform in the constitution of our Civil Courts If this should be conceded, he was prepared to move for the appointment of a Select Committee to enquire and report on the subject, with instructions to report progress monthly to the Council till its labors on the subject were completed. In the course of six months, he thought, the Committee would have ample materials from which to prepare a law, which, he believed, might be perfectly satisfactory to Government and the public. He did not think the Code of Procedure would answer. Its elaborate provisions were not necessary, and they must adopt a much more simple procedure. The present system was unsuited to the genius of the people and was far beyond them. They were not prepared for the niceties of our judicial system.

Under this view of the subject, he should feel it his duty to oppose at present the second reading of this Bill.

MR. PEACOCK said, every one who knew anything of the Courts of Justice in this country must be anxious to see them improved. The constitution of new Courts presented various and great difficulties, not only on financial considerations, but also on account of the materials from which the Courts must be composed. But he had no doubt that these difficulties would eventually be got over. The Select Committee on the Civil Procedure Bill had anxiously considered this question, but had not come to a final conclusion.

He was surprised however to hear the Honorable Member for Bombay speak as he had done, when he expressed a wish that some one should introduce a Bill to force on a consideration of the question Such a speech might have come from one who had not been a Member of the Select Committee on the Civil Procedure Bill, but the Honorable Member was a Member of that Committee. Why the Honorable Member had changed his opinion, since that Committee presented their Report, he (Mr. Peacock) knew not; but he found it stated as follows in the Report of that Committee:—

"The important subject of the constitution of the Civil Courts has been much considered by us, and various schemes (chiefly concerning Bengal and the North-Western Provinces) have been proposed for consideration; as yet we are not prepared to report upon this subject, and we do not think it necessary to delay the Report on the several Bills and the further progress of this Bill, through its subsequent stages, until schemes have been matured for all the Presidencies, and until sanction has been attained for the increased expenditure which it seems probable will be necessary whatever schemes may be ultimately adopted. When the Bills relating to Criminal Procedure have been revised by Select Committees, and when it has been considered in what mode and among what Courts jurisdiction in Criminal matters should be distributed, and also to what extent Appeals in Criminal cases should be allowed, the subject of the constitution of the Courts and the several schemes devised may be more conveniently discussed in the form of a separate Bill. The Bill prepared by us, as it now stands, provides a form of Procedure fitted equally to the Civil Courts at present established, and to those which may hereafter be substituted for them."

Now the Honorable Member had signed that Report. Had he since changed his views? Why did he now wish some one to force on a consideration of the matter and that this Bill be postponed? The Council could not provide for the constitution of the Courts without consulting the Executive Government, and probably the Home Authorities, upon the financial question necessarily involved in it. The Select Committee had therefore thought it better that the Code should not be delayed on this account. The Honorable Member for Bombay, however, who had signed the Report of that Committee, and who had agreed to it, with one exception (he, Mr. Peacock, believed), now came forward to propose a postponement of the Code of Procedure, and to say that that Code was cumbrous. Why did he not oppose it, when the Bill was in Committee? He (Mr. Peacock) should have thought from his speech that the Honorable Member had not been a Member of that Committee.

He was glad to see this Bill brought forward. He was an advocate for passing the former Bill "for the more easy recovery of small debts and demands." But such strong objections had been made to giving Moonsiffs final jurisdiction even to the extent of fifty

Rupees, that he did not press the third reading of that Bill. Her Majesty's Commissioners had about the same time reported that, if the Code of Procedure were passed, there would be no necessity for Small Cause Courts.

This Bill would enable the local Governments, with the sanction of the Supreme Government, to establish Small Cause Courts, and, without waiting for sanction, to invest certain existing Courts with Small Cause jurisdiction. It enabled the local Governments to appoint better Judges than now existed for the trial of small causes where such Courts might be considered most necessary, and it gave them final jurisdiction under fifty Rupees. Under these circumstances he was determined to give the Bill his support.

He could not think it necessary, after what the Select Committee had stated in their Report, to appoint another Committee to consider the constitution of the Courts. The Honorable Member for Bombay could bring the question again before the Select Committee, or if he wished to press the whole Council to a decision upon the subject, he could bring in a Bill of his own. There was nothing to prevent him from adopting that course.

[Mr. LeGeyt.—The Select Committee was discharged.]

The Select Committee had not been discharged so far as the question of the re-constitution of the Courts had to be considered, as he (Mr. Peacock) understood it. It was easy for the Honorable Member to introduce a Bill. Why should he wish that some one else should do that which it was competent to himself to do?

Mr. Ricketts said that, after the good reasons given by the Honorable and learned Member (Mr. Peacock) for the delay in bringing forward the general question of the re-organization of the Courts, it was useless for him to say anything on the subject. They were all aware how anxious all classes were that the question should be pushed forward. Only a few days ago, a paper had been communicated to the Legislative Council by the Government of India, being an extract from a letter addressed by it to the Bengal Government, relative to the necessity of relieving the Sudder Court of a large mass of its least important business, in order to allow the regular number of Judges to dispose of the most important portion satisfactorily and without falling into arrears. It had lately been determined that the system of full benches for hearing special appeals should not be interfered with. Of course expense was augmented by that system; but seeing that all parties—pleaders, suitors, Judge, and Government—had expressed approval of it, it was not thought proper for the sake of a small saving to alter it. It appeared from the Report of the Select Committee on the Civil Procedure Bill that the question of the re-organization of the Courts was postponed on the ground of expense; but it was very desirable that the re-organization of the Courts should be effected without any delay that could be avoided.

Mr. Harington said, he would endeavor to answer the objections of the Honorable Member for Bombay, first thanking the Honorable and learned Judge on his left (Sir Arthur Buller) and other Honorable Members for the favorable notice taken by them of his humble efforts in bringing in the present Bill.

The charge made by the Honorable Member for Bombay against the Bill was the same as had been brought against other measures introduced by him, namely, that it was piecemeal legislation, but he apprehended that all legislation partook more or less of that character.

If he had understood the Honorable Member rightly, he did not object altogether to the Bill so far as it went, but he considered that it did not go nearly far enough. Now it was just this objection of not going far enough which had been the means of depriving the North-Western Provinces and the Lower Provinces of the Presidency of Bengal at least, for the space of nearly four years, of the great benefits which might have been expected to result from the establishment of Courts of Small Causes in those Provinces, and which, if the views of the Honorable Member for Bombay were adopted by a majority of the Council, would, he ventured to predict, have the further effect of postponing the establishment of Courts of that description for an indefinite period. The same objection had already proved itself in one instance a fatal apple of discord, and, if acted upon in respect to the Bill under discussion, such, he feared, would again be its character.

In the year 1854, Mr. Mills and himself were engaged, under the orders of the Supreme Government, in preparing a Code of Civil Procedure for the use of the Courts of the East India Company in the three Presidencies, but knowing how urgent was the demand throughout the country for Courts which should have power summarily to dispose of petty actions of debt and the like according to a simple mode of procedure, they put aside for a time the work on which they were specially employed, and drew up a Bill for the more easy recovery of small debts and demands which they at once submitted for the consideration of the Governor General in Council, and which, on the establishment of this Legislature, was transferred to it exactly, he believed, in the form in which it had been prepared by Mr. Mills and himself.

In that Bill it was proposed that the Government should have power to constitute separate Courts of Small Causes for the trial of the simpler classes of suits, wherever the amount of litigation promised to afford sufficient employment for the Officers appointed to preside in those Courts, and, where such was not the case, to invest any of the Judges of the existing Courts with Small Cause Jurisdiction, who might be reported by the Sudder Courts qualified in all respects to exercise the same. This provision for the gradual introduction of a system of Courts of Small Causes, as fitting instruments could be found for successfully carrying it out, met with the cordial approval, he believed he might say, of nearly all the local authorities who were consulted at the time, and who must be regarded as amongst those best qualified to give an opinion on the subject. Amongst the authorities who supported the proposition of Mr. Mills and himself, were the present Lieutenant-Governor of Bengal and the late Lieutenant-Governor of the North-Western Provinces, Mr. Colvin. The Select Committee, however, to whom the Bill was referred for report, took a different view. They thought that the Bill did not go far enough, and they accordingly recommended, and a Committee of the whole Council adopted their recommendation, that the Section which Mr. Mills and himself had introduced should be struck out, and that a new Section should be substituted for it by which the Court of every Moonsiff in the Country without distinction would, simply by the passing of the Bill, have been constituted a Court of Small Causes for the trial of suits up to the amount of fifty Rupees.

The opinion of the public on this amendment was invited by the republication of the Bill, and as was noticed by him in the remarks which he had ventured to address to the Council in introducing the present Bill, the result of the invitation was an almost unanimous verdict in favor of the Section proposed by Mr. Mills and himself; and against the amendment adopted by the Committee of the whole Council on the recommendation of the Select Committee. He would not take up the time of the Council to-day by reading again the opinions elicited on this point. Those opinions were embodied in the printed papers which were in the hands of Honorable Members, and any Honorable Member could refer to them if he pleased.

Before the subject again came under discussion, the Code of Civil Procedure prepared in England by Her Majesty's Commissioners for the use of the Civil Courts in this country was received in Calcutta, and as the framers of that Code declared that the procedure which it prescribed would, in the simpler classes of suits, be equally expeditious and economical with that followed in the Courts of Small Causes at Calcutta, Madras, and Bombay, a plausible ground presented itself for postponing the further consideration of the Bill before the Council, and it had continued quietly to slumber in the Office of the Clerk of the Council from that time to this, nor did he think that, in so far as the particular amendment of the Select Committee to which he had been referring was concerned, its repose would ever be disturbed, for he could not conceive that in the face of the strong and decided opinion, which had been so generally pronounced against the amendment in question, the Council would insist upon it as a condition of any Bill of this nature which might be passed that it should be enforced at once throughout the country. As had been remarked by him on a former occasion, he did not think that this course would consist with their duty to the public.

Had the original proposition of Mr. Mills and himself been allowed to stand, and looking to the very favorable reception which it had so generally met with, he certainly did think that it was a subject of deep regret that it had been put aside for the amendment proposed by the Select Committee on the Bill, there could scarcely be a doubt that Courts of Small Causes would long since have been established at the Sudder Stations of the different Districts and in all the principal Towns and Cities in the interior to the great benefit of the people residing in those places; but the objection mentioned by him was raised, and what had been the consequence? Why, at the end of 1858, instead of the greater part of the country being covered with Courts of Small Causes, they were engaged in debating only whether a Bill, for the establishment of Courts of that description, should be allowed to be read a second time.

The Honorable Member for Bombay in the speech which he had just delivered, had given them a sketch of the Courts which he was anxious to see established, but without further information, and indeed until the plan of the Honorable Member had assumed a more definite shape, it was difficult to form an opinion as to its merits. If, however, the Honorable Member would bring in a Bill embodying the scheme of Courts which he was disposed to prefer to the plan proposed by him (Mr. Harington), he promised to give it his best attention, and to divest himself, as far as possible, of those feelings of favoritism which every parent was supposed to entertain for his own offspring, in order that he might subject the measure of the Honorable Member to a fair and impartial comparison with the Bill introduced by him, and should the result of that comparison be favorable to the scheme of the Honorable Member and that scheme should appear to him suited to the part of the country which he had the honor to represent, he would at once abandon his own Bill and support the Bill of the Honorable Member. But he begged the Honorable Member to bear in mind the great length of time that the subject of the future constitution of the Courts in this country had been under the consideration of the Council, and that up to the present time little, if any, progress had been made towards the solution of this very difficult question. If therefore the Honorable Member really contemplated introducing a Bill, he must be allowed to express a hope that no time would be lost in bringing it in

It was scarcely necessary for him to add that this was not a final measure. He had never pretended that it was. It was a beginning only; but, as remarked by the Honorable and learned Judge on his left (Sir Arthur Buller), it was, he believed, a beginning in the right direction, and to show the extent to which it went, it was sufficient for him to say that it was calculated that in the North-Western Provinces at least sixty per cent of the entire civil business arising within those Provinces would be cognizable under the provisions of the present Bill should it pass into law; so that, although the Bill certainly professed to deal with little suits only, he thought that the Honorable Member of Council opposite (Mr. Ricketts) would admit that it was not a "little Bill". This brought him to the observations which had fallen from the Honorable Member of Council in respect to the large amount of business which now devolved upon the Sudder Courts, and here also the Bill brought in by him would operate most beneficially, since it proposed to cut off the right of special appeal to the Sudder Court in all cases of debt and the like, cognizable under the Bill, in which the amount or value of the property in dispute did not exceed the sum of five hundred Rupees. In every such case, under the present system, however trifling in amount, the parties might prefer a special appeal to the Sudder Court, and the relief therefore which the Bill would afford to that Court would be very large.

The Honorable and learned Member of Council on his left (Mr. Peacock) had fully answered the objections made by the Honorable Member for Bombay to the Code of Civil Procedure which had recently been settled by a Committee of the whole Council, and, as regarded that Code, he would merely repeat what he had formerly said that, although, no doubt, some of its provisions were not suited to cases of the simple character to which the present Bill was intended to apply, he still thought that the Code contained sufficiently simple and summary rules for the trial and determination of the simplest classes of suits.

The Honorable Member for Bombay considered that the Bill left it uncertain who were to be appointed to preside in the Courts which it was proposed to constitute, and whether the Judges were to be Europeans or Natives, and he also seemed to think that there would be some difficulty in finding fitting men for the appointment. He (Mr. Harington) did not anticipate that the difficulty noticed by the Honorable Member for Bombay could arise; he had no doubt that, if adequate salaries were given, there would be no want of qualified candidates from amongst whom suitable selections might be made. He hoped to see some of the appointments filled by English Barristers, and with more liberal salaries, he thought that after a little time it would be found that better educated and altogether a superior class of natives would be induced to join the Judicial branch of the public service. But if it was really the case that competent Judges were not obtainable for the Courts which he wished to see established, notwithstanding that the Government might be willing to pay them liberally, all that he could say was that it was useless their attempting to reform the subordinate Civil Courts. He had certainly no intention of excluding natives from sitting as Judges in the Courts on which the task of carrying out the provisions of the Bill would devolve. This, he thought, was clear from the second Section, which gave the Government power to invest any of the existing Courts with Small Cause jurisdiction, and he need not tell the Honorable Member for Bombay that a very large proportion of the Judges presiding in those Courts were Natives. With regard to the reconstitution generally of the Courts in this country not established by Royal Charter, with a view to their improvement, he might observe that the great difficulty with which they had to contend arose out of the present state of the public finances, which it was feared would prove a serious obstacle in the way of the adoption of any scheme which they might consider themselves justified in recommending. The Honorable the Lieutenant-Governor of Bengal had proposed a plan of Courts which had been generally approved by the Select Committee on the Civil Procedure Bill; but it was calculated that to carry it out effectually it would cost ten lakhs of Rupees at least over and above the existing judicial charges of the Presidency of Bengal alone, and it seemed almost hopeless to expect that the Government would assent at the present time to this additional expenditure in a single branch of the public service.

He believed that he had now noticed all that particularly called for remark in what had fallen from the Honorable Member for Bombay, and it only remained for him to press his motion for the second reading of the Bill.

RYOTWAR ARREARS (MADRAS PRESIDENCY).

MR. FORBES moved that the Council resolve itself into a Committee on the Bill "for the better recovery of arrears of Revenue under Ryotwar Settlements in the Madras Presidency;" and that the Committee be instructed to consider the Bill in the amended form in which the Select Committee had recommended it to be passed.

Agreed to.

Section I provided for the repeal of Act XXIII of 1856.

MR. CURRIE said that Act XXIII contained a provision for indemnity for previous acts. In repealing that Act, it would be well to save the indemnity. He therefore moved the addition of the following words :—

"except so far as relates to indemnity for any thing done before the passing of that Act."

The motion was carried, and the Section then passed.

Section II provided as follows:—

"Whenever the Revenue or rent of any such lands is withheld beyond the day on which it falls due according to the Kistbundy or other engagement, or where no particular day is fixed, then beyond the time when such Revenue or rent becomes payable agreeably to local usage, the Collector shall have authority to proceed for the recovery of such arrears by the distress and the sale of the moveable property or the sale of the immoveable property of the defaulter wherever found."

MR. RICKETTS said, he wished to add a Proviso to this Section to the following purport—

"Provided that standing crops, bullocks necessary to the cultivation of a tenant's holding, ploughs, and implements of husbandry, and the tools of artisans shall not be subject to distraint or sale."

The existing laws excepted all the articles above enumerated, except standing crops, from liability to distraint or sale. By Section IV Regulation XXVIII. 1802 it was enacted that—

"The ploughs and implements of husbandry, the cattles actually trained to the plough, and the seed-grain of under-farmers, tenants, or ryots, shall not be distrained for arrears of rent or revenue, so long as other property may be forthcoming equal to the discharge of such arrears; distrainers deviating from this rule shall be punished by an award, to the party aggrieved, of damages adequate to the injury sustained, with costs of suit."

The same provision was contained in Section IV Regulation XVII. 1793, as modified by Section XIV Regulation V. 1812 of the Bengal Code; and in Regulation XVII 1827 of the Bombay Code. Unless therefore good reason was shown, it would be well to make a similar exception in this Bill. It could not be good for Government to be concerned in cutting, carrying, reaping, and storing crops. Enquiry would show the expenses attending such proceedings to be a great objection. In a Bill relating to the recovery of Government Revenue, he could not think it becoming to give powers to sell the implements of husbandry and tools of artisans when they were withheld from others.

MR. FORBES said, he was sorry he could not agree to the proposed amendment. The old laws provided for the sale of the crop after it had been reaped and gathered, and he could not see any reason for saying that the Collector should not sell a standing crop if he could reap and thresh it and then sell the out-turn. It must be remembered also that the present Bill enabled the Collector to sell the land of a defaulter, and if necessary to imprison him, and it was not clear of what advantage it would be to a man to be left in possession of his bullock and ploughs when he had no land to cultivate. Although the Bill empowered a Collector to sell the bullocks of a defaulter, there was nothing in it which would oblige him to do so if, all things considered, he determined that it would be inexpedient to do so. He (Mr. Forbes) hoped that this consideration would induce the Honorable Member not to press his amendment.

MR. CURRIE said that, by Section VI, standing crops could only be distrained and sold when fit for reaping and gathering. The crop was the main security for the Revenue; and he thought it would never do to except standing crops from distraint altogether, for that would be to give the defaulter the opportunity of making away with them.

The motion was put and negatived, and the Section then passed.

Sections III and IV were passed as they stood.

Section V provided for the withdrawal of distress on tender of arrear and expenses "in the presence of two credible witnesses."

MR. RICKETTS moved that the words above quoted be omitted.

The motion was carried, and the Section as amended then passed.

Sections VI to XIV were passed as they stood.

Section XV was passed after verbal amendments.

Section XVI was passed as it stood.

Section XVII was passed after a slight amendment.

Sections XVIII to XXIII were passed as they stood.

Section XXIV provided for the arrest of the defaulter where arrears could not be liquidated by distress.

Mr. RICKETTS said, he had a few words to add to this Section. In discussing the Code of Civil Procedure, the Council had lately decided that persons should not be imprisoned for long terms for small sums. Adopting this principle he would move the addition here of the following words :—

"But no person shall be imprisoned on account of an arrear of revenue for a longer period than two years, or for a longer period than six months if the arrear does not exceed five hundred Rupees, or for a longer period than three months if the arrear does not exceed fifty Rupees.

Mr. FORBES explained that this Section provided only for cases where the debtor had been guilty of wilful concealment, or of some fraudulent transaction. Practically speaking, it was a power which would hardly ever be exercised. There was this difference between the part of the Civil Procedure Code to which the Honorable Member had referred, and the present Section. The Section of the Code of Civil Procedure provided for the case of a man who could pay his debt but could not, while this Section was to refer to those who could pay and would not.

The motion was put and carried, and the Section as amended then passed.

Section XXV was passed after a slight amendment.

Sections XXVI and XXVII were severally passed as they stood.

Section XXVIII was passed after a slight amendment.

Sections XXIX to XXXI, and the Preamble and Title, were severally passed as they stood.

The Council having resumed its sitting, the Bill was reported.

SALES OF LAND FOR ARREARS OF REVENUE (BENGAL).

Mr. GRANT moved that Mr. Ricketts be added to the Select Committee on the Bill "to improve the law relating to sales of land for arrears of Revenue in the Bengal Presidency."

Agreed to.

SMALL CAUSE COURTS (MOFUSSIL).

Mr. HARINGTON moved that the Bill "for the establishment of Courts of Small Causes beyond the local limits of the jurisdiction of the Supreme Courts of Judicature established by Royal Charter" be referred to a Select Committee, consisting of Mr. Peacock, Mr. LeGeyt, Mr. Currie, Mr. Forbes, and the Mover.

Agreed to.

NOTICES OF MOTION.

Mr. CURRIE gave notice that he would, on Saturday next, move the second reading of the Bill "to amend the law for the trial of Officers of the Bengal Pilot Service accused of breach of duty."

Also the third reading of the Bill "for making better provision for the care of the persons and property of Minors in the Presidency of Fort William in Bengal."

And for a Committee of the whole Council on the Bill "for the amendment of the law relating to Merchant Seamen."

IMPRESSMENT OF CARRIAGE AND SUPPLIES FOR TROOPS (BENGAL).

Mr. LeGEYT moved that a communication, received by him from the Bombay Government, be laid upon the table and referred to the Select Committee on the Bill "to amend the law regarding the provision of Carriage and Supplies for Troops and Travellers, and to punish unlawful impressment."

OATHS AND AFFIRMATIONS.

Mr. CURRIE moved that the draft of the letter to the Government of India and the local Governments on the subject of Judicial oaths and affirmations (which was circulated by the Clerk for approval) be adopted.

Sir JAMES OUTRAM moved that the following words be inserted after the word "persons" in the 1st paragraph of the letter :—

"European or Native, selected for their knowledge and experience, without reference to class or position, and whether Government employés or not."

Agreed to.

SIR JAMES OUTRAM moved that the following question be inserted in the letter, namely :—

"Is it desirable that false testimony by witnesses after simple affirmation or warning should be liable to the same penalties as now assigned to perjury under oath?"

After some conversation, the motion was by leave withdrawn.

MR. LEGEYT moved that the following question be inserted in the letter, namely :—

"Is it desirable that every Court before which a witness is judicially examined should have the power of inflicting summary punishment for wilful false testimony?

"Is it desirable, in the event of summary punishment being sanctioned for false testimony, that the present penalties for perjury should be restricted to fine for lesser, and to a moderate imprisonment and fine for more serious cases?

"Is it desirable that there should be a right of appeal against such convictions, or would it be preferable to provide that all sentences should be subject to the confirmation of the next Superior Court?"

MR. CURRIE said, these questions were not directly connected with the questions upon which the Council had determined to ask for information, and they had not been brought under the consideration of the Council. He felt some difficulty, without further consideration, in expressing any opinion on them, but his immediate impression was that it would be very unadvisable to give to every Court the power of punishing summarily any witness who, it might think, was giving false testimony. The subject, however, was altogether distinct from that before the Council, and he thought that it should not be mixed up with it.

THE VICE-PRESIDENT agreed, and said that the questions had reference more properly to the Code of Criminal Procedure.

The motion was by leave withdrawn, and the letter, as amended on Sir James Outram's motion, adopted.

The Council adjourned.

Saturday, December 4th, 1858.

PRESENT.

The Hon'ble the Chief Justice, *Vice-President,* in the Chair.

Hon. J. P. Grant.	E. Currie, Esq.
Hon. Lieut.-Genl. Sir J. Outram.	Hon. Sir A. W. Buller.
Hon. H. Ricketts.	H. B. Harington, Esq.
Hon. B. Peacock.	and
P. W. LeGeyt, Esq.	H. Forbes, Esq.

PILOT COURTS (BENGAL.)

MR. CURRIE moved the second reading of the Bill "to amend the law for the trial of Officers of the Bengal Pilot Service for breach of duty."

THE VICE-PRESIDENT said, he must for himself say that, although he had no desire to interfere with the second reading, he did not think the Bill provided the best tribunal for the trial of Pilots. The original constitution of the Court was based on the principle of composition of forces. Certain Merchants were to be Members of the Court, because, as Merchants, they were interested in shipping and in the safe navigation of the river and port. Certain Pilots were to be Members of the Court, because, as Pilots, they were interested in seeing that no member of the service suffered injustice. Certain Ship Captains, both because they were interested in seeing that no ships, through negligence, were run ashore, and also because they might be supposed to bring to the enquiry that professional knowledge which was so necessary. The Honorable Member for Bengal now proposed to leave out the Pilots, to which he (the Vice-President) had no great objection, if they were found to have too great a bias; and he proposed to retain two Merchants and one Captain. He thought there was no great use in retaining so much of the mercantile element. As far as his experience of

Calcutta went, the Merchants were not very fond of giving their time to this kind of enquiry, and he did not think that the interest which theymight be supposed to have in shipping was any reason for calling on them to give their time and to assist in enquiries of this nature. The sort of assistance which the President required was that of persons skilled in navigation generally, conversant with the management of the ships, and having some knowledge of the difficulties of this river, and, therefore, capable of assisting the Judge or the other Judges in weighing that conflicting evidence as to tides, currents, shoals, and the manœuvres of the vessel, which a trial of this kind seldom failed to exhibit.

He should have thought that, at the Bankshall, men might be found with the necessary qualifications and free from the imputation of bias. But if it were deemed desirable to have men with less connection with the Pilot Service, he would rather have recourse to Ship Captains than to the Merchants. As the Bill stood, there would be one Member of the Court with the special knowledge that was requisite, and two who did not possess that knowledge, and he thought that the working of the new tribunal, if its constitution were not altered in Committee, would not be satisfactory.

MR. PEACOCK said, it was not his intention to oppose the second reading, but he agreed with the Honorable and learned Vice-President in thinking that the tribunal provided by the Bill was not the best that could be devised. In the first place it was objectionable that the Judge should select his own Jury. In the next place, only the number of Jurors actually required for the trial was to be summoned. If these persons should not attend, they could be fined. But suppose one of them should be ill or unable to attend, the Court must be adjourned. It appeared to him that that was a mistake which should be rectified.

He agreed with the Honorable and learned Vice-President, that two Merchants and one Master of a Merchant Ship would not constitute the best tribunal for trying a case of negligence or misconduct in piloting a vessel. In England the Admiralty Court was assisted by two elder brothers of the Trinity House. The Judge did not select them as Jurors; they were only Assessors to assist him. But in this Bill three Jurors were to be selected by the Judge. This, and probably other points, would require consideration in Select Committee.

He did not approve of Section XIV, which provided as follows:—

"If it shall appear to the Judge of the said Court that the verdict of the Jurors is manifestly contrary to the evidence, or that the trial is otherwise insufficient, the Judge, instead of passing sentence on the accused person, or declaring him acquitted, as the case may be, may certify the same to the Lieutenant-Governor of Bengal. If the verdict of the Jurors be a verdict of acquittal, the said Lieutenant-Governor may either direct that no further proceedings shall be taken in the case, or may order a new trial before another Jury, as he shall think fit. If the verdict be a verdict of conviction, the said Lieutenant-Governor shall order a new trial before another Jury."

Under this Section there seemed to be no option given to the Lieutenant-Governor, in the case of a conviction, as there was in the case of an acquittal, of ordering a new trial or not. In the case of a conviction, the Lieutenant-Governor would be compelled to order a new trial; whereas, if the conviction should be manifestly contrary to the evidence, and there was no new evidence to be adduced, he could not see the benefit of ordering a new trial.

Then, as to Section XII, which authorized the Lieutenant-Governor, with the sanction of the Governor-General in Council, to prepare a schedule of offences and punishments for the guidance of the Court, he was not sure whether the punishment had not better be left to the Judge instead of leaving it to the Lieutenant-Governor to frame a schedule of offences and punishments. The schedule referred to was not a Code of Criminal law, otherwise he should have doubted how far the Council had power to sanction such a provision; but it was merely a case of dealing with servants of Government by reducing their rank or pay, or suspending them from employment for a limited period.

SIR ARTHUR BULLER said, there should be some provision giving the party accused a right of challenging the Jurors. It was obviously extremely likely that there might not be a good feeling between all Merchants and all Pilots.

MR. CURRIE said, he was far from supposing that the proposed Jury was, in all respects, the best tribunal that could possibly be devised; but it appeared to be the one most in accordance with the opinions which had been given by those who had recommended a reform of the Courts. Objection had been taken by his learned friends to the mercantile element. At present the Courts consisted of two Ship Captains, two Pilots, and four Merchants: it had been said by the former and present Presidents of Marine Courts that the only independent Members were the Merchants; and in all the suggestions which had been made, the retention of Merchants had been proposed. It had, therefore, seemed to him that, in constituting a Jury whose verdict should be according to the opinion of a majority, it was desirable that the Merchants should have a preponderance. He believed that the employment of Merchants on this duty originated with a proposal of the Chamber of Commerce. He concurred generally in what had been said by the Honorable and learned Vice-President, and in introducing the Bill, he had stated that his individual opinion would have been in favor of a Judge and professional Assessors. That was the plan upon which he had originally prepared the Bill; but the Lieutenant-Governor, whose opinion, from his long experience of the business of the Marine Department, was deserving of all respect, was strongly opposed to the plan of Assessors, and he had altered the Bill accordingly.

With regard to the objection of his Honorable and learned friend (Mr. Peacock), that it was not right that the Judge should select the Jury—as the law now stood, the Superintendent of Marine, who was, in fact, the Prosecutor, and not the Judge, had the selection. Surely it was better, if it rested between them, that the selection should be with the Judge rather than with the Prosecutor. Objection was also taken because the Bill did not provide for summoning a larger number of persons than would be necessary to form a Jury, inasmuch as the trial would be delayed if the attendance of one of them was prevented by sickness. But it seemed to him that there were great objections to summoning more persons than were really necessary. The number of Jurors prescribed by the Bill was very small; notice being given to each person that his attendance would be required on a future day, the Judge would be able, in case of any one signifying his inability to attend, to substitute another person.

As to Section XIV, he was not sure that he rightly apprehended the objection taken by his learned friend. If the verdict was one of acquittal, and the Judge thought it erroneous, a discretion was reserved to the Lieutenant-Governor; and this, he thought, was right, because, notwithstanding the opinion of the Judge, the Government might think further proceedings against the accused unnecessary. But if the verdict was one of conviction, and the Judge thought it contrary to the evidence, the Section allowed no discretion to the Lieutenant-Governor, but required him to order a new trial. This, he thought, was no more than what justice to the accused demanded.

MR. PEACOCK explained his meaning to be that, when the Lieutenant-Governor agreed with the Judge in thinking a verdict of conviction erroneous, it would be sufficient to stop the proceedings. He did not think that the Lieutenant-Governor should be obliged to order a new trial.

MR. CURRIE proceeded. With regard to Section XII he would only remind the Council that the punishment of Pilots for breaches of duty had, from a long course of years, been regulated by a Code framed by the Executive Government. Many suggestions had been made for revising and improving the Code, but no one had proposed to dispense with it altogether. The Section did not make it imperative that there should be such a Code; it merely recognized any Code which the Executive Government might think proper to frame, the punishments being exclusively of a kind which a master may inflict on his servants. He could see no objection to continuing this power to the Executive Government.

The motion was then put and carried, and the Bill read a second time.

DELHI TERRITORY.

MR. PEACOCK moved the third reading of the Bill "to repeal Regulation V. 1832 of the Bengal Code, and to make certain provisions rendered necessary by the transfer of the Delhi Territory to the administration of the Chief Commissioner of the Punjab."

The motion was carried, and the Bill read a third time.

RYOTWAR ARREARS (MADRAS PRESIDENCY).

MR. FORBES moved the third reading of the Bill "for the better recovery of arrears of Revenue under Ryotwar Settlements in the Madras Presidency."

MR. RICKETTS said, when this Bill was in Committee, he had endeavored to induce his Honorable friend, the Member for Madras, to introduce a proviso exempting standing crops and other articles from distraint or sale. But the Honorable Member was opposed to his amendment, and the Council rejected it. He felt quite sure, however, that he was beaten, not because the cause was a bad cause, but merely from the weakness of the advocacy. It was not—it could not be a bad cause. The subject had been considered by the Legislature of this country no less than five different times. First, in 1793, by Regulation XVII of the Bengal Code, ploughs and implements of husbandry, cattle actually trained to the plough, and the seed grain of under-farmers, ryots, and talookdars were exempted from distress. That exemption was adopted by the Madras Government in 1802, was again considered and adopted by the Government of the North-Western Provinces in 1803, and again reaffirmed in Bengal in 1813, and again in Bombay in 1827, which was the fifth time. Surely, Lord Cornwallis, Lord Wellesley, Lord Minto, and, above all, Mr. Elphinstone, were not all mistaken. He found in the Bombay Law (Regulation IV. 1827)—

"Such implements of manual labor, and such cattle and implements of agriculture as may, in the judgment of the Court from which the process issues, be indispensable for the defendant to earn a livelihood in his respective calling or cultivate any land that he may hold for the purpose, shall be exempt from attachment."

Those were words worthy of the great and good man who framed the law. They applied to process for the recovery of arrears of revenue, as well as to process in execution of decrees. Surely, after this indulgent and considerate policy had been approved by the Legislature five times in half a century, some reason should be assigned for reversing it. The matter might have been considered by the Select Committee, but there was no evidence that it had attracted their attention. It might seem a very little matter, but it was not a little matter to deprive a man of the means of earning a livelihood. The Honorable Member for Madras said that, as the defaulter was to be imprisoned and his lands sold, it could not much benefit him to exempt his cattle and implements of trade and agriculture. But they would be useful when he came out of Jail, and he could arrange for their safe custody meanwhile. He thought it probable that he should divide alone, but he could not attach his name to the third reading of this Bill without the insertion of the exemption in question. He hoped the Council would allow the Bill to be re-committed. He would not press for the exemption of standing crops; but the exemption introduced into previous laws should, he thought, be introduced into this Bill. He moved, by way of amendment, that the Bill be re-committed.

MR. FORBES said, he would at present offer no opinion on the Honorable Member's proposed amendment. The question now before the Council was—"Shall the Bill be re-committed or not?" As the youngest Member of the Council, it would ill become him to say what course should be followed with regard to the Honorable Member's amendment. But he thought it a very bad precedent now to establish that a question once decided by vote should, particularly without previous notice or intimation, be brought forward for re-consideration. It was not every Member that could attend all the meetings. Some had arduous duties elsewhere, which prevented their regular attendance. Those Members, when they saw by the Orders that a particular question was to be brought forward, might make a point of attending, and might then presume that the question was settled and would not be brought forward without previous intimation. As a matter of convenience, it was not right that questions should thus be re-opened. If the motion were carried, he would have an opportunity of replying to the arguments of the Honorable Member of Council.

MR. RICKETTS said that he did not wish to move the re-committal, but only to oppose the third reading.

MR. CURRIE said, he just wished to observe that the intended motion was not quite the same as that proposed at the last meeting. His objection to that motion was, that the exemption included standing crops. It made an important difference, that the amendment now proposed did not extend to them. He therefore thought that the Honorable Member was quite regular in moving for a re-committal.

THE VICE-PRESIDENT thought that it would be very unwise for the Council to lay down a rule against reconsidering a matter on which a vote had once been taken. Their object was to make their Bills as perfect as possible; and upon many subjects of debate Honorable Members might be found to alter the opinion which they had previously expressed. The question, however, could not now be said to have arisen here, for the Honorable Member's proposed amendment was different from that upon which the Council had voted at the last meeting.

MR. PEACOCK said, he thought that the Honorable Member was quite regular, if he wished it, to move for re-committal. He thought it very desirable that the Honorable Member should adopt that course in the first instance, instead of opposing the third reading upon a point which might possibly be amended. The vote of the Council had not been taken upon the simple question, whether implements of trade should be liable to be distrained; and he thought it would be better that that question should be discussed separately, without being encumbered by the question as to standing crops, with which it was mixed up in one motion at the last Meeting.

The amendment being put, the Council divided :—

Ayes 8.	*Noes* 2.
Sir Arthur Buller.	Mr. Forbes.
Mr. Currie.	Mr. Harington.
Mr. LeGeyt.	
Mr. Peacock.	
Mr. Ricketts.	
Sir J. Outram.	
Mr. Grant.	
The Vice-President.	

So the amendment was carried.

The Vice-President then retired from the Council Chamber, and Mr. Grant took the Chair.

MR. RICKETTS moved that the following proviso be added to Section II :—

" Provided that bullocks necessary to the cultivation of a tenant's holding, ploughs, and implements of husbandry, and the tools of artisans, shall not be subject to distraint or sale."

MR. FORBES said that the Honorable Member, in bringing forward this motion, had said that it would not be right to pass a law in opposition to laws passed by such eminent statesmen as Lords Cornwallis, Wellesley, and Minto, and Mr. Elphinstone. He (Mr. Forbes) however thought that that was hardly a sound argument, for it would equally apply to the amendment of any law, since every law had been passed in the time of some great man. The Council would recollect that a similar motion had been brought forward by the Honorable Member for Bombay, when the Code of Civil Procedure was in Committee, and rejected. He did not see why the Government should be in a worse position in the collection of their Revenue than the ordinary creditor was in the realization of debts due to him. It was true that hitherto the Madras law had exempted cattle and implements of trade and agriculture from sale. But that law was passed, not for the realization of the Government dues, but for the collection of arrears of rent due to zemindars by their ryots, the same law having been applied to collections by Government under Ryotwar Settlements.

It was reasonable to say that a zemindar should not have the power, for he probably would not be guided by

Mr. Forbes.

the same liberal principles as the Government. This Section did not make it imperative, and the Officers of Government would still be left with a discretion which, he had no doubt, they would use safely. He would therefore vote against the amendment.

The motion being put, the Council divided :—

Ayes 7.	*Noes* 2.
Sir Arthur Buller.	Mr. Forbes.
Mr. Currie.	Mr. Harington.
Mr. LeGeyt.	
Mr. Peacock.	
Mr. Ricketts.	
Sir J. Outram.	
The Chairman.	

So the motion was carried, and the Section as amended then passed.

The Council having resumed its sitting, the Bill was reported.

MR. FORBES moved that the Bill be read a third time and passed.

The motion was carried, and the Bill read a third time.

GUARDIANSHIP OF MINORS (BENGAL).

The Order of the Day for the third reading of the Bill "for making better provision for the care of the persons and property of Minors in the Presidency of Fort William in Bengal" being read—

MR. CURRIE moved that the Bill be re-committed to a Committee of the whole Council, for the purpose of considering proposed amendments therein.

Agreed to.

Section III provided as follows :—

"Every person who shall claim a right to have charge of property in trust for a Minor under a Will or other Deed, or by reason of nearness of kin, or otherwise, may apply to the Civil Court for a Certificate of administration ; and no person shall be competent to institute or defend any suit connected with the estate of which he claims the charge, or to give any legal discharge to the debtors of such estate, until he shall have obtained such Certificate."

MR. CURRIE moved for the omission of the word "other" before the word "Deed."

Agreed to.

MR. CURRIE moved for the substitution of the following for all the words after the word "administration" :—

"And no person shall be entitled to institute or defend any suit connected with the estate of which he claims the charge until he shall have obtained such Certificate. Provided that, when the property is of small value, or for any other sufficient reason, any Court having jurisdiction may allow any relative of a Minor to institute or defend a suit on his behalf, although a Certificate of administration has not been granted to such relative."

He said he might mention that, after the re-publication of the Bill, he had endeavored to obtain opinions from persons capable of judging as to how it might be expected to work in practice. One of the Judges of the Sudder Court had kindly favored him with some remarks. His opinion was very favorable: he said :—

"I reckon this one of the most useful Acts we have had for long."

With regard to this particular Section, he said :—

"Perhaps the latter part of Section III is too strictly prohibitory. Cases may arise in which it should suffice, without enforcing the general provisions of the Bill, to empower a near relation or friend to sue or to defend a suit on behalf of a Minor. I think power should be given to the Courts to appoint a manager for the purpose of carrying on a suit (and no more) on the Minor's behalf."

A native gentleman of experience had also taken the same objection to this Section as it stood, especially where the Minor's property was of small value, in which case the trouble and expense of obtaining a certificate might be quite out of proportion to the value of the property.

For these reasons, he begged to move the present amendment.

MR. PEACOCK said, he thought the proposed amendment a great improvement, especially as regarded defendants.

The motion was carried, and the Section as amended then passed.

Section VI provided for an enquiry being made by the Civil Court on application for the appointment of a fit person to take charge of the property and person of a Minor.

MR. CURRIE moved the addition of the following proviso:—

"Provided always that it shall be competent to the Civil Court to direct any Court subordinate to it to make such enquiry and report the result."

The motion was carried, and the Section as amended then passed.

Section XI provided for the appointment of a Guardian.

MR. CURRIE said, the two other amendments which he had to move had been suggested by some remarks of his learned friend opposite (Mr. Peacock), when the Bill was before in Committee. He seemed to think that the functions of the Guardian and the Administrator were not defined with sufficient precision. He now moved the addition of the following words to Section XI:—

"The Court may also fix such allowance, as it may think proper, for the maintenance of the Minor; and such allowance, and the allowance of the Guardian (if any), shall be paid to the Guardian by the public Curator or other person as aforesaid."

Agreed to.

MR. CURRIE then moved the insertion of the following new Section after Section XVII:—

"Every person to whom a Certificate shall have been granted under the provisions of this Act, may exercise the same powers in the management of the estate as might have been exercised by the Proprietor if not a Minor, and may collect and pay all just claims, debts, and liabilities due to, or by, the estate of the Minor. But no such person shall have power to sell or mortgage any immoveable property, or to grant a lease thereof for any period exceeding five years, without an order of the Civil Court previously obtained."

Agreed to.

The Council having resumed its sitting, the Bill was reported.

MR. CURRIE moved that the Bill be read a third time and passed.

The motion was carried, and the Bill read a third time.

MERCHANT SEAMEN.

MR. CURRIE postponed the motion (of which he had given notice for this day) for a Committee of the whole Council on the Bill "for the amendment of the law relating to Merchant Seamen."

PENSIONS.

MR. PEACOCK moved that the Report of the Select Committee on the project of a law for applying the provisions of the Government Order of the 1st December 1857, which affect Military Pensioners, to Pensioners in the Civil Department, and to the holders of rent-free lands, be adopted.

Agreed to.

RYOTWAR ARREARS (MADRAS PRESIDENCY).

MR. FORBES moved that Mr. Ricketts be requested to take the Bill "for the better recovery of arrears of Revenue under Ryotwar Settlements in the Madras Presidency" to the President in Council, in order that it might be submitted to the Governor-General for his assent.

Agreed to.

GUARDIANSHIP OF MINORS (BENGAL).

MR. CURRIE moved that Mr. Ricketts be requested to take the Bill "for making better provision for the care of the persons and property of Minors in the Presidency of Fort William in Bengal" to the President in Council, in order that it might be submitted to the Governor-General for his assent.

Agreed to.

DELHI TERRITORY.

MR. PEACOCK moved that Mr. Ricketts be requested to take the Bill "to repeal Regulation V. 1832 of the Bengal Code, and to make certain provisions rendered necessary by the transfer of the Delhi Territory to the administration of the Chief Commissioner of the Punjab" to the President in Council, in order that it might be submitted to the Governor-General for his assent.

Agreed to.

DRAINAGE OF CALCUTTA.

SIR ARTHUR BULLER said that, seeing his Honorable friend, the Member for Bengal, in his place, he would take leave to put to him a question which he believed would not wholly take him by surprize. He wished to ask him what steps had been taken to carry out the promise of the Act XXVIII of 1856, to give them, "with the least possible delay," an efficient system of drainage. In so doing he was quite aware that his Honorable friend was not in any way responsible for what had or had not been done, or was at all bound to answer any question that he might take upon himself to put to him. But he asked him the question, because he knew of no one who was so able to give information on the subject, or who was so ready, on all occasions, to impart what information he possessed.

The Council would recollect the animated discussion which took place in the Committee on the Municipal Bill upon the subject of drainage, and the jealous determination with which many Members, but especially his Honorable and learned friend on his left (Mr. Peacock), insisted upon an adequate provision being made for that important purpose. This provision was embodied in the 25th Clause of the Act, whereby it was enacted as follows :—

"The Commissioners shall carry out, with as little delay as possible, such a complete system of sewerage and drainage within the said town, as shall be directed by the Lieutenant-Governor of Bengal, with the sanction of the Governor-General in Council, subject to such alterations as may, from time to time, be ordered by the said Lieutenant-Governor with such sanction ; and until such system of sewerage and drainage has been completed, and all the expenses thereof defrayed, and all monies borrowed for the payment of such expenses, on the security of the rates and interest thereon, have been repaid, shall set apart for the purposes above mentioned an annual sum, not less than one hundred and fifty thousand Rupees, out of the proceeds of the rate provided by Section IX of this Act."

The Act was passed in December 1856, and certainly, at that time, there was every reasonable hope of the promise being speedily fulfilled, for it appeared that, so far back as that time in the preceding year, namely, in December 1855, a scheme of drainage had been submitted to the Lieutenant-Governor, and by him referred, in March 1856, to a Committee for their report; and on referring to their debates in June of that year, he found the Honorable Member for Bengal expressing his hope that that report would soon be ready.

But, nevertheless, by one of those fatalities, which seemed to be the too common lot of reports in this country, the report in question was not made till June 1857. He had not that document before him, but he believed there was no doubt that it substantially adopted the scheme of 1855, and he presumed that it was intended to act upon it at once; for in that same month an establishment was proposed and sanctioned for the purpose of carrying it out at a cost of upwards of two thousand Rupees a month. No blame would seem to attach to the Commissioners, for they at once set to work, getting out machinery and collecting raw material, and making other preliminary preparations, which would be indispensable to whatever scheme they were eventually ordered to carry out. Many months ago, he believed, they were in a condition to begin, but there was no scheme to begin upon; and now they had so thoroughly completed their preliminary arrangements, that there was nothing else that they could do but begin upon the scheme, and still there was no scheme to begin upon. The engines were compelled to be idle, and the establishment was compelled to be idle too, and he believed their own invention could suggest no better occupation than to sell the bricks which they had made, and which were not only useless now, but very much in the way.

But what all this time had become of the scheme? They left it in the hands of the Government of Bengal in June 1857, favorably reported upon by the Drainage Committee. From that time up to April 1858 it seemed to have remained unnoticed. At all events, he could not learn that anything was done towards its advancement. In April, however, it was referred to Mr. Rendel, an English Engineer of reputation, who happened to be in Calcutta, and Mr. Rendel took it to England to consult his brother, an Engineer he believed of still higher reputation, promising to send back a report by return of post. Post after post had returned, but no report, and he understood that the last that had been heard on the subject was that Mr. Rendel was ill, and that all his Indian business was stopped. In the mean time, as he had before said, the engines were standing still, and the establishment at two thousand Rupees a month was standing still, and the cold weather months, in which the best work was always done, were fast slipping away. Could, then, the Honorable Member tell him what their prospects were likely to be? Could he answer him these few questions? He owned they were difficult ones. Suppose Mr. Rendel's report came out some fine day, was it to be referred again to the Commissioners, and then again to a Committee? And, then, could he tell him how long it was likely to remain with the Government of Bengal before it obtained the preliminary sanction of the Lieutenant-Governor? And, again, if it got through that stage, how long it was likely to remain with the Governor-General in Council before it received its final permission to come into existence? He apprehended that, however doubtfully the promises of the Act had been kept as to the "carrying out the complete system of drainage," they had been most scrupulously observed as to the levying of the tax; and that every fraction of the heavy impost which it sanctioned, had been unmercifully realized. He should be glad therefore to be informed, if the Honorable gentleman was able to inform him, whether the lakh and a half required by the Act to be annually set apart for the purposes of drainage had been so set apart; and if set apart, how set apart? Whether it had been spent, or more or less left to accumulate; and finally, if spent, how spent; and if left to accumulate, how much had accumulated, and how it was proposed that the accumulation should be applied?

As one who was a party to the Act of 1856, he was anxious to have these questions answered, for, when he found things, now in December 1858, much in the same state as they were in December 1855, it was impossible not to have some misgivings as to the wisdom of their legislation.

The public, moreover, he was sure, must desire to be enlightened on this subject, for all they at present knew was that nothing had been done, and

Sir Arthur Buller.

that for that nothing they had been compelled to pay—he thought he was not using an inappropriate figure of speech—most handsomely *through the nose.*

MR. CURRIE regretted that it was not in his power to give any further information than the Honorable Member had already communicated to the Council. Having brought in a Bill for the Municipal taxation of Calcutta, and carried it through Council, he was *functus officio*—he had no official information of any thing that had transpired since. He was aware, from the same sources as the Honorable and learned Judge, that the report of the Drainage Committee had been submitted to Government about eighteen months ago. He knew also that the Municipal Commissioners had lost no time in setting to work, and in making preparations for an efficient commencement so soon as Mr. Clarke's scheme had been approved. But what was the present cause of delay, he was not informed. The Act required the scheme to receive the sanction of the Lieutenant-Governor and of the Governor-General in Council—whether the Bengal Government had submitted the scheme with the report, approving of it, to the Supreme Government, he was not aware; nor did he know how the reference to Mr. Rendel originated. He agreed with the Honorable and learned Judge that it could hardly have been necessary to call for Mr. Rendel's opinion. Mr. Clarke was a professional Civil Engineer of considerable experience in drainage matters; his report had been submitted to scientific men, and after long and careful examination had been approved by them. The better plan would, he thought, have been to have commenced operations at once.

As to what had been done with the money raised by the increased taxation, he knew only from the published reports. Considerable sums had been paid for machinery and other things, and the remainder had been set apart in the Bank of Bengal under a separate account for drainage. There had, he supposed, been some accumulation, but the current expenses had been considerable.

He was asked, if Mr. Rendel's report should recommend any material variations from the proposed scheme, what course would be taken? He confessed he was unable to answer that question. He thought it was to be regretted that opportunity had been given for the occurrence of such a contingency.

MR. GRANT said, perhaps if the Honorable and learned Judge would put the same question to himself or to any Member of the Executive Government at the next meeting, he might have such information as could be obtained on the subject from the Government records.

The Council adjourned.

Saturday, December 11, 1858.

PRESENT:

The Hon'ble the Chief Justice, *Vice President*, in the Chair.

Hon'ble J. P. Grant,	P. W. LeGeyt, Esq.,
Hon'ble Lieut.-Genl. Sir J. Outram,	E. Currie, Esq.,
Hon'ble H. Ricketts,	H. B. Harington, Esq., and
Hon'ble B. Peacock,	H. Forbes, Esq.

PILOT COURTS (BENGAL).

THE CLERK brought under the consideration of the Council a Petition of Mr. John Higgins, Branch Pilot in the Bengal Pilot Service, against the Bill "to amend the law for the trial of Officers of the Bengal Pilot Service for breach of duty."

MR. CURRIE moved that the above Petition be referred to the Select Committee to be appointed on the Bill.

Agreed to.

CANTONMENT JOINT-MAGISTRATES.

MR. HARINGTON presented the Report of the Select Committee on the Bill "for conferring Civil Jurisdiction in certain cases upon Cantonment Joint-Magistrates, and for constituting those Officers Registers of Deeds within the limits of their respective jurisdictions."

NABOB OF SURAT.

MR. LEGEYT moved the first reading of a Bill "to amend Act XVIII of 1848 (for the administration of the Estate of the late Nabob of Surat, and to continue privileges to his family)." He said, the object of this Bill was to modify Act XVIII of 1848, so as to give a right of appeal to the Judicial Committee of the Privy Council from any order of the Governor of Bombay in Council made under that Act. The Act (XVIII of 1848) was passed, in order to settle the family disputes of the late Nabob of Surat, who died in 1842. During the late Nabob's lifetime a law existed, by which he and his family enjoyed an exemption from the jurisdiction of the Civil and Criminal Courts of the East India Company. The exemption ceased on his death, and his heirs and the other members of his family were very desirous that it should be continued to them. In 1848 an Act was passed, giving the Governor of Bombay in Council the power

"To act in the administration of the property, of whatever nature, left by the late Nabob of Surat, in regard to the settlement and payment of the debts and claims standing against the estate of the said late Nabob at the time of his death, and to make distribution of the remaining property among his family;"

the Act further declaring that

"No act of the said Governor of Bombay in Council, in respect to the administration to, and distribution of, such property, from the death of the said late Nabob, shall be liable to be questioned in any Court of Law or Equity."

In execution of the power thus conferred upon it, the Government of Bombay appointed the Agent to the Governor at Surat to investigate all claims on the Estate of the late Nabob, and to report thereon to the Government. He did so, and reported to Government the manner in which he proposed that the property should be distributed, which was confirmed by the Government of Bombay. Some of the immediate heirs, however, were discontented with his award, and appealed to the Governor in Council for a reconsideration of the Agent's decision. Their prayer was refused, and they thereupon presented a petition of appeal to Her Majesty in Council. The Judicial Committee of the Privy Council, after hearing arguments on both sides, delivered judgment as follows:—

"Their Lordships are of opinion, however, that the intention of this Act was not to create a Court; that the intention of the Act was to delegate, either arbitrarily, or subject to certain limitations of discretion, the administration and distribution of the Nabob's property, but in such a way that the administration and distribution should not be judicially questioned. The expression, it will be observed, is not 'shall be liable to be questioned in any other Court of Law or Equity,' but 'shall be liable to be questioned in any Court of Law or Equity.' It may seem an anomalous and extraordinary proceeding to vest powers of this description, not liable to be checked by any ordinary course or powers of law, in any individual or in any body, but the Indian Legislature had power over the property; they might, in the exercise of that power which is inherent in Legislation, have given the whole property at once to any stranger, or devoted to any purpose, and whether with moral justice or not, is not the question. Instead of doing that, they do what to their Lordships appears substantially the same thing; they vest the power of dealing with it in a particular individual or a particular body, and declare that its acts shall not be liable to be questioned in any Court of Law or Equity.

"Their Lordships, therefore, consider that, in the ordinary exercise of their functions, they are without jurisdiction to interfere. They are of opinion, that the proceeding of the Governor of Bombay in Council has not been an act of a Court, Judge, or Judicial Officer within the meaning of the third Section of the Statute 3rd and 4th, Will. IV., C. 41, but has been the act of a person or body not in any sense Judicial, delegated and authorized to perform a particular function as to the responsibility for the exercise of which, or as to any appeal from that exercise, they were exempted by the Legislature which created them."

Subsequently the Government of Bombay received further advice on the subject from England, and had forwarded to him, for the purpose of being brought before this Honorable Council, an opinion of Her Majesty's present Attorney-General and Solicitor-General, which stated as follows:—

"We are of opinion that, having regard to the obvious necessity that the matters referred to in the petition of Jafur Alee should, if brought before the Judicial Committee of the Privy Council, be heard by them in the presence of all the parties interested, the best mode by which to obtain the opinion of the Judicial Committee would be that pointed out in the letter of the India Board of the 19th of January 1857, namely, that the Court of Directors should instruct the Government of Bombay to take steps for procuring a modification of the Act of 1848, so as to give a right of appeal to the Judicial Committee of the Privy Council from any order of the Governor of Bombay in Council made under that Act."

This opinion was forwarded by the Honorable the Court of Directors to the Government of Bombay in a Despatch dated the 1st September last.

It was, therefore, expedient to seek for an alteration of the law from the Indian Legislature. He had, accordingly, prepared a Bill which proposed to repeal that portion of Section II of the Act of 1848 which barred the jurisdiction of the Courts; and to re-enact it with a modification. Accordingly Section III provided that the orders of the Governor in Council, made under Act XVIII of 1848, should, like orders made by Government in suits against the first-class Sirdars of the Deccan, under Regulation XXIX. 1827 of the Bombay Code, be open to appeal to Her Majesty in Council.

He proposed next Saturday to move the second reading of the Bill, and would consider, in the meantime, whether it would then be necessary to suspend the Standing Orders with a view to proceeding with the Bill forthwith.

The Bill was read a first time.

FRAUDULENT TRANSFERS AND SECRET TRUSTS.

MR. PEACOCK (in the absence of Sir Arthur Buller) postponed the first reading of a Bill for the prevention of Fraudulent Transfers of Property and of Secret Trusts.

STAMP DUTIES (BENGAL).

MR. PEACOCK postponed the motion (which stood in the Orders of the Day) for the third reading of the Bill "to amend Regulation X. 1829, of the Bengal Code (for the collection of Stamp Duties)."

MERCHANT SEAMEN.

MR. CURRIE moved that the Council resolve itself into a Committee on the Bill "for the amendment of the law relating to Merchant Seamen;" and that the Committee be instructed to consider the Bill in the amended form in which the Select Committee had recommended it to be passed.

Agreed to.

Sections I to III were passed as they stood.

Section IV defined the general business of Shipping Masters.

MR. CURRIE said, he had an amendment to propose in this Section. The Section was taken from the English Act, but somewhat abridged. In making the necessary alterations, certain words had inadvertently been omitted, which he thought it important to retain. The English Act made it the duty of Shipping Masters not only to superintend and facilitate the engagement and discharge of Seamen, but also "to provide means for securing the presence on board, at the proper times, of men who are so engaged."

He now moved that these words be added after the word "mentioned" in the 6th line of the Section.

The motion was carried, and the Section as amended then passed.

Sections V to XVI were passed as they stood.

Section XVII was passed after a verbal amendment.

Sections XVIII to XXX were passed as they stood.

Section XXXI prescribed rules regarding the production of agreements and certificates of competency or service for Foreign-going ships.

MR. CURRIE said, he had one or two amendments to propose in this Section, which had been suggested by the Governor of the Straits Settlement, in consequence of there being no Collectors of Customs at the Stations in that Settlement. He begged to move the substitution of the following words for the word "and" in the 33rd line of the Section:—

"Or if there be no Collector of Customs, to the Officer whose duty it is to grant a Port-clearance."

THE CHAIRMAN asked, what was the state of things in the Straits, since the Clause went on to say:—

"And if any such ship attempts to go to sea without a clearance, any such Officer may detain her until such certificate as aforesaid is produced."

Who was to detain her?

MR. CURRIE said, he apprehended that, in every Port, there was some Officer whose duty it was to grant Port-clearances or documents of some kind, without which ships could not go to sea.

MR. GRANT said, that no Port-clearance was required at all in the Straits.

MR. PEACOCK suggested a general provision to the effect that, in places where there was no Collector of Customs, the duties imposed by the Act on Collectors might be performed by any Officer appointed by Government.

MR. CURRIE withdrew his motion, observing that the amendment was proposed by the Governor of the Straits Settlement, who ought to know what local circumstances required, and stating that he would make enquiries on the subject, and propose such amendments as he might find to be necessary before the third reading.

The Section was then passed as it stood.

Section XXXII was passed after an amendment

Sections XXXIII to XXXVII were passed as they stood.

MR. CURRIE moved the introduction of the following Sections after Section XXXVII :—

ALLOTMENT OF WAGES.

"All stipulations for the allotment of any part of the wages of a Seaman during his absence, which are made at the commencement of the voyage, shall be inserted in the agreement, and shall state the amounts and times of the payments to be made. All allotment-notes shall be in forms sanctioned by the local Government, and shall be made for the benefit only of a relative of the Seaman or some Member of his family, to be named in the note, and shall be payable to the Shipping Master on account of such relative of the Seaman or Member of his family. Such allotment shall not, in any case, exceed one-third of the wages of the Seaman.

"The Owner or any Agent who has authorized the drawing of an allotment-note shall pay to the Shipping Master, on demand, the sums allotted by the note, when and as the same are made payable, unless the Seaman is shown in manner hereinafter mentioned to have forfeited or ceased to be entitled to the wages out of which the allotment is to be paid; and in the event of such sums not being paid to the Shipping Master on demand, the Shipping Master may sue for and recover them with costs. The Seaman shall be presumed to be duly earning his wages, unless the contrary is shown to the satisfaction of the Court or Magistrate, either by the official statement of the change in the Crew, caused by his absence, made and signed by the Master, as by this Act is required, or by a duly certified copy of some entry in the Official Log-book, to the effect that he has died or left the Ship, or by a credible letter from the Master of the Ship to the same effect, or by such other evidence, of whatever description, as the Court or Magistrate trying the case considers sufficient to show satisfactorily that the Seaman has ceased to be entitled to the wages out of which the allotment is to be paid.

"The Shipping Master, on receiving any such sum as aforesaid, shall pay it over to the person named in the allotment-note. All such receipts and payments shall be entered in a book, and all entries in the said book shall be authenticated by the signature of the Shipping Master, or his Deputy; and the said book shall be, at all times, open to the inspection of the parties concerned."

He said, the reasons for striking out the Sections relating to allotment of wages were stated at length by the Select Committee in their Report. They intimated at the same time that, possibly, it might be found advisable to replace them. The communications since received seemed to render it advisable that they should be replaced; or rather that provision should be made for the allotment of wages on the same principle as was provided for in the existing Local Act, the payment being made through the Shipping Master. The Sections, the introduction of which he had now to move, were taken partly from the Merchant Shipping Act 1854, and partly from the Local Act.

The Sections were severally agreed to.

Sections XXXVIII to LIX were passed as they stood.

Section LX was passed after a slight amendment providing for the case of the Straits Settlement.

Sections LXI to LXIII were passed as they stood.

Section LXIV was passed after an amendment providing for the case of the Straits Settlement.

Sections LXV to CII were passed as they stood.

Section CIII was passed after an amendment.

Sections CIV to CXV, Tables A and B, and the Preamble and Title, were passed as they stood.

The Council having resumed its sitting, the Bill was reported.

DRAINAGE OF CALCUTTA.

Mr. GRANT said, on the last occasion a question had been put by the Honorable and learned Member who was absent to-day; on which he (Mr. Grant) had promised to obtain some information. It related to what had been done in the matter of the Drainage of Calcutta. The Honorable and learned Member had referred to the Report of the Messrs. Rendel, and the Honorable Member for Bengal, he believed, mentioned that it was expected immediately. He (Mr. Grant) had since learnt that a letter had been received by the last Mail, from which it appeared very probable that the Report in question was on board the steamer now expected.

He had promised to make some enquiry as to the expenditure of the money which had been set apart for the purpose from the proceeds of the House Rate. The following was the information which had been kindly furnished to him on this head:—

Drainage.

Collected and set apart specially for the purpose, up to 1st September 1858 ...	2,35,600	0	0
Expended in Stock and Plant, Machinery, Brick-field, and Engineer's Establishment...	1,76,078	0	0
Balance in hand to meet the cost of further Machinery ordered out from England, making Bricks, and setting up Establishment ...	59,522	0	0

Water Supply.

Collected and set apart for 1857 ...	30,000	0	0
Ditto for part of 1858 ...	16,000	0	0
	46,000	0	0
Purchase of Land, Excavation of Tank, Ghats, and Railing in Chowringhee ...	35,000	0	0
Balance to be added to further Collections for a Tank in the Northern Division of the Town ...	11,000	0	0

PILOT COURTS (BENGAL).

Mr. CURRIE moved that the Bill "to amend the law for the trial of Officers of the Bengal Pilot Service for breach of duty" be referred to a Select

Committee, consisting of Mr. Grant, Sir James Outram, Mr. Peacock, and the Mover.

Agreed to.

The Council adjourned.

Saturday, December 18, 1858.

PRESENT:

The Hon'ble J. P. Grant, in the Chair.

Hon'ble Lieut.-Genl. Sir J. Outram,	P. W. LeGeyt, Esq.,
Hon'ble H. Ricketts,	H. B. Harington, Esq., and
Hon'ble B. Peacock,	H. Forbes, Esq.

DELHI TERRITORY; RYOTWAR ARREARS (MADRAS PRESIDENCY); AND GUARDIANSHIP OF MINORS (BENGAL).

THE PRESIDENT read Messages informing the Legislative Council that the Governor-General had assented to the Bill "to repeal Regulation V. 1832 of the Bengal Code, and to make certain provisions rendered necessary by the transfer of the Delhi Territory to the administration of the Chief Commissioner of the Punjab;" the Bill "for the better recovery of arrears of Revenue under Ryotwar Settlements in the Madras Presidency;" and the Bill "for making better provision for the care of the persons and property of Minors in the Presidency of Fort William in Bengal."

OATHS AND AFFIRMATIONS.

THE CLERK presented to the Council a Petition from Mr. Macleod Wylie, Barrister-at-Law, praying that the Council will not pass the Bill "concerning Oaths and Affirmations," but will, on the contrary, abolish all oaths and solemn affirmations in judicial proceedings, and pass a law to provide a summary punishment for perjury, and such other laws as experience may suggest for the discouragement of existing malpractices of a like nature.

MR. FORBES moved that the above Petition be printed.

Agreed to.

THE CLERK reported to the Council that he had received a communication from the Secretary to the Government of the North-Western Provinces, forwarding copies of letters addressed to the Sudder Court and the Sudder Board of Revenue on the subject of judicial oaths and affirmations.

MR. FORBES moved that the above communication lie upon the table.

Agreed to.

FRAUDULENT TRANSFERS.

MR. PEACOCK (in the absence of Sir Arthur Buller) postponed the first reading of a Bill for the punishment of Fraudulent Transfers of Property and of Secret Trusts.

NABOB OF SURAT.

MR. LEGEYT moved the second reading of the Bill "to amend Act XVIII of 1848 (for the Administration of the Estate of the late Nabob of Surat, and to continue privileges to his family)."

The motion was carried, and the Bill read a second time.

STAMP DUTIES (BENGAL).

On the Order of the Day for the third reading of the Bill "to amend Regulation X. 1829 of the Bengal Code," (for the collection of Stamp Duties) being read—

MR. PEACOCK moved that the Bill be re-committed to a Committee of the whole Council, for the purpose of considering a proposed amendment therein.

Agreed to.

MR. PEACOCK said, since giving notice of amendments in Section III of this Bill, he had spoken to his Honorable friend on his right (Mr. Harington), and it appeared to them that, under the Section as it would stand if amended as proposed, a review of judgment would necessarily be admitted on the application of any party considering himself injured by the decision of a Court by which any deed, instrument, or document was rejected upon the ground that the same was not stamped within the meaning of the Rule which this Act proposed to repeal. He would not, therefore, move the amendment in the precise terms proposed, but he would move an amendment by which it would be left to the Judge to grant or not the application for a review. Unless he was satisfied that the deed, instrument, or document, if admitted, would have led to a different decision upon the merits of the case, he would not grant the application. This appeared to be more satisfactory than if the application for review were to be granted as a matter of course. He, therefore, begged to move that all the words after the word "may" in the 7th line of Section III be omitted, and the following words substituted for them :—

"Obtain a review of judgment if the application be made within six months from the passing of this Act, and if the Court to which the application is made be satisfied that the deed, instrument, or document, if admitted, would have led to a different decision upon the merits of the case."

The motion was carried, and the Section as amended then passed.

The Council having resumed its sitting, the Bill was reported.

Mr. PEACOCK moved that the Bill be read a third time and passed.

The motion was carried, and the Bill read a third time.

CANTONMENT JOINT-MAGISTRATES.

Mr. HARINGTON moved that the Council resolve itself into a Committee on the Bill "for conferring Civil Jurisdiction in certain cases upon Cantonment Joint-Magistrates, and for constituting those Officers Registers of Deeds within the limits of their respective jurisdictions ;" and that the Committee be instructed to consider the Bill in the amended form in which the Select Committee had recommended it to be passed.

Agreed to.

The Bill passed through Committee without amendment, and was reported.

REGISTRATION.

Mr. FORBES said, when his Honorable friend, the Member for the North-Western Provinces, brought in a Bill for conferring Civil Jurisdiction in certain cases upon Cantonment Joint-Magistrates, and for constituting those Officers Registers of Deeds, he also stated that he believed that he (Mr. Forbes) had a measure in contemplation for amending the general Law of Registration. He had had such a measure in contemplation for some time—before even he had had the honor of a seat in the Legislative Council ; and, although the longer he had contemplated the measure the more he was convinced of its very great importance, he had at the same time become also more aware of the many difficulties by which it was surrounded. But these difficulties, great as they were, he had no doubt, would be surmounted if the consideration and experience of several minds were engaged together upon the subject. Instead, therefore, of attempting, single-handed, to grapple with a question which had already been unsuccessfully essayed by far abler men than himself, he proposed to ask for the appointment of a Select Committee to consider and report upon the subject.

He had received a communication from the Madras Government, submitting a report from the Sudder Court, suggesting improvements in the present system of registering Assurances, together with the draft of an Act for affording protection to rights on property ; and he now moved that these papers be referred to a Select Committee, consisting of Mr. Peacock, Mr. LeGeyt, Mr. Currie, Mr. Harington, and the Mover.

Agreed to.

NABOB OF SURAT.

Mr LeGEYT moved that the Bill "to amend Act XVIII of 1848 (for the administration of the Estate of the late Nabob of Surat, and to continue privileges to his family)" be referred to a Select Committee, consisting of Sir James Outram, Mr. Peacock, and the Mover.

Agreed to.

STAMP DUTIES (BENGAL).

Mr. PEACOCK moved that Mr. Ricketts be requested to take the Bill "to amend Regulation X. 1829 of the Bengal Code (for the collection of Stamp-Duties)" to the President in Council, in order that it might be submitted to the Governor-General for his assent.

Agreed to.

The Council then adjourned, on the motion of Sir James Outram, till Saturday the 8th of January 1859.

INDEX

TO

THE PROCEEDINGS

OF THE

LEGISLATIVE COUNCIL OF INDIA.

VOLUME IV.

A.

E.

P.

CPSIA information can be obtained
at www.ICGtesting.com
Printed in the USA
LVHW101225100123
736788LV00002B/22

9 783375 131210